DARK MAGIC SERIES BOOK 3

QUEEN
OF THE
SHADOW
MENAGERIE

J. E. HARTER

This is a work of fiction. All of the characters, organizations, and events portrayed in this novel are either products of the author's imagination or are used fictitiously. Any resemblance to actual events, locales, or persons, living or dead, is coincidental.

Copyright © 2024 by J. E. Harter

All rights reserved.

No portion of this book may be reproduced in any form or by any electronic or mechanical means, including information storage and retrieval systems, without written permission from the author, except for the use of brief quotations in a book review, as permitted by U.S. copyright law.

Cover Artwork: Miblart

Editing: Erin Young

Map Design: Alec McK

Paperback ISBN: 979-8-9886106-7-0

Hardcover ISBN: 979-8-9886106-8-7

AUTHOR'S NOTE

The book contains subject matter that might be difficult for some readers, including extreme fantasy violence, blood, gore, war, language, torture, explicit sexual content, depressive thoughts, references to rape (consent withdrawn) and sexual abuse, depiction of miscarriage

CHAPTER 1

MARAI

Reality was a smear of noxious nightmares. Only in dreams could Marai escape the horror.

She'd find herself bathed in sunlight, wrapped in strong arms beneath soft sheets. Ruenen's voice filled her ears with music, laughter, and declarations of adoration. Her family, whole and healthy, waved to her from the door of their little cottage. Kadiatu, round face beaming, flowers in her hair. Leif giving Marai that smug smirk she both loathed and loved. Thora and Raife, hand in hand, while Aresti stood gleaming in golden armor.

A calloused hand slapped Marai's face.

Sharp, stinging pain wrenched her from a drug-induced sleep, her only place of refuge.

Disoriented, she gasped, groggy from the metallic powder's effects, as the throbbing pain of the slap burrowed into her teeth and jaw.

Marai took in the burned, leering visage, inches from her own.

"There's those wild eyes," Slate said, but his voice held no fondness. It was cold, rough, seething with anger.

Marai rapidly blinked away the blurry film over her eyes. Slate, her old demon, crouched next to her within the dark recesses of the ship that held her captive. She tried to move, to strike him back, but the hefty chains on her wrists and ankles rattled, holding her to the wooden floor and wall of the ship. Marai had no strength. No weapon.

One terrible word echoed in her mind: *Prisoner.*

Slate didn't back away. The puckered, red scar that traveled from his lip to his outer cheek looked more grotesque up close. Marai had given him that scar, and ruined his pretty face forever. That, and the shiny, fibrous burns all over his body, the thin, branch-like lines on his neck and face, and patchy golden hair, made him look more like a child's nighttime terror than the dashing pirate captain he once was. He latched onto her scalp with clawed fingers and yanked her forward. Marai wheezed as her windpipe crushed against the iron collar ensconcing her throat.

"I lost everything because of you," Slate hissed, fisting her hair. His breath was hot against her ear, and she cringed at the sensation.

"How are you still alive?" she rasped.

She'd electrocuted him, sliced his face open, and left him stranded on a floating inferno. That was enough to kill a normal man. But not Captain Slate Hemming.

"You should've made sure to finish the job."

She already regretted this mistake, especially when his slick tongue licked up the column of her neck. It wasn't out of lust. Slate knew how toxic his touch was to Marai. This was to remind her who had control, and with his hold on her, Marai couldn't jerk away.

"I'd love nothing more than to kill you," he said.

Marai gnashed her teeth at his throat. "At least death would spare me from having to look at your hideous face."

Despite being imprisoned, helpless against his cruelty, Marai wouldn't let Slate see her fear. She wouldn't give him that power. He'd taken far too much from her already.

Slate's blue eyes blazed in the lantern light dangling above his head. "So eager to die? I'm not going to make it quick. That would be a mercy you don't deserve. No, I'm going to make you suffer—"

"Leave her alone," ordered a hoarse voice at Marai's side.

Keshel was conscious, chained next to her in the hull of a ship like pigs set for slaughter. Pointed ears peeked out from the long black hair hanging limply over his shoulders. His dark angular eyes speared Slate with a stern glare Marai was familiar with. She'd been on the receiving end of that glare often as a child. It was effective, even in Keshel's vulnerable state.

Slate's lip curled, but he released her tangled blonde hair, and stood.

Marai coughed, gulping down air. "Where are you taking us?"

Slate sniggered, and shook his head with disdain. "*I'm* not taking you anywhere."

Surprise and relief flooded through Marai. *He's not in charge.* He wasn't the one who'd kidnapped her. *At least he's not my jailer.* The thought provided her some solace.

She'd destroyed his ship, killed his crew. All of his bounty lay on the bottom of the ocean floor. *Now Slate must degrade himself by serving on someone else's ship.* It was the purest form of humiliation for a captain—to be demoted to a mere sailor, taking orders from another. Slate had once been the most feared pirate on the Baurean Sea. Now, he was nobody.

Marai couldn't stop her smile from spreading. "It must be painful—your fall from power. You're as mangy as a flea-bitten cur. A penniless nobody—"

Slate stomped on her left knee.

Marai grit her teeth, trying not to yell, as her eyes bulged from the agony. The bastard dislocated her kneecap; a round lump formed on the outer side. Marai wasn't a stranger to blood and gore, but the sight of her own kneecap in that crooked position sent her stomach roiling. Adrenaline submerged most of the pain for now, but it would rear its ugly head the minute Marai settled down.

Keshel tried to reach for Marai in his heavy chains, but the shackles held him back. "Stop, please!"

Marai wasn't used to hearing Keshel plead, to hear desperation saturate his words. He was normally too proud for that. He stared at her injured knee with pure fear shining in his eyes.

Slate assessed Keshel coolly, glancing at his pointed ears. "Another freak like you, I see. What happened to that other milksop who was so besotted with you? Did you set him on fire, as well?"

Marai bristled at the mention of Ruenen from Slate's treacherous lips. "He's King of Nevandia now."

Slate barked out a laugh. "And I'm Laimoen, King of the Universe."

Marai grimly wondered if perhaps Laimoen, God of War and Destruction, *wasn't* pulling the strings of fate here.

Slate's face turned serious. "What did you do with it?"

"With what?"

"My *ring*. The one you stole from me."

"Oh. That piece of junk?" A dark smirk stretched across Marai's face. "That ancient faerie queen's curse you told me about? It was real. I'd tell you to ask Rayghast's soldiers about it, but they're dead now."

Meallán's bloodstone ring wasn't on Marai's person. She hadn't wanted to get rid of the connection to her past, to fae history, so she'd left her ancestor's trinket in her room in the castle of Kellesar. Big mistake.

Slate glared at her. "You're fortunate. You'd have been thrown overboard days ago if this was *my* ship. I would've sliced you up into tiny pieces and watched the sharks devour you." A cruel smile brewed at his ruined lips; he delighted in the image. "But alas, you're my employer's quarry. Only a fat load of coin is preventing me from damning his wishes and killing you right now."

"Who's your employer? Is it Koda?" Marai asked, desperate for any information on their current state.

"Regrettably for you, I'm not at liberty to say anything." Slate sauntered to the stairs leading to the upper decks. "Enjoy the trip, Marai. We'll have plenty of time to play later."

He disappeared to the floor above.

"That was him," Keshel said, watching Marai intently. "The pirate who . . ."

Raped her? Manipulated her? Used her?

"Yes."

I'll kill him. I'm going to chop off his hands and watch as they flop onto the deck. Then I'll slice out his filthy tongue. Lastly, I'll wrench out his black, worthless heart.

The murderous thoughts calmed her, settling her mind into its usual pinpoint focus.

Marai surveyed the cavernous hull. The ship was large, larger than Slate's *Nightmare,* and relatively clean. No musty, foul odors; just the briny scent of salt water and damp wood. Crates, barrels, and trunks were tied in organized bunches with ropes, stacked against the walls. It was bright down there; overhead lanterns swayed with the rocking waves. She didn't even spot a single rat.

But this was still a jail, where she and Keshel remained its prisoners.

I will not surrender.

Marai thrashed against the chains. The shackles were firmly secured to her body and the surrounding wood. They were strong, made of thick iron. New. Not a single speck of rust. Impossible to break. She winced as the movement drew a sharp pain through her knee, but she'd rather damn the leg entirely in order to acquire freedom.

"Stop, you'll hurt yourself," Keshel said. He'd barely moved since Slate left, as if he'd already succumbed to their situation.

Marai ignored him.

I escaped the dungeon of Dul Tanen. I escaped The Nightmare. *I can escape this.*

She snarled as she tried to remove the collar from her neck, cracking and breaking fingernails in the process. Her panic flared as she discovered that the indentation she felt wasn't, in fact, a keyhole. The collar was otherwise smooth all around, welded together somehow. She studied the one around Keshel's neck from a distance. His, too, had a strange marking upon it: an archaic symbol etched into the foreign metal that Marai didn't recognize. A three-pronged object, like a pitchfork. The sight of it made Marai shiver for some reason.

How do the collars come off? Perhaps she needed a special key to remove it.

Or magic.

She reached into her well, searching for an ember of power, a spark, but it was just out of reach. Not gone, but . . . snuffed out, tamped down by some unknown force. Marai tried to pull from the well of magic, but the collar shocked her. A cold, charged bolt skittered through her blood and bones, like it had before, as if using her own magic against her.

"It's no use. Look at your wrists, Marai. You're bleeding," said Keshel, watching her struggle with a sad shake of his head. "Koda will return soon. Maybe he'll be willing to talk."

"For someone so wise, I'd have thought you'd come up with a better plan," she snapped at him. "I won't sit here and do nothing."

She had to get free. She had to return to Ruenen, to her people back in Nevandia. Thora, Raife, and Aresti must be terrified.

"What do you think you can do?" Keshel challenged, but without much strength behind the words. "Our magic is smothered by these collars, our bodies chained and weakened from that drug. Even if we were to free ourselves, Koda has the unique ability to immobilize us with a snap of his fingers. I'm sorry to say that we're stuck here. Let me try to speak to him."

Marai glared at him, at his nonchalance, at his acceptance of their miserable fate. "You think negotiating with your friend Koda will help us? That he'll let us go once you've utilized your *profound* logic and convinced him. Oh, yes, maybe this has all been one big misunderstanding."

Keshel leaned his head back against the wall and closed his eyes. His skin was more moon-pale than usual, thin and papery like pages in the books he loved. A sheen of sweat coated his forehead and upper lip. Marai was used to the listless tilting and swaying on the water, the creaks and groans of a ship. Keshel wasn't.

He let out a long, resigned sigh. "It's my fault we're here."

Surprise sluiced through Marai, then a wave of anger, like the ocean crashing against the hull, filled her chest.

"How could you trust him so blindly? You should've told me about Koda straight away." Her tone was as venomous as a desert rattlesnake.

But the truth was, she'd been foolish, too. She hadn't brought her dagger to Ruenen's coronation. She never went anywhere unarmed, but that night, she'd be sloppy, caught up in the romantic fairytale. She should've been more wary of Koda; reached for her magic faster. The Lady Butcher would have. Marai was as culpable for their circumstances as Keshel.

However, instead of admitting this, she sent all her guilty poison at him. "You never should've kept his existence a secret from the rest of us."

Us. Thora, Raife, and Aresti . . .

But not Kadiatu. Not Leif. They were dead. Marai barely had time to mourn them. It hadn't been long since the final battle between Nevandia and Tacorn. Only a few days after she'd watched Kadiatu and Leif die, their blood coating the Red Lands' grass. She hadn't put flowers on their graves yet. Her heart could barely ache at their loss, not at this moment. Not when her mind was buzzing with panic, anger, and calculations.

"I'm sorry," Keshel whispered. "You're right. I was a fool. I was *excited* to learn that there were other fae in the world. I didn't want to feel alone anymore, especially after Leif and Kadi . . . I didn't think about our safety. I didn't think about Koda's motives. I barely thought to question him at all."

Marai imagined how Keshel must have felt, heartbroken and full of sorrow from the loss of his family. When Koda appeared, he was probably as amazed as she was when she'd first met the part-fae male on the dock of Cleaving Tides. After a lifetime of loneliness, thinking they were the only faeries alive after the massacres, another had appeared with the promise of magic and camaraderie.

"The worst part is that I'd seen this coming."

A wave slammed against the ship's hull. Marai went cold as her stomach churned. "What do you mean?"

Keshel opened his eyes, staring distantly at the support beams in the supply chamber. "I told you before . . . I saw you in chains."

Marai remembered that conversation, now seeming so long ago. Keshel had warned her that Ruenen would be the ruination of the fae, the whole of Astye. But Ruenen had *saved* Nevandia. He'd won against King Rayghast of Tacorn, brought peace and hope to a war-torn country. He had, indeed, altered Astye forever, by creating a safe haven for magical folk. Ruen wasn't the Ruin of everything . . . he was the Ruin of Marai.

"Everything led us here, despite how I sought to avoid it," Keshel continued. "You meeting King Ruenen in the North brought you to Koda, one way or another. We're exactly where fate wanted us to be."

"I don't believe in fate."

How could any of this be Lirr's plan? Why would the Goddess of Creation, of Life and Light, inflict such pain on people? Marai stared at her bloody fingernails, wrists, and ankles. She still wore the emerald and aureate gown she'd worn to Ruenen's coronation. It was ripped and dirty, stained with her blood. She'd lost her heeled slippers somewhere. Hours, or days ago, she'd felt so nervously happy. Her heart had fluttered in her breast like a hummingbird's wings when he'd walked her down the aisle at Ruenen's coronation. When Ruenen, newly crowned, had kissed her in the hallway. Danced with her, smiled at her.

Oh, how easily happiness can slip away.

"Perhaps, but you *do* believe in prophecies," Keshel said, reminding her of the one he'd previously made that had sent them to Nevandia in the first place.

"I believe you see things and interpret them in your own way. Your visions are sometimes unreliable. They're possible outcomes, not set in stone. Have you *seen* anything since we arrived on this ship?"

Keshel pointed at the collar around his neck, giving her a flat look. "Not a thing." He sighed again. "I've never gone this long without a vision. It's as if I've gone blind."

Marai knew how he felt. Without her magic, she felt empty. Powerless. How could someone seal away magic? And for what purpose?

"Who *is* Koda?"

"He told me he was originally from Yehzig," said Keshel. "His mother fled the fae massacres on Astye years ago and settled there. Koda's half, like us."

"But why kidnap his own kind? That makes no sense. Is he holding us for ransom?"

Koda had somehow known about Ruenen's secret: that Ruenen wasn't the true King of Nevandia. He wasn't King Vanguarden and Queen Larissa's son. Was all this for blackmail?

Whatever Koda wanted, Ruenen would pay. Marai knew he'd empty Nevandia's coffers for her safe return. He was probably frantic right now . . . Marai's heart clenched at the thought of how confused, how hurt he must be. Did he think she'd left him willingly? That she'd run away from him again in fear of intimacy? Of what they'd shared together, what Ruenen had been planning to ask her . . .

I have to get back to him.

"I sense something more sinister," Keshel said. "There'd be no reason to set sail if they were merely after coin. No, this is a larger operation."

"He's taking us to Andara," said Marai, the pieces fitting together.

Andara, the mysterious country far out to sea that no one traveled to, or returned from. Marai and Ruenen had once wanted to go there, but it had been a flimsy dream of gossamer smoke, as foolish as believing she might have found happiness and love at last.

"Something is happening on Andara," Keshel said. "I believe Koda when he says there's magic there. But what kind? His employer must be powerful and

QUEEN OF THE SHADOW MENAGERIE 9

wealthy. Sailing to and from Andara is no easy endeavor. He must've paid handsomely for the crew and a boat of this size."

Marai's brain whirred with strategy. "Koda's not a fighter. He used his magic and a drug to incapacitate us instead of bodily force. If I could swipe the keys, I know I could overpower him. Then I'll portal us home to Nevandia."

"You don't think he'll be expecting you to try something?" Keshel asked, frown deepening.

"Talking about me?" came a jocular voice from the stairs. Boots clomped with a jaunty gait, and Koda came into view. He smiled when he saw his prisoners, as if nothing brought him more joy than to see Marai and Keshel trussed up in chains.

Marai was resistant to admit that the fae male was strikingly handsome, with starlight-silver eyes that glowed with fae magic. He leaned casually against the support beam in the center of the hull. He'd taken off his knit cap, fully revealing his thick, wavy, black hair and pointed ears. Clearly, he wasn't concerned with anyone onboard the ship knowing his true heritage.

"What are we doing here?" Marai asked him with vehemence.

Koda blinked, acting surprised at her question. "My employer wants to meet you: Meallán's progeny, heir to the faerie throne. A woman with tremendous magical power. And you, Keshel, a seer, another rare ability."

"Are you going to sell us?" Keshel paled further. "As slaves?"

"You're destined for greater things," said Koda with a flippant hand.

Keshel put on his authoritative airs, sitting up straighter, setting his face into a mask of calm. "You're one of us, Koda. Brethren. Kin. We fae should stick together. I'm certain we can negotiate an agreement which benefits us both if you let us go."

He hoped to speak reason into the male. Marai scoffed inwardly—if her hands were free, she would've just punched Koda in the face.

Keshel jerked his chin at her. "Whatever you want, she can ensure you get it. She has the King's favor."

Koda chuckled, and said to Marai, "You think the Nevandian King will bail you out? I'm sure he would, tulip, but I'm no idiot. You'll kill me the second I let you go. You weren't called the Lady Butcher for nothing." He winked, all jolly like she was a beautifully wrapped gift someone had presented him. "Those chains are already digging into your flesh, Marai. I suggest you relax and enjoy the ride to Andara."

"*Fuck you*," Marai snarled, pulling on her chains, only making Koda chuckle again.

"You are a fearsome thing, aren't you? You live up to the nickname you earned, and you'll live up to your new title as Queen of the Fae."

Is that what this is about? That I'm related to Meallán?

Marai's ancient relative had been a powerful faerie queen who'd been murdered by her own human slaves, but not before she'd cursed them. The bloodstone ring Marai stole from Slate had been the cursed object Meallán intended to use to bring about the downfall of man. That hadn't come to pass–Marai had used up the ring's magic against King Rayghast of Tacorn and his dark magic. She'd controlled the curse, and focused it only on Nevandia's enemies. Meallán's curse was gone.

"I have no desire to take the throne. Tell that to your master," said Marai.

Koda twisted his mouth, pondering his answer. "I'm going to let my employer speak to that. He is, after all, the one who wants to meet you both so badly."

Keshel's stomach gurgled. He sagged against the wall, a look of torment streaking across his face. Unlike Marai, he wasn't used to this kind of hardship. She'd learned how to go days without food and how to survive when the entire world wanted her dead.

How long has it been since we left Nevandia?

Marai's stomach was a hollow pit, her throat dry as the Badlands desert, but she couldn't think about those things. She had to keep her focus on escaping.

"Hungry, I see. We can rectify that," Koda said. "I need to keep you both hale on this journey. Since you so enjoy his company, I'll have Hemming bring you food and water, although I can't promise he won't spit in it."

"You can't trust him," Marai said. "Slate will steal anything he can get his hands on. He'll charm the crew, create a mutiny, kill you without a second thought."

"Never fear. We're old *friends*, Slate and I," said Koda, dripping with sarcasm. "I know all his foul tricks. He's no threat to me."

"Dangerous men are made worse when they have nothing left to lose," Marai said, tone as edged as her missing blade, Dimtoir. Her father's sword; another thing Marai had lost that day on the Red Lands moor.

Koda slid his hands into his pockets, and walked back towards the steps. "Oh, Hemming has something to lose. He values his life, no matter how small and insignificant it is now."

"*Wait,*" Marai called.

Koda stopped halfway up, and turned back over his shoulder.

"How many days since the coronation?"

"Three. We'll be in the Yehzig port of Qasnal in four more days," said Koda. "Best you both hunker down and get excited for Andara. It's the fae's ancestral home, after all."

With one final grin, he disappeared whistling.

Three days. Marai's stomach plummeted. Koda must've had the ship waiting for him at the Syoton port of Baatgai, ready to sail. There was no way Ruenen could have caught up to them in time. He'd have no idea where to look for her.

I won't give up.

Marai struggled against her chains, harder this time, trying to pull them from their anchor in the wall and floor. Iron bit into her flesh. Crimson blood dripped down her hands onto the green silk of her gown. Her kneecap hammered with agony.

"Stop, Marai," Keshel said, voice taking on an emotional urgency she'd rarely heard from him. "I can't bear to watch you bleed. Let's try to be patient."

Desperation filled Marai's lungs like water. It clouded her mind. It sped up her pulse to a frenetic gallop. "Every moment we're on this ship, the further we sail from safety."

And from Ruenen. If she could just get the collar off . . .

Of course, there *was* another way. The dark thought wormed its way into her mind, like it had been planted there, although she'd sworn never to use it again.

Did she dare? Did it matter? She'd damn her soul, but Marai couldn't remain a prisoner. What choice did she have left?

Keshel looked sharply at her. "Whatever you're thinking, stop."

"I'm not thinking about anything but escaping."

"You can't use dark magic to solve our problems. Nothing good can come from it."

Marai slumped against the wall, bringing her right knee to her chest; the left kneecap was so swollen that it wouldn't bend. "Don't worry. I won't call upon it."

"*Promise* me."

"I promise."

She was as blind as Keshel. Marai had no plan. No power. She was alone, adrift in a sea of peril and uncertainty.

"We'll find a way out of this," Keshel said, but Marai heard the doubt in his quiet voice. "Your King, along with Raife and Aresti will search for us." He kept his intense gaze pinned on her face. "And I believe in you."

Marai snorted, shaking her head. "Your faith in me is unfounded."

She only made things worse. Marai was the hand that dealt death. A dark shroud hovering over everyone else. In life, she'd gone from one horror to the next. It never seemed to end. Was this what life was? Suffering?

Keshel reached for her hand. The chains prevented him from touching her, but the gesture moved her all the same.

"I've watched you do astounding things, Marai. Things no one should be able to do. I've seen you brave the horrors of this world, fight off monsters both inside and out, and appear on the other side, stronger than before. I *know* you can find a way." Keshel gave her a wisp of a smile, softening his gaze. Those dark eyes had always been the most human part of him. Faerie genes didn't manifest the same way in every part-fae. His eyes didn't glow like Marai's did. They didn't swirl with living magic, but never before had Marai seen them filled with so much warmth. "I stand by my faith in you."

Marai swallowed the lump in her throat. Now wasn't the time to get emotional, to lose faith in herself.

She would set them both free. She'd find a way home to Ruenen.

Even if she had to destroy every soul onboard the ship, including her own, in the process.

CHAPTER 2

RUENEN

The world sloped away as his eyes scoured the rolling hills. His ears remained vigilant for the slightest sound, listening for her voice, for the call of his name. *Ruen.*

But all he heard was the wuthering, whispering wind through bushes and heather. All he saw were leagues and leagues of mist, craggy rocks, grassy valleys, a sapphire lochan, and the small village of limestone thatched cottages.

Ruenen wouldn't allow hope to leave him. He clung to it, gathering the threads that tethered his soul to hers.

Marai is alive.

Yet, every day, hope slowly drained from him like pus from an oozing wound. Each passing hour seemed an eternity.

They'd searched Kellesar so thoroughly, Ruenen had learned every street, tavern, and back alley in his city. He'd climbed down into cellars and hidden tunnels. He'd visited the small towns nearby, traversed across highland moors, ventured into caves and hovels. Spoken to dozens of his citizens, but not a single one had seen Marai or Keshel. No travelers had come through with prisoners, except for his own soldiers escorting Tacornians to the dungeons. Ruenen had sent men to search up and down the country, and within neighboring Tacorn.

It didn't matter how many hours, how many leagues, how many soldiers. Five days after her disappearance, Ruenen was left standing with empty arms and a tormented heart.

Marai had vanished into thin air; opened her portal, as Nosficio surmised, and disappeared with Keshel and the other strange magical presence the vampire had scented that night.

Not even the beauty of the flourishing highlands on a spring day could wrench Ruenen from his anguish. Nevandia's lands burst with life and color. Clusters of crocuses and primroses, heather, gorse, and broom dappled the lush, verdant grass. Farmlands were recovering; the soil fertile enough to produce the first good harvest in years. The pristine, clear blue sky seemed to celebrate.

King Rayghast of Tacorn was dead, and his dark magic had disappeared, no longer siphoning life from Nevandia as it had for decades. Ruenen's people showered him with praise and gratitude. He'd earned their staunch loyalty after winning the war, but not even this newfound joy for his country could vanquish the fear and longing inside him for Marai.

Hooves approached from behind. Someone cleared their throat.

"It's late, Your Grace. We should return to Kellesar."

The Captain of the King's Guard and Commander of the Nevandian Army appeared alongside Ruenen's horse. Avilyard's gaze bored into Ruenen beneath his visor. The older man read the emotions Ruenen hid beneath the guise of a king; an urbane mask Ruenen wore in each public moment.

Avilyard pressed in his deep voice, "I don't want you out here after sunset, Your Grace, not with Tacorn loyalists still on the loose. If we leave now, we can make it to Kellesar by nightfall."

Although the war with Tacorn was won, peace remained a far-off fantasy. Tacorn soldiers, commanders, noblemen, and peasants formed a rabble of never-ceasing attacks on Nevandian lands and citizens. They usually carried out these skirmishes at night, and while they didn't have the numbers to overtake Nevandia, they caused enough mayhem to keep Ruenen and his small, exhausted army busy.

"A few moments more," Ruenen replied, though he knew there was little point to this search.

They'd ridden south that day across the border into Tacorn. Avilyard and Holfast had wondered if a Tacorn loyalist might have kidnapped Marai and Keshel, but Ruenen knew this was folly. They'd already deduced someone with magic had taken them, but who else besides the fae had strong enough magic to overpower Marai?

Unless that someone was using *dark* magic . . . another fiend like Rayghast who harnessed forbidden power.

A warm breeze swept Ruenen's chestnut hair into his eyes. He watched his golden-armored soldiers question the Tacornian villagers, search their cottages, wade into the shallows of the loch. At least the villagers were eager to help, aware that the king who'd recently defeated their own lingered in the hills above them.

With disappointed shakes of their heads, his soldiers retreated from the village, returning to their mounts. They rode up to meet Ruenen on the hill where he and Commander Avilyard sat upon their steeds.

"We'll find her another day, Your Grace," Avilyard said. His rumbling voice, usually so reassuring, showed signs of fatigue and doubt.

Five endless days. Ruenen's nerves were coiled tight as a spring. Every hour he wasn't searching or presiding over meetings, he was in the training ring sparring, or in the monastery praying. It had been years since he'd prayed regularly to the gods. Back when he was a small child, Monks Amsco and Nori made him attend services several times a day. Ruenen knew the ancient invocations. He repeated them, over and over, until his voice grew hoarse and knees sore from kneeling.

Please, Lirr, Goddess of Light, bring Marai home. Bring her back to me.

But the goddess had yet to answer his prayers.

At Avilyard's continued insistence, Ruenen turned his white horse around, back northeast towards Kellesar. He galloped onwards through the open valley, following the snaking Nydian River, winding through the hills, leading him home, but farther from Marai.

Night blanketed the highlands in darkness. It was a moonless eve, but the city of Kellesar, a beacon of radiant light, floated up from the valley. Its moonstone marble walls reflected the torches and firelight within its buildings, illuminating the castle perched upon the hill. The spires reached up towards the Gods' city of Empyra and a blanket of stars. Ruenen was always struck by the beauty of this city, but its splendor had dimmed in Marai's absence. The stars above reminded him of her peaceful face when she stared up at them, mesmerized by the expanse of the sky.

At least I'm home.

Ruenen hadn't realized when he'd started thinking of Kellesar as home, and the sloping landscape as his own. Home had been a foreign word to him for his whole life, not until he'd taken his place as King. But Marai was part of that equation. No home was complete without her.

His horse's hooves clopped across the cobblestones as he and his men rode through the main city gate. Ruenen loved the way the tightly-squished buildings leaned forward, as if sheltering him from the outside world. The streets were alive with activity, lanterns ablaze. Music floated out of a nearby tavern, along with the scent of dinner and locally-brewed ale. Laughter and conversation brightened these once desolate avenues and alleys. Ruenen wished he could sit with his people, kick back with a stein, and sing alongside them, but he was King now. Holfast reminded him daily that kind of interaction was no longer allowed with "average citizens."

Ruenen had lost part of himself when he'd become King; the carefree, reckless, jovial part. He had to discover who this new Ruenen was. He needed to understand the person beneath the crown.

People waved and bowed as he passed through the winding, narrow streets. Ruenen tried to greet them, but there was no joy in his smile. Even the woman who owned the hand pie shop, Ruenen's favorite store in the city, couldn't bring a true smile to his face when she handed him a freshly baked meat pie with a flaky, buttery crust.

He did, of course, devour it straight away, though.

Cantering through the castle portcullis at the highest point of the city, weariness tugged on Ruenen's neck and shoulders. He rubbed at a muscle spasm beneath the back of his skull, as he brought his horse to a halt. He leapt off, and handed the reins to a groom.

Another team of soldiers were also dismounting their steeds in the courtyard.

Hope flared, bright as a sunburst, as Ruenen strode directly to the group's leader. "Anything?"

Raife bowed, then removed his golden helmet. Sandy-blond curls tumbled past his shoulders. Sweat plastered his dirt-stained, freckled face. "Nothing, Your Grace. We gave the sentries at the Syoton border the posters Thora made. They hadn't seen anyone matching Marai or Keshel's likenesses, although I'm not sure how much I trust their word. I would've gone further into Syoto, but I know our forces are stretched thin as it is, with so many out searching."

Or wounded or deceased from the final battle. Nevandia had lost so many good men, young and old, soldier, miner, and farmer, on the Red Lands. It would take decades to replenish the loss of life over the forty years of war.

Disappointment flooded Ruenen's heart, but he placed a hand on Raife's shoulder. "Thank you, my friend. You made the right call."

Raife gave a weak smile; his luminous emerald eyes shimmered with the emotion Ruenen wouldn't let himself show. Raife was Marai and Keshel's kin—maybe not by blood, but they were family, nonetheless. Their abduction had been hard on him, too, especially so soon after the death of his twin brother, Leif.

"I spoke to the guards," Raife said, gesturing to the golden pillars of men standing by the massive castle doors. "Aresti's team still hasn't returned."

"Are you worried about her?" Ruenen certainly was.

Aresti had barely been beyond the Kellesar walls. Before that, she'd spent her entire life in a cave in the Badlands with Raife and the other fae. She was new to this world.

Raife cocked his head to the side in an avoidant way. "She can take care of herself. And she has the weres with her."

Tarik, Brass, and Yovel were most enthusiastic to assist in the search. They hardly knew Marai, but for some reason, the coal-mining werewolves from Ain were already intensely loyal to her.

"What about Nosficio?" asked Raife.

"No word," said Ruenen, and Raife's face darkened.

Nosficio the vampire hadn't been seen since the night Marai and Keshel had been taken. His superior sense of smell was a valuable tool for tracking, and Ruenen could only pray that the vampire's absence meant he was still hot on the trail. An unlikely ally, Nosficio was also strangely dedicated to Marai, perhaps because he'd known her ancestors, Queen Meallán and King Aras, centuries ago.

Regardless of Nosficio's loyalty to Marai, he gave Ruenen the creeps.

"Go home," Ruenen told his exhausted friend. Raife would stay up with him all night if Ruenen asked, drinking ale somberly in the royal apartments. "Get some sleep, and give Thora my best."

"Make sure *you* get some rest, too," replied Raife, giving Ruenen a pointed look.

"I'll give it a good try."

Raife heard the lie, but bowed again wordlessly before dashing off through the portcullis into the street. He'd been gone for over four days, and was probably anxious to see Thora.

She must be sick with worry.

Without Raife and Aresti present, Thora was the only fae left in Kellesar; her whole family shattered and scattered. At least she could have Raife back for a night.

Ruenen walked on wobbly limbs into the castle. Hours and days of riding made his legs sore and stiff, but the sight of the resplendent entrance took his breath away. Frescos and stained glass, gold-painted tiles, moonstone marble. Ruenen remained slightly mystified at his newfound good fortune. Not long ago he was a penniless bard wandering the continent, running from Rayghast. Now he was a king, and this beautiful building was his home.

Bassite, Master of Household, greeted him with a deep bow at the towering doors.

"Your Grace, so happy to have you back safe and well," the white-haired man said in earnest. Ruenen liked Bassite. He kept the castle running in tip-top shape and had even hired newly widowed women to work there with decent wages. It was a small step forward for equality that Ruenen was more than pleased to encourage. "Shall I have dinner sent up to your chamber?"

"Yes, thank you, Bassite," Ruenen said, exhaustion, like marrow, filling the bones in his body. He slowly climbed the grand marble stairs to the second floor. His feet dragged as he reached the royal apartments. Two golden-armored King's Guard opened the massive oak double doors for him.

"Welcome home, Your Grace," said one of the soldiers. His voice was youthful, chin covered in a patchy beard. His eyes ignited with admiration as Ruenen passed.

"Thank you, Sir Nyle," he replied.

"Glad to have you back," said Nyle's best friend, Sir Elmar. The two King's Guard youths barely went anywhere without the other.

Another face bobbed into view at the open door. "Your Grace!"

Mayestral pulled the cape from Ruenen's shoulders and draped it over his arm. The balding Groom beamed at his King, but his smile faded as he took in Ruenen's slumped posture.

"Another rough day, I take it?"

Ruenen nodded.

"I shall have a bath prepared at once, Sire."

Mayestral gestured to a servant waiting at the door. He disappeared in a flash as Mayestral ducked into the wardrobe, hung up the cloak, and pulled out a silk, green robe.

"All well in the South, my King?" he asked, putting on a bright tone for the sake of his sovereign.

King. Ruenen was still getting used to the title. The word seemed to curdle the more he heard it. It didn't suit him, not when his hands yearned for his lute. Nothing could have soothed him more in Marai's absence than long hours playing music. He could get lost there, share his sorrows and fears through notes and lyrics that he dared not speak to others.

But alas, like Marai, music was lost to him right now.

Ruenen collapsed into an armchair and yanked off his smelly boots. "As well as can be expected."

Mayestal's face fell. "I take it, then, that there's no news of Lady Marai and Lord Keshel?"

Ruenen couldn't muster the words again. The same question, and the same answer. He closed his eyes.

Mayestral got the message. The Groom said with false optimism, "I'm sure they'll turn up soon, Your Grace. Perhaps this is all one big misunderstanding."

Doubtful. Nonetheless, Ruenen appreciated the effort.

After his bath, and whilst eating dinner, Ruenen penned a letter to each of the other six rulers on the Continent of Astye. Nine kingdoms, now only eight monarchs. It was Ruenen's first official correspondence with some of these rulers since he'd become King, and what a subpar introduction it was. The letter he copied over and over again, beseeching the kings and emperors to aid him in his search for his two missing countrymen. He begged them, like a starving man would for bread, to respond with even the most insignificant news or details. To the King of Henig, he pleaded to send men to the docks at Cleaving Tides to question the sailors and merchants. He sounded too desperate and juvenile, but Ruenen didn't care. He *was* desperate.

The seventh ruler on Astye, Queen Nieve of Grelta, was still currently housed in the Kellesaran castle. An integral part of Nevandia's win over Tacorn, Nieve remained Ruenen's guest. She allowed her own soldiers to patrol and search with Nevandian troops. Her forces held control of the fortress at Dul Tanen in Tacorn, King Rayghast's castle. Nieve was a powerful ally, and had taken a strong liking to both Ruenen and Marai.

He should have joined Nieve for dinner that evening. That would have been the hospitable, kingly, thing to do. *Another thing to feel guilty about.*

Ruenen set down his quill once the sixth and final letter was inked, and its wax had cooled.

"Please send out these letters immediately," he said, handing the pile to Mayestral.

"Is there anything else I can do for you, Your Grace?"

"No, thank you. I'm off to bed."

"Sleep well, Your Grace. Ring if you need anything," Mayestral said with a gentle smile, crinkling his brown eyes.

The tallow candle on Ruenen's desk had nearly burned down to the wick. He blew it out as Mayestral exited, and climbed into his overly-large bed.

Lying there, in the dark quiet of night, was when he missed Marai the most. The bed was too vast, night too silent, memories too vivid that merely recalling the effervescent scent of her, the wildness of her eyes and hair, made him ache with a pain so severe it threatened to tear him apart. He squeezed his eyelids closed so tight that he gave himself a headache.

Only five days without her, and he already missed her more than he could bear.

What would happen as the number of days doubled and tripled? What would happen if he never found her?

Ruenen pounded a fist onto his mattress.

No. I'll find her. If I have to search this entire continent. If I have to sail across the ocean.

I will find you, Marai.

The council chamber was full to the brim with Witenagemot and guards, already in heated discussion when Ruenen entered. Raife stood alone to the side in newly gleaming armor. Thora must have polished off the grime when he'd returned last night. He still received wary, disgruntled, even disgusted looks from members of the Witan and the other guards. As the only fae in the room, he stood out amongst the King's Guard, but Raife remained poised at all times. He never flinched at the looks some councilmen shot him. Ruenen could only imagine how difficult it must have been for Raife to be without Marai, Keshel, and Aresti, let alone his brother, Leif, and recently departed Kadiatu.

Lord Koven Holfast, Steward of the Throne and highest ranking official in Nevandia, came to Ruenen's side. The man looked tired. Ruenen bet Holfast slept as restlessly as he did, and he swore he counted at least two new wrinkles on the Steward's face.

"Good morning, Your Grace. I'm pleased to see you. We weren't sure you would make it today," he said. Ruenen could hear the held-back scolding. Holfast had been running the country for years as Steward, and kept Ruenen busy with tasks and a royal education. He didn't want Ruenen riding through the countryside looking for Marai and Keshel. It wasn't "kingly," he said.

"What's on the agenda today?" Ruenen asked, taking a seat on his bone and gold throne with a stifled groan. His legs and lower back still hurt from riding.

The black-robed Witan members sat around the long table in the center of the room. Ruenen was adjusting to seeing two former Tacornian councilmen at the table. Wizened Lord Cronhold had immediately pleaded for leniency after Rayghast's defeat, and cunning Lord Wattling exposed the depths of Tacorn's wealth. They'd both pledged their loyalty to Nevandia, claiming they wanted peace between the two countries.

Ruenen had been reluctant to forgive them so easily. The two lords had buoyed Rayghast's cruelty for years. They'd *let* him torture innocent people.

"We must unite Nevandia and Tacorn," Lord Vorae had said. He was a heavy-set, bald man with an impressively groomed beard, who always seemed to be in the grumpiest of moods. "The best way forward is to bring their old council members onto the Witenagemot. Give them some leniency, show them that we respect their knowledge. It will make the transition easier for both countries. We don't have the numbers to position ourselves across Tacornian lands. We must be willing to make some sacrifices, and focus our attention on bettering Nevandia."

Ruenen had relented then. Thus far, both Cronhold and Wattling had been rather helpful in providing insight into Tacornian politics, customs, and finances, although Cronhold was so decrepit that Ruenen doubted the man would last the year.

Holfast interlaced his thin fingers upon the table, ready to begin the litany of duties he'd set aside for Ruenen. "We must discuss the land negotiations with Ain and Beniel. Several trades-worker guilds are petitioning to take over Tacornian contracts. But first, we need to decide what to do with Queen Rhia and Princess Eriu."

"They're still here?" Ruenen asked. He'd thought Rayghast's widow and her younger sister had been sent back to their home country of Varana days ago.

"We've been waiting for you, Your Grace," Lord Corian said, eyes shifting between the other Witan members, "but you've been . . . distracted."

Vorae and Fenir exchanged a glance. Another member of the Witan nodded in agreement. They believed the search for Marai and Keshel was unnecessary. A hindrance. To the Witan, Marai and Keshel were insignificant compared to Nevandia as a whole.

"Lady Marai and Lord Keshel are valuable members of this Witan; ones I instated, myself. Kidnapped members of my Witanagemot should be a top priority for all of us," said Ruenen with a warning edge, heat traveling up his spine. "Would you want me to stop searching for *you*, Lord Corian, if you should be taken prisoner?"

Corian's expression soured, but he didn't dare respond.

Ruenen continued. "If it wasn't for Marai and Keshel, none of us would be alive. Their fae magic *saved* this country, don't forget."

"None of us have forgotten, Your Grace," Holfast said, leaping in before Corian could reply. Ever the peacemaker, Holfast settled the room with a stern look. "We're all hopeful for their safe return, and continue to support your efforts in finding them."

"We should keep the, uh, Varanese princess here," Cronhold said, as if he hadn't heard the last few moments of conversation. "Use her as leverage over Emperor Suli."

Jittery Lord Fenir nodded. "That would teach Varana to think twice before standing against Nevandia in the future."

"Princess Eriu is a child, not a hostage," snapped Ruenen, and Fenir sunk back in his seat. "I won't utilize Rayghast's tactics of terror. We shall return the princess back to Varana with a full escort as a show of good faith."

"A noble thought, Your Grace, but what about Queen Rhia?" asked Vorae, a challenge in his voice and in the rise of his eyebrows. "Should we hand Rayghast's widow over to someone who was once our enemy, too?"

Ruenen scowled and twisted his mouth in a swallowed retort. He truthfully didn't know what to do with Rhia. She'd gone ballistic in the castle halls, terrified of the fae and werewolves wandering around, and since then, she'd been locked in a cell in the dungeon. Although Rhia wasn't a physical threat, she *was* still Queen of Tacorn. If released, citizens could rally behind her. But sending her back to Varana with her younger sister might also provide Emperor Suli with a claim to Tacorn's lands and throne.

Ruenen's headache strengthened across his forehead and behind his eye sockets. "I've made no decision on Queen Rhia yet. Let's settle this matter another day. What's next on the agenda?"

After tireless discussions about Ain, Beniel, Tacorn lands, and Nevandian guilds, Ruenen dismissed the Witan, and hurried outdoors before Holfast could shove more work at him. Raife, in his clanking armor, caught up to him as they turned right once out of the courtyard, approaching the dirt training ring. Ruenen shed his crown, jacket, and vest on a nearby bench, and untucked his shirt.

I need to beat something. No music could comfort him in this moment.

He grabbed hold of a broadsword and held it out, silently requesting Raife join him in the ring. The faerie male removed his helm and unsheathed his blade.

Ruenen attacked. His blade slammed into Raife's, sending a jarring sensation up his arms. His moves were sloppy, propelled by frustration. Raife blocked and parried, taking the brunt of Ruenen's anger, of his mounting fears and hopelessness. With each attack, Ruenen's strength began to fail. He'd wasted his energy too early; a novice mistake, one that Marai would reprimand him about. Raife disarmed Ruenen easily with a somber expression.

"I should be out there looking," Ruenen said, chest heaving.

"You're doing everything in your power to find them," said Raife.

"Not enough. I don't have time to search, but I don't have time to sit in endless meetings, either. As King, I have everything I could want, except the *freedom* to do what I want."

Raife approached, his face lined with worry. "You're only one man. This isn't your burden to bear alone. Our resources are limited right now, but Aresti and Nosficio are out there. Perhaps they'll learn something. It's only been a few days. We must keep our faith that Marai and Keshel will return to us."

"I'm afraid I'm beginning to run low on faith these days."

"I won't give up," Raife said. "I won't lose any more of us. I'll do what must be done."

He'd lost his brother, and a younger sister in Kadiatu, and yet somehow, Raife managed to wake up each day and fight for a future. If he could keep going without them, then Ruenen couldn't be weak. He couldn't lose faith. He had to keep fighting. For Marai.

Ruenen sighed. "I should go back inside and work, but Lirr's Bones, I can't concentrate. I'm not the king the Witan wanted for Nevandia."

"Maybe not, but you're the king the *people* need and love. That matters much more."

Only around others did Raife treat Ruenen as his King. In private, Raife spoke to him candidly, as a friend. Ruenen and Raife shared a smile, but they quickly dropped their camaraderie as a new figure emerged into the ring.

With her blazing red hair, silver crown, and pristine white dress, Queen Nieve looked immensely out of place on the dusty training grounds. Three silver Greltan guards trailed behind her. Hips swishing with each step, Nieve carried a letter in her bejeweled hand.

Raife bowed, and Ruenen took the Queen's pale hand in his own and kissed it.

"Your Grace, ready for a sparring match?" he asked with a cockeyed grin.

Nieve's blue eyes flashed, a smile spread slowly across her lips. The Queen of Grelta loved to play. "And ruin my gown? Not today, King Ruenen. Perhaps another time."

Ruenen winked. "I'll hold you to it."

Flirting with Nieve was easy, meaningless, and distracting. She could read him like a book—she knew he meant nothing by it.

"To what do I owe the pleasure of your company, Queen Nieve?"

"Please, dear, call me Nieve. We're allies now. Friends," she said. Her face fell as she tapped the letter with her finger. "I regret to say, however, that I must take my leave of you and your beautiful country. I received news that my husband has taken ill and is bedridden. I must return home at once to be at his side. I've been away long enough."

Ruenen remembered the Greltan King's frailty. King Maes had some kind of degenerative illness, one that limited his mobility and made it difficult for him to speak, which was why Nieve ran the country in his stead. She'd been the face of Grelta for years.

"I'm tremendously sorry to hear that King Maes is unwell," Ruenen said. "Please give him my best regards, and wish him a speedy recovery."

Nieve gave Ruenen a hard stare. "I'm always astounded by your sincerity, Ruenen. You haven't yet been tainted by wealth and power. It's refreshing."

"I don't intend to be infected by such desires. My only aim is to do the best I can for my people and country."

Nieve kissed Ruenen on the cheek, taking him by surprise. He couldn't help but blush; she was a beautiful woman and smelled of heady floral perfume. "Make sure you do just that. You're inspiring change throughout Astye. Other rulers are looking now to Nevandia to see what you do. I admire your youthful audacity, and I think you'll be an excellent influence on those too stuck in the mud to change."

"Thank you," Ruenen said. Her words brought a volcano of emotions to the surface. That was what Ruenen *wanted* to do for Astye, but he was currently floundering in the loss of Marai.

"Sweet, dear lad, all will be well. I look forward to the havoc you will reap on the status quo." Nieve smiled devilishly for a moment before her countenance shifted, dropping the flirtatious act. "Will you let me know once Lady Marai and Lord Keshel return?"

"I'll send word immediately."

"I shall leave a few regiments of my soldiers here to help maintain the peace. Your army is not yet ready to take on that full burden."

"That's far too generous of you, Your Grace, when you've already done so much for Nevandia already."

"*Nieve*," she urged again. "If you see that vampire, though, tell him he owes me a debt."

Nosficio and Nieve had a complicated relationship. Ruenen wasn't sure it was love, but there was certainly a deep connection there, one that kept driving the queen and vampire back together despite troubled events of the past.

"I'll do my best, Nieve," Ruenen replied with a smile.

"Very good." Nieve patted his cheek, then turned on her heel, gliding back towards the castle. Over her shoulder she shouted, "And that faerie woman . . . Aresti? She can come visit Grelta whenever she wants."

Raife chuckled as Nieve and her guards disappeared around the corner. "Perhaps the Queen is biting off more than she can chew?"

"I think she's very capable of handling things herself," mused Ruenen.

He was glad that, even in the midst of this chaos and uncertainty, he had a friend in Queen Nieve of Grelta.

Raife held out Ruenen's sword. "Another round?"

Ruenen took the blade and began again, this time hearing Marai's voice in his head, instructing him, guiding him, telling him to focus.

He disarmed Raife in a few moves.

"You're getting better," his freckle-faced friend said. "Marai would be impressed."

She would, but Ruenen knew that she'd also have dozens of adjustments for him to make. He needed that person in his life. The one who strived for him to be better.

Marai, where are you?

CHAPTER 3

MARAI

Her ears picked up the recognizable sounds of a busy port: chattering voices, gulls cawing, sloshing water, the loading and unloading of heavy equipment and goods. The ship must have docked in Qasnal, the first and only port along the route to Andara.

Marai had been in the Yehzigi port city before, onboard *The Nightmare*, back in her days as a pirate. She'd stolen a magical artifact there for Slate—a dented chalice, from the Sultan, no less. Marai had barely made it back to the ship before getting caught. She was a wanted woman in Yehzig. If the authorities in town knew she was there, she'd instantly be arrested and hanged.

The black worm himself climbed down into the hull of the ship carrying bowls of slop, the same meager, nauseating food he'd been giving Marai and Keshel the past four days. Slate dropped the bowls of congealed bread and mashed peas unceremoniously next to Marai and Keshel with a sneer, most of the food spilling onto the floor. He shoved a bucket of warm water into their reach. Keshel sniffed his slop, lips curling into a disgusted grimace, but Marai downed her bowl in a few bites. She'd learned never to pass up food, no matter how mushy and revolting.

She needed to keep her strength up in order to escape.

"Koda says you're allowed upstairs for air on deck," Slate announced, sounding both bored and bitter. "I told him it was a bad idea, but he seems to think you docile enough." Slate dangled a set of wrought-iron keys in front of Marai's face. "I get the pleasure of taking the bitch for a walk."

Marai waited, watching as Slate unlocked her chains from the wall.

Grab him. Kill him.

But five more sailors appeared on the stairs. Slate knew what she'd intended to do, he knew her mind. He jeered at her furious expression, then stepped back quickly, holding onto the length of her chains. A leash. Another sailor unlocked Keshel, who put up no fuss.

Marai got slowly to her feet. Her body ached as the weight of the chains around her wrists, neck, and ankles pulled her downward. She hadn't moved in a week, except to relieve herself in a bucket hidden behind a support beam. Her swollen knee throbbed, making her limp. She'd already shoved her kneecap back into place days ago, and had wrapped it with a strip of fabric from her gown. Weak legs trembled with each laborious step she took up the stairs, but finally, she caught her first whiff of glorious, salty, humid air. She sucked in a deep breath, filling her lungs to the brim. Ocean wind whipped hair into her face and stung her eyes as seagulls laughed and swooped overhead. The afternoon sun was bright and inviting, warming her pale skin and making Marai squint.

Slate kicked the back of her legs, pushing her further onto the deck so Keshel and the other sailors could get up the stairs. As she trudged, dragging her bare feet across the wooden planks, she searched for weapons. The sailors didn't carry swords on their hips the way Slate's crew used to. Some had utility knives, but Slate yanked Marai away from them before she could reach out a finger.

"Don't even think about it," he snapped. "Be an obedient dog and keep walking."

Marai snarled like the beast he claimed she was. "I will enjoy killing you."

Slate pulled on her chains harder in response, causing Marai to stumble and slam into the deck. Her already injured knee blazed in fiery pain. She caught a glimpse of Keshel behind her, a glower etched deep across his face. He didn't want her antagonizing Slate, and he didn't like seeing her hurt and abused.

She stood again, holding her shoulders back. *Never show your weakness. Don't let him win.*

Hobbling along behind Slate, Marai took in details of the vessel that had become her prison. *The Arcane Wind* was clean and sturdy, powerful, relatively new; one of the largest ships Marai had seen. The sails were tan, recently mended. No splintering wood. No ripped rigging. No chipped paint. In order to sail the treacherous waters to Andara, a ship needed to be substantial in order to survive. This one just might make it.

The crew was a mixture of young novices and old sea-dogs, but none of the men were quite as gruesome as Slate's gang. They smelled only slightly pungent, and none seemed inebriated. They ignored Marai and Keshel as they passed, going about their work diligently. There was order on this vessel. Organization.

Koda was nowhere to be seen.

"How long are we docking here?" Marai asked Slate, hungrily surveying the Qasnal port.

Grand Harbor was circular, with a mouth-like opening for boats to pass through. A towering lighthouse stood on the far right edge, gazing out to the Eastern Ocean. On the left side, a pentagonal stone garrison sat, armed with patrolling soldiers on its ramparts.

"Just for the night to resupply and rest up for the journey," Slate said.

One night. This was the last port, the only land before endless days at sea to Andara. She had to find a way off the ship tonight. Since she couldn't access magic, Marai would need to escape the old-fashioned way: stealth and thievery.

But she'd need to remain inconspicuous in order to get that chance to escape. She regarded the harbor with feigned curiosity. Marai spotted the obelisk at the center of the city of Qasnal which demarcated one of the Sultan's royal palaces. A massive angular temple sat on a hill, surrounded by palm trees. Across the Dedeen Strait, visible from Grand Harbor, was Yehzig's smaller island of Bursgami.

If she could figure out which boats were heading back to Astye . . .

After two laps around the deck, Marai allowed Slate to bring her downstairs. She slouched, faking exhaustion, and Slate came closer, pulling her towards the wall. As he passed, Marai's hand darted towards his pocket where the jangling keys were hidden.

However, the chains on her wrists were loud and bulky, and there was nothing sleight about her sleight-of-hand. Slate felt her touch before she barely caught the keyring on her finger.

He backhanded her across the face. Keshel shouted as Marai crashed into the wall and slid down.

QUEEN OF THE SHADOW MENAGERIE

"Try that again, and I'll make sure all you drink for the rest of this journey is piss," Slate said. He locked her back up, then pulled out a knife, placing it under her left pinky. "You think you're so clever, sitting there ruminating on ways to outsmart me. You forget that I *know you*, Marai. I know your mind. I know your body—"

Marai spit in his face.

Slate bared his teeth, letting the saliva drip down his mutilated cheek. "I'll take a finger every time you fight back."

"That's enough, sailor," came Koda's stern, authoritative voice from the stairs. Marai hadn't seen him in two days. His expression was serious; she'd never seen him as anything but casual before.

Slate glared as Koda approached. "Are you going to tolerate her insubordination? She's trying to escape. Such behavior would be punished on *my* ship—"

"We're not on your ship, and you are not the captain," said Koda, coming to Slate's side. They were about the same height, and Marai enjoyed watching the power-struggle between the two.

"Neither are you," Slate bit back. "You're a paid lackey, just like me."

Koda bristled. "You forget your place, *sailor*. I may not be Captain, but as long as I'm onboard, I'm in charge of this ship and this crew. Our employer wants her unharmed. We can't bring him spoiled goods. Any physical harm that befalls either of these prisoners will not only force me to dock your pay, but perhaps I'll need to take a finger from *you*."

A cruel smile curled the corners of Slate's lips. "I'd like to see you try."

In a physical match-up, Marai placed her bets on muscular, agile Slate. He was one of the best swordsmen she'd ever seen. He'd taught her everything she knew about fighting.

Koda lifted one hand. His thumb and middle finger met, ready to snap. "Don't test me. I'll always be faster."

No solitary human could defeat magic on their own. Slate was smart enough to understand that. Marai could see threats and strategies swarming the pirate's brain. Koda, however, didn't seem phased by Slate's aggressive expression. The half-fae male knew he had the upper hand. Slate grumbled under his breath, staring daggers at Koda, but he backed away in defeat.

Koda turned his unusually serious face to Marai. "I must ask you not to fight us anymore. It does you no good."

"I will if you keep *him* away from me," she said, chin jutting towards Slate.

Koda glanced back at the glowering ex-captain and nodded. "Fine. Hemming will no longer be in charge of your care. I'll have someone else watch after you, but if you continue this ill behavior, I'll be forced to separate you and Keshel."

Marai didn't want that. At least with Keshel by her side, she knew he was alive and unharmed. Remaining together would make escaping easier. Beyond that, she had company, someone to pass the long hours with. Not that Keshel was particularly garrulous—he'd spent most of the past week in sullen silence, pondering whatever it was he pondered. The secrets of the universe, perhaps.

Koda ordered a sailor named Curly to keep watch down in the hull. Curly was a broad man with a thick head of poofy brown hair and hands the size of dinner plates. He kept his brow furrowed, but his face lacked the animosity of Slate's.

Perhaps he might be an easier mark . . .

However, Curly stayed vigilant all through the day they were anchored in Qasnal. He sat on a crate of dry goods and whittled away at a piece of wood, silent as stone. He ignored Marai's requests for more food and water by acting as if he didn't hear her . When night fell, he stood, stretched, then stomped back above deck.

"I have to get that knife from him," Marai whispered to Keshel once the sailor was out of earshot.

Keshel sighed through his nose. "He'll never get close enough for you to try."

Marai scowled at him, at his pessimism. Even if he was right, she resented him for his lack of vigor. "What have you been thinking about all this time?"

"What Koda said the other day . . . about Andara being the ancestral home of the fae."

Anger sparked up Marai's spine, heating her chest. "*That's* been your focus? Not finding a way off this ship?"

"Forgive me if I don't have experience breaking out of prisons," replied Keshel blandly. He reached for the bucket of water and took a long chug.

With a huff, Marai leaned back against the wall. He had a point. "And what are your thoughts on Koda's statement?"

QUEEN OF THE SHADOW MENAGERIE

"It goes against everything I read in my histories. Fae accounts made it seem as if our people were always on Astye, since Lirr created them. If what Koda says is true, the ancient fae weren't as ancient as we suspected. It means that Andara's records go back even farther than Astye's."

Marai recognized the glint in his eyes. Keshel swore by his beloved books. They were practically religious texts to him.

"Too bad you never got the chance to visit the Nine Kingdoms Library in Kaishiki," she said offhandedly. "They might have had more accurate manuscripts hidden away somewhere."

"Yes, if only our kidnappers had been more considerate in their timing," said Keshel with a slight smile. After a long moment, he said, "Tell me about it. The library."

Marai's anger dissolved, grateful for the distraction. "I've only seen inside it once." But for someone who rarely picked up a book, Marai had been amazed. "Ten floors of books and manuscripts. Rows and rows, organized by author and topic, supposedly from the earliest days of the written language. The highest ceiling I've ever seen, painted blue like the summer sky. Balconies on every floor, looking down into the main room full of tables and armchairs, surrounding fireplaces."

Keshel's face took on a dreamy look. "Sounds marvelous."

"There are people whose only job is to organize and catalog tomes and volumes. Historians spend days slumped over piles of ancient manuscripts, scribbling down their notes, so they can write their *own* books."

"People are paid to do that?" Keshel's eyes opened wide as Marai nodded. "I might faint."

Marai laughed, bringing a smile to Keshel's pale face.

But as quickly as his joy came, it vanished. He lifted his arms, gazing at his shackled wrists. "Now, I may never see it. Too bad, indeed."

"Don't think like that. We'll get out of this," Marai stated firmly.

"And go home to what? A country that's terrified of our kind? That thinks of us as monsters? Lesser beings?"

"We were making progress. Think of the Treaty."

"Now that Nevandia's won the war, they're focusing on themselves. On re-building. Not the Treaty. It will take decades to heal the fissures between humans and magical folk."

"It's worth the effort, Keshel. We'll still deal with prejudice, but maybe future generations of magical folk won't. Besides, Ruen is fighting for us. If we put in the hard work now, there will be a better future for our . . . children."

Future generations. Children. The ones Thora and Raife would undoubtedly have one day. Would Marai ever have her own? Even if she escaped from Koda and the ship, her future was so uncertain. Would she become Ruenen's mistress? Bearing his bastard children while he married another woman? She cringed at the thought. Marai didn't know if she even *wanted* children. She wasn't maternal. She'd barely interacted with a child before. *What example could I set for them? That it's acceptable to become a killer? How can I be a mother when I have so much blood on my hands?*

But then she thought of a little boy with Ruenen's dimpled smile, and something about the image tugged at her heartstrings.

Keshel stared at her, as if he could read where her thoughts had gone. "What is it about King Ruenen that keeps him constantly on your mind?" His posture grew stiff. "I'm surprised that you trust him so willingly."

"Hasn't he proven himself a good man? An ally of our people?"

"It's more than that, Marai," Keshel said. "You love him. I suppose I'm merely wondering why."

The personal question brought heat to her face. Marai bit the inside of her cheek. She didn't want to talk about her feelings for Ruenen, especially since Keshel was only asking because of *his* feelings for *her*. Thora had once said Keshel was jealous of Ruenen, of Marai's relationship with him. Clearly, that jealousy hadn't disappeared.

Keshel seemed to piece together that Marai wouldn't answer that question. "We've sacrificed so much. Kadiatu and Leif . . . look where it got us. Imprisoned on a ship, setting sail to a country we know nothing about. That for all we know may be *worse* than Astye." Grief swept over Keshel's face. "I think about them constantly. I have nothing better to do, nothing to take my mind off them. I replay

QUEEN OF THE SHADOW MENAGERIE   35

those moments . . . when the earth swallowed Kadi, and that blade pierced Leif's heart."

Anguish tore through Marai at the memories. She'd never forget the sound of Kadiatu's pleading. Her scream as earth engulfed her. That one small hand reaching out for Marai to save her. The fire fading from Leif's emerald eyes as he'd nobly sacrificed himself for Thora and a few wounded humans.

"I failed them," Keshel said, his voice growing rough as he hung his head. "Their parents entrusted *me* to keep them safe, and instead, I watched them die."

"Then I must take half the blame, as well, because *I* was the one who encouraged them to leave the cave. I knowingly put them in harm's way. I couldn't save them. For all the power I supposedly have, I failed to protect them."

Their deaths would haunt her forever. *Two more for the tally, Butcher,* she thought bitterly.

"If we'd stayed in that cave . . . who do you think we'd be?" Keshel asked.

Marai pondered this question, picking at her ragged fingernails. "Mere shadows of the people we *could* become."

Keshel released a hum of agreement. "Do you think Thora and Raife would have eventually admitted their feelings to each other?"

"You *knew*?"

"Of course I knew. I'm not blind. In fact, I consider myself highly observant," Keshel said with a chuckle. "They weren't that good at keeping it a secret."

Marai snorted. "No, they weren't. I don't think they would have confessed how they felt if they'd stayed. Thora needed to feel safe. I doubt she ever would have felt safe enough in the Badlands to allow her heart to open fully, and Raife would never have put that pressure on her."

Keshel looked at Marai, unblinking. "I'm glad they found their happiness together. In the end."

Marai turned away from his intense stare, her cheeks heating again as she read everything he thought in his dark eyes. What Keshel felt for her, Marai didn't truly understand. Was it love? Attraction? Intrigue? Marai could never return those feelings, and she couldn't encourage them, either.

Keshel would always be her family, an older brother. Possibly even a friend. But he wasn't Ruenen, and Keshel knew that.

Curly returned, bringing with him the scent of grilled, peppered meat and ale from his dinner in the Qasnal port. The thought of spiced kebabs and herbed rice made Marai's mouth water.

"We'll make you a deal, Curly," Keshel said, trying his negotiating tactic again. "If you let us out of these chains, we'll take you back to Nevandia. We're members of King Ruenen's Witenagemot, and he will reward you handsomely for saving us. Anything you want, he'll give you. Maybe even a title. Would you want to be *Lord* Curly?"

The not-Lord Curly didn't glance at Keshel. The sizable sailor fell asleep after a while, his head tilting back against the support beam, letting out a grumbling snore. Koda's boss had somehow hired a loyal crew, or the mysterious employer was wealthier than a king.

Marai edged as close to Curly as her chains would allow; her toe barely reached the hem of his pants. *No use.* Unless the man toppled from the crate and landed directly in front of her, she'd never get the knife or the keys.

"Face it, Marai, we're doomed to ride this out," Keshel said gloomily. He closed his eyes, shimmying into a comfortable sleeping position. "Perhaps if we're good and quiet, they'll give us better food."

"Doubtful."

The next day, *The Arcane Wind* set sail for Andara, and they lost their last chance for freedom.

Curly never answered their questions or comments. As the days dragged on, Marai and Keshel had taken to pretending he wasn't there. They shared stories of their childhood; when Leif got stung by a scorpion and bawled like a baby until Thora healed him. The first time eight-year-old Kadiatu used her magic, how thorns had sprouted up in Keshel's bed, stabbing him while he wrote in his journal.

"It was as if someone had shoved thirty forks up my rear," Keshel said with a chuckle. "Thora had to heal my wounds in private. We were all utterly mortified by the experience."

"Kadi was much more careful with her magic after that. Remember when I put that dead vulture in Aresti's bed?" Marai was proud of that prank, and the memory of it still made her laugh.

Keshel scowled. "She nearly created a tornado there in the cave, and Raife and I had to physically separate you two."

"We were wild back then."

"Back then?" Keshel repeated. "You're both *still* wild, with tempers to match Laimoen, himself."

The distraction of the past was helpful to Marai in more ways than one. She didn't want Curly to know that her thoughts were always about how best to dispose of him. How to escape. She kept conversation relatively light and unsuspicious, and Curly remained silent, passively doing his job.

Eventually, Koda graced them with his presence again, bringing with him a bundle of fabric and watery mush, which Marai and Keshel gobbled up like it was butter-roasted pheasant.

"It's a forty-day journey 'til we see land again. We've had fair sailing so far while we're in the Eastern Ocean, but once we cross into the Northern Sea, that will change quickly," he told them, leaning against the support beam in that indifferent way. His bright eyes locked on Marai, swirling with magic. "Curly says you've been decently behaved. You have experience on a ship, correct?"

"Experience burning one down, you mean?" She grinned at the memory of *The Nightmare* bursting into flame.

Koda wasn't amused. "*Working* one."

"You already know I was on Slate's crew."

Koda reached out a hand and Curly placed the wrought-iron keys into his palm. "I'm going to bring you both upstairs, and you're going to be put to work. Listen to everything Curly or Captain Brelioc tells you to do. I'll be watching. Work hard, and you can have dinner, too."

Marai and Keshel hadn't had more than one bowl of slop a day for at least two weeks. They'd been fed only enough to keep them alive. Merely the word *dinner* sent Marai's stomach growling.

"We understand," Keshel said before Marai could reply negatively.

Koda unlocked their chains as Curly hovered behind him, eyes narrowed, watching for signs of disobedience, but unless Marai could get a weapon, there was nothing she could do against Koda's magic or the collar.

"You'll be wanting a change of clothes," Koda said, handing Marai the bundle of cloth. "Can't be distracting my men while you're wearing that slip of a dress."

Marai ducked behind a support beam and stack of crates to change out of her ruined gown. It was nothing but rags now. She tugged on a billowy shirt and too-loose pants that she tied up with a strip of rope around her hips.

Curly had Marai and Keshel swab the deck, which was particularly nasty since the cook had recently gutted some fish, and made even more difficult with their ankles and wrists manacled. It slowed them down, and prevented Marai from maneuvering easily, thanks to her injured knee. They wiped down the sides of the ship, removing caked on dried bird poop. Curly ordered them, in a deep giant-esque voice, to wash Koda and Captain Brelioc's laundry. It was a full day of chores, but she and Keshel were used to such labor. Keshel had been a hard worker in the caves, and Marai had spent three years aboard *The Nightmare.* Neither of them complained as the sun beat down, baking the skin on their backs, and sweat dripped beneath their collars.

At the end of the day, Marai was so exhausted she collapsed against the wall of the hull, glad for sleep. Her knee ached and stomach growled, throat dry and scratchy. As promised, Koda delivered bowls of fish stew. It was a small portion, but the protein filled up Marai's stomach and stopped the pangs.

Koda watched her slurp down the stew like he was studying a foreign object. "How are *you* possibly the last Faerie Queen?"

"You'll need to ask my ancestors that question."

"You're the most unlikely person: a skinny little half-fae murderess. You have no manners, no proper upbringing, no aspirations of leadership."

Marai scowled at the insults. All true, of course, but she wouldn't admit that. "Doesn't change what's in my blood. How did you know about Ruenen?"

Koda's eyebrows rose. "You mean the pretend prince?"

Keshel's head snapped to Marai. He knew nothing about the lie she, Holfast, Vorae, and Fenir had concocted to put Ruenen on the throne.

"Blackmail is a powerful tool," Koda said, smirking. "Find the right person, discover their breaking point, their tongue loosens, and *poof*—the answers are yours."

"Who snitched?" Marai asked, jaw muscles clenching.

"Unlike them, I'm better at keeping secrets." Koda winked. "Speaking of King Ruenen, I expect you to keep behaving, or I'll be forced to send a message to some furious Tacornian lords, letting them know the truth about your King."

Marai tensed. "We're in the middle of the ocean. You can't get messages out to anyone."

"Oh, I have my ways." He jauntily climbed back above.

The minute Koda was out of earshot, Keshel turned to Marai. "What—"

"Not now." Marai's mind reeled. Who had Koda blackmailed in Nevandia? There were only four possibilities, other than herself. Ruenen would die before revealing the truth, and for better or worse, Marai trusted Holfast to put Nevandia's future first. That left Vorae and Fenir, and of the two lords, Fenir was clearly the weaker and most jumpy. If Marai had to place a bet, she'd put her money on him being the snitch.

Would Fenir tell others? Would Ruenen be overthrown in Marai's absence?

This knowledge was now out there in the world. Anyone could discover the truth, and Ruenen would be killed because of it. Koda used this as a threat over Marai's head, and he must have some magical way to pass information along. He could unveil the truth at any time.

I need to escape.

Things changed once they entered the Northern Sea.

Skies darkened, and the sun disappeared behind ominous clouds. Rough, indigo waves slapped against the side of *The Arcane Wind*. The ship listed and jolted, making it nearly impossible to stay upright for long. Harsh wind tore through the sails. Captain Brelioc, a bearded, pox-marked man, forced Marai to climb the rigging and dangle dangerously to patch the tears. It was the only time they unshackled her ankles, but she learned to navigate climbing with the ones around her wrists. A rope secured her to the mast, so that if she ever did fall, she wouldn't go overboard.

Keshel, however, wasn't quite as useful; he spent most days turning sickly green and vomiting over the railings.

Koda and Slate had clearly warned the crew to be wary of Marai. No one came close enough to her with weapons or keys, frustrating her immensely, but at least Slate was no longer loitering nearby. He did shoot her nasty glares from across the deck, and muttered insults whenever he passed by, but the crew was focused on manning the ship, vigilant at all hours. Surviving the journey required every person to do their job right.

In the evenings, Keshel ticked off another day on the hatch-marked calendar that he'd scratched into the wooden hull wall. Eighteen days. Twenty-two. Twenty-nine.

Marai had never sailed this far out to sea before. Slate and *The Nightmare* had once traveled to Andara without her, but when she was with him, he'd preferred to loot in the Southern Baurean Sea. The ex-captain now skulked around *The Arcane Wind*, uneasy, flinching at powerful waves. White-knuckled, he'd grip the railings whenever the ship would dive from the crest. He'd never been a nervous sailor before, at least to Marai's reckoning . . .

Then the first storm hit.

Marai had never experienced such a gale, such violence and strength of the ocean. The towering, rolling waves looked like mountains, reminding Marai of the dark, earthen one that had devoured Kadiatu. Each gigantic undulation of the sea sent the ship crashing downwards. Water swelled over the sides of the ship, sweeping sailors off their feet. The dark sky churned with mauve and black clouds. Rain pelted her face, drenching her to the bone. Thunder boomed. Lightning that wasn't Marai's own cracked across the sky.

Captain Brelioc bellowed out orders, standing at the helm, holding to the wheel tightly. Koda was tucked safely inside his cabin—he wasn't a sailor and apparently far too important, despite the fact that his fae magic could have assisted.

The sea surged over the side of the ship. One of the crew was washed overboard—there was no chance to save him. Marai tied a length of rope around her waist, the other end attached to a metal loop on the railing, to prevent herself from meeting the same fate.

Any moment, a mast could crack. The Northern Sea battered the ship with such force, Marai wondered if it might split in two.

Keshel slammed hard onto the deck as a wave swept his feet out from under him.

"Send Keshel back downstairs," Marai begged to Curly, who was pulling on a rope to steady the sails. "Please, he'll be killed!"

Curly nodded absent-mindedly, then returned his full attention to the sails.

Marai called to Keshel over the howling wind and lashing rain. "Go down!" She gestured to the stairwell.

Keshel shouted something back, but Marai couldn't hear him. He turned and climbed carefully down the stairs into the hull, safe for now. Marai then returned her focus to Curly. His muscular arms bulged as he wrangled the unruly ropes.

Distracted.

Marai stumbled as the ship lurched, knocking into him. Her slender fingers reached into his pants pocket and swiftly pulled out the keys.

Curly didn't notice.

Marai's heart pounded, sensing freedom at her fingertips.

From the other end of the ship, however, silver eyes locked on hers.

Koda.

She ducked beneath the stairs of the main deck. The collar had to come off. If Koda caught her, she could do nothing with it subduing her magic. Her hands trembled as she tried to find the right key to unlock the collar. *There must be a trick to get it off.* A magnet. An inner chamber. Something to do with the archaic symbol.

A stormy sea of panic roiled inside her. This was her chance to escape. She had to get the collar off.

Desperately, she tried the keys again, but nothing worked. She roared into the raging wind as fury ripped through her. She tried to call her lightning, but the collar sparked painfully against her skin.

Koda's head appeared under the stairs, wet black hair plastered to his face.

"I thought you'd try something like this," he said, yanking the keys away from Marai. "No key can remove this collar. Only my employer can take it off, and I don't think he'll be doing that, especially with your temper. Once it's on, it's on for good. Now get downstairs like a good girl."

Marai bared her teeth as the ship listed. She shoved against him, knocking Koda onto his rear. With a flick of his fingers, Koda had Marai immobilized, frozen by his strange magic.

She couldn't blink. Couldn't breathe. The air grew incredibly cold, as it had the last time he'd used his power on her. Rain turned to sleet against her face. Marai knelt, still as a sculpture, unable to stop Koda from calling over a few sailors and dragging her across the deck by her arm, like a little girl's rag doll. They hurled her down the stairs, and Marai crashed onto the floor, pain blazing up and down her side.

"Chain her up," Koda commanded below and tossed the keys to someone Marai couldn't see. Koda's magic released its hold on her and she breathed again. Someone pulled her backwards and locked her into the chains next to Keshel.

Slate stepped back from her. His blue eyes were wide, hair and clothes disheveled; his patchy skin was the color of whey.

"What's wrong with you?" Marai asked, unable to help herself. "Sea sick?"

"Nothing's wrong with me. I've been instructed by that bastard Koda to guard you," he said, but something about the twitch of his shoulders, the shakiness of his voice, screamed false to Marai.

He's afraid.

Slate ran his hands through his ratty locks, then cringed as the ship plummeted from the top of a wave. He clung to the support beam to keep from being tossed about the hull. Marai's heart dropped into her stomach as the ship smashed into the water again. Keshel groaned into a bucket. Water flooded down the stairs.

The ex-captain slid down the beam and sat, glaring at the slippery floor. *Why is Slate so afraid of the storm?*

Marai remembered a story he'd told her ages ago about the hurricane that ravaged his home as a boy. He'd lived in a fishing village off the Astyean coast. He'd lost everything that day, including his family, when the hurricane hit. The event had propelled him towards his life of piracy. He'd claimed that he wanted to conquer the ocean that had destroyed his life.

Now that she thought of it, Marai couldn't remember seeing Slate on deck of *The Nightmare* during a storm. He must've hid in his cabin until the weather calmed each time. All those years together . . . how had she never noticed before? Of course, none of the storms in the Baurean Sea were like this one.

For a long time, Marai had been afraid of *him*. Slate Hemming had been her hurricane.

But not anymore.

Slate was reduced to nothing more than a trembling leaf in the breeze. For all his bravado, all his cruelty, he'd never grown past that little boy in the storm.

The ship listed. Waves crashed against the side, unrelenting. Thunder roared.

The Arcane Wind might not make it to Andara. Marai and Keshel could drown in the perilous waters. Koda and the crew acted as if this was routine, as if they'd done this dozens of times before. Maybe they had.

In her days as a pirate, Marai once thought her death might come at sea. Then, as the Lady Butcher, that it might greet her at the edge of a blade.

She rubbed a hand across the metal of the collar, fingertips tracing the etched symbol, thinking about the man who created it. The man awaiting her at the end of the journey.

But now . . . Marai guessed her death would come on Andara, one way or another.

CHAPTER 4

CAVAR

Fog hung low, veiling the wooden planks of the dock in a thick blanket, a natural repellent to foreigners who decided to come snooping.

Andara did not welcome visitors.

Cavar stood on the lip of the dock, lured there in the dark hours of morning by a call from across the sea. Waiting. Watching.

He wasn't alone. Franulovic had joined him. He and the harbormaster hung back near the barrier. Small fishing boats were docked at the far end of the harbor, their owners already returned from their morning runs. Cavar had watched the fishermen unload their quarries and drag them into the market. No ships were currently at anchor. The season for trade amongst the other Andaran port cities was only just beginning. Crews had the winter off.

But someone was coming.

Her magic vibrated through the earth, sending ripples of power across the water.

The ship was still days away, but Cavar could *feel* her approaching. Weak as she was, even with the collar, the Faerie Queen was powerful. The amulet around his neck heated against the skin beneath his shirt. Black smoke swirled in chaotic circles within the confines of the sleek, black stone that sat inside the elegant bronze bezel setting.

Soon, Cavar said to the amulet, grasping it in his fist. The power inside pulsated, throbbing with its own heartbeat, as if enlivened by the Faerie Queen's impending arrival.

Koda had done well. When he'd sent his first message on the wind months ago about the girl, Cavar had been curious. Now, he was obsessed. He and the magic within his amulet wouldn't have to wait much longer; the winds had been favorable.

Cavar left the docks, flanked by his hulking guard, Franulovic.

"Lovely to see you, Governor," said the harbormaster, clutching his record-book to his chest. He gave Cavar a bootlicking smile.

Cavar passed through the barrier, a thick curtain of mist and fog concealing the city beyond. Only those native to Andara could freely pass in and out. Cavar had designed it that way, but even though it was his creation, the sensation when traveling through felt suffocating, heavy.

Once on the other side, he walked through Bakair's organized, pristine streets of identical stone buildings the color of sand; their conical roofs topped with red clay shingles. A charm of seashells and gull feathers dangled above each doorway, an Andaran superstition, to ward off magic. It was early morning, but Bakair's markets were already bursting with life. Merchants haggled from their stalls, dripping with beaded necklaces and sausage links. The fishermen had sold their fresh catch to merchants, who thrust fish into the faces of passing customers. Red-vested Peace Keepers patrolled the streets, curved blades at their sides, keeping order.

Citizens on the inclined streets quieted, dipping their covered heads in reverent greeting to Cavar as he passed.

"Governor, sir," they said, giving Cavar the same smile as the harbormaster.

He was the most recognizable figure in town. Cavar exuded importance, from his buckled shoes, his clean, manicured fingernails, to his expertly cut graying hair. Not an *unkind* man, but he didn't have time today to stop and chat with the rabble.

His office and townhouse resided in the Central Quarter at the top of the hill, along with other buildings of power and government. They were the only multi-storied structures in Bakair. The bank, the House of Justice, Trade Administration, and several other political offices surrounded his own in the cobbled square, where employees were headed off to work.

Cavar's middle-aged assistant, Tulum, leapt to his feet when his employer entered the office.

"The shareholders have arrived, sir," he whispered, face alert and tense. He took Cavar's floor-length brocade coat and felt hat embellished with pearls. "As well as the Guardians. I've already sat them in your office."

Cavar walked past Tulum's organized desk, noting that the five wooden chairs that normally sat in the waiting room weren't present. He was right on time for their meeting, but those of worth on Bakair were loath to wait for anyone or anything. If a function didn't start early, it was considered late. Any minor inconvenience to a Guardian was deemed the highest insult.

His office was indeed packed with interested parties. Eight chairs weren't enough—several people were standing impatiently, tapping their toes, but everyone leapt to respectful attention when Cavar entered the room. The sight of such crowded disorganization irked him.

"My friends, I'm sorry to have kept you waiting," he said, skirting around them and finding his place at his large desk. Every piece of agarwood furniture was polished to gleaming perfection. The elegant woven rug on the floor had been an expensive purchase from Yehzig. The portraits on the wall of the Andaran landscape were commissioned from the most celebrated artists. On the shelves sat leather-back books, and labeled samples of rocks, crystals, and gemstones.

His "friends" were powerful people in Bakair, and across all of Andara. He knew everyone of worth, because he'd *put* them in those positions.

"*The Arcane Wind* is making excellent time. My assistant Koda assures me that he will be in port within the week," he continued.

A quill on his desk was crooked. Cavar put it back in its place.

"My amulet became rather warm this morning, Governor," said Mistress Blago, a shareholder, whose husband was a high-level politician outside the city in more rural Togir. She was a severe looking woman with a thin face and brown skin. Her wrists were adorned with gold bangles that matched her dangling earrings. The bronze amulet around her neck, secured by a matching chain, was the least flashy accessory she ever wore. "Does that have something to do with the package onboard?"

"That's correct, my dear Mistress. The magic within the amulets is reacting to our prize. The nearer she becomes, the more I expect the magic to respond."

Mistress Blago looked positively appalled. "And should I expect to be scalded by my amulet, Governor? I thought these things were safe."

"My dear Mistress," Cavar soothed with his practiced charm. "Never, in all my many years of wearing it, has my amulet brought me harm. Our prize is a powerful creature. It's only natural that the magic in our amulets should respond to her kind."

"Is it wise to bring a creature of such power here?" asked bald Gamal, Minister of Commerce. His nose was long and pointed, eyes shrewd beneath bushy, slanted eyebrows that made him look constantly furious. "I don't want to deal with another one on the loose."

"Will she be properly contained?" asked Kovacevik.

"Naturally, Ministers, my men will take extra precautions with her, especially within the city limits. Koda assures me that the collar is working as it should. Her magic is thoroughly suppressed. She's as harmless as a butterfly."

Guardian Kovacevik scoffed. "Faeries aren't harmless, especially their queens, and Meallán was the worst of all, if the histories are true."

"Queens can be overpowered," Cavar said with a grin. For hundreds of years, humans on Andara lived in fear of the magical creatures that shared their lands. Thanks to the amulets, humans fought back, gaining control. Cavar stopped fearing magical folk a long time ago. "Human slaves on Astye brought down the royal fae, let's not forget. They didn't have the power we have now. Koda will keep the Faerie Queen secure."

Kovacevik, Gamal, and others nodded their approval.

Cavar's grin widened. "Once we announce her arrival to the public, our pockets won't be deep enough for the windfall headed our way. People across the country will travel far and wide to see the last Queen of the Fae."

He grabbed a small gold bell from his desktop. Three tinkling rings and a woman slithered into the room from a hidden door behind his desk that led upstairs to Cavar's townhome. Chains around her feet clinked and scraped against the floor, ruining the haughty aroma in the room. She had olive skin, dark eyes, and lips the color of dahlias. Across her jawline and forehead were bold, black tattoos in patterns of dots and lines, currently shielded by long, dark hair.

"Innesh, you're in charge of ensuring the new arrivals are situated. Instruct Gunnora and Anja to help you prepare," Cavar ordered imperiously to the woman. "You'll no longer be serving me here in Bakair. You're to attend Guardian Kozina, instead. I'll send Yelich with you back to camp."

"Yes, Governor," said Innesh in a monotone voice. Her face remained blank. A beautiful woman, but hardened and dulled at thirty. She backed out of the hidden door, closing it with a snap behind her.

"That Yehzigi woman is an eyesore," said Mistress Blago with a disdainful look at the door. "She's been around for ages, and has never once smiled politely in anyone's direction. If *my* servant was that aloof, I'd have her whipped. Your guards are far more amiable." Her eyes darted to the doorway where Franulovic stood. Mistress Blago's gaze devoured the guard's muscular arms and thick neck, his imposing stature, and uniformed embroidered red vest and cap. She ran a slow tongue across her lips in approval.

"That's because they're well paid, Mistress," Gamal said with a scoff. "Unlike that woman, who's merely a slave."

"True, true, Minister. Thralls aren't known for their loyalty or jovialness." Cavar stood and smiled once again at the room. "We are the prime of this city, of this great nation, and our business is essential. It reminds our people that we alone can protect them. Nothing, not even faerie magic, can touch us, because we are its masters. We've been granted *power*. And now, my friends, we shall tame the most powerful of all fae. Soon, we shall surpass being mere humans. Soon, we will become immortal *gods*."

That was what the magic inside the stone had promised Cavar on the day he'd found it.

Soon, I'll leave these shores and spread my glory elsewhere.

"Our glory," nudged the stone's cobwebbed voice.

Indeed, Cavar replied.

The Guardians in Cavar's office got to their feet and chanted, "Hail to the power of the amulets. Hail the Guardians."

The onyx stone within Cavar's amulet pulsated, warming against his chest, as the magic inside twisted and swirled, awaiting the Faerie Queen.

CHAPTER 5

MARAI

When Marai was a pirate, a tiny thrill used to kick-start her pulse upon seeing land. After days or weeks at sea, knowing that port, dry land, and civilization were mere hours away gave her a sense of completion. Satisfaction.

But now it was Andara that loomed on the horizon.

It wasn't thrill that quickened her heartbeat. It was apprehension. The uncertainty of what was to come. Of who would greet her at the port, and the potential dangers that lurked there.

Marai and Keshel stared at the shadowed mass of land ahead of them from the bow of the ship. Koda had given them a break from laundry duty once Andara came into view.

"Ready to see your ancestral homeland?" Their captor seemed eager for them to see it, keenly watching their reactions.

From this distance, Andara looked like any other country. Not mysterious. Not magical. Just earth, beaches, trees, and hills. Marai spotted shrouded mountains further inland. A row of massive, fanged teeth, the peaks were rugged and spiked.

The woolen quilt made of mist hugging the shoreline must have been the magical barrier Slate had told Marai about, veiling whatever lay beyond the dock.

"You've explained nothing about how Andara is the fae's homeland," said Keshel.

"You'll learn the truth soon enough." Koda grinned, wind sweeping black hair across his face.

Keshel scowled, and lifted up his manacled wrists. "You've made it quite clear that we're not here for tourism and history lessons."

Koda mimed locking his mouth shut with a key.

The immature gesture and dismissive statement irked Marai. "Is this employer of yours worthy of your devotion? Is his good favor worth kidnapping your own kind?"

Koda's face darkened. "My employer gave me a job when no one else would. Me, a beggared half-fae. He took me under his wing, and for that, I owe him my allegiance."

No matter how kind this employer had been to Koda, it wasn't an excuse to imprison others. Koda was complicit in these atrocities, all for the sake of one person's approval.

"I sent him a message on the wind, letting him know our scheduled arrival date," continued Koda.

"Message on the wind?" Keshel repeated, as if Koda was speaking in riddles.

"I can do more than immobilize," said Koda. The wind spun around him, rustling his hair and clothes. It shimmered, almost visible, smelling of brine. Certainly not a normal wind like Aresti's. "I can send messages—words—to anyone I want on a gust of wind. It's quite useful in communicating across continents. That's how my employer knew of your existence in the first place: I sent him a message about you, and he was immediately interested." Koda settled his magic, and the wind disappeared. "You could send messages this way, too. Well, if you weren't wearing the collars."

No individual faerie had the power to control every element; Marai, herself, could only utilize wind and fire, in addition to whatever magic allowed her to harness lightning. Koda, it seemed, also channeled the power of wind, as well as the magic that allowed him to freeze a person's central nervous system. Marai had grown up believing in set magical rules. There were things faeries could and couldn't do. But she'd learned by now that magic didn't always make sense. Some fae were gifted with something *extra*. She, Keshel, and Koda were proof of that.

A million grievances on her tongue, Marai glared at Koda, but Slate's surly approach drew the half-fae's attention away.

"When do I get paid?" Slate asked him.

Koda pulled Slate aside, speaking in a hushed voice. Whatever Koda said in response, Slate didn't like the answer. His volume rose, and Marai chose to drown him out.

"Any visions of what's to come?" she asked Keshel, even though she knew the answer.

"If only," he said with a disappointed sigh. He'd never gone this long without a vision before. Marai guessed it must have left him feeling as adrift as *The Arcane Wind* in the storm, tossed around, searching for purchase.

Marai scooted farther away from Koda and Slate's heated debate. Keshel followed her lead.

"Once we hit land, we should try to escape." She'd said this for the past forty days, to which Keshel's mouth always twisted in cynicism. If they could get away from Koda, they'd have a fighting chance. They could hide out somewhere, find a blacksmith, and get the collars off. Then Marai could try portaling to Northern Grelta, the closest landmass to Andara. It was a risk—she'd never tried traveling that far via portal, over a large body of water, but she'd do whatever she had to in order to get home to Ruenen.

"You don't get to make demands, sailor," Koda snapped, his argument with Slate reaching a climax. "The Governor won't take kindly to your insubordination. Be careful, or you'll find yourself without a job."

Slate's lip curled into a horrific sneer as Koda turned his back on him and addressed Marai and Keshel.

"Let's get you both back below deck. Hemming, Curly, see to it that our guests are secure in the hull until *The Arcane Wind* pulls into port," said Koda.

Slate's strong hands latched onto Marai's arms.

"Worried you'll be cheated out of your pay?" she asked, giving him a saccharine grin. "You used to do the same thing with your own crew. How does it feel, now that the boot is on the other foot?"

Slate pulled her, jarringly, into his chest. His mouth lingered at her ear as he said, "Perhaps I should take an extra share now? Throw you over a crate and have my way with you."

"You said I was lousy," Marai said, calling his bluff. "After what I did to you and your precious ship, I know you don't want to touch me."

Slate huffed a laugh as he walked her back towards the stairs. "You repulse me, but I think I can stomach one or two thrusts before we make port. Consider it my repayment."

"I doubt your employer, this *Governor*, would be pleased." Marai would give Slate hell if he tried anything, but she knew he wouldn't. Not with the threat of money dangling over his head. He wouldn't risk not getting paid for a few brief minutes with her.

"You think you're so clever," Slate hissed as he chained her to the wall. "You think you're still in control. Well, *this* has been the pleasant part of your imprisonment."

A tingling sensation ran up and down her spine. A distant buzz tickled her inner ear.

Magic.

But not hers.

Keshel's head snapped up, meeting her gaze. He sensed it, too.

The magic didn't belong to Koda, either. Something about it seemed . . . different. Complex. Rich, and heavy, and alluring. Not fae. Marai had a strange suspicion that she'd felt this before. The answer was on the tip of her tongue.

Slate read the concern on her face and smirked. "Rutting around with you isn't nearly as pleasurable as the idea of you rotting away in a cell for eternity. I'll pray to Laimoen that you meet such a fate."

He sauntered up the stairs, whistling.

Marai stewed in silence, glaring at the wooden floorboards.

"How are you able to face him?" Keshel asked after a while. "After what that monster did to you, how can you look at him? Speak to him without falling apart?"

Marai met Keshel's burning gaze. "Because I know my worth. He cannot harm me anymore. That's all in the past."

Keshel stared at her. "It's rather remarkable . . . your resolve. For you to overcome such trauma . . . well, I admire your constant courage, your belief in your own strength. A few weeks ago, when I looked at you, I only saw the rebellious girl from the cave. But not now. Now I see the resilience of a queen."

"I'm not a queen," she said with a grimace, earning a smile from Keshel.

"You are, in every way that matters."

Koda clomped down the stairs into the hull an hour later.

"Ah, can you feel it?" he asked, taking in the tilt of Marai and Keshel's heads and alert postures.

The magic had been growing stronger the closer they got to land. It was now impossible to ignore the sensation.

"That's the barrier," Koda continued. "It spans the entire perimeter of Bakair and its pebbled beaches, protecting Andara from unfriendly, foreign visitors."

Curly, Slate, and the other sailors appeared to unlock Marai and Keshel from the wall. They held onto the lengths of chain, leashes for their pet fae.

Koda leaned in, nearly cheek to cheek with Marai. "I'll be taking you to my employer now. There, you can ask him all those aching questions of yours. Any fuss, and the Governor won't take kindly. I expect you to walk calmly and quietly through the streets. Don't interact with anyone you see. They won't help you, anyways. They're terrified of faeries."

Koda and the others led them upstairs to the gangplank, connecting the bobbing ship with the dock.

If there was one sliver of sunlight in the situation, it was that Slate wasn't allowed to go past the docks. If Lirr was at all considerate, Marai would never lay eyes on his face, hear his slick voice, again. She'd tackle whatever would come in Andara, but at least her greatest demon wouldn't be there to watch, punishing her with every glance and word.

Slate stepped in front of Koda's path. "We're here. Mission complete. Where's my payment?"

What had Koda promised Slate to incur such desperation? Was Slate really that single-minded?

Koda's muscles clenched in irritation. "My employer's accountant will be by shortly. You'll wait for him here on the dock, and once everything is settled up, you'll head back to Astye with whatever remains of the crew."

Some of the crew, the burlier, heavy-browed ones, were disembarking, bags slung over their shoulders. *Locals,* Marai assessed. Andarans. Marai watched them shake hands with some people on the dock, shouting greetings, then disappear through the thick veil of fog past the planks.

Slate went pale, making the pink scars more stark on his skin. "Back to Astye? But we've only just arrived. I thought I'd be welcome in Andara for making this crazy voyage and risking my life. I thought you'd provide lodgings for your crew, and you mentioned an amulet—"

He doesn't want to go back on those waters. Marai couldn't blame him. Every crossing was a danger, a chance he wouldn't make it to the other side. *So that's where his desperation comes from.* Slate wanted to make a name for himself here on Andara, and never go back across the Northern Sea again.

"You thought wrong, Hemming," Koda said with a bite. "You're nothing more than a hired grunt. You'll accept your pay, and then be off. Andara doesn't need criminals and lowlifes sullying our country. Cavar would never waste an amulet on *you.*"

Marai and Keshel exchanged glances.

Amulet? he mouthed to her, frowning.

Koda brushed past Slate, who whirled around, fist pulled back to strike.

A single snap, a burst of chilly air, and Slate froze.

Koda walked down the gangplank with casual confidence, whistling again. He didn't release Slate until he was safely standing amongst the guards on the dock.

Slate staggered forward, face red and angry with humiliation. Marai snorted as she passed him.

"Goodbye forever, Marai," he said before she could step onto the strip of wood connecting the ship to the dock. Malice laced Slate's blue eyes. His scarred face perverted into a hideous sneer. "I'm sure whatever awaits you in this country, it will be exactly what you deserve."

Marai smiled sweetly. "I hope you drown on the way back."

Slate gave her one final scowl before he backed away, and Marai was ushered down the gangway.

Five hulking men waited for them on the docks, wearing red vests embroidered with that same symbol on Marai and Keshel's collars. Matching felt caps sat on their heads. Their olive and brown-skinned arms were as thick as Marai's whole torso, and they even edged out Keshel in height. They were also rather hairy; most sported bushy mustaches, long, pointed goatees, or chin-straps. Marai guessed these were Koda's mysterious employer's men. Everything about them shrieked dangerous and imposing, including the curved swords at their belts.

Marai hoped the opportunity would present itself to grab one of the blades and free herself.

"We have an escort." Koda showed off his toothy grin.

The men stared stoically back. Marai couldn't tell if they were always so serious, or if they merely didn't like Koda. Whatever the case, the five brutes towered over Marai as if she was nothing more than an ant beneath a thicket of trees.

Four men took hold of the chains binding Marai and Keshel, while the fifth led in front of Koda. Curly and the other non-native sailors remained on the dock, turning their backs on Marai and Keshel without a final glance.

Forty-seven days together without even a goodbye? Marai thought snidely.

With each step she took, a sense of foreboding skittered across Marai's skin, prickling the hairs on her arms. The swirling low, gray fog across the wooden planks encircled Marai and Keshel, seemingly alive and interested in their presence. The magical barrier between the harbor and the city beyond was nothing like Keshel's. A thick wall, Marai sensed enormous pressure and stifling air as she passed through. But again, this magic didn't seem to be from anyone with fae blood. It didn't feel *elemental.* Dark tendrils curled around her, lingering on her exposed skin, as if it savored the sensation of touching her.

Once on the other side, Marai's eyes widened as the sights, sounds, and tingles of magic flooded her senses.

This could have been any seaside city in Ain or Henig, with its immaculate, identical sandstone buildings and cobbles, although the cooler temperatures reminded Marai more of Grelta this late in spring, situated on the same plane as the Greltan capital of Lirrstrass.

Marai shivered as a crisp breeze ruffled her hair. *At least it's not snowing.*

The city of Bakair was situated on a hill. The inclined streets were incredibly clean, and lacked any vegetation or nature besides the flower boxes beneath window sills or manicured topiaries next to doorways, alongside clay urns and vases.

Marai caught whiffs of spices, grilled meats, and baked sugared pastries that made her mouth water and stomach rumble with want. Jasmine and incense filled the air, the same scent as Koda.

The amount of buildings and people rivaled Syoto's populous capital city of Kaishiki. The streets were packed with humans going about their day. Not a single faerie, vampire or werewolf in sight. The people here looked healthy, well-fed, clean, and generally content in their light-colored embroidered linens. They wore hats and head coverings, adorned with seashells, feathers, and beads, showing no skin but their hands and faces, as they laughed, haggled, and discussed, but Marai didn't catch a single raised voice. No children running amok, playing in the streets. She also didn't see any beggars or seedy back alleys, no one causing trouble. The city seemed far too peaceful to be real.

Perhaps it had something to do with the dozens of red-vested guards patrolling the streets. Adults and children bowed their heads respectfully, voices quieting, as they passed, indicating a strict, regimented governance of the city. Their eyes trailed Koda and his entourage, some pointed and whispered, but no one threw anything. No one shouted nasty words and insults Marai's way. Koda wasn't hiding his pointed ears. The people knew what he was.

But Koda said they were terrified of faeries . . .

If anything, the people seemed fascinated by their arrival. Whispers in a language Marai didn't recognize trailed her jangling footsteps.

That strange magic was stronger on this side of the barrier, and Marai sensed it following at her heels like a loyal dog.

Some of the citizens she passed wore identical bronze necklaces, displayed proudly on top of their clothing. These individuals were dressed more elaborately, more fashionably than the common folk, obviously people of importance with the way the others backed respectfully away.

"Why do some people wear those pendants?" Keshel asked Koda who was walking next to them with his jaunty, confident gait.

"Oh, those are amulets, and their bearers are Guardians," he said over his shoulder.

Guardians? Marai stared at one woman in an elegant silk dress wearing the bronze amulet. She gave Marai a haughty sniff in return. That woman didn't look strong enough to lift a sword, nonetheless guard anything.

"Exactly what are they guarding?" Keshel pressed further, craning his neck to get a view of everything. Despite their predicament and worries, Keshel was enraptured by the city. He gobbled up every detail, every scrap of knowledge he could gain. Marai had missed that sparkle in his eyes.

"Why, Andara, of course," Koda said with a chuckle.

"What do you need protection from when you have that barrier encompassing your port?" questioned Marai. No foreigners could enter Andara; not Slate and the other sailors, or even an invading army.

For the first time, Koda's smile slipped. "Not everything here is as peaceful as it seems. I didn't lie when I told you there are fae on Andara. They're here, sequestered up in the Northern Hinterlands, along with the rest of the magical folk." He gestured to the steep, jagged mountains in the distance.

Interest piqued, Marai drew closer to Koda, nearly tripping over her shackles. "So you also have vampires and werewolves?"

"They're not native to Andara like the fae, but there are more species of magical creatures out there than you know." Koda gave Marai a raised-brow look that suggested *something,* but she didn't know what he meant.

Other species? Marai glanced over to Keshel, who looked as mystified as she was.

"The fae don't leave their hideout in the Hinterlands," said Koda as they kept climbing the main thoroughfare. "They erected their own magical barrier that they call the Veil, to keep themselves in and the rest of us out. They have their own little world up there, lording over the other magical folk. Although, they'd probably *love* to meet you, Faerie Queen."

"That's where you're truly from. The Northern Hinterlands," Marai said, trying to piece everything together, such as why a half-fae like Koda was willing to kidnap others of his kind.

"Me? No, I'm from Yehzig, as I said. I've never seen what's beyond the Hinterland's Veil. I've never even gotten close. For the most part, magical creatures that aren't behind the Veil stay away from humans, but sometimes they stray into our towns. That's why we have the Guardians. The magic in their amulets ward off attacks from the folk."

Humans and magical folk didn't get along on Andara, either. *No different than Astye. Why is it so difficult for everyone to coexist?*

"Where did these magical amulets come from?" Marai asked, eyes narrowing with suspicion.

Humans couldn't use magic. What were these amulets? How could a mere trinket give ordinary humans power? Something dark and sinister tapped against her skull, and crept through the recesses of her mind. She didn't trust those amulets, nor the supposed "Guardians."

"Governor Cavar created the amulets and gave them out to those he deemed worthy of leadership. It's the Guardians' duty to keep Andara safe and functioning properly. They run all aspects of government. Every city and town has a Governor and several lesser Guardians. Bakair is the Capital, and largest city on Andara."

A human man *created* magical amulets? That wasn't possible. The ominous feeling intensified within Marai, despite the bright sun, delicious scents, and normalcy around her. This Governor should not be able to *create* magic.

"He made Andara what it is," Koda continued, as if he'd said nothing unusual. "Not long ago, it was a disorderly country, with no cohesion or government, sectioned off into factions. Governor Cavar united Andarans under one flag. He's the most highly respected and powerful leader in the country, and Cavar's recently been re-elected for his tenth term."

"Ah, the bloodhound has returned," came a heavily accented man's voice. "Is this them?"

Koda halted his retinue, and greeted a bald man flanked by several other men and women. They all had those bronze amulets around their necks, and reeked of patronizing importance.

"Guardian Gamal," Koda said with a bow, although Marai noticed that his dark hair shielded a rictus grin.

Not friends, I suppose.

"These are indeed Governor Cavar's elite guests," Koda continued. "Allow me to introduce you to Keshel, seer of the future, and Queen Marai of the Fae."

Marai stiffened and glowered at Koda. "I'm not a queen."

"Oh, but you are. You're the last remaining descendant of any royal fae, and you have the magic to prove it. Not that we'll let you, of course." Koda smiled at Guardian Gamal, who looked Marai up and down with a judging eye.

"She looks human. She's too gangly and smells dreadful," he said with a disappointed sneer. "She'll never pass for a queen. For goodness sake, she has no wings, and her ears aren't even pointed. The people won't buy it. At least the male looks faerie enough and has a useful skill, but I can't believe Cavar wants *her*. Seems like a risk, if you ask me, and not just a financial one."

Marai leapt towards the pompous man's face, letting out a snarl. "You have no idea how many ways I can kill you." Her chains snapped taut as the guards pulled on them.

The bald man jumped back, clinging to his amulet with a sweaty hand. Black smoke swirled at his feet, then erected a dark fog barrier between them. Marai was hauled backwards by the guards and only stopped fighting against them when she stared at the familiar smog, saw it writhing around Gamal's amulet. The pit in her stomach grew wider at the scratch of pepper in the back of her throat. Her head swum at the subtle scent of sulfur.

Dark magic.

That was what she felt when walking through the barrier, what had been trailing her through the streets.

Marai rapidly scanned the man's brown hands and neck. His exposed skin was normal flesh, not blackened like Rayghast's had been, or the tips of her own fingers.

Somehow, Governor Cavar and the Guardians could harness dark magic and *use* it without any noticeable negative effects.

"My apologies, Guardian Gamal, she hasn't yet learned her position here," Koda said with a scathing glare at Marai, "but I assure you, she'll be house-trained soon enough."

The smoke-barrier around Gamal dissipated as he released his hold on the amulet. "Creatures like her shouldn't be out here amongst the citizens. You'd better hurry on to Cavar's office before she hurts someone."

Koda and Gamal exchanged several more words in the Andaran language, then Koda flashed his false, toothy grin. The man and his entourage passed by, giving Marai a wide berth.

"You're making me look bad," Koda growled as he grabbed her arm and pulled her along the street.

The chains around Marai and Keshel's ankles scraped and clanged against the cobblestones. More whispers and fingers pointed their way. Marai may not have understood the language, but she guessed what they were saying, regardless.

"I thought you said Andarans fear magic," she said through clenched teeth as two children gaped, mouths open like fish sucking in algae. A third child stuck out his tongue.

"They *do* fear it, but don't we always have a fascination for the things that scare us?" Koda posed.

Marai and Keshel exchanged another dubious glance. Dark magic was terrifying, but she was desperate to learn more about it, to figure out how it worked, and where it came from. Only then could she stop it completely.

They walked into a large circular forum. The largest and grandest buildings in the city seemed to be in this central area, towering over the one-story houses and shops. Wrought iron embellished the doors, along with gold and silver filigree. Marai noticed a higher concentration of magical amulets in the forum, as well, around the necks of wealthy citizens passing between the offices.

Koda and the guards stopped at the ornately carved wooden door of a building; the sign above said something in a curly, dotted language Marai couldn't read. Painted below the letters was the three-pronged symbol Marai had come to recognize as an emblem of Andaran power. Koda opened the door, shoving Marai and Keshel inside what appeared to be an office lobby.

A man sitting at a desk burst to his feet, eyes wide. He had long, thinning light brown hair and wore a pointed cap. He smoothed out the front of his buttoned jacket with trembling hands. Marai noticed he didn't have an amulet.

Obviously not important enough to earn one.

He stammered out a brief conversation with Koda, gaze flicking to Marai every other word, before disappearing behind another door.

Marai quickly scanned the desk, searching for a letter opener or sharp quill she might use to stab Koda and the guards, but the desk was virtually spotless with only a few documents. Too clean. Too organized. Nothing within reach.

All too soon, the door reopened and the anxious assistant stepped out. He said something to Koda, then slid out of the way against the wall, avoiding getting close to Marai and Keshel as they were once again shoved through the doorway.

Marai thought the assistant was being a tad dramatic. No one, not even she, could be as dangerous as the older man standing before her now.

Engraved into the glossy, onyx stone positioned in the middle of his amulet was the same symbol on her collar and the sign above the door.

This man was undoubtedly the Guardian who'd tamed dark magic and could use it freely without consequences.

CHAPTER 6

RUENEN

"I'm sorry to have returned empty-handed, Your Grace." Aresti clenched her fists, face awash with shame.

Her search team consisted of three werewolves—Tarik, Brass, and Yovel. They'd been gone since the morning after Marai and Keshel were taken. That was forty-seven days ago, and Ruenen had barely heard from them, except for a hastily scratched note weeks ago from Aresti stating she'd gone across the Varanese border. Now, covered in mud and sopping wet, the team slumped with exhaustion in their chairs.

Thora, the shortest in the room by far, had brought her bag of medicinal remedies with her. She assessed Aresti first, then the weres, searching for injuries. Her sable locks tumbled down her back as she passed a gentle hand over a blistering rash on Yovel's neck. His hazel eyes lit up when it disappeared from his skin, and he kissed Thora quickly on each bronze cheek, making her whole face blush.

"You tried," Ruenen said to Aresti as she hung her head. He hated seeing her so defeated. "You gave everything you had, and returned home safe. That's what matters."

The words were true, but disappointment sank deep within Ruenen, and fear coiled itself around his heart.

"Not a word, not a sign," said Aresti, running a hand through her short black hair. She'd shaved the sides since Ruenen had last seen her, and she had a new piercing in her left eyebrow, amassing seven total. Her beautiful face was tense and furrowed, dark angular eyes shimmering with worry. "Searching is pointless. We *know* they took Marai's portal. They could be anywhere!"

Aresti wasn't wrong. Brisk responses to Ruenen's letters had been trickling in from the other kings and emperors of Astye. None of them had seen Marai and Keshel, nor did they seem to care that they were missing, providing Ruenen with their meager "condolences."

"We won't give up," Raife said, placing a hand on Aresti's shoulder. "We'll find them, or they'll escape and come home to us."

Aresti closed her eyes tightly, perhaps holding back tears. Keshel was her cousin, as close as any brother, and even if Aresti wouldn't admit it out loud, Ruenen knew she cared about Marai just as much.

She pulled away from Raife and sniffed. "I should go back out there. I should keep looking."

"You'll do nothing of the sort," said Thora in her stern, motherly tone. In a room full of warriors, Thora's presence soothed their wired nerves. "We knew this would be difficult, and Marai and Keshel would be so pleased to know how hard we've been looking, but they wouldn't want us to do anything imprudent or dangerous. Nor would they want us to lose focus on our other main objectives in Nevandia."

The long list of tasks made Ruenen cringe: stabilizing Nevandia, eliminating the rebellions, figuring out better ways to integrate magical folk into human society, creating equality and harmony between Nevandia, Tacorn, and magical folk, etcetera, etcetera . . .

Ruenen absorbed Thora's comforting words, but they didn't help ease the knot of burning anxiety in his chest. He turned to the three weres. "I'm eternally grateful for your assistance. You could have been home with your people by now, but you chose to stay after the battle and help us find Marai and Keshel. Please, let me know how I can repay you."

Tarik exchanged looks with Brass and Yovel. "You owe us nothing, Your Grace. We're more than willing to search for Lady Marai and Lord Keshel. They're important to the cause, after all," the leader of the weres explained. "If it would be acceptable to you, we'd like to stay on and continue to aid in the effort of magical acceptance. I think you'll be needing us more than before without their presence."

Tarik had arrived from Ain with his band of five werewolves to fight alongside Nevandia and the fae. He'd lost three of his men in the Battle of the Red Lands, as people were now referring to it. The werewolves had come because they'd heard of Ruenen's stance of opening Nevandia up to magical folk, but he never would have done so without Marai and Keshel's orchestration.

"Don't you have families to get back to?" asked Thora.

"Nah, Mistress, we're bachelors for life," said Tarik with a gruff laugh. The dark-skinned were had a new scar that traveled up the length of his left bristly jaw. "No pups waiting for us, neither."

Ruenen clapped a hand on Tarik's muscular shoulder. "You're very welcome to stay for as long as you wish. Nevandia is your home."

Thora was absolutely right about everything she'd said to Ruenen, yet it was far easier said than done to focus on things other than Marai and Keshel.

Marai would be furious if I neglected my duties. But the thought didn't make Ruenen feel less lost and confused when he met with his Witan later that day.

"Do you still intend to leave for Dul Tanen today, Your Grace?" asked Holfast once the Witan was assembled and seated.

Raife and Aresti stood in their gleaming armor against the wall like the others in the King's Guard. Ruenen was glad to have Aresti back again to help balance out the fae and humans. She was also the only female in the room—not that it was easy to tell, since she was as tall as some of the men, and indistinguishable in her armor.

"Yes, I think it's time I speak with the people there," said Ruenen. "They need to know that they aren't my enemies, that they're now Nevandian citizens, and therefore, my people, too."

He didn't truly want to go to Dul Tanen. The fortress held terrible memories for Ruenen of almost being tortured to death by Rayghast, of nearly watching soldiers rape and murder Marai. The thought of going back there, even as the ruler of the newly conquered kingdom, made him squirm with disquiet.

"Lord Vorae says that hostile Tacorians still remain in the city," Fenir said. They'd stationed Vorae in Dul Tanen to oversee things weeks ago. He'd been able to quell several uprisings, thanks to the Greltan soldiers Queen Nieve had left behind. "You must take the full King's Guard with you."

"Commander, please send another squad of riders to search the Southern borders," Ruenen said to Avilyard.

"We don't have the extra men to send to Ain, Your Grace," Corian said with an impatient huff.

"I think we can spare a few . . ." But Avilyard didn't sound pleased at the prospect.

Ruenen got to his feet, ready to leave for the day-long trek to Dul Tanen, but Holfast held up a silent hand. His face remained placid, but Ruenen spotted the pursing of the Steward's lips, the tell-tale sign that he had something to say that he knew Ruenen wouldn't like.

This should be fun . . .

"Your Grace, before you leave, there's an important matter we must discuss."

Ruenen sat back down on his throne, crossed his legs, and gestured for Holfast to continue. The Steward cleared his throat and stood, addressing only Ruenen.

"We've put this off for as long as we can, Your Grace, but we need to settle the matter of your marriage."

Ruenen's gut twisted. Holfast had tried to speak with him about it at his coronation. The Lord Steward had told *Marai* what he expected of Ruenen. It felt wrong then, but even worse now, to discuss marriage without the one person Ruenen truly wanted to be with.

"Don't we have enough to worry about?" Ruenen asked, letting the irritation seep into his tone in a very un-king-like manner. "We're rebuilding two whole nations. Tacornian rebellions are brewing. We're struggling with human-magical relations and initiatives. We haven't decided what to do with Queen Rhia, *and* Lady Marai and Lord Keshel are still missing. Marriage is the *last* thing on my mind."

"A worthy marriage could improve some of those issues, my King," said Lord Goso, a rather quiet and small man on the Witan. He was the Ambassador to Grelta, and had only returned from his long stint there a week ago. He worked hard to ensure the alliance between Nevandia and Grelta stayed strong, and trade between the countries was booming thanks to him.

"We know you're torn in many directions, Your Grace, but that is the job of a king," Lord Corian said. "You've been distracted by Lady Marai long enough. She

QUEEN OF THE SHADOW MENAGERIE

may or may not return, and even if she does, her presence doesn't affect choosing your future wife."

Ruenen bit back his retort. *But she is my future wife.* Or, at least, he wanted her to be. He'd never gotten the chance to ask her. Ruenen didn't know if she would've said yes . . .

"Who do you have in mind?" he asked as a muscle in his jaw ticked. He didn't want to talk about other women, but Ruenen knew he wouldn't be able to leave this meeting without first listening to his counsel.

Holfast pulled a lengthy piece of parchment closer to him. Ruenen recoiled at the sight of dozens of names.

"There is, of course, King Maes and Queen Nieve's daughter, Princess Elurra, of Grelta—"

"She's thirteen," said Ruenen. "I won't marry a child."

Nieve had also said she wouldn't marry Elurra off for political gain. *At least Nieve has a conscience.*

"I suppose that rules Princess Eriu of Varana out, then," said Wattling as Holfast scratched two names off his list.

Eriu was even younger than Elurra. The thought made Ruenen cringe with disgust.

"I agree about Princess Elurra. Our ties are already strong enough with Grelta. It would be better to make an alliance with another kingdom," Goso said lightly.

"There's the King of Beniel's granddaughter," suggested Fenir. "She's fifteen, and quite pretty, I've heard. Good, noble stock. As our new neighbors to the West, this might be a beneficial union."

Out of the corner of his eye, Ruenen saw Aresti roll her eyes and Raife elbow her. He couldn't help but feel similarly.

"What about, uh . . . Queen Rhia?" came ancient Cronhold's voice from the far end of the table. "You said it yourself, Your Grace . . . you haven't yet decided what to do with her. Why not marry her yourself?"

Ruenen had to stop his jaw from dropping at the suggestion. Was there any worse humiliation for Rhia than to be married off to the man who'd killed her husband and conquered her country? She'd already suffered enough at the hands of Rayghast.

"That *is* an interesting idea . . ." Corian mused, scratching his chin.

Ruenen got the impression, though, that this wasn't the first time the men of the Witan thought of this match. In fact, they leaned forward, looking at him with expectant eyes. They *wanted* Ruenen to choose Rhia.

"It would certainly help our relations with the Tacornians," continued Corian.

"And the Varanese," Fenir added, with a hopeful, overly enthusiastic smile

"I won't be marrying Queen Rhia," Ruenen stated firmly.

"Don't make such hasty decisions, Your Grace," Corian said. "She is perhaps the best option we have, and she's as pretty as any other woman you might find."

"Any king in your position would marry her," Wattling said, nodding his head profusely. "Rhia is the torch of unification we've been searching for."

Ruenen fixed each man at the table with a razor-edged glare. "Queen Rhia refuses to see me. The last time we tried to relocate her from her cell, she threatened to claw Sir Nyle's eyes out. She was horrifically wounded and abused by Rayghast's magic, and has declined all offers to be healed by Thora, my Royal Healer. The Queen wants nothing to do with me or Nevandia. Do you truly think, in her current state, that she would be a good symbol of unification? Can you see her standing peacefully next to me at a wedding altar?" Ruenen flung a hand at Holfast's long parchment. "I've never met any of the women or girls on your list. None of them can be my wife." *Because they aren't Marai.* "I'll marry when I'm ready, not be forced into some arranged marriage to benefit trade."

Holfast blinked slowly, thoughts and warnings swum in his dark, focused eyes. "Leave us, please."

The Witan stood, their chairs dragging on the tiled floor, and the chamber emptied of all except Holfast and Ruenen.

Holfast took a deep breath and faced Ruenen without any of the pretense he often presented in public. "This is about more than just trade, Ruenen," he began in his usual leveled tone. "This is more than forging alliances. This isn't even about Lady Marai, whom I know you miss and care for. This is about securing your *lineage.*" Holfast lowered his voice. "If anyone should discover that we put a false king on the throne, Nevandia would be ruined. You and I would be executed as traitors. Right now, we're vulnerable. The best way to secure our safety is for you to marry a woman of royal blood, such as Queen Rhia, then your children will truly be in line for the throne. Every day that goes by without a royal heir, your position weakens."

"Is that all a crown is?" Ruenen took the gold and emerald circlet from his head. "I thought I was meant to lead. I didn't realize that my real duty was to ensure a bloodline."

"A crown is those things, and more, Ruenen," Holfast said, in a gentler voice. "The stakes are far too high for us to delay any longer. You must beget a legitimate son."

"Why do we need to hurry? Besides us, only Vorae, Fenir, and Marai know the truth of my bloodline." That he wasn't of the royal bloodline, and instead, the son of Queen Larissa's sister Morwenna and her husband Rehan Ashenby.

Holfast shifted on his feet and gave Ruenen a firm stare. "How do we know Lady Marai was truly taken against her will?"

The muscles in Ruenen's body constricted. Veins in his neck grow taut. If Holfast meant what Ruenen thought he meant . . .

"Marai would *never* tell anyone," he said, stepping close to Holfast. "She's not out there selling my secrets for money or power, if that's what you're implying. I trust her completely."

"Even if you do, we cannot be so sure that she'll keep your secret under the threat of torture."

Ruenen's anger ebbed away as the image of Marai being repeatedly struck, blood trickling from her mouth and nose, crept its way into his mind. The thought of someone using her to get information on him . . . perhaps it was possible, but Ruenen knew.

"She'd die before revealing any information that would cause me harm."

Was that why no one had seen any signs of her whereabouts? Had she already been disposed of by her kidnapper?

No. I'd feel it. Ruenen knew his own heart would stop beating the moment hers did.

"Please, consider the options, Ruenen," Holfast said. His usually stoic expression broke. Concern was etched into the wrinkles on his forehead, around his baggy eyes, and his pursed lips. "Let's speak with Queen Rhia, arrange some daily meals and walks with her. I'm certain she'll see reason. She does not wish to spend the rest of her days in that cell."

"This is my *life,* Holfast. It's my choice who I spend my life with. And I'm sure I'm the last person Queen Rhia wants to marry."

"Then make a choice. I will not choose your bride, but she must be someone from the list."

Ruenen shook his head and backed away. "I cannot do this without Marai."

Holfast sighed, pinching the bridge of his nose. "We've already discussed that you cannot marry her. She isn't of royal or noble blood, and she's *fae.* The Witan and your people won't allow it, no matter how much you might feel for her. If we find her, and you'd like to keep her as your mistress, very well, but—"

"She *is* of royal blood." While it wasn't his truth to tell, Ruenen didn't want to withhold it any longer. "Marai's last in line for the faerie throne, the only surviving heir. She's Queen of the Fae."

Holfast blanched. Ruenen could have laughed—he'd never seen the Steward so utterly shocked.

"Keshel had records, and Nosficio knew Marai's ancestors Queen Meallán and King Aras. He says she has the same powers as Meallán."

"Well, that's . . . certainly news," said Holfast. "However, it doesn't change the problem at hand."

"Why not?" asked Ruenen. "You said I had to marry someone of royal or noble birth—"

"Who's human, not the *Faerie Queen*. Ruenen, I know you care for her—"

"I *love* her."

Everything stopped. Time stood still. The wuthering in the bushes and the chirping of the birds ceased. Ruenen's heart alone galloped with the might of a hundred horses.

He'd only said the words to her once before. He'd planned to say them a thousand more times the night of the coronation. He'd intended to beg on his knees, grovel at her feet, serenade her with love songs, until she agreed to marry him. His confession then had been dismally insufficient to the millions of ways she'd stirred his soul.

Although he knew Holfast had already guessed his feelings, it was so terribly wrong to announce such things without Marai there to hold his hand.

Holfast's face fell in disappointment. He knew this battle with Ruenen was lost, at least for today. "I'm grateful to Lady Marai. I respect her, and I'm naturally worried for her safety, but you cannot marry her. I don't say this out of my own prejudice. I say this knowing what will happen with our countrymen, with our allies. We'll be shunned for having a faerie queen. Other kingdoms may use it as an excuse to proclaim war upon us."

"We're trying to create equality and harmony between humans and magical folk," Ruenen said. "What better way to show the world we're serious, that we cannot only cohabitate, but *thrive* together, than for me to marry Marai?"

"Our top priority isn't magical folk. It's Nevandia. You must remember that a good king doesn't put himself first. He puts his *people* first."

"My parents married for love, didn't they?" Ruenen didn't mean Vanguarden and Larissa.

Holfast's eyes softened again. "They did, yes. They'd met at a ball, and courted each other for months before their parents agreed to a marriage. But they were a rarity in our society. I, myself, did not marry for love. I met my wife once before exchanging vows with her. She was a complete stranger. It's our duty to protect our family trees. Lineage matters a great deal in this world."

"But are you *happy*?"

"My wife resides in our country estate. I see her during important functions that require her presence. Marriage is not the fairytale in your mind, Ruenen. It's a business deal, but there are many ways to make it work for both parties." Holfast rolled up the parchment with the dozens of inked names and handed it to Ruenen. "Now, you must depart for Dul Tanen. Look this over tonight. Consider what future you want our nation to have. I look forward to hearing how your visit goes."

Ruenen hadn't seen Dul Tanen when he'd been dragged through on horseback months earlier by Commander Boone and his black-armored men. A burlap sack had covered his head, his wrists and ankles had been bound. But riding in this time, with his full retinue of golden guards, Ruenen could sense the difference. The citizens were subdued, standing along the streets, watching as he passed. Ruenen expected their hands to be full of rocks, mouths full of curses, like the last time, but instead some only wore expressions of disdain. Others gaped in astonishment. Several bowed. A small, gangly child gave Ruenen a polite wave.

Lord Vorae came into view once Ruenen turned into the cobbled castle courtyard. The councilman stood on the fortress steps, surrounded by a mixture of Nevandian and silver Greltan soldiers. "Your Grace, I hope your journey here was uneventful."

"It was fine," Ruenen said as he dismounted, followed by his King's Guard. "How have things been here, Lord Vorae?"

"Small skirmishes from some remaining Tacorn soldiers and loyalists. We still have a curfew in place at night, but things seem to be settling down. The dungeons are full, and trials are dealing out the appropriate forms of justice per sentencing."

How many Tacornians had gone to the executioner's block? Ruenen had hoped to avoid more death, but there was only so much room available to house all the rebels and instigators.

Ruenen then gestured to the castle gates where hundreds of people stood, ogling at him through the bars. "Allow the people into the courtyard. I'd like to address as many as I can."

"Are you sure that's safe, Your Grace? You never know who might be in the crowd," said Avilyard.

"I'm not going to hide behind castle walls," Ruenen replied. "I want the people of Tacorn to know that I come in peace."

Vorae opened his mouth, then thought better of disagreeing. He ushered Ruenen to the top of the fortress steps as Nevandian and Greltan guards allowed Tacornian citizens to file in beneath the portcullis, and fill the somber gray-stone courtyard.

"Good afternoon," Ruenen said, putting on his kingly veneer. His throat suddenly became dry, tongue thick. He still wasn't used to addressing so many people as King, especially when half of the faces looked like they wanted to murder him.

If I had my lute in my hands, this would be much easier.

QUEEN OF THE SHADOW MENAGERIE   73

But he hadn't played any music since Marai had disappeared. Her kidnapper had snatched away Ruenen's joy, along with his heart.

"This is a tumultuous time for us here in the Middle Kingdoms. You've lost your king, and Nevandia has gained a new one. I'm not blind to the fact that many of your men died on the battlefield fighting against us, and I'm truly sorry for their loss. I never wanted to harm Tacornians or go to war. I have no desire for conquest. I would've preferred if King Rayghast and I came to an agreement, but that was never in his plan. And so, here we are, trying to rebuild and find peace between our nations. This won't be easy, but we must work together to unite our countries. I promise that I will treat all Tacornians with the same love and respect as my own people. I welcome your thoughts, today and always, on how we can heal the wounds of the past."

Scoffs and grunts of dissent echoed in the air as the crowd shifted on their feet.

"But these rebellions must stop," demanded Ruenen. "No more blood spilt in the Dul Tanen streets when we have already suffered so much. No more men need be jailed when we should be sharing our grievances and trying to find a solution."

"Where are the faeries?" a man cried, prominently wearing the Tacornian crossed-sword emblem pin on his coat.

The entire courtyard went silent.

Ruenen's body tensed. He'd been dreading this question. Raife and Aresti stood somewhere behind him in the mix of King's Guard. They weren't outwardly recognizable as fae with their helmets on, thankfully, and they made no move to implicate themselves.

"You're allowing magical folk to live on your lands," another man yelled, pointing an antagonizing finger at Ruenen. "We've seen what kind of destruction and death they cause."

"*Abominations,*" shrieked a woman, turning to others in the crowd. "How can we trust Nevandia? You can't trust *anyone* with magic!"

The dissents grew louder as bodies pushed closer towards Ruenen in their outrage.

"No faeries in our streets!"

A rock narrowly missed Ruenen's head.

Behind him, metal armor shifted as his King's Guard took steps towards shielding their monarch. Greltan guards within the courtyard closed in, hands on their weapons.

Ruenen raised his arms and his voice, setting his face in steely authority. "Yes, we have several faeries living and working in Nevandia, as well as werewolves and one vampire. I'm fortunate to call them my friends. They are loyal, valued citizens, and they, like you, only want peace and prosperity—"

The crowd lurched forward, anger palpable, and the silver-armored Greltans closed in, unsheathing their swords, knocking people to the ground, arresting others. Women and children ran screaming out of the courtyard to avoid the impending eruption.

I'm losing them.

"King Rayghast was also of faerie blood," Ruenen shouted, unwilling to show a flicker of fear before this mob. "Your own King lied to you, and hid his powers!"

"We didn't know about that until the battle," said one of the men near the front, shoving against a King's Guard. "Doesn't make us want to trust another king."

"Your Grace, come inside," Vorae said, pulling on Ruenen's arm.

These people are scared. Ease their fears.

"I understand that such a catastrophic breach of trust makes you weary of those in power," Ruenen shouted, shaking off Vorae. "You remember the horror. The violence. The charred, desiccated bodies that used to hang from these ramparts."

He looked behind him at the walls of the intimidating, impenetrable fortress. The eyes of the crowd glanced up, too, remembering the bodies that used to sway there. The crowd quieted. Those who'd turned their backs on Ruenen slowly faced him again.

"You didn't know then what Rayghast was doing, but he used dark magic to torture prisoners in this very fortress, including his commander, Heqtur Boone. Lord Wattling and Lord Cronhold informed us of the full extent of Rayghast's evil. Queen Rhia was a victim of Rayghast's sinister powers, as well. She's currently in our protection in Kellesar, healing from the wounds he gave her. Queen Rhia even claims that Rayghast admitted to killing his own father, King Talen, with those dangerous black flames. You lived in fear of your king. That one wrong move, one whispered word, would see you strung up in the dungeon. That's no way to live. That's no way to *rule*."

The silence roared, pressing down on Ruenen's shoulders. Sweat trickled down the back of his neck. But people were listening. He had to hold their attention. He had to restore their trust.

"I admit that not all who wield it use magic for peace, but it *can* be used for good. Our Royal Healer saved the lives of countless Nevandians on the battlefield. She healed me after Rayghast shoved a blade through my side, and she healed Tacornian men on the field, as well. I've seen magic bring vitality back to dying soil so that crops can thrive again. I trust the magical folk in my company. That's why I placed two of them on my Witenagemot. Their hearts are brimming with passion to heal the wounds of the past. For too long we've lived opposing one another: Tacornians and Nevandians, humans and magical folk. Why not bridge the gap? Why not try to understand the other? I believe this world would be a much better place if we *listened* and *learned* from each other. This change won't occur overnight, but I'm asking you to try, my friends. I'm asking you to help us."

Again, silence.

Perhaps I'm asking too much of them.

But eventually, frowns eased. People lowered their angry fists.

"Perhaps His Grace would be willing to hear from those we elect to speak on our behalf?" asked a well-dressed man on the far side of the crowd; a merchant or some kind of official.

"King Ruenen and the Witenagemot don't have time—" began Vorae.

"We will *make* time," Ruenen said. "Lord Vorae will gladly speak with your representatives, and bring your concerns to the Witenagemot. He'll ensure your voices are heard."

Vorae shot Ruenen a brief look of annoyance at this new responsibility.

Ruenen smiled at the crowd, then turned toward the dark fortress behind him. He shivered when entering, taking in the oppressive atmosphere of the cold, stone hall. It contained an air of emptiness, with its sparse decor that had none of the grandeur of his own castle in Kellesar. The walls and floors were the same gray stone as the courtyard and cobblestoned streets. No portraits or tapestries lined the halls, and very little natural sunlight lit the corridors.

This was a fitting castle for Rayghast's darkness. At least Vorae had already burned the dozens of faerie wings that had once been nailed to the walls . . . Rayghast's trophies from the fae massacres.

Directly above the fireplace in the throne room was a foreign letter, or some archaic sort of symbol, painted in black on the stone wall. Ruenen had never seen such a thing before. It reminded him of a three-pronged pitchfork with arrowheads on each tip. The bottom end of the staff curled like a pointed scorpion's tail. What in the hells did it mean, and why had it been placed in such a prominent spot?

A ripple of cold undulated down Ruenen's back. Something felt *strange* about the symbol, a chilly prickling at the back of his neck, as if he'd just received terrible news, or was wandering around alone in a dark forest.

Is Rayghast's ghost haunting me? Ruenen wouldn't be surprised. He couldn't stop his eyes from gazing about the room, searching for the dead king's transparent figure.

He refused to sleep in Rayghast's bed, so instead, Ruenen slept in a guest chamber on the opposite side of the castle. He was anxious to get back to Kellesar to see if there was any news of Marai. That chilly feeling he'd had earlier . . . could it have been a premonition? He tossed and turned, Rayghast haunting his dreams like a ghoul in the corner.

"You're a pathetic excuse for a king," the dead man said, eyes black as voids. *"You're weak, and failing your people. Mine will never bow to you."*

Memories of Marai strung up in the dungeon below flashed in Ruenen's mind. Rayghast stood next to her, black stained arms wreathed in black flames and blood.

"Ruen, help me," she sobbed, eyes nearly swollen shut, face battered and bruised.

"The Faerie Queen will never escape her prison. You failed her, too. All she will ever know is suffering."

Those black flames ensnared Marai's body, devouring her as she screamed and screamed.

Ruenen jolted up out of his sheets and ran a shaking hand across his face. *Gods, I need to get out of this place.* No sleep would come for him as long as he remained in that terrible fortress.

The next morning, Ruenen dressed quickly and bid a brief adieu to Vorae.

"Have some breakfast before the journey home, Your Grace," the councilman pushed.

But Ruenen's stomach churned and his palms were clammy. The sight and smell of eggs made him gag, and he couldn't shake the lingering, grim nightmares. The sense that something bad was going to happen to Marai.

"That symbol above the fireplace in the throne room . . . any idea what it means?" he asked Vorae hesitantly.

The councilman rolled his eyes. "Your Grace, I've stopped trying to make sense of anything Rayghast did in this godsforsaken fortress."

Ruenen leapt onto his horse to begin the long ride back to Kellesar. He sensed something following him; Rayghast's phantom, maybe, kicking him out of his city. Ruenen barely noticed where his horse was going. As the road cleaved through the forest, he pushed his mount harder, whizzing past trees and villages.

Marai's screams chased at his horse's hooves. Ruenen was so lost in thought, to the echo of that wretched sound, that he didn't notice the shouts of warning from his men behind him. He barely registered the twitching of his horse's ears, of her hesitant gait, until she stopped sharply. The horse reared with a frightened *neigh,* and Ruenen nearly fell from her back as he tried to steady her.

For Empyra's sake . . . but his horse continued to protest.

As his mind cleared, the air came alive with shouts and commands. Ruenen's heart thumped at the sound, and he wheeled his mount around to face whatever had suddenly appeared.

Tacorn rebels?

No, a shadowed animal, the size of a bear, bolted from the thicket.

It let loose a skin-crawling growl as it rammed into the two Guards who'd leapt protectively in front of Ruenen.

The men were flung from their mounts. One of the horses fell on top of its rider's leg, crushing it. The other man's helmeted head smashed against the trunk of a tree.

Lirr's Bloody Bones . . .

The animal certainly wasn't a bear.

It was a shadow creature.

CHAPTER 7

MARAI

The Governor was not at all what Marai imagined he'd be.

He was as tall as the doorframe Marai was standing in, with curling gray hair, tanned skin, and alert, light eyes. His thin figure wore finely tailored breeches, silk hose, and a mauve vest with a swirling vine pattern.

This man with the easy smile was the villain who'd brought her to Andara? Around his neck sat the bronze amulet, but none of the other Guardians had that black stone. *His* amulet was special. And that three-pronged symbol . . . it connected the stone to Marai's collar.

He opened his arms, as if greeting an old friend. "Welcome to Bakair." His smooth, accented voice grated against Marai's ears. As he came around to the front of his polished desk, she shifted protectively closer to Keshel. "What a pleasure to make your acquaintance. I'm sure Koda has already told you, but I am Jakov Cavar, Governor of this fine city."

There was something rather rehearsed about him, as if everything he did and said was a front, a false persona. Marai didn't know what kind of control he had over dark magic, but if he was the creator of the amulets, he was more powerful, knowledgeable, and dangerous than he pretended to be, and she had an inkling that the glossy stone played a part in it.

Governor Cavar gestured to the two empty agarwood and leather chairs before his desk. "Please, have a seat. Make yourselves comfortable."

Marai and Keshel didn't move. They stood stiffly in the doorway with the massive guards behind them.

"We'd be more comfortable if you took these manacles off," said Marai with a glare.

Cavar merely chuckled. Another practiced, false sound.

With a shove forward from Koda, Marai and Keshel trudged toward the chairs, chains dragging on the expensive rug. Marai didn't take her eyes off Cavar as he sat in his own upholstered armchair behind the desk and steepled his hands.

"I'm sure you both have many questions for me."

"Why have you brought us here?" Marai blurted with as much venom as she could muster.

"Yes, might as well start with the big one," Cavar said, eyes dancing over Marai's bedraggled appearance. "Koda said you had quite the temper. A bright fire within you. I admire that, Marai. A faerie queen such as yourself *should* be formidable."

Marai bristled at the title, and repeated for the hundredth time, "I'm not a queen."

Cavar's fake smile grew. "But you *are*, my dear. You're Queen Meallán and King Aras' descendent. The royal fae on both Andara and Astye are dead, except for you. You are singular. You are precious."

Marai didn't like the manic, possessive glint in his eye. It reminded her of how Slate used to look at her in her youth onboard *The Nightmare.*

"You didn't answer my question," she said, leaning forward, fingers curling into fists in her lap.

The glint in Cavar's eyes vanished, becoming colder and harsh. His smile dipped, revealing the true face of the Governor.

"What kind of rocks are those?" Keshel asked, catching both Marai and Cavar off guard. He pointed with his shackled hands at the window, to the labeled and categorized rocks, of various shapes and sizes, sitting on the sill, glistening in the sunlight. "I once read a book on geology, but those focused entirely on ones found in Astye. I'm curious about the native stones found on Andara. You're clearly a collector."

Cavar considered Keshel for a moment.

"I'm more than a mere collector." He stood in one swift movement, and sauntered to the window. He lifted a pink quartz, shifting it in his hand, studying it. "Long before becoming Governor, I was a geologist. I was fascinated with how rocks and gems were made—especially those formed by compacting heat and pressure."

"A fellow scholar," said Keshel, tinting his voice with interest. "I admit I'm surprised that a mere geologist became Governor of such an important city. Unfortunately, where we come from, those with studious, inquisitive minds are not often so esteemed."

Marai sensed what Keshel was doing. *Keep Cavar talking. Flatter him.* Perhaps such tactics would work better than Marai's blunt questions and fury.

Cavar took the bait. "From what I know about your leaders in Astye, they're only given power thanks to their blood lines. Kings and emperors do not *earn* their positions, as I have. I suppose you could say I used to be something of an alchemist, searching for fame and glory, as I began experimenting with pulverized materials, hoping to create gold with basic minerals."

Keshel nodded. "I've heard about alchemy. I've never tried it, myself, but I did read about a researcher in Beniel who'd devoted his entire life to alchemy, but was, sadly, unsuccessful."

Cavar chuckled again. "As was I. Alchemy is a rather wooly subject of study. However, it seems almost like fate that I stumbled upon a stone far more valuable than gold."

Marai's pulse spiked. She tried not to appear too eager. At her side, Keshel kept his passive facade in place.

Cavar removed the amulet around his neck, holding it up to the sunlight flooding through the window. "Whilst foraging for gems in the Hinterlands, something caught my eye. I found a strange black stone at the base of a tree. Glossy and smooth, except for one small carving of a strange symbol I'd never seen before. I was distracted, mesmerized by this new stone and the strange thrum of power I felt from it. I didn't notice the creature, one of the magical folk, until it grabbed me from behind. The stone came *alive*. It warmed in my palm and black flames shot out, burning the beast to cinders. I realized then what I'd found—a weapon."

Marai's mind wheeled. The stone itself contained dark magic? *Impossible.* Her eyes scanned Cavar's body, searching for the tell-tale signs of dark magic, but his skin, like Guardian Gamal's, was unstained.

"How can you wield such magic freely?" asked Keshel.

Cavar's performative smile returned. "I merely need to think, to *will* it. As long as I grasp the amulet, it does my bidding effortlessly." He pointed at Marai's blackened fingers in her lap. "Koda told me that the Astyean King, Rayghast, used similar magic, but at a physical price. It seems you also tried to wield it, Marai. You of faerie blood—magic already runs in your veins. You were greedy in thinking you could take more when you already have immense power."

"You don't think attempting to turn rocks into gold for the sake of fame and glory isn't greedy?" asked Marai.

"I never said I wasn't. But I believe the magic in our world has its own designs. The stone was sent to me in an effort to balance the scales. Humans are not born with magic, so the universe sent us a tool. You see, back in those days, magical folk didn't have the Veil distancing them from us. The beasts used to come into our villages and kill anyone in their path, leaving nothing but destruction and sorrow in their wake. As weak humans, armed with mere swords, pitchforks, and rage, we could do nothing to stop them . . . until this."

He stroked a reverent finger across the tripointed symbol on the stone. Cavar didn't understand how dangerous that stone was. Being in the same room as that dark power made Marai uneasy. She remembered its silky, sinister voice beseeching her like a lover. She never wanted to hear that voice again, to feel those filmy, smoke-like hands on her body.

Marai glanced at Koda in the corner, staring at the amulet with envy clearly written on his face. He didn't wear one. Perhaps he wasn't important enough in Andaran society to. Or maybe it was his faerie blood that prevented Cavar from giving one to him.

"You shouldn't use it," said Marai to the Governor. "There are always consequences."

"Perhaps for you," he replied with a pointed stare.

Marai ground her teeth. Yes, she *had* been greedy. Greedy, and desperate, and wrong to reach into that darkness, but she'd learned her lesson.

"This stone grants me the ability to do anything I want, the same magic the fae used when burning our villages and tormenting my people." Cavar's face darkened. "I lost many friends, including my own parents, to those monsters.

Thanks to this stone, I was able to ward off an attack from a horde of faeries threatening my village. I saved my sister's life."

A little voice wormed into Marai's ear. *Is that magic really so terrible?* Thus far, Cavar hadn't admitted to using the stone for anything but self-defense. Marai couldn't blame him for retaliating against those who attacked him, for protecting his loved ones.

"Despite what you may believe, I don't despise magic," Cavar continued. "No, I find it *fascinating*. I am, at my core, a student of the natural world around me. This includes magic. It's part of everything, existing around us in the very air we breathe, the earth and skies. I harnessed this magic for myself. Although I searched for more of these stones, this was the only one. The original. Destined for me. I used its mighty power to replicate its properties and create the amulets. They sell for a high price, as you can imagine. It has made me a rather wealthy and powerful man."

"But you don't give those amulets to everyone," Keshel said. "Poorer individuals are left defenseless while you amass the power."

"Not at all. You see, once you're given an amulet, you become a Guardian. Our duty lies in protecting our people. It's an immense responsibility and honor to be named a Guardian. There are now hundreds across Andara. One Guardian governs every major city and town." Cavar ran a hand through his gray curls. "This stone bestowed another gift on me—it slowed down the aging process, ensuring that I will lead for years to come. I may not look it, but I'm over one hundred years old."

"Lucky you," Marai bit out, lip curling in anger.

"Your kind lives for centuries," said Cavar. "Perhaps not part-fae, but those of full-blood can live up to a thousand years, I'm told. This stone provides me a balanced form of immortality. It's only fair."

Marai's heart pounded against her ribcage. Swirling tendrils of black smoke whirled around the bronze of Cavar's amulet, as if sensing Marai's presence, her anger. Yet again, confliction gnawed at her. Nothing Cavar had said so far was exactly villainous. Elitist, yes, but he spoke like many powerful men Marai had encountered on Astye.

"Did you bring us all the way here to kill us? To get further revenge on the fae?" she asked.

Cavar strolled over to stand before Marai and Keshel. He smelled of a spicy, rich cologne. His cold, pale blue-gray eyes narrowed slightly. "The amulets have made magic accessible to us humans. It fascinates not just me, but all of us, and while average people may not be able to purchase an amulet themselves, I've found a way to bring magic to them."

Icy dread gripped Marai's lungs as his long fingers reached out to touch her. She jerked backwards in her chair, nearly tipping it over, then smacked his hand away with her heavy chains. *"Don't touch me."*

Three hulking guards dashed to her side, restraining her in the chair before she tried to run or attack.

Marai tunneled deep inside herself, digging through the haze of snuffed out magic. She called to the power within her, but it didn't stir. Whatever was going on with Cavar and his stone, Marai wanted no part of this. That amused glint in his eyes returned as he watched Marai struggle for her magic. The metal collar tightened around her neck the more she tried to reach for that spark.

"These collars have never been tested on someone as powerful as you. I was a little worried they wouldn't work as well, but I'm beyond pleased with the result," Cavar said with delight.

He waved off his guards as Marai slumped into her chair; their grip on her arms and shoulders would leave bruises. Cavar then dug into his vest's breast pocket to produce a small notebook and stick of charcoal. He jotted a few sentences as he spoke.

"This metal isn't iron. It's a compound I created in my experiments. With the help of the stone, I designed a collar that entirely cuts off a magical creature from its power, granting *me* complete control."

Keshel's face went paper-white. "What do you mean?"

"I can decide when and how much magic you use at a time," the Governor said. He finished his notes and returned the book to his pocket. His voice pitched lower, more threatening. "I can make you do things. Perhaps things you normally won't or can't do." He grasped his amulet, and dark smoke seeped out through his fingers. "For example."

Blacklight flared from the stone.

Suddenly, Keshel gasped, eyes going wide, glazing over in a distant way. Marai recognized that look. After days without a vision, he was finally *seeing*.

Marai clasped his hand. "Keshel!"

He didn't respond. Didn't acknowledge that he'd heard her. He was lost in a vision, growing deathly pale. A bead of sweat dripped down his temple into his matted black hair. The muscles in his jaw tightened until it was locked together in a pained grimace.

"Stop it," Marai snarled at Cavar, getting to her feet. She leapt towards the Governor, stained fingers reaching to tear off his face.

Cavar's eyes flashed, he whispered a word, and dark magic came alive inside his stone again.

Lightning surged through her veins. Marai collapsed onto the floor, seizing with pain, as the collar used her own magic against her. Icy, electric poison stabbed every nerve in her body.

Keshel remained rigid in his chair, entirely frozen, locked in the collar's grasp, unable to break from the vision.

"Release him," Marai managed to shout without biting off her tongue from the seizures.

Cavar dropped his amulet, and Keshel was released. He let out a pained breath, then slumped against the back of the chair. Keshel's hands shook at his sides, staring at Marai while she panted and writhed on the floor from the electric shocks circulating through her nervous system.

"We do not fear your kind any longer," said Cavar, glaring down at Marai. Cold control seeped into every syllable. Gone was his cordial performance and false smiles. "We are *gods* compared to you. Your folk are scattered, unorganized, fighting against each other, but with *you*, Marai, they could rally together. You could start a war."

"I have no intention of leading a war against Andara," she grunted. Marai barely had control over the spasming muscles in her jaw. "I don't care about being Queen."

"Your mere existence holds power for your kind," said Cavar. "The royal line ends here. No more Faerie Queens or Kings. Your freedom is mine. Your *power* is mine."

He grabbed a sleek knife from his desk, its handle bejeweled with rubies and sapphires. Marai tried to squirm away from him on the rug as he knelt next to her.

"Keshel is unique. His gift of foresight will be very enticing to patrons. They'll pay any amount of coin in order to see their futures." The Governor twirled that knife between his fingers.

Patrons? Marai could barely think of anything but the effects of the collar's shock waves traveling through her.

"You?" Cavar reached down and roughly clasped Marai's chin with his fingers. "They'll be *enthralled* by you, Queen of the Fae. My crown jewel." He frowned. "But you don't look anything like what I expected. They'll doubt your authenticity if I present you as you are now."

In one swift move, Cavar sliced his knife upwards across Marai's forearm. She barely flinched at the cut—the pain was nothing compared to the collar.

"What are you doing?" she asked him weakly, trying to get to her knees. Crimson dripped down her arm, between her fingers . . .

"I'm going to awaken your dormant blood," Cavar said.

"But she's only half-fae, like me," came Koda's voice from behind the chairs. He sounded awed, almost worshiping, corrupted by the power of the amulet.

"The stone can do anything," stated Cavar, closing a fist around the amulet, while the other hovered over the cut on Marai's arm. "Even bring forth the sleeping magic in her blood."

The air shifted and cooled. The flames in the fireplace flickered and danced, growing brighter, taller. Cavar's amulet pulsated with luminous blacklight. Sulfur invaded Marai's nostrils.

This frightened Marai more than Rayghast ever had. Cavar had unchecked power in his grasp, to which she had no defense. She tried to wrench her arm away, but something, whether it was the collar or Koda's power, held her in place.

Marai watched in terror as Cavar's hand hovering above her arm glowed in the same eerie black way.

Magic coursed through her; ripping, stinging, burning, *pulling*. Marai screamed. Blood pounded in her ears. Her body was on fire, as if her skin was being turned inside out. Every ligament, shard of bone, blood cell within her came alive, searing, torturing her.

She was aware of nothing but pain. Her fingers scraped the rug. She pulled and scratched, trying to crawl away, away from the agony. There was a twinge in her ears, something she barely noticed before her back split open.

Gods, no!

Had Cavar sliced open her back with the knife?

No, her skin and muscles were *tearing*.

The only sounds Marai heard were her own screams.

Is this how I die? She'd rather die than feel this torment one moment longer. It would be a blessing.

Were the gods delivering their justice upon her for the lives she'd taken? Was this torture earned? She'd endured the heartbreak and humiliation of Slate. She'd lost so many people she loved, and she'd nearly given her life to save the rest. Hadn't she been punished enough?

But the torture continued, and Marai clung to the final thread of light within her.

Ruenen... his face swam into view behind her eyelids. In her agony, she could barely remember the sound of his voice. She couldn't replicate the color of his eyes in her memory. She'd never kiss his lips again. She'd never smell his woodsy, smokey scent. The longing, and heartache, and pain brought tears to her eyes. They spilled down her cheeks as she thrashed.

Then suddenly, the burning and ripping stopped. Gone in an instant.

She collapsed onto her stomach. She couldn't move. Her throat was ravaged. Her blurry eyes closed. Warm blood trailed down her body, seeping into the rug.

Before she disappeared into the darkness, Cavar leaned in, his breath warm against her ear.

"Welcome, Your Majesty, to the Menagerie."

CHAPTER 8

RUENEN

Every shadow creature Ruenen had seen was the image of a thousand nightmares.

This creature had the head of a buzzard, but with razor-sharp teeth, no feathers, and no wings. Its body was covered in rust-colored, fleshy hide. Black spikes protruded from the knobs of its vertebrae.

Why did they all have to be so hideous? *Can't they take the form of something cuter?*

The monster roared, and Ruenen's horse bucked, throwing him off. He crashed to the ground on top of his left arm, the jarring impact reverberating in the nerves of his teeth. White-hot pain shot up his arm.

The King's Guard raised their weapons high upon their steeds. Raife's bowstring creaked as he pulled back, aiming his arrow at the creature's eye. Two swords gripped tightly in her hands, Aresti moved protectively in front of Ruenen.

The creature's frightening gaze was locked on Ruenen, as if he, alone, were its intended target.

Ruenen stumbled to his feet and clutched the handle of his broadsword with his good arm. One of the guards on the ground had an injured leg, bone protruding through the skin. The other was lying supine on the ground, unconscious. *Or dead.*

"Hold," Ruenen ordered his guards, and walked past Aresti on her horse.

"What are you doing?" she hissed, latching onto his good shoulder to pull him back.

He remembered what he'd heard on the moor weeks ago the last time he'd confronted a shadow creature, when Marai and Nosficio had been there with him. The creature had *spoken* some strange, guttural language, which had stirred unease within Marai. Although the buzzard-hybrid was monstrous, it was still a magical creature . . . perhaps it could be reasoned with.

This is probably a very bad idea.

Ruenen raised his hand (the other arm wouldn't move, it was most likely broken,) and he addressed the creature, inching closer through the forest duff. "Why did you attack us?"

The creature huffed and blinked its reptilian eyes at him, making no sign that it understood the question.

"Who are you? Why are you here?" Ruenen asked slowly, enunciating every word.

The buzzard-creature cocked its head and took a step closer to Ruenen. His Guard drew further in as the creature's bulbous eyes grazed from Ruenen's boots to his crown. It didn't stare at him with hunger the way an animal would. No, the monster regarded Ruenen as if it was observing, making judgements, gaining knowledge. Its eyes slid to each member of the King's Guard, taking in their weapons.

"Your Grace, there's no way that thing possibly understands you," Avilyard said.

But the shadow creature gave its reply in the same guttural language Ruenen had heard before. Its voice was harsh and low, sending a chill across Ruenen's skin, as it spoke directly to him.

"We can leave each other in peace," Ruenen replied when it quieted. Desperate to be understood, he gesticulated with his right arm as he spoke. "There's no need to harm each other. See? We'll go. You go. No killing."

The creature didn't agree with Ruenen's plan. It tossed its fowl head back and forth. Black smoke twirled around its human-esque fingers. Ruenen recognized that magic. It reminded him of Rayghast.

Oh, fuck.

The smoke burst into black flames, crawling up the creature's hands and arms.

Lirr's Bones. Dark magic had spawned this creature, but could they now also utilize its power?

"Get back, Your Grace!" Avilyard raised his sword as Aresti finally managed to tug Ruenen behind his mounted Guard.

The creature growled in response to the movement, and sent a wave of black flames crashing towards Ruenen. With a stroke of her hand, Aresti's wind sent the flames swirling back towards the beast.

Ruenen heard the twang of a bowstring as Raife's arrow soared through the air, but it disintegrated when it tried to pass through the black flames. Raife tried again, this time igniting the tip of the arrow in his own magical fire. The flaming arrow pierced a hole through the beast's magic, and lodged into its shoulder.

"It's easier to bring one down with magic," Raife told Aresti. He'd also battled a shadow creature before with Leif and Keshel. Swords and arrows *could* kill the creatures, but Ruenen remembered how Marai's lightning had made quick work of one.

The buzzard-creature shot more black flames his way. Aresti summoned her wind and swept the attack aside like a curtain, but holding that dark power back required all her focus. Within seconds, a sheen of sweat broke out across her forehead.

Raife shot three more flaming arrows in rapid succession, only one hitting its mark in the creature's gut. The carrion beast barreled forward towards Ruenen, reaching out its fingers.

One more flaming arrow hit the beast in the chest. Its black magic receded, and the creature stumbled backwards, allowing Ruenen to quickly approach.

Avilyard tried to pull him back, but Ruenen slipped through his grasp. "Your Grace, don't!"

Ruenen ran forward, lifting his sword with one arm, and sliced across the monster's chest. The creature roared and fell onto its rear, its eyes wide as it sensed death approaching. Ruenen then cut off the vile creature's head. Black, bloody viscera sprayed across his face and clothing.

How many more of those things walked the Middle Kingdoms? It was impossible to know the amount Rayghast had spawned in his lifetime.

Will we need to fight them forever? Ruenen was already exhausted by the prospect. What protections could he put in place for his people so they wouldn't be harmed by these creatures?

"Your Grace, are you injured?" asked Avilyard breathlessly, running to Ruenen's side, looking him over.

"I'll be fine." It was silly to make a fuss when the two soldiers on the ground were in worse shape. "Help them, Commander. We're still hours away from Kellesar."

The Guard set about crafting two gurneys for the injured guards from branches.

Aresti gave Ruenen a hard look. "That thing was after *you*."

Using only his good arm, Ruenen busied himself with tying the makeshift gurneys to the backs of the horses, avoiding Aresti's gaze.

"It didn't seem to care about the rest of us," she pressed, helping him with the rope when he struggled. "Why do you think it wanted you?"

"How am I supposed to know? It's not as if I could understand it," Ruenen said. "Perhaps because I'm King, and it somehow knew that."

"It used dark magic, like Rayghast could. Did you know they could do that?"

Ruenen sharply tightened the final knot. "No."

The men were lifted gently onto the gurneys. Avilyard had dressed their wounds as best he could.

With a furrowed brow, Raife tossed his magical flame onto the deceased creature, burning the body. Ruenen gave him a quizzical look.

"I want to be sure it doesn't rise up from the dead," Raife explained. "I'm beginning to learn that nothing, especially dark magic, stays down for long."

Ruenen and his Guard took twice as long as usual to return to Kellesar, with the gurneys dragging behind them. Ride too fast and the injured men would be tossed off. Ruenen was beyond bone-weary by the time his retinue arrived inside the grand, white-moonstone entrance to the castle.

"Send for the Royal Healer," Avilyard told a passing servant.

Mayestral, ever the attentive shadow, rushed over the instant Ruenen's feet touched the tiled floor.

"Are you injured, my King?" he asked, brown eyes wide as he took in the way Ruenen cradled his left arm.

"Thora will mend it in a heartbeat," Ruenen replied, although the arm hung at a weird angle, and the pain had increased during the long hours of riding.

"Our King was *very* brave," Aresti said. Ruenen could tell by her edged tone that she wasn't pleased with his recklessness. "He took down a shadow creature."

Mayestral gaped. "Brave *and* skilled, Your Grace!"

Ruenen frowned. He hadn't felt particularly brave or skilled killing the creature. It was just something that had to be done.

He then turned to Raife. "Be sure Thora heals the men first. They're in worse condition than me."

Raife and Aresti disappeared as Avilyard shed his helmet and thick gloves.

"I hope your visit to Dul Tanen was a success, Your Grace," Mayestral said, bobbing behind Ruenen as he walked towards the stairs. Candles flickered in their sconces, lining the staircase. "Despite your injury, of course."

"As good as could be expected. Any word on Lady Marai? Lord Nosficio?" Ruenen asked.

The Groom's anxious expression fell into a sincere, empathetic frown. "No, my King, and I'm sorry for it."

"Avilyard, keep sending out scouts," Ruenen called over his shoulder as Mayestral ushered him upstairs towards his chamber. "Send as many as can be spared. I'll take a team out to search tomorrow."

His commander sighed and shook his head, but said, "As you wish, Your Grace."

Perhaps it was foolhardy, spreading his soldiers so thin while the relationship with Tacorn remained so tumultuous, but Ruenen hoped that his visit had at least accomplished some goodwill.

He asked Mayestral to send up dinner, and some time after he collapsed into a plush armchair in his room, Thora and Raife appeared at the door. She carried her leather medicine case, a gift from Ruenen when he'd awarded her the title of Royal Healer.

Damn, I was kind of hoping it was dinner.

"Are my men okay? Did the unconscious Guard wake up?" Ruenen asked as soon as she entered the room.

"Yes, both are fully healed and alert, Your Grace," Thora said, and sat on the floor in front of him.

"When we're in private, you can call me Ruenen," he reminded her for the thirtieth time.

Thora was more hesitant than Raife or Aresti to speak so informally with him. A hand grazed over his injured arm as she assessed his condition. "This is a bad break."

Closing her eyes, blue healing light radiated from Thora's hands, seeping into Ruenen's skin. The magic numbed the pain as he felt the bones snap back together, reforging like a broken blade.

"Raife told me you put yourself at risk by killing a shadow creature on the road," she said as Raife hovered by the fireplace.

Ruenen scowled at the male behind her. "I handled it fine."

Raife put his hands up in defense. "She pulled the details from me. I didn't have a choice."

"Pushover," Ruenen muttered in jest, flashing a smile at Raife, who tried and failed to suppress a chuckle. "That thing was after *me.* I didn't want anyone else to get hurt because it made me its target."

Thora's stern, ginger gaze pinned Ruenen in place. "Marai would be furious if she knew you put yourself in harm's way like that when you had plenty of guards around you."

"Well, Marai's not here." The words came out clipped. The despair, caught in Ruenen's chest for days, tumbled from his lips. "She's not here, and no one but us seems to care. No one else is worried about her or Keshel. Every day I feel like I'm farther away from her, from the person she wants me to be. The person *I* want to be."

"You're doing good work, Ruenen," Raife said. "Progress takes time—"

"I'm tired of being patient," snapped Ruenen, yanking off his crown and throwing it onto the chair. "I'm tired of everyone telling me what to do, who to marry." His gaze darted to Raife by the hearth, then back at Thora. "And I'm not helpless without Marai. I *can* defend myself. I don't need her or anyone to protect me. What I *need* is for her to be *here*. I need her to be alive."

He instantly regretted his terse tone as a wave of hurt flashed across Thora's face. She, too, was frightened that Marai and Keshel were lost for good. That two more people she loved had been taken from her.

"I'll never give up hope, because I *know* they'll return to us. Marai will . . . she'll do whatever she has to in order to get free. I swore on Kadi and Leif's graves that Marai and Keshel would come home," Thora said, silver lining her eyes. Then that hurt and terror transformed into determination. "But you must also be *alive* to greet them when they do, Ruenen. We understand that you're upset and frustrated, but you cannot make rash decisions."

Thora had never scolded him before. It reminded him of Mistress Chongan, when she'd chastise him and the boys for swiping food before dinner, or trailing soot from the forge into the house. Thora was so steadfast in her belief that she loosened some of the tension in Ruenen's heart. He needed to be strong, as well. Everyone in the kingdom was relying on him.

"I'm sorry," he replied in a softer tone, ignoring the stinging in his eyes. "I've always been reckless. Marai used to hate that. It was wrong of me to take out my anger on you. But the truth is that I'm *terrified*, Thora. I'm scared I'll never see Marai again, that she's somewhere suffering, and I can't help her." Ruenen took Thora's small hand in his own as he released a quavering breath. "But you're right—Marai and Keshel will come home. I won't give up, and neither will they. Marai will fight forever if she has to."

Thora smiled and squeezed his hand back. Ruenen then noticed a thin metal band around her troth finger. He stared and stared at it.

Thora's cheeks turned a rosy pink. She pulled her hand from his grasp. "We should, um . . . get going. You've had a long day."

Raife cleared his throat and avoided Ruenen's eyes as he extended a hand to Thora, lifting her off the couch.

A strange, hollow pain gushed through Ruenen, seeing their entwined fingers. *They deserve happiness,* he thought. *This shouldn't bother me.* Thora and Raife had suffered so much loss and hardship. Marai had told Ruenen that the two faeries had loved each other for a long time, but never felt safe enough to act on those feelings. They'd finally found security in Nevandia, and Ruenen was glad that they were beginning a new journey together. That love could still exist when things seemed bleak.

But Ruenen couldn't stop the ache from spreading; the loneliness and longing for the woman who'd vanished on him twice. Would he get to place a ring around Marai's finger? To openly display his affection for her?

He swallowed down the lump in his throat, and forced himself to smile. He flexed his fingers and moved his arm—completely healed thanks to Thora's power. "Thank you, Thora. I'm feeling much better now. Go home with her, Raife. I'll see you in the morning."

Raife slung Thora's medical bag over his shoulder, and gave Ruenen an embarrassed sort of smile. Ruenen caught a glint of metal around Raife's troth finger, as well.

When had they married? Did Aresti know?

And why didn't they tell him?

You know why. They didn't want to upset you. Ruenen was a mess these days, barely holding it together. *Lirr's Bones, I've snapped at my closest friends tonight.*

As the door closed behind them, he released a heavy sigh.

You can't stay sad forever. Pull yourself together.

Thora was correct: Marai would be furious if Ruenen squandered precious time. No matter what, Thora tried to improve relations with humans through her healing practice. She hadn't lost focus. She woke up each dawn determined to make a difference.

Ruenen had important work to do in order to heal the fissures in his war-torn nation. And then there were the things he knew Marai wanted him to do, such as finding ways to empower women, to create equality between humans and magical folk.

The world needed to change, and Nevandia would lead the way.

Ruenen had to get to work.

CHAPTER 9

MARAI

How am I still alive?

Marai's body was utterly ravaged, but the pain in her back was the sharpest and deepest, slicing into muscle and bone.

She waded through the haze of dark mist within her mind. Her head lolled on her shoulder, but Marai eventually came to. The brain-fog cleared, allowing memories to come flooding back.

Where am I?

Marai opened her eyes to find that she was sitting on cold, patchy grass inside a tent that smelled of cat pee and mold. Her hands were tied around a wooden pole behind her back. Something heavy sat between her shoulder blades—an unfamiliar weight pulled down on her muscles. Dried blood crusted her baggy sailor's clothing. The cool metal of the collar was still firmly ensconced around her neck, and iron shackles remained locked around Marai's ankles. However, nothing but the wooden pole was holding her down.

And she was alone.

Where's Keshel? Her pulse galloped. Had Cavar tortured Keshel after he'd finished with Marai?

She struggled, wincing from the strain on her back, and tried to get her feet beneath her in order to stand. If Marai pulled the pole from the ground, her arms would be free, and she could run to find Keshel.

Marai turned her head to look behind and assess the pole situation.

She gasped, heart skipping a beat.

Her father's dazzling lavender and cerulean wings were attached to her back.

No, not attached . . .

They were *hers,* sprouted from her own body. She *felt* the tingle of cold through them. The tickle of grass as they drooped on the ground. They were exactly how she remembered them on her father's back; the hues of blue and purple bled together like paint in water, with swirls and dots of lavender around the edges. But unlike her father's, a jagged white line sliced down the center of both forewings, shimmering and electrified. A matching pair of lightning bolts.

Marai's head spun, suddenly lightheaded.

How? How is this possible?

Only pure-blooded faeries, like her father, were born with wings. How could she suddenly have *wings* growing from her back?

But then she remembered—Cavar had summoned her "dormant blood" using his amulet. Somehow, he'd changed her. A prickle in the tips of her ears told her that they were now pointed, as well. She could hear with greater clarity than before; the sound of someone coughing far off in the distance, the flutter of a bird's wings, the soft breath of wind stirring a leaf.

Her eyesight had also sharpened. Marai stared in wonder at the grains and grooves in each blade of grass, at the uneven stitching of the tent's canvas, at the dozens of shades of white and yellow in the strands of her hair.

And the wings . . . she had to admit that they were beautiful. Seeing them again after so many years brought a dew of tears to her eyes. They didn't *feel* monstrous
. . .

Marai scolded herself for her brief fascination. *Dark magic formed them.* If the stone could bring out her dormant blood, she couldn't help but wonder what else Cavar could do with its power?

I need to get as far away from here as possible. I need to go home to Ruen.

She reached for her magic, and lightning struck within her veins, sending a wave of searing pain through her. Shocked, as usual.

Marai tried to lift her wings. The muscles in her back screamed at the weight, the unfamiliar usage. She barely got one wing off the grass before she broke out into a sweat.

The tent flap opened.

Marai froze, expecting Cavar or Koda coming for more torture. She steeled herself, ready to fight, no matter how weak and restrained she was.

Instead, two women entered, and Marai had to stop her jaw from dropping.

The first was far shorter than Marai. Brown curls framed her large forehead, and her blue eyes rounded at the sight of Marai tied to the pole. She carried a bundle of gauzy, silk fabric in her small, pale arms.

The second figure's skin was dusty-pink, hair an odd lavender-gray, with vibrant white eyes, and *wings*. Tall and thin as a twig, the winged female carried a wooden washbowl and cloth in long, boney fingers. In all of Marai's travels, she'd never seen anyone like her.

Am I dreaming?

The pink-skinned female wore a familiar metal collar around her neck, marking her as one of Cavar's prisoners. The human woman, however, wore no chains.

Marai openly stared at them as they stared back.

The shorter woman coughed politely, interrupting the silence, and gave Marai a smile. "We're here to clean you up, Your Grace."

"Don't call me that," Marai croaked, voice rasped from her earlier screaming.

"Well, what do you want us to call you?" asked the shorter woman. "I know you lot enjoy your respectful, flourishing titles."

Not me.

Marai scowled. "You work for Cavar?"

"May we approach, Your Grace?" pressed the shorter woman. "Or Your Majesty. Or O Mighty Queen. Take your pick, I have more."

Marai would've normally snorted at the woman's cheek, but the shooting fire in her back reminded her that no one who worked for Cavar could be trusted.

"Are you employed by the Governor?" she asked, punctuating each word.

The short woman exchanged a glance with the winged female, whose face crumpled with shame as a boney, pink finger touched her collar.

"No, we're like you . . . his property . . ." The accent in her voice was heavy, and it took Marai a moment to fully understand her.

Why was Cavar taking people prisoner? Marai could *possibly* understand why he'd trap magical folk, but the human woman's presence didn't make sense. What did he do with his prisoners?

"Where's Keshel? My . . . companion. What has Cavar done with him?" Marai questioned, leaning forward and pulling on her bindings.

"He's well and unharmed, a few tents over," the short woman said. "We just came from tending to him. He's very worried about you."

At least Keshel's okay. Or so the women said. Marai knew she shouldn't trust the word of these females, but the sorrow on the winged one's face was so plain, so deep, she couldn't help but feel minutely eased by their presence.

"I'm Gunnora," the shortest said, "and this is Anja." She blinked at Marai expectantly.

"Marai."

Anja, in a ratty homespun dress, dipped into a polished curtsy, making Marai's cheeks heat. "It's an honor to be in your presence, Your Grace." Her translucent wings, longer and thinner than Marai's, fluttered with zeal.

"No need to curtsy," Marai said. "I'm not a queen."

No, she was an ex-pirate, ex-mercenary, who may have led troops into battle and defeated an enemy king, and was once loved by the King of Nevandia, but was now nothing more than a prisoner in a piss-smelling tent.

However, Anja looked up, tears welling in her striking white eyes. "After all of these long decades, waiting for a faerie queen, here you are. When Koda told us about you, all of us in camp got very excited. I couldn't wait to meet you, and seeing you here now . . . well, it means a lot to me, Your Grace, even if you are a prisoner, like us."

Her words were filled with a reverence Marai couldn't understand. *Why? Why does Anja, Cavar, or anyone for that matter, care so much that I have royal blood?*

"You're not exactly what I was expecting for a faerie queen," said Gunnora dryly, giving Marai a skeptical look. "I thought you'd be a little more . . . regal."

This time, Marai did snort under her breath. There had been one moment where she'd felt regal. She'd been wearing a queen's gown, her arm looped through the arm of a king, who'd led her down an aisle, in front of hundreds of eyes, and kissed her in a hallway. If she hadn't been taken from Ruenen's side, what might have happened? Would she have stayed in Nevandia, and become his mistress? Or would she have set out on her own, searching for meaning in her newfound title as Queen?

"What camp is this? Where are we?" Marai asked, shoving thoughts of Ruenen aside.

"One step at a time, Your Grace," Anja said in a soothing voice. "Please, if you'll allow us to approach, we'll clean you up and give you this change of clothes."

Marai had no reason to fear these females. They were in the same predicament as her: slaves to a greedy madman. She nodded and Anja smiled, teeth pearly white against her unusual skin tone. She stepped forward with a washbowl, and sank to her knees at Marai's side.

Dipping the cloth in the water, she said, "There are rumors going around camp about what happened. You have so much blood on you." Anja's smile disappeared as the cloth turned from white to rust-colored. She gently wiped blood from Marai's back, and Marai flinched. Anja jerked her hand away. "I'm so sorry, Your Grace."

Marai clenched her teeth as a ghastly stinging and burning radiated from the wounds where the wings had punctured through her skin. "No, it's fine. Keep going."

Anja's lip trembled. "Is the pain . . . unbearable?"

Marai's back throbbed and smoldered; she could deal with that, but something deep and vital had changed within her. Tiny, charged needles in her veins jabbed at her from the inside. If the collar wasn't dousing her magic, Marai wondered if it would be even stronger than before. Her body, while aching, felt entirely new.

She shook her head, clearing away the wonder. Marai had already wasted too much time sitting in that tent, chatting. She needed to grab Keshel and find a way to escape.

"Can you get me out of these chains?" she asked Anja.

The female's face fell further as she wiped blood and grime from Marai's face and neck. "We have no way to break the chains, and only Koda carries a set of keys to unlock them. He'll be here soon; he's speaking with Cavar."

"I doubt he'll take the chains off your ankles, though," Gunnora said with one raised eyebrow. "Heard you gave the boys trouble in Cavar's Bakair office. I believe the term going around camp is that you're a 'wild stallion that must be broken.' He won't let you loose until he trusts you not to kill him."

Well, that will never happen.

Gunnora must have read the thought on Marai's face because a smirk bloomed on her lips. "I'd love nothing more than to see you give Koda a well-deserved pummeling, but I must warn you to be careful. Cavar's guards patrol the camp at all hours, and they have whips and weapons, not to mention Koda can freely use his magic."

"What kind of camp is this?"

Anja began wiping down Marai's arms. Her gentle touch reminded Marai of Thora's healing hands. "You're now part of Cavar's Menagerie."

Marai vaguely remembered the Governor saying so before she passed out in his office. "What exactly is this Menagerie?"

"Cavar collects magical folk and puts us on display. We . . . we perform for paying customers. Humans on Andara travel far and wide to watch us."

Bile rose in Marai's throat and churned her stomach. She'd never heard of a more disgusting thing. Wealthy Astyeans would trap and house exotic birds for sport, calling that their menagerie, but this was different. Cavar was enslaving *people*. The fae massacres on Astye were horrific, but Cavar had come up with a new type of reprehensible persecution. Marai would rather be dead than imprisoned.

"Cavar finds and enslaves magical folk on Andara, and then sends that bastard Koda off into the world, searching for others." Gunnora's face contorted with vehemence as she gestured to her small body. "Doesn't matter if you're magical or not, if you're labeled as 'different' or 'unique' then you're shipped off to the Menagerie. We're his little freak show."

A circus. Marai remembered Thora mentioned the term before. She'd read it in one of Keshel's books, apparently.

"How long have you both been here?" Marai asked.

"Seven years," said Gunnora, lifting a shoulder.

Seven years. The number seemed astronomical. Marai had been Cavar's prisoner for over a month, and that was already far too long.

Anja sighed. "I was taken thirty years ago."

Everything went cold and dark within Marai. Anja and Gunnora's nonchalance, their acceptance of this lifelong incarceration, tugged on her heartstrings.

"At first the Menagerie was a small handful of folk, but it grew steadily each year," continued Anja. "Cavar added more and more of us, growing bolder in his ways of entrapment, and started imprisoning more powerful folk and creatures. None of the original folk from those early days are still alive. As of now, I'm the longest-serving member. I think the only reason I've survived so long is because I'm fae, and we're . . . sturdier, thanks to our magic."

"You're really fae?" Marai asked.

Anja didn't look anything like the full-blooded fae from Marai's childhood. Even with wings and pointed ears, they'd looked mostly human. None of them had had such vividly colored skin, and Anja's wings were pointier, paper-thin like a dragonfly's, not the rounded butterfly wings sprouting from Marai's own back.

"I'm Andaran fae, Your Grace, quite different from you," Anja said, smiling again, happy to explain. "Andaran faeries have never bred with humans, therefore, our blood is entirely pure, harkening back to ancient times. Astyean fae, however, coupled with humans centuries ago, which explains why you and Keshel have such human characteristics." Anja's white eyes grazed over Marai's face and wings, as intrigued by what she saw as Marai was of Anja. "To be honest, I've never seen an Astyean faerie before. How *human* you look! So different, Your Grace, and yet, the same magic runs in our veins. The same ancestors: Lirr and Laimoen."

It took Marai a second for Anja's words to settle, to work out their meaning. Anja believed that fae were descended from the gods?

Don't think about that now. She needed to find Keshel. She needed to escape this monstrosity of a Menagerie.

"How can I get out of this camp?" she asked.

Anja and Gunnora's wrists and ankles weren't bound. They were free to move around as they pleased, however, both females frowned at Marai's eager tone.

"I'm sorry, Your Grace, but even if we had the keys to unshackle you, you wouldn't make it out of here," said Anja.

"Cavar has a magical barrier erected around the entire Menagerie," Gunnora explained. "Others have tried to escape before, but no one can pass through the fog. It's impossible."

Like the barrier on the docks . . .

Anja shook her head. "I think the only way we'll ever be free is if the barrier comes down—"

"And Cavar would never willingly do that," chimed in Gunnora. "You'd have to *kill* him to get that barrier down, or somehow steal his amulet—"

Marai's resolve returned with blazing fire. "Then that's what I'll do."

She'd tear Cavar limb from refined limb with her bare hands if necessary.

Anja grabbed hold of Marai's arm in a panic. "You can't, Your Grace! Cavar's too strong, and if you try, he'll punish you severely. I know you're powerful, but no one can compete with the amulets, especially his, due to the black stone. Cavar isn't often at the Menagerie, so it would be hard to get your hands on him. Acacia, Koda, and the guards keep things running here."

"But Cavar's at the Menagerie right now," Gunnora said with raised brows. "Goes to show how important you are to him, Your Grace, that he came all the way out here to ensure your transition goes smoothly."

If I could just get my hands on him . . .

"Guardians and investors from around the country are arriving to see you, as well, which means that there will be dozens of amulets present this week," said Anja. "Your Grace and Keshel are the most exciting additions to the Menagerie that Cavar's had in decades."

"You don't have to treat me like royalty," Marai said with a grimace. "I'm shackled to a pole. It doesn't matter who my ancestors were. It didn't before, and it certainly doesn't now."

Anja pursed her lips. "But it *does* matter. You're not aware what it means to those of us in this camp to have you here. What it means to *me* that a faerie queen of a bloodline long thought dead, still lives. You are a symbol of hope and strength, Your Grace. A symbol that after all the atrocities committed by humans against our kind, your bloodline has managed to survive. And so shall we, because you're going to lead us."

The way Anja was staring, eyes shining, face alight with adoration, reminded Marai of Kadiatu. Anja had the same gentle spirit. Had Kadiatu, from the Underworld, sent Marai this female to befriend her? To guide her to a more purposeful existence? To *save* these people, as Anja seemed to believe?

Marai didn't know how to help Anja, Gunnora, and the other folk in the Menagerie. She didn't know how to save herself and Keshel. How could she lead these people to a better life when she was a prisoner?

The tent flap was brushed aside again, and Marai stiffened at the appearance of the stranger in the entryway. It wasn't the bold tattoos across her face that caught Marai's attention. No, it was her eyes. Veiled. Hard. As if this woman had seen and done far too much. As if she'd overcome tremendous hardship and still said "fuck you" to the world.

Unlike Anja and Gunnora, her ankles were clad in iron shackles. Marai guessed this labeled the woman as "untrustworthy," and for some reason, she found herself instantly more interested in the stranger.

"Koda's coming," the woman said in a thick Yehzigi accent, but her voice was hollow. She gazed at Marai with none of the warmth Anja and Gunnora had, as if kindness and joy had been stripped from her. It was like looking through a mirror at Marai's old self, the Lady Butcher. The woman's empty eyes snapped back to Anja and Gunnora. "Finish cleaning her up. She's a mess. Koda will take a whip to you both if the job isn't done before he arrives."

Anja and Gunnora jolted into action. Within moments, they'd cleaned the blood from her, but Marai still felt its crusty residue on her skin. Her hair remained matted with blood, despite a brief rinse.

Then Koda entered the tent.

He didn't bother to announce himself. His arrival sucked the air right from the space as he stared at Marai. Gunnora and Anja stepped away from her, lowering their heads meekly in his presence.

The other woman, however, glared at Koda with so much hate that Marai was surprised the half-fae male didn't burst into flames. The woman didn't fear him. Didn't respect him. Marai saw a potential ally in her.

Koda's silver eyes flicked to look at the woman, as if surprised she was standing there, glaring at him so ferociously. Marai expected to hear a reprimand, but Koda turned his attention back to his newest prisoner. "How are you feeling, Marai?"

She spat at his feet. Marai heard Anja's tiny gasp, and watched Gunnora's mouth twitch at the edges. The other woman's expression didn't change.

Koda heaved a heavy, disappointed sigh. "I was hoping you'd be more amiable now that Cavar awakened your dormant blood and gifted you those beautiful wings." His eyes glowed with molten envy.

"Why would I be pleased? He *tortured* me with dark magic," Marai growled. "He changed me when I didn't want to changed."

"For the better, Marai. Cavar's taking an enormous interest in you, sparing no expense." Koda's voice sounded strained, like the thought displeased him. "Now you're no longer half-fae, torn between two worlds. Your blood is pure. Well, not as pure as Anja's, but isn't it the dream of all part-fae to fully belong? Don't the wings make you happy?"

Marai felt quite the opposite. Looking at her father's wings, drooping forlornly against her back, made Marai incredibly sad. She missed him, missed watching his stained-glass wings flutter and shimmer in the sunlight, and glow like a beacon of hope in the darkness. Marai missed the safety of his arms when she was a toddler. His laughter. His stories. She wished her father was *here*.

It was Koda's dream to be a pure-blooded fae, not hers. Marai had never wished for such a thing. That would require removing her mother's human blood from her veins. Removing her from Marai's past.

Koda knelt at Marai's side, gaze sliding over her wings and pointed ears one final, envious time. "I'm going to unbind your hands, and I want no fuss." He finally glanced up at the harsh woman. "Make sure she's presentable to Cavar. She needs to look like a queen when she walks into that office."

The tense narrowing of her eyes was the woman's only response.

Watching Marai carefully, Koda removed the rope around her wrists and tent pole.

"There now, that's better, isn't it?" he asked, all jolly, once Maria's hands were free. "You'll need to show off your wings. Cavar will be expecting perfection."

"I can't move them." The only movement Marai could produce was a slight twitch, and it hurt like hell.

Koda frowned. "Anja will need to work with you on strengthening those muscles. It can't be that hard, could it? Faerie wings are quite light."

"I'm sure Cavar could do the same for you," Marai snapped in his face, "torturing you from the inside-out."

Koda smirked, leaning away. "Governor Cavar would never waste such a gift on me."

For a moment, Marai saw a split-second of regret in Koda's handsome face, but it was gone as quickly as it came when he stood up and faced the woman, Anja, and Gunnora.

"Put her in that dress. Brush her hair again, too. She's a godsawful mess." He then turned back to Marai. "I'll step out to give you privacy, but make sure you behave. Don't bother trying to call on magic; you know by now the collar will use your own against you. Any commotion, and I'll take out your punishment on Keshel."

Marai bared her teeth.

Koda made to exit the tent, but the woman stood in his way like a statue.

"Move aside, please, Innesh," said Koda. A muscle feathered his jaw as he stared her down.

Finally, the woman, Innesh, moved, and Koda strutted from the tent.

Innesh gestured to Anja and Gunnora, who stepped forward again and assessed Marai's pitiful condition. Her shirt was in tatters, especially where her wings had ripped through. Her pants were covered in dried blood. Marai could barely stand without their aid; she winced and hissed at the pull of the wings between her shoulder blades.

Anja ran out and returned with clean, fresh water in her bowl. She dumped the whole thing over Marai's head, and scrubbed out the blood, but Anja couldn't remove Marai's shirt because it snagged on her wings.

Innesh stepped forward, took the shirt in her hands, and ripped it right off Marai's body. Marai quickly wrapped her thin arms across her chest, but Innesh, Anja, and Gunnora weren't as self-conscious as she was. Anja brushed through Marai's matted locks as Gunnora placed the bundle of clothes she'd been carrying at Marai's feet.

"Step into this," she ordered.

The dress had no back and slid across Marai's skin like a soft breeze. The material was flowing, ethereal, the color of a summer forest, with a pink-flowered applique sewn along the hem that only touched Marai's knees. A scandalous length back on Astye. Far too revealing, even more so than the dress Ruenen had given her for his coronation. Gunnora pulled down Marai's pants, tossing them aside, and produced pink silk slippers.

QUEEN OF THE SHADOW MENAGERIE

Marai shivered in the chilly air, hugging herself to keep warm. *Couldn't they give me a sweater or a dress with longer sleeves?* Wet hair dripped down her back like melting icicles.

When Marai was deemed presentable, Innesh ushered her outside the tent to Koda, who was leaning, bored and aloof, against a tree. Marai didn't pay much attention to him; she was too engrossed in the sight of the camp.

Rows of tents, not unlike the Nevandian war camp, were packed in closely next to large iron cages. *Did all the magical folk live here together in these tents?* She didn't see any others yet, as if they were hiding within. Cavar's red-vested guards, however, were everywhere, skulking through the rows with surly expressions, probably keeping folk at bay with their whips and swords.

Where's Keshel?

There were a few scattered trees and bushes. A creek. And of course, that towering wall of dark fog. Craning her neck up, Marai glared at the barrier as it domed protectively around the entire camp.

However, there was one side of the camp free of the barrier. The back of a three-story, rounded, black sandstone building served as the fourth wall. It looked out of place compared to the sparsity of the rest of the camp. The structure was imposing and ominous; a prison without a roof.

That must be where we're put on display. But Marai's mind went through fast calculations as she studied the structure. *That's the breach where I can escape from.*

"You're dismissed," Koda said tersely to Anja and Gunnora, jerking Marai back to the present. "Innesh, Acacia wants you, so you're to come with us inside."

Innesh merely glared back at him.

Koda rolled his eyes, then took hold of Marai's arm and quickly blindfolded her.

"Why bother?" she asked through gritted teeth, tossing her head as he tried to tie it.

Koda smacked her upside the head, and Marai stilled instantly, more shocked than hurt.

"You need to be inducted into this new world slowly. No sense overwhelming you with everything at once."

Now he's trying to be thoughtful?

"Also, I know you're crafty. We're not taking any chances with you," he added.

Fuck. But Marai still had no idea where Keshel was. She couldn't leave without him, even if she managed to get the chance.

Marai let Koda lead her through the rows towards the building. Her new fae ears picked up the scuff of Innesh's slippers, the rattling of her shackled feet, as she trailed behind. It didn't take long to reach the door where Koda whipped off Marai's blindfold.

Up close, the circular building wasn't as big as she'd thought—it appeared that way because it was the only structure in the vicinity. Its black stone walls climbed upwards, curving, more like an amphitheater. The main entrance must have been on the other side, because Koda ushered Marai through a small back doorway. Cavar would never allow his patrons to view the grim, dingy tent-city of the creatures they paid to see. That entrance, on the other side, was where Marai would make her eventual escape.

Up a set of simple stone stairs, Koda brought Marai to another wooden door on the landing. The half-fae male knocked twice.

"Koda with the Queen," he said cheerily. It was a voice, Marai realized, that Koda reserved only for his employer.

"Enter," came Cavar's smooth voice from inside, and Marai was once again face-to-face with her newest enemy.

CHAPTER 10

CAVAR

The sight of her made his pulse quicken.

Not with attraction, but triumph.

When Koda had discovered the girl's lineage, the little voice inside Cavar's head had become consumed with the idea of her. Of *possessing* her.

"Bring her here," it had urged Cavar, and he'd complied, all too eager to please the magic in the onyx stone that had granted him such god-like power.

The Faerie Queen stood in the doorway of his office at the Menagerie. She'd been cleaned up, dressed up, and brought to heel, although her face remained a mask of hatred. Her eyes were as wild as an out-of-control blaze. He'd have to do something about that before presenting her to the other Guardians and investors later that evening. Marai's newly-formed wings drooped against her back; it would take some time before her muscles adapted and strengthened to lift them. Cavar marveled at their iridescent color and shine, so many shades of purple and blue in swirls that were reminiscent of brushstrokes, as if a painter had used them as his canvas.

Next to Cavar, Acacia clapped and giggled. "Oh, she's *perfect!* We'll have lines out the door for decades."

Lady Acacia Kozina's eyes sparkled as she gazed at Marai, who, unsurprisingly, glared back at the woman Guardian. Acacia was Cavar's niece. Well, *distant* niece—he'd been alive for over one hundred years. She was the great-granddaughter of his deceased sister. Acacia was also one of his business partners in the Menagerie, and ran the show in his absence.

Next to her stood a major investor, Lord Sheerek Greguric, a surly Northern Andaran Governor and Guardian of the rugged alpine city south of the Hinterlands. He'd seen his fair share of magical folk; his whole family had been murdered by a goblin creature. Greguric held no fascination for the folk, didn't care about the spectacle of the Menagerie, maybe not even the money. No, Greguric simply wanted revenge.

His dark, beady eyes narrowed as he approached Marai. She stiffened and tried to pull away, but Koda had a vise-like-grip on her arm. Innesh hovered, a morose silhouette blocking the doorway.

"Where are the bindings for her wrists?" Greguric asked Koda.

"She's no threat as long as we have her companion, Keshel, whom you inspected earlier," Koda replied, then his eyes snapped to Cavar. "Unless, of course, Governor, you'd like me to put them back on."

Cavar waved him off. "Unnecessary. As you said, her feet are bound, so she can't run, and I have control of her magic. She's harmless."

As if to prove him wrong, Marai thrashed in Koda's grip.

"I've killed a dozen men with my bare hands," she growled. "There's nothing harmless about me."

Greguric scowled. Despite wearing an amulet, his hand stroked the hilt of a knife at his belt. He was perhaps the most reluctant Guardian to use magic. Cavar had learned the other Governor preferred the action of a physical brawl—he was an accomplished boxer and regularly trained.

"That's no way for a queen to behave," Acacia scolded, walking straight up to Marai. She was only three and twenty, but Cavar saw great promise in her. One day, he planned to hand off his business here in Andara to her so that he could pursue opportunities abroad. Acacia pulled and tugged at Marai's dress, one she'd picked out herself, and examined the material. "You're passable in that *unique* way. Not pretty, but interesting to look at, like a little forest faerie. She'll need a crown of woven flowers or vines, I think. Do a twirl for me."

Marai's face detonated with rage and shock.

Acacia wasn't known for her patience, and slapped Marai across the face. "I said *twirl*, girl!"

A red mark blossomed across Marai's cheek as she bared her teeth at Cavar's niece. "Touch me again, and I'll bite off your hand."

Cavar certainly couldn't have that, and Acacia, in the stubbornness of youth, drew her hand back to strike the Faerie Queen again.

"Acacia, allow me, dear." Cavar took hold of his amulet. It warmed beneath his skin, and the magic came alive, excited to do his bidding. The magic *wanted* to touch her.

Cavar forced his will upon Marai, and she spun in a dainty, perfect circle, with the grace of a well-practiced dancer. Her dress fanned out around her, and for additional effect, golden specks of light and dust trailed behind her wings.

Acacia clapped again, positively delighted. "Fantastic! See, Sheerek? She's harmless. And the gold light, Uncle, was an excellent touch. We shall have to call it . . . *faerie* dust!"

Cavar released Marai from the stone's will, and she stumbled in disbelief. Her freedom, her *control,* had been snatched away easily. Cavar grinned as understanding darkened Marai's face—she could rebel all she wanted, but the truth, Marai began to discover, was that Cavar could *make* her do anything. As long as she wore that collar, she was his marionette.

"She'll be the main act?" Greguric asked.

"The grand finale," Cavar replied. "Our crown jewel. Queen of the Menagerie."

He'd always been an ambitious man. While mentally stimulating, the life of a scholar didn't line his pockets. He knew what the people craved. Andarans were as mesmerized by magic as Acacia was of Marai. They wanted spectacle. They wanted to be *dazzled* by the magical world, but from a safe distance.

Since Cavar had first used the stone's power to create the other amulets and distributed them amongst the wealthy Guardians, Andara had enjoyed sixty years of peace. Sixty years since the Hinterland's Veil had been erected and the folk sequestered themselves away. Most Andarans alive had never seen a magical creature, except at the Menagerie.

"We'll need to raise the price of admission," Greguric stated.

"Already in motion, Governor," Cavar said, clapping a hand on Greguric's back. "We have fliers being posted in the nearby towns, and I shall give you some to bring back home with you. I expect the news will travel fast that we've captured an elusive Faerie Queen. Now, my friends, I have some things to discuss with Marai, but please join me this evening for a celebratory banquet. Everyone else will be here by then."

"Mistress Blago is coming? Uch, that woman is insufferable," Acacia said, then planted a quick kiss on Cavar's cheek before she made for the exit. "I'll make sure everything looks magnificent for tonight, Uncle."

Innesh slid out of her way, and Acacia gave the Yehzigi woman a revolted look before leaving; Greguric skulked after her.

"Wait outside, and close the door," Cavar ordered Innesh. "I'll speak to you separately."

Innesh glanced at Marai, then disappeared into the hallway.

"How dare you treat me like a puppet," Marai spat, struggling against Koda's grasp.

Her face evoked murder. If she got her hands on him, Cavar knew the Faerie Queen would rip out his throat and devour his heart for dinner. There was a part of him that feared her, that dangerous glint in her luminescent eyes, because Cavar also knew that if the day ever came when she got her hands on his amulet, at the magic inside the stone, she could destroy his whole empire. She'd already turned thousands of enemy soldiers to ash. Lady Butcher Marai was the most powerful creature on earth.

But she was no goddess. Her magic wasn't limitless, like the magic in the stone. *Cavar* was limitless. *He* had the power of a god. And the Faerie Queen belonged to him.

"And me," the stone's little voice reminded him.

"You need to control your temper. I won't tolerate disrespect," Cavar said, polished politeness gone with his niece and Greguric. He leaned against his desk, crossing one foot over the other. She might be a queen, but to him, Marai was only a girl in a costume.

"You used dark magic on me," she said. "You *changed* me."

"The stone's magic never entered you. It pulled forth what was already in your blood, making you into what you're supposed to be. Half-bloods can't be Faerie Queens."

QUEEN OF THE SHADOW MENAGERIE

"I don't *want* to be Queen of the Fae."

Cavar launched off the desk and prowled towards her, gripping his amulet again. "Every time you disobey me, you will be beaten. You cannot win here, so stop fighting, and practice your best smile."

"I will *never* concede to you. I'll fight you until the very last breath leaves my body."

Cavar had to admire her bravery. If only she was willing to work *for* him instead of against him . . . but her vexatious attitude was beginning to bore him.

"Think about King Ruenen."

Marai's eyes widened, swirling with magic and fury at the mention of the newly crowned Nevandian King. "What about him?"

"Koda tells me you're close with him, and that the young monarch has *quite* the secret." Cavar relished the fear in Marai's face. It wasn't her own bodily harm, or even that of Keshel's . . . it was her love for the Nevandian King that Cavar could use to control her. "If it was revealed that he isn't the *true* King, he'd be imprisoned for the rest of his life, or more likely, hanged as a traitor. You wouldn't want that to happen, would you? Because all I have to do is write dozens of missives to spread around Nevandia and Tacorn, and there'd be a mob at his door demanding his head. The boat back to Astye hasn't left yet . . . I'm sure Slate Hemming would be more than happy to ensure the missives reach their intended audience. I've been meaning to introduce myself to the leaders of Astye for some time now, anyways."

Marai paled and swallowed. The threat hit its mark.

Cavar created a small barrier around himself. To Koda he said, "Hold her still."

Koda snapped and Marai froze. It was tremendously valuable, Koda's gift. Fascinating and useful how thoroughly he was able to immobilize someone. At Cavar's insistence, Anja had trained young Koda in the art of Andaran magic when he'd first arrived.

The room grew colder, saturated with Koda's magic. Cavar dropped the barrier that had protected him from Koda's power. He took a pair of shears from his coat pocket, then grabbed hold of one of Marai's delicate wings. It was smooth and soft as silk, paper-thin between his fingers. With surgical precision, Cavar clipped a portion away from her right hindwing.

Once finished, he signaled to Koda. With another snap, Marai was released and collapsed to her knees, gasping in pain, although this time, there was no blood to stain his expensive rug. Faerie wings, Cavar had learned from studying Anja's, were made of a thin, membranous layer of chitin and tubular veins and bones, like a lowly insect.

Using the bell on his desk, Cavar signaled for Innesh to re-enter, then turned to his half-fae assistant. "Take her to the cage. It's already sitting in the banquet hall."

Koda took hold of Marai again. She seemed too stunned and weak to fight back or say anything.

"And Koda—good work, son."

His assistant beamed at the compliment. "Thank you, Governor."

Innesh's dark eyes narrowed at Koda, and Cavar didn't miss the look of contempt on her face. Neither did Koda. Their eyes held for a brief moment, and something like regret passed over Koda's face. Then it was gone, and he yanked stumbling Marai from the office.

Koda was still so much like that young orphan boy who'd appeared on the dock of Bakair fifteen years ago, seeking refuge from the cruelty of his past on Yehzig. Seeking *love* and respect. Cavar had given that boy those things in exchange for his loyal service.

And clinging to the boy's side had been a Yehzigi girl. She, however, had never sought Cavar's love. She didn't have Koda's gift or heritage, but the faerie boy had begged for the girl to stay near him. Childish Koda had been in love with her, and sometimes, Cavar thought his right-hand still was.

Innesh's face was removed of malice as she stared at Cavar.

"Make sure that faerie is ready to perform in three days. I'll take your hand if she embarrasses me in front of patrons."

Innesh's jaw tightened. "Yes, Governor."

"Help Acacia set up for the banquet tonight. It must be perfect for our important guests."

"Yes, Governor."

Yes, Governor. Innesh rarely said anything different. She'd had her earlier defiance beaten out of her. Now, she was a walking shadow.

The banquet hall on the second floor sparkled with diamonds dangling from the chandeliers and earlobes of the fashionable aristocracy present. The room was lit by a thousand candles. Spring flowers of every color decorated the centers of the tables and backs of chairs. Guests held glasses of gold, sparkling wine in their bejeweled fingers. Dozens of stones pulsated around the necks of Guardians; the amulets reacted to each other's presence.

Cavar stood before them upon the mini-stage erected for the occasion, Acacia at his side, dressed in billowing bright purple.

"My friends, welcome, welcome back to the Menagerie!" He'd prepared this speech days ago. It was memorized, burned into Cavar's brain and branded on his tongue.

The audience applauded.

"I started this Menagerie fifty years ago with only a handful of creatures, a makeshift stage, and twenty patrons. Now, I have this beautiful amphitheater, dozens of investors, and over twenty acts. What makes this Menagerie special is that we have the most diverse display of folk, and we're always finding new additions. That's what keeps people lining up at our ticket booth. Our performances never get stale, and we're always improving. For fifty years, we've been providing education and much-needed entertainment to the people of Andara. We've taught our countrymen that magic can be tamed, creatures can be captured, and peace is but a stone's throw away."

Cavar winked, indicating his amulet. The audience laughed.

"We Guardians carry a heavy burden, the safety of Andara around our necks, but I'm glad that tonight we can revel in our success. We need no longer fear the rising of the faerie folk. I have in my possession the final blot in the royal bloodline. The last loose thread, now tied up securely in a knot. I give you, Queen Marai of the Fae!"

Koda and three red-vested Peace Keepers wheeled in a dark iron cage. Marai stood against the far side, trying to bend the bars with all her might, lavender eyes wide with fear.

Foolish girl. Her life belonged to Cavar now.

The crowd parted, and the cage was brought to the center of the room.

"Isn't she fascinating?" Cavar asked his fellow Guardians. "Please, have a closer look."

Voices floated up to him on the dais, like the bubbles in his wine glass. Guests closed in on the cage. Some of them dared reach a hand inside to poke and prod at Marai, who cursed and hissed at them like an angry cat.

"Look at those wings!"

"Is it magic making her irises swirl like that?" a gentleman asked another.

"She's ghostly pale. Does she have fanged teeth? I've heard some of them do. Faeries are such strange creatures."

"Acacia, did you choose her dress? It's lovely," preened one of Acacia's wealthy friends.

Marai darted away from their touch, but there were too many outstretched hands and faces pressing in at her. She dropped to the floor of the cage, bringing her knees into her chest.

Mistress Blago's politician husband, as oily a man as Cavar had seen, approached him on the dais. "Well done, Governor. She's exquisite." His glass clinked the rim of Cavar's and he smoothed out his mustache with a finger. "Will she be available for perusal soon?"

Cavar met Blago's dark, insistent gaze. "In due time, my friend. She's brand new, and I'm not yet certain how she'll operate. But I promise that you'll be the first to know. I'm certain she'll be quite the *spark*."

Blago smiled his oily smile and returned to his wife, who pointed at Marai with a disgusted, curled lip.

Marai sat in her cage the entire banquet, scowling, curling inwards as a small girl would to shield off bad dreams. She sent a crude gesture to Cavar, and Koda rapped on the bars with a cane.

Cavar expected the best. He did not like to be disappointed, but thankfully, spirits were high. The guests were happy, knowing how much richer they'd be by month's end. The food and drink were sublime, music excellent, and at the end of the night, Innesh and the other slaves would ensure that every speck of dirt and debris would be cleaned from the hall.

All in all, it was a splendid reveal, and a successful evening. He hoped to have many more such evenings after he partnered with the rulers of Astye. Country by country, Cavar would expand his Menagerie across the world. He'd have a foothold in every aspect of commerce, and by selling his amulets to the wealthy, he and his stone would have power and control over them all.

Cavar would bring Andara out of the shadows, make it the leader of the known world, with him at its helm. Magic was money, and Cavar planned to become the richest man on earth.

And the stone would have its prize in Marai.

"Take her back to her tent," he told Koda, "and make sure she gets punished for her behavior this evening." Although, Cavar suspected that her wildness only made Marai more enthralling to his guests and shareholders.

Koda and the Peace Keepers dragged the cage away, Marai cursing at them and threatening to pull out their entrails.

Cavar's ground his teeth. *She needs to learn to control that tongue before I have it removed.*

Acacia kissed Cavar on the cheek, wiping away his irritation. "She's a menace, that one, but she'll settle in. I won't stand for such ill behavior. I promise, Uncle, that the Menagerie is in good hands with me."

"I trust you, my dear."

But he didn't trust Marai. Not yet. Not until she'd realized she was thoroughly beaten.

CHAPTER 11

MARAI

Marai had suffered through humiliation before, but nothing compared to the soul-crushing indignity she'd experienced in that banquet room.

For hours, she'd been prodded, pulled at, sneered at, and inspected like a horse at auction. One man had licked his lips while staring at her, as if imagining how she'd taste, picturing the things he'd do to her if the cage's bars hadn't separated them.

Marai sat there and watched the Guardians and Cavar's wealthy friends gorge themselves on food and sparkling wine, enduring the indignity of their scrutinizing gazes. Their faces lacked any kind of compassion for Marai's entrapment. Not a single one of them regarded her with expressions of apology or concern. She was no better than a pet bird in a cage.

When the event was over, Koda and another guard named Yelich yanked her from the cage roughly by her wings. Marai cried out from the pain, then Yelich struck her across the face with the handle of his whip.

"That's for your poor behavior tonight," Koda said coolly.

Blood dripped from Marai's mouth as Yelich blindfolded her. His meaty fingers latched onto her wings again, and dragged her outside the theater. Walking backwards, Marai stumbled through rows of tents, feet catching on rocks and tree roots, ignoring the whispers and comments, too exhausted and mortified to care. Yelich shoved her into her tent and removed the blindfold, leaving her alone with Koda.

She could still feel the possessive touches and ogling stares, leaving a greasy, dirty film across her body that no amount of scrubbing could remove. Marai wanted out of Andara more than anything, but at the same time, her body craved sleep. She couldn't focus on an escape plan. She couldn't focus on anything but the weariness, the chasmic disquiet of her mind, and the sharp sting in her right hindwing where Cavar had clipped away a portion, leaving her feeling unbalanced.

I truly am a caged bird. Her heart ached for the loss of flight—something she'd never imagined doing before, but for a few glorious minutes, Marai had wondered if she could fly straight home to Ruenen. Now she never would.

With a furrowed brow, Koda watched her assess the damage to her wing. "You'll get used to life here."

Marai glared up at him. *Used to it?* She didn't want to get *used to it.* Because then that would mean she'd given up, and Marai would *never* give up. "Why are you doing this? Why allow those bastards to make a mockery of your people? When they insult me, they're insulting *you,* as well."

Koda's face shuttered. "I have no people." He turned his back on Marai, and disappeared back outside.

She wanted to kick something. Rip something apart. Run and run until her lungs collapsed and there was nothing before her but ocean.

Innesh slipped into the tent. Marai had watched her in the banquet hall, serving those imperious cretins with an expression of indifference. She'd been forced to wipe up spilled wine on the floor, on her hands and knees. To clean food from a man's boot. To carry Acacia's white poof of a dog around. Marai expected her to say something about their shared degradation.

Instead, Innesh tossed a moth-eaten bedroll onto the ground, as well as a patchy blanket, nightgown, skin of water, and a wooden bowl and spoon. Eventually, she said in a voice devoid of feeling, "Bring that bowl and spoon with you to the commissary twice a day. If you lose it, you don't get another."

"Where's Keshel?" Marai asked, ignoring the meager supplies and stepping towards the quiet, stone-faced woman.

Innesh blinked once, then turned and exited the tent.

Marai's scowl deepened. *Not friendly, then.* She'd thought, perhaps, to find some camaraderie in the human woman who so clearly despised her captors, who stood tall and unafraid, unaffected, despite her circumstances.

Perhaps there was no such thing as friendship in a place like the Menagerie, where everyone was only looking out for themselves, hoping to survive to the next day.

Marai tried to lift and spread her wings to get a better glimpse of the damage done, but her back and shoulders cried in protest.

How do I strengthen muscles I've never had to use before?

Marai sighed and closed her eyes. What was the point of trying to use her wings when she'd never be able to fly anyways? She'd spent years honing her body, training to become a fierce warrior. She'd been agile, grounded. She'd known exactly how her body moved, how each muscle worked. Now, she'd been forced off-balance.

I'll need to re-learn how to fight with these.

But that was for another day.

Marai didn't want to be awake. She didn't want to hurt, to feel, to live in this nightmare. She slowly unfurled the bedroll and climbed beneath the musty blanket, but her damned, cumbersome wings kept getting in the way. She tossed, flaring her wings out the best she could to lie on her back, but one kept curling the wrong way under her. She hissed as stinging pain shot straight through her wing and up her spine.

"How the *fuck* am I supposed to sleep?" she bellowed in frustration, slamming her fists against the bedroll.

Someone laughed melodically at the opening of her tent. Marai turned to see Anja peeking her colorful head in. Anja's face brimmed with a pitiable smile as she held up a small lantern, illuminating the tent in wan light.

"It takes some getting used to," the fae female said, "but I promise, you'll sleep again. May we enter?"

Marai nodded, sitting up in her bedroll.

Anja stepped inside, followed by a tall, thin someone with haggard, angular eyes.

Marai bolted out of her bedroll and threw her arms around his tapered torso.

Keshel emitted a soft *oof* when she slammed into him. He wrapped long arms around her, holding her the way he had in the Badlands that first night, when she'd cried against his chest, so lost and broken. Seeing him now, unharmed and clean, in a long wool coat, brought Marai some semblance of calm. A trickling stream of relief coursed through her.

At least she still had *him*.

"They wouldn't let me see you," Keshel said, releasing a shaky breath. "Koda used that metallic powder on me in Cavar's office. The last thing I heard was your scream before I went under, and when I woke up in my tent, you weren't there. That dour woman with the tattoos kept watch over me for a while. I wasn't sure . . . she wouldn't say . . ." His arms around her tightened.

Marai pulled away, allowing him to see her fully. To inspect her. "I'm alive. I'm . . . okay."

Keshel's attention immediately snapped to her wings and pointed ears, his expression shifting from confusion, to horror, to curiosity. "I don't understand. How is this possible?"

"Cavar, he . . . brought forth my dormant faerie blood."

Darkness and rage contorted Keshel's usually impassive face. "That's impossible." Marai could see the wheels turning in his brain, perhaps thinking back on passages from his favorite fae history books, mentally flipping through pages. "I'm sorry that I couldn't help you."

"There's nothing you could've done to stop him. Not while Cavar has that stone."

"I don't understand any of this," said Keshel, which was a rare admission. "But that stone . . . it's made from dark magic, isn't it?"

Marai nodded with a grimace. "You and I both knew that we'd have to face it again. We knew that dark magic was still out there, despite Rayghast's death."

Back in Nevandia, before they'd been captured, Keshel had a vision. Marai remembered that conversation they'd shared on the garden bench after she recovered.

"Dark magic isn't gone," Keshel had said. *"This land may be free of it, but elsewhere in the world, others are using its power. Darkness will keep spreading, but we cannot stop it if we don't know how. Something is coming. A war is brewing between light and dark."*

"It seems we've found another source," continued Marai.

"Or it found *us*." Keshel arched one eyebrow. "I think I'm beginning to find some links between earlier visions. I think I've *seen* Cavar's stone before. And the symbol . . ." He pointed to the three-pronged engraving on his collar. "It was on those chains you wore in that vision I had a while back. I've been writing all my past ones down—" He pulled a tattered book out from his coat.

"You've had that this entire time?" Marai asked, stunned.

Keshel's precious journal had traveled across the world with him, full of his notes and thoughts, tucked away from his captors.

"You need to learn about the world if you're going to live in it," he said in response as he jotted down a quick note.

"Have you had another vision since . . ." Cavar's office.

Keshel shook his head. "No, my mind's been clear." He glanced over her shoulder at her wings again. "May I?"

Marai shrugged, and his dark eyes lit up as Keshel gently lifted her top left wing, lips parting in fascination.

"Did you know that faerie wings are an intricate system of tiny scales that are genetically inherited? That's how you get the color and pattern variations. Like a butterfly."

Marai snorted. Of course she didn't know that. Who else but Keshel would know such random facts?

He stepped away, frowning. "I'm sorry, I shouldn't be staring, considering how terrible this is, considering what happened to you . . . but I'm also truly amazed."

"Ever the scholar," Marai said with a lopsided smirk. "You wanted to learn about magic on Andara, right? Well, we've certainly learned *something* to add to your journal."

A gutted look flashed across Keshel's face. "I never wanted this, Marai. I should've expected Andara to be another dark place like Astye, but I wanted to *believe* that there was a better world out there. What Cavar did to you—"

"I know," Marai said, putting a hand on his arm. She'd hoped for that, as well. Not only in Andara, but in Nevandia. For magical folk. With Ruenen. She'd let herself believe. "I'm glad you're okay. Cavar didn't do anything to you, did he?"

QUEEN OF THE SHADOW MENAGERIE

"Not after he forced that vision from me in his office. I'm allowed to remain unshackled, except for the collar. Thanks to Anja, I've been fed, clothed, and cleaned."

Marai had nearly forgotten the female was there.

Anja's already rosy cheeks turned fuchsia as she dipped her head and smiled. "It's the least I could do, but it's time for curfew now. It's mandatory to be in your tent after light's out. The Peace Keepers will come around and check in a few minutes." She picked up Marai's nightgown. "Let me quickly help you with your wings."

Keshel waited outside as Anja helped Marai into her slatted nightgown, buttoning the back, giving her advice on how to sleep with wings.

"The Peace Keepers patrol at all hours of the night. Sometimes they'll burst into your tent if they 'suspect' foul play—" Marai stiffened. Anja noticed. "—But you don't need to worry about them touching you, at least in *that* way. Cavar has very strict rules for employees of the Menagerie. If there's anything you need, let me or Gunnora know. My tent is right next to yours."

Despite the dreadful circumstances, Anja was a blessing disguised in pink skin and diaphanous dragonfly wings. Marai didn't know how to properly thank her for her kindness, but it seemed Anja understood when Marai opened and closed her mouth and no sound emerged. Anja smiled and swept from the tent, allowing Keshel to reenter.

He looked Marai over, in her sepia-colored, thin nightgown, limp wings poking out the back. In the dark of the tent, his eyes shimmered with sorrow and affection. His throat bobbed as he said, "Goodnight, Marai."

"Goodnight, Keshel" she replied, exhaustion sweeping over her. Would her body ever feel strong again? Would her soul? "We need our rest if we're going to mount an escape."

Keshel turned to leave, but his hand stalled on the tent flap. He looked back over his shoulder. "For what it's worth, I'm glad it's *you* I'm stuck here with."

He disappeared outside, leaving Marai alone in the dark. Alone in the silence. Alone with her oppressive thoughts of how best to tear the Menagerie apart.

She climbed into her bedroll. Closed her eyes. Breathed deeply.

Reaching out her mind in hopeful prayer, Marai whispered one final thought.

"Goodnight, Ruen."

"We thought, perhaps, you'd appreciate a tour of the Menagerie, since it's now your new home," Gunnora said to Marai the next morning, and crossed small arms across her chest. "Did Innesh not bring you a coat?" She sighed. "She's as sensitive as a piranha. I'll find you something. Andara is always cold, except for the three summer months when the temperatures become somewhat reasonable. You'll freeze to death in that nightgown."

Marai's exposed skin was already numb from the chill. She felt a sharp pang in her chest when she remembered how she used to be able to create bubbles of warmth around her when she slept outside in the forests. But the cold was the least of her worries. Gunnora stepped back outside the tent as Anja turned to Marai.

"I'd be happy to work with you later on strengthening your wing muscles, Your Grace."

"Thank you, but please call me Marai."

Anja's eyes widened. "That would be disrespectful—"

"Marai isn't one for formality," Keshel said, popping his head inside. "She'd just as well be your friend than be your Queen."

Anja smiled. "I could always use another friend. Those are . . . rare around here. I must warn you, Marai, that the others in camp may not be as quick to dismiss your title. As I said earlier, they're eager to meet Meallán's heir."

"Are there more fae here?" asked Marai, pulse suddenly quickening. She was going to meet other magical folk. Perhaps Keshel had rubbed off on her, because she felt slightly *electrified* at the idea of meeting fellow fae.

Anja's face fell. "No, alas, it's only me. Cavar did have another once, but she . . . didn't last long." Whatever had happened to the other faerie, Marai guessed it was something tragic and painful, based on Anja's heartbroken expression. "Most faeries stay behind the Veil, content with life in the court. Magical folk on Andara are subjects of fae regency. Even though we haven't had a monarch for centuries, the faerie nobles who govern the Hinterlands still abide by those old ties. All of us magical folk respect what once was."

"What is the faerie court in the Hinterlands like?" asked Keshel, and took out his small, tattered notebook from his coat. He opened to a blank page and plucked a piece of charcoal from his pocket. "Can you enlighten us about Andaran history?"

Marai could have laughed. *Always learning. Always researching.*

"I'd be happy to tell you, but I don't think now is the time," said Anja, staring at the notebook in confusion.

Keshel pressed on. "Tonight perhaps? Or tomorrow?"

Anja smiled, charmed by his interest. "Are you a writer?"

Keshel shook his head. "A scholar, I suppose. A lover of history and lore."

Gunnora returned then with a red cloak. "It's the best I could find. That bandit Cyrill is hoarding coats in his tent. I had to pry this out of his spindly fingers."

Marai tied the itchy, wool cloak around her shoulders, but the back stuck up at an odd angle because of her wings.

"I'll alter some clothes for you to accommodate them," Anja said, turning around to show Marai the two slits and buttons in her own coat that allowed her wings to slide in and move freely.

"Yes, and I'll get a better coat for you from Cyrill later," Gunnora said. "For now, let's show you both around our little slice of paradise."

The minute Marai stepped outside her tent, activity stilled in the nearby area. There were so many creatures she'd never seen before in her life. Folk of all sizes, shapes, and colors. Their eyes went wide, and they dropped whatever they'd been doing to approach her tentatively.

Marai's gaze immediately latched onto two creatures standing right in front of her. With the lower bodies of horses, and upper bodies of men, the creatures stole the breath from her lungs.

Shadow creatures!

Marai reached for her nonexistent sword, bent her knees into a defensive stance, ready to battle.

But the horse-men looked nothing like the gruesome beasts Marai had grown accustomed to in the Middle Kingdoms. Their faces held no animosity. They were almost . . . beautiful.

"*Centaurs,*" Keshel whispered at her side.

Marai had never heard the word before.

The two centaurs, both males, regally bowed from the waist. They sported trimmed beards and long, silky hair. One centaur's body was brown and white spotted, while the other was midnight black.

"Your Grace," the spotted centaur said in a deep, rich timbre that reminded Marai of Avilyard, Captain of the King's Guard. "It brings us joy to be in your presence."

"Thanks . . ." Marai said, unable to think of anything more clever or respectful to say.

"This is Wilder," Gunnora said, indicating the spotted centaur, "and that's Dante."

Dante, the darker, more rugged of the two, took Marai's hand and kissed it. "Should you need anything, please don't hesitate, Your Grace."

"Er . . . thank you," Marai said again, cursing her awkwardness and the heat that burst into her cheeks.

I'm not meant for this kind of attention. How had Ruenen handled this with such poise and confidence? Even when he doubted himself, he was far better at being royal than Marai. The thought of him, his dimpled smile, his kiss, his arms holding her to his bare chest, made her deflate.

She changed the subject. "Are you both from the Hinterlands?"

"Oh, yes," Wilder said, smiling. "Our kind live in the forests near the border. Most of us come from many different parts of the Hinterlands. It's quite a large, diverse country."

Interesting. The Hinterlands considered itself a separate country from Andara. How big was Andara, and the court beyond the Veil? She wanted to learn more about the centaurs and their homeland, but they both bowed again, then clip-clopped away, making room in the ever-expanding circle around Marai.

I wonder what Ruenen would say if he was here to see this.

QUEEN OF THE SHADOW MENAGERIE

"'Lo, Athelstan," said Gunnora to a wisp-thin man to their right. "We're giving Queen Marai a tour."

Athelstan had the look of someone who had once been large and muscular, but had lost all of his strength. He was grizzled and shaggy-haired, with dark bruises of overripe fruit under his eyes, but Athelstan managed to eke out a smile when she faced him.

He quickly grasped Marai's shoulders and planted a kiss on both cheeks. "May Lirr bless you, My Queen."

Marai's face burned. Next to her, Keshel chuckled.

"Athelstan is a werewolf," Anja explained.

Marai recognized the tell-tale signs of a werewolf in him: the scars, low-set ears, thick hair on his arms and chest.

"We knew werewolves back on Astye," she said, heart heavy. She'd barely gotten to know Tarik, Brass, and Yovel before she'd been taken.

"Oh, aye, I'm from Grelta, like Miss Gunnora there. My pack lived near the Cliffs of Unmyn. Both Miss Gunnora and I were captured by Koda on the same trip," Athelstan said with a slight Greltan lilt in his voice. That meant he'd been in the Menagerie for seven years, like Gunnora.

"What exactly does Cavar make you *do* in this Menagerie?" Keshel asked the werewolf. He'd been taking secretive notes in his journal as they spoke. His attention was particularly hooked on the fog barrier around the camp.

Athelstan tapped the iron collar around his neck with a shaking finger. "We all do something different, depending on our abilities. I, for example, am forced to turn."

Air *whooshed* from Marai's lungs. "Without a full moon?"

Athelstan nodded solemnly. "Almost every night for the past seven years." He gestured to his sickly body. "Can you believe I'm only four and thirty?"

No, Marai couldn't. Athelstan looked closer to four and sixty with his graying hair and sagging skin. No wonder the poor man seemed so cadaverous; Marai couldn't imagine how debilitating, how strenuous, that constant transformation was on his body.

Cavar wasn't simply housing magical folk against their will. He was making them use *magic* against their will, as he had to Marai in his office when he'd forced her to twirl. Her stomach roiled at the memory of the sensation. She'd had no choice—every muscle in her body went lax and loose. Although her mind screamed against it, she had no control, as if Cavar had removed her from her own body. What must it feel like for Athelstan to transform against his will, against his *nature*? Marai's fists clenched so tight she lost feeling in her fingers.

He won't live much longer. The signs of deterioration were prevalent, and yet Athelstan smiled with a warmth that proved this werewolf, a magical creature, had more humanity than Cavar, himself.

Marai quickly became overwhelmed by the similar plights of the other residents of the Menagerie. Groups of tiny, scrunched-faced hobs, and gnomes with pointy hats shook and kissed Marai's hands. They juggled balls, tumbled, and danced on demand for the Menagerie, but at least none of them had collars on.

A shrouded Banshee, who didn't show her face beneath the hood of a brown cloak, bowed low to Marai. Her voice was high-pitched and grating when she spoke. "We're glad to have you among us, Your Magnificence."

She swooped away, and Marai caught a glimpse of long white hair in the wind.

"Don't worry, Bellaya hasn't shrieked in months," Gunnora said to Marai, patting her arm.

"What do you mean?"

"Well, she's a banshee. When you hear a banshee shriek at night, it means someone you care about is doomed to die." Gunnora brushed away Marai's concern with a hand. "The last time Bellaya foretold anyone's death, it was a really old gnome. She's not that scary, despite ominous appearances."

A towering, green-skinned ogre with a jutting jaw grunted a greeting to Marai, while an oni with fangs, horns, and bluish-gray skin clapped in delight.

So many interesting faces and accents. Marai had never felt more ignorant of the world than she did meeting the members of the Menagerie. There was so much for her to learn from them. Beyond the Veil in the Hinterlands was a rich, vibrant society filled with folk she could only conceive of in dreams. Marai had traveled all over the continent of Astye. She'd sailed to the countries of Yehzig, Casamere, Listan, and Ukra, but there was so much more to discover. *This world is far vaster than I ever imagined.*

Marai was reluctant to admit that Cavar had truly created a magical Menagerie. It was, indeed, an impressive sight to behold when all those species of folk gathered together.

Keshel looked like he might faint from the excitement.

Anja and Gunnora then guided Marai and Keshel past a cloudy water tank that housed a mermaid named Eno with umber skin, aquamarine hair, and shimmering salmon scales on her tail. Sadly, the tank was too small for her to do anything more than float morosely in place. She gave Marai a somber wave as they passed by.

"She only speaks Mermish. We've never been able to fully communicate with her," said Gunnora, returning the wave, "but I think she understands us fine."

Anja pointed out the diverse hoard of caged creatures Cavar had acquired. A beautiful, glowing white unicorn was tethered to a tree, chomping on a meager patch of grass. A massive, eagle-headed griffin prowled in its cramped, barred cage, similar to the one Marai had been in the previous night. A phoenix cooed sadly as it cleaned its bright red-and-yellow feathers on a perch, while a winged lion with a scorpion's tail called a manticore could only gather the energy to blink at Marai as it lounged on the bottom of its cage.

"Are there dragons here?" asked Keshel, furiously writing in his notebook. "I've read about them, but I thought they were a myth."

"There aren't many dragons left, unfortunately," Anja said. "Only a few remain beyond the Veil. Cavar has never had one in the Menagerie, since they never leave their caves within the peaks of the Hinterlands Mountains."

"Not sure where he'd store one, either," Gunnora added with raised eyebrows.

"Most of the residents you see are performers, but some of us are merely slaves, such as Innesh, Gunnora and I," Anja explained, giving Marai and Keshel a remorseful look. "I've been 'retired' as the faerie spectacle now that you're both here."

"What will you do instead?" asked Keshel.

"Whatever duties Koda assigns me," said Anja. "We prepare food for the animals and clean their cages, sweep the theater, mend, and do laundry . . . not just for the folk, but for Koda and the Peace Keepers, as well. I don't mind, though.

It's hard work, but I would rather be helping my fellow folk than dancing and twirling for gawking humans."

Marai agreed. Nothing could be worse than being stared at by hundreds of hungry, judging eyes, knowing that their entertainment was Marai's misfortune.

I'd rather clean up griffin shit than perform in the Menagerie.

"Is that her?" came a nasal, yet gravelly voice from down the row.

Another creature Marai had never seen came creeping towards her. It had long, spindly limbs and copper skin, a nose like a carrot, and bulbous black eyes. On its pointed chin was a black goatee.

"Wearing my cloak, I see," the creature said, eyeing Marai and her short, red cloak. "I suppose I have to be generous to the Queen of the Fae."

"I think the Queen of the Fae deserves a better coat than that shabby thing," snapped Gunnora with a shake of her head. "Marai, this is Cyrill, our resident hoarder and skinflint."

Cyrill drew himself up to his full height, which wasn't much taller than Marai. "I beg your pardon, Madam, but I'm a collector and preserver. That cloak is at least twenty-and-five-years old, and I snagged it straight from the shoulders of a guard's wife. What are you goggling at, wingless?" His eyes flashed in Keshel's direction.

"Forgive me," Keshel stammered, "I've never seen anyone like you before."

Cyrill scoffed. "Well, I've never seen a wingless faerie before, but you don't see me staring rudely at *you*. First time for everything, boy." He crossed his gangly arms. "I imagine you don't get many goblins in Astye. We hate the water. Not good swimmers, we. My kind would never dare cross that sea."

A goblin? Marai thought they were a myth, a bedtime story parents told their children so they'd keep their rooms tidy. Her own mother had told her that goblins would sneak into young Marai's room at night and steal her toys if she didn't put them away. *Seems you weren't that far off, Mama.*

Marai used to be a bedtime story, too. Parents used the Lady Butcher as a threat to misbehaving children. Perhaps she and the goblin weren't that different, despite appearances.

"For a queen, you don't look like much," Cyrill said in a disappointed tone, circling and examining her. "The color red does nothing for you. Red is a color of power. You look about as weak as a lamb."

Marai glowered at him, but before she could speak, Keshel jumped in.

"I wouldn't rile her, goblin," he warned. "She could strangle your thin neck in a heartbeat if she wanted to. Marai used to be a mercenary before she learned she was Queen of the Fae."

Cyrill took a step backwards, drawing his arms to his chest, and gave Keshel a contemptible look. "You, sir, I don't like."

"I know it's in your nature, but don't be rude, Cyrill," said Gunnora with a long-suffering sigh.

The goblin narrowed his eyes, then focused back on Marai. "You're Queen now. You must act like it. Hold your head high, put those shoulders back. Show us that you're here to lead. Even if you can't save us, you need to bring us together, make us different creatures feel like one. Otherwise, you don't deserve to wear the color red."

He gave Marai a final sniff with his long nose, then skittered back down the row.

"Don't mind him," Gunnora said with a dismissive gesture in Cyrill's direction. "He's always grumpy and unpleasant, but he means well. Cyrill's been here almost as long as Anja has."

Gunnora and Anja then brought Marai and Keshel to meet Desislava.

Although she was already pale, as most vampires were, there was a chalky quality to Desislava's skin, a thinness to her pitch-black hair, and tremendous hunger in her gaunt face. Desislava was the only one of the folk chained up; the collar around her neck was attached to a metal encasement around the trunk of a large tree, tethered like the unicorn. An animal. But Desislava was far less innocent. She struggled against the chain, and inhaled the air as Marai approached, savoring the scent of that effervescent blood Nosficio was so infatuated with. Saliva dripped from her fanged mouth.

"You're the Queen everyone's been talking about," Desislava said. Her glowing red eyes reminded Marai of the friend she'd left behind, but Desislava's were pained and feral. The vampiress reached out a pale claw-like hand. "Come closer. Please. I only wish to pay my respects."

Marai recognized the signs of starvation in Desislava's emaciated cheeks and desperate tone. She'd never had much fondness for vampires, especially before Nosficio, but it broke Marai's heart to see the vampiress in such a state. She didn't think proud Nosficio could have borne the suffering and humiliation.

"It's not her fault, but stay away from her," whispered Anja in Marai's ear. "They only feed her a small amount of animal blood. It's enough to keep her alive, but she killed a guard, brand new on the job, two weeks ago. Bellaya didn't get the chance to shriek before it happened."

Keshel took a purposeful step back.

"They dragged his body away before I could get more than a sip," moaned Desislava, her face crumpling. "The taste of his human blood still lingers on my tongue, like a divine echo."

"Cavar uses Desislava to scare the patrons." Gunnora shook her head so that her brown curls bounced around her face. "Shock-value and a little fear, he claims, makes the show more interesting."

"Every story needs a villain," growled Desislava in disdain. Her lips curled and she closed her eyes, sorrow washing over her expression.

She wasn't a villain. Not by her own intentions.

"I hate this place," Marai stated, anger rising within her, a kettle about to boil over. "I want to burn it down."

"We all do," replied Gunnora, "but don't you think someone would have done it already if they could? I'd slit the throat of Cavar's goons without any hesitation, but it would do no good. I'd still be stuck here."

The rage inside Marai cooled. Gunnora had a point.

"All of these creatures come from the Hinterlands?" asked Keshel as they walked away from Desislava. He was still taking notes, pondering a million thoughts in his never-tiring brain.

"Many of them come from behind the Veil, yes," Anja said. "For one reason or another, they wandered out from behind the protective barrier, and were caught by Cavar. But Eno was captured from the waters around Ukra, and Desislava, like Gunnora, Athelstan, and you, is from somewhere in Astye."

Right, because werewolves and vampires are only native to Astye.

"Is that how *you* got here?" Marai asked Anja. "You came from behind the Veil?"

Anja's pale eyes twinkled, like two sad stars burning out. "I was once a noble lady in the court, and I made the mistake of believing myself in love with someone my family did not approve of. We agreed to run away together, outside of the realm, but after I left the Veil and all I knew behind me . . . my lover didn't follow. Once you pass through the Veil, you cannot ever go back, no matter how much you plead. No matter how much you regret. It didn't take long for Cavar to find me."

"That's unfair," said Keshel.

"That's how it's been since the Veil was erected. Leadership believes it's for everyone's protection."

"Sounds like you need new leadership," Marai said, without thinking.

Anja gave her a pointed look.

Oh. That would be me.

"Let's move on, shall we?" asked Gunnora. She led Marai and Keshel to the end of the row where the stone theater stood at the edge of camp, and gestured wide with her arms. "This is where the magic happens. Not yours, of course. All the magic is Cavar's." She shot Marai a wry smile.

"The audience enters on the other side, where the gates and ticket booths are," said Anja.

Sitting in the middle of a grassy field, the amphitheater was nowhere near as impressive as the Kellesaran castle, Glacial Palace, or Nine Kingdom's Library.

The edges of the sprawling field where the camp and theater sat were supposedly surrounded by dense pine forests and a nearby town. A red-pebbled path snaked through the grass, from the town to the theater gates, but Marai couldn't see anything beyond the barrier.

"I only know because sometimes I'm ordered to do chores outside the theater: sweep the walkways, clean the ticket booth . . ." said Gunnora, trailing off.

Keshel nudged Marai and pointed upwards to the curved fog ceiling. "I think there's at least four overlapping layers to the barrier. Even with access to our magic, I'm not sure you and I could break out or dismantle it."

Marai slightly lifted an ankle, showing off her shackles. "With these on, we wouldn't get far . . ." *But that doesn't mean I won't try if given the chance.*

"Do you see any weaknesses in the barrier?" Keshel asked. "Any unguarded areas?"

Marai shook her head. She'd been studying it all morning during the tour.

"Cavar's shields are far stronger than mine." Another rare admission from Keshel.

"Because they're not made of *his* magic. He's only borrowing from another source, just like Rayghast."

Cavar was a leech. He had no real power without that stone.

"There's no show tonight," Anja said, breaking up their hushed conversation. "We only do performances on Third Day to Sixth Day. Cavar wants you both to watch the show tomorrow night, and then you'll start on Fourth Day."

"What exactly are we expected to perform?" Marai asked, crossing her arms and glaring at the building. It wasn't as if she had some practiced dance routine, and she certainly couldn't juggle.

"It's different, depending on what our gifts typically are, but oftentimes we're merely paraded around the stage so the audience can gape at us," said Anja with a bite. "I'm sure Koda will give you instructions when it's time."

"What if I refuse?" Marai asked as two red-vested guards skulked past, glowering at her. She sent a rude gesture their way, which they ignored, as if her impudence wasn't worth their time.

"You won't have a choice, I'm afraid. They'll force you, using the amulets," Anja said.

All of Marai's lethal focus honed in on the amphitheater. *We'll see about that.*

Gunnora escorted Marai and Keshel to the small creek that ran on the far side of camp, where she pointed out that the end closer to the amphitheater was for bathing. A smooth rock the size of a bush indicated the section further upstream that was for drinking and cooking water only. Gunnora then showed them the commissary, which was merely a larger tent than most of the others with a fire pit set up out front. A tripod of wooden posts was erected, where a large cauldron dangled over the flames and a hunched man stood stirring the contents.

"That's Bobo, one of the few employed workers in the Menagerie," whispered Gunnora. "Old as the damned hills, and as sour as he looks. Comes in every morning from the village to cook the most godsawful slop imaginable."

Bobo sneered at Marai and Keshel as they passed, then hacked up a loogie and spit on the ground.

Charming.

That evening, Marai and Keshel ate Bobo's stew of gray animal innards while huddling around a campfire with Anja, Gunnora, and Athelstan. The food was truly no better than what they'd been served on *The Arcane Wind,* but at least it was warm. Marai clung to the red cloak around her shoulders against the brisk wind.

While she ate, Peace Keepers and magical folk alike passed by to get a look at Marai. It heated her skin as she ducked her head low, trying to avoid their avid stares. The folk kept trying to give her extra pieces of bread. A hob offered her his entire, untouched bowl of stew.

"Forgive them," Anja said, smiling as Marai declined the hob's offer. "They'll grow used to you in a few days."

"It's not every day you see a Faerie Queen, practically back from the grave," Athelstan said with a chuckle. "Not that you were dead, I just mean that no one thought any royal line had survived."

Marai turned to Keshel, who sat quietly eating the flavorless mushy green and brown stew, made of nettles, hardtack, and offal.

"Are you sure you never saw any of this?" she asked, voice low, leaning into him.

Keshel set down his spoon and massaged his red, cold fingers. "I saw you in chains. I saw us making a journey across the sea, but in that vision, I never saw beyond the docks. I wonder if the barrier prevented me from seeing anything else . . ."

"What does this symbol mean?" Marai asked Anja, indicating the engraving on her collar. "Is it Andaran?"

"I'm honestly not sure," said Anja. "It's not something we have in the Hinterlands. As far as I know, the symbol was already engraved on the stone when Cavar found it."

"It's a dark mark, whatever it is," Gunnora said gravely. "A *devil's* mark, I think."

Keshel repeated her words under his breath, contemplating. He flipped through his journal. "It reminds me of Laimoen's symbol."

A twisted symbol of a dagger. The three-pronged symbol on the collars *did* bear a resemblance to the God of Destruction's mark, with its curled, pointed tail. A devil's mark . . .

"What did you see in Cavar's office?" Marai asked Keshel. "When he forced that vision on you."

Keshel winced at the memory of that invasion into his mind. "I saw . . . golden light and glittering darkness."

Marai's stomach clenched. "Was it dark magic?"

"No, the vision wasn't hostile, with the usual black flames and smoke. The magic I saw reminded me of the night's sky, speckled with stars. It seemed almost like the golden light and glittering darkness were magically entwined somehow, twisting together to become a stronger, unbreakable bond."

"Balance," Anja chimed in. The others had quieted to listen in on their conversation. "You saw the golden light of Lirr, and Laimoen's power."

"You believe in the gods, as well?" Keshel asked, eyes brightening to learn something new. "I assumed, because of the distance, Andarans wouldn't—"

"Of course! While the humans on Andara worship no gods but themselves, Astye was founded on Andaran fae beliefs. As I mentioned before, we believe Lirr and Laimoen are our ancestors. That they're fae, themselves. We have many lesser gods, as well, like Seol, Goddess of Knowledge, and Rialbe, God of Music and Art. To us, Lirr is the Goddess of All Things. She is light, and Laimoen is dark. Life and death. Day and night. All things require balance."

Marai had always liked the idea of Lirr and Laimoen, mates and partners, as the natural give-and-take of life, that with darkness comes the light. She'd always struggled with that balance inside herself.

"What do you think such a vision means?" asked Athelstan to Keshel.

"I'm not certain," Keshel replied. "It was brief, and usually my visions build off each other in some way. That's the only vision I've had in nearly two months." He took a reluctant bite of his stew, then pouted at its woeful taste.

QUEEN OF THE SHADOW MENAGERIE

"Guess it's no use asking you, then, if I'm ever getting out of here…" Athelstan said as a weak joke that no one laughed at.

Keshel frowned further and apologetically shook his head. "I wish I could tell you anything at all. I'm not used to being so blind."

Marai heard the note of shame in Keshel's voice. She felt it, too—the uselessness. Without magic, Marai was merely a short woman with a sharp tongue and deadly sword-skills that she couldn't use. She was powerless.

"We've never had a seer in camp before," said Gunnora. "You're probably as exciting to Cavar as Marai."

In response, only one side of Keshel's lips twitched.

He and Marai bid the others goodnight after dinner. It was curfew, when folk had to return to their tents and stay quiet.

Keshel walked Marai to her tent first. "I've been thinking about the onyx stone. I think it's a conduit. That's why Cavar doesn't suffer any physical ramifications for tapping into dark magic. The magic never enters his body, and no shadow creatures are spawned. It's exactly the same as when you used Meallán's cursed ring."

Marai's body went cold. "You think it was dark magic inside Meallán's ring?"

"What else could make such a curse? I saw a vision of Meallán once, when she shrouded herself in darkness and created the curse as humans battered down her door. She called upon the darkness, but it was too late for her to use the ring herself."

"My skin didn't turn black when I released the curse because the ring was a conduit," Marai finished for him.

"Because Meallán already paid the ultimate price for tapping into that forbidden power." Keshel pursed his lips. "If we could get your magic back, I think you'd be able to tear through Cavar's barriers. You're stronger than I am."

Marai grunted in reply. That *if* was a large ask. She didn't know how to get the metal collar off her neck, even if she did somehow manage to incapacitate Cavar.

"We'll get out of here," she said, faking the certainty in her voice. "I promise you. We'll be home with Thora, Raife, Aresti, and … Ruenen soon."

A surly guard, Sirco, passed by. "Curfew. Get into your tents, maggots."

Marai flipped him off.

"Goodnight, Your Magnificence," Keshel said, a snarky smile on his lips as he bowed to her.

"Don't make me punch you."

He chuckled, then turned, heading for his own tent.

Keshel and the rest of the Menagerie believed Marai could help them. Unify them. Maybe even *save* them. She didn't know how, and she didn't have a plan.

But Keshel was counting on her, as were her family back home. Across the sea, *Ruenen* was counting on her.

Marai had to find a way. She couldn't let them down.

CHAPTER 12

RUENEN

"Queen Rhia has agreed to take a walk with you," Holfast said.

Ruenen's boots had barely touched the painted, gold sunburst tile in the castle entryway. His Steward had been waiting for him at the bottom of the white-marble stairs, arms full of papers, tapping his foot impatiently while he waited for Ruenen to emerge.

"A walk?" Ruenen repeated, groggy from continued lack of sleep. The shadow creature's horrific visage had haunted him all night. In his fitful dreams, the creature's beak dripped with Marai's blood as it pecked away at her gaping stomach wound. That image of her lying dead in the woods was hard to shake, and it left Ruenen sweating and shaking in his tangled bedsheets.

Fifty days now without her. Almost two months with no word.

"To be civilized. To get to know one another," pressed Holfast, giving Ruenen a sharp look that said *please try.*

Ruenen's eyes narrowed. "Why would we want to get to know each other?"

Rhia had made it perfectly clear that she wanted nothing to do with Ruenen or Nevandia. He rubbed at a sore muscle in his shoulder. Although Thora had healed the break, his arm and side were still bruised and smarting from falling off his horse.

Holfast sighed as if trying to reason with a stubborn toddler. "She agreed to speak with you in exchange for more comfortable accommodations, and time with her sister before Eriu's departure back to Varana. Remember, this isn't about you. It's about the future of Nevandia and Tacorn."

"You released her from the dungeon?" Without Ruenen's consent.

"Earlier this morning. If you'd been awake, you could have done it, yourself."

Ruenen was about to retort when Queen Rhia and Princess Eriu appeared from the hallway. Both Varanese princesses curtsied, well-trained and elegant, keeping their eyes to the floor in Ruenen's presence.

"Your Grace," Rhia said, voice cool and distant. Ruenen bet that was the same voice she'd used when addressing Rayghast: respectful, emotionless. The right side of Rhia's face was covered with a white cloth patch to hide her disfigurement. Her long, silky black hair had been styled to cover that side.

She still refuses Thora's help . . .

"Thank you for the private chambers. You are a generous and merciful king." Rhia was a polished queen who knew exactly what to say. Her eyes met Holfast's from across the grand entryway, a quiet understanding between them.

Ruenen shot his Steward a glare, but then plastered on his smile and bowed to Rhia and Eriu. "I'm glad to hear the rooms are to your liking."

"Eriu also wishes to say her thanks, seeing as how she returns to Varana this afternoon," Rhia said, giving the little girl a gentle shove forward.

Eriu fumbled a curtsy again. "Thank you for your hospitality, King Ruenen. I shall tell my father of your generosity, and I will be forever grateful that you sheltered me in my time of need. Varana looks forward to renewed friendship with Nevandia."

She said this with a rehearsed quality, as if Rhia had instructed her on what to say. She probably had.

"I, too, look forward to mending the fractured bonds between our two nations," Ruenen said to the little girl. "Safe travels, Princess. I hope your journey home is uneventful."

"It will be *boring*," Eriu muttered under her breath.

Rhia tapped her on the elbow in reprimand.

Ruenen leaned forward towards Eriu with a sneaky smile. "I told our cook to pack you desserts for the road. The extra delicious kind." He winked.

Eriu tried to suppress a grin and failed. A servant led the little princess away down the hall.

Holfast jerked his chin towards the gardens.

Ruenen kept his strained smile as he turned to the stone-cold queen, and proffered his arm. "Would you care to accompany me on a turn around the gardens?"

"What a marvelous idea," Holfast said. "It's a beautiful morning."

"I would be honored, Your Grace." Rhia's pale hand slipped through Ruenen's arm.

He led her out the back double-doors, but not before shooting Holfast his most aggrieved look, which his Steward completely ignored.

White clouds dappled the strikingly blue sky, looking like fluffy pillows for the gods to rest their heads as they surveyed the world below. The verdant spring air filled Ruenen's lungs as the sun warmed his skin. Pollen tickled his nose. He hadn't spent much time in the magnificent garden. It was a place of peace and sanctuary for his court. Head Monk Baureo walked with Fenir and Wattling, discussing Lirr's blessings on Nevandia. Lord Corian's wife sat reading on a bench beneath the shade of a willow tree. Their gazes trailed Ruenen and Rhia down the pebbled pathways.

But Ruenen didn't desire such peace. Mostly, he wanted to search and search until his legs gave out. Until he'd traversed every corner of the world to find Marai.

The garden had fully transformed since he'd first arrived in Kellesar. The grass, no longer brittle and brown, was lushly green. Colorful flora and fauna bloomed and sprouted from every vine, bush, and bed. The sight reminded Ruenen of sweet Kadiatu, when she'd sniffed at her first-ever scent of grass on her fingertips. How she'd shrieked in delight at the wonder of nature.

"You do me an honor, Your Grace," Rhia began, "one I'm not certain I deserve."

"Oh?" he asked, eyebrows raising. "Why not?"

"You don't need to be kind, Your Grace. I'm very aware of the commotion I caused in my first days here," she said tersely, as if admitting that cost her something. "Please, forgive me. It was unrefined and unbefitting of a queen."

For a moment, Ruenen was at a loss for words. Truth be told, he didn't feel like Rhia had to apologize for anything.

"You'd suffered greatly at the hands of your husband. You'd lost your kingdom, your freedom—"

"I lost my freedom many years ago, the moment I was born a female," snapped Rhia, then puckered her lips, controlling herself. "It was difficult, yes, and upsetting, but you and your Witenagemot have been kind to me, and especially to Eriu. She's the most precious thing in the world to me." She lifted her dark eyes to his face for the first time. Despite the patch covering her wounded face, Ruenen couldn't help but find Rhia quite beautiful. She had smooth, delicate skin, and full, pink lips. She used beauty as both a weapon and a shield. Those full lips pouted as she said, "If you hadn't sheltered Eriu, let her stay safe behind your borders, she would have been married to a vile man, and might have been executed by Rayghast. No matter my personal feelings on the company you choose to keep and employ . . . I thank you for protecting my sister."

"You're most welcome. Eriu is an innocent—no child should be forced into marriage, especially with someone as heinous as Lord Silex." Ruenen grimaced at the thought of King Rayghast's staunch supporter.

"I suppose marriage is the reason why you and I are taking this walk," Rhia said pointedly, cocking an eyebrow in a coy manner.

Ruenen opened his mouth, closed it, startled by her straight-forward comment. "Yes, I suppose that's what my Witan most desires."

They continued walking in silence, around the bend in the path where vines and wisteria made a tangled bridge over their heads. Ruenen hated silence, especially the awkward kind.

"I used to live in Varana, you know," he said. "It's a beautiful country. I really loved it there."

"How interesting," stated Rhia with a genuine smile. "Where did you live?"

"Chiojan."

Her smile immediately wilted. "Before or after Rayghast destroyed it?"

"Before. During." Ruenen shut out the memory of the city in flames, of the Chongan's mutilated bodies strung up in the square. "Rayghast was searching for *me*. That's why he invaded Varana. I'm sorry to have thrust your country into a forced alliance with him."

Rhia's face tightened slightly. "If not you, it would have been for some other reason. Rayghast saw weakness in my father, and had always intended to control him. He wanted to conquer the kingdoms, one by one. Varana was the first and easiest target."

Ruenen stopped walking. "I must be honest with you, Your Grace, because I don't want to string you along when you've already suffered so much at a man's hands. I'm not ready to marry. Two members of my Witan are missing, one of whom is my closest friend—"

"You think that really matters to your council?" asked Rhia. "Royals have far less choice in such matters than you might think. I, for one, had no choice when I married Rayghast, and from what I'm learning now, I have little choice once again."

"But you do have a choice. You can say no."

Please, say no.

Rhia released a soft laugh. "It has been made quite clear that my status here is less than secure. You and your Witan have taken your time trying to figure out what to do with me. I'm well-aware that the best way to unite Nevandia and Tacorn is for us to wed, and make myself useful."

"And you're okay with this?"

She giggled, then looked him up and down, biting her lower lip. "Who would say no to marrying a king?"

Once upon a time, Ruenen might have been swayed by such flirtation. If Marai never existed, then Ruenen might find the thought of marrying Rhia appealing. But Lirr's Bones, if Marai never existed, Ruenen wouldn't be alive, and Rayghast would be ruling Nevandia. The fact was, no woman, no matter how beautiful, how cunning, could remove Marai from his heart. She was lodged in there so thoroughly that the organ now only beat because of her. She was the spring breath that filled his lungs.

"You don't need to flatter me. I'd rather us speak candidly," he said.

Rhia's flirtatious expression disappeared, replaced by one of calculation. "If it means I'm not executed or imprisoned for the rest of my days, then yes. You are a young, handsome, and kind king. I could do far worse, and already have. We could have a perfectly amiable marriage—perform our duties to each other, and then live life comfortably and separately. We don't have to be lovers, or even friends. I would consider myself the most fortunate Queen in all of the Nine Kingdoms to have a *partner* in the business of matrimony."

That was what Holfast had suggested in an equally straightforward fashion. Why was everyone so content on ignoring Ruenen's objections to marriage? For making choices for him?

"What about the fae?" Ruenen asked. "They're my friends, and I trust them with my life, but I know you have rather strong opinions on them."

"Strong opinions" was putting it lightly. Rhia abhorred any mention of magic. She'd been positively feral in her early days in the Kellesaran castle, ranting and screaming that the fae would use magic and kill everyone in the kingdom. It hadn't been good for morale.

As expected, Rhia crinkled her nose in disgust. "As long as they do not come near me and don't use magic in my presence, then I won't say anything further about them."

"How can I trust that you won't try to undermine my rule the way you did with Rayghast? Sending out those secret messages through your ladies and servants . . . not that I blame you in that circumstance, of course, but how can I trust that you won't start spreading lies and dissent about me or the fae?"

Lines of concentration appeared between Rhia's brows, but then she looked up at Ruenen through her long eyelashes. "I'm a survivor, Your Grace. I did what I had to do to stop an evil man from destroying me and everything around us. If you agree to keep your *faeries* at bay, and if I'm well-treated, then there will be no need to turn against you."

Ruenen's heart sunk, growing heavier and heavier. "So you would agree . . . to marry me."

Rhia's chin dipped once. "I'm a queen, Your Grace. I would like to remain so."

What excuse could he use now? The Witan was already ravenous to have Rhia as Queen before she consented, and now, Ruenen would be lucky if he could make it another week before the chiming of wedding bells.

I don't love this woman. I don't want this woman. Things were spiraling out of his control. Holfast was already making plans, and Rhia was accepting them.

"Thank you for your honesty, and for your company, Your Grace," Ruenen said, giving Rhia a cordial kiss on the hand. He barreled back inside the castle, trying to keep the anxiety at bay, past Mayestral hovering at the door.

"Would you like me to fetch your lute, my King?" he asked. The thoughtful Groom could read Ruenen's emotions.

Before Marai disappeared, Ruenen would have begged for his lute. But not now. There was no music in his heart to play.

Holfast caught up to Ruenen as he dismissed Mayestral and made for the courtyard.

"I hope you and Queen Rhia had plenty to discuss."

"It doesn't matter if we did," Ruenen said, swinging around to face his Steward. "It doesn't matter if we despise each other. You and the Witan have made it perfectly clear that you will arrange this marriage with or without my consent. All you needed was hers, which she feels she *must* give, or she's left adrift in the world."

The corners of Holfast's eyes pinched. "I'm doing my job, which is the best I can do. As I have *always* done. You may disagree now, but once peace has settled across our newly acquired lands, you'll realize that it was the correct decision."

"And what of Marai?"

"We have poured far too many resources into finding her and Lord Keshel, and while I regret the loss of them both, we must move forward and admit that they are probably dead—"

Ruenen clenched his fists so tight at his sides that his knuckles cracked. He bit his lip so hard he drew blood. He'd never once resorted to violence, and he certainly wasn't going to start pummeling an aging man in front of a courtyard of guards and servants, but what Holfast had said was more painful than Rayghast's sword gouging a hole in Ruenen's side.

"I will *never* give up on her," Ruenen said as tears stung his eyes.

Holfast's face softened a fraction at the pain he heard in Ruenen's voice. "It's time to let her go."

Ruenen's knees nearly gave out. He wanted to damn everything and throw his crown at Holfast's feet. To grab a horse from the stable and ride out of the city. But Holfast's words were more potent than Ruenen had thought, because suddenly, the hope he'd been cradling for weeks ripped from his body, leaving a gaping, bleeding hole.

The truth Ruenen had tried to ignore was now as excruciating as a thousand swords plunging into his soul.

She would have come back by now if she was still alive.

Feet skidded on cobblestones behind him.

"I'm sorry to interrupt, Your Grace," came Raife's voice from the portcullis.

Ruenen schooled his features back to neutrality, shielding his broken heart, then faced Marai's adoptive brother.

Raife was out of breath, sweaty, with his helmet tucked under his arm.

"Do you have news?" Ruenen asked, closing the distance between them. Hope, like a candle, once again lit up inside him.

Raife's emerald eyes twinkled in the sunlight as he said, "Twenty-two fae are standing outside the city gate."

Ruenen approached slowly, as if they were skittish deer in a quiet wood.

The grouping of faeries stood at the other end of the bridge spanning the Nydian River, out of range of the archers standing along Kellesar's wall walk. They huddled together protectively, reminding Ruenen of when Marai brought her own people to Kellesar. Most wore cloaks and hoods to disguise themselves, hiding their pointed ears, despite the warm weather. Heavy, bulky bags were strapped over their shoulders and dangled from their fists.

But Ruenen blanched when he spotted colorful wings.

Full-blooded fae. Ten of them.

Marai had once told him that all full-blooded fae were killed in the massacres. Ruenen had never seen one before, and the sight was truly magnificent. Their wings reminded him of a butterfly's; a mosaic of bright colors and patterns, indicating a family line or clan, perhaps. A subtle light, a glint of magic, radiated from each wing. It would be impossible to hide those wings, to blend in with humans, but somehow, like Marai's people, this group had managed to survive against all odds.

QUEEN OF THE SHADOW MENAGERIE   147

A baby wailed in its mother's arms, and three other small, fae children peered out from behind the adults. Ruenen had never seen fae children before, either. One little boy's prominent, pointed ears protruded from beneath his shaggy brown hair, and he stared at Ruenen in wide-eyed innocence. His eyes, like his wings, glistened in the sunlight, reminding Ruenen of Marai's electric irises, swirling with magic.

Raife, Aresti, Thora, Tarik, Brass, and Yovel accompanied Ruenen to the bridge as his welcoming committee. Ruenen didn't think bringing the rest of his human King's Guard would display the tolerance and unity he was aiming for. He'd instructed Aresti and Raife to keep their helmets off so that the visitors could see they were also of fae blood.

"Friends, welcome to Kellesar," he called to them with the biggest smile he could muster.

The fae made no sound, no movement forward. They returned Ruenen's greeting with stoic, suspicious stares. The full-blooded male in the front of the pack, with wings of swirling green and vermillion, must have been their leader. He was the tallest, with a sword at his hip, and a crossbow strapped to his back. His tawny hand sat on the bone hilt of his sword.

"I'm King Ruenen Avsharian. You're all welcome here."

Again, none of the fae moved. It was Raife who stepped around Ruenen and began to cross the moonstone bridge. The group took several frightened steps backwards. Raife halted mid-way, hands submissively in the air.

"My friends, we wish you no harm. Magical folk are safe in Kellesar," he said, face lighting up like the sun. "I'm Raife, part-fae member of the King's Guard."

The fae leader's gaze scanned over Raife's features. "We've traveled a long way, risking our lives in the process. Forgive us if we don't accept your word without assurances."

Raife nodded. "I understand how it feels to uproot yourself from safety, but you're here now, and we're so happy you are."

The boy with brown hair stepped out from behind the leader. His small hand tugged on the leader's tunic.

"Papa, that's the *King*, and he has a *faerie* on his royal guard," he said. His wings were identical to the leader's.

"Actually, there are two of us," Raife said to the boy, then gestured behind him. "Aresti is also part-fae. And that's my wife, Thora. She's King Ruenen's Royal Healer. Tarik, Brass, and Yovel are werewolves and friends."

Murmurs bounced around the fae pack like a babbling brook. Ruenen saw the anxiety in their bodies loosen. He took another step towards the fae, and this time, they didn't retreat.

"You must be exhausted. Please, follow us up to the castle and I shall have some food and rooms prepared for you." Ruenen turned to Sir Elmar, who'd been lingering at the gate, and ordered him to alert the servants in the castle.

The young knight dashed up the cobblestone streets, through the crowd of people gathering, and out of sight.

"We don't trust so easily. Not even our own kind," the fae leader said in a gruff tone once Elmar was gone. He corralled his son behind him once again and gave Ruenen a hard stare. "We'd heard rumors that magical folk fought in the battle alongside you. But most importantly, we'd heard from a vampire that a faerie queen was amongst those here. Is that true?"

Ruenen swallowed. He couldn't get his mouth to form the words.

"Marai—*Queen* Marai—isn't here," Thora stated, after Ruenen hesitated. "But she is indeed Queen Meallán and King Aras' descendent. She saved this kingdom from Rayghast's dark magic, and helped pave the way for the acceptance of magical folk and gave us a home here. Human, fae, werewolf, and vampire alike."

"Where is she, then?" asked the little boy, popping out again.

His father heaved a heavy sigh in response.

Aresti walked over to where Raife stood, mid-way across the bridge. "She was kidnapped. Taken almost two months ago, along with my cousin, Keshel, a fae member of King Ruenen's Witenagemot."

Chatter and concern flooded the group of fae. The leader's face darkened with further suspicion.

"We leave," he ordered to his people, then turned back to Raife and Aresti. "If anyone tries to attack us, we have no qualms about using whatever means necessary to survive."

Meaning magic. *Fuck.*

"Why do you want to leave?" Raife asked, reaching out, desperate to make them stay. "You've come all this way—"

"Did you kill the Faerie Queen?" the leader asked, glaring straight at Ruenen, defensively blocking his son and the winged female with the baby behind him. "Did you use her power and leverage against Tacorn, then discard her when she was of no more use to you?"

"What? *No.*" Anger rushed through Ruenen at the accusation. He hastened to Raife's side as the fae backed quickly away, well-clear of the bridge. "Marai was taken, *kidnapped,* by someone, and we don't know who or why, but we've been searching every single day since she and Lord Keshel were taken."

"We'd be dead if it weren't for Marai," came Tarik's deep voice as he joined Ruenen on the bridge in a show of solidarity. "Not everyone here in Nevandia kisses our boots, that's true, but they know what Marai did for us. She held off Rayghast's forces. No one from Nevandia would've dared harm her after she freed the country from his dark magic."

Tarik's statement didn't thaw the ice in the fae leader's face, but some of the others were moved. The redheaded female with the baby whispered something to the leader.

"Queen Marai is my friend. I . . . care for her." Ruenen took an unsteady breath. "A piece of me dies every day she is gone."

A hand slid its way into his. Ruenen looked down to see Thora, eyes red and watery. Raife clapped a hand on Ruenen's shoulder while Aresti and Tarik stepped closer around him. They were one unit. Not royalty, or fae, or werewolf.

The fae leader studied them as the female at his side beamed with delight.

"She exists," she said. "I believe you. And we will help you find her." The female nudged the leader in the back, forcing him forward.

The male sighed and came back to the edge of the bridge. "Can you guarantee our safety? That we won't be shot the instant we step through that gate?"

Aresti snorted the way Marai always did. "Pretty sure we said the same thing when we first arrived. We have a formal, written decree here in Nevandia, signed by the human Witenagemot, King Ruenen, and all of us you see before you. Harm to magical folk is punishable by law."

"It goes both ways, though. We must also abide by those rules," Tarik said.

"We came here to meet the Queen of the Fae," said the leader, expression unreadable, "but my partner is right. If she's missing, then it's our prerogative to help you find her. She's a symbol of hope for us, that the fae may rise again."

Ruenen's body sagged in relief. He hadn't realized how much he'd been sweating. He held out his hand to the leader. "I will gladly accept any aid you're able to provide in the search for Queen Marai and Lord Keshel."

The leader eyed Ruenen's outstretched hand, as if touching a human was the last thing he wanted to do, like he might contract a disease from it.

Ruenen added, "Guests are safe within these walls. You may stay as long as you like."

At long last, the leader bridged the gap and shook Ruenen's hand in a firm grip. "I'm Braesal."

Up close, Braesal's eyes were the color of sunsets, and his short brown hair was as curly as Raife's. His son bounded across the bridge to his father's side, followed by the pretty redheaded female with the baby.

"This is my partner, River, and our children, Holt and Fina."

Thora approached River and tickled baby Fina's chubby arm. "Does anyone in your party need medical assistance?" Fina issued a gurgling giggle that made Thora grin.

"No, we made it here in one piece, thank Lirr." River's irises seemed to ripple like water. They matched the shimmering wings at her back, which looked to be composed of every shade of blue imaginable. "Though it took us far longer than expected since we mostly traveled by night. Wings are difficult to hide."

"Well, you don't have to hide who you are here," said Thora.

River grasped Thora's hand as tears lined her eyes. "This place is like a storybook to us. A dream come true." She kissed Thora's cheek. "Don't mind Braesal. He's an overprotective father."

Thora laughed. "Yes, we had one of our own. He's very much like our beloved Keshel, whom we greatly miss." Thora's face fell briefly, but then brightened once again. "Come, I'm sure your baby needs changing."

"I'm hungry," young Holt announced.

"Let's get you inside to remedy that," Ruenen said.

"And then we can discuss finding our Faerie Queen," said Braesal pointedly.

QUEEN OF THE SHADOW MENAGERIE

He whistled over the rest of the fae, who were far more at ease now. They gave Ruenen smiles, respectful nods, bows, and curtsies, gaping up at the castle walls with re-ignited intrigue.

For the first time in weeks, an ember of a different kind of hope brewed within Ruenen as he led the fae through the cobbled, winding streets of Kellesar, past the colorful shops and houses. He reveled in the feeling that something genuinely *good* was happening. That Marai and Keshel's mission to create a safe place for magical folk was truly coming to fruition.

And Ruenen couldn't shake the sensation that when Marai and Keshel returned, they would be proud of what had been achieved in their absence this day.

That Marai would look at Ruenen in admiration, because even though his heart yearned and ached for her, he still kept trying to make the world a better place.

As she always said he would.

CHAPTER 13

MARAI

B ile surged up Marai's throat.

Violence against magical folk was bad enough. But exploitation? Degradation? Treating living, sentient beings as if they were nothing more than animals to be ogled at?

The Menagerie was a blight. A cancer. And Marai couldn't stand for it.

Not as Koda and the Peace Keepers placed Marai and Keshel backstage, in the wings behind the black velvet curtain, forcing them to watch each "performance."

There was no roof on the amphitheater. It was the first time Marai had seen the sky, inky and clouded, since Bakair. Moonlight, and dozens of flickering sconces illuminated the stage, shrouding everything in cryptic shadows. If Cavar was aiming to set a vibe of mystery and subtle danger, he'd done it well. Rows of ravenous audience members, their faces veiled by darkness, were packed into seats and benches, shoulder to shoulder. Marai could almost hear their erratic pulses racing in anticipation of what they were about to witness.

It was nearly pitch-black in the wings, but Marai's fae eyesight observed the ropes, counterweights, and pulleys, every tool and possible weapon at the belts of the two stagehands running back and forth behind the crossover. There was only one door backstage, leading into the stairwell with the offices and banquet hall. There were two other doors at the back of the audience. No windows.

Escaping would be difficult, but not impossible. Cavar's barrier stopped at the amphitheater. Marai studied the smooth, interior stone walls, covered by posters advertising the Menagerie creatures. If she could get free from Koda and the guards, she could climb a rope to the top of the curtain rigging, then scale the walls the rest of the way to the top. From there, though, she didn't know how to get down on the other side and grab Keshel.

She'd need someone else to help her incapacitate Koda. The Peace Keepers she could handle, but Koda would need to be taken by surprise, paying special attention to his fingers. Marai glanced at Keshel, his thin arms, his drawn face. He wouldn't be much help. She'd need someone ruthless and brave.

Desislava was hauled onto the stage, wrapped in chains, by two guards dressed in black, their faces covered by white clay masks. Desislava snarled and struggled against her bindings as her captors dragged her center stage. She was incredibly strong, despite her severely weakened and malnourished state; the guards' boots skid across the wooden planks as they tried to restrain her.

Marai didn't feel much pity for vampires, but this was gut-wrenchingly painful to witness.

"And now, the most fearsome creature we have in our collection: Desislava, vampire from far off Astye!" Arcturius, the Master of Ceremonies, painted an exotic picture for the audience. Koda translated his Andaran for Marai and Keshel. As one of Cavar's human employees, Arcturius reveled in the sound of applause. He wore a black and white striped coat with black pantaloons and a black felt hat. His face was painted pure white, with kohl around his eye sockets and lining his lips, making him look like a ghoul.

A drummer and fiddler to the side of the stage, dressed and styled similarly, played an intense melody.

Arcturius and his curly mustache bounded closer to Desislava, dancing just out of her reach. The vampire's crimson eyes burned as the smell of his human blood flooded her starved senses. The shadows cast across her pale face made her appear all the more vicious and terrifying. Desislava snapped her jaws, revealing those lethal fangs, and the audience gasped and clasped their hearts in fear and fascination.

"Isn't she marvelous?" Arcturius asked the crowd with glee. "Notice her immense strength. Lethal fangs. The glowing, soulless eyes. She'd drain everyone in this room faster than you can say 'fiddlesticks' if she got free."

Further gasps from the audience. People shifted in their seats. A small child wailed. But no one left the room in fear, disgust, or shock. The audience remained, positioned on the edge of their seats, drinking in the show as Desislava might sip on their blood.

Her starvation was their spectacle, and anger throbbed behind Marai's eyes.

One day, I hope she does rip out their throats.

Arcturius released a melodic chuckle. "Not to worry, my friends. The Menagerie knows how to handle our beasts. Desislava is only one of many wonders from the Nine Kingdoms."

The black-attired guards heaved Desislava offstage, their muscles bulging as she continued to thrash in a hunger-induced rage.

"We have yet another creature of the night," Arcturius said, twiddling his white gloved fingers and swathed his voice in mystery. Marai had to hand it to him—the man knew how to hold an audience's attention. "He may look human enough, but at the full moon, he becomes a ferocious monster, capable of eating your children and snapping a grown man in two!"

Athelstan shuffled out next, walking without an escort or shackles across the wooden boards of the stage. He, too, wore all black. The music changed to another ominous tune as the audience leaned forward, waiting to see his transformation.

Grinding her jaw, Marai hated their wide eyes and gaping mouths. *How can no one care how sickly he is?* Didn't it bother any of them to see living beings treated this way?

Athelstan's frail figure took center stage, his face a sagging mask of forlorn defeat. He clenched his fists, and his collar pulsated with black lambency.

"I present to you: Athelstan, man-eating werewolf!"

People screamed as Athelstan's body contorted and crunched. Bones and muscles snapped and expanded. His form lengthened. Fur sprouted across his face and arms. Claws protruded from his gnarled fingers. He roared, showing off his viscous maw.

Werewolf transformations were traumatic on the body, even when it only occurred once a month on the regular full moon. But to do this every night for *seven years* . . . Marai shut her eyes and turned away. She'd never witnessed a transformation before. Now she never wanted to again.

Keshel grabbed her hand and squeezed, breathing in staccato bursts.

QUEEN OF THE SHADOW MENAGERIE

Marai had no idea what Athelstan did on that stage, or any of the others after him. She couldn't bring herself to open her eyes again. Words and sounds became muddled in her ears. Her head swum, and she felt dangerously close to keeling over. The only thing keeping her standing was Keshel's grip on her hand.

Something began to shift inside her. A flame ignited in her core, a spark of defiance and power that had nothing to do with magic.

These beings had families and friends who loved and missed them back home, like Marai. It wasn't just Keshel she wanted to rescue anymore—it was *all* of them. The entire Menagerie of folk and creatures Cavar had forced into this life of torture. As much as she wanted to get back to Ruenen, Marai knew that he would never leave these folk behind. Ruenen wouldn't stand for this. He'd find a way to rescue them.

She didn't entirely accept the royal blood that coursed through her veins, but Marai was becoming aware of a building sense of responsibility to the members of the Menagerie.

Marai didn't notice when the show ended. She buried herself deep inside, to the part of her that still remembered what it was like to be free, to be held in Thora and Kadiatu's arms, safe, and warm, and loved. She distracted herself by remembering the way Ruenen's hair flopped over his gold-flecked eyes. By the sound of his pounding heart against Marai's palm as he kissed her with soft lips–

A rough hand on her arm wrenched her from those memories.

Koda frowned at her, fingers digging into her skin. "Get used to it, Marai. That will be you tomorrow night."

Marai spat in his face. "You're a pathetic, ass-kissing louse."

Koda wiped off her saliva with his sleeve, scowling. "Don't make this worse for yourself. Remember, if you misbehave, it won't be only you who suffers punishment." His silver eyes flicked to Keshel.

Emotions shoved against Marai's ribcage, wanting release. Screams of rage threatened to claw up her throat. "How can you stand by and let Cavar do this?"

"Maybe because I don't want to be in those chains, too," said Koda with vehemence. "In this world, it's survival of the fittest. I'm respected here. Trusted. Isn't that better than getting a collar molded around my neck?"

Rage seared across her skin. White, lightning fury streaked across her vision. "You're a *disgrace* to your people. To the fae who birthed you. To the magic you were gifted!"

Using all her strength and flexibility, Marai kneed Koda in the groin.

Volgar, the Peace Keeper holding Keshel, punched him in the face in retaliation. Keshel tumbled to the ground with a *thud*. Marai froze as Volgar grabbed Keshel by the front of his shirt and aimed a hairy-knuckled fist at him again.

"Think wisely before you say another thing," Koda growled, hunched over from Marai's attack. "It's not only Keshel we'll hurt. That servant, what's her name? *Gunnora*. She's just a funny little human freak that makes the audience laugh when they see her. We have gnomes and hobs that can do that, and plenty of more useful servants."

Marai threw her head back and breathed deeply. Frustrated tears welled in her eyes, but she refused to let them fall. She could not show such weakness, not only in front of Koda or Keshel, but to the other magical folk. If they were looking to her as a symbol of strength, she had to keep it together.

Marai allowed rough hands to grab and hold her still. No one helped Keshel as he staggered to his feet, blood dribbling from his nose.

"Now that we're all calm . . . let me explain your roles here at the Menagerie," Koda said with a satisfying wince as he moved. "Patrons will pay extra to have a private reading with Keshel. A tent has been set up outside of the amphitheater."

Keshel's brow pinched. "That's not how my visions work—"

"It is *now*, thanks to the collar."

Koda's gaze then slid to Marai, standing again with his usual swagger. "And the Faerie Queen will be a delicate, *silent*, dancing puppet."

Marai released a groan of disgust.

"Now, now, cheer up, tulip, it'll be fun," Koda said with a grin. "You'll have hundreds of admirers throwing flowers at your feet. You'll forget all about the Nevandian King."

After being ushered back to her dark tent by the guards, Marai howled in rage. If she'd had access to magic, she would have turned the entire camp to cinders. Instead, she threw her wooden bowl and spoon to the ground. She kicked her bedroll into a lump. None of that was satisfying, so she yanked off the idiotic silk dress she was wearing and ripped it to shreds.

Someone pushed through her tent flap.

Marai halted her rampage, suddenly aware that she wore nothing but a gauzy shift.

Innesh stared her down. She'd probably been sent by Koda to keep an eye on Marai.

"I heard you kneed Koda in the cock."

Marai nodded, drawing herself up to hear the condemnations, to accept whatever punishment was in store.

A slow, conspiratorial grin spread across Innesh's tattooed face.

Silently, Innesh slithered back out of the tent, once again leaving Marai alone in the darkness.

Strange as it was, Marai found herself smirking, too.

"I won't fucking wear that."

Marai stood against the far side of her tiny tent with her arms crossed tightly over her chest. Anja held out a frilly white monstrosity of a dress, undoubtedly picked by horrid Acacia.

"Why can't I wear black like everyone else?"

"The other dress was definitely less hideous, but since you shredded it, you'll have to wear this now," Gunnora said. "Unless you'd rather go on stage naked. What a rousing first performance *that* would be."

Marai's body coiled tighter. "I'm not stepping foot on that stage."

Anja frowned. "I'm afraid you have no choice. Cavar's still here. He's going to watch you tonight and program your collar."

"*Program?*" Marai repeated.

"Cavar sets the limit on what magic you're able to use in the show. Athelstan's collar is programmed to force his transformations. Keshel's will allow him to have visions, cutting off access to his other magic," said Anja. "Since you're the most powerful of us, I'm imagining your programming will take more effort than usual."

Marai cringed. "I don't want him touching me."

"Oh, he doesn't have to," Gunnora said. "He'll use that stone in his amulet to control you from backstage. He's the only one who can, since the other amulets don't have as much power."

"Please put the dress on, Marai," pleaded Anja, holding out the white eyesore. "If you don't, they'll whip you. Sometimes it's better to accept defeat than suffer further pain . . ."

Marai groaned, then snatched the dress from Anja's hands. It was, after all, just a dress. The worst part of the evening was yet to come.

The dress was even more horrendous on Marai's body. Its frothy, white frills climbed up her neck, hiding the collar, and itched insufferably. Plate-sized applique white roses covered the hem of the knee-high dress. The ensemble was completed with matching slippers and a flower crown of white gardenias.

"If this is what Acacia thinks is fashionable, she has the intelligence and maturity of a toddler," Marai said with a scowl as she looked down at the outfit. "And why is everything black and white?"

Gunnora laughed. "Not sure Acacia has any idea what a faerie queen would wear, neither do I, for that matter, but you do look remarkably like a frosted cake."

"Black and white are the Menagerie colors," explained Anja. "Cavar believes the monochrome palette looks mysterious."

Marai scratched at the fabric on her neck as she exited the tent, coming face to face with Keshel. Heat coursed into her face as Keshel blinked repeatedly, seemingly stunned by her ridiculous doll-like appearance. He glanced at Anja, as if searching for the joke.

"You look . . . cheerful, Marai," he said, biting his lip to stop from smiling. A large bruise had formed on his face from Volgar's punch.

At least I can distract him from this misery and make him smile.

"Why does Keshel get to wear something normal?" Marai asked, noticing his clean white tunic, vest, and black britches.

"They want me to wear this cloak and put the hood up to look mysterious," he replied blandly, indicating the dark fabric slung over his arm. The sewn-on jewels looked like stars against the night sky.

Marai scratched at the lace again. "Maybe it *would* be better if I went onstage naked."

Keshel turned beet red and cleared his throat. "I . . . um, guess we should get going."

"We'll walk with you. We've been instructed to clean Acacia's room while she's busy at the show," said Anja, reaching for a bucket of soapy water by the tree.

Gunnora got to it first. "I got it." At Marai's questionable eyebrow, she said, "I'm stronger than I look," then hauled the bucket into her arms.

The camp at night was always dark; no sliver of moonlight could seep through the dense fog barrier, but the darkness seemed heavier inside the camp, thicker, more complete. Gunnora and her human eyesight tripped over a rock, sloshing the water in the bucket. Marai tried to walk through the row with as much dignity as she could muster, sensing the eyes of dozens of slaves and magical folk. Marai, Keshel, Anja, and Gunnora walked towards the amphitheater, passing two Peace Keepers, Yelich and Sirco, managing the folk entering the building.

Sirco stuck out his leg, tripping Gunnora.

She fell, face first, into the dirt, slopping the sudsy water on Sirco's boots. Yelich roared with laughter.

"Watch where you're going, *freak*," Sirco snapped at Gunnora, who slowly lifted herself from the ground.

Marai's nerves were already frayed. She whirled around, standing protectively in front of Gunnora, fists raised. "If you *ever* touch her again, I'll cut out your tongue."

"She's not a performer. She's a slave," said Yelich.

"She soiled my boots. On purpose. She needs to be punished," Sirco said, pulling a leather whip from his belt.

"It was only water," Gunnora whimpered, but she turned around, and braced herself for the pain.

"Move aside," Yelich sneered to Marai.

Marai didn't move. "Don't you *scum* have other work to do?" She could feel the collar tightening, waiting to shock her. Her own magic must have been swirling around inside, rising with her anger. She lifted her chin in defiance. "You're making us late, and Cavar won't like that."

"We're instructed to punish those who disrespect or disobey us," Sirco said, drawing his arm and the whip back. "Get out of the way."

"Then whip me instead," said Marai.

A collective breath was held. Yelich glanced at Sirco. Keshel gaped at Marai. Gunnora shook her head, eyes wide.

"We don't take orders from you," Sirco said, and tried to shove Marai out of the way. "Get inside the theater."

But Marai held her ground. "Do it." She turned, offering him her back; her wings still drooped sadly. "I'll accept whatever punishment you believe Gunnora has earned."

She could handle the pain. It would hurt more to see them flay Gunnora's back open.

Sirco hesitated. He didn't move.

"What's going on out here?" came Acacia's nasal, superior voice. She appeared in the amphitheater doorway, dressed elaborately in shades of pink with a ridiculous feathered hat on her head. "Why are you raising a whip at my performer?"

Innesh hovered behind her, watching the scene unfold with interest.

"The little one spilled water on me, ma'am, and *this one* refuses to move, saying she'll take the whipping instead," Sirco explained, jerking his head to Marai.

Acacia scoffed. "They're *late*. Keshel should already be out front greeting patrons. You can whip her after she cleans my room." She snapped her gloved fingers at Gunnora and Anja. "It had better be spotless by the time the show's finished."

Anja and Gunnora rushed inside and up the stairs, heads bowed.

Acacia turned to Yelich. "Take Keshel out front. Uncle Jakov is there, and every second Keshel is delayed is money we aren't making. There's a line waiting."

Yelich grabbed Keshel's arm and dragged him inside. Marai didn't get to say goodbye to him before Acacia turned her blue eyes on Sirco.

"I won't have you marring my uncle's prized pet before a show. She needs to look perfect, and a whipping would ruin her dress and hair. There will be none of that tonight. Now, both of you, get inside and do your jobs."

Sirco dipped his head. "Yes, ma'am."

Marai stepped around him and entered the theater on her own. She'd won the battle. This time. Next time, it wouldn't end so painlessly. Gritting her teeth, Marai walked up the stairs, into the dark backstage, and heard the sound of excited babble from the front of the amphitheater. The audience was getting into their seats.

Koda and another Peace Keeper appeared from the other side of the wings.

"Time for your debut," he said with a snide tone.

Acacia brushed him aside as she examined Marai, up and down. "Acceptable, but something's missing . . . ah!" She reached into the pocket of her voluptuous silk gown and procured a small jar. Acacia dipped her finger in, revealing a red powder.

Marai jerked her head away as Acacia's finger neared her face.

"Hold her still," Acacia ordered Koda without glancing at him.

He grabbed Marai's face and held on as Acacia swiped a red finger across Marai's cheeks and lips.

I'd rather have the ghoul makeup, Marai thought with a grimace.

Acacia stepped back to observe the finished product. "Much better. Now, do you know what to do?"

Marai didn't reply. She put all her hatred into the glare on her face.

Acacia sighed. "No matter. My uncle will ensure you dazzle tonight." She then turned to greet Arcturius with a kiss on each of his painted cheeks.

Marai's heart pounded as the musicians began their prelude. The stagehands pulled on their ropes. The curtain parted. Arcturius took to the stage with a sweeping gesture, and the audience hooted and hollered.

Time trudged on. Act after act went and finished.

Finally, nearly two hours later, the juggling gnomes bowed to their applause, and Sirco removed the shackles from Marai's ankles.

Arcturius then began his new introduction, and Koda translated for her.

"We have come to the final act of our Menagerie. The one I know you all have come to see. Tonight, you will witness her flawless beauty and poise. Her glittering, radiant magic. Without further ado: Marai, the last Faerie Queen!"

Marai momentarily forgot how to move. She stepped backwards, aiming to flee now that her feet were free of the chains, but Sirco grabbed her, pushing her forwards.

She twisted and ducked, getting loose from his muscular arms. She barreled towards the backstage door.

A shockwave of pain rushed through her. The collar heated against her skin, stabbing her with tiny needles of lightning. Marai seized, collapsing to the ground before she could reach the stairs, gasping for breath. Cavar's buckled boots appeared by her face.

"Get up, and don't embarrass me."

Cavar grasped his amulet, black light bleeding between his fingers, and Marai was shoved out of her body.

She stood up against her will. Even as she tried to fight against it, her slippered feet tread gracefully past the black velvet curtain and onto the stage. She was powerless against the compulsion, against the strength of the magic within Cavar's stone. Her mind pounded a fist against the glass wall trapping it, cutting off her brain's communication to the rest of her body.

Candles had been placed in a circle across the floor. Marai stepped inside them. Her muscles twitched as a vapid smile was forced onto her face. Her wings lifted and fluttered, making Marai's back shriek. Perhaps if she wasn't so horrified and sickened, she might have marveled at the beauty of those wings in the candlelight, so very like her father's.

She was only dimly aware of Arcturius' narration, the audience's *oos* and *ahhs,* their applause, their cheers. A numbness settled over her. Distorted sounds and sensations. Marai felt entirely detached from herself, as if she was watching everything from high above. Cavar compelled her arms and legs to move in a choreographed routine. Each time she spun, golden sparkles spewed from her fluttering wings.

Arcturius shouted something enthusiastically in Andaran. Marai guessed he said, "Faerie dust!"

QUEEN OF THE SHADOW MENAGERIE

The audience clapped.

Her hands whirled around and around, and warmth reached her fingertips. *Magic.*

For a moment, Marai wondered if it was her own power finally coming back to life. But her hope dissipated quickly when tiny, winking stars appeared in her palms. Cavar had her toss them into the crowd, and the stars dissolved like snowflakes on the faces of the patrons.

Next, she created pink flames and ignited a row of lanterns placed along the front of the stage.

Foolish parlor tricks. Marai's real magic was far more impressive.

But the audience didn't care that she had the power of queens in her veins. They only cared about the pretty flower petals she scattered across the stage as she twirled.

With one final sprinkle of faerie dust, Marai's body curtsied as the audience rose to its feet. Applause thundered through the wooden planks beneath her feet. She daintily dashed off stage as Arcturius ended the evening with a fanfare from the musicians.

Once in the dark seclusion of backstage, magic released its hold and Marai was thrust back into herself. A jarring impact, as if she'd fallen from a tree branch and crashed to the ground, or been yanked out of violent ocean waves just before drowning. She could once again feel the ground beneath her feet. The nip of cold at her nose and cheeks. Humiliation and anger rose within her, but her body had been drained by the invasive magic. She barely had the strength to keep herself standing.

Cavar appeared at her side. His eyes glittered, probably envisioning the mountains of gold he'd soon be earning. "I own you, Marai. Never forget it."

She hated him. More than she'd despised Rayghast. Possibly as much as she hated Slate. But Cavar also scared her, because he had the advantage. Because, as he said, he *owned* her, and there was seemingly nothing she was able to do to prevent the stone's dark magic from seizing control.

I'll fight it. I will fight it every time, even if it's to no avail.

Cavar turned to his niece. "Come, Acacia, the Guardians and investors are meeting in the banquet hall for a celebratory drink and to discuss the expansion."

"So many parties, Uncle! We should capture Faerie Queens more often."

They strode away, arm in arm.

Koda's mouth contorted. His brows furrowed, perhaps upset that Cavar hadn't asked him to join.

A dog begging for attention from its master, Marai thought bitterly.

Cavar didn't care about Koda any more than he cared about Marai or the other magical folk. Koda was a loyal pawn, and that was all he'd ever be.

Koda must have been more put out than she knew, because he didn't bother to escort her back to camp. Marai stumbled at the top of the stairs. Innesh latched onto her arm, keeping her upright.

"Thank you," Marai mumbled.

"The first show is always the hardest," said Innesh's gravelly voice. "Get some rest."

"I will, once I see Keshel."

Innesh nodded, then disappeared in the dark, swirling mist.

Struck by the woman's sudden kindness, Marai waited outside Keshel's tent. It didn't take long for him to appear. He staggered, eyes partly closed, but when he caught sight of Marai, he straightened, and took on a confident gait.

He's forcing himself to appear strong in front of me.

"How did it go?" Marai asked, her voice strained.

Keshel swayed, and Marai reached for him. A cold sweat dappled his forehead; his eyes bleary and bloodshot.

"I'm fine," he said, righting himself, brushing hair from his face. He gave Marai a wan smile. "Everything went fine. I'm merely tired."

"You don't need to pretend," Marai said with a scowl. "Not for me."

For a moment, Keshel didn't answer. He closed his eyes, as if trying to steady his breathing.

"I'm used to my mind being invaded by visions. It's always strange, but tonight was the first time where I felt my mind truly wasn't my own." Keshel's throat bobbed. His hands shook. "When I'd finished the whole queue of patrons, and the amulet's power released me, I had a hard time deciphering what was real. It took a few moments to realize that I was no longer in a vision. I was disoriented, so much so that I retched onto the grass."

Marai's stomach clenched. No matter how miserable, how humiliated she was, Keshel's experience had been far worse than hers. "Did you see anything important in your visions?"

Keshel grimaced. "It was mostly silly things about money or someone's love life. Insulting, really—my visions used to have meaning, but now I've been degraded to being a mere sideshow fortune teller. And I hate it, Marai. I *hate* how angry I feel." His hands clenched at his sides. "I want to tear this place apart."

"I understand," she whispered, because hatred and anger were the only things keeping her standing.

"Although . . . I suppose . . ." Keshel's brow pinched in concentration. "Tonight, there were always these hazy images in the background of the visions. If I looked past the main story, I could see that same golden light, swirling with a glittering blackness. And a wisp of auburn hair."

Marai crossed her arms. "Your visions are being vaguer than usual."

Keshel returned her sardonic comment with a flicker of a smile. "How was your evening?"

"I'd rather not recount it, if you don't mind."

Keshel nodded, and turned to enter his tent before curfew.

Shame pooled in her stomach. Marai grasped his arm. "I'm sorry that I'm not strong enough to get us out of here. I'm sorry that you must remain here. That you were taken to begin with."

Keshel gently took Marai's hand in his own. "You're not to blame for any of this. I'm beginning to believe that Lirr wanted us to come here."

"To be slaves?"

"To learn something." Keshel leaned his head down, pressing his forehead to Marai's. She allowed the intimate gesture, sensing Keshel needed the comfort, but still her face flushed. "I may not agree with her methods, but I believe Lirr wants us to stop Cavar and destroy the amulets. I don't think this is a punishment. I think she *needs* us."

Marai pulled back from Keshel. "How can you believe that? How can you have such faith in beings we don't even know exist?"

She'd stopped believing in the gods as a young girl, after her parents were massacred. But if Lirr and Laimoen *were* real, how could they allow the Menagerie to exist? How was this awful place *not* a punishment? Had they sat back and watched this tragedy unfold for fifty years from their heavenly city of Empyra, and now wanted Marai and Keshel to clean up their mess?

And why had they created that stone, granting unlimited, dark power to a villain like Cavar?

Maybe they didn't. Maybe someone else did.

It was an idea that had been growing in Marai's mind since Keshel mentioned that the stones were conduits. Marai couldn't imagine that Lirr, Mother of Life, if she existed, would create something so forbidden and heinous as dark magic. It went against everything the goddess supposedly stood for. Monk Baureo claimed that the gods *loved* all creatures, therefore, it seemed unconscionable that even Laimoen would do such a thing, despite being the God of Destruction.

Dark magic didn't balance the scales. It only brought corruption and terror.

Keshel slanted a thin-lipped smile. "I'd rather have faith that my life has purpose than lose myself to hatred and despair."

"You mean like me?"

"No, Marai, you're not like that at all. There's a bright light inside you. It's a power that has nothing to do with magic. What you did for Gunnora tonight is proof of that." His lanky body curled downwards, and Keshel kissed the top of her head, stunning Marai into silence.

His finger twirled around one strand of her wavy hair. The darkness of night made his eyes appear black as ink, but they were warm, no longer shards of cold, distant steel.

And for the first time, Marai looked at Keshel and saw his beauty.

It was a soft, refined beauty. Smooth as ice.

He'd always been handsome, as most fae were, but Marai had never truly noticed *him* before. His gentleness. His inner strength. His mind. Keshel was her brother. A stern father-figure. But he was only a few years older than her. He was still a young man, trying to find his way.

Marai didn't know how to respond, so she stalked back to her tent and shed the ugly dress, leaving it in a crumpled ball on the ground.

She could still feel Keshel's forehead pressed to her own, his lips in her hair. But she couldn't help but wish it was Ruenen's forehead and lips touching her, his presence sheltering her.

"Good night, Ruen. I promise I'll find my way home. Wait for me."

CHAPTER 14

CAVAR

After the final guest left or went off to bed, Cavar poured himself another glass of wine. He struck a match, lit a candle, then sat down at his desk. He opened the wooden chest, filled to the rim with bronze coins, and began to tally the earnings from the evening.

He couldn't have asked for a better premiere. Every seat had been filled. It was the largest audience he'd had in months, and thanks to the extra coin from Keshel's fortune telling, Cavar raked in the most money he'd ever earned in a single evening. The expense and hassle of bringing Marai and Keshel to the Menagerie was worth it, and the income would only increase as word spread across the country.

Marai's Menagerie image had been curated to appear like she was a pure, ethereal damsel. The rest of his Menagerie was dark and sinister in nature, or comical, thanks to the gnomes and hobs. But Marai was to be its angel, clad in white.

And, as Cavar had hoped, its sexual potential to audience members.

Salivating men and women cornered Cavar at the end of the show, pleading for a night spent with the Faerie Queen. They'd practically shoved coins into his hands, but Cavar knew Marai wasn't ready for that yet. He didn't trust her. But soon.

"I promise, gentlemen, ladies, that after she's acclimated to the Menagerie, each of you will get your turn with her," Cavar had said.

"Sure, and I bet you want to take her for a test ride, yourself, first," came the snarky voice of the Minister of Justice.

QUEEN OF THE SHADOW MENAGERIE

Cavar had stopped his lip from curling at the disgusting thought.

The Governor had plans. *Major* plans. On the world stage, he wouldn't remain anonymous much longer. He'd been exchanging correspondence with the Sultan of Yehzig, and Cavar was gaining ground in establishing a second Menagerie in Qasnal. The Sultan and Yehzigis despised magic and wanted none of it in their country, but Cavar had slowly, over several years, worn the Sultan down, illuminating the financial benefits that the Menagerie could offer Yehzig. Cavar proposed to split half the profits with the Sultan, and hoped to then establish a trade of amulets to affluent Yehzigis.

Then, he would set his sights on Astye.

There was a knock at the door, and Koda popped his head inside the office. "May I come in, Governor?"

Cavar gestured for him to enter, barely glancing up from his ledger and the bronze coin between his fingers.

"Pleased with the results of the evening?" Koda asked, slipping through the door and coming further onto the rug.

"Quite pleased. It seems our idea works."

Koda beamed. "I had a feeling it would. When I saw her open a portal that day in Cleaving Tides, I knew you'd love to have her. And yet, Governor, sir, forgive me, but I'm a trifle concerned."

Cavar's gaze darted up from his ledger. "Why is that?"

"Marai is trouble. She has no regard for authority, and takes pleasure in threats and violence against us. The camp adores her, and I can see them rallying behind her in a rebellion if we're not careful."

"Then punish her. Don't let her walk all over you," Cavar said, annoyance rising. Koda was distracting him from his counting.

"I've been doing this, Governor, but Marai's stubborn, with a fiery temper and an even wilder tongue." Koda's face darkened. "And sometimes, when her anger is stoked, I can feel her power in the air."

Cavar's eyes narrowed at his assistant. "Are you saying my collar isn't working properly?"

Koda instantly back-tracked, smiling. "Oh, it's definitely working, Governor. We'd be dead if it wasn't. I'm merely saying that we need to be wary of her. Her power is unpredictable. I don't think Marai knows the full extent of what she can do."

Cavar pursed his lips. He didn't like Koda doubting his creation, the collars, in this way, but his assistant may have had a point.

When Cavar was programming Marai's collar during her performance, he'd felt a slight pushback of magic. Not enough to cause concern, but Cavar had never felt that before from the other folk. Not Anja, or Keshel. He'd tasted the crackle of Marai's fury on his tongue, and a static pulse skittered across his skin.

Perhaps Koda was right. Perhaps Cavar *did* need to be cautious.

"She'll never overpower you," the little voice in his head told Cavar. *"She's not stronger than me."*

Me. Cavar didn't know who the voice belonged to, the mysterious soul stuck inside the stone, but it had never steered him wrong in sixty years. He trusted the stone's power and knowledge.

"Keep a close eye on her," said Cavar, returning to his ledger. "Do whatever you need to in order to subdue her. Make sure the camp sees her as nothing more than another prisoner. Increase the whippings. Cut off a hand from someone unimportant. I don't care."

Koda bowed, noticing Cavar's dismissive tone. "Of course. You can put your faith in me, Governor."

Cavar waved him away, focusing once again on his calculations. Koda's attention-seeking presence was irritating him. He wondered if one day the faerie would curl up, panting, at Cavar's feet beneath the desk.

Koda's face drooped in disappointment. As he made for the door, Koda shot over his shoulder, "Congratulations, Governor. The Menagerie is a marvel."

Then he finally exited.

The only reason Koda wasn't performing with the rest of his kind was because he was easy to manipulate, eager to please. The minute he stopped being useful, Cavar had no qualms about putting a collar around him, as well.

CHAPTER 15

RUENEN

The arrival of Braesal and the new fae was not as warmly received as Ruenen had wanted. Tensions ran high in Kellesar. The following day, a large caravan of Tacornians arrived, seeking their own new life in Nevandia, and an all-out brawl had almost occurred in the streets when the Tacornians came face-to-face with a few of Braesal's people. Luckily, Raife, Aresti, and Avilyard had managed to quell the arguments before things got out of hand.

"Some of the things the Tacornians shouted . . ." Raife shuddered later that afternoon in Ruenen's private office.

Ruenen hadn't been there, but he could only guess at what terrible, derogatory insults people had shouted.

"Makes me wonder if Braesal's people should really stay," continued Raife. "Maybe we're moving too fast."

"If they leave, hate wins," said Aresti with a severe expression. She leaned against the windowsill, looking down into the city, fiddling with a gold hoop in her ear. "It would show everyone who dislikes us that we can be easily removed. Tacornians shouldn't get to decide what happens in Nevandia."

Ruenen agreed with her. "If Braesal's people give up, there's no hope for that peaceful future we envisioned." What Marai envisioned and Keshel helped orchestrate. He couldn't let them both down. "We'll make it work. We have to."

"Perhaps we could host some assemblies, where the fae and werewolves meet with citizens to answer their questions," said Avilyard. "Educate people on magical folk. Fear and hatred is often based on ignorance and misunderstandings."

"That's a good idea, Commander," Raife said, "and I'd be happy to participate, but what about the Witan?" He arched his sandy eyebrows at Ruenen.

The Witan had been equally upset by Braesal's arrival. Holfast had merely closed his eyes and pinched the bridge of his nose while Wattling and Corian's raised voices echoed off the marble walls of the chamber.

Cronhold had shaken his feeble finger in the air. "Not since the raids have I seen so many faeries gathered together. The last time, they tried to kill me!"

"That's because you were slaughtering *them*," Ruenen reminded the uproarious table.

While Nevandia's previous kings had begun hunting down the fae decades ago, it was Tacorn and Rayghast who'd finished the job, massacring hundreds, nearly wiping out faeries on Astye entirely. Cronhold had participated in that, as a member of Rayghast's counsel.

"We already have enough faeries here," Lord Corian said.

"We opened our lands to magical folk," Ruenen had shot back. "We promised them safety. Citizenship. Homes."

"We promised *Lady Marai's* people those things. I don't recall us agreeing to let any faerie with a sob story bang on our door." Corian scowled and crossed his arms.

"We don't know these people," Fenir had said with a shaky voice, his eyes round. "We don't know what their purpose is in being here. It could be *sinister*."

Ruenen had rolled his eyes. "I'd assume, considering that they brought all their earthly possessions with them, that their purpose is to *live* here. They traveled with *children* halfway across Astye, for Empyra's sake. They're not a threat."

"You can never be too careful, Your Grace," Fenir said, eyes darting around the room in a shifty, anxious manner, as if he expected Braesal to pop up and assassinate him.

"They want to help us find Marai and Keshel," said Ruenen. "Perhaps with the fae's assistance, Marai can finally come home." His stern facade faltered, and he knew Holfast spotted the pain displayed in his face.

"Good. Let them," said Wattling, not noticing Ruenen's hurt. "Make themselves useful. Then our soldiers can focus on their *real* jobs." He shot Ruenen a look.

Corian groaned. "We'll be overrun with magical folk before the New Year."

It was nearing the Summer Equinox. New Year was seven months away. If that many magical folk appeared in Kellesar, it would be a miracle. *Let's hope Marai is home by then . . .*

"When you're King, Corian, you can decide whatever you want," Ruenen had said, "but since *I* am currently King of Nevandia, magical folk are welcome in my lands."

That had been the end of that conversation. For the moment.

"Maybe I should lead a group of Braesal's people on a search of Cleaving Tides?" asked Raife now, bringing Ruenen back to the present. "You said you wanted a team to go there, and Commander Avilyard can't spare more men."

"If they'll go with you," Avilyard said, looking skeptical, "but Sir Raife is correct, Your Grace. With several teams still out searching for Lady Marai and Lord Keshel, I can't send anyone else until they return. I need—"

"I understand, Commander," Ruenen said, running a hand across his jaw. He had six small groups of soldiers and volunteers spread out across the continent searching, not including Nosficio. But that wasn't enough. Unless the whole Nevandian army was out there searching, it would never be enough. Perhaps the fae could find Marai. Maybe they could do what Ruenen couldn't. "Go ahead and ask Braesal for his thoughts, but I don't want you leaving, Raife. I need you here." He turned back to Avilyard. "I have an idea, Commander. Our army could certainly use new recruits, right?"

"We do, Your Grace, but integrating faeries into the army might be difficult," Avilyard said with a frown, guessing what Ruenen was thinking. "It was difficult enough for the King's Guard to accept Sir Raife and Dame Aresti. I doubt you'll garner support for arming more."

Aresti let out a rough laugh. "They have *magic*—they're already armed, as it is. Giving them a physical weapon won't do more harm."

"Bringing faeries into the army will be no more difficult than integrating them anywhere else in the country," Ruenen said. "However we can incorporate them into society here will be beneficial for everyone. And yes, Avilyard, your idea of an assembly or two is an excellent idea. I'll ensure the Witan begins organizing it."

Raife scanned Ruenen's face, observing the strain and evidence of sleepless nights. In an optimistic tone, he said, "There are two vacant cottages in Grave's End. Rundown, of course, but we could put Braesal's people there. They're across the road from ours."

Grave's End still remained one of the poorer neighborhoods in Kellesar, but Thora had been busy cleaning it up. She maintained Kadiatu's garden, and planted more flowers and vegetation in front of the cottage and along the street, while Raife helped the neighbors mend their broken-down houses and sweep up the trash in his spare time.

"Although, if more fae move in, the rest of the neighborhood might up and leave," said Aresti with a tone that suggested she wouldn't mind that happening. "More room for us. Would be nice to have my own place."

"The people of Grave's End have tolerated us, haven't they? What's a few more folk?" asked Raife. "Families, even. It's good for the neighborhood."

"I've been meaning to speak with you about that, actually," said Ruenen, standing from his desk. "I'd like to show you something later on, if you and Thora would accompany me."

Confusion swept across Raife's expression. "Of course, Your Grace."

He and the others bowed, making for the door.

"I feel as if I haven't thanked you three enough," announced Ruenen, causing them to halt. Aresti, Raife, and Avilyard were the most loyal to him, out of the entire guard and Witan. He could count on them, speak to them in ways he didn't even dare with Holfast. "You've gone above and beyond the past few months, since the moment I first arrived in Nevandia. I know you've spent far more time working than resting, putting in countless hours searching for Marai and Keshel, battling cantankerous Tacornians, and trying to better Nevandia. I appreciate all that you do."

Avilyard's hazel eyes twinkled. "There is no greater honor, Your Grace, than to serve a righteous and noble King."

Is that what Ruenen was? Sometimes it was hard to tell. He'd been cranky and listless since Marai's abduction. When he woke up in the morning, he certainly didn't feel righteous or noble. Mostly, he felt as if every day he was treading water, trying not to make a mistake, not to cause another war, not to get anyone killed. Ruenen's emotions swayed like a pendulum between guilt and frustration, loneliness and heartache, back and forth, swinging and swinging.

"Don't get sentimental on us, Your Grace," Aresti said with a cringe. "Not sure I can handle another man crying in front of me today."

"Who did you make cry?" asked Raife warily.

Aresti heaved a heavy sigh. "Fenir dropped some papers in the hallway—notes or something—I picked them up to hand back. You would've thought that I'd threatened to rip out his liver and eat it for dinner."

"He's been on edge since the end of the war," mused Ruenen. He'd noticed the councilman growing paler and slimmer by the day. His long brown hair seemed thinner, and there were a few patches of scalp showing, as if he'd ripped out some strands.

"I think we're all adjusting to peace," said Raife. "Perhaps Lord Fenir needs more time to feel secure."

Ruenen understood that. Sometimes, he'd wake in the middle of the night and forget where he was, forget he was King, expecting to be sleeping on a pile of hay in some stranger's barn. But then he'd settle into his sheets and remember: *life is different now.*

Ruenen had asked Raife and Thora to meet him on the corner of Birch and Hyacinth streets. It was a higher-class neighborhood, full of merchants and lower-ranking officials and nobles. Elmar and Nyle trailed behind, keeping a respectful distance from the conversation.

"Is someone ill here, Your Grace?" asked Thora. She'd brought her medical bag along, having come from several house visits.

"Not exactly," Ruenen said with a playful air of mystery. He gestured up at the multi-storied house before them. Its shutters and wooden beams were painted a cheery yellow, but its window-boxes were empty of flowers. There was an air of vacantness about the place. It was larger than their cottage, but like most of the houses in Kellesar, it was squished between two similar-sized buildings. "The previous owner perished in the battle, and with no beneficiaries, it's been sitting vacant for months." He clapped a hand on Raife back. "It's yours."

Raife blanched. "What do you mean?"

Ruenen's smile spread across his face at Thora's wide eyes. "I purchased the property in your names. It's my wedding gift to you. I would give you lands, as well, and a lordship if I could, but I think that would be difficult to do right now. But I intend to do it in the future."

Thora and Raife stood speechless. They stared at Ruenen as if he'd sprouted an extra head and started speaking gibberish.

"Are you . . . certain?" stammered Raife. "That's a very generous gift . . ."

"There's no one more deserving. You've stood by me through so many battles, risked your lives to keep me on the throne, helped me forge a better Nevandia, and comforted me in my darkest moments. You are the best friends I could ask for. Since I couldn't throw you an enormous wedding, I've had to find another way to show you both my gratitude."

Silver lined Thora's eyes. "You're not . . . upset at us?"

"Why on earth would I be upset at you?"

"Because of Marai."

Ruenen went cold. *Am I that transparent?* It was true that he'd felt resentful when he'd first seen their troth rings. He'd wondered why *they* were allowed their happy ending, while he and Marai were constantly torn asunder, as if they were parallel lines fated to never intersect.

He smiled. "Not at all. It's more important than ever to find happiness and love. You two waited a long time to be together. Marai would be thrilled. I only wish I could have been there to celebrate with you."

"It was a private ceremony," said Raife sheepishly. "We only told Aresti a week after she returned from her scouting mission. She wasn't pleased that she missed it."

Ruenen plopped a small key into Thora's palm. "Welcome home."

Thora burst into tears and threw her arms around Ruenen's neck. She sobbed a few incoherent remarks into his shirt.

"Thank you," Raife whispered, and then joined in on the embrace.

Ruenen watched with a melancholy smile as Raife and Thora stepped into their new house. They ran their hands over the door frames, the wooden banister, the small gilded mirror that hung on the wall in the foyer.

"So many rooms," Thora said, looking up at the stairs to the second floor.

Raife took her hand and kissed it. "We'll fill them soon."

They'd create a big, beautiful family, and Ruenen couldn't help but feel that tug on his heartstrings again. Gods, he wanted that for himself, too.

Thora kissed Raife then, and the ache in his heart grew so heavy that Ruenen had to step away. He hadn't lied—he was beyond happy for his friends. He wanted them to have this life together, to build a family. But at the same time, it tore open the Marai-shaped wound in Ruenen's chest every time he saw them smile, hold hands, or kiss when they thought he wasn't looking.

He turned up the street to head back to the castle, Nyle and Elmar clanking at his heels.

A large, dark shape flew high above the castle spires, passing in front of a cloud.

Ruenen froze. There was no mistaking the silhouette. The wings. The human-like form.

The shadow creature from the Red Lands battlefield.

What in the Unholy Underworld is it doing here?

It had soared above the battle during Ruenen's fight with Rayghast, birthed from the King's usage of dark magic. The creature had simply watched the fray from above, like it had been waiting for *something*, then disappeared once Marai's magic had unleashed. Now it was back, circling the castle like some evil bird of prey. Was it after Ruenen, like the vulture-creature had been? Was it searching for Marai? Or merely taking a pleasant flight to stretch its wings?

"Your Grace?" Elmar's voice startled Ruenen from his staring. "Everything alright?"

"Do you see that thing?" Ruenen pointed at the figure soaring between the white spires.

Nyle scratched his wispy beard as he gazed up at the flying shadow. "Pretty big bird. An eagle, perhaps?"

"Or a massive bat," replied Elmar, cocking his head to the side in examination.

"It's a shadow creature," said Ruenen.

Elmar's jaw dropped. "They can fly now? Lirr have mercy . . ."

"Should the archers shoot it down, Your Grace?" asked Nyle.

"Arrows won't reach it."

"Should we call for Sir Raife?" Elmar asked. "I bet his fire could—"

"No, let's leave it alone for now," said Ruenen. He didn't want to cause unnecessary alarm in the city. Chances were that they wouldn't be able to reach it, anyways, and he also didn't want to bother Raife, to pull him from his newlywed bliss unless he had to. "I guess there's no harm in it *flying* around. But I want every guard and soldier in the city watching it until it goes away. If it attacks anyone . . . kill it."

"We should return to the castle then, Your Grace," said Elmar, his youthful face darkening. "I don't like the idea of you being out here with that thing circling above, especially when the last one we encountered tried to kill you."

Something was going on with the shadow creatures. If another one came for him, Ruenen would be ready.

"You also don't want to be late for your dinner with Queen Rhia," added Nyle.

Ruenen fought back a groan. Holfast had arranged for him to eat dinner with Rhia for the past few days. He'd said it was only polite, since Rhia was technically considered Nevandia's royal guest, but Ruenen knew Holfast's ulterior motive.

Rhia was already waiting in his private dining room when he arrived. Ruenen hadn't had time to change, not that he would have. He didn't feel particularly compelled to put on his best for a woman who clearly had no attraction to him.

Rhia curtsied gracefully. "Your Grace. You look well this evening."

Ruenen almost laughed at her rehearsed lines. His hair was wind-tousled, boots scuffed from traipsing through the city all day. But Ruenen refused to be impolite. He knew this wasn't enjoyable for Rhia, either.

"Thank you, Your Grace. You look lovely, as always."

And she did. Rhia was dressed in traditional Varanese attire: a deep violet robe-like dress with long bell sleeves and silver sash. Her hair had been coiled upon her head, threaded with sprigs of heather from the moor and sparkling diamonds. Her lips had been painted a deep, luscious red. The only flaw in her appearance was that she still refused to allow Thora to heal her facial wound. The bulky patch covered her right jaw and cheek.

Ruenen and Rhia sat in their chairs across from each other at the table. Servants entered and placed platters of food before them. Red wine from Ain was poured into goblets. Ruenen gathered grouse and bread sauce onto his plate.

"Excellent weather today," he said into the stifling silence. "Late spring on the moor is extraordinarily beautiful. Not too hot yet."

Most evenings since Marai's disappearance, he'd eaten with Raife, Thora, Aresti, or the werewolves, and there'd always been things to discuss. Rhia, however, had no problem with the silence. In fact, Ruenen guessed she rather preferred it.

"Yes, Your Grace." She took a bite of food and chewed, then winced. Rhia often winced while eating, but tried to hide it.

Why does she continually choose to suffer? Thora could heal that in two minutes.

Annoyed by her prejudice, Ruenen couldn't help but prod. "What do you think of the new fae arrivals?"

At that, Rhia's fork halted near her lips. "As long as they don't come near me, I have no opinion on the subject."

"I'm thinking of employing some of them here in the castle."

The corners of Rhia's dark, almond-shaped eyes tightened. "This is your castle, Your Grace. You may hire whomever you please."

"And if you happen to run into a faerie in the halls? Will that upset you?"

Meaning, would she throw a tantrum like she had after first arriving in Nevandia? He couldn't have that. Magical folk needed to be treated with respect, especially under his own roof. If Rhia accosted any of them, it would cause a major problem, and encourage others to act similarly.

"I'd appreciate it if you'd keep them away from my chambers, but I understand that I may . . . see one or two of them sometimes, the same as I do your King's Guard." Rhia's chest rose as she took an anxious breath.

She's holding back a thousand critiques and admonishments.

"If I'm to remain here permanently, as your Queen, I should like to interview my own ladies and servants—"

"I don't believe I've asked for your hand," said Ruenen sharply. He instantly regretted his rude tone, but didn't regret the words.

Rhia's gaze bored into his. "Lord Steward Holfast has made it quite clear that it's to happen. I only ask for the ability to build my own staff—"

"The Steward doesn't speak for me, especially in these matters. I already told you that I'm not interested in marriage at this time."

"If Lady Marai were present, you would be," sniped Rhia.

Ruenen gripped his knife and fork until his knuckles turned white. *Calm down. Don't retaliate.* He took several deep breaths, curbing the frantic pulse in his neck.

"My apologies if I spoke out of turn, Your Grace," said Rhia, ice seeping into her tone. "I clearly misunderstood." She looked back down at her plate.

They didn't speak again for the remainder of dinner, and Ruenen couldn't exit the room fast enough. He gave a terse "goodnight," then stormed up to his chambers. He should've been more polite, more understanding of Rhia's plight, but he hated how Holfast had his whole life planned out without consulting Ruenen. He hated how everyone knew his feelings for Marai ran deep, yet no one cared enough about them because she was fae, thus unworthy of his hand. He hated Rhia's prejudice and stubbornness.

But most of all, he hated the sensation of stagnation, of being unable to fix any of those issues. Of losing himself. Of losing Marai.

He reached for his lute, fingers stalling on the strings, as he'd done so many times now. He sat in the plush armchair in front of the fire, and waited for the music, the inspiration, to come. Where were the melodies that used to echo in his ears? Had his fingers forgotten how to strum the courses? He didn't even have the heart to hum a familiar tune.

Ruenen didn't recognize himself. He never snapped at women, never felt so trapped, even when Rayghast had been hunting him. And never before had he been unable to play music . . .

I need to be a better person. I must be grateful for what I've been given. Be kinder and more understanding. I need to find my way back to my old self. Otherwise, I don't deserve to be King. I don't deserve Marai's praise or faith in me.

I need to be worthy of her.

Movement flashed outside his window.

Ruenen's heart stuttered. *Nosficio?* The vampire had entered through a castle window before . . .

Shoving his lute onto the chair, Ruenen dashed to his broadsword hanging on the wall. He pulled it down, and came to the window.

It wasn't Nosficio.

There, floating in the star-speckled sky, wings beating in midair, was the shadow creature.

It didn't bother to hide as it blatantly gazed at Ruenen and his sword. How long had it been hovering there?

From this distance, Ruenen could see details he hadn't before. The creature's long hair, white as snow, fanned out around it in the spring breeze. It looked almost like a human man, except for its glowing yellow eyes and the red-striped markings across its face and arms. Ruenen had seen other shadow creatures with similar markings, but each had different colors and patterns. Did the markings possibly indicate different breeds? Clans?

The creature wore human clothing—black britches and a billowing black tunic. Where had he gotten those? From his victims?

"What do you want with me?" Ruenen shouted. He was tired of all this: Holfast, Rhia, Tacorn, faeries, missing Marai, shadow creatures . . . couldn't he have one evening without drama? Without fighting for his freedom or someone else's?

He raised his sword and pointed it at the creature. "Leave or I'll cut you down!"

Ruenen's grip on his sword tightened. *I don't know if I can fend it off on my own.*

The creature quirked an eyebrow. His feathered hawk wings flapped in a steady rhythm as he crossed his arms.

Does it . . . understand me?

He gave Ruenen a bored, judgmental look.

If he truly was trying to kill me, he would've done so already.

Ruenen lowered his sword slightly. "Why are you in Kellesar? Are you loyal to Rayghast?"

The creature blinked. He opened his mouth, revealing pointed teeth, and spoke, but not in a language Ruenen could understand. His words were the same guttural language the other creatures had uttered, but this creature's voice, while harsh and cold, didn't sound like a beast. His gestures, facial expressions, and pattern of speech seemed incredibly human.

Had he been *studying* humans? Was that why the creature stalked the city?

The creature beat his wings and flew closer to the window. Ruenen lifted his sword again and leapt backwards, ready to defend himself, but the creature merely observed him. His forehead pinched as he thought, then he pointed a long, pale finger at Ruenen. He spoke again, not with menace, but as if trying to explain something.

Ruenen's face contorted in confusion. "I don't understand you."

The creature rolled his eyes and groaned. Unlike the other creatures who'd exhibited such animalistic violence, this one wanted to *communicate,* but that didn't mean Ruenen trusted him. He'd tried communicating with the beast in the forest and it had nearly killed him.

"I'm King Ruenen," he said, pointing to himself.

"Ruenen," the creature repeated, then replied with his own three words. Perhaps one was his name?

This is crazy!

With one powerful flap of its black and brown wings, the creature suddenly bolted into the night sky, far too high for Ruenen to see in the darkness. He practically toppled out the window as he leaned over the sill, trying to see where the creature went. After a few minutes without a sighting, Ruenen shut the window latch and raked a hand through his hair.

Even though the land had healed, the shadow creatures were here to stay. Dark magic wasn't gone. *Could Marai's disappearance have something to do with this? Are they targeting me because of her?*

Ruenen needed to speak to Braesal about the creatures. He wondered if the new fae knew of dark magic's existence. Braesal needed to be brought up to speed, in case the shadow creatures became more of a consistent problem.

Ruenen sat heavily on the edge of his bed, head in his shaking hands.

"I need you, Marai."

She would know what to do. With the creatures, the faeries, and the Tacorn transition. She'd restore balance to the Witan. Bring music back into Ruenen's life, and make him laugh again with her sass. Most importantly, Marai's touch would fill the massive hole in his soul.

Overwhelmed, Ruenen looked up at the ceiling. "Can you hear me, Marai? Wherever you are, does your chest also ache with the same heavy emptiness?"

He didn't expect a reply, but he couldn't stop the words from spilling from his mouth in a fervent prayer.

"My arms search for you in the night, in my dreams, desperately grasping at air. I wake each morning, ribs bruised from wishing so hard, with a thousand things to tell you. Then I remember that you're not here."

Tears stung his eyes. Ruenen was used to loss—everyone he'd known from his childhood, everyone who'd cared for him, was dead. His parents, Monks Amsco and Nori, Master Chongan and his entire family. But this time was different. *Marai* was different.

Ruenen let the tears flow freely. "Come back to me. As a ghost, as a dream. I beg you, my love, come home."

CHAPTER 16

MARAI

Word of the newly discovered faerie queen had spread across Andara.

Four performances in, and people were traveling from other towns and cities, fascinated to see this "mythical being." Marai couldn't believe that *she* was apparently the premier form of entertainment for Andarans.

They must have pretty boring lives if they have nothing better to do than watch me spin around for ten minutes . . .

It was a frenzy that rivaled the Desert Beach Equestrian Race in Beniel or Wrestling Championships in Syoto, two of the biggest sporting events on Astye. Bobo told Gunnora that the inn in his nearby town had no vacancies. Taverns and businesses were packed. Patrons were being turned away at the Menagerie's ticket booth, unable to snag a seat. They were told to come back and get in line earlier the next night.

Their pleasure was Marai's torment, as every night, her body was invaded by Cavar's magic.

Not that the Governor himself was there. After her first performance, Cavar had returned to Bakair, probably to count his gold, kiss his stupid rocks, and reorganize his bookshelf. The collar he'd programmed with his magic worked in his absence. Marai had hoped it wouldn't, that the magic might weaken without him there, but the wretched thing had the power to subdue her entirely.

Marai fought with all her strength before being propelled onto that stage, despite the shackles kept on her wrists and ankles. She'd given Koda a black eye, Yelich a bloody nose, and Volgar had purple bruises dotting his shins. Acacia or

Koda would backhand Marai across the face until the collar's magic took over and she became a compliant doll.

"You should stop struggling so," Anja said as Marai held a cool, wet cloth to her swelling cheek. Anja sat on a log around the campfire, darning socks for members of the Menagerie. "Others are following your lead now. Eno glared at the audience with her arms crossed the whole show tonight. And two of the gnomes faked an illness to get out of performing."

Marai's jaw ticked as she scowled at the flickering flames of the campfire. "I'm aware. I tried to take their punishments."

She'd tried to stop Sirco from whipping the tiny gnomes, who were even smaller than Gunnora. Marai had knocked the whip from his hand.

"Strike me, not them," she'd said defiantly to the guard.

Sirco wasn't allowed to whip Marai and draw blood before a show, so he'd instead punched her in the stomach. She hadn't been able to stand for a few minutes after that, and had been forced to watch as Sirco flayed open the gnomes' backs.

"I tried to protect them, and I couldn't," Marai said bitterly to Anja. "Folk are rebelling because of me. I didn't ask them to do it, but they are. It's only fair if I do what I can to protect them." She winced at the tender bruise on her stomach.

"It matters to them that you *tried*," said Anja, "but Koda knows this rebellion is your doing. Soon you won't get a scrap to eat, and you'll be so black and blue that Acacia's makeup won't hide it."

Koda had begun restricting her food intake as punishment, which Bobo heartily enforced. Marai didn't mind, since eating Bobo's disgusting food was its own form of torture.

Cyrill strolled over with his awkward, tip-toeing gait. He leaned into the conversation as he scoured Marai's face.

"One day there will be an opening," Marai said, lowering her voice. "One day, Koda and his thugs will make a mistake. The collar won't work, or something else will happen, and I'll break free. So no, Anja, I won't stop. I won't stop until we're freed." *Not until Keshel and I are home. Not until I see Ruen again.* "And if everyone in this wretched camp stands up to Koda and Acacia, refuses to perform, fights back, then maybe we can overpower them. We're stronger together."

Anja looked horrified by the idea, but Cyrill narrowed his black eyes.

"Your wingless friend is back," was all he said before he kept walking.

Marai rushed to Keshel's tent, one row over from the campfire. He was later than usual returning from the Menagerie that night. The minute she walked in, she knew he wasn't "back" yet.

At least Marai's mind still belonged to her as she danced, twirled, and formed shimmering stars in her hands. Keshel returned to his tent more lost and confused than the day before. Marai sat with him in those disorienting moments as he spewed nonsensical fortunes, standing so utterly inert with that eerie, distant glaze.

"Lady Pashmina's husband will die. Fret not, as gold will rain down upon her. The puppeteer beckons."

Marai's stomach clenched with concern as she tried to guide him to the bedroll. "Lie down, Keshel—"

"The girl dances in a field of fireflies."

"Do you want some water? Food? I saved some bread for you."

He'd lost his appetite. His skin was deathly pale, and Marai hated seeing the harsher contours of his face and neck as he lost more weight.

"Guardian Parvuk is soon to be Governor. A great promotion. The man is doubly marked, but the key. She will have six babies."

Marai released a harsh exhale. It was convoluted nonsense. She didn't know how to fix this, to remove the images from his brain, and it pained her to be so helpless. She simply had to wait it out.

Finally, Keshel's eyelids blinked rapidly, and the sheen on his corneas disappeared. He recognized Marai, but squeezed his eyes shut, blocking out the world, as if he didn't want to see her. Keshel then gagged, reaching for his wooden bucket.

"Is there anything you can do to keep yourself grounded? Or to fight back?" she asked as he vomited into the bucket.

Keshel slumped down in his bedroll, bucket in his lap. "Is there anything *you* can do to keep the magic out of your body?"

All magic has limits, Keshel had once told her. *We just need to find out what its limits are.*

"What if we steal Acacia's amulet while she's sleeping?" Marai posed.

"And what would that accomplish, other than you getting captured and whipped?"

"I *was* a mercenary, Keshel. I know a thing or two about stealth. We could use her amulet to get these collars off, I bet. Then you could study it. See how we can destroy them."

Keshel cringed. "I have no desire to touch those amulets." Vomiting now ceased, he set his bucket to the side of his bedroll. "I dream the visions now. I see them in the corner of my eye, following me in my waking hours. I'm not sure removing the collar would stop them at this point."

Marai reached for his hand, but Keshel, with the countenance of a trapped animal, snatched it away.

"You can't touch me."

"Why not?" she asked, stunned by his frightened tone.

"I don't want to see things. About you." Keshel's abilities never relied on physical contact alone, but touching skin-to-skin made his visions clearer, more visceral.

"It's after show-hours. Surely the collar isn't working right now."

Keshel shivered and pulled his moth-eaten blanket towards him. "The magic doesn't turn off, as Koda kindly reminded me. The visions are always with me. They never leave." He lay down and turned in his bedroll so that his back was to Marai.

Marai picked at her stained fingernails. The bowl of fish broth she'd been allowed that night for dinner curdled in her stomach. "Ignore Koda. He's playing games. Don't let him break you."

Eventually, after no movement from Keshel, Marai left his tent. She stared up at the amphitheater as guards blew out the torches for the night.

I can get in. I just need to figure out which room belongs to Acacia. Marai had never been allowed on the upper floors of the theater, but she knew Cavar, Acacia, Koda, and the Peace Keepers had apartments there.

Tonight. It would be quiet. The guards were exhausted and grumpy from the little rebellions in camp. Marai doubted they'd be on high alert that evening.

But then, Koda appeared at the end of the row, jauntily walking towards her. His hands were in his pockets as he whistled a merry tune. The act was part of his game, to make him appear powerful.

Rage rose quickly up Marai's throat as she thought about Keshel, about her hatred for the Menagerie. She couldn't get to Cavar, but Koda was right there in front of her. *An opportunity.*

She ran, best she could with shackled feet, and launched herself at Koda.

He was so caught off guard by Marai's sudden attack that she knocked him down before he could snap his fingers. She wrapped the chain of her shackles around his wrists and held them above his head.

Then Marai snapped the bones in his fingers.

Koda howled. He didn't know how to fight, and couldn't shove Marai off. His legs flailed, but Marai had him pinned. He relied far too heavily on his magic. He was *weak.*

With a roar, Marai buried her knee into his stomach, over and over, losing herself in the fury. Maybe this was her opening. Her way out.

Curious heads peered out of tents. A group of gnomes, two of the ones she'd tried to protect, pointed and clapped, urging Marai onwards. Cyrill hovered, a creepy, bent shadow, watching with rapt attention.

"*All hail the Queen,*" shouted someone. A chorus of support followed.

Feet pounded the earth behind her. A swarm of Peace Keepers appeared. Time was up.

Muscular arms twined around Marai's middle and yanked her off of Koda.

"You're a monster," she shouted as Yelich restrained her, dragging her backwards. "We're people, not cattle. We're not experiments. Not entertainment. Keshel is losing his mind in there. You're killing him!"

Koda sat up, wincing and hacking, staring at his twisted, gnarled fingers. Yelich said something to him in Andaran. Marai recognized the word *Cavar.*

"Does it look like I can send a message right now?" Koda snapped at the guard, hands trembling in pain. "I'll do it after Acacia heals me." He then looked up at the crowd of magical folk who'd materialized during the brawl. "Show's over. Get back to your tents before we take a whip to each of you."

The folk glowered, but disappeared quickly at the arrival of more guards. Koda said something to Yelich and Sirco in Andaran, and the two guards hauled Marai to another area of camp. In the middle of the row stood a solid, black, metal crate, large enough for a person to sit inside. At first glance, Marai thought it was for storage.

Koda smirked as the realization hit Marai. "Welcome to your new accommodations, Your Grace."

Marai flailed, trying to twist out of their grasp, but Sirco landed a brain-rattling punch to her jaw. The fight left her as stars exploded in her vision.

Yelich lifted the heavy lid of the crate and pushed her inside. Marai slammed into the metal bottom on her left shoulder and wing. Sirco lowered the lid, engulfing her in complete darkness. A key scraped into a lock.

No! Please Lirr, no!

No prison was worse than this. Not the one in Dul Tanen when Rayghast nearly tortured her and Ruenen. Not Slate's cell onboard *The Nightmare*. Not even his bed.

The silence inside was so complete, so oppressive, Marai couldn't hear a sound but her own rapid breathing. Her wings were painfully crumpled beneath her. She pounded and pushed against the lid of the crate, but it was firmly locked. She yelled until she was hoarse, hammered until her fists were bloody. No light seeped through the cracks. It was as dark as if she'd been transported to the Underworld itself. Tiny holes along the bottom edge allowed her to breathe, but barely.

There would be no show for two days. How long would she be forced to stay in such confinement, and what would happen to Keshel in the meantime?

Eventually, exhaustion pulled her under and Marai lay against the cold metal, drawing her legs into her chest.

The sound of rattling keys. A creak. Bright sunlight poured in.

Marai squinted, her eyes accustomed to the darkness. The light burned and blinded.

Koda's disgusted face swam into view. "Uch, you smell horrible."

Marai hadn't been granted use of a privy. She'd been lying in her own filth for an unknown number of days.

Koda pulled her from the crate, his fingers entirely healed. Marai's muscles were horridly stiff; her bones cracked and ached after spending so much time curled inwards. She stumbled once her bare feet hit the grass, falling to her knees like a newborn foal.

"Move. Cavar's ready to see you."

Koda showed her no sympathy as he dragged her through the rows of tents and onlookers. A crowd of folk gathered again; Marai spotted Anja, Gunnora, Athelstan, and Cyrill amongst them, but Keshel was absent. Panic clutched at Marai's racing pulse—had they done something to him?

Marai tried to make eye contact with Anja and Gunnora, but Koda pressed her onwards. Dante and Wilder trotted behind her, as if they were in Marai's personal retinue, watching out for her.

Innesh, steely-eyed stone of a woman that she was, planted herself in Koda's path. "She needs to eat something first."

Koda halted. "Cavar said now."

"Oh, yes, Master's calling," Innesh sneered with venom in her Yehzigi accent. Koda's fingers encircling Marai's bicep tightened. Innesh pulled a plump carrot from her pants pocket and held it out to Marai. "Eat it on your way."

Marai reached for it, but Koda grabbed the carrot first. "She hasn't been given permission to eat."

"There's a show tonight. She's had no food or water for two days. Do you want her to pass out on stage? Cavar's magic can't keep her conscious." Innesh glared daggers at Koda and crossed her brown arms. "That would be a pretty embarrassing incident for Cavar's precious audience to witness."

Why is she helping me?

Innesh had shown no interest in Marai, or any of the magical folk, before. She was always aloof, hard at work doing whatever it was Acacia or Koda instructed her to do.

Is it because of Koda?

Marai had attacked and wounded him more than once. She wondered if she was earning some form of respect from the Yehzigi slave woman. Both of them were the only two in the Menagerie from Yehzig, and it was clear that Innesh utterly despised Koda, even more than Cavar. Koda's feelings towards her were more conflicted, more difficult for Marai to assess. His eyes softened whenever Innesh was in his presence, and he removed most of his superior manners.

After a tense staring contest between Koda and Innesh, he finally thrust the carrot into Marai's dirty hands. "Eat and walk."

Marai bit off the tip of the carrot, mouth exploding with its sweet, earthy taste. Koda shoved her forward past Innesh, giving the woman one final look. The vegetable crunched delightfully as Marai chewed slowly. She'd endured longer periods without food before, but for some reason, this simple carrot was the most satisfying thing Marai had ever eaten. By the time they reached the amphitheater, she'd devoured it.

Koda rapped twice on Cavar's office door. The Governor's smooth-toned voice beckoned him inside.

Cavar was seated at his desk, surrounded by neat stacks of papers, writing something. Dressed in his usual refined attire, he didn't look up as Marai and Koda entered.

"I hear you've been a constant nuisance, Marai," he said as he scrawled. "What was it about this time?"

"Keshel, Governor," said Koda, putting on the airs he only wore in Cavar's presence.

"He'll die if you keep forcing those visions on him," Marai croaked, vocal chords ravaged from yelling in the crate. She didn't have the energy to imbue the words with her normal rage.

"He won't *die*," said Cavar, dipping his quill in a pot of ink before returning it to the paper, "he'll merely lose his sanity."

Marai sucked in a ragged breath.

"The magic in the collar will keep him doing his job, even if his brain turns to mush."

Tears stung Marai's eyes. "How can you be so callous? So hateful?"

Finally, Cavar put down his quill and said, in a voice full of ire, "I despise magical creatures."

He called for Sirco, who came into the office dragging a limp and battered Keshel with him.

Marai squirmed in Koda's grip. Keshel's face was mottled with swollen bruises and lacerations, and he stared at Marai with mournful eyes. Sirco turned Keshel around, showing off his back with sick glee. Bloody lines seeped through the fabric of Keshel's shirt.

Fury detonated within Marai. He'd been whipped. At least five lashings.

"I hear you've been thinking of yourself as some kind of leader, a saint begging to take the punishments of other folk," sneered Cavar. "That's going to stop. Look at what you made us do, Marai. His suffering is *your* fault. But I can see in your eyes that you still have too much defiance left in you. Very well."

The Governor clutched his amulet as it pulsed with power. Smoky tendrils drifted from the stone across the room, crawling like hands, closer and closer.

Smoke shot up Keshel's nostrils. He released a strangled gasp, then groaned, clutching his stomach.

Marai's fury turned to horror. Dark magic was *inside* him.

Keshel vomited onto Cavar's expensive woven rug and collapsed into the puddle of sick, writhing and bleating in agony.

"*Stop,*" Marai shrieked, thrashing.

Dark magic would destroy Keshel from the inside out.

"Say you'll be a good girl, and I'll make it stop," said Cavar.

She reached out to Keshel, but Koda's grip on her was strong.

Cavar's voice was glacier cold as he said, "*Say it,* or I'll make it worse."

Keshel's face and fingers contorted in torment. He let out a howl of pain as his body spasmed.

Marai's blood froze to ice. She couldn't let this torture go on. "All right, I'll stop."

The words stole something from Marai. Her freedom. Her strength. Her pride. Giving up was worse than defeat. It was failure and submission.

"Stop what?"

Marai's teeth sank into the inside of cheek to suppress the real words she wished to say. "I'll stop fighting against you, Koda, and the guards."

Cavar's lips cut into a cruel line. "You'll be a good girl and won't complain?"

Marai nodded once.

"Say those exact words for me."

Marai barely moved her jaw as she said, "I'll be a good girl."

Cavar approached her slowly, a wolf stalking its prey. His face was close, so close Marai could spot every wrinkle and liver spot on his skin.

He's not ageless. Not immortal. Cavar's days were numbered. Maybe not soon, in another one hundred years or so, but he wasn't a god. He *would* die, and if she still lived, Marai would dance on his grave.

"If you *ever* strike one of my men again, I'll cut off Keshel's fingers," said Cavar. "And if that doesn't get through to you, I'll remove other unnecessary parts of him, one by one."

Marai wouldn't, *couldn't*, be the cause of Keshel's pain. Although she trembled from head to toe, she remained stationary, subdued, until Cavar released his hold on Keshel.

Black, writhing smoke was sucked out from his nostrils and returned to its home within Cavar's stone.

Keshel groaned, sagging into the rug, lying prone and still. Marai's eyes traced his body, searching for any signs of the dark magic on his skin, but she didn't see any stains similar to her own fingers. He hadn't used dark magic, himself. Perhaps he wouldn't be stained.

But what internal damage was done?

"Get her cleaned up and ready for the show tonight. Acacia has a new dress for her. Have Innesh deliver it." Cavar returned to his desk and picked up his quill. "I look forward to your cooperation, Marai."

Sirco laced his arms under Keshel's shoulders and dragged his limp body from the office. Marai followed in a daze. Volgar helped Sirco carry Keshel back to his tent. They deposited him there on his bedroll, dumped like a corpse. Keshel's eyes hadn't opened. He hadn't moved.

Koda gave Marai one last look. "Don't fuck up again. His life is in your hands." He swaggered away, whistling again.

Alone at last, Marai took hold of Keshel's face in her hands.

"Keshel, wake up," she urged in desperation. His eyelids twitched. "*Please.*"

One dark eye cracked open. "Marai."

She sighed with relief. "I'll get you some water and bandages—"

But Marai didn't have to. Innesh pushed aside the tent flap carrying a basket of medical supplies, a skin of water, and rolls baked with nuts and berries. Marai also spotted cream fabric at the bottom of the basket; another of Acacia's gods-awful dresses.

Without a word, Innesh knelt in front of Keshel. Marai watched her work in silent gratitude. The Menagerie had no designated healer, therefore, many of the folk learned to treat wounds and illnesses on their own. Innesh wiped the blood from his face and lacerated back, cleansed his cuts and dabbed them with ointment, wrapping his back the best she could. Her touch was gentle, despite her austere countenance.

Innesh got to her feet and addressed a weary Keshel, "You have two hours before showtime. Get some rest, and don't move for a while."

"Even if I wanted to, I can't move from this spot," he grunted back.

Innesh tossed Marai the rumpled dress, and exited the tent.

"Thank you," Marai said, chasing after the slave woman. "For helping Keshel. And the carrot."

Innesh's brown eyes flashed to where Koda was standing two tent rows away. She stepped closer to Marai. "Learn to turn them off. Your emotions. That's how you survive fifteen years here."

She then stalked away, iron chains rattling in the dirt.

Marai returned to Keshel's tent. She had no desire to bathe and get ready for the performance. Instead, she watched Keshel sleep. He lay on his stomach, pale and still as the dead.

"This is my fault," she whispered, hanging her head.

"No, it's not." Keshel opened his eyes and turned his head to look at her. "No one can avoid Lirr's will."

Marai scowled. "If this place is her will, then she's a cruel goddess."

Keshel lifted his head, face suddenly stern. "You mustn't say such things about Lirr, Marai. She listens to everything we say, and she's already disappointed with you."

"Along with everyone else these days . . ."

"It was *supposed* to be you."

Marai's brows furrowed in confusion. "What do you mean?"

Keshel's long fingers reached out and grasped her hand. His eyes immediately glazed over, overcome with a vision, staring distantly into space. Marai tried to pull free, but his grip only tightened.

"You aren't the One." Keshel's voice took on a cryptic, monotone quality that he used when seeing. A bead of sweat trickled down his jaw. "You gave into the darkness. You called upon it. You're impure."

Marai glanced down at her stained fingers. *Impure.* She'd used dark magic in her panic months ago, afraid of being touched, of being intimate, of the haunting nightmare that was Captain Slate Hemming.

"The auburn haired girl comes." Keshel blinked, as if surprised by this statement.

Marai finally yanked her hand away from his. "You're not making any sense."

Keshel's visions were never entirely concrete, but they were more unstable now because of his battered mind.

His head collapsed onto the pillow, eyes rolling backwards. Keshel slurred out, "She can defeat the darkness."

He went unconscious with such finality that terror rushed through Marai. She splashed water on his face, called his name, shook him, but Keshel didn't budge. His chest still rose, heart still beat. The dark magic from the stone made him sicker, less stable.

What had those visions meant? Marai had mistakenly let dark magic in, that was true. She'd made a grave error when calling upon its power, and while she didn't plan to use it again, there was something larger at play that she didn't understand. Cavar's stone was part of it.

Anja's face peered in through the tent flap. "Forgive me, but Koda instructed me to make sure you get ready in time."

"Tell that bastard that Keshel can't go on tonight. He's unconscious from the injuries," Marai replied, getting to her feet, scraping off the grass stuck to her kneecaps. "Let Koda know that I'll be obedient. I'll do what's asked of me, but he needs to give Keshel time to heal."

One night off wasn't enough to cure Keshel's mind or body. Those lacerations from the whip would take weeks to heal. He'd be in agony for days, so Marai would do her best to earn the time he needed to recover.

She stomped to the creek and submerged herself in the brisk water. Marai scrubbed the filth from her body and hair. Her ugly frilly dress was ruined, and she didn't bother trying to clean it. She rushed back to her tent, put on the new one, brushed her wet hair, and did as Innesh instructed.

She locked away her emotions.

Walls up, shields up.

The sensation was familiar. Once again, she froze her feelings, tucking them away deep inside, where she used to store them as the Lady Butcher. But now she held no sword. Wielded no magic.

As she walked towards the amphitheater, Cyrill caught up to her with a red scarf in his hand.

"You can wear red now, I suppose."

"I don't want red," Marai said, setting her face into a glower as she counted the number of windows and floors from the outside. "Get me everything you have in black."

CHAPTER 17

RUENEN

Braesal and his people hardly left the safety of their cottages in Grave's End. They were far more hesitant to integrate than Raife, Aresti, and Thora had been, perhaps because they didn't have someone like Marai guiding and pushing them. Ruenen had offered them everything they needed to start fresh, but Braesal had refused. He did, however, send a small group of part-fae adults to Cleaving Tides, at Raife's suggestion. Most of the adult fae had volunteered, which was a testament to their dedication in finding Marai, but Ruenen had hoped for more camaraderie.

"Let them be," Holfast said when Braesal didn't show up for the scheduled meeting to discuss the assemblies and sign the decree. The Steward rolled the thick parchment back up into a long tube. "If they don't want to participate, you cannot force them."

"Yes, but they need to sign the agreement," pressed Fenir, fidgeting in his seat. "We can't have any rogue faeries running around. They have to understand the *rules* of living in our country."

"They aren't *rogue*. They're nervous," Ruenen said. "They don't feel welcome yet, and can you blame them? None of you could drum up a friendly word to them when they arrived."

"They're making *us* nervous," Corian grumbled to his neighbor. "They've been here for ten days, and they already caused a brawl in the streets."

"Tacornian transplants started that," Ruenen said with a warning edge. "Braesal's people were defending themselves, as is their right."

That brawl had nearly cost Ruenen more than he could explain: relationships with the fae, with the Tacornians, the Kellesaran citizens . . .

Ruenen stood from his throne, and the Witan, in a rippled wave across the table, got to their feet. "Give it to me, and I'll get them to sign it." He held out his empty hand to Holfast.

"Your Grace, there's no need for you to do this," replied Wattling. "You aren't responsible for going down there and hand-delivering that document. You'll be coddling them like children."

Ruenen released a long-suffering sigh. He was tired of the infighting. Of the small jabs. Of being told what not to do. "I *am* responsible for them, Lord Wattling. As King, I'm responsible for all citizens of Nevandia, and now Tacorn, too. Braesal's people have lived the past two decades hiding in a cave in the White Ridge Mountains. Perhaps they need a gentler hand. The assemblies that Avilyard has arranged should help with that, but only if Braesal's people show up."

Holfast gave Ruenen that stern gaze, the one that meant he had opinions, but still, the Steward handed over the rolled-up decree.

Ruenen tucked it into his pocket. "I'll bring it back safe and sound."

"Make sure you bring a horse, Your Grace. Kings don't stumble around in the streets," the Steward said.

Ruenen almost never rode his horse when he went into the city. It was a small rebellion that greatly irked Holfast. As always, when Ruenen left the castle, he was flanked by two golden guards. This pair was younger than Elmar and Nyle, only in their third week on the job. They didn't have Elmar and Nyle's friendly, buoyant smiles. This new pair were serious, intensely focused on their task to protect Ruenen. It was admirable and appreciated, but they made for terribly boring company.

Fresh air filled Ruenen's lungs, along with the scent of the wisteria that climbed up the castle walls. Hot rays of sunshine beamed down upon the courtyard. The trees were filled with birds, chirping and singing in their happiness.

If only to please Holfast, Ruenen gathered his horse from the stables and meandered down the winding, cobbled Kellesar streets, past the wealthy nobles' houses, the markets and town square, towards the city wall and Grave's End.

People were so used to seeing Ruenen outside of the castle that they didn't crowd around him the way they used to.

"Good day to you, Your Grace," shouted a cheerful carpenter, hanging a new door on someone's house.

Women waved and curtsied; children marched behind his horse, pretending that they were part of his guard, but people no longer made a huge, riotous fuss. Ruenen liked that things had settled down, that he could feel somewhat normal. That Kellesarans considered him one of their own.

At the end of the long street in Grave's End, Ruenen spotted faerie children playing a game of chase. They stopped when they saw the horses and armed guards approaching, rushing back inside their cottages, Holt's wings glittering in the sunlight.

Braesal and two other males came to the doorway, faces etched in stone. They looked ready for a fight, knives and hammers in their fists.

I wish Raife and Aresti were here. Both of them were helping Avilyard train the new recruits near the army barracks outside the city limits. Tarik, Brass, and Yovel, who lived in the cottage next door, were also nowhere to be seen. Ruenen had no idea what the werewolves did during the day when they weren't with him.

"Greetings, friends. I hope all is well," Ruenen began lightly, dismounting his horse.

Braesal crossed his arms in response, but at least he'd put down the knife.

River poked her head out from behind her partner. "Your Grace!" She swatted at Braesal with a dish towel. "Get out of the way, you big lump. You can't leave a king standing in the street!"

Braesal and the two other males moved aside to let Ruenen into the cottage.

"Sorry it's such a mess, Your Grace," River said, sweeping potato peelings on the table into her palm. "We're so busy settling in here, and we were about to make some lunch."

"I don't mean to intrude, and I certainly didn't mean to come unannounced," said Ruenen. He scanned the small cottage that had once housed Marai before it became solely Raife and Thora's. It was clean and tidy, despite what River said, and packed to the brim with bodies and wings.

River ushered Holt and his two friends out the back door into Kadiatu's garden. Ruenen caught a glimpse through the door and smiled at the variety of color. Everything was in bloom and well-cared for. Kadiatu would be delighted.

Braesal took a seat at the small, wooden kitchen table. He gestured for Ruenen to sit opposite him as River set down a cup of water and a plate of strawberries.

"Have you heard from your people?" Ruenen asked, starting with an easy subject. Braesal's search team had left four days prior.

"Not yet, but if all is proceeding according to plan, they'll be at the Ain border by now," Braesal said. "They're moving slowly, so as not to attract attention. I'd go, myself, but . . ."

"You're worried for the safety of your people here," Ruenen finished for him. "I understand. Please let me know when you hear from them." Ruenen pulled out the decree and unfurled it upon the table. "I brought this for you to read and sign. It's something we require for magical folk to reside here in Nevandia."

"Do you require all of your citizens to sign such a decree? Or the ones moving here from Tacorn?" asked Braesal with a cocked eyebrow.

"No," replied Ruenen, the heat of shame creeping up his neck.

"Then why should we? We're no less trustworthy than those Tacornian barbarians accosting us on the streets," the fae leader said, sunset eyes pinning Ruenen in place. "We came here for the promise of a new life, but right after we arrived, we were attacked. We don't feel safe, except within our homes, which we know we can fortify and protect."

"I apologize for that incident. I should have anticipated it. We should have better prepared both you and the Tacornian transplants, but we're rather overwhelmed at the moment," Ruenen said, and hated the excuses pouring from his mouth. "I wish it had been a smooth transition for everyone. Mistakes were made, but I'm hopeful that we can move forward."

"By signing this, what will that accomplish?" asked another male. Ruenen thought his name was Zorish. "Will people stop shouting curses and slurs at our children?"

"All magical folk must sign the decree, set forth by Lord Keshel and the Witan. If you sign this, it means that we can hold those accountable for any injustices set upon you. I can't guarantee that you won't still experience prejudice and difficulties, but until you sign this, you aren't under the decree's protection. This is the best way to keep your children safe."

River brought over a quill and pot of ink, dropping them right in front of Braesal. "Well, I'll sign if he's too stubborn."

She dipped the quill tip into the ink and scrawled her name below Tarik and the weres. Ruenen stopped his gaze from latching onto Marai's tight, hasty signature next to Keshel's. River passed the quill to the brunette behind her. Slowly, the adults signed the document. Braesal, last to sign, grimaced as he did so.

Ruenen let the ink dry, then rolled the parchment back up. "Thank you. I know this isn't easy, but we can make progress if we work together. And that brings up my next order of business." *Uch, I sound like Holfast.* "There are positions open at the castle—"

"For servants," Braesal said.

"Yes, and in the kitchens. Commander Avilyard could also use more enlisted men. Food and lodging are provided for castle staff and military personnel, as well as decent wages. In both instances, you'll be under my personal protection."

"Working for humans, serving humans . . ." muttered one of the other winged males, Finneagal, standing behind Braesal's chair. Ruenen had watched him write his name on the decree.

"You're welcome to try your hand in business, mining, farming, or in the tradesmen guilds," said Ruenen. "Lirr knows we need those workers, too, but I can't help you get those jobs. The positions at the castle and in the military are open now, and they're under my jurisdiction. You'll be treated fairly and equally."

Braesal and the males around him exchanged looks. Some genuinely seemed interested in the idea, but others crossed their arms, like blond-haired Finneagal, shaking their heads, faces taut with tension.

"Give us some time to consider," River said, sensing her partner's hesitation. She placed her hands on Braesal's shoulders. "All of us deserve to choose the paths that are right for us and our families. Don't you agree, Braesal? I, for one, would be very interested in finding some meaningful work." Her fingers tightened on his muscles.

Braesal rolled his eyes. "Yes, love." He took one of her hands in his own, and brought it to his lips. It was the most tender gesture Ruenen had seen from Braesal. He was a husband and father trying to do his best to protect his people.

River slanted a smile at Ruenen, fully aware of her power.

"One last thing before I leave you to lunch in peace, and this is perhaps the most important and most difficult to explain," Ruenen said.

Braesal leaned forward in his chair; that ease he'd just displayed with his partner disappeared.

"What do you know about dark magic?"

The reaction was instantaneous. Eyes flashed open wide, a female gasped, and Zorish flinched.

Braesal's face grew dangerously severe. "Very little. It's forbidden, so how does a human king know about its existence?"

"It's a long story," said Ruenen, "but one you need to hear in order to understand that there are dangers." He launched into a recounting of when Marai tapped into its power in Cleaving Tides. "She didn't know it existed until she'd called upon it. A residue of dark magic lingers here in the Middle Kingdoms. I was attacked by a shadow creature not long ago, and recently, I was visited by another one—"

"A what?" River asked. Whispers filled the room like water hissing from a hot stone.

But a new voice cut through the disquiet.

"One was *here*?"

Ruenen turned around in his chair to see Thora standing in the doorway, medical pack slung over her shoulder. She rushed into the cottage, smelling of astringent medicinal herbs, worry knitting her brow.

"Why didn't you tell us sooner?"

Ruenen avoided her stern stare. He hadn't said a word to anyone about the "conversation" he'd had with the winged creature.

"I haven't seen him since, and trust me, I've been searching." Every night before bed, Ruenen scoured the skies before locking his bedchamber windows and drawing the curtains. Whenever he set foot outdoors, his head automatically tilted back to scan the clouds and castle spires for any sign of the creature.

"Excuse me, but what *are* these creatures you're talking about?" River asked, putting her hands on her hips. At the back door, Holt's round face peeped inside, tipping his pointed ear closer.

"Shadow creatures are created from dark magic," explained Thora matter-of-factly. "Whenever anyone uses its power, a creature is born from black flames and smoke. They're grotesque, vicious combinations of animals, humans, and evil."

A mahogany-skinned male at Braesal's side, named Beck, Ruenen thought, looked ready to faint. "I've never heard of such a thing . . ."

"Is someone using that power here?" Braesal asked, body wound tight as a snake ready to strike. Ruenen bet the fae leader would pack up his people and run for the hills at the first sign of dark magic.

"No, I killed the madman responsible," said Ruenen, and shuddered as he told the story of the battle, when Rayghast called upon the darkness. "He used dark magic for years, and we're still cleaning up his mess. These shadow creatures are the last remnants of that power. We've been killing them off as we find them, but they're a real nuisance to fight. It took Raife, Aresti, and me combined to take one down. Magic seems to be the best way to dispose of them. It's only a matter of time before another one shows up and threatens our safety."

"Not to mention that they seem to be after *you*," Thora added, eyeing Ruenen.

Braesal studied Ruenen, too. "Why are they targeting you?"

"I don't know, but I'm inclined to think it has to do with Marai," said Ruenen. "She's their greatest threat. Marai was the only person able to kill a shadow creature on her own. Without Marai, I'm . . ." Lost? Useless? Ruenen was treading water, barely keeping himself from drowning. He took a deep breath. "Perhaps they want to get rid of me in an effort to weaken her."

The shadow creature's interest in Ruenen must have meant that Marai was still alive. He *had* to believe that.

Beck scratched his stubbly jaw. "We could hunt the beasts down, but our two best trackers are heading to Cleaving Tides right now to look for the Queen."

"What's she like?" asked a small voice from the garden door. Holt blinked eagerly at Ruenen. "The Faerie Queen."

Ruenen's mouth went dry. He cleared his throat, unable to find the right words.

Thora, reading his silence, said, "She's a survivor. Marai won't want you to treat her any differently than you do each other. She has a nasty temper, and can be standoffish, blunt, and restless. She's been known to curse and pick fights, and gods help the person who forces her into a dress."

The fae exchanged another round of confused and skeptical glances, while little Holt at the door giggled.

"But she'll always fight for you. She stands up for us all, and says the things no one else will. Her loyalty knows no bounds." Thora's eyes glistened as she took hold of Ruenen's clenched hand sitting on the table. "And when she welcomes you into her heart, she will protect you with an unmatched ferocity and blazing courage."

Ruenen took another shaky breath and squeezed Thora's hand back. He couldn't have described Marai better himself. He felt a gushing affection for Thora then, at her subtle strength, and obvious love for Marai.

Braesal studied Ruenen, dissected him so thoroughly that Ruenen wondered if the fae leader could see into his soul.

"Very well, then, Your Grace," he said. "We'll come to your assemblies and do our part in the community. And when we find Queen Marai, we'll help her defeat the shadow creatures."

He reached across the table, calloused hand open and inviting. Ruenen shook it, feeling the power in Braesal's strong, capable grasp. He had the hands of a man who would do whatever it took to protect his people. Hands that would work hard to better things for magical folk; a good ally for Ruenen to have, and a good leader for the country.

Maybe I should give him a place on the Witan?

It wasn't the time to mention such a thing, but it was definitely something to consider in the future.

Ruenen stood and cleared his throat again. "Thank you for your hospitality. Anyone who wishes may come to the castle at any time to seek employment. Ask to see me. I'll ensure you get everything you need."

He stepped outside, followed by Thora and Braesal, and shoved a foot inside the stirrups of his horse.

"You're in love with the Faerie Queen."

Ruenen nearly toppled from his saddle. His face seared with heat, but he was well past the point of denial. "Is it that obvious?"

From the ground, Thora tried to hide her laugh.

"Your Grace, I'm married," Braesal said, and the corners of his mouth twitched. "I deeply love my partner. It was easy to spot those same feelings on your face the minute you mentioned her name. It's rare for any human to love one of us, but it seemed especially impossible for a king. My apologies for underestimating you."

"No apologies necessary. Marai would certainly have some snarky remarks, though."

Both Braesal and Thora chuckled.

"I look forward to meeting her . . . when she returns." Braesal's face went serious again, his eyes as luminescent as Marai's, swirling with magic.

"Today marks two months since Marai and Keshel went missing," Thora said, whole body slumping.

"You can rely on me to do whatever I can to find them. When things stabilize here, I'll go out to search, myself," Braesal said.

Ruenen could only show his gratitude with a stiff nod.

"Come, Mistress Healer," said Braesal, turning away from Ruenen. "I believe my wife was hoping to proposition you for work."

"Proposition me?" repeated Thora as Braesal escorted her back inside the cottage.

"To accompany you on your daily patient visits . . ."

Their voices trailed off once the cottage door closed with a creak, and Ruenen lurched his horse forward up the street.

Two days later had Ruenen and Bassite, Master of Household, greeting three of Braesal's people in the castle's grand entryway. Two coltish, part-fae sisters gaped up at the crisscrossing beams and painted ceilings. Both shockingly pale with hair lighter than Marai's, Braesal explained that they were orphans. The youngest, Lilly, couldn't have been older than fourteen, while the other, Daye, was around Kadiatu's age of seventeen.

The third was a wrinkle-faced older male with gray streaking his hair. Other than Rayghast, Ruenen had never seen anyone with fae blood reach advanced years. Quinton didn't appear much younger than white-haired Bassite. In fact, he could have entirely passed for human if his eyes weren't glowing turquoise.

"Too old for the army," Quinton said, adjusting the strap of the bag on his shoulder. "Figured I'd best make myself useful here. Those cottages are too cramped with all them children and wings."

"We shall find an appropriate place for you," Bassite said, then turned his attention to the sisters' pointed ears. With a slight frown, he addressed them professionally. "And what skills do you two have?"

"Daye's a good cook, but she can't talk," explained younger sister Lilly.

"She can't, or she won't?" pressed Bassite, frowning deeper.

"A farmer cut out her tongue," Lilly said with a toss of her long hair.

Ruenen couldn't help but stare at Daye. She hung her pale head as her sister told the tale, as if she was ashamed, frightened of the reaction she might receive from Ruenen and Bassite, but instead, fury rushed through Ruenen. Orphaned and starving, he didn't blame Daye for trying to feed herself and younger sister.

"No one here will harm you, Daye," he said, far sterner than he intended. "You shall have work and a home in this castle for as long as you desire."

The girl's head raised and her amber eyes were wide, as if she'd never heard such words uttered from a human's mouth before. Daye slowly nodded; Ruenen guessed that it wasn't easy to brush aside the shadows of her past.

Like someone else I know. In fact, Daye reminded Ruenen so much of Marai that he felt the strong urge to protect her, to shelter her away from the callousness of the world, where even in Nevandia, Daye would still be subjected to stares and harsh whispers.

"You enjoy cooking?" he asked her.

Daye nodded vigorously.

"Bassite, please find her a place in the kitchens," said Ruenen, then turned to the younger sister. "And what about you?"

QUEEN OF THE SHADOW MENAGERIE

Lilly contorted her face into a pondering expression. "I can do any labor you want, Your Grace. Cooking, cleaning, mending, running errands, working the stables—I can do it all, and better than any boy." She shot Ruenen a look of fiery confidence as she jutted out her small chin.

Ruenen laughed. She also reminded him of Marai, but instead of her vulnerability, it was in the girl's strength, her unwavering tenacity.

"You strike me as someone who's very brave," he said, stroking his chin as if he was sizing her up.

Lilly straightened her posture. "Little frightens me, Your Grace, and when it does, I'll fight on through it."

A mischievous, and probably very bad idea, came to Ruenen. "I have just the job for you." Bassite raised a curious eyebrow as Ruenen turned to him. "Please see Master Quinton and Miss Daye settled in their posts, Bassite."

Bassite bowed grandly, then guided Daye and Quinton down the hallway to the servant's staircase below. Ruenen gestured to Lilly to follow him, instead. The faerie girl's russet-brown eyes glistened with eagerness as she trotted behind Ruenen, up the main staircase, and down to the far end of the hallway.

Harmona, Marai's old maid, was about to knock on a door when she spotted Ruenen approaching. The girl squeaked, and curtsied so low, Ruenen was surprised that she didn't topple over.

"Your Grace, how may I help you?" she asked in her tiny mouse voice.

"I was hoping you'd be willing to have Lilly here shadow you," he said. "She's new, and requires a learned instructor to train her."

"You want *me* to train her?" asked Harmona. Her eyes darted to Lilly's pointed ears, and Harmona grew paler. "But—"

"I'm sure she'll be a fast learner. Perhaps she can start with you now."

"I mean, yes, Your Grace, but I don't know—" stammered Harmona. The young chambermaid had always been afraid of Marai, of the fact that she was fae. It had taken her weeks to look Marai in the face. Perhaps it was a bit cruel of Ruenen to make Harmona so uncomfortable, but she had to get over her fear, and Lilly seemed brazen enough to teach her. They'd hopefully be good influences on each other.

However—

"What's taking so long?" came a voice from inside the room. "I can hear you chatting out there."

Harmona jumped as Rhia whipped open the door. The Queen glanced from Harmona, to Ruenen, to Lilly, then Lilly's ears. She narrowed her eyes, two chips of ice, at the fae girl. The room suddenly grew colder.

"What is that doing here?" Rhia asked, voice clipped.

"This is your new chambermaid, Lilly. She'll be assisting Harmona from now on," Ruenen explained lightly as Lilly curtsied effortlessly, mimicking Harmona.

This was a gamble, of course. Reckless. He should have spoken to her first before putting Lilly in her service, but Rhia's prejudice infuriated him. As a guest, she couldn't dictate who Ruenen hired as her servants. She may have been a queen, but she certainly wasn't *his* queen.

If she throws another tantrum about the fae, the Witan will hopefully stop pressuring me to marry her.

"Take her away," snapped Rhia, "I won't allow her to set foot in my chambers."

"You said you wanted more staff."

"I told you I wanted to hire *my own people.* She's—"

Ruenen turned to Lilly and Harmona, still frozen in their curtsies, unsure of what to do. "Harmona, why don't you show Lilly around? Come back in ten minutes. Thank you both."

Harmona dipped another curtsy, and scuttled down the hall, Lilly at her heels, already asking questions.

Rhia glared at Ruenen with such resentment that, for a moment, he wondered if he'd truly stepped over a line.

"I won't let that creature near me."

"And *I* won't tolerate hateful language to my staff," he said with a locked jaw, standing firm. "You have no right to treat her as if she's anything less than a person."

"She isn't human! All those with magic are abominations," Rhia shouted, chest heaving as emotion consumed her.

"She has human blood in her veins, same as you and me. She's only part-fae, and probably has little command of magic," Ruenen explained, "which you would know if you'd attend the assemblies Commander Avilyard has organized."

A delicate hand lifted to the patch on Rhia's face. "I *know* what magic does. I know its pain better than anyone. What if she uses it on me?"

The Queen quivered as she curled inwards on herself, and Ruenen's anger melted away. Tears streamed down Rhia's pale cheeks as she backed away inside her room.

Ruenen softened his voice and features. "She isn't Rayghast, Your Grace. She's a young, orphaned girl, looking for a fresh start. I don't believe Lilly, or any of the fae, would ever hurt you. They hold life in higher regard than most humans I know. Please, give her a chance. Treat her as you do any other servant, and if you truly do have issues with her performance, let Bassite or me know." Rhia didn't stop shaking, so Ruenen placed a hand over his heart. "I won't let *anyone* harm you, Rhia."

Perhaps it was the promise, or maybe it was merely the use of her name, but Rhia finally looked at him. Her body settled as she searched his face for the lie, for the manipulation, the darkness she had grown accustomed to with Rayghast.

But she couldn't find it in Ruenen.

"You're under my protection," he continued now that he had her attention. "You're safe."

"And what if you change your mind and decide to get rid of me?" she asked, the fear on her face making her look much younger than nineteen. "Will you cast me out in the street? Imprison me? Execute me?"

"Regardless of what happens between us in the future, you'll always have a home in Nevandia. You'll be taken care of."

Rhia swallowed. Ruenen watched the terror melt away in her eyes.

"Fine," she said, drawing herself up to her usual hauteur, "but that maid had better not be a nuisance." She closed her chamber doors with a snap, leaving Ruenen alone in the hallway.

Well, that's some progress, at least.

Three faeries were employed in the Kellesar staff for the first time in history, one directly serving a queen. Five others had enlisted in the military, including one female to join Aresti. River was assisting Thora, and the other adults sought work elsewhere. Even the influx of Tacornian transplants were settling into life in Nevandia.

Things seemed to be falling into place.

Ruenen smiled, at ease for the first time in days. He entered his own quarters further down the hallway, only to be pounced upon by Mayestral.

"Your Grace, a letter has arrived for you."

On Mayestral's silver tray, the letter sat, made of fine parchment, in elegant looping writing. Ruenen recognized the sigil on the blue blob of wax: a roaring bear. He ran his thumb under the seal and unfolded Queen Nieve's letter.

His mood plummeted as he read. Nieve's letter, as with the others he'd received from her, was concise, without frills, nor ego.

"Your Grace?" asked Mayestral, brow furrowing at Ruenen's reaction. "Is all well in the North?"

Ruenen sighed, running a hand through his hair.

"King Maes is dead."

CHAPTER 18

MARAI

She bided her time.

Marai spent days studying the rotations of the Menagerie's guards. Which paths they took. How often they passed by her tent, the amphitheater. She memorized the sound her manacles made on the dirt, and the stone stairs. She listened to the creak of the amphitheater door when it opened and closed.

Using those mercenary and thievery skills she'd developed thanks to Slate and years as the Lady Butcher, Marai deduced which window belonged to Acacia, and how many stairs it would take to climb, how long it would take her to get in and out of Acacia's room.

All the while, Marai pretended. She behaved. She let Koda and the Peace Keepers believe her submissiveness, that their threats had truly taken root inside her. They removed the shackles off her wrists. The hounds were finally off the scent.

"I'm doing it tonight," she announced to Keshel at the creek. They were washing their bowls and spoons after dinner. The black curtain would rise in less than an hour, and Keshel would once again be lost to visions and Marai's body would be invaded by foreign magic. They'd suffered and endured long enough. It was time to end this.

"Doing what?" Keshel asked, rubbing the inside of his bowl with a rag in a rhythmic, circular pattern. He moved slowly, as if every slight action drained him. He reminded Marai of a walking skeleton; he'd lost so much weight, and his hair lost its glossy shine. Now his daily retching included black, tainted blood; his body was trying to rid itself of the dark poison inside him. Keshel often forgot conversations that he and Marai had hours earlier, but he'd always, without fail, remember the visions that plagued him. A kind of chant, he mumbled them under his breath, and scratched notes down in his journal.

Cavar was right—Keshel was losing his grasp on reality, diving deeper and deeper into the complex labyrinth of his mind.

Marai lowered her voice. "Stealing Acacia's amulet."

Keshel's head snapped to her. "You're insane if you think you can get in there without being noticed."

"You didn't know me in my days as the Lady Butcher. I can, and I will, get that amulet."

She'd had tougher commissions before, with less time to prepare. Her mark, Acacia, wasn't physically strong enough to overpower her without the amulet; Marai wasn't afraid of her waking. The Peace Keepers weren't terribly bright or observant. She could outsmart them. As long as Koda didn't randomly have duty that night, Marai was *certain* this would work.

Keshel's expression, however, was etched in dread. "Don't do it, Marai. Don't risk yourself that way. No good can come of this."

"No good? We need to get these collars off, and the only way is with those amulets. You and I can then dismantle Cavar's barrier, and we can finally get out of here."

"I wish you'd stop putting yourself in danger. No amulet is worth you getting punished." Keshel searched her face, eyes flashing briefly to her lips. His tone took on a new urgency. "I can't bear to see them beat you again. To stuff you in that box. It was terrible, Marai, knowing where you were, but not being able to help you."

Marai cringed at the memory of being trapped for days in that dark, cramped prison. She hadn't thought about how it must have been for Keshel, seeing Koda and the Peace Keepers locking her inside.

I won't go back in there.

"I have to do something. None of us can keep living like this." Marai gazed around the camp. She watched the majestic manticore pace back and forth in its too-small cage, Desislava groan in hunger, leaning weakly against the trunk of her tree, clutching her stomach.

On the path, Gunnora stumbled, carrying a basket of laundry that was more than half her size and far too heavy. She dropped a garment in the dirt, and Volgar, passing by, snickered and called her something derogatory in Andaran that made Gunnora flinch. She hastily picked up the garment, bowing and apologizing. Volgar's hand lingered on his whip, but he kept on walking.

Marai had a responsibility to the folk of the Menagerie. They looked to her for leadership, whether she accepted that fact or not. A searing, intangible need to protect them rushed through Marai. An undercurrent of roiling storm clouds, of lightning in her veins, far more powerful than the title of Faerie Queen. It was an innate *need* to help them. Marai always had a twisted sense of justice, but this time, the right thing to do was so obvious, she didn't have to think about it.

I'll do whatever I can to free them.

The burden was on her shoulders, and she refused to fail them.

That night, Marai let herself be ushered to the amphitheater as usual. She didn't resist as Acacia fussed with her hair and makeup, and straightened her flower crown. Marai studied the bronze chain's clasp at the top of Acacia's spine; how she could unhook it and swipe the amulet without Acacia noticing in her sleep.

The collar's magic took hold of her, and guided Marai onto the stage. She'd stopped noticing the audience. Her ears muted the cacophony of their applause to a dull hum, the musicians and Arcturius' speech to mere reverberations. She didn't feel much of anything while she performed. Not the temperate summer breeze on her exposed skin. Not the flicker of candle flames as she controlled their color and intensity. Not the pinprick of two hundred ravenous eyes watching her. Marai could have been sleepwalking.

The performance ended. The curtains closed. The audience vacated their seats, and began the trek back into town. The sconces and torches were snuffed out, and Marai returned to Keshel's tent. With the assistance of a disgruntled Yelich, he staggered in moments later, eyes glazed.

"Lirr's watching you," Keshel warned dazedly to no one in particular.

Yelich made a face of indignation and left.

Marai guided Keshel into his bed, and stroked dark strands of hair from his pale face.

"I wish I was the one you thought of when you stare at me like that," he mumbled.

Marai's breath caught. She'd been thinking about Ruenen, how she longed to touch him, to sweep the hair from his eyes. How soon she'd be with him, if all went well.

Keshel fell instantly to sleep, released from his visions for the night.

"This isn't goodbye," she whispered into his pointed ear. "I'll be back for you, and then we'll run out of here together."

She made sure the guards saw her return to her tent. One of them always passed by and lingered outside. She yawned, cracked her neck from side to side, slumped her shoulders, as if exhausted, then entered her tent. Marai pulled on her nightdress and crawled into the bedroll, curling up on her side in order to not crush her wings, which she was finally gaining control over, thanks to working with Anja.

The scuffed footsteps outside her tent grew farther away as the camp quieted.

Marai's eyes snapped back open. She counted the minutes. Then hours.

Finally, it was time to move.

She lifted her bedroll and found the black garments Cyrill had compiled for her. He hadn't questioned her about the clothing, but he'd given her a look that suggested he knew she was up to something. Marai first bound her wings against her back, making them as flat as possible. She couldn't wear pants with shackled ankles, so she donned a long black mourning dress. She tucked her braided hair up under a black cap and pulled it down to her eyes, then wrapped a dark purple scarf around the lower half of her face and neck.

The Lady Butcher returns.

The chains were a problem. They rattled with every move, so Marai carefully wrapped them double in another thick, dark scarf. The knobby material dampened the sound as much as possible, but Marai had another idea up her sleeve. She knotted a long sash around her waist, then tied one end to the middle of the chain, lifting it from the ground. It wasn't ideal, but at least it wouldn't drag on the dirt or stone.

QUEEN OF THE SHADOW MENAGERIE

Before leaving, she stuffed her clothing into the bedroll in the shape of a body. Not completely convincing, but if a Peace Keeper poked his head in, he'd see a dark mound and probably pass by.

Koda would be harder to fool, but he wasn't scheduled for duty that night.

Marai had earlier made an incision in the back of her canvas tent. She crawled out slowly through the tear, only large enough for her small body. Her eyes and ears remained alert as she oriented herself in the darkness. Tent by tent, she crept, using only the balls of her bare feet. Twice she had to duck out of sight of a guard behind a tree and Bobo's canteen. But eventually, she made it to the amphitheater door.

That had been the easy part.

She pulled a pin from her hair and went to work on the lock. Marai had done this a million times—another skill learned from Slate. Finally, it clicked, and Marai slowly opened the door a crack. Sucking in to make herself thinner, she slithered inside and closed the door again. The stairwell was as dark as pitch, but Marai had studied it. She knew how many steps it took to reach the stairs. With her hand on the stone wall for guidance, Marai climbed. One staircase and the first landing. Then the second set. Third.

She'd never been up here before, where the apartments were. Members of the Menagerie weren't allowed, except for Innesh, Anja, and Gunnora, who cleaned the apartments and brought Acacia food. But Marai counted the windows and paces she'd mapped out on the ground below for days. Eventually, she came to the room that belonged to Acacia. It was the only window that was consistently illuminated by candlelight, regardless of which guards were on duty.

Marai tried the door handle. Locked. The pin did its job again, and Marai gently pushed the door ajar, only a sliver.

Lace and jewels bedecked Acacia's room, and everything from the curtains, to the upholstered furniture, to the rugs, had pink flowers sewn into the pattern. Roses and green leaves were painted onto the walls. A large, open armoire housed elaborate hats, dresses, and cloaks. Dozens of silk and pearled slippers lined the bottom of the closet. On her vanity, necklaces and rings littered the tabletop. A jeweled tiara was perched upon a stand.

And there, in an enormous four-poster bed, lying like a snoring, sleeping princess, was Acacia, bronze amulet resting innocently upon her chest.

For a moment, Marai's vision blurred and all she saw was red. Bloody red fury at this woman's blithe attitude towards the suffering of the people in the camp below her. At the extravagance she lived in while others were whipped and starved, living in a piss-smelling tent. Acacia was a villain. A greedy, spoiled brat of a villain.

Marai tip-toed over to the side of the bed. She could kill Acacia right then and there. All it would take were her own two hands wrapped around her captor's delicate neck.

But Marai stilled her hands.

It's not the moment. She had to get in and out quickly without drawing attention. Acacia would make some noise. Koda was just down the hall. He'd hear with those pointed fae ears. And the death of a Guardian would cause too much of an uproar. A stolen amulet, though? Possibly misplaced or lost? That was easier to hide if Acacia were to wake before Marai used it.

Marai hooked a finger around the chain and gently turned it so that the clasp came to the front.

Acacia snorted and snuffled in her sleep. Marai froze.

The Guardian then turned over onto her side, shifting the amulet's clasp. Marai rolled her eyes and suppressed a groan as she moved to the other side of the bed and tried again.

With the lightest of touches and the fingers of a thief, Marai undid the clasp and pulled the amulet from Acacia's neck.

The Guardian's hand shot up. Marai stopped breathing.

But Acacia merely scratched at her neck, still quite asleep.

Marai backed away and stuffed the amulet into her dress pocket. She then closed the door, and went back the way she came, stopping at a hallway window to peer down and assess. Sirco was turning into fourth row, which meant Marai only had a few minutes to get downstairs and out the door before he came by the theater and saw the open lock. Going faster and louder than she should have, Marai bolted down the stairs and slipped from the door, latching the lock once more, barely avoiding Sirco as he approached. She hid around the curve of the theater, back pressed against the stone, as Sirco and his lantern meandered around

QUEEN OF THE SHADOW MENAGERIE

for several minutes by the door. He hacked up phlegm and spit on the ground. He kicked at pebbles. Sniffed, and wiped his nose with the heel of his palm.

Then he left, starting his route again down the first aisle.

Marai dashed in the darkness, not back to *her* tent, but to Keshel's. She slithered through the flap and shook him awake.

His eyes flew open, wide and terrified at the black-adorned stranger above him.

Marai covered his mouth with her hand and pulled down the scarf, then dangled the amulet into his face with a triumphant grin.

"Oh, Marai, you didn't," Keshel whispered, shaking his head.

"I told you I could get it. No one saw me. All it took was careful planning." She handed Keshel the amulet. "Here, you try it."

"I don't like this," he hissed, eyeing the amulet warily. "I can feel dark magic pulsating inside."

So had Marai. While it had been in her pocket, the amulet heated and sent vibrations through her bones, like it was *happy* she picked it up.

Keshel shoved the amulet back at her. "Why can't *you* use it first?"

"Because I'm worried that using it will trigger something in me. You've never once used dark magic. I might be too . . . susceptible to its allure."

The way it called to her, *wanted* her. It could be very dangerous to use. She wasn't sure, since she truly knew nothing about that power, but Marai didn't want to take any chances with their only chance at freedom.

Keshel frowned, but set his face with determination. He took the amulet in his hands and closed his eyes.

"Cavar said all he had to do was *will* the magic to do what he wanted," Marai reminded him with hushed anticipation.

The amulet's magic flared, brightening the tent. Keshel quickly shoved it beneath his blanket, dousing the black light.

"What did you ask it to do?"

"Nothing yet. It . . . knew who I was," he whispered, eyes frantic. "I don't know, Marai, that light might be a warning signal to the other amulets—"

Marai said through gritted teeth, "Fine, give it to me."

Damn the magic. If it calls to me, I'll ignore it, like the last time. As she had on the battlefield in the Red Lands.

Keshel passed her the chain and Marai held the amulet in her grasp.

Unlock my collar. She pushed the thought into the stone. *Release me.*

"Ah, there you are," it cooed back. A filmy finger stroked across the recesses of her mind. *"I will have you, Marai, one way or another."*

She jolted and dropped the amulet into the dirt.

"What happened?" Keshel questioned; his rapid breath sawed in and out.

Marai shivered. "It recognized me, too. It said it intends to have me. Whatever that means."

Keshel pursed his lips. "He wants to possess you."

"Who?"

"The Lord of the Underworld."

Ice snaked under Marai's ribs. The tent grew darker. Night closed in around her, alive, pressing, constricting.

As far as she knew from the teachings of monks and priestesses, the Underworld had no ruler, no inhabitants other than wandering, deceased souls. But what did anyone truly know about it? It wasn't as if anyone visited the Underworld and returned.

The shadow creatures. They came from the Underworld, birthed from dark magic, which Keshel had already guessed came from the world of the dead. Someone down there must be creating them. Someone must have control.

"Have you seen this Lord of the Underworld in one of your visions?"

Keshel nodded solemnly. "Dozens of times. He aims to have the Chosen One for his own, because then He will truly have the power to escape."

The Chosen One? "What do you—"

Too late, Marai heard the footsteps outside the tent.

She and Keshel went utterly still.

The flap parted, revealing the shadowed, serious face of Innesh. Her eyes went from Marai to the amulet, and grew more severe.

"You fool," Innesh snapped in a hush, coming fully inside. "I saw a shape moving amongst the camp. I had a feeling it was you, but never did I imagine *this.*"

"Back away, Innesh," Marai warned, letting danger edge into her tone. "We're going to get these collars off and—"

"Do you think the other Guardians haven't felt the reaction to their own amulets? They're all connected. Cavar and the hundreds of other Guardians sensed something's wrong by now. Let's say you get this collar off, and somehow take down the barrier, where do you intend to hide? Guardians will swarm this field come morning. Daybreak is only two hours away. You won't get far, not with Keshel in his condition."

Innesh had a valid point. Keshel was in no shape to run the leagues necessary to truly escape the Menagerie and get back to the docks in Bakair. Not only that, there was no way Marai could free the others in camp. If she left, she'd be abandoning everyone else.

But Marai couldn't give up.

"Once the collar is off, I can fight back. I'll have use of my magic again, and I know I can defeat those Guardians."

"Maybe one or two, yes, but do you truly think you can beat the dozens that will come, using their amulets against you? Plus Cavar, himself?" Innesh's face was as livid and wild as a tornado in the Badlands. "Who do you think Cavar will punish if you *do* get away? You'll get innocent Menagerie folk killed. Are you, their Queen, going to abandon them? You won't get far. Cavar will catch you, and you'll be tortured and imprisoned in that crate for life. Unless you're able to kill him, it's useless to try."

Marai grit her teeth, seething with rage. She *hated* that Innesh had a point. Unless Cavar was there and Marai killed him, there'd be no way to stop the Guardians from hurting Keshel, Anja, Gunnora, and other members of the Menagerie to punish her.

Innesh held out her hand. "Give it to me now. I can't let you use it."

A furious female scream pierced the air.

Boots scrambled outside past the tent, running towards the amphitheater.

While Marai was distracted, Innesh launched herself at the amulet. The slave woman was larger than Marai, and elbowed her in the face. Keshel frantically shushed them as they tussled, and the sound of another set of boots ran past.

Innesh yanked the chain from Marai's fist, and disappeared out of the tent faster than a blink.

Fuck!

Marai forced her feet to move, darting and weaving past tents as the camp came alive with activity in the dull, gray light of morning. Eight Peace Keepers and Koda were at the door to the amphitheater, where Acacia stood in her nightgown, flailing her arms dramatically as she shouted in shrill Andaran.

Along the way to her tent, Marai shucked off the black clothes, piece by piece, stuffing them into the hollow of a tree, and tossed her cap into a nearby, low-burning campfire. She barely made it into her bedroll before her tent flap was wrenched open by Koda. She squinted her eyes, playing the part of an innocent, slumbering maiden.

Koda's silver eyes sparked with accusation.

"Can I help you?" Marai asked as Koda grabbed her arm, dragging her from her bed.

He flung her blanket and pillow across the tent, lifted her bedroll and shook.

"Open your hands," he ordered.

Marai lifted her empty palms.

"Mouth."

She opened wide with an exaggerated huff and stuck out her tongue. Koda's cold hands raked up and down her nightdress, and Marai stiffened at the unwelcome sensation.

Still not satisfied, Koda got into her face, nearly nose to nose. "Where is it?"

"Where is *what*?" Marai asked. "You haven't told me what this is about."

"You took Acacia's amulet."

Marai crossed her arms, having flashbacks of a similar conversation with Slate onboard *The Nightmare*. "I've been fast asleep here all night. Maybe Acacia lost her amulet, and doesn't want to admit that she's careless."

Koda glowered. "Where did you put it? Is it in the creek? Did you dig a hole somewhere? Stuff it up your ass?"

Marai cringed away from him, at the thought that Koda might actually *search* for it there. "Firstly, I don't know which room is Acacia's. Secondly, I'll remind you that my ankles are shackled. There's no way I could have done such a thing without someone noticing."

Which is, unfortunately, true. Innesh had noticed. Eagled-eyed Innesh. Which got Marai wondering—what was *Innesh* going to do with the amulet? Would she give it back to Acacia?

"If anyone could have pulled off this little stunt, it would be you," Koda said.

He dragged her outside, where a group of Peace Keepers and Acacia waited. The female Guardian's curly black hair was tousled, robe hanging open, not even tied around her waist. Without her usual glamorous makeup, Acacia looked ordinary.

"Did you find it?" she asked Koda.

"Not yet. Search thoroughly," he told the red-vested guards.

Sirco and another burly man ducked inside Marai's tiny tent and began tearing it apart. They searched the lining and stitching, the hole at the bottom where the pole was planted.

"*You took it,*" Acacia shouted at Marai, and thrust a shaking finger at her chest. "You demon. You ugly little brute."

Marai expected a backhand across her cheek, but Acacia was far too invested in watching the guards search.

After a thorough hunt, Sirco came up empty-handed.

"Could she have disposed of it?" Acacia questioned. "Swallowed it? Given it to another?"

"Check Keshel's tent," ordered Koda, and the Peace Keepers flocked over there, yanking Keshel outside as they tossed around his belongings.

Still, nothing. They checked Anja and Gunnora's, too.

Koda scrutinized Marai, who continued to make her face look innocent, confused, and tired. Well, she didn't have to feign exhaustion since she'd been awake the entire night.

"We know you took it."

Marai shot back, "If I'd wanted that amulet, I wouldn't have thrown it away. I wouldn't have destroyed it. I'd have used it to get this collar off. But since it's still on, and I'm standing here, I obviously didn't steal Acacia's stupid necklace."

Acacia stomped her feet with a scream. "My uncle will be furious. He'll have your head for this, little vermin!" Receiving no further reaction from Marai, Acacia cooled her wrath. She tossed her hair and gave Marai a superior look. "No matter. My uncle will make me a new one. Worry not, girl, I'm going to make your life miserable."

Marai held back a snarky retort.

Acacia tossed her head with a *humph,* and marched back to her apartment inside the theater, leaving Marai alone with Koda.

"Am I free to go back to bed now?" she asked him. Not that she could—her tent was in shambles on the ground.

"You might think you've gotten away with this, but rest assured that I'll be watching you," Koda said, lips rearing back to reveal pearly-white teeth. He left Marai, gathering up the Peace Keepers at the end of the tent row into deep conversation.

The sun was rising now; its rays muted and dimmed by the fog barrier, creating the usual gray pallor over the camp. Everyone else was awake and had been peering out of their tents at the spectacle.

Marai met their gaze, one by one, and was surprised to see a black scarf around Athelstan's neck, a long dress draped over Dante's back like a blanket.

They'd collected her hastily discarded clothing while Koda and the guards had been preoccupied. They'd covered her tracks. She wanted to thank them, to tell them how sorry she was that she'd failed, but Koda was still watching her, over his shoulder, from a distance.

Keshel came to her side, expression hard and disappointed. It was one Marai used to see on his face when she was younger. At least his vexation was familiar. It was better than his sad, confused resignation.

"Have you had enough now?" he asked, voice as tight as his crossed arms. "Are you done?"

"Never. I'll think of something else next time."

Keshel grasped her shoulders, looking her straight in the eye. "Please. This is folly. They'll separate us if you keep going. Marai, I can't lose you." His voice cracked as those normally so impassive, dark eyes shimmered with emotion and desperation.

"And I can't lose *you*!" She wrenched away from him. "You're dying. Can't you see? I'll do *anything* to save you. This goes beyond just you and me, Keshel. All of the folk here deserve a better life. Even if I fail every time, I'll continue to try

QUEEN OF THE SHADOW MENAGERIE

and free us. That's what matters—choosing to fight. Showing Cavar that he may have taken my freedom, but he cannot destroy my heart."

Marai turned her back on Keshel and skulked to the creek. She plopped down onto the bank and tucked her knees to her chest, wrapping her thin arms around them. She sat there all morning, having nothing else to do. She wasn't hungry for breakfast, and the atrocious smell wafting from Bobo's commissary was enough to make her gag.

Footsteps and the sound of dragging chains indicated Innesh's arrival behind her. The Yehzigi woman waded into the shin-deep creek and splashed water on her brown arms.

"What did you do with it?" Marai asked.

Innesh's dark eyes flicked to assess the location of Koda and the guards further up the row. At first, Marai wasn't sure the woman would respond.

"I disposed of it," Innesh said curtly.

"Why not give it back to them?"

Innesh stopped scrubbing her arms, and pierced Marai with a dueling stare. "I owe those people nothing. Not loyalty. Not respect. If I didn't believe in the terrible retribution that would come our way, I would've let you have it."

"I can protect myself."

"Perhaps, but can you protect all of them?" Innesh gestured to the bustling camp.

Anja and Gunnora were watching Marai and Innesh at the creek curiously. Keshel stood with them. Anja tried to get him to eat the bread in her hand, but Keshel shook his head.

"What do you care about the others? You don't go out of your way to show kindness," said Marai, as Athelstan lumbered over to join her friends in conversation.

"And you do? The Queen who would have abandoned her people to save herself?"

"I wouldn't have abandoned them," Marai snarled. "I would have fought for them, which is more than you do."

Innesh took a seat next to her on the bank. "I wasn't taught kindness. You don't know my past. You don't know me."

"Oh, I know you," said Marai, "because you're the same as I used to be."

Innesh stiffened. "My parents sold me to the Skelm as a girl; a gang of grifters known for using children as runners and pickpockets. They left their mark on me." She stroked a finger across the tattoos on her jaw. "The streets of Yehzig aren't kind to girls. My next meal was determined by how many people I'd swindled that day. My profit was given to the Skelm. That was the life I knew, one of running. Lying. Surviving."

Her face and rigid posture then softened. "One day, a new boy arrived. He was nothing like the other gutter rats. I'd never seen anyone with pointed ears before. I'd never heard of a faerie. But Koda showed me that there was magic in the world. He was the Skelm's new prized pet, better than me at pickpocketing, and he never had issues sucking up to those of higher rank. But he regarded me as if *I* was worth something more than the things I stole, and I'd never been looked at that way before."

"You loved him?" asked Marai.

"I cringe at the very memory, but Koda showed me that my hands could do more than reach into a stranger's pocket. They could touch with gentleness and affection. They could hold onto another. Koda heard rumors of traders going to Andara, and we snuck aboard their ship. When we landed on the docks, the minute Cavar spotted Koda's pointed ears, he knew what he was. And Koda, so eager to *be* someone, to be respected, finagled his way into a position at the Menagerie. Cavar said I could work there, too, but unlike Koda, who was useful and eager, I was shackled and forced into a life of slavery even worse than the one I'd left on Yehzig."

"If Koda loved you, why didn't he stand up for you? Free you?"

"Because Cavar promised Koda something better: power and prestige," Innesh said bitterly, "and for a half-fae orphan, who'd never had a father, who was offered a better life, that promise far overshadowed the one Koda and I had made to each other."

Marai thought of Ruenen then. Of the promise he'd almost made to her. Of the promise she knew now she would have accepted. Despite being King, Ruenen wouldn't have chosen power or wealth over her. When listening to Innesh's story, and remembering Anja's from before, Marai felt a surge of overwhelming sorrow and bittersweet affection.

I'm lucky to have been loved by Ruen. Even for a short time.

Innesh's expression of steel returned. "If I get the chance, I'll kill Koda, myself. His betrayal of a young girl's heart, my freedom, is worse than what Cavar has done to me."

"When we succeed in getting out of here, I'll happily leave Koda for you," said Marai.

Innesh stood and brushed the dirt from her pants. "Acacia will get another amulet, and they'll watch you more closely than before. So here is my advice for you, Faerie Queen—survive. Endure. Do not let them take anything else from you. It isn't winning, but it's better than giving them the satisfaction of defeating you."

CHAPTER 19

RUENEN

Ruenen found himself on the Northern road inside of an ornate, gilded carriage. A pile of paperwork on the seat next to him provided endless hours of distraction during the journey to Lirrstrass. Holfast would at least be happy—Ruenen was now caught up on reading and signing all the things he'd been putting off.

Nieve had invited him to the funeral celebrations for King Maes, and Ruenen immediately accepted her invitation. With the King dead, no one was certain whether the Greltan council would allow Nieve to remain in power, or if someone else would take over as Regent until Prince Hiver came of age. Ruenen had to make sure the alliance between Grelta and Nevandia didn't weaken.

"Nieve saved us on that battlefield," he'd told Holfast when the Steward protested. "Grelta is our strongest ally and friend. It's important that we're there for the Queen and future King in this time of grief."

"That's a long way to travel," Holfast replied. "Two weeks there by carriage, and back again. You'll be gone an entire month."

Honestly, that was one of the major draws for Ruenen going at all. Other than a few excursions to Tacorn, he hadn't left Nevandia since taking the throne months ago. He'd been itching to go across Nevandian borders to search for Marai and Keshel. He didn't think they were in Grelta, but each time they stopped at a town to rest, Ruenen, Raife, and Aresti questioned people in hopes of gleaning some kind of information or clue.

An added bonus was that there wasn't any dreadful snow and whipping, icy wind up north at this time of year. Now Ruenen had to deal with the sticky heat of summer.

"Any interest in joining me?" Ruenen had asked Holfast, who certainly looked as if he could use a vacation.

His hair was almost entirely gray now, and he always seemed to have dozens of things to do. The Steward worked harder than anyone Ruenen had ever met. He went from meeting to meeting, spending hours in his private office next door to Ruenen's, drafting proclamations, proposals, and laws. Holfast gave his all for Nevandia every day, and Ruenen admired him for it.

The Steward gave Ruenen a wry smile. "No, thank you, Your Grace. I promise that I will keep things running smoothly while you're away."

"Oh, I'm sure you will," said Ruenen, then winked at the Steward. "I'll be sure to bring you back a trinket from abroad."

Holfast had actually given Ruenen a rare chuckle for that. "I prefer sweets."

Ruenen's kingly caravan crossed into Greltan territory, and began its ascent towards the city of Lirrstrass, up the hilly terrain. The highest peaks were further north in the White Ridge Mountains, but Lirrstrass was located far above sea level.

Inside his carriage, Ruenen was barefoot, his pants rolled up to his knees, and shirt sleeves rolled to his elbows, top unbuttoned. It was oppressively hot inside. The seat beneath him was velvet and leather, making his bottom-half sweat, and the walls and ceiling were covered with stifling brocade fabric.

He used a piece of paper to fan himself as he glanced out his jostling window. They were in the midst of a central forest road. Green trees towered over his caravan, but they weren't the only ones traveling. Summer was always the ideal time for people to travel in Astye. Ruenen passed several other carriages, wagons, riders, and pedestrians along the way.

Raife and Aresti pulled up alongside his window on their horses.

"Looking forward to seeing your friend the Queen?" Ruenen asked Aresti. He was hinting to their previous visit to Lirrstrass, when Aresti had spent a mysteriously passionate night with both Nieve and Nosficio. She'd never said a word about it, but Ruenen knew it happened, and couldn't help but tease her a little bit.

"I'm looking forward to a good meal and a cold bath," she replied irritably. "And getting off this damned horse. My rear is bruised and sore from this journey."

Of his retinue, Aresti was the only one besides Lord Goso who'd been to the Glacial Palace on Ruenen's previous visit. Goso, Ambassador to Grelta, sat in the carriage behind Ruenen's with his twitchy assistant, and seemed anxious to return in order to conduct business with the Greltan counsel. He'd been particularly aggrieved when Ruenen told him of King Maes' passing. Goso had been doing business with him for much of his reign.

"Besides," Aresti continued, "the Queen will be in mourning. It wouldn't be appropriate for me to . . . divert her."

"Perhaps a diversion might be what Queen Nieve needs," said Raife with waggling eyebrows.

Aresti didn't respond, but instead urged her horse forward, up to where Tarik was riding. Ruenen thought Nieve might enjoy meeting the werewolf, since they'd never been properly introduced, and Tarik was eager to go.

"It's important that I represent werewolves abroad," he'd said with jocular swagger. "Be an ambassador of sorts. To build more understanding of my people's plight. There are quite a few were packs in the White Ridge Mountains."

To round out Ruenen's retinue, Lord Wattling also joined the excursion. Holfast had been the one to persuade him, telling Ruenen that it made Nevandia appear stronger to have the ex-Tacornian councilman there in solidarity. And of course, there was Ruenen's constant shadow, his Groom Mayestral, and a few other members of the serving staff. Elmar, Nyle, and ten more members of the King's Guard surrounded Ruenen's carriage on all sides.

They were a recognizable caravan as they passed through the city of Lirrstrass, and perhaps the people had been expecting him. Citizens waved and shouted, throwing flowers in the path of the horses and carriages. The last time Ruenen had seen this city, it was covered in snow, and the people had worn thick, bulky furs. Now, they were dressed in lighter linens, appearing more like humans and less like bears. No longer so desolate and bleak, signs of life were everywhere in

Lirrstrass. The city's surrounding forests were lushly verdant, and lambs in the paddocks nursed from their mother ewes.

The Glacial Palace reminded Ruenen of a fairytale. Its turrets and towers were no longer coated in icicles and snow, and the obsidian rock glimmered like black ice in the sun. However, the Greltan flags that usually flew high above the towers were now at half-staff, and replaced with ones of dark blue. Panels of the same color had been hung from each of the castle's windows, indicating the passing of the King. Homes and businesses in town hung those same panels out their own windows, and some people wore the mourning colors.

Ruenen wasn't used to seeing the Queen of Grelta in anything but white or pale shades. Dressed in a blue so dark it was almost black, but with red hair blazing, Nieve stood on the steps of the castle in greeting, her son Hiver and daughter Elurra standing at her side. Ruenen also spotted her mysterious, masked Master of Spies lurking in the background by the main castle doors.

The horses slowed to a stop, and a castle servant opened Ruenen's carriage door. He clambered out, grateful to stretch his legs after hours of sitting. He walked stiffly to the stairs, meeting Nieve halfway.

"Your Grace, I'm so sorry for your loss," he said, kissing her outstretched, black-gloved hand. She still wore several glittering jewels on her neck and fingers.

"You're very kind to make the long journey here, King Ruenen," Nieve said solemnly. She was paler than the last time Ruenen had seen her in Nevandia, and were those strands of gray he saw in her hair? "I didn't expect you to come, but Maes would have been honored by your presence. You honor us. You remember my children? Crowned Prince Hiver and Princess Elurra."

The young redheaded royals dipped into respectful bows and courteous greetings, but sorrow swum in their blue-gray eyes. They'd lost a father at a young age. Ruenen understood how they felt, having been stripped of three father-figures in his life before he'd turned sixteen.

"How are you both?" Ruenen asked them.

Hiver looked up, surprised at the question. "Tolerable, Your Grace. Thank you for your concern."

Elurra sniffled. "Yes. Tolerable." Her trembling voice told Ruenen that she was certainly *not* doing tolerably.

Nieve glanced at Aresti, who'd climbed down from her horse and was handing the reins off to a stableboy. Aresti and Nieve's eyes locked for a moment, but Nieve broke the contact and instead focused on Tarik.

"I remember you, Master Wolf. You were quite brave and fierce against the Tacorn army."

"Tarik, Your Grace. My condolences to you about the late King," Tarik said, lowering to a knee. His voice took on a lofty quality Ruenen hadn't heard from him before. "Your home is beautiful, but you far outshine even the most magnificent of structures. I think the true gem of Grelta is, in fact, its Queen."

Nieve regarded him with her usual coy interest, trailing over his muscular forearms and broad chest. She looked at Ruenen and mouthed, "I like him."

Ruenen's shoulders shook with suppressed laughter. *Perhaps Tarik will be added to her rotation.*

"You are most welcome, Master Wolf. Please, my esteemed guests, come inside for some refreshments."

Nieve escorted Ruenen and his retinue through the towering castle doors and into the entrance hall. Despite the obsidian rock on the outside, the interior of the castle was bright, with white-washed walls, and silvery blue winter mountain landscapes painted upon them.

Servants were waiting with goblets of wine and small bites of meat and cheese on silver trays. Ruenen took a goblet and shoved a piece of ham into his mouth.

A massive portrait of a young King Maes stood in the middle of the hall, draped in translucent dark fabric. Even in his earlier years, Maes seemed frail, but certainly better than when Ruenen had seen him months ago, when he'd barely been able to walk or speak. He had a kind smile, the type most rulers lacked or refused to show. The smile of a man who'd trusted his wife to rule in his stead when he'd become too ill to do so. A rare king, indeed.

"The funeral ceremony will take place tomorrow morning. My people have already come to pay their respects to Maes during the past few weeks," Nieve explained in the hall after cordial introductions between Ruenen's company and the Greltan counsel. "His body has been lying, encased in ice, within the monastery since his death, open for all to view. As is our tradition. Tomorrow, we will bury him in the crypt, and enjoy a grand feast in his honor. Tonight, we'll have a modest dinner."

"How are you holding up, Your Grace?" Ruenen asked once Goso and Wattling were pulled into conversation with Greltan ministers.

Like her son, Nieve blinked, as if surprised Ruenen should ask such a question. He wondered if anyone had asked her yet; Nieve always put on a show of such strength. She searched his face with her piercing blue eyes. "You're a sweet thing, to look so concerned for me. I'm doing as well as can be expected. I knew this was coming for a long time, but . . . it doesn't dull the loss. I hate to know that Maes' body lies in that frozen tomb down the hall." She took a long sip of wine. "To be honest, I'll be glad when this is over, and his body is laid to rest in the royal ice catacombs beneath us. But I suppose he's at peace now."

"Please let me know if there's anything I can do, for you or your children."

Nieve gave him a sad smile and placed her gloved hand to his cheek. The maternal gesture was her way of thanking him. She then pulled Ruenen further to the side, away from the men conversing nearby. "What of Lady Marai?"

"The search continues." Ruenen heard the sorrow in his own voice, the bitterness and frustration.

"I'm sorry, Ruenen. She's special, to be sure. I like her, and not because she's fae and destroyed half of Rayghast's army. Astye needs more resilient, no-nonsense women like her."

Yes, Astye *did* need Marai. So much potential for change was just out of reach, but with her, Ruenen knew it could all be possible. Nieve understood that, as well.

"I sent out my Master of Spies on a few excursions, hoping he might be able to dig up some information," Nieve said, "but I'm sorry to report that he heard nothing across Grelta."

"I appreciate you trying," said Ruenen.

"I'll keep trying until she's back in your arms. And Nosficio?" she then asked, glancing away, as if to deny interest, like it was normal conversation to ask about one's vampire ex-lover.

"I haven't seen or heard him since the night Marai was taken."

"He hasn't given up on finding her, I know it," Nieve reassured. "Nosficio cares for very few, but he definitely has a vested interest in Marai. He'll search until he has an answer. That vampire is incredibly determined and stubborn when he wants to be." For a moment, Nieve's eyes softened, thinking of Nosficio, but she quickly snapped back to her regal countenance. "You must be tired, Your Grace. We shall speak more at dinner."

Ruenen retired to the same stylish room he'd slept in before, when he'd visited the Glacial Palace as a prince instead of a king.

Mayestral was there, ready to assist. "A bath, my King?"

Ruenen nodded, aware of the greasiness of his hair, the smell of his traveling clothes, and the overall sticky feeling of his skin after traveling in the heat of summer.

Dinner that evening was a subdued affair. Nieve's children, also dressed in dark colors, picked at their plates. Elurra sniffled, her eyes red-rimmed, while the Queen drank several glasses of wine in rapid succession. Conversation was quiet around the table between the other lords, ladies, and council members. Aresti, standing in the corner, didn't take her eyes off of Nieve the entire night.

"I've heard rumors of your impending nuptials," Nieve said as Ruenen chewed on his sturgeon and asparagus. "Is it true that you're to wed Queen Rhia?"

Ruenen nearly spat out his food. He forced himself to swallow and keep his face polite. "Those rumors are incorrect, Your Grace. While my council has certainly been urging towards that decision, that won't be possible."

Nieve gave him a penetrating stare. "You have to wed sometime, and Rhia *would* be the smartest choice for you. If I was on your counsel, I'd advise you the same thing. However, I think love is a remarkably powerful thing, and couples marrying for love is even more astonishing. I've never been truly in love, myself, but I can see it plainly in others. I saw it openly displayed on your face when Lady Marai walked into a room. And I saw it in *hers* when you two danced at your coronation. I imagine that she's the reason for your reluctance?"

"My counsel has instructed that even if Marai returns, I won't be allowed to marry her. She isn't *proper* enough, according to them," Ruenen said with acid on his tongue.

"Oh, fie on your counsel," scoffed Nieve. "You're King, aren't you? You decide the rules."

Did he? Ruenen had been feeling like an employee to his own crown. Maybe he hadn't been staunch enough in his stance. Everyone else bowed to a king's whim across Astye—why shouldn't his own Witan?

He picked at his asparagus with his fork. "Holfast said that marrying a faerie would entice other countries to invade us out of hate. Marai could only be my mistress, he said, despite her being Queen of the Fae."

Now it was Nieve's turn to choke on her wine. "Is she really?"

Ruenen nodded.

The Queen smiled, cat-like. "What a remarkable and *delicious* turn of events. I wasn't aware royal faerie lines still existed."

"She's the last."

"A rare jewel, to be sure," Nieve said, arching an eyebrow. "Well, I for one, would be beyond pleased to have a Faerie Queen on the throne in Nevandia. We need to shake up the status quo. I think we're on the cusp of something great and meaningful on this continent."

Ruenen hoped that was true. He *wished* for it, to pave the way for lasting change. He was willing to work hard to achieve it, and his heart ached at the mere *idea* of having Marai sit on a throne next to his.

"You poor man," said Nieve, drawing Ruenen's attention back to her. "It must be hard to be without her, and not know if she's well."

"There's no one else on this earth, not a single other soul that lives and breathes, I could bind myself to," Ruenen said. "Every part of my being belongs to her."

Nieve's grin grew. "You're a poet, Your Grace."

"Musician, actually," Ruenen said, smiling back. "And what of you? Your son?"

Nieve let loose a brisk sigh. "Hiver is too young to rule. He's only fifteen, and has his father's gentleness. I'll remain Queen until he comes of age, and even then, only step down when he feels ready."

"Will you remarry?"

Nieve laughed loudly. "Good heavens, no! Not if I can help it."

Heads at the table turned to see why Nieve was suddenly so jovial.

Ruenen blinked. "But won't your counsel force you to?"

"They know better than to try," she said. "I'll be in mandatory mourning for two years, anyways. I care far too much for my freedom to be tied down to another man; one who may not be as kind and lenient with my eccentricities and experimentations as Maes was. My heart has always been my own, and I don't intend to share my power with another man, either."

"Who needs husbands, anyway?" Ruenen asked, raising his glass.

"You're my favorite royal, did you know that?" Nieve replied, clinking her glass to his.

Ruenen had witnessed so much death, but had never once been to a funeral in his twenty-two years of life. And certainly not one for a king.

The ceremony in the monastery was austere and somber, with the Greltan Head Monk and His Priestesses chanting traditional religious texts. The windows were draped in the same dark blue fabric, candles lined the room, incense formed curls of smoke in the air, wafting its heady scent up Ruenen's nose, making him lightheaded.

King Maes' body lay beneath a shroud of silver and white, entombed in a block of ice that dripped puddles onto the floor. The monastery itself was quite cold, despite the heat of summer past its doors. One by one, guests were invited forward to view his body and place one alpine rose, a local flower to the Greltan mountains, atop his body. Nieve and the children stood next to him, accepting condolences.

Ruenen began to sweat. His heart thumped within his chest. *I don't want to see any more dead bodies.* After witnessing hundreds of his men slaughtered on the Red Lands, Master Chongan and his family's mutilated corpses, the thought of gazing upon the dead king made Ruenen queasy.

I must do this for Nieve. With leaden legs, Ruenen waited his turn in line to gaze upon the body. Thanks to the shroud and thick ice, it was impossible to see Maes' face beneath, but the encasement did nothing to hide the small, thin outline of his body.

Ruenen's thoughts turned to Marai. Cold undulated through him as a vision of *her* funeral, *her* frail body encased in ice, flashed through his mind.

Don't think about that. She isn't dead.

His hand shook as he placed his alpine rose upon the King's chest, alongside the others. *Be at peace, Your Grace.* Ruenen kissed Nieve's hand, as well as Princess Elurra's. To Crown Prince Hiver, he inclined his head, then returned to his seat.

After the ceremony, it was time for the processional. The ice tomb was lifted by several silver-clad Greltan King's Guard, and must've weighed a ton. Nieve, Elurra, and Hiver followed Maes' body from the monastery and down into an arched stairwell, ending in the royal ice catacombs where previous monarchs of Grelta were laid to rest deep beneath the castle.

Ruenen didn't follow into the catacombs. Instead, he took some air in the castle garden. He was emotionally exhausted and physically taxed, but still needed to attend the massive feast. He'd barely stopped shaking all day, because that vision of Marai was burned into his mind. What if she *had* been killed? What if her body was lying somewhere, discarded and buried without honor? The thought of leaving a flower on an unmarked grave sickened him.

"Is something wrong, Your Grace?" asked Mayestral when Ruenen returned to his chambers to change before dinner. "Are you ill?"

Shake it off. She's alive. You'll find her.

At the banquet, he sat at the table next to Nieve, who was dressed in midnight blue again, with tiny diamonds littering the bodice. It was traditional for the feast to be a happier affair than the funeral, meant for celebrating the achievements of the departed. In fact, in Grelta, Ruenen heard that the festivities would go on for days.

Nieve disappeared from Ruenen's side at some point. He hadn't been paying attention—his eyes barely left the musicians in the corner of the great hall, singing tales of King Maes the Benevolent. Needing air, Ruenen excused himself to Prince Hiver and Princess Elurra, who seemed to be having a miserable time. Their young faces were splotchy, noses red.

Ruenen spotted Nieve at the front doors, staring up at the star-studded sky. He turned around, aiming for the gardens, instead.

Nieve looked over her shoulder and waved him over. "I wanted a moment of quiet reflection, but I could use the company."

Ruenen stood at her side, watching the wheeling stars overhead. "It was a beautiful ceremony."

"By the book, although I think Maes would have preferred something far more intimate if he'd had a choice." Nieve gave Ruenen a doleful smile. "I was married to Maes when I was fourteen. Can you believe that? We were children, but our marriage was more than amiable. He was my best friend, a good husband, and an excellent father."

"When did he . . . ?"

"The first signs of his illness occurred in his early twenties, but I think the signs were there earlier. Small, subtle things that we overlooked. Sadly, there was nothing to do to stop it progressing. But despite his decline, despite losing the ability to do *anything*, he always smiled. He never complained. At least not to me. If I'd been in his position, I would have given up ages ago. Or at least been intensely bitter about it."

"I'm blessed that I was able to meet him," Ruenen said. "I wish I could've known him better."

"Oh, he would've liked you. Maes loved a good joke, and back when he was younger, he was quite the chatterbox," said Nieve. She released a shuddering laugh, as if trying to hide her sorrow.

Ruenen took her hand. He wished he could say, *You don't always have to be strong, Nieve. You're allowed to grieve.* But he didn't want to patronize her. She already knew it.

"I'll miss him every day," she said. "He'd been there for so much of my life, that I'm . . . not sure what life is without him."

They stood there in silence for a while, staring at faraway stars.

Nieve's shallow breathing eventually calmed. She patted Ruenen's hand and released her hold. "I'm ready to go back in now. Thank you for your company."

"Forgive the intrusion," came a voice of silk and hemlock.

Ruenen whirled around, heart hammering at the recognizable sound.

From a dim corner of the hall, as if borne from twilight and shadow, strode a figure. He prowled towards Nieve and Ruenen, crimson eyes burning as they latched onto the Queen. He pushed back the hood of his velvet cloak, revealing his gray-hued face, covered in splotches of black ichor.

A grin slid across Nosficio's lips, revealing two sharp fangs. His uncanny eyes then met Ruenen's as he said, "Good evening, Your Grace. I have a lead for you."

CHAPTER 20

CAVAR

"Is she ready yet?"

Minister Blago's finger tapped erratically on his knee as he sat across from Cavar's desk, hair slicked back with some foul-smelling oil. He'd arrived at the Menagerie and demanded a meeting with Cavar before the show. The Governor, himself, was getting ready to leave for Bakair. He'd been constantly torn away from his duties within the province due to Marai. His bags were packed, carriage ready, and he was moments away from leaving when Blago interrupted him.

"You promised that I would be the first to sample her. It's been several weeks now, and I've watched her perform countless times. She seems entirely under your control," the Minister continued, taking Cavar's silence for confusion. Blago had indeed watched countless performances since Marai arrived.

Cavar would know, he counted the man's money again and again. He couldn't remember the Minister being so interested in the Menagerie before.

"Yes, I remember our conversation Minister, however, I'm not sure she is docile enough for your taste," said Cavar.

Blago liked his entertainment boneless as a dead fish. The man wanted no dominance, no dithering or pushback, which created quite a problem for Cavar. Even shackled and threatened, Marai would never let Blago touch her willingly. She'd kill the Minister in seconds, but not before insulting the man with every curse in the dictionary.

Blago set down a full pouch of rattling coins onto the desk. "That's double the amount I paid for the pink-skinned one."

QUEEN OF THE SHADOW MENAGERIE

Cavar pulled the pouch towards him and uncinched the string. Inside were shiny bronze coins, far more than what Cavar would normally charge. Blago must have been desperate, and it made Cavar dislike the man more. The Minister's sexual appetites were appalling.

I'm glad I'm not governed by such boorish desires.

"What about power?" the voice in Cavar's head prodded.

Cavar chose to ignore it.

Blago licked his lips as he waited for Cavar to consider. The Governor sighed. He would need to program her collar to restrain that stubborn faerie in a new way.

"Very well. Tonight, it is." Cavar glanced at Koda standing by the door. "Go retrieve Marai, and have Innesh prepare a room for the Minister."

Koda hesitated, brows pinched, but exited silently out of the office.

Blago's smarmy grin slid across his thin lips. "Excellent. I look forward to it." The man was perspiring in anticipation. He dabbed at his forehead with a handkerchief. "Will she be . . . pliant?"

"She'll be whatever you desire, Minister," said Cavar, voice smooth and cordial to appropriately hide his disgust. He couldn't comprehend why anyone would want to bed a magical creature, but a shockingly large number of people enjoyed the exotic experience, and paid handsomely for it.

Blago got to his feet, twirling his felt cap in his hands. He ran a pinky across his upper lip, smoothing out his mustache. "Nice doing business with you, Governor."

"Is the Mistress here tonight?" asked Cavar innocently. "Should I prepare a room for her, as well?"

The Minister's face fell into a grimace. "Blessedly, no. My wife's at home, and I don't have to see her sour face for at least another two days."

"Give her my best when you do see her," Cavar said, always feigning politeness to his clients. He swept the pouch of coins from the table and into a drawer.

Koda returned with Marai in tow. She had on a white gown and usual surly expression, but Blago didn't seem to mind. His hungry eyes darted across her body, as if he already owned her. Well, he'd paid, so he technically did, for one whole evening.

Marai flinched away from his possessive gaze.

"Until tonight," Blago said, then hastened from the office.

Marai accosted Cavar the moment the door snicked shut behind the Minister. "What did he mean?"

"After tonight's performance, Koda will escort you upstairs to the guest apartments, and you will entertain Minister Blago until sunrise."

Marai went white as a ghost. "I'm not your *whore.*"

"You think you have a choice?" Cavar grasped his amulet, and sent his iron will into the stone.

She is my puppet. She will do whatever I say.

The swirling magic was all too willing to comply. *"As you wish,"* it crooned, a smile to its voice.

Marai went rigid under the stone's influence. Magic cocooned around her in a smoky haze as Cavar strained, pushing his will harder than he ever had before. There could be no mistakes.

"You will be silent unless he craves a sound from you. *Moan.*"

The sound of pleasure was ripped from Marai's throat. It seemed wrong coming from her frozen mask of horror.

"You will let him touch you any place he chooses, and use you however he'd like."

Magic pushed Marai backwards into the wall. Cavar commanded her to raise one arm, then the other, as if in bondage.

"You won't fight back, and you'll do as he says. The collar will ensure it."

"Yes, yes!" The stone's voice grew louder in Cavar's head.

When Cavar released her, Marai stumbled forward, cheeks blazing, fury contorting her face. "I will not be sold! I won't let some perverted swine *touch* me—"

"Oh, he'll do more than touch you, Your Grace. He will command you. All Blago has to do is say a word, and your collar will react."

The Faerie Queen swayed where she stood, a sickly fog coming over her. Her anger was palpable in the static raising the hair on the back of Cavar's neck, but he enjoyed her expression of dawning realization that there was nothing she could do to stop the event from happening. She was powerless.

QUEEN OF THE SHADOW MENAGERIE

"If he enjoys you, then you'll do it again on his next visit," continued Cavar, "and for anyone else who wishes to pay."

"I'd rather die," Marai snarled, clinging to the infinitesimal threads of control she thought she had left.

Cavar pinned her with his cool gaze. "I won't *let* you die. You and I will continue this dance for decades, Marai. We have all the time in the world."

"She's ours forever," the voice said.

Marai swallowed, her expression a canvas of terror.

Cavar pulled on his coat and adjusted his hat. "You're excused."

Koda shoved Marai out the door, and she put up no protest.

"Are you sure this is wise, Governor?" asked Koda once the door was closed again. "After the amulet incident, and all . . ."

"What's the worst thing she can do? She cannot overpower the collar, which I've programmed to force her submission. She won't be able to move unless Blago makes her. She won't be able to speak unless he asks. From now on, we can command her with a mere word. If she begins to rebel, the collar will stop her. I've taken away her free-will."

"Forgive me, Governor, but why didn't you remove her free-will before? Could have saved us a lot of hassle—"

"Every day I discover more of the stone's true potential. A decent scientist always performs several trials of an experiment. I tried the commands on Anja earlier today."

Koda didn't appear convinced. He shifted on his feet, mouth twisted in doubt.

"You need to stop fearing her," Cavar told his assistant. "You cannot let Marai think she has control, because she *doesn't*. Stop treating her like she's some explosive weapon."

Koda dipped his head. "Of course, Governor. I merely want to be cautious, is all. I'd hate to see anything tarnish the Menagerie's, or your reputation."

Cavar smirked. "Nothing will, because nothing can compete with the stone. Now, I'm off for Bakair. Don't bother me unless it's something truly important. I'm sure Blago will let me know if he's pleased."

"When will you be back again, sir?"

"I hope not for several weeks. The security of the Menagerie is in your hands. I expect perfection, Koda, or I'll put one of those collars on *you*."

His fae assistant swallowed, then placed a hand to his heart. "You can count on me, Governor."

CHAPTER 21

RUENEN

Nosficio stood in Ruenen's guest room in the Glacial Palace, leaning casually against the fireplace mantel. He took his time removing his gloves, finger by finger, and then his cloak. He hadn't bothered to clean the black blood from his face, and other than those specks upon his gray skin, he looked immaculate. No dirt, no windswept hair. Ruenen had rarely seen the vampire in a state of dishevelment.

"Are you going to speak or stand there all night?" asked Nieve with a huff. She sat, stiff-backed, in a poofy armchair nearest the fire. But Ruenen wasn't fooled—her eyes raked over Nosficio with something primal glinting in her ice-blue eyes. "I'm abandoning my husband's funeral banquet for this."

Raife, Aresti, and Tarik had been fetched by Mayestral from the great hall. They stood behind the couch where Ruenen was seated, waiting to hear what the vampire had discovered.

Nosficio folded his arms over his chest. "I've had a long day, Your Grace. I'm merely gathering my strength."

Ruenen rolled his eyes. Nosficio had a flair for the dramatics.

"Where did the blood come from?" asked Aresti.

Nosficio tossed a few roped dreadlocks behind his shoulder. "You should be thanking me. I encountered a shadow creature outside the city limits." He looked at Ruenen. "It was following your trail. Closely. If I hadn't killed it, you might be dead now."

Fuck. Ruenen glanced at Raife and Aresti. That made three shadow creatures targeting him. Ruenen had no idea that they were so organized . . . which got him wondering if someone was perhaps controlling them. *But who?*

"Please, Lord Nosficio, we're desperate," said Raife, his face a storm of emotion. "Whatever you've learned about Marai and Keshel's disappearance, we must hear it now."

Nosficio's eyes narrowed briefly, irritated by the demand. "There are networks across this continent, as your Master of Spies is well aware of, Your Grace." He jutted his chin out at Nieve. "I've been hunting them down, hoping to link anyone to our Faerie Queen's disappearance. I was directed to the port city of Cleaving Tides. You see, there's a part of the story that has never quite clicked for me. Months ago, the werewolves met a faerie male on the road, traveling to Nevandia, who up and vanished with the wind upon arrival in the Middle Kingdoms."

"You already asked me about him before you left," said Tarik. "He said he didn't want to participate in a battle, and left us outside the Nevandian army encampment."

"But hadn't he been interested in the other fae?" Nosficio pressed.

Tarik nodded vigorously. "Oh, quite surely. Said he was looking forward to meeting them."

"Then why did he vanish?" asked Nosficio, standing up straighter. "You said you met him in Ain. Why go all the way to Nevandia? That's a long way to travel and then decide not to at least introduce himself to the fae." Nosficio's eyebrows were high on his forehead as he regarded Tarik. "The description you gave me was that of a handsome, lean, brown-skinned male with black hair, pointed ears, and unusually bright silver eyes."

"What's your point, exactly?" asked Aresti, putting her hands on her hips.

"It appears that very same male was seen in Cleaving Tides, about four months ago."

Wind rushed from Ruenen's lungs, as if he'd been punched in the gut.

"Isn't that right around the same time you and Marai were dallying on that pirate ship?" Nosficio asked him.

Dallying? Ruenen scowled. They'd been kidnapped by Slate. It certainly hadn't been a pleasure cruise.

Tarik's physical description of the fae male could have fit hundreds on Astye, but no one had silver eyes like the man who'd rescued Ruenen from Rayghast's bounty hunters. His eyes were memorable—molten silver, almost as if they were alive with starlight. Or *magic*.

"I've met this male before, on the docks after Marai used her portal to return to the Badlands," said Ruenen, brows knit with thought.

After she'd run away in terror, haunted by Slate Hemming's toxic touch. Ruenen was left to the mercy of the hunters, but before he'd been dragged away, the faerie male appeared and helped Ruenen escape their clutches. At the time, he'd thought the stranger was merely being generous, but now Ruenen doubted his intentions.

Had the male helped him because of Marai? Because he knew Ruenen would eventually lead him back to her?

"So he has a connection to Marai," Aresti said, biting on her thumb fingernail.

"I don't know if Marai met him before, but he was there on the docks. He probably saw her and guessed she was fae," said Ruenen. The male probably saw her open the portal.

"Apparently, this stranger had been searching for a few new crew members to sail to Andara, but no one wanted the job, despite the large amount of money offered for such employment," Nosficio continued. "His ship, he told the sailors, was anchored in another port. The only ship that sails to and from Andara leaves from—"

"Baatgai," Tarik cut in, eyes wide. "In Syoto."

"Why Baatgai? Why not somewhere in Varana or Grelta further north?" asked Raife.

"No one sails out of Grelta," Nieve said. "Our waters are too treacherous, and eastern beaches too rocky and inclined. The few ports we have are for local travel only."

"I've heard of that ship," said Tarik. "We would occasionally bring coal up from Ain to Baatgai to send off to Yehzig. That ship regularly sails there, and would sometimes carry our quarry to Yehzig, what with Baatgai being the closest port to Qasnal."

"When the faerie was traveling with you, did he mention Marai?" Raife asked the werewolf.

"He did, now that you mention it," said Tarik. "Talked non-stop about some blonde faerie girl he'd met, and knew she'd made her way to Nevandia. He seemed lonely and excited, so I didn't judge or think anything weird about it."

"What was his name?" asked Aresti.

"Koda."

Nosficio had smelled a strange magic in the courtyard the night Marai and Keshel were taken. Koda, another faerie, was the only plausible explanation.

"If he indeed kidnapped Lady Marai and Lord Keshel, where did he take them? To his ship in Baatgai?" asked Nieve.

"*Queen* Marai, I think you mean," Nosficio said pointedly at Nieve, "and yes, I believe so. My guess is that he forced Marai to open her portal. He wouldn't have been able to get far on foot or horseback with two captives."

Ruenen stood and began to pace. His pulse ratcheted up. None of the search teams, including Braesal's, had gone to Baatgai. Ruenen had foolishly overlooked the port. "Did you go there? Baatgai?"

The vampire's eyes tracked Ruenen's steps, back and forth across the rug. "Not yet. I meant to go straight there after I spoke to the sailors, but I heard . . ." Nosficio's tone changed. He softened, eyes only for Nieve. "I heard about King Maes' death, so instead, I rushed here."

Nieve and Nosficio stared at one another, as if there was no one else in the room. A spark traveled in the air between them, so potent that it made Ruenen's arm hair stand on end.

"Why would another faerie kidnap his own kind?" asked Raife, running a hand through his curls and breaking their connection.

"Rival clans?" posed Tarik. "That happens with werewolf packs. Sometimes, we'll take females from other packs to help diversify the population of our own. We'll even take the children of strong warriors."

"That's terrible," Aresti said, nose scrunching up in disgust. "Sounds like Rayghast and Tacorn."

"My people wouldn't have to do such things for survival if we were treated as *real people* on this continent . . ." said Tarik with a dangerous edge.

"I don't think there are any faerie clans," Raife said. "We didn't even know others survived the massacres, but then Braesal's group showed up, so clearly we didn't know anything at all."

"A vendetta?" Nieve offered with a shrug. "Jealousy? Power? Why does anyone attack another? Sometimes, there's no rhyme or reason for villainy. Sometimes, people merely want the world to burn."

"And what about Andara? Why take them there?" Raife asked. "Marai mentioned it once to us a while ago, before we left Ehle, as a place we might be able to settle should we want to leave Astye. But she didn't seem to know much about it, either."

"No one does," added Nieve.

"When I first met Marai, I hired her to get me to Cleaving Tides so I could board a boat to Andara," Ruenen said.

"But boats to Andara don't sail from Cleaving Tides—" began Tarik.

"I know that *now,*" Ruenen said in exasperation, "but at the time I was working with faulty information."

Slate Hemming had told Ruenen he'd give him passage to Andara on his ship. He'd lied, and actually kidnapped Ruenen with the intention of selling him to Rayghast for the bounty on his head.

Why did everything always come back to Andara? It was as if the mysterious country was pulling Ruenen there, through its own form of magic. He couldn't remember when and how the idea of going to Andara had popped into his brain, but from the first moment he'd thought of it, the idea propelled him forward. Straight into his fated meeting with Marai.

Fate wanted me to meet Marai. It wanted her to go to Andara. This thought sent a chill up Ruenen's spine.

"Have you been there?" he asked the ancient vampire. "Andara?"

Nosficio was as old as Marai's fae relatives, Queen Meallán and King Aras. Surely, in his many centuries alive, he'd traveled to Andara.

"Vampires don't cross oceans."

"Not a good swimmer?" Ruenen cocked an eyebrow. He and Nosficio had never gotten along. The only reason the vampire hadn't killed Ruenen yet was probably due to his loyalty to Marai. But that didn't mean Ruenen wouldn't still poke and prod.

Nosficio glowered back at him. "Would you want to be trapped onboard a ship for an extensive journey with a vampire? I cannot travel over water, Precious King, because I'll devour everyone on board. Then who would sail the ship? I've never left Astye, but I've heard whispers for years about Andara. Secrets. Hidden magic." His crimson eyes flashed. "*Other* creatures."

Thanks to Nosficio, they had a solid lead. Hope swirled within Ruenen. He could barely keep his heart contained within his chest. There was no time to waste.

"We should leave for Baatgai immediately," he stated.

I'm coming, Marai. Hold on a little while longer.

"Slow down, Your Graceless," Nosficio said. "Let's say your Witan lets you go on this voyage, that you get to Baatgai and survive the treacherous waters to Andara. What will you do when you get there? We know nothing about that country. How large it is, its cities, its inhabitants. We wouldn't know the first place to start looking for our favorite little queen."

Ruenen clenched his fists. "But at least we'd be there. At least, I would finally be on the same soil as her."

"Use your brain, not your heart," snapped Nosficio. "It would be suicide to sail there without knowing what awaits you. Koda obviously has strong magical abilities to kidnap both Marai and Keshel, and I doubt he was acting alone. Maybe not another faerie, but he said he had a whole crew of sailors."

Raife's hand appeared on Ruenen's shoulder, forcing Ruenen to look at him. "I know you want to run off and find Marai and Keshel—trust me, so do I—but we need to be smart about this. We need to gather more intel."

Ruenen shrugged him off, retracing his path on the rug again. Blood rushed in his ears, concern gripped his stomach. "What if Marai doesn't *have* time? We don't know why they took her and Keshel. The longer we delay, the more danger they're in. I have to find her. I'll have no peace until I bring her home!"

Nieve got to her feet in one smooth movement. She walked to Ruenen and took hold of his restless hands. "Stay through tomorrow night. Breathe. Make a plan. You've already traveled a long way, and your people and horses need rest. But you must leave for home soon. I only wish I had a ship and a crew to assist you in this endeavor. All I know about Andara is that it's a place you don't go to. It's far too dangerous to cross the Northern Sea, even now in the calm season."

"Agreed," said Aresti. "We can't run off to Baatgai without a plan. Let's get some rest and return to Nevandia. From there, we can gather our people and *all of us* can go find Marai and Keshel."

Ruenen didn't want to wait. He wanted to dive head first into the Northern Sea and swim until he reached Marai.

Nieve placed a hand against his cheek. "All will be well, Ruenen. You'll be with her again soon enough. Forgive me, but I must return to the feast below. I've been gone far too long, and my guests will be wondering where I am. I hope you'll come back downstairs, Ruenen. You've hardly touched food all day, and the festivities may take your mind off of Marai." Nieve made for the door, but her hand froze on the handle. "Although, later tonight, I will not be opposed to some company."

Her piercing gaze landed on Nosficio, then Aresti, then Tarik. She exited; silks swishing at her ankles as she disappeared from sight.

Tarik grinned, clearly eager to please his new friend, the Queen of Grelta. Aresti pretended like Nieve's comment didn't affect her, but Nosficio eyed both her and Tarik jealously.

I guess the vampire doesn't like sharing, Ruenen thought sardonically.

"I must depart, as well," Nosficio said curtly, and raised the hood of his cloak. He stepped towards a window, unlatching the lock. "If you need me, I'll be enjoying a private dinner. The Queen forbids me from feasting on Lirrstrassian cuisine, so I must find sustenance elsewhere." With a departing fanged sneer, he disappeared through the window and out into the night.

"You should return to the celebrations," Raife said to Ruenen. "The Queen's right—a distraction would do you well. Then you should get some sleep."

Ruenen continued to pace. "How can I possibly sleep?"

His body felt as if he'd been electrocuted by Marai's lightning; every part of him tingled with apprehension, his blood spiked with adrenaline. Ruenen was alive and awake in ways he hadn't been for weeks. He couldn't stop moving, could barely think straight.

"How can I lie there in bed, and wait, when we're so close to finding her?" he asked Raife, Aresti, and Tarik. He looked imploringly at Mayestral, a ghostly shape in the corner of the room, who'd listened to every word spoken that evening. Ruenen had forgotten he was there.

"You're closer, Your Grace, but I think you still have far too many unanswered questions," said the Groom, stepping forward onto the rug. "I can get you a sleeping draft to help you rest."

"No," Ruenen said, "I don't intend to rest until we have those answers, until we have a plan and I'm on a ship headed to Andara."

Aresti's dark eyes glinted in the firelight, the flames casting severe shadows across her face. "Oh, we'll get those answers, and when we do, nothing will stop us from rescuing Keshel and Marai." Her beautiful face contorted into mirthless rage. "And we'll kill *everyone* who had a hand in this."

CHAPTER 22

MARAI

*W*alls up, shields up.
     Endure.

Marai stepped out of Cavar's office and tried not to spill the meager contents of her stomach all over the hallway. She considered clawing her hair out, gouging her face with her fingernails, if it made her less appealing. The thought of a strange man's hands touching her, *penetrating her* in any way, was a nightmare revisited from her time with Slate.

Acacia appeared at the bottom of the stairs. "What are you standing there for? Don't you have somewhere to be?" She clasped her amulet, reminding Marai that with a mere word, Acacia could force her to do anything, or prevent her from inflicting such bodily harm to herself.

Cavar wanted Marai to feel small and insignificant, and he knew exactly how to do that: take away her freedom, her power, her fight, and now her bodily autonomy. She'd be a slave in every way possible. Cavar intended to rip away her soul, piece by piece, until there was nothing left of Marai. Until she was a hollow ghost.

She wordlessly obeyed Acacia, taking her place backstage, fretting about the horror that awaited her after her performance. Koda and Acacia hovered, studying her for signs of rebellion. Marai stepped onto the stage, beneath the flickering candlelight, hearing the boisterous awe of the crowd and Arcturius' inane prattle, as if from very far away.

The man who'd paid for a night with her was sitting somewhere in those seats. Sitting and anticipating the ways he'd devour her. Marai knew he wouldn't be kind or gentle. He wouldn't be understanding. She was his for the whole night, this stranger who had laid claim to her.

A cold, numb smog settled over Marai's mind as her puppet-body moved.

Don't feel.

She'd been so close to freedom, with the amulet in her grasp. So close, she'd practically heard Ruenen calling her from across the sea. And because she'd hoped, she'd let herself imagine. Like a fool, Marai imagined the moment when she'd finally encircle her arms around his neck. Run her fingers through his soft, chestnut hair. Gaze into those beautiful, warm brown eyes and count the golden flecks.

It hurt to have those images ripped from her, leaving behind nothing but a ragged, gaping hole she was desperate to fill with the entirety of him. As if she'd lost Ruenen all over again. Was there any hope in getting back to him?

Slate had left terrible wounds on her soul, ones that had taken years to heal. What wouldn't the Menagerie take from her, and what scars would she gain? Each day, parts of herself shriveled away and died. Would Ruenen want her anymore if other men had her?

Perhaps Innesh was stronger than her, because Marai's erected walls and shields crumbled, scattering debris across her heart, the more she thought of Ruenen. There, on that stage, she couldn't stop herself from feeling. A bevy of emotions and pain rushed through her, swelling inside like the cresting of a wave.

If only I could see him one last time.

Overcome, Marai closed her eyes to hold back the tears.

Strange.

She'd never been able to voluntarily move, not a blink, while the collar had control. Perhaps she would have pondered it more seriously if she wasn't drifting off, dreaming upon more pleasant things.

A dull, fizzy sensation tickled her neck, but she took no notice as the world slipped away beneath her feet. Marai swam through puffy, golden clouds. Past rivers of glistening stars. She parted gauzy curtains of burnished light, and there he was.

This conjured image of Ruenen sat on the edge of a bed in a room she didn't recognize. His head hung into his hands, his knees bounced anxiously, and

Marai's heart clenched. Why did this dream version of him look so defeated? She'd wanted the radiance of his smile. The sound of rolling laughter from his chest. His soulful voice as he sung to her.

"Ruen," she whispered, hoping the mirage would change.

And it did.

He froze. Her fae ears captured his stuttering breath. Slowly, Ruenen raised his head.

His whole face changed as he looked at her. He *saw* her, and Marai's heart sprinted.

"Marai?"

She smiled at the sound of breathless longing in his voice, as if her name itself were magic. She drank in the sight of him as he got to his feet. He looked weary, strained, and pale, but his shoulders were broader, his arms more muscular. He wasn't wearing his crown. His eyes shimmered with a fervor Marai knew was reflected in her own.

How did one speak to people in dreams?

"Hello," she said, and cursed her awkwardness. *Even in my own hallucinations I'm hopeless.*

"Are you . . . real?" Ruenen asked, and the hope in his expression was a tangible thing. "Or am I going insane?"

Marai glanced downwards at herself. Nothing had changed since she'd closed her eyes. She was wearing the same flowing dress, another of Acacia's designs. Her hair cascaded loosely down her back, past her watercolor wings. "As real as someone can be in a dream, I suppose."

But this dream-Ruenen wasn't embracing her. He rubbed his eyes, then stared at her like she was an apparition. His eyes traveled from her face, to her pointed ears, to her wings.

She wanted nothing more than to touch him, so Marai offered Ruenen a hand. "Come. Dance with me."

At that, Ruenen's mouth twitched. "This must surely be a dream, because the Marai I know wouldn't voluntarily dance with anyone."

Her smile widened. "Or say please, but here we are."

Ruenen closed the distance between them, reaching for her hand. His fingers passed right through her own, as if she truly was a ghost.

But again, it was strange—she could feel his warmth. His breath on her skin. A light, subtle sensation at her hip indicated that he'd placed one hand there.

Marai's free hand grazed the length of his corded arm. Ruenen shivered.

"I can almost feel you," he said into her ear. "Gods, how I've longed for you, Marai."

She closed her eyes again, leaning into the slight warmth. Even if she couldn't touch him, they could pretend. They could dream.

Their feet tread the steps along the rug. Marai remembered that dance at the coronation, and she could still hear the melody. Their bodies flush together, they swayed.

This is all I need. I could die here. I hope I do. Ruenen made it so easy to fall further into the dream. Marai wanted to cling to this moment for as long as she could.

"Dream-you has wings?" Ruenen asked, amusement in his tone.

"Real-me does, too."

Ruenen stopped swaying. "What do you mean?"

"It's a long story, one that you should already know, since this is *my* hallucination. Now, dance again before this disappears and I wake up."

"Marai, where are you?" Ruenen asked, brows furrowed.

"I'm right here."

Why was dream-Ruenen being so serious? His forehead touched her own, or would have if he hadn't been a mirage, but she still felt the tiniest connection. A spark.

"I've been searching for you. I haven't given up. I never will until you're home safe." His voice took on an aching desperation. "Where did Koda take you?"

"I don't want to talk about Koda. This is supposed to be a happy dream."

Ruenen bit his lower lip, then shook his head. "I don't think this is a dream."

There was a distant sound, like the roar of a crowd. Marai felt a tug on her shoulders. Something itched at her neck. No, not itched . . . prickled.

I'm not ready to leave yet.

"Your Grace," came a new voice. One from within the dream.

QUEEN OF THE SHADOW MENAGERIE

Ruenen's head snapped up, looking into the foggy world behind Marai.

"The Queen is waiting for you to return to the celebrations," continued the voice.

The Queen. Marai's stomach plummeted. The warmth she'd gathered drained away, and the dream began to crumble.

"I'll be with her in a moment," Ruenen said impatiently to the voice, eyes not leaving Marai's face.

This dream-Ruenen had married another? *This is supposed to be happy. An escape.* Why was her mind ruining this moment? Marai's eyes stung with unshed tears.

The tugging on her body became stronger. The yelling louder. Cracks began to appear at the corners of the dream, like ice breaking on a frozen lake.

"What's happening?" Ruenen asked her, growing immediately tense. He hadn't let go of Marai, his hand hovering in her own.

Someone wrenched Marai out of the dream. It felt like falling from a high cliff. Disorientating. Head-spinning.

Suddenly, the world was dark, and loud, and chaotic. Marai blinked rapidly, trying to focus, to come back to reality. She felt her feet on the solid ground, then the spark of the collar traveled up her spine. Lightly, at first, but grew stronger with each passing second.

Ruenen remained there with her, a hazy specter in the middle of the Menagerie stage. Her mind must have still been partially in the dream.

The audience was shrieking, barreling out of their seats. Peace Keepers ushered them from the amphitheater, swords drawn. Where was the danger?

Marai's body seized as the collar's punishing electrocution took over. She collapsed on all fours, and Ruenen screamed her name.

"We apologize for the disruption," Arcturius said, but his usually confident voice wavered as he wrung his gloved hands. Sweat dripped down his face, black kohl streaking the white paint. "We promise that this will be fixed for tomorrow night. Come back and see us again!"

Yelich's enormous hands hefted Marai to her feet, and dragged her offstage, away from Ruenen's mirage. She guessed then what had occurred, although it was hard to believe.

Marai had stopped moving.

The collar had lost its control on her while she'd daydreamed. Impossible, and yet, it was the only explanation. Somehow, for a few moments, Marai had gained control of her body.

Dream-Ruenen stood in the middle of the stage, whirling around, taking in the amphitheater with wild, terrified eyes. "Marai, where are we?"

Don't leave me, Ruen, she wanted to say. *Don't let them take me to the back room. Don't let that man touch me!*

But she couldn't speak. The collar's electrocution had fried her voice.

Koda appeared, marching like a man on a mission, and struck her in the face. A muscle jumped in his jaw as he stared, bug-eyed, at her. He struck her again, on the other cheek. He then whipped out the little box of metallic powder, and blew some in Marai's face.

Ruenen yelled again, but his outline grew dimmer. The dream was disappearing as she began to lose consciousness. She reached out one hand to him. *Stay!*

Her hand and body went limp in Yelich's arms. Koda locked manacles around Marai's ankles, and then snapped a set of them around her wrists.

"What the fuck did you do?" he demanded.

"I was daydreaming," she replied sluggishly. Her vocal cords hurt.

Ruenen called her name again and again, reaching for her. He was barely visible now. She gave him one final smile as her vision darkened. Her head drooped onto her chest.

Then, all went black.

Marai woke up to darkness. In fact, she wasn't sure if she was truly awake when her eyelids first fluttered open, but the total, oppressive obsidian could only mean one thing—she was back in the metal box.

She'd been stuffed in there, unconscious, for gods-knew how long. Her stomach rumbled. Her throat was dry and scratchy from dehydration. Her wings had been crushed beneath her, stuck in that uncomfortable position for hours.

QUEEN OF THE SHADOW MENAGERIE

She'd grown used to this box. To the complete, void-like blackness of its interior. To its stark silence.

How, *how,* had she gained control? It hadn't been a long period of time, but Marai had somehow overpowered the collar's programming without even trying. Had it been more than a daydream?

Ruen didn't think it was a dream.

He'd looked so shocked, so frightened. Why would her mind play such tricks on her?

But if it *was* real, she'd somehow *traveled* to Ruenen's room.

Was it because I was missing him? Because I wanted to see him that badly?

None of it made sense.

And then something wormed its way into her mind. A seed of heartbreak implanted itself there.

If it *was* real, then Ruenen had married his Queen. Holfast and the Witan had swiftly married him off to whomever they saw most fit. It was never going to be Marai. Even if she wasn't trapped in a metal box on Andara, Ruenen was always going to marry a proper, human woman. Someone flawlessly beautiful and well-mannered, whose father was either a lord or a king.

Marai released a sob as a deluge of tears rushed down her cheeks.

Because she realized something in that darkness, and it tore her in two, trampling her hope.

She wasn't going to leave Andara.

The Menagerie was her only future.

CHAPTER 23

RUENEN

What in Lirr's Bloody Bones happened?

Ruenen marched back and forth across his guest room in the Glacial Palace, dragging hands through his already rumpled hair and the stubble on his jaw. His mind roared, pulse stampeding a wild beat as panic consumed him, remembering what he'd seen.

Was that real?

The vision, dream, whatever it was, dissolved right as those enormous men dragged Marai, unconscious, away. Something had made her seize from unseen magic, as if her own lightning was being used against her. Ruenen had tried to go after her. He'd tried punching a guard, but his fist had gone straight through the man's head. He'd been confined to the limitations of the dream, forced to watch, and then disappear when it ended.

And Koda was there. Koda, her abductor. Ruenen seethed, remembering how the male had struck Marai.

The bones of her sternum and wrists were too prominent, and the hollowness of her cheeks caused Ruenen physical pain. She was still beautiful, of course, with her unusual, ethereal allure, but that new-Marai was beautiful in a delicate, almost paper-thin way. As if one gust of wind could snap her bones. And she had *wings*.

Ruenen's mind spiraled. He had to help her. Now. *How* could he help her?

He couldn't catch his breath. He gulped down air, chest heaving, heart fighting within. His hands shook uncontrollably. As his vision blurred, he felt like he might pass out.

"Your Grace, is something wrong?" Mayestral appeared in the door, rushing to Ruenen's side. He took Ruenen's shaking hand in his own. "Are you ill? You're very pale. Shall I fetch a healer?"

Ruenen removed his hand from Mayestral's. "I saw her. Marai. She was here. And then I was there!"

A crease formed above the Groom's nose. Then he said gently, "I'm not sure I understand, Your Grace, but you seem distraught. Perhaps you should sit down for a moment?" He tried to guide Ruenen over to the armchair.

"You didn't see her? She was standing right here, on this very rug." Ruenen refused to budge, his voice getting higher and more strained with each word. "And then I saw . . . I don't know *what* I saw, but I think I know where she is now."

"I didn't see anyone in here except you, Sire." Mayestral's expression grew concerned, as if he worried that his King had suddenly gone insane.

Maybe I have. Maybe none of that was real, and it was a figment of my imagination.

No. He'd been wide awake. Not even slightly drowsy.

He'd felt her. Maybe he hadn't been able to touch her, but Ruenen had sensed that spark in the air that only Marai exuded. The building he'd been transported to, a theater of some kind . . . he could never have imagined that space. It looked nothing like any place he'd been. Ruenen knew, with every fiber of his being, that Marai had truly visited him.

"Perhaps some water?" Mayestral suggested with enthusiasm, walking to the pitcher on the table.

"Go find Raife and Aresti, and Nosficio, too," he ordered to his Groom. "And send Queen Nieve my apologies—I cannot return to the festivities because I've had news of Lady Marai."

Mayestral opened his mouth, then held back the comment. He gave Ruenen that confused, concerned look as he bowed low and exited the room. The double doors closed behind him with a *thud*.

Once again alone, Ruenen closed his eyes. He'd never been good at clearing his mind, but like a sieve, everything except thoughts of Marai emptied from his brain. He settled, hoping to reestablish the connection through space and time.

Marai, I'm here. I'm listening. Please, come back, my love!

But she didn't reappear. Ruenen must have stood there for a while because eventually, a knock came at the door, startling him. Ruenen wrenched it open to reveal Aresti and Raife; Mayestral hovered behind them, fidgeting with his tunic.

"What's going on? I thought you were going to meet us down in the great hall?" asked Raife.

Ruenen stepped back to let them in, then closed the door.

Aresti arched a skeptical eyebrow at him. "Mayestral said you had a hallucination about Marai?"

"It wasn't a hallucination," Ruenen replied. "I saw—"

"This had better be important."

While Ruenen's back had been turned, the vampire had snuck in through his window without a sound. Nosficio sat on the window ledge, one leg crossed over the other, posture erect and regal.

"I was enjoying the company of a young fop in the castle gardens," Nosficio continued, glancing at his talon-like fingernails. He'd cleaned the black ichor off his face.

"I thought Nieve has rules about you drinking blood in Lirrstrass," Aresti said with a glare.

"She does, but the boy was quite willing, and he tasted divine." Nosficio smirked back at her. "Besides, the Queen was otherwise engaged and not paying any attention to *me.*"

His eyes sparked with jealousy. Not at Aresti, however. Nieve must have been flirting with Tarik, and Nosficio decided to take out his annoyance in a way that he knew would grab Nieve's attention.

Ruenen had no time for that petty nonsense tonight. "Marai visited me. Here, in this room."

The silence in response was saturated with doubt. Nosficio looked like he might burst out laughing, while Raife and Aresti merely blinked at him. Mayestral pouted in the corner.

Yes, he definitely thinks I've lost my mind.

"While you were napping?" asked Aresti.

"I wasn't sleeping, or dreaming," said Ruenen. "She was here, a spectral blurry version of herself, with wings and pointed ears, as if she'd suddenly become *more fae,* if that's possible. She asked me to dance, and I could *feel* warmth from her, but I couldn't touch her—"

"Sounds like you nodded off, Your Graceless," Nosficio said with an impatient wave of his hand. He made for the window, brushing dreadlocks away from his face. "I'm sure you pleasured yourself to her image most enthusiastically—"

"Fucking *listen* to me," Ruenen roared.

For the first time, Nosficio was utterly speechless as he spun back around, mouth ajar as if scandalized. He glared at Ruenen; a muscle in his jaw feathered. Mayestral flinched at Ruenen's yell, lowering his head as if his King admonished him. Aresti and Raife exchanged silent glances. Ruenen didn't typically raise his voice at anyone, especially the four people in the room with him, and his outburst had filled the room with more unease.

Ruenen schooled his features into a mask of calm. "I'm not crazy. I'm not imagining the things I want to see. Marai was standing right here, and she's being treated like an animal over there, and she's so frail. If you'd seen her, you'd be terrified, too. You wouldn't be able to calm down, either."

He was so genuinely scared for her that Ruenen didn't know if he could hold himself together much longer. The threads of his control were coming loose, strand by strand, unraveling.

Nosficio stepped further into the room, standing where Marai's image had been. His nostrils flared, pupils dilated. He sniffed twice.

"It's peculiar, and very subtle, but I think I . . . *smell* her," he finally said. "A summer storm."

Aresti blanched. "How did she . . . did she make a portal?"

"I didn't see one. I don't think she was *really* here," said Ruenen. "I'm fully aware of how absurd this sounds, but it was as if her soul traveled to visit mine. Her body was elsewhere. In that place."

"Can fae do that?" Raife asked Nosficio.

"Don't look at me, boy," the vampire said with a shrug. "I'm not an expert on faeries. *However* . . ." Nosficio now had everyone's rapt attention. "Maybe Marai is more like Meallán than I originally suspected."

"Explain," Ruenen demanded, patience for the vampire's secrecy running low.

"Meallán could dream-speak."

"Which is . . . ?" asked Aresti.

"She could communicate with others by either visiting them in their dreams, or in their subconscious. Meallán dream-spoke to me several times. She'd appear like an apparition, as if she were present, but not truly whole." The vampire's face darkened, his red eyes drifting into some far-off thought. "She did it the day of the first human rebellion . . . to let me know that Aras had been killed."

Ruenen often forgot that Nosficio had a past. One that he rarely spoke about, but had been filled with love and pain, like any human being's. The vampire pretended he felt nothing, yet Ruenen sensed that Nosficio felt rather deeply and tried to cover up those emotions with his sexual and violent antics.

Nosficio's sorrow cleared. Back to business again. "I've never heard of another faerie who could dream-speak before. Meallán was an extraordinarily powerful Queen, so much so that Aras and I always joked that she'd been blessed by the gods. It's possible Marai inherited the ability to dream-speak from her, as well as Meallán's other gifts."

Raife scratched at his neck. "I've never heard of such a thing before, but I suppose, with Marai, anything is possible."

"When she visited me, she had this . . . collar around her neck," said Ruenen, "with a three-pronged symbol I've *seen* before painted on a wall in Rayghast's castle."

Aresti gasped. "The shadow creatures. Rayghast, and the symbol . . . do you think it's all connected?"

"To dark magic?" asked Raife, putting the pieces together, too. "You think someone else is using it?"

"It's possible." Aresti looked back to Ruenen for confirmation. "But it still doesn't help us figure out where Marai and Keshel are."

"I saw it," Ruenen stated. "I guess I got carried along with Marai, because I was transported somewhere else."

"Somewhere else?" Aresti repeated, eyes wide.

"She brought you into her world," Nosficio said, stroking his chin and nodding. "She gave you a glimpse of where they've been keeping her."

"Not intentionally," said Ruenen. "I don't think she was aware she was dream-speaking. Marai thought it was a hallucination, herself."

"Did you see Keshel there?" Aresti asked. She took a few steps closer to Ruenen, her face an open book of *want*.

"No, but I did see Koda." Ruenen recoiled again from the image of him striking Marai across the face, then shackling her like a prisoner. "He was exactly how I remembered him. The room was dark, a kind of circular, stone theater. It had a stage in front of a full audience of humans. And that metal collar did something to Marai. It hurt her. She seemed utterly powerless against it, and then Koda blew a dark powder into her face. A drug of some kind."

For a moment, all was quiet as everyone pondered Ruenen's vision. Aresti fiddled with the piercing in her bottom lip, and Mayestral continued to fidget away at his fingers and tunic near the door.

"You said it was a theater?" came Nosficio's voice, quiet and pensive, as he stared out the window into the dark sky. The cacophony of music, clapping, and laughter, meant the funeral celebrations were still in full swing below. "Go deeper into what you saw."

Ruenen bit the inside of his cheek as he tried to remember the details. It was difficult, everything had happened so fast, and had this blurry sheen to it. "The room was dark, mostly black stone. There were posters on the walls, and candles on the stage in a circle. Huge men in black clothing with white masks. One had a whip. Another had a long, curved knife at his belt. The audience was trying to get out of the building, rushing the doors. They looked frightened. Whatever Marai had done was a disruption. Possibly dangerous."

In the blink of an eye, Nosficio appeared at Ruenen's side. Ruenen jolted backwards, surprised by the sudden movement and having the vampire so close to his face.

"The posters . . . what did they say?" Nosficio pressed.

"I wasn't exactly close enough to read them, but they were written in a language I didn't recognize," explained Ruenen. "There were drawings on them. Of creatures. One of them looked like Marai."

Nosficio froze, crimson eyes widening. "Can you draw the symbol you saw on Marai's collar?"

"Do you know this place?" asked Ruenen, breathlessly searching for a piece of paper and quill. He sketched the three-pronged symbol and handed it to Nosficio.

The vampire's eyes devoured the image, then he began to pace, retracing Rue-nen's exact steps on the rug in slow, purposeful strides. "Over a decade ago, a vampiress disappeared. Her name was Desislava. We didn't run in the same circles, by any means, but I knew her vaguely. I'd see her from time to time at the Den."

The Den was a hidden town of criminals in the southern Greltan forest. Marai had taken Ruenen there once, although she'd called the town Iniquity. That's where they'd first met Nosficio, and Nieve's Master of Spies hired Marai to give the vampire a "message."

Since Nosficio was currently standing in Nieve's castle, and had been drinking blood from one of her subjects moments ago, that message clearly hadn't been properly received.

"Vampires disappear sometimes," he continued. "Some go underground, for one reason or another. Some are staked and killed. But Desislava was *taken*."

"Taken?" asked Raife, who'd sat down on the couch, dragging his hands through his sandy blond curls.

"Disappeared without a trace. There were rumors in the Den that she was kidnapped, but it's not easy to subdue a vampire, as you know." Nosficio's eyes flashed at Ruenen.

"Why would someone kidnap a vampire? Or two faeries, for that matter," questioned Aresti, crossing her arms. "It makes more sense for a human to simply kill them. They've certainly had no problem doing that in the past."

"I believe a werewolf was also mysteriously taken a few years back," Nosficio said. "No one knows by whom, or how, or where they go, but another vampire, Grimure, searched Desislava's last known location, and smelled magic in the air. He also found a ripped piece of paper with a drawing of a winged lion-creature on it. And this symbol. The words weren't written in the common tongue. After some questioning and research, Grimure learned it was advertising some sort of show on Andara."

"Do you think they're connected? Dark magic, and the disappearance of the vampire, werewolf, and then Marai and Keshel?" Raife asked Nosficio, getting to his feet.

"I think it's a very odd coincidence if they're not. I became curious about Andara after speaking with Grimure. It worried me. But such a show doesn't exist here on Astye, not even in the spy ring, so I stopped searching for it. I only heard it whispered about once on one particular dock."

Ruenen didn't need Nosficio to say the name. He already knew it.

Baatgai.

"We leave at first light," Ruenen said to Aresti and Raife. "Mayestral, alert the staff to pack tonight. We make haste for Baatgai."

Mayestral stammered, caught off guard, then hastened from the room as Ruenen began throwing his clothes into a trunk.

"We still don't know *where* Marai and Keshel are. If they're truly on Andara or Yehzig, or somewhere we've never heard of," said Raife, coming to Ruenen's side. "We'll need more information in order to find them. It would be a waste for us to go all the way to Andara and find out this show doesn't exist anymore."

Nosficio grabbed Ruenen's arm, halting him from his packing. His grip was a little too strong—his fingers squeezed Ruenen's muscle. "What happened to the bloodstone ring?"

Marai's ring, the one her ancestor Queen Meallán had cursed, a dark jasper stone speckled with red.

"I don't know. She wasn't wearing it the night of the coronation," Ruenen replied, shaking loose of Nosficio's grip. "Why?"

"Because a powerful magical item such as that might be useful," said the vampire. "All magic leaves traces."

"Marai told me that it called to her, on Hemming's ship. That's why she stole it in the first place."

"It's connected to her, for better or worse. I have a hunch that a ghost of our Faerie Queen's power lingers within the ring, and it will continue to call for her. I'm wondering if it's possible for us to use the ring to track her." Nosficio stepped back towards the window again. "Return to Kellesar. Find that ring, and get more men while you're at it. This won't be an easy rescue. You'll need all the magical manpower you can get. Besides, your Witan would be petrified if their King suddenly voyaged to Syoto without their knowing."

Ruenen didn't want to go to Kellesar and listen as Holfast told him dozens of reasons why he shouldn't go to Baatgai. He didn't want a single person to scold him, or prevent him, or proclaim he was wrong, or crazy, or emotional. Not for the first time, Ruenen wished for the freedom he'd once had as an anonymous bard.

"What will *you* be doing?" he asked the vampire.

"I, precious King, will travel ahead. There's much information I can gather from the sailors at the port in the meantime, and you'll require a ship, so I will also take it upon myself to secure both a vessel and a crew."

"Thank you, Nosficio," Ruenen said, and was surprised to hear himself say it. "I appreciate your efforts."

Nosficio also seemed surprised by the gratitude. He narrowed his eyes, as though suspicious of Ruenen's honesty. "I'm not doing it for you. I'm doing it for Meallán and Aras' heir. Put away those moony eyes and get ready to empty your pockets. We still have a long way to go."

With a dramatic sweep of his cloak, Nosficio leapt from the window and into the night.

"It would be nice to see him trip once," mused Ruenen dryly.

"Do you really think we can find them?" Raife asked. His emerald eyes pleaded for the answer, searching Ruenen's own. The same burning hope in Raife's face was now reigniting within Ruenen, himself.

They had more than a lead now. They had something tangible. And the world seemed brighter, more beautiful than it had for months. Even the night sky itself glistened with possibility as a million stars winked in the distance. A melody stirred within Ruenen's chest, and for the first time since Marai had vanished, his fingers yearned to touch the strings of his lute.

Ruenen's heart slowed to its normal rhythm. A resolute calm filled him. "Absolutely."

A smile broke across Raife's freckled face, a smile Ruenen shared. Gods, none of them had had much to smile about for a while. Ruenen was relieved to feel it stretching across his lips, to see it on the face of his friend.

"Hate to break up this tender moment, but may I remind you that the hard part will be *getting* to them," added Aresti with a cynical frown.

"Then we'd better get started," said Ruenen. His steps were lighter with new-found confidence as he returned to packing.

Figures arrived at the door, interrupting him from his task again. None of them looked particularly pleased by Ruenen's actions.

"I heard that the King of Nevandia is readying to leave immediately. Right now? In the middle of the night?" Nieve asked, her piercing eyes accusatory.

Behind her, Wattling, Goso, and Nieve's second-in-command on the council waited with impatient expressions, crossed arms, and tapping toes.

"My apologies, Your Grace, it's not my intention to be rude, but I've had some very important news about Lady Marai and Lord Keshel, and we must be on our way at dawn," said Ruenen.

"What news could possibly be more important than finishing our diplomatic stay here?" asked Lord Wattling, whose face was turning redder by the moment. Based on his slurred words, it seemed he'd been partaking in a fair amount of wine. "We only arrived yesterday, and I've no desire to get back in that carriage so soon."

Ruenen told them everything, barely taking a breath the entire story. Nieve's face shifted from disappointment to genuine surprise. Wattling looked as if he'd swallowed something unpleasant, like a slug. Always the quiet, introspective one of the Witan, Goso scratched his head in confusion, though his brown eyes were round.

"I see," Nieve said once Ruenen finished. "I'll be sure my staff knows to ready your horses and carriages at first light. Everything will be prepared for your departure, including a light breakfast for the road."

"This is preposterous!" Wattling stomped his foot, reminding Ruenen very much of Lord Vorae, who was still governing Dul Tanen. Or an angry tomato. "Never, in all my years, have I heard such a ridiculous story. Back in Tacorn, none of us on the council would have—"

"Be careful what you say, Lord Wattling. You're speaking to your King," Nieve said with a warning edge, and fixed the lord with her piercing gaze. "A king, may I remind you, who won't torture you in his dungeon for speaking against him, the way your previous monarch would have. We know that you would *never* have gone against Rayghast's word, no matter how cruel or violent."

Wattling swelled up like a toad waiting to croak, but he slammed his lips together and said not a word more, glaring off down the hallway.

Returning her cool focus back to Ruenen, Nieve asked, "You're personally going after Marai and Keshel, then?"

"I'll entrust no one else to this task. It's time I stop making others do my work for me."

Nieve gave Ruenen one of her rare, genuine smiles. The kind that made her seem less like an imperial Queen and more like an ordinary woman. "How gallant you are. I suppose I feel a tad jealous. You would go to the ends of the earth and back to rescue your lady love."

"To be very fair, Marai has rescued me countless times. I think it's time I return the favor," Ruenen said with a smirk.

"Take five of my men with you for the voyage. Please, don't bother arguing, Your Grace. My mind is set. I'll worry for your safety the entire time, and I'll feel better knowing you have every protection possible. Ensure that both the Queen of the Fae and Lord Keshel come home safe and sound."

Wattling murmured "Queen of the Fae" under his breath, looking repulsed by such a thing.

Ruenen kissed Nieve's gloved hand. "You are a true friend, Your Grace, and the pinnacle of generosity and grace."

"Come now, stop your flattery or I shall blush," Nieve replied with a flirtatious wink. "Let me know the instant you've returned from your long journey. I'll be anxiously waiting, and I promise to pray that the winds are swift, waters calm, and any enemies you face will be easily disposed of. Oh, and I expect an invitation to the wedding."

Ruenen felt the color rising into his face. This only pleased Nieve more as she pinched his cheek with a laugh.

"Godsspeed," she said, then turned to the group of men behind her. "Come, gentlemen, let's return to dinner and enjoy more of that excellent wine. Servants will take care of your packing, not to worry. Lord Wattling?"

The cranky, red-faced lord shot Ruenen a frown, but held out his arm for the Queen. Nieve looped hers around his, and escorted him from the room, laughing falsely at something he muttered.

That seed of hope Ruenen had been nurturing, deep inside for months, sprouted. Curling vines and sturdy branches of faith shot through him, forming a towering tree, a pillar of unwavering confidence.

I'll see Marai soon.

He placed a steady hand on both Raife and Aresti's shoulders. They copied his move, the three of them conjoined, their arms as sturdy as tree branches.

Grinning, Ruenen said, "Let's go get our family back."

CHAPTER 24

CAVAR

Koda's message on the wind didn't catch up to Cavar until early morning, surrounded by waving fields of wheat and barley. Between the Menagerie and Bakair was nothing but sprawling farmland, dappled with the occasional sandstone cottage, but the entire province was under Cavar's jurisdiction.

He'd fallen asleep in his carriage, the curtains closed, and the message couldn't get in. He'd also, foolishly, removed his amulet, tucking it inside the lock-box with his coins and jewels, hidden beneath the seat. Cavar didn't take any risks with highway robbers who might snatch the amulet from around his neck while he slept.

If he'd been wearing it, he would have felt the amulet's scalding heat and the warning that accompanied it.

Cavar stepped foot outside the carriage in the pale dawn to stretch and relieve himself.

Koda's unwanted voice instantly assaulted him. *"Marai overpowered collar, but it remains attached and unbroken. Frightened everyone inside when she stopped listening to its commands. I subdued her and shut her within the crate. Night with Blago didn't happen. He's furious. Audience demanding refunds. Acacia frantic. Please return in all haste."*

Cavar couldn't believe his ears. It took a moment for the words to settle before he kicked at a rock in the road, spewing brown dust in the air. He released a raging snarl, setting his hat askew.

"Governor, sir?" asked the timid voice of the carriage driver.

QUEEN OF THE SHADOW MENAGERIE 271

Franulovic, the largest of Cavar's Peace Keepers, stared mutely at him, mouth slightly open, unsure what to do. There never was much happening in that pea-sized brain.

Cavar was halfway to Bakair where other urgent business awaited. He was Governor, for fuck's sake. He had to attend the monthly Meeting of the Ministers. There were hearings, and hours of other work ahead of him.

But behind him lay massive failure. A breach in his air-tight control. An event he never planned for, and couldn't imagine being true.

It was impossible for Marai to beat the collar and overpower Cavar. The stone had never failed him before. *Is its magic weakening?*

Cavar grasped his amulet. It warmed, black smoke writhing inside the stone. Magic leapt to his will, behaving as usual.

"It was a fluke. A glitch," the little voice said, but Cavar detected a bite of anger in its tone. A tinge of worry.

Perhaps the magic had weakened because Cavar had taken the amulet off for several hours . . .

Well, I certainly won't make that mistake again, he thought. The stone would never leave his neck, as long as Marai lived.

Cavar had to make a choice—turn back to the Menagerie, or go forward. Both choices left him weakened, open to accusations of negligence.

"Save your image," the voice said. *"Pretend everything is fine. Go about your schedule as if nothing is amiss."*

With another snarl, Cavar hastily penned a message for Acacia, instructing her to refund everyone with a complaint and allay their concerns about the Menagerie's safety. She was to state that the incident was a small, magical glitch while Cavar made "adjustments" to the collars. That would hopefully snuff out concern and suspicion.

As for Marai, Koda was to keep her locked away until Cavar's return.

He handed the letter to Franulovic. "Deliver into Acacia's hands, then return to me in Bakair."

Franulovic rode off in a cloud of brown dust, back towards the Menagerie.

Cavar would head to Bakair, attend to his meetings and work, and return to the Menagerie later in the week. Then he'd question Marai, and ensure such a catastrophe never happened again.

The Governor balled his hands into fists within his coat. *If she thinks she knows what suffering is, she's about to realize she has no idea.*

CHAPTER 25

RUENEN

Morning crawled across the sky with hesitant blue light, as if the sun didn't yet want to be awake, but was being hauled out of bed reluctantly. Robins and thrushes screeched out their morning greetings as Ruenen's caravan hurtled and jostled over the highland road into the city of Kellesar. They'd pressed hard to make it home from Grelta in less than two weeks, resting for no more than a couple hours in towns along the way.

Under the portcullis and into the castle courtyard, Ruenen didn't wait for the porter to open the door. He leapt from the carriage, spewing orders as he went into the castle. His retinue scrambled from their horses, trying to keep up with him. There was no time to waste, and much to do before he departed again.

Raife and Tarik were sent to gather Thora, Braesal, Brass, and Yovel, then to return to the castle as soon as possible. Mayestral and Aresti trailed at Ruenen's heels as he took the stairs two at a time, and headed straight to Marai's old room.

Ruenen hadn't been in here since the night before the coronation. He hadn't wanted to be reminded of those moments they'd shared in this very room. The sight of the bed brought memories surging back to him, so potent that he had to look away. He'd kissed Marai in that bed, touched her, worshiped her, confessed his love. Slept next to her in a peace so profound that he didn't think he'd sleep soundly again unless she was curled at his side.

Marai hadn't left many personal effects here, other than a few miscellaneous items of clothing. The room itself had always seemed too large for her. Now, it felt charmless and deserted without her.

Ruenen tore open the drawers in the vanity, and there it was—the bloodstone ring. A deep green jasper stone, freckled with red dots, the ring felt completely normal to Ruenen as his fingers plucked it from the drawer. No tingle, no electric spark. He'd expected it to be heavier than an average ring. Warm, maybe. But he was human. Perhaps the magic of the ring couldn't be sensed by someone without fae blood.

He offered it to Aresti. "Do you sense anything?"

She took the ring from Ruenen's palm. Immediately, her eyes widened and Aresti sucked in a breath, placing a hand to her stomach. "Well, that's odd."

Ruenen then remembered the curse placed on that ring by Meallán. "What do you feel?"

He'd thought Marai had used up its magic on the battlefield, but maybe it was still cursed.

"A pull. As if someone was tugging on a rope tied around my waist."

"But you don't feel anything sinister in it, right?"

"Nothing that indicates the curse still exists." Aresti spun around and stopped, facing Northeast, where the cold fireplace hearth stood. "The pull is coming from that direction."

Andara.

"Nosficio was right, then. We can use this to track her once we arrive on Andara," Ruenen said, his spirits buoyant. He was certain this would work. Aresti tried to return the ring, but Ruenen pressed it back into her hand. "You can feel it calling for her. I'm entrusting this to *you* to help guide us to Marai and Keshel."

Aresti nodded, and stuffed the ring into the leather pouch she wore at her hip.

Sir Nyle appeared at the door. "Your Grace, the Witan and Commander Avilyard have been alerted of your arrival. They'll meet you in the chamber in an hour's time. There's also a letter for you."

Ruenen took the paper from the guard's hand, and broke the wax seal as he turned to Mayestral. "Please, begin packing. Lightweight, athletic attire. Nothing too flashy and cumbersome. I'm not traveling to Andara as a king."

To the Groom's credit, he didn't balk at Ruenen's orders, and immediately directed two servants to bring Ruenen's luggage up from the carriages.

Ruenen then turned his attention to the letter.

Your Kingliness,

I've arrived in Baatgai, and asked around the port. At the mention of Andara and the Menagerie, the harbormaster (after much persuasion) kindly remembered two unconscious people fitting our Queen and Councilman's descriptions being loaded onto a ship. The vessel in question, The Arcane Wind, is the only known ship that sails to Andara, with a stop in Yehzig along the way. It only makes this voyage once every two or three years, and usually returns to port after about four months. It's not allowed to linger in Andaran waters, and the rest of the time, it sails to transport goods along the Astyean coast and Yehzig. As it happens, The Arcane Wind left for Andara several months ago, and is due back in Baatgai any day now. If it arrives before you do, I shall ascertain the price of hiring the crew to set sail again.

Yours forever in darkness,

Nosficio

Ruenen held back an eye roll. Even in a letter, Nosficio found a way to irk him, but Ruenen could scarcely wait to join the vampire in Baatgai. He wanted to question the crew, himself, but first, he needed to bathe, eat, and meet with his most-assuredly surly council.

An hour later, he sat on his throne before a full table. Not only was the entire Witan and King's Guard present, but the fae and werewolves had appeared at Ruenen's summons, as well. Holfast, as expected, gave Ruenen a steely-eyed stare. He and Fenir had been talking with Wattling when Ruenen had walked in the room. No doubt, they'd been apprised of Ruenen's intentions. Fenir was sweating, and had sunk low in his chair, as if to hide from the very thought of his King venturing to Andara.

"We're glad you've returned, Your Grace, and so soon," Holfast said, and Ruenen caught the subtle icy tone. "However, Lord Wattling and Lord Goso have brought to my attention something that is quite concerning."

"I won't skirt around it, my lords. While in Grelta, I was finally contacted by Lord Nosficio, who discovered that Queen Marai and Lord Keshel were kidnapped, and taken to Andara. She's in a terrifying state. Marai's being abused and starved, and she won't last much longer. I'll be traveling there to retrieve them personally," Ruenen said, addressing everyone in the room.

"You cannot go, Your Grace," stated Corian, voice cutting through the responding din like a knife. "If you feel determined to find Lady Marai and Lord Keshel, then by all means send a team of faeries to Andara. I'm sure *their* people would be glad to volunteer. You, as our sovereign, cannot go on such a dangerous mission."

Aresti, Braesal, and Tarik shot Corian looks of contempt. Thora bit her lower lip.

"I don't believe I was asking for permission," Ruenen said with cold authority.

"You could *die,* Your Grace," Corian pushed back. "We know the stories of the Northern Sea. It's violent even in the best of weather. Your ship could founder, and then what would we do? You have no queen, no heir, no next-of-kin. We'd be right back to where we were before you arrived."

"Then it's lucky we have such a competent Steward of the Throne," said Ruenen, looking now at Holfast.

"Let's say, for argument's sake, that you survive the journey there and back again," the Steward said, steepling his fingers, elbows on the table. "An absent King, for any amount of time, could stoke an uprising. If there's a whiff of this journey revealed to the public, someone might try to steal the throne from you while you're gone."

"Tell no one outside of this council where I am," Ruenen said. "Say I'm ill. Or so caught up in my duties that I cannot be seen in public."

"You'd be gone for over three months," said Holfast.

Ruenen put on his most serious, regal expression. "It's your duty, as my Witan and trusted council, to keep the people's faith in their King."

Fenir, who'd remained remarkably silent on the issue, paled as he slid further down in his chair.

"Perhaps we table this discussion until *after* you've wed Queen Rhia and sired a son," Wattling said, placing his hands on his large stomach. He received a few mumbles of agreement. "We could arrange the wedding for next week if you're in such a hurry."

QUEEN OF THE SHADOW MENAGERIE

Ruenen ground his teeth. *Don't rise to the bait.* "Marai and Keshel are in grave danger."

"What exactly is your evidence that Lady Marai and Lord Keshel are in Andara?" Holfast asked politely, tentatively, knowing that negative mentions of Marai always set Ruenen off.

Ruenen hesitated. He didn't think his Witan would believe his story about Marai dream-speaking to him. Instead, he said, "Lord Nosficio came to me with a true lead. We have plenty of evidence to suggest their whereabouts are in Andara, specifically in a place called the Menagerie."

At this, Fenir emitted a choked squawk, drawing eyes to him. Biting down on his lip, he looked like a man ready to combust.

"Lord Fenir?" asked Goso to his left, and patted the man on the back. "My dear fellow, what's wrong?"

Fenir exploded, wailing up at the ceiling. "It's true, it's all true!" He then ducked his head, and hid beneath his long, stringy brown hair.

The councilman was well-known for being high strung, but Ruenen had never seen him fall apart in such a way.

"It was blackmail," Fenir continued through gasping sobs, "and he told me not to say anything, because he knew King Ruenen and the others would go after them—"

Holfast's face spasmed for a moment, hiding his shock, then returned to its usual stoic countenance. He addressed the rest of the table calmly as he said, "Would you all mind waiting in the hallway? I think Lord Fenir is overcome and requires a smaller audience at this time."

"Should I stay and tend to him?" asked Thora.

"We'll call you if we require your services, Mistress Healer," Holfast said. "I'm sure it's nothing a simple conversation cannot fix."

With disgruntled and concerned looks, the rest of the table stood, chairs scraping and groaning. Raife, Thora, and Aresti looked questionably at Ruenen, and he pretended not to see them. He didn't know what Fenir was talking about, but it definitely wasn't good. The Witan, fae, and werewolves departed, leaving Ruenen and Holfast alone with Fenir.

"Who blackmailed you?" Ruenen asked, getting up from his throne. Heat crept up the knobs of his spine, burning at the base of his neck.

"*Him,* that silver-eyed faerie. Koda." Fenir stared up at Ruenen from his chair.

Towering over him, Ruenen's hands curled into fists at the mention of the male's name.

"He forced me to tell him everything I knew about Lady Marai and Lord Keshel," said Fenir. "He tortured me, trying to get any leverage he could over them, and I let some things slip—"

"What things?" asked Holfast very slowly and severely.

Fenir's owlish eyes flickered to Ruenen and then back to Holfast, and Ruenen saw the realization hit the Steward at the exact same moment.

Fenir had told Koda that Ruenen wasn't the true King.

That explained how Koda was able to overpower Marai. Ruenen would've bet his life that Koda threatened to expose the secret, and Marai went along with him in order to protect Ruenen.

Fuck, fuck, fuck, fuck.

Fenir shook from head to toe as he leapt from his chair and collapsed at Ruenen's feet. "Please, spare me, Your Grace! I had no choice. He cut off my ear and threatened to do worse if I didn't tell him everything he wanted to know." He pulled back his curtain of hair to reveal a rough hole on the side of his face where an ear had once been. Judging by the jagged, uneven flesh that remained, the ear hadn't been taken in one swift slice.

"Why didn't you tell us months ago?" Ruenen asked the supplicating lord.

Fenir squeezed his eyes closed tight. "He used magic on me—froze me solid like a statue in my own apartments right after the battle. He said no harm would come to you or Nevandia as long as Lady Marai and Lord Keshel were quietly abducted. He only wanted the information as leverage over Marai." Fenir pulled at the hem of Ruenen's traveling cloak. "I did what I had to do, Your Grace. My only love is for Nevandia. My loyalty is to you, I promise."

Ruenen wrenched his cloak from Fenir's shaking hands, then returned to the dais. He sat down heavily on his throne, and massaged his forehead, thinking.

Holfast did not show mercy in the hard lines of his face. "It's clear that this Koda studied which members of the Witan were the weakest."

Ruenen released a long-suffering sigh. *Treason was not on my agenda today.*

Holfast turned to Ruenen. "What would you like to do with him, Your Grace?"

"I won't say anything, I promise, Your Grace. I'll work harder, d–d–do whatever you want." Fenir groveled, pressing his forehead to the cold marble floor. "Please, don't hang me!"

Ruenen reached over and tugged on a golden tassel next to the throne. A bell rang out distantly somewhere, and two guards re-entered the room. "Lord Fenir will be confined to his quarters until further notice. He'll have no visitors, be under constant surveillance, and his correspondence shall be examined by Lord Holfast."

Fenir appeared ready to faint with relief. "Thank you, Your Grace. Thank you, truly. I am blessed to have such a merciful King. I promise that I shall prove to you my loyalty."

The guards pulled him to his feet and ushered Fenir from the room, as the rest of the Witan, King's Guard, and magical folk peered inside the chamber, confused and appalled.

"I'm surprised by your leniency," Holfast said, coming to stand at Ruenen's side on the dais.

"Not many people can stand up to torture," Ruenen said, remembering how frightened, how resigned to death he'd been while in Rayghast's dungeon. He'd luckily never been tortured, but he'd been close, and he knew he would've said almost anything to get out of it. He might not have been able to hold his tongue, either, if Koda had sawed off his ear.

"Regardless, circumstances have changed," Holfast said in a low murmur as everyone slowly returned to their seats at the table. "The secret is out there. I'm inclined to agree that we must go after Koda, in order to guarantee that such information never reaches the wrong ears. I know it's pointless to persuade you to stay behind. I'd turn my back for a second and you'd be climbing out the window."

Ruenen gave his Steward a crooked smile. "Am I that predictable?"

"You're *desperate*," Holfast said with a resigned shake of his head. "I'd chain you to your bed frame if I thought that would work."

"What's happening with Lord Fenir?" asked Corian. "Why is he confined to his quarters?"

"He's unwell," Holfast said. "The poor man is suffering from some kind of fit. Overworked, perhaps. King Ruenen and I decided that it was best to give him some time off, for both his health and the good of Nevandia."

Thora scowled at both Ruenen and Holfast, obviously seeing through the ruse. Ruenen would need to speak with her about this, and beg her to continue the lie. His brain danced around thoughts of Marai in shackles, Fenir's ear, Koda's blackmail, and other splendid things.

He wiped his sweaty palms on his trousers, thrust his shoulders back, and addressed his Witan with as much authority as he could muster. "It's been decided. For the sake of Nevandia's future, and for our missing friends and colleagues, I'll be going to Andara."

"Your Grace, this is ridiculous," Corian said, slamming a fist onto the table.

Ruenen looked down his nose at Corian. "I am the *King*. I don't need your permission to do *anything*, Lord Corian. The only reason I wear this crown is because of Marai. She saved Nevandia, and now it's my turn to save her. To bring her and Lord Keshel home. Steward Holfast has agreed, and will of course lead the country in my stead until I return. He knows my mind, and I trust he will impose my will."

"You can count on us, Your Grace," said Goso, getting to his feet. "We of the Witan are here to serve you."

Commander Avilyard stood next. "You have the loyalty of the army behind you, Your Grace. My soldiers will protect the people, and keep our lands safe until you return."

Slowly, reluctantly, the rest of the Witan got to their feet and murmured their own pledges of loyalty. Ruenen noted the tight-lipped, red-faced Wattling, and Corian's furrowed brow. They'd be troublemakers in his absence.

"Who will you take with you, Your Grace? You cannot go alone," Avilyard said.

"I cannot ask anyone to join me on such a dangerous mission. If you choose to travel with me, it must be your decision."

Aresti was the first to move, kneeling before Ruenen's dais with a bowed head. "I will gladly join you, Your Grace, to rescue my cousin and Marai."

"You shall have us, as well," Tarik said. He and Yovel stood and thumped a hairy-knuckled hand to their broad chests. "We owe you and Queen Marai for giving us werewolves a new home, for fighting for our kind. Yovel and I will come, and Brass will stay behind to watch over things here."

"Marai *isn't* a queen," Corian grumbled. "She certainly won't be Nevandia's Queen."

"Oh, but you're wrong, Lord Corian," said Holfast before Ruenen could open his mouth. "Marai is the last living descendant of the royal fae. She is, indeed, a queen in her own right."

Ruenen couldn't hide the shock from his face. Holfast had never once stood up for Marai before in front of the Witan. Corian gaped as if Holfast had smacked him in the face with a dueling glove.

Avilyard's voice was a deep rumble as he said, "I would come with you, Your Grace, but—"

"I need you here, Commander," said Ruenen. "Nevandia must continue its path towards peace and progress with Tacorn. If I'm to leave, I need to know that my country is in safe hands, and that the army can be deployed if necessary. I trust you to make those decisions without me."

Avilyard seemed torn. "Then please accept at least twelve of the King's Guard."

"That, plus the five soldiers Queen Nieve sent," Aresti reminded Ruenen.

"I think six will do, Commander," Ruenen said. "We need to travel lightly, inconspicuously."

"You can put, uh, as many well-trained soldiers on that ship as you want," said Cronhold, "but that won't stop a boat from sinking in those, uh, waters."

The old man had a point.

It was Braesal's turn to stand now. "I cannot stop a storm or calm a sea, but my elemental expertise is water, Your Grace. Two others of my group are also water-workers." He gestured to full-blooded Finneagal and half-fae Beck at his side. "We can perhaps make things a little less tremulous for crossing the sea."

"And with my control of wind, we can navigate there swiftly," added Aresti, smirking from ear to ear. She was practically vibrating with anticipation. Ruenen saw in her the same, shared frenzied excitement to begin.

The one person who hadn't moved yet was the one that Ruenen was most surprised by.

Raife sat hand in hand with Thora at the table, whispering back and forth to each other, frowning.

"Very well," Holfast said. "This is to be your official party, Your Grace. Lord Wattling, I believe our King will require a vast amount from the treasury to support this journey. Perhaps we can also secure some assistance from the Emperor of Syoto. I'll write him a letter, Your Grace."

Ruenen dismissed the meeting with a wave of his hand. Only those who had volunteered for the mission remained, along with penitent Raife and Thora.

"Forgive me for not volunteering," Raife said, rushing over to Ruenen. "We didn't want to talk about it in front of the Witan. I would join you, of course, you know I would, and I'd planned on it, if not for . . ." He trailed off, looking at Thora for assurance.

She took his hand and faced Ruenen with as much determination as she had when facing an army of Tacornians. "If not for the fact that I'm pregnant."

Aresti gasped and covered her mouth. The words clanged through Ruenen. It was certainly not what he'd been expecting Thora and Raife to say.

"Obviously, I cannot travel with you and become a liability," said Thora. "My stomach is rather volatile these days."

"And I cannot bring myself to leave her, not for any reason, especially when we're splitting up and spreading our forces so thin. Thora and my child's protection is paramount to me, no matter how much I wish to see Marai and Keshel again," Raife said, eyes begging for forgiveness. "This was not an easy decision, and the guilt I feel is—"

Ruenen smiled. "I'd do the same, if I was in your position." And he would have. If it had been Marai, *their* child . . . "I cannot fault either of you for not wanting to take this journey. You must stay and take care of things here. Avilyard will need your assistance." He grabbed Raife and pulled him into a bear-like embrace. "Congratulations, my friend. You will make an excellent father."

Raife hugged him back. "Bring our family home." He tried to hide the crack in his voice with a cough.

Ruenen released him, then kissed Thora on both cheeks. "You two and your secrets! First, you hide your marriage. Now, this?"

"I only just found out while you and Raife were away," she stammered, obviously missing Ruenen's playful tone.

"I'm jesting. How long until the little one arrives?" he asked.

Thora's face brightened. "Oh, months yet. You should be back in time before the baby is born." Her face fell, happiness drooping at the thought.

If we survive...

No. We'll survive. Marai and I will both be here to celebrate the birth.

The next morning, early and under the cover of darkness, Ruenen met Elmar, Nyle, and four other King's Guard in the courtyard, plus Nieve's silver-clad men. They were to leave quietly, so as not to draw attention to Ruenen's absence.

The rest of his retinue appeared through the portcullis: bright-eyed, pointed eared faeries Aresti, Braesal, Beck, Finneagal, and Zorish, and the hulking werewolves Tarik and Yovel, all on horseback. Raife would travel with them and a few extra King's Guard to Baatgai, then return to Nevandia. The Witan, along with Thora, Brass, and the rest of Braesal's group had come to see them off.

Mayestral, as well, had packed his own bag, along with a few other servant volunteers.

"You don't need to come, Mayestral. Tend to things here," Ruenen said, but the loyal Groom shook his balding head.

"My place is at your side, Your Grace. Where you go, I go." Mayestral nudged the sides of his horse to align directly behind Ruenen's.

"Wait, please," came a young, female voice from the doorway.

It was Lilly, with Daye trailing behind her, carrying a sack over her shoulder. They came up to Ruenen's horse and curtsied.

"Daye is volunteering to come along as your cook, Your Grace," said Lilly.

"It's far too dangerous for you," Ruenen replied, looking at Daye, who met his gaze with a resolute stare. "You don't know where we're going."

The servant volunteers were only told basic information about the length of the journey.

"She knows there will be risks, Sire, but she wants to serve you and the Faerie Queen. I'd come, too, if my duties to Queen Rhia didn't keep me here."

Ruenen smiled, and spoke to Daye. "Thank you. I'm happy to have you join us." To Lilly, he said, "Please take care of Queen Rhia . . . I'm sure she'll be rather upset with the situation." He leaned over in his saddle, towards Lilly's ear. "But you mustn't tell her anything, or Harmona and the other servants, either. This trip is secret, at least for now."

"You can count on me, Sire," she said, and saluted him.

Ruenen waved goodbye to Holfast, standing morosely on the steps. He lifted one hand in farewell to his King. They'd spoken at length about the running of Nevandia in Ruenen's absence. Goso, Cronhold, Avilyard, Raife, Thora, and Brass had been present as Ruenen laid out his orders. He needed those remaining in Kellesar, the people he trusted most, to know his wishes, his hopes for the future, so that if something were to go awry on his mission, Nevandia and its citizens would be taken care of.

On the moor, Ruenen took one final, longing look back at Kellesar. He whispered goodbye to his beautiful city as the first rays of sun hit its spires. This could be the final time he ever laid eyes on it. His heart ached when he turned his back on the city and his people, moving his retinue forward up the road towards the glen and path to Syoto.

Ruenen knew that if he didn't return with Marai, he wouldn't return at all.

He shed every emotion except determination and gritty optimism.

I'm coming, Marai. Hold on a little longer. Stay alive.

CHAPTER 26

MARAI

All she'd known for days, weeks, months, was darkness. Endless silence. The smell of her own refuse.

Once a day, Volgar, Yelich, or Sirco opened the lid of the crate and tossed her a half-empty waterskin and scraps of food: rinds of fruits and vegetables, the heels of stale bread, bones with barely any meat on them. Marai ate the meager supplies slowly, savoring each miniscule bite throughout the hours. Her captors never spoke to her. Koda never once showed his face.

Marai's mind was a hive, buzzing with thoughts. She had plenty of time to think in the void.

About Ruenen and his new Queen. About Keshel and his visions, his fragility. About the others in the Menagerie that she was letting down. About the sinister cobweb of a voice she'd heard when she held the stone. The echo of its words wouldn't leave her alone, even in sleep.

About how, for mere moments, Marai had overpowered Cavar's collar.

How had she blocked its pull on her strings? Even if her "visit" to Ruenen was nothing more than a daydream, her magic had briefly overpowered Cavar's. Perhaps, if no one had stopped her, she might have broken free entirely.

Magic had risen within her, dulled by the collar, but the spark through her blood, itching at her neck, was unmistakable. That sensation of power surged into every crevice, every hole, that had been aching with loss for months, and now that she was empty once again, Marai craved it. She tried and tried, over and over, to reach and drag it up from the depths of herself, but the magic wouldn't come. The collar's chokehold remained suffocatingly strong.

But Marai had beaten it once. She could do it again.

That thought, alone, gave Marai fortitude enough to endure the everlasting darkness of the box. It kept her from breaking entirely.

I can survive this. Darkness has always been my friend.

Marai shifted positions in the box as she let out a grunt of discomfort. One arm was numb, having been trapped beneath her. She turned onto her other side. Slowly, the pins and needles returned as blood surged through the limb.

Flexing her hand, she thought back to the moment she'd been on stage, trying to remember every detail. *How had it happened? What had been the catalyst?*

She'd been missing Ruenen.

No, not missing him. Aching, *burning,* for him.

Then there was fear.

The fear of her fated rendezvous with Cavar's perverted patron who'd bought Marai for the night. At least she'd escaped that particular torture for now. She'd rather be jammed inside a box than whored out to the wealthy.

Love for Ruenen and fear. That formidable combination of emotions had happened to her before.

The thought of seeing Ruenen, touching him, had been the key, a switch. A longing and terror so strong that magic welled up inside her and had to escape.

He's always been the key to unlocking my trapped potential. That day in the Tacornian woods, when Marai had first used lightning and scorched the earth, it happened because Ruenen had held her hand. The thought of dying alongside him, of being tortured and raped, had awakened that mighty power. Later, in the dungeon, Marai had *opened a portal* in order to save them both from Rayghast's menacing devices.

Ruenen gave her courage. He brought her strength. He taught her to believe that she was more than a mercenary, more than the scars that tainted her.

Suddenly, the lid of the box opened.

Light flooded in. Marai shielded her eyes, blinded by the overcast sun.

Koda stared down, his expression grave. "Get up."

Marai didn't have the energy to fuss, much less climb out of the box unassisted. It took her several minutes, but eventually she was able to hike up a leg, then roll her body over the edge and onto the grass. The food and water she'd been given had barely been enough to sustain her, and that small amount of movement left her drained. There was no way she could get to her feet.

Koda heaved an irritated sigh, then called over Yelich and Sirco. He didn't want to touch her, himself. She knew she smelled rank, and Marai had an inkling that Koda was a little afraid of what she'd done that night on the stage.

Cavar's thugs dragged Marai's body up the row of tents. Her head lolled on her chest, dizzy, starving, nauseous, and overwhelmed. She didn't want to look up to see the faces of the Menagerie watching their supposed Queen be carted off to her punishment. She could only imagine their expressions of disappointment. She hoped Keshel wasn't watching.

She didn't have to open her eyes to know where she was headed.

A door opened with a creak. Her toes skated across stone. Up a flight of stairs where her bare feet slammed into each stone step. Another door opened.

Yelich and Sirco flung Marai onto the rug of Cavar's office, then backed away.

Acacia gagged from somewhere in the room. "Uch, she smells *awful!*"

Marai didn't lift her head, didn't raise her body off the ground when Cavar's silk and leather shoes came into view from around his desk.

"No one has *ever* been able to cancel out the collar before," he said, but it wasn't a compliment. Not in that tone of gelid fury.

Cavar wanted to be as powerful as a god, stronger than the fae, and Marai had proved that he wasn't. To him, no greater offense could be given.

"We've been too gentle with you," he continued.

Marai snorted. *Gentle?* Using all the energy she could muster, she gave Cavar the finger. "Piss off."

Acacia gasped. One elegant, pearl-studded shoe kicked Marai in the stomach.

"How dare you!" Acacia kicked her again, aiming higher. This time, Marai felt a rib crack. "She's far too defiant, Uncle. We cannot stand for this a moment longer. And now my shoe is soiled by her filth."

Cavar placed a hand on Acacia's shoulder, pushing her behind him. The Governor crouched down next to Marai's face. His pale eyes were as sharp as a razor's edge.

"Do you have any idea how much money you've cost me? I had to refund *every single one* of those audience members. Attendance has been down since. People are afraid that the Menagerie isn't safe anymore, that I'm losing my touch. You created a stain on the Menagerie, on *my* spotless reputation."

Money and power. Why did people always throw away their humanity to obtain it? Cavar was no different than Rayghast, or Emperor Suli of Varana.

Marai hissed at the pain as she lifted head and bared her teeth. "This is what happens when you hold the Faerie Queen captive."

"You, a piddling little faerie, are no queen."

"You *made* me into this," Marai growled at him. "You brought this upon yourself the second you had Koda kidnap me. Your own people, along with the magical folk, know me as the Faerie Queen. *I have power now.*"

Cavar reeled back, as if she'd struck him with more than words. He recovered, settling back into his rage. "You don't get to take things from me. You cannot compete with my power."

Marai made sure he saw her eye roll. "It doesn't belong to you. You're only borrowing magic from the stone. Put me back in the box. I can handle it. But you'll only be making the folk more loyal to me, and give me more reasons to tear down your empire."

Acacia huffed and harrumphed in the background, hands on her hips.

Cavar's expression cleared. He stood and smoothed back his curling hair. He adjusted the lapels of his long coat. "Oh, I'll put you back in that box, Marai, but first, I need you to understand that you are *nothing.* That you will never leave the Menagerie. I promise that you will never again know a moment's peace or a life without pain."

He grasped his amulet. Black light from its stone bled through his fingers.

Acacia gasped, clutching her chest. "Ouch, Uncle! That burns." Her amulet was overheating; Marai smelled the scent of burning flesh. Acacia removed her amulet and dangled it away from herself.

Cavar ignored his niece. The stone kept pulsating, the light growing brighter.

Then, from the ground itself, between the pores in the stone and woven threads of the rug, black smoke rose from the Underworld.

As it had with Keshel, the smoke whirred and writhed, slinking across the floor towards Marai.

Her heart sprinted. Her throat went narrow as ribbons of smoke ran filmy hands up her legs and hips, her torso and neck. Marai flailed on the rug, trying to shake off the smoke, but it climbed higher, undeterred, until it plunged into her mouth and nose.

Marai coughed relentlessly, gagging, but it didn't matter.

Dark magic was inside her.

It slithered down her esophagus like a serpent, and flared to life upon reaching the cavity of her chest, spewing cold fire into every organ, bone, and vein.

That voice, that horrible voice, laughed in triumph.

A thousand knives tore and stabbed, but *inside* her. It was the worst pain Marai had ever felt, unlike anything she'd experienced. Worse than when Cavar had freed her dormant blood. Worse than when she'd spent nearly all of her Life Energy on the Red Lands battlefield.

The darkness was an army of maggots eating away at her, charring her with black flames from the inside out.

Marai couldn't think, except to beg it to stop.

Everything she'd feared about dark magic, that it would one day consume her, destroy her, was happening. Her heart beat so fast she thought it might actually explode.

She may have pleaded out loud. *Stop! Make it stop!* It may have only been inside her mind, but she was certainly screaming.

And then the smoke, the darkness, was sucked back out of her body, back into Cavar's stone, dispersing in wisps, as if it had never been there. The stone's pulsating light dimmed back to normal, and Cavar dropped his hand from the amulet.

Marai panted. Raw and ragged, she vomited where she lay; black blood with the slick sheen of oil. Moaning, she curled inwards, tucking her knees to her chest.

This is what Keshel experienced that day. But Cavar had let it go on far longer with Marai.

"I left some in there," Cavar said. "A constant reminder of your weakness."

Dark magic left dirty handprints throughout her body, but when glancing at herself, Marai saw no physical evidence. Nothing had changed; the tips of her fingers remained stained. The damage was internal, leaving Marai to wonder how long she had left to live with it skulking around inside.

"Get rid of her," Cavar ordered to his guards with disgust. "And burn this rug. It's soiled."

Marai was hauled from the office, body limp. She was deposited outside the amphitheater door, dress hiked up her hips, left to lie on the dirt and grass as an example. It wasn't that cold, but Marai couldn't stop the shivers from consuming her. She couldn't move except to vomit more black blood. Couldn't open her eyes.

A blanket was laid over her.

"Quick, help me get her into her tent," Anja's voice said.

Arms lifted Marai again. She cried out in pain at the jostling.

"Be careful," Anja fretted.

A deep male voice replied, "I'm trying."

The arms cradled her body to a strong chest. Hooves clopped on the ground. Snippets of whispers reached her ears.

"Is there anything I can do?" came a new male voice, kind and nervous.

"Keep the others away, Athelstan," Anja said. "She wouldn't want everyone to see."

Marai heard the rustle of the tent flap, and then she was laid on a scratchy bedroll. She squinted to see the hooves and midnight legs of a horse, then Dante's torso and grave expression. Anja hovered behind him, and Gunnora peeked around Dante's rump.

"Marai!" Keshel stumbled into the tent, but there was no room for him. It was too crowded with Dante's body taking up most of the space.

"Let me know if the Queen needs anything," the centaur murmured to Anja, and then quit the tent.

Keshel collapsed at Marai's side, clutching her hand. "She's frozen. Marai, can you hear me?"

"We need to get nourishment in her," Anja said. "Gunnora, steal whatever you can from Bobo. Maybe ask Gruper to help you—he has light fingers."

The flap opened and closed. Footsteps came in and out. Keshel didn't let go of her hand. Marai could feel him shaking. Or maybe that was her.

"What did they do to her?" asked a female voice, sharp as a knife.

Keshel's cold fingers were gentle as he lifted the blanket. His gaze raked across Marai's body. "Cavar used the stone on her."

A heavy silence saturated the tent.

"But she doesn't *look* injured," Anja whispered.

"The magic is inside her," said Keshel, voice wavering. He placed his hand on Marai's cheek. "It's a cold burning. I feel it, even now, days after Cavar used the amulet on me, but I think what he did to Marai was worse."

"What can we do to help her?" asked Innesh, kneeling beside him.

"Rest. Food. That's all you can really do. I don't think . . . I don't think there's a way to stop it from destroying us, slowly, inch by inch." Keshel's thumb stroked Marai's cheek. "It's a disease."

"You shouldn't be out of bed, either," Anja said. "You look no better than her."

"I'm staying," Keshel stated.

Anja didn't press him again.

Gruper, the squash-faced hob, appeared shortly after with water, his small pockets full of berries, mushrooms, and a bannock. "This is all I could snag."

"That's plenty for now, thank you," Anja said. "We need more blankets from Cyrill. Can you speak with him, please?"

Gruper bowed his head quickly at Marai. "My Queen." Then he was gone.

Sometime later, Gunnora returned, her expression secretive, glancing behind her outside. "I grabbed some of this." She held out her palm to reveal a sweaty clump of dark, metallic powder.

Anja gasped. "How did you get this?"

"Koda was in Cavar's office, so I told Volgar that I'd left a dirty rag in Koda's room. I whipped inside and took a pinch. Not enough to get noticed, of course."

"If you'd gotten caught—"

"Well, I didn't. Volgar's an idiot. Here." Gunnora sprinkled the powder into Keshel's trembling palm. "Marai's been fighting for all of us, day after day. It's time we stand up and fight for *her*."

"Thank you, Gunnora. I'll give it to her," said Keshel.

"Not all at once," Anja warned. "Just enough to let her rest."

"Make sure you both eat that," ordered Gunnora, pointing at the small pile of food on Marai's bedroll. "Gruper didn't risk getting whacked by Bobo's ladle for you both to starve."

The tent emptied, save for Keshel. Marai watched him slowly chew on a berry, then heave and spit it out. He couldn't keep much food down.

"I saw him," Marai finally said through her ravaged throat.

Keshel started, surprised by her consciousness. "You shouldn't waste your energy speaking."

"I saw him, Keshel."

"Eat something, and then I'll give you this powder so you can sleep."

"Stop . . . telling me what to do and listen," Marai said with as much bite as she could muster.

Keshel's lips twitched. "Who did you see?"

"Ruen."

Keshel's eyes widened.

"That's why they did this. Because my magic overpowered Cavar's collar. They're scared of me."

Keshel squeezed Marai's hand, face pained, skin the color of whey. "I've been so worried, Marai. I didn't know if they'd let you out again."

"I'd rather be in there than lying here with dark magic infesting my body."

Keshel's frown deepened. "You saw King Ruenen? How?"

"I don't know. But I almost did it, Keshel. I almost got the collar off. But I don't think now . . . I'll be able to."

Not with the mutilation caused by dark magic. Marai had never felt so ill, so weak before.

"Don't worry about that. I know you'll think of something," Keshel said, giving her a slim smile. "Close your eyes."

Marai did as he instructed. The burning sensation was so great inside her that it would keep her awake without the aid of the narcotic powder. Keshel blew the substance into her face, and she coughed as it entered her lugs.

Marai then went quiet for a while. Keshel must have thought she'd drifted off, because he jumped when she asked, "How long do you think we have to live?"

Keshel didn't meet her eyes. "I don't know, Marai. I just don't know."

He stroked her hair, over and over, with his long fingers. He closed his eyes, and began to chant. Marai recognized its comforting tones from years ago. Keshel used to chant in the language of the gods, ancient fae, when she couldn't sleep at night. In those early days, she'd have nightmares of the massacres. Of watching black-armored Tacornian soldiers cut down her neighbors and friends, of the blood and gore. The last glimpse of her parents before Keshel hid Marai away. He'd sit at her bedside, no more than a child, himself, and lull her to sleep. The language reminded Marai of her father, and the tune was a comfort.

The sound of Keshel's voice had soothed her pain then. It did so again now. Marai lapsed into a light sleep, but even the powder couldn't dull the hurt.

Innesh returned at some point. "It's time for the show."

"They're not going to force her to perform, are they?" asked Keshel.

"No, but you must report to your usual station."

"I'm not leaving her here alone."

"Go, before Cavar punishes you in the same way," ordered Innesh as if she was a general commanding a soldier. "He's in a violent mood tonight. I'll watch after Marai. She won't be alone."

Marai didn't know if Keshel returned that night. She didn't know if Innesh stayed. Sleep was agony. Being awake was agony. She was on the precipice of both, and knew that the only way to rid the suffering was death.

Two days later, Marai's condition hadn't improved. She hadn't left her bedroll, but apparently, Cavar's patience had grown as thin as a frozen lake in springtime.

"Get her up, cleaned, and dressed," Koda demanded from outside the tent. "Cavar wants her onstage tonight."

"She can't stand, Koda Sir," Anja demurely mumbled. She, Gunnora, Innesh, and Keshel had been at her bedside nonstop. "I don't think she's well enough to perform. She continues to vomit this strange bile—"

"That's what the collar is for," snapped Koda. "You have an hour to get her ready."

Anja roused Marai by splashing water on her face and yanking her into a sitting position. "There, now. Move slowly."

"Everything hurts," groaned Marai.

Sorrow flashed across Anja's face, but then it cleared as she smiled, lifting a spoon of stodgy mush to Marai's lips. "Our people beyond the Veil will be celebrating the Solstice. It was always my favorite time of year. The Court parties last for a week, with music and dancing, decorations, and the most delicious food. I didn't sleep for days, sometimes. I never wanted to miss a moment."

She coaxed the spoon into Marai's mouth and forced her to swallow. Marai's stomach churned, and she leaned over to empty the contents of her stomach.

"In the Hinterlands, we find ways to celebrate the small things," Anja continued, scooping up another spoonful of mush. "Our people try to find joy wherever they can, especially when the royal fae lines died out. The Hinterlands changed. Without true leadership, our country broke into warring factions. The nobles of each fief are constantly fighting, but Solstice is one time of year when we put away the chaos and celebrate together with the rest of the folk."

"Sounds like you have as many troubles as we do on Astye," Marai mumbled, wiping the bile from her cracked lips.

"That's why we're so glad you're here. Us folk are used to being set against each other, but a true Faerie Queen could unite the fiefs and stop the fighting. You could provide the guidance we so desperately need."

If Marai had the energy, she would have told Anja to stop hoping. To stop believing Marai could make anything better. But she said nothing because she ended up vomiting and moaning into the bucket.

"Come on, Marai," Anja said urgently with a glassy sheen in her eyes. "I know it's hard, and I know it hurts, but please try. You need your strength."

Marai finally swallowed down some water with her assistance, and managed to eat one bite of the mush without it coming back up again.

Gunnora entered sometime later, and muttered, "How are we going to make her look less like a corpse? She's nothing but skin and bones."

"You think those horrid people care how thin she is?" Anja asked. "None of them care if we're on death's door. They'd probably cheer if one of us expired right there on stage."

They delicately washed Marai's body. She didn't mind that they saw her naked; she was beyond prudishness, beyond self-consciousness. They dressed her in another abominable outfit, and guided her from the tent. Each step was torturous, stealing more and more strength from her. Anja and Gunnora handed her off to hale Innesh, who carried Marai's full weight like she was nothing but a coat draped over her arm.

The entire camp had come out of their tents. They marched behind Marai and Innesh, a unit in her failed army.

"I can't endure this," Marai admitted softly to Innesh. "I can't help them."

Innesh's grip around her hip tightened. "You *will* endure this, for as long as you must. You're their Queen."

Marai felt nothing but pain. Even her love for Ruenen, and Keshel, Thora, Raife, and Aresti had been nibbled away by the darkness inside her, as if it could also consume her soul, as well as her body.

"I'm not worthy of that title," she whispered. "I don't think I ever was."

Innesh's jaw ticked, but she ignored Marai's sorry confession.

Once backstage, Innesh gently lowered Marai into a chair. The show had already started. Wilder and Dante cantered around the stage like prized horses. Cyrill came next, hovering creepily in the shadows of the curtains, making the audience whisper with intrigue. He pretended to swipe a doll from a little girl, and actually took a felt hat off a man's head and put it on his own bald one. The audience laughed, but Cyrill kept the hat.

Marai mused blandly, *Is that how he gets ahold of his clothes?*

Cyrill stopped by Marai's chair when he finished and looked down his long nose at her.

"Whatever you do, don't give up."

He adjusted his new felt hat and snuck away.

The collar's magic took over, straightening Marai's marionette body from the chair, as if an iron rod had been inserted along her spine. Her wobbly legs were barely able to support her weight as she twirled onto the stage to hesitant applause.

Cavar's customers were still unsure about her. There were vacant seats in the audience, something Marai hadn't witnessed before, and the first three rows were empty. People who were in attendance eyed Marai with suspicion. Arcturius, off to the side of the stage, bit his gloved thumb and observed her every fake move. As her regular routine continued, however, the atmosphere eased, the audience relaxed in their seats.

All the while, Marai's head spun, stomach heaved, body screamed in agony, but her mind was barren of thought. Her heart devoid of feeling, as if she truly was a corpse in a dress. A puppet they'd attached to strings and forced to insipidly smile.

The performance finished without a hitch. Somehow, the magic prevented Marai from vomiting.

Arcturius dabbed his painted brow with a hankie, relieved, and the audience roared with their usual applause.

"Isn't she marvelous, folks?" he proclaimed with a giant grin. "See? As harmless and beautiful as a damselfly. Tell your friends and family that all is well here at the Menagerie. Come back and see us again soon!"

Marai curtsied, spun offstage with a flutter of her wings and golden faerie dust, and instantly collapsed in a heap on the floor. Without the magic's hold on her, she could've been a puddle of rainwater. She vomited black bile onto the floor.

Innesh appeared with a mop. Her eyes snapped from Marai to the two Peace Keepers backstage, standing with their bulky arms crossed.

"Is no one going to help her?" Innesh asked them.

"You get to take out the trash tonight," Franulovic replied. He was Cavar's personal favorite guard. If he was present, that meant Cavar had remained behind at the Menagerie to watch Marai's performance.

Innesh handed the mop to Franulovic. "Then you can clean up her mess."

She hoisted Marai onto her feet, and dragged her back through the rows of tents.

"Take me to Keshel's," Marai said.

Keshel hadn't returned yet when Innesh dropped her off, so Marai climbed into his bedroll. He used to smell like leather and old parchment, like the dry desert air of the Badlands. Now, Keshel's bedroll smelled of sick, must, and mothballs.

Marai waited for a long time.

Keshel eventually stumbled in, guided there by Yelich. His glazed expression meant that Keshel was lost to his visions.

Gods, he's so much worse now, Marai thought as he stood there, inert, in the middle of his tent. She proceeded to watch him for another full hour until the visions cleared.

He blinked, realizing she was there, lying in his bedroll. Keshel then promptly vomited into his bucket.

How does he have anything left inside him? Marai certainly didn't, but somehow, the black blood was constantly coming up.

Once finished, Keshel crawled into the bedroll beside her, fully clothed, forgoing all pretense.

They lay on their backs, staring up at the canvas ceiling, Marai's wing splayed out beneath him. It didn't hurt to have him lay on it; Keshel barely weighed anything now.

Marai listened to his strained breathing. Tears welled in her eyes.

"I never asked for any of this," she said. "I never asked to be heir to the faerie throne. I never wanted to have this title, this responsibility. I only wanted to *live,* so why does life have to hurt so much?"

Keshel took her hand; his skin as ice cold as her own. "You and I were built for a higher purpose, Marai. You were Chosen. Lirr never meant for us to find happiness, to live like the others. We were created to stop the darkness, and we both failed."

"But we're not disposable," Marai shouted as hot tears rolled down her cheeks. "We're not here as experiments or her meaningless sacrifices. Perhaps I could've done the right thing if I'd known. If she'd cared enough to give guidance. Why must we be perfect? Can we not make mistakes?"

Marai once thought that Lirr had stopped her from taking her own life after leaving Slate and *The Nightmare.*

"Why? Why would you make me this way?" Marai remembered shouting at Lirr and the heavens. *"Why give me life just to let me suffer?"*

But a bright ray of sun had cast itself across Marai's face, and she'd paused long enough to reconsider. She'd thought it was Lirr's hand of light, showing her another way, another path, but if Lirr had indeed halted Marai's blade, it hadn't been because the goddess loved her. It was because Lirr had a "higher purpose" for Marai.

Keshel turned his head to look at her. "I think I was created to guide you. I was supposed to be your eyes, but *I* failed you. I was . . . too scared not to read the signs. Too stubborn to believe what they implied."

Was that why Keshel had the powers he had? In the magical world, he was as unique as Marai. She lifted a hand and touched her fingertips to Keshel's eyelids. His lashes fluttered beneath the pads of her fingers.

"I suppose it doesn't matter anymore," she said. "You said I can no longer defeat the darkness because I chose to call on it. That I'm *impure*."

Instead, it was going to devour her, body and soul.

"Once you let it in, the darkness has power over you. You forged a connection with the Lord of the Underworld that day. The fate of this world is no longer up to us," said Keshel. "The girl with the auburn hair will do what we couldn't. Darkness will continue to spread until she arrives and saves us."

"Will Lirr abandon her, too, if she fails? Will this auburn-haired savior be allowed a chance at life and happiness?" Would she succeed where Marai had failed? Marai suddenly felt a tremendous protectiveness for this unknown girl. From the moment of her birth, she'd have no choice but to carry the weight of the world on her shoulders

Don't forsake her, Lirr. Love her as you couldn't love me.

Keshel stared back up at the ceiling. "The girl is only one of those pieces. There must always be four. Lirr needs all four in order to succeed. That's where we failed."

"Four what?"

"The light, the dark, the eye, the shield. When they combine, evil will yield." Keshel said these words in a rhythmic chant, distantly, as if the goddess herself was speaking through him.

Marai scowled. "Nothing you say makes any sense."

Keshel suddenly smiled. "Has it ever?"

She squeezed his hand tighter. "Tell me she won't be alone, Keshel. This girl."

He brushed away a stray tear sloping down Marai's cheek. "She'll never be alone. I promise." Keshel reached beneath his bedroll and pulled out his tattered journal. "I've been writing everything down for her. A guidebook. I used to think I was a scholar, but that was never what I was supposed to be. I won't be there, in her time, but at least I can be *her* eyes. She can read this, and *know*."

Marai let out a sob. It was relief coursing through her now, relief that this girl wouldn't go into this world blind. That this beautiful soul who hadn't yet been born would know her purpose and wouldn't fail. There was hope for her. Keshel's words would lead her through to the light.

"You have to promise me, Marai, that you will get this book to her. Somehow, find a way to put it away for safekeeping."

"No, you'll do it, yourself."

"More of me dies every day," Keshel whispered into the night, holding the journal to his chest. "When I open my eyes, I feel the darkness inside, and I lose."

Marai sensed it, too. If Keshel died, she would depart shortly after; then no one would get the journal to the girl.

She didn't promise him then. She didn't want to lie.

"Can I stay here tonight?" asked Marai instead. "I don't want to be alone."

Keshel nodded and tucked the journal back under his bedroll. He wrapped his arms around her, nestling Marai close.

After a few moments of silence, he said into the night, "I mourn for us, Marai. I mourn for the people we might have been."

CHAPTER 27

RUENEN

The journey to Baatgai was fraught with summer storms, complete with flooding, hailing, roaring winds, and breaking down. Ruenen's nerves were frayed from their crawling pace traveling from Nevandia through the neighboring Empire of Syoto.

But whenever lightning struck, Ruenen thought of Marai.

The scent of petrichor, of humid, rain-drenched air, of ether and wild skies, filled his lungs and reminded him of her.

I'm coming, he'd whisper into the storm.

Then, as the tempestuous clouds broke apart and sunlight finally kissed their clammy faces, the port of Baatgai came into view.

Unlike Cleaving Tides, this port wasn't situated on a beach. Baatgai was a fishing village that had virtually no coastline. The gray and brown slatted buildings came right up to the water's edge, raised up on wooden posts hammered into the wet sand. Old men in conical hats sat on their porches, dipping fishing lines straight into the sea. Most of the boats docked at the port were small fishing vessels, rowboats and canoes; although a few were larger, built for commuting trade along the Eastern Astyean coast, and to the closest other land mass of Yehzig.

One ship, however, eclipsed the others. Ruenen spotted its three masts from a league away. It was the largest boat he'd ever seen, sturdy and new, twice the size of a regular merchant ship.

The Arcane Wind had returned.

QUEEN OF THE SHADOW MENAGERIE   301

Ruenen dressed in unassuming traveling clothes. His crown was packed at the bottom of his bag, currently slung over Mayestral's shoulder. He didn't want to draw too much attention, but his caravan attracted fascinated eyes no matter what he was wearing.

Unlike Cleaving Tides' diverse and colorful population, Baatgai was a homogeneous community. Everyone had black hair, dark eyes, and sun-hardened skin, except for the occasional traveling sailor. People in town came out to gawk at the Nevandian strangers, and the fae, with their wings and pointed ears, stood out the most. Ruenen doubted if the Baatgaians had seen a full-blooded faerie before.

Two dozen horses halted at the edge of the village. Baatgai's streets were too narrow and inclined for the horses to traverse in a group, so Ruenen decided to continue on foot. Guards and servants leapt from their mounts and tied them up outside the village limits.

"Wait for me here," Ruenen instructed them.

Despite the drizzle and shrouded sun, it was the middle of the day, therefore Ruenen was immensely surprised to see a dark shadow waiting at the village gate. Nosficio, covered head-to-toe in pomegranate velvet so that not a sliver of his skin was showing, greeted Ruenen as he approached the wooden fence. The vampire bowed with a nauseating swirl of his wrist. Only his red eyes were visible beneath his mask and hood, appearing both menacing and comical at once.

Ruenen almost smiled. *Marai will be shocked to learn how far Nosficio is going to get her back.*

"Your Grace, glad you finally made it," the vampire said.

"The storms delayed us," Ruenen said, stretching from side to side, stiff from hours on his horse.

Salty sea air filled his nose. The humidity had dropped since the latest rain. Raife's hair had been a bramble of frizz and curls the entire journey.

"Quite the entourage you have," Nosficio said, watching as Tarik and Yovel, then Braesal's group of four dismounted. The vampire's eyes shimmered with interest at their water-color wings.

Overhearing, Braesal gave Nosficio a darting glance, placing his hand on the pommel of his sword in warning, but he dipped his head in greeting to the vampire, who'd directed them to Nevandia in the first place.

"Is that *The Arcane Wind*?" Ruenen asked, drawing Nosficio's attention back to him.

"It arrived four days ago. The locals here have been very hush hush about it. I think perhaps they're frightened of its crew and owner."

"Or you," Ruenen said. He also bet that these simple people had never dealt with a vampire before, and Nosficio was highly intimidating in his current swathed getup. "You're more terrifying than whoever works on that boat."

"Perhaps." Ruenen heard the sly smile in Nosficio's voice, hidden from view by the mask. "I've tried to approach the crew, but they're about as chatty as a cadaver. I've offered them money in exchange for information, and they refused. I then offered to hire them and charter the ship, and they finally deigned to respond by saying flat-out that I couldn't afford it." Nosficio gave Ruenen a pointed look. "I didn't tell them it was the King of Nevandia who wanted their employment."

Ruenen was about to march down to the ship and speak with them, when Nosficio grabbed his arm.

"There's one sailor who's been quite willing to speak to me, however. Seems to find me fascinating. He's asked me as many questions as I've asked of him. Doesn't appear to have much loyalty to the owner of the ship. In fact, he became quite garrulous the more coin I passed his way."

"Can you take me to him?" Ruenen asked. He wanted to hear everything with his own ears. Before following Nosficio, he turned back to Mayestral. "Find us accommodations for the evening, and then send the horses back to Nevandia. I don't intend to linger here long."

"Of course, Your Grace," Mayestral said, and gathered the staff together to delegate. Some would return to Kellesar with Raife and two other King's Guard.

"I suppose it's time to part ways, then," Raife said somberly. His emerald eyes gazed off to *The Arcane Wind* below in the dock, as if longing to set sail, himself. "Please, stay safe, my friend. Thora and I won't be able to sleep until you're home."

"Watch over Nevandia for me. Keep my Witan on task." It was improper for a king to hug one of his guards, but Ruenen didn't care. He held onto his friend for a moment.

"Tell Marai and Keshel that I'm . . ." Raife chewed on his words, conflicted. "Tell them that I'll be waiting for them. That I love them. That I can't wait to raise a toast in their honor, and celebrate their return."

Ruenen smiled. "I will."

Aresti threw herself at Raife, wrapping long arms around his neck in a tight embrace. It didn't seem like she wanted to let him go, but Raife's face was turning a tad purple. He whispered something into Aresti's pointed ear, and she released him with a sniffle.

Raife then shook hands with the rest of the team, and gathered up the horses. "Safe travels to you all."

"And safe travels to *you*, Sir Raife," Tarik replied with a thumping fist to his chest. "Take care of that wonderful wife of yours."

Raife returned the gesture, thumping his golden breastplate.

Ruenen watched as Raife led the much smaller caravan away from Baatgai, back home to Kellesar. When Raife was nothing more than glinting armor in the sun, Ruenen, Aresti, Tarik, Braesal, and Elmar followed Nosficio through the tiny, hilly streets of Baatgai down towards the water. Ruenen was impressed with how clean and quaint the village was. Everyone seemed to have a job, a purpose. Even the children were engaged in activities, weaving fishing nets, shucking oysters and mussels, mopping porches.

Nosficio led the group to a small seaside tavern on the dock, serving fresh-caught fish, crab, and rice wine. One entire wall of the tavern was open to the sea.

A man sat at a table, back to the door. He had a jug of liquor in front of him that he drank straight from. His patchy blond hair stuck up at strange angles.

"I hear you're a man who knows things," Ruenen said as he approached the ramshackle table.

"Depends how much you're willing to pay for what I've got to say."

The slick voice sounded familiar. Ruenen's heart jumped, and he couldn't explain why. Not until he sat down opposite the man at the table.

He was severely scarred from fire, lightning, and blades, but that didn't stop Ruenen from recognizing those blue eyes immediately.

Slate Hemming's grin spread across his distorted lips. "You again."

Ruenen couldn't find the words. He didn't know how to steady his raging pulse. His fingers curled into fists in his lap.

Hemming was supposed to be dead. Ruenen had watched Marai set fire to his ship, *The Nightmare*. He'd abused Marai during her days as a pirate and member of his crew. He'd made her believe she was nothing but a tool, an object for his pleasure and gain.

How had this cockroach of a human being survived?

Hemming glanced from Nosficio to Aresti, then Tarik and Braesal. Elmar remained outside to stand guard at the door. Hemming was fully surrounded by magical folk, but that only made the captain's eyes glisten with interest. Marai had told Ruenen that Hemming was obsessed with magic, envious of those who could wield it.

The pirate sat back in his chair, crossing one leg over his knee, nonchalant. "Figures it'd be you asking about Marai. She has you wrapped around her little finger, doesn't she?"

"You know where she is," Ruenen said as heat rose up his neck.

"You escaped Rayghast's clutches?" Hemming asked evasively.

Ruenen had to play his game. He wouldn't let Hemming slither away. He calmed his breath and crossed his arms, mimicking Hemming's casual attitude. "More than escape, I'd say. You hear that Rayghast's dead? That his kingdom has been integrated into Nevandian territory?"

"What happens between these Nine Kingdoms doesn't matter to me," said Hemming with a flippant wave. "Politics are trivial. My life is at sea, where no one rules."

"I'm sure the idea of kidnapping Marai appealed to you."

"I didn't kidnap her. Although, I won't lie and say I didn't enjoy the sight of her in chains."

Hemming's crooked, demented grin had Ruenen seeing red. *Don't let him goad you.* But Ruenen didn't have to admonish the pirate. Braesal did it for him.

"That's our Queen you're speaking of." He stepped closer, towering over Hemming with his full height, breadth of shoulders, and splayed wings.

"Queen?" Hemming burst out laughing. "If you think that little bitch is your Queen, then you've been deceived."

QUEEN OF THE SHADOW MENAGERIE   305

Aresti withdrew one of her short swords and stabbed it into the table, right between two of Hemming's fingers. The ex-captain froze as Aresti growled into his face.

"Tell us what you know about Andara and the Menagerie, and I'll let you keep your hand. I'm not opposed to taking *smaller* parts, as well." Her dark eyes dipped to Hemming's pants.

Hemming slid his hand off the table, but didn't bat an eyelash. "You're a fun one, aren't you?"

Aresti spat at the foot of his chair in response.

Ruenen didn't want the situation to get out of hand. He needed Hemming's cooperation, and hurting him wouldn't get them any closer to Marai. "You heard her. Tell us about the Menagerie."

"I'd say more, but my throat's gone dry . . ."

Ruenen's jaw tightened, but he gave Tarik a coin, and the werewolf returned a moment later with a new jug of rice wine, setting it down in front of Hemming.

"Talk, or we'll let Aresti have her way with you," he said.

Hemming took a long swig. "It's a freak show, the brainchild of my employer, Governor Jakov Cavar. A place where he's gathered magical creatures and puts them on display."

Ruenen watched this statement ripple down the line of his magical companions. The words "freak show" sat heavily on their brows. Nosficio's eyes glowed a violent crimson. Ruenen's stomach knotted at the thought of Marai and Keshel locked up in cages. It must have also been the fate of that other vampire, Desislava.

"This Governor . . . is he fae?" asked Tarik. His facial muscles were tense. For a man usually so jovial, he looked ready to murder someone.

"Human, as is most of the population of Andara."

"How is a human able to keep those magical creatures imprisoned?" Aresti asked. "Especially Marai, with her abilities."

Hemming tapped his neck. "A special collar. Cavar's creation—it negates magic. Makes Marai as weak as a kitten."

Ruenen ground his teeth.

Hemming took another swig of the liquor bottle and observed the change in Ruenen's demeanor. With a smirk, he said, "It was a delight to see her so powerless. After what she did to me, it's exactly what she deserved. Marai couldn't stop me from touching her, stroking her soft skin, grabbing fistfuls of her hair, from dragging her across the deck like a *dog*—"

Ruenen leapt across the table, knocking Hemming backwards off his chair. All he felt and saw was white hot, searing rage. He pummeled Hemming's face with his fist four times before Tarik and Braesal could pull him off. The barman shouted, demanding they stop or leave the premises.

"No more fucking games, Hemming," Ruenen said, stepping away. "You tell us exactly where this Menagerie is or I swear to the gods I'll arrest you and make your life a living hell."

"Arrest me?" spat Hemming, along with his mouthful of blood. He wiped away the dribble and got to his feet. "On whose authority?"

Nosficio's nostrils flared at the scent of blood. His eyes honed in on Hemming, and the ex-captain noticed, stiffening.

"Mine." Ruenen shot Nosficio a warning glance, then stood taller as he again addressed Hemming. "By order of the King of Nevandia."

Hemming laughed incredulously. "Oh, sure, *you're* the King of Nevandia!" He stopped, studying the stoney faces of Ruenen's companions. He finally noticed the growing number of Ruenen's armed men waiting outside the tavern door. Hemming's rubicund face fell. "You've got to be kidding me."

Aresti pointed her sword's sharp tip at Hemming's shriveled heart. "Address him as 'Your Grace,' you worm."

"Come to think of it, maybe I *should* arrest you for kidnapping me months ago," Ruenen said. "Or I could let Aresti skewer you right here. No one would miss you. But I think I'll give you a chance to redeem yourself. Sit down and tell me everything you've learned about Koda, Andara, the Menagerie, and this Governor Cavar."

Hemming fumed, but sat back in his chair. For an hour, he recounted every detail he'd learned. The others pulled up chairs, clinging to the ex-captain's words.

The scope of the Menagerie, of Cavar's power and control, horrified Ruenen. From getting past the barrier and into Bakair, sneaking around the Guardians, and then getting into the Menagerie, itself, would take precise planning. The amulets were the biggest issue. Even if they succeeded in locating Marai and

Keshel, they'd need to overpower Cavar and his Guardians, and remove the collar around Marai and Keshel's throats.

Ruenen began to sweat. *I'll need to come up with an airtight plan.* He tossed a pouch of coins across the table.

"Half now for getting us to Andara. The rest when we return safely with Marai and Keshel."

Hemming's greedy eyes widened. "I have no control over when that ship sails again. That's up to Captain Brelioc."

"Not if I buy the ship and the entire crew," Ruenen said. He'd had Wattling dig deep into Nevandia's coffers, which the churlish lord had been reluctant to do. "If Brelioc won't make the journey, then I'll name *you* Captain of *The Arcane Wind*. Does that seem like a fair deal?"

"He doesn't deserve that," growled Aresti.

"No, he doesn't," Ruenen said, glaring at Hemming, "but getting Marai and Keshel home is all that matters. Once we get to Andara, you can plunder whatever goods you can find, especially if owned by our friend the Governor. What say you?"

Hemming's blue eyes gleamed as he pulled the pouch of coins towards him. A slow, sinister grin bloomed on his scarred face. "Let's get going then, shall we?" He drained the remainder of his liquor and stood. "I'll introduce you to Brelioc and the crew."

As Hemming led them from the tavern, Aresti pulled Ruenen aside. "You can't possibly put this bastard at the helm of our mission."

"We need him. We need this ship and the crew. We have no other choice." But Ruenen hated it, too. It felt like a betrayal to hire the man who'd scarred Marai's young soul.

I will do whatever I must to bring her home. Even if it meant allying with a snake.

Ruenen and his team met with the crew and Captain Brelioc onboard the deck of *The Arcane Wind*. Hemming hovered to the side, picking at his fingernails with a superior, smug expression.

"I refuse," Captain Brelioc said after Ruenen offered to pay more than what Cavar was already paying the men. He was a bearded old sea-dog, face wrinkled and hardened like old leather. "I don't want to incur his wrath. You have no idea how powerful the Governor really is. That magic in his amulet . . . why do you think I've made the journey all these years? I'm terrified of what will happen to me if I get on his bad side."

Ruenen understood the old captain's refusal. He wasn't going to force him to sail, especially since Hemming was waiting to swoop in from the wings.

Half of the crew also could not be tempted by money. The ones who remained only seemed persuaded because Ruenen was a king, and knew there may be more reward on the backend once the journey was completed. Ambitious men like Slate Hemming. Those not making the journey gathered up their things with grumbles and glares, and disembarked *The Arcane Wind*.

"Do we have enough men to sail?" asked Mayestral, watching the men disembark from the gangway.

"If your people help and don't laze about the whole trip, then we should be fine." Hemming rolled up his sleeves. His arms were as burned as his face, and Ruenen noticed that his old water dragon tattoos were virtually indistinguishable. Hemming immediately took charge of the remaining crew, pushing out his chest. "Get her ready to set sail tomorrow morning, lads."

His hand reached for the captain's quarters door handle, but Tarik latched onto Hemming's arm.

"That'll be the King's quarters, now."

Hemming glared daggers at the werewolf, but Tarik didn't balk at the grotesque face. Cursing under his breath, Hemming settled into the smaller officer's cabin down the hall. Mayestral and the remaining Kellesar staff went to work cleaning Ruenen's cabin, setting up his minimal belongings inside. Daye went below deck to take stock of the supplies and food. There was a noticeable nervousness in the air as the servants worked. Ruenen doubted if any of them had ever left Nevandia, nonetheless traveled by boat abroad, but they'd volunteered to come to please their King.

On deck once night fell, Nosficio removed his mask, gloves, and cloak, fully revealing his face and fangs. "This is where I leave you."

"Are you sure you don't want to come along?" Ruenen asked.

The vampire's wit, speed, and strength would be highly useful in sneaking onto Andara.

Nosficio gave him a wry smile. "Standing on this boat now is the closest I will get to sailing." He then grew serious. "I'm entrusting Marai's safety to you, precious King. I expect her back on these shores within ninety days."

Ruenen nodded. Nosficio cared about what happened to Aras and Meallán's heir. It had become his self-proclaimed duty to watch over Marai. Ruenen couldn't help but ask him, "What will you do in the meantime?" The vampire always made him incredibly curious.

"I left our Greltan Queen at a time of immense turmoil. I shall return to assist in alleviating her grief."

Ruenen caught the meaning. "I could also use your help with the Witan. I'm nervous about leaving Nevandia for such a long time. I'm hoping I can trust you to keep my reign secure." He removed a letter from his vest pocket, and handed it to Nosficio.

"What's this?" He stared at the green blob of wax with the royal sunburst seal.

"I'm officially declaring you a member of my Witenagemot."

Nosficio blinked. "I'm surprised to know that you trust me with such a tremendous responsibility."

"I promised you a seat on my counsel in exchange for your help delivering messages to Nieve during the war," Ruenen said. "Now is your chance to make some waves."

Nosficio arched a pleased eyebrow. "I'm not sure your Witan will be grateful for my presence, but I think I'll enjoy frightening those old men."

"And please help the remaining fae and Brass with the shadow creatures," Ruenen added. "There's one with wings who's been stalking around Kellesar. Keep an eye out for him and others."

Although, it was possible the creatures would leave Kellesar alone and follow Ruenen to Andara. He wondered if they could swim . . .

Nosficio rolled his eyes. "I'm not your errand boy."

"No, but you *do* care about what happens to Astye. Keep it safe for Marai, for when she returns." Ruenen held out his hand. "Thank you for getting us this far."

Nosficio stared at the hand. Slowly, he shook it. Ruenen felt the power in his grasp, and the vampire's long nails scraped against his skin. *He could destroy me in seconds.*

Instead, Nosficio simply said, "Good luck," and disappeared in a blur of wind, off to do gods knew what, but Ruenen felt more at ease leaving Nevandia, knowing that the vampire would be watching over it.

As soon as the sun rose the next morning, splashing peach and orange paint across the sky, *The Arcane Wind* set sail with Captain Slate Hemming at the wheel, a look of triumph on his face.

Ruenen would need to watch him closely, but for now, Ruenen stood at the bow, staring at the reflection of the foreglow on the water. A breeze ruffled his hair; his heart lighter than it had been in ninety-five days.

I'm coming, my love. I'll see you soon.

CHAPTER 28

MARAI

She lost track of the days and hours.

Marai ate. She retched it back up. Black blood coated the inside of the bucket.

She bathed in the creek. Dressed. Walked to-and-from the theater. Disappeared into a daze while performing. She couldn't recall anything from those nights.

Marai caused not a ripple of tension. Koda and the Peace Keepers observed her every move, but even they could see that her fire had been smothered.

She'd become a mere fading cinder of who she once was. An echo of a being.

Marai's nights were spent in Keshel's tent, sleeping at his side, watching him toss and turn as vivid dreams and visions flickered against his eyelids. She studied the cliffs of his cheekbones in the darkness. The shape of his furrowed brow. The taut muscles in his neck. The sound of his slowed heartbeat.

In the mornings, fear would grip her. He would lie there, so still . . .

Will Keshel wake up today? Because one day, Marai knew he wouldn't. One day his eyes wouldn't open, and she would be alone.

But in the morning, he'd blink away sleep and turn to face her in the bedroll. Perhaps he worried the same thing about her, that she'd be gone when he awoke. Keshel would pull out his journal from beneath the bedroll and scratch down whatever he'd seen whilst he slept.

"I don't know who this Lord of the Underworld is, and why no one has heard of Him before, but in my visions, He's a figure of smoke and black flame. I can never see His face, but dark magic lives within Him, in Cavar's stone, accessible through the earth at our feet. It's because of Him that it exists."

Him, with a capital "H." It was Him who spoke to Marai, with that sinister, smokey voice. Him, who wanted to lure her away.

"I think He's trapped in the Underworld, and is trying to use you and Cavar, even Rayghast, to get out," Keshel explained.

Marai barely spoke. Movement caused her pain. Dark poison corrupted her from the inside out. Her mind was a chasm of torment and nausea. Thinking of Thora, Raife, and Aresti back home only brought her agony, so Marai closed the door on them. There was no hope in seeing them or Nevandia again. She'd lost everything—her home, her people . . .

And the man she loved. Ruenen was married now. He had a *wife*, and that was the deepest pain of all.

Summer began its slow transition to autumn. The world inside the barrier never changed, due to a stabilizing magic in place throughout the camp to ensure temperatures stayed within a reasonable range. But Marai smelled autumn's earthy decay in the air. Saw it in the golden, slanted light of the sun. Nights grew colder. The grass beneath her turned yellow and brown. Cyrill gave her and Keshel an extra blanket.

She saw Cavar in passing only once, his office door ajar when Marai was ushered through to the backstage. He sat at his desk, counting coins, jotting down numbers in his ledgers. His eyes snapped up to meet hers for an instant, then returned to his work.

Cavar believed the rebellion was over. That he'd won. That he'd tamed the most powerful faerie and become an untouchable, god-like being.

He was right.

Marai had nothing left to give, except her life, which was slowly draining away.

CHAPTER 29

RUENEN

R uenen had never sailed on the open sea before.

Marai loved the vastness of the ocean. She'd told him that sailing signified freedom. That standing on a beach felt like she was on the edge of something powerful.

Ruenen felt that now, too.

The waters were calm in the Eastern Ocean. No rain, no storms. Ruenen grew to enjoy the gentle rocking of the ship. The constant sound of waves and seagulls. The dazzling reflection of the sun and moon on the water at different times of the day. The taste of salt on his lips.

While the massive ship was the size of a small village, it was still a constrained place. Whenever Ruenen felt the tickle of restlessness, or the tapping on his brain of being trapped, he'd pick up his lute and play.

Music once again flooded his life with melodies. Ruenen saw lyrics in every sunset, a harmony in each chorus of laughing gulls.

He'd forgotten who he was. He'd gotten lost in his gilded crown and marble halls, his life set off-course by a royal title. He may be King of Nevandia, but his heart belonged to a bard and the fire of a forge. His fingers held the quill that signed a treaty, but also plucked the strings of a lute to bring music, memory, and stories to life. His hands held the hammer that shaped a refined blade. They held a sword that protected those he loved.

At night, Ruenen donned the hat of Ard the Bard, and played for the crowded deck. The crew listened in, hanging from the rigging, sitting on boxes and crates, and some joined him with instruments of their own.

Aresti roared with laughter at Ruenen's first original tune, "The Lady Butcher."

"That's the most ridiculous song I've ever heard," she said, clutching her stomach as she nearly toppled from the crate where she was seated.

"I'll have you know that it's a very popular song in the taverns across the East," Ruenen replied, mildly affronted. "Don't forget, that was who Marai was for a long time."

He fondly remembered those first few days after meeting her, hiring the Lady Butcher to get him safely across Astye to Andara. When he didn't know what she looked like, or that she was half-fae. When she spoke to him in grunts and demands.

How ironic that he was sailing to Andara now to find her...

"You know, in Ain we'd heard tales of the Lady Butcher," said Yovel. "Within our clan and the towns nearby, her name was feared."

Tarik leaned back against the wall of the ship, staring up at the stars. "Strange to think that that same ghoul of a woman is actually the Faerie Queen."

Ruenen smiled. *Strange, indeed.*

Tarik raised his eyebrows at Ruenen and made a sweeping gesture with his hand. "'The Ballad of the Faerie Queen.' Good title, no?"

As glad as Ruenen was to have both Tarik and Yovel along for the journey, he'd completely forgotten about the full moon.

"We need a safe place to shift," said Tarik, pulling Ruenen aside after their brief stop in Yehzig, "and you need to keep everyone away from there until dawn."

It was actually Hemming who came up with the idea. He led Ruenen and the weres into the deepest part of the hull, down several flights of stairs, to an area mainly used for storage. Several sets of new, sturdy chains were anchored to the floor and wall.

Yovel examined them, yanking as hard as he could on the chains. Nothing budged. He nodded in approval. "These will work well. Where are the keys?"

Hemming pulled them from his pocket and tossed them to Tarik. "They've secured many magical creatures before, including other werewolves. I know they'll hold."

Ruenen grimaced. He didn't need to ask if Marai and Keshel were also chained up there.

The next evening, Ruenen and Hemming locked the door to the hull, and Ruenen prayed that those chains wouldn't break with the strain of two werewolves, and that the door wouldn't come crashing down. All through the night, in his cabin several levels above, he heard their howls and snarls, the sound of the chains rattling. He couldn't sleep, not with the threat of a werewolf bursting into his room and devouring him whole.

But the sun rose, and the chains held.

Then the winds changed. The sky grew darker. There was nothing ahead of *The Arcane Wind* but expansive, churning ocean. They were alone.

Water-workers Braesal, Beck, Finneagal, and Zorish stood at the bow, sensing the waves beneath the ship, and diminishing any that grew too large or rough. Their job would only get harder the further north they traversed.

When the first storm hit, *The Arcane Wind* was prepared. Aresti did her best to redirect the high winds away from the boat, by pushing her own magical gusts against them. Braesal, Beck, Finneagal, and Zorish planted themselves on the wooden deck, arms stretched wide. Through the pelting rain, Ruenen saw their magic at work, streaks of turquoise cutting through waves, halting another from crashing into the ship. Braesal was the strongest of the four, and gathered up the falling rain around the ship and sent it spewing back into the sea. Ruenen had witnessed impressive magic before, but he'd never seen someone so utterly in control of the elements around him. Braesal was a master. A god of the sea.

"Your Grace, you should remain in your cabin," he said without an ounce of fear as he cut a charging wave in half.

Ruenen slipped as the ship tilted forward, and slammed his knee into the deck. He hissed with pain, but staggered back to his feet again. "I won't hide away when everyone else is risking their lives for this mission."

He helped the crew the best he could, although he had no real understanding of how things worked on a ship. He spent most of the storm getting tossed from one end of the boat to the other, nearly going overboard at least five times. His eyes darted to the wheel, and widened when he didn't see Hemming standing there. First-mate, Curly, manned the ship.

Lirr's Bones, where on earth is Hemming? Everyone, besides Mayestral and the other servants, were on deck helping in any way they could. Ruenen couldn't remember the last time he saw Hemming. Before the storm hit, maybe . . .

Eventually, the gray, tumbling clouds dispersed to let in a few rays of sunlight. The downpour weakened to a drizzle, and the wind stopped ripping through Ruenen's hair and clothing. With the storm subsided, he went in search of Hemming, and found the captain in his cabin, huddling on the floor next to his cot. It was a jarring sight, to see such an arrogant villain be reduced to this quivering man.

"Get up," Ruenen said without an ounce of pity. He was drenched to the bone, sore, and exhausted after the hours-long watery siege.

Hemming sent him a weak scowl in return.

"Do you intend to spend the rest of the voyage cowering in here? You're a *captain*. An experienced sailor. You've done this before. I'm paying you to do your job, but perhaps I should pass it off to Curly, since he was the one *man enough* to steer the damn ship."

Hemming staggered to his feet. "And here I thought you were a spineless whelp. I suppose I shouldn't be surprised by your callousness. You bested Rayghast, after all."

Ruenen didn't take the comment as a compliment. If it was anyone but Hemming shaking in fear of the storm, Ruenen would never force them out, but with the Captain, he didn't feel bad about it. Not after what he'd done to Marai. Not after he'd tried to sell off Ruenen to Rayghast.

After that day, Hemming commanded the wheel during every storm. He truly was an expert, and well-worth the reputation he'd forged. He plunged headlong into gigantic waves, held the wheel steady, but his hands still shook on the spokes, and each giant wave that swelled from the sea made Hemming's eyes nearly pop out of his head.

Thanks to Aresti's wind, Braesal's water-work, and Hemming's navigation, they made excellent time across the Northern Sea. The trip from Yehzig to Andara was usually around forty days.

They were arriving after only thirty-two.

Andara's misty landmass came into view early in the morning, and Aresti held up the bloodstone ring between her fingers.

"Oh, Marai's definitely here, all right," she said. "This thing's vibrating like a rattlesnake's tail."

A giant screen of dark fog, as tall as the walls surrounding Kellesar, blocked the view of the city that lay beyond. All Ruenen could truly glimpse was an unprotected harbor.

He called a meeting in the dining cabin with Hemming, the fae, the weres, and those of the King's Guard who would help retrieve Marai and Keshel on land. Mayestral hovered behind Ruenen's chair, but the staff and crew would remain on *The Arcane Wind.*

"How do you intend to get through the barrier?" Hemming asked Ruenen. "No use planning further if you can't get past the dock."

"Can't we go around it?" Ruenen asked. "Are there other ports we can try?"

"On either side of the barrier is rugged, inclined terrain that's difficult to scale," said Hemming. "Bakair is located high above sea level. The only clear path is through the city. I've never seen other ports, but I don't believe they're close or easily accessible. We'd waste valuable time searching, and they'll erect other barriers if they see us in the water."

Ruenen looked to Braesal, sitting on his left. "Anyone able to dismantle barriers?"

Braesal shook his head. "That's a rare ability. Never seen anyone do it before."

At his side, Zorish nodded in agreement.

Damn. If only Keshel were not the one in need of rescue . . .

"You'll need an amulet, then. Or you'll need to get one of the Guardians to dismantle it for you," said Hemming, leaning back in his chair and crossing his arms.

Ruenen studied the Captain. "Sounds like we'll have to lure them out from the city."

"How?" asked Hemming, unimpressed.

"You and the crew. Stay on the dock, demand more money, cause an uproar. Tell them that Brelioc was attacked in Baatgai and half the crew taken prisoner. *Lie.* You're good at that."

Hemming cocked an eyebrow. "Let's say they go for this story. One of the Guardians comes out to negotiate. What do you want us to do next? Threaten them? Put a knife to their throat?"

"Exactly," said Ruenen. "Distract them, and someone else can come up from behind and secure their hands so they can't reach for the amulet."

"Once the barrier's down, we need to stay hidden. Try to sneak our way to where the Menagerie is," Aresti added. "We won't succeed if we have half the city chasing us."

"The Menagerie isn't in Bakair," said Hemming, shaking his head. "I don't know exactly where it is because I've never been allowed past the barrier, and Koda didn't say a word to me about it, but the crew think it's farther inland, somewhere below the Hinterlands."

"Hinterlands?" asked Braesal.

"It's where all of *you* come from," replied Hemming, gesturing to the fae. "It's up in the mountains, surrounded by its own impenetrable barrier." He spread out a rough, hand drawn map across the table. It wasn't to scale, and only pointed out the major landmarks and roads within Bakair. "I snagged this from Brelioc. As you can see, there are four main roads out of the city. One of them should take you directly to the Menagerie. Problem is: which one?"

The table leaned forward in their chairs to study the map. There was a large causeway through the city, which then branched off in four directions.

"I'm assuming those giant, shadowy mountains that we saw in the distance are the Hinterlands," Ruenen said. "They're to the Northeast of Bakair. This main causeway ends at the Central Quarter. From there, two of these roads lead in the direction of the Hinterlands."

Aresti met Ruenen's gaze from across the table. She made a face, eyes darting to her pants pocket. *The ring.* It would guide them down the right road. They didn't need a map—Marai's magic would draw the ring straight to her location.

They had a plan. They had a route.

This will work. It must work!

Hemming shook his head and rolled up the map. "You're exceedingly optimistic about your odds. Maybe if Marai, herself, were among you, I'd be inclined to agree with your optimism. But even you—" He jerked his chin at Braesal, "Won't be able to go up against those amulets and win."

"Let us handle that," Ruenen said. "Your job is to lure a Guardian out to the docks and subdue them."

The ship slowly pulled into the harbor, much to the surprise of a few fishermen bobbing off the coast. They gaped as the ship passed by their tiny vessels.

Ruenen's body was electric, wired, ready to run and fight. He trilled his antsy fingers upon the railing as the crew began to collect on deck. Braesal, Finneagal, and Zorish waited below, while Aresti and Beck covered their pointed ears with wide-brimmed hats.

Once *The Arcane Wind* was safely at anchor, Hemming confidently strolled down onto the dock from the gangplank.

"What's the meaning of this?" guffawed the harbormaster with a thick accent Ruenen had never heard before. *Andaran.* The man's ample stomach strained at the buttons on his long waistcoat. He flipped through papers in his ledger, utterly baffled. "You're not due back. No return date was set by the Governor. Where's Brelioc?"

"We had some trouble on Astye. Brelioc and half the crew were taken prisoner. A band of criminals tried to take the ship, too, but I sailed her here," Hemming said with an ease suggesting he was quite practiced in lying.

"You idiot," the harbormaster said with a superior look. "You sailed all the way here with half a crew? What if you'd wrecked the ship? You should have anchored in Yehzig. Whatever got in your brain that you should return without Governor Cavar's permission?"

The fishermen nearby quickly abandoned their work and disappeared through the dense fog barrier. They sensed something was about to happen, and clearly didn't want to be around when it did.

"We were pursued to Yehzig. Only way to outrun them was to sail here," said Hemming. "Look, we've got grievances. We want more money. We risk our lives each time we sail, and now we've got people on Astye and Yehzig who know our employer's wealthy. If we go back there, they'll try to ransom us. They'll commandeer the ship."

More of the crew had skulked down the ramp. Curly, the largest, crossed his burly arms and loomed over the squat harbormaster.

Realizing the threat before him, the harbormaster's dark eyes darted from sailor to sailor. "You'll need to wait here. I'll reach out to the Governor, and see what he has to say. Until I receive directions from him, you should keep to the ship, sailor—"

"I'm the captain of this ship now," Hemming said with a smirk, "and I wait for no one. Go get Cavar, or we may not remain very patient." He took a threatening step towards the harbormaster.

The paunchy man jolted backwards. "I'm afraid the Governor isn't in town right now."

Ruenen's lips twitched. *That's a relief.* If he wasn't in the city, that would make their infiltration much easier.

Hemming's boot tapped against the dock. "Then bring me someone else. Someone with authority who can fix the situation." He then leaned in slightly and whispered something to the harbormaster.

The harbormaster bit his lip, then sighed. "I shall return shortly." He turned on his heel and marched through the barrier on the other side of the dock. The fog swallowed him; the magic in the barrier moved and swirled like smoke.

An uneasy feeling rose the hair on Ruenen's arms. He didn't trust Hemming's secretive comment. Ruenen, Aresti, Tarik, Brass, and Yovel hustled down the gangplank, joining the crew.

"What did you say to him?" Ruenen demanded of Hemming.

The Captain shrugged. "Nothing, except a final threat."

Ruenen met Aresti's skeptical gaze.

Not long after, the harbormaster reappeared with ten people in tow. Most were red-vested guards, but two of them sported identical bronze necklaces. The first was a severe-looking woman, bedecked in gold bangles. The other was a bald, grumpy man with an enormous mustache.

They'd only planned on one Guardian coming, not two, and certainly not a handful of guards.

Hemming had warned them.

Fucking double crosser. So much for sneaking into Bakair...

The woman Guardian grasped the amulet at her neck. "So it's true—invaders! Stand back, you brutes!"

Before she could attack, Aresti knocked the woman down with a fierce gust of wind. The female Guardian screamed as she rolled backwards, dress flying over her head, revealing her undergarments. Tarik and Yovel charged the male Guardian, knocking him to the ground before he could reach for his amulet. King's Guard and fae clashed swords with the guards.

In the chaos, Hemming ripped the necklace from the woman's neck as she shrieked something in Andaran. Hemming rushed to escape into a docked rowboat. He fumbled with its ropes, long enough for Ruenen to pounce, knocking him to the ground.

Ruenen set his blade against the Captain's throat as fighting continued around him. "Don't even try."

Hemming struggled, grabbing at Ruenen's shirt. "You'll never beat Cavar. You're as good as dead, and Marai will spend the rest of her life a slave."

Ruenen pressed the edge of his sword harder, cutting a thin line at Hemming's throat. The pirate stilled, face red and livid. Ruenen snatched the amulet from his fist, and called over Elmar and Yovel.

"Lock this filth up in the storage room."

As Elmar and Yovel carted Hemming off below deck, Aresti cut down the final red-vested guard. Two of the ship's crew were dead, and the dock dripped with slippery blood.

Ruenen turned to the two Guardians, both fuming and red-faced, held captive by Curly and Tarik. "How do we lower the barrier?"

The bald man cracked first as Curly's chokehold on him tightened. He whimpered, sweat trickling down his temples. "All you need to do is hold the amulet and force your will upon it."

Force my will? Ruenen's fingers tightened around the bronze amulet. *Dismantle the barrier. Let us pass through.* With every ounce of focus he had, he pushed the thought into the amulet.

It pulsed against his palm with warm blacklight. The foggy barrier dissolved into wisps of smoke, revealing a bustling, clean city of identical sandstone buildings beyond. The Andaran people behind the barrier froze in the middle of the streets to stare.

Ruenen whistled. Braesal and Finneagal emerged from the deck, hopping over the railing, wings fluttering as they landed effortlessly on the dock. The female Guardian let out another yelp, before she fainted in a puddle of silk skirts on the wooden planks.

"How do we get to the Menagerie?" Ruenen asked the bald man.

"Follow the main road. It's a two-day ride by carriage from Bakair," the Guardian said, spewing spittle as he spoke. "But once Cavar hears about this, he'll stop you. You'll never make it to the camp."

Ruenen turned to Curly and the crew. "Hold them both on the ship in the cell with Hemming. Search them for weapons and information, but swear to me that no harm will come to them."

"Yes, Your Grace," grunted Curly.

They hoisted the unconscious woman and male Guardian onto the ship.

"There's a good chance other Guardians may arrive," Ruenen said to Nyle and Zorish, who'd elected to stay behind and watch over the ship with the Greltans, Mayestral, and staff. Ruenen tossed one of the amulets to Nyle. "Use this only in defense. See if you can get a barrier up around the ship. Maybe move it somewhere along the coast. I'm leaving you both in charge." He leaned into Nyle's ear. "Don't let Hemming or the crew get their hands on it."

Nyle bowed. "I won't fail you, Your Grace."

Ruenen gathered his team: Aresti, Tarik, Yovel, Braesal, Beck, Finneagal, Sir Elmar, and four other disguised King's Guard dashed into the city of Bakair.

The tawny-skinned citizens panicked in the absence of the barrier. Realizing there was a foreign invasion occurring, they scattered like mice towards whatever shelter they could find. They seemed particularly frightened by Braesal and Finneagal, with their wings on display.

These people weren't a threat. Ruenen saw no amulets. No weapons. These were common folk, and Ruenen felt guilty for terrifying them and their children. Andarans shouted and squealed in their native language, tossing stones, household items like kitchen knives, and fishing tools as Ruenen's team passed. Ruenen narrowly missed being struck by a hammer, thrown by a cursing man who chased him up the street.

Do they have no army?

They weren't Guardians, and Ruenen didn't see any of the red-vest guards, either, while tearing up the main thoroughfare.

At least, not until they reached the Central Quarter.

It was a large square, surrounded by the tallest and grandest buildings in the city. A governmental and business hub, Ruenen guessed. The men and women standing out in the streets were dressed in fine clothing, gold and jewels. Several wore amulets like the one in Ruenen's fist, but some of them cowered behind others, clearly not used to violence. Ruenen had to wonder if these well-dressed Guardians had been in a real battle before.

Well, he wasn't taking any chances.

Create a barrier around us, Ruenen ordered the amulet. It pulsated again, glowing, before a dark, dense mist formed around him and the rest of his team. The acrid scent of sulfur lingered in the air.

Two of the bravest Guardians in the square sent a barrage of magic into Ruenen's barrier. Shards of onyx ice, high winds, and black flames crashed against the mist. Ruenen recognized those black flames. Could taste the pepper on his tongue. How could he ever forget? Rayghast had used those flames on the battlefield, as easily as he'd controlled the earth.

No wonder Cavar was so powerful. The amulets contained dark magic.

Ruenen nearly dropped his amulet. *He'd* used dark magic.

Yet none of the Guardians had stained skin like Rayghast and Marai. Ruenen glanced down at his own hands, searching for the signs, but his skin remained the same. Somehow, the amulets allowed its users to access that power without any repercussions.

But he couldn't focus on that. More Guardians joined in, launching into another round of attacks. However, Ruenen's will must have been stronger than theirs, because his barrier held. Their attacks burnt out on contact with the mist.

These people, these *Guardians,* weren't fighters. They didn't react fast enough. They all stood in a row, completely untrained and unaware of battle tactics, and their moves were hesitant, unsure, uncreative.

With a sweep of his hand, Braesal drenched them in a wave of water from the fountain in the middle of the square. A handful of Guardians collapsed to the ground, drenched and deterred.

Aresti made a throaty sound of approval before releasing her own gust of wind, blowing two Guardians backwards. They crashed through a window. Shards of glass went flying. A massive topiary toppled over onto a man, crushing him.

Two roads came into view. Aresti stopped running, clutching the bloodstone ring in her hand. She faced one road, then the other, then back again. Finally, after a minute of trial and error, the ring made its decision.

Aresti pointed to the road that branched off to the right. In the distance, the spiked summits of a jagged mountain range rose from the earth.

Follow the road. Don't stop.

Ruenen's feet pounded the dirt beneath him. Adrenaline coursed through his body, keeping his legs and arms pumping, the breath filling his lungs.

Bakair guards and the bravest townspeople gave up chasing Ruenen and his team when they reached a sprawling wheat field outside the city. They had a full, open road ahead of them now, amongst leagues of crop fields and patch-work plains.

"Keep checking that ring," Ruenen shouted to Aresti. "I don't want to go off course."

A few days and one road until he saw Marai.

I'm coming. Stay strong and wait for me.

CHAPTER 30

MARAI

Time passed.

Marai didn't count the days.

Marai didn't care.

CHAPTER 31

CAVAR

"Everything has been going smoothly, Uncle," said Acacia at breakfast.

In the banquet hall, light streamed in from the Southern-facing windows, but not from the north. Never from that side of the room, where the barrier clouded the sun and the image of the jagged Hinterlands in the distance. Cavar had arrived the previous evening to watch the performance and observe Marai. As Acacia said, the Menagerie was running as it should.

"Audiences are coming back, and the Faerie Queen has been reduced to nothing but a walking shadow. Although, I think you may have overdone it with the stone's magic, Uncle. She's constantly vomiting that vile black sludge, and I'm tired of having people clean it up."

"No," Cavar said, taking a bite of his smoked fish on toast, "we cannot underestimate her again."

Yes, the Menagerie was recovering well, but that was why they needed to avoid complacency. Stay the course.

"Won't she die from the damage inside her? She's a major investment. That would defeat the purpose of bringing her here."

"It won't kill her for a while," said Cavar, swiping a pad of salted butter across another piece of bread. "I'll remove it in a week or two, but by then, she'll be so broken that she'll never cause us trouble again."

Acacia frowned, but kept slicing her orange into dainty, minuscule pieces.

Then Cavar's amulet heated.

An abnormal, searing heat, bleeding through the fabric of his shirt and vest. The stone pulsed out a dark warning.

Acacia's emitted the same steady pulse. She dropped her knife with a hiss, removing her amulet before it burned her. "What on earth is going on?"

"You think I know?" Cavar snapped back, staring into the writing black smoke of the stone. "I'm sitting right here with you."

Acacia recoiled. He never admonished his niece, but she was sometimes a brainless ninny.

Cavar didn't wait to ask further foolish questions. He stood from the table, stalked out of the hall, and into the camp. Everything was quiet. Calm. Most of the creatures hadn't yet risen, but he wasn't worried about them. He sought out the Faerie Queen.

Marai sat at the bank of the creek, wings drooping down her back. Thin arms pulled her knees to her chest. The collar remained secure around her neck, and she didn't notice Cavar standing on the path behind her.

The amulet's reaction wasn't because of Marai. Something else was happening, *somewhere*.

Koda approached with a grin, hands in his pockets, performing his regular rounds of the camp. "Good morning, Governor. Nice to see you out here."

Cavar didn't venture into the tent city if he could help it. It stank of animals.

For his amulet to heat and pulsate in this way, it meant that either several other Guardians were using theirs at once to fend off an attack, or a singular person was using a tremendous amount of magic. The only one who ever used that kind of complicated, intense magic was Cavar, himself, when making more amulets or programming the collars. His was the only amulet powerful enough to do those things, thanks to the stone.

Acacia rushed to his side. "Uncle—"

"Not here." Cavar didn't want the creatures to know, especially Marai. She could use this as ammunition against him. "Franulovic, Yelich, with me."

He rushed back into his office, Acacia and the guards at his heels. She closed the door behind them all.

"Do you think there's been an attack?" she asked, breathless.

Cavar didn't know, and he hated not knowing. Usually he was the informed one, apprised of all happenings on Andara, but he didn't even know where the problem was occurring.

Calm down. Think.

It couldn't be folk from the Hinterlands. Cavar had sentries posted around those mountains. If there'd been a massive movement from beyond the Veil, someone would have noticed and sent word. Faeries were crafty, but couldn't become invisible.

What's happening? he asked the stone.

"Danger," it replied, as if its attention was focused elsewhere.

Cavar's blood ran cold. That one word was enough.

Governor Greguric burst through the door. "What in the blazes is going on?"

Cavar wasn't expecting him, but he was mildly amused by the coincidence of Greguric's appearance, since he lived near the Hinterlands.

"Greguric, what a surprise."

"I want to know why my bloody amulet is burning me." Greguric parted the buttons of his shirt to reveal a red welt on his chest. "I was riding to Bakair. Had to rip the damn thing off."

The Meeting of the Governors. The bi-annual meeting was three days away. Governors from across Andara would be congregating in the capital city of Bakair. It would explain why multiple Guardians were using their amulets at once, if they were in the same place, but who would dare attack such an event?

"Is it the fae?" asked Greguric darkly, eyes filled with murderous intent. "Did those beasts sneak past us somehow?"

"Surely not. We'd have to be blind not to notice a grouping of them skulking around—they don't exactly blend in. And there hasn't been a faerie attack for decades," said Acacia, wringing her hands.

"I'm in the dark, same as you, and until I ride for Bakair, I'll know nothing more." Cavar yanked on his coat and hat, snatched up his traveling bag, and headed for the door, left ajar by Greguric.

It was a two-day journey to Bakair. By the time he arrived, he may be too late to stop whatever was happening.

No, the amulets will win. The Guardians stationed in Bakair will quell the attack, even without me there.

"Will you be needing your carriage, Uncle?"

"I'll ride faster on horseback." Cavar faced Franulovic and Yelich by the door. "Both of you come with me to Bakair. No time to gather your things. We leave at once."

The group of them, Cavar, Acacia, Greguric, Franulovic, and Yelich, prowled through the theater, up the aisle, and out the front entrance to the stables.

"Heighten security here," Cavar told Acacia. "Take no chances. Place all guards and Koda on duty until I've sent word."

With that, he nudged his horse forward, off to battle whomever tempted to disturb his regimented rule.

CHAPTER 32

MARAI

"Something's going on," Innesh mumbled, unusually urgent.

The females in camp had gathered for their daily wash in the creek. Marai had been sitting there for hours, staring at the frigid water. The temperature grew chillier as early fall settled in, and the few trees in camp began to shift their leaves from green to blazing reds and oranges.

"What do you mean?" Gunnora asked Innesh, edging closer. "Nothing ever happens here. Especially now that Marai . . ."

She darted a quick glance at Marai, who stood silently in the creek splashing water on her face, wiping away the residue of black blood on her lips.

Marai could finish the sentence for her. *Now that Marai is dying.* She'd stopped caring weeks ago what happened in this camp. She'd stopped feeling much of anything. Whatever was going on, it didn't matter, because it certainly wasn't going to bode well for the folk of the Menagerie.

Innesh lowered her voice further, talking in grave, conspiratorial whispers with Gunnora and Anja. Their discussion was a distant buzz in Marai's ears. She didn't care enough to listen in. Marai remained silent as she wrung out her dripping hair. It had grown so long now that it reached her hips, and the wild tresses got in the way every time Marai vomited that black blood.

She stared at her rippling, wretched reflection in the water. She'd ventured so far from who she was that Marai didn't know herself anymore. She hated the deadness in her violet eyes; could no longer see her mother in her gaunt features. Marai doubted if even Ruenen would recognize her now.

"What do you think, Marai?" prodded Anja, dragging her back to the present.

QUEEN OF THE SHADOW MENAGERIE

It doesn't matter what I think.

Marai staggered from the creek, and trudged back to her tent, shivering. She dressed with aching slowness, as her body groaned from the movements. She sat down, head between her knees, until her brain stopped spinning. Marai's fingers were stiff and clumsy, and it took ages to lace her slippers, and the lower back of her dress.

"Time to go," Koda grunted, appearing at her tent flap.

Marai didn't ask why he was there to escort her, something he hadn't done since Cavar had tortured her with dark magic. Koda's grip was tight on her skeletal arm as he escorted her to the theater, and back again later after the show.

Security remained heightened throughout the next day. Every Peace Keeper employed by the Menagerie was on duty, day and night, and they watched Marai closely. What could she have possibly done? She had no strength, no willpower, no fire left in her veins.

Innesh wasn't the only one who'd noticed the tense atmosphere. Backstage, folk gathered in the wings, hissing to each other. Cyrill's bulbous black eyes slid to Marai.

Perhaps Cavar had decided to get rid of her. Perhaps he'd smother her with dark magic as a grand finale. Marai wouldn't flinch. If black flames consumed her, she'd rejoice and let death come for her. A swift demise was better than the slow agony of her current deterioration.

Marai sat in her chair, staring at the floor, the show continuing on as normal.

Magic took over when it was time for her finale. Right on schedule, Marai walked out onto the stage, eyes blurry in the flickering candlelight, struggling to focus. The audience applauded as usual.

Marai did a pirouette, sending golden sparkles into the faces of those in the front row. They "oooo'd" as if she'd done something impressive. Her wings fluttered, emitting a radiant glow.

I am nothing. This is all nothing.

Volgar, who'd been prowling up and down the aisle, disappeared out the exit door. He didn't return.

The show was almost over. Only a few more moves, and she'd be released or killed.

Were those yells from outside? *Doesn't matter.*

Sirco rushed up the aisle. Arcturius squealed and ducked behind the velvet curtains. The musicians abandoned their instruments and joined him in hiding.

The sounds of a brawl. Steel clanged. Boots scuffed on stone. Curious heads of the folk peeked out from the wings of the stage. The audience stopped paying attention to Marai when they turned around in their seats; their murmuring almost drowned out the sounds of the brawl.

Marai's body continued its movements. Whatever was happening outside hadn't affected the collars. Nothing would, unless Cavar died. But that . . . that was impossible.

A shadowy figure appeared at the top of the aisle, where the exit doors were located. In the dim candlelight, Marai's faerie eyesight noticed the sword in its hand; fat droplets of blood dripped from the blade. The figure had the build of a man, and his chest heaved. The scabbard of another sword poked out from behind the man's back.

Heavily armed.

Marai's body glided across the stage, arms fluidly swaying; the picture of grace. The collar pressed on. Unstoppable. Inescapable.

The figure started down the aisle, sword ready in his hand.

Come to kill me?

A calmness settled over Marai, imagining that blade at her throat. Almost grateful, she thought, *I'm ready.*

"Marai!"

Everything within her stilled.

That voice. She'd know it anywhere.

Another hallucination.

She forgot how to breathe. How to blink.

It's just another vision. She was imagining him, out of pure longing, before her impending death robbed her of her memories of him.

The shadow raced down the aisle. Heads in the audience turned to watch him, probably wondering if this was part of the show.

"Marai!"

Even in the darkened aisle, she'd recognize the shape of him. The way he moved. The way he said her name. The melody and cadence of his voice.

Marai froze.

Move! Move! The collar commanded, but its pull on her muscles lessened. Its voice became a dull order in the background as Marai's heart surged into her throat.

Her fingers trembled as she raised her arm, reaching, reaching for the figure.

It had to be a daydream.

Even if it is, let me touch him one last time.

Sirco appeared up the aisle and raced towards the shadow, sword drawn, releasing a warrior's war cry. The figure dodged the strike, in a maneuver Marai recognized, one she'd seen him do a dozen times. He then sliced through Sirco's stomach, spewing blood onto nearby audience members.

That was when people finally screamed, realizing this wasn't part of the Menagerie's performance. The audience leapt from their seats, crawling over one another, and stampeded for the exits. Politeness thrown aside, they shoved others out of the way, knocking women and children down onto the ground. Arcturius, the stagehands, and musicians leapt into the escaping crowd. It was pure pandemonium.

Then the shadow stepped into the flickering light cast by one of the nearest sconces.

Marai's body shook. She observed his bloody, sweat-drenched face; his wide, frantic eyes.

Tears cascaded down her cheeks, distorting her vision. *This can't be real.* Tingles pierced her skin. A ghostly charge she hadn't felt in ages slowly climbed up her spine. A welcome sensation after months of emptiness.

Power filled every crevice of her. A building power she couldn't and wouldn't contain.

She reached for the man, still calling her name.

He was her key. Her magic, locked away for months, awakened at the mere sight of him.

Because he was real, and she was stronger with him.

White sparks created fissures in the collar. Iron cracked. More galvanic light burst forth as a name traveled up through her larynx, as though ripped from her very soul.

"Ruen!"

The collar shattered into pieces across the stage, and Marai's lightning exploded.

Remaining audience members shrieked, diving to the floor to avoid being struck by a wild bolt of white-hot power.

The theater illuminated in blinding light. Power snapped around Marai's ears. *Her* power. Suddenly, she was alive again. Every cell within her reanimated.

The curtains were on fire. Wood and stone from the rim of the open ceiling fell into the vacant seats. Scorch marks marred the stone. Flames curled the edges of the posters on the walls.

But not a single strand of lightning had touched the man now leaping onto the stage.

As quickly as it came, the lightning vanished. Marai had used up the remaining strength she had stored away. Her trembling legs, made of crepe paper, gave out, as she reached for him.

But Ruenen caught her before she hit the ground.

He clung to her. She could feel him shaking. Marai only had the strength to raise one arm and gently stroke a strand of sweaty chestnut hair from his face.

She had a million questions, but could only ask, "How?"

Ruenen pressed his forehead to hers. Their noses touched. He was *warm*. He was *real*. Ruenen was *here*.

"You showed me," he finally said. His voice was strained, as if trying to keep his emotions in check. "When you visited me, you dragged me back here with you."

"That was real?" she asked, crying once again in amazement as Ruenen nodded.

"Get away from her," said a sharp female voice from behind them.

Ruenen reached for his sword.

"No, wait," Marai said, unable to shout. Her throat was rough from barely speaking in days.

Innesh stood over Marai and Ruenen, holding an amulet in one fist and a small, tin box in the other, her face blazing with ferocity. Marai understood then. Innesh had never gotten rid of Acacia's stolen amulet. She'd kept it safe, hidden, for a moment like this.

"This is Ruenen," she told Innesh.

Understanding dawned in Innesh's dark eyes.

"Where's Koda?" asked Marai, suddenly remembering the chaos. If Koda appeared and used his powers, Ruenen would be dead.

"Unconscious," Innesh said, and held up the tin box. "Gave him a little of his own medicine. He should be out for a while." She then addressed Ruenen. "You need to stand back so I can remove the darkness eating away at her innards."

Ruenen sucked in a sharp breath, glancing to Marai for confirmation. She dipped her chin, and Ruenen backed away, seemingly reluctant to let her go.

Innesh held up the bronze amulet. She closed her eyes, muttered something under her breath, and the amulet glowed within her fist.

Darkness was sucked from Marai's body, like one might suck venom from a snake bite. Swirling streamers of black smoke exited her body through her mouth and nose, as it had entered, and returned to its home within the stone. Marai hacked and coughed at the sensation. No black blood came up as she coughed. Her lungs fully filled with air.

The darkness was gone. It couldn't hurt her anymore.

She sagged in relief as Ruenen's arms encased her again. His expression shifted between dozens of emotions and questions. He opened his mouth, but Innesh cut him off.

"Did you see Governor Cavar out there? Men with amulets like this?"

"A few rode by on horseback this morning," Ruenen said. "We hid in the bushes off the road, and they didn't see us. They seemed quite determined to get to Bakair. We *may* have caused a disturbance there."

Oh gods, Marai had missed that playful smirk of his.

"We don't have much time. He'll return as soon as he senses I used the amulet," said Innesh.

"I have one of those, too," Ruenen said, drawing out his own amulet and chain from his pocket. "We brought down the barrier in Bakair."

"Where's Keshel?" Marai asked, grabbing Ruenen's hand. "His fortune teller tent is right outside the—"

"He's fine," Ruenen said, raising Marai to her feet again. "Aresti already grabbed him."

Marai choked up. "Aresti's here?"

Lirr's Moldy Bones, since when had she become so weepy?

Ruenen nodded, smiling.

"Talk about this later," snapped Innesh, pulling out a set of iron keys. She bent over and unlocked the shackles around her own ankles. They *thunked* to the floor, and the room itself seemed to breathe with Innesh. For the first time in fifteen years, Innesh took an unshackled step, a fire smoldering at the fringes of her eyes. "What's your plan, Your Graces?"

Marai and Ruenen exchanged looks. *Your Graces.* The titles stirred something within her. It was a reminder. A reminder of her promise, her responsibility, her destiny.

Ruenen sheathed his sword. "I have a ship waiting in Bakair that will take us back to Astye."

Who else had traveled across the treacherous Northern Sea to Andara? Were Raife and Thora onboard? Tarik and Nosficio?

Marai turned towards backstage.

The magical folk had been hovering, watching from the wings as the curtains smoldered around them. Cyrill, the gnomes, hobs, oni, Athelstan, Dante, and Wilder stepped out onto the stage, watching as Marai and Innesh freed themselves of Cavar's control. Not everyone from the Menagerie was present, however. Eno's tank was still backstage, along with the griffin, manticore, and phoenix in their cages. Anja, Gunnora, Desislava, and others remained oblivious of the night's turn of events from within the camp.

Ruenen's gold-flecked eyes swum with curiosity at the sight of the unique creatures before him. "Who are they?"

"They're my people." Marai drew herself up, and addressed the folk on the stage, her voice still hoarse. "You're free. Get as far away from here as you can. But if you want to leave Andara, start a new life someplace where folk like us are treated as citizens, follow King Ruenen of Nevandia outside."

None of the folk said a word. Most likely in shock, their eyes shone with fear and wonder.

"And where are you going?" asked Innesh, lancing her with a hard stare.

"Back into the camp to get the rest of us." Without the darkness eating away at her, some of her strength had returned. Her legs felt steadier than they had in weeks.

Ruenen brought Marai's hand to his chest. "I don't want to leave you, not for a second."

Marai placed her free hand on his cheek. "There are things I must do first. Please, get my people organized and ready to leave. I'll be quick." She then backed away, dropping her hands from Ruenen. There was important work to be done. "Someone will need to help Eno in her tank."

"Eno?"

"She's a mermaid," Marai said, "and also free the griffin, manticore, and phoenix."

Ruenen blanched. "Oh. Right. Well." He looked to the folk, and beckoned them. "Follow me, please. Be careful of falling, flaming debris."

With that, the other folk quickly followed Ruenen up the aisle.

Cyrill shot Marai a departing smirk. "Excellent work, my Queen."

Marai turned to Innesh once the room was clear. "I need your help."

Innesh immediately dashed backstage, and Marai followed, past Koda's unconscious body sprawled on the floor. They ran through the hallway, past Cavar's vacant office, down the steps, and burst into the camp. A crowd of the remaining folk had gathered near the door. They bombarded Marai and Innesh the minute they stepped outside.

"What's happening?"

"There's smoke coming from the theater!"

"Are we in danger?"

"*Calm down,*" Innesh shouted, then gestured for Marai to speak. "Listen to our Queen."

That silenced everyone. Anja's jaw dropped as she noticed the absence of Marai's collar, and the change in her demeanor.

"My friends from Nevandia have come," Marai announced, and the folk inched closer. "They have a ship in Bakair ready to take us home. Those who wish to stay on Andara are free to go where they please, but if you choose to come to Astye with me, you must leave now."

"We're . . . free?" asked Anja.

Marai nodded.

The crowd of folk released shrieking gasps and sobs. They embraced each other and applauded, leaping into the air, howling into the night. Gooseflesh prickled her arms, and Marai felt as if she was soaring.

Innesh raised the amulet chain above her head in triumph. "We're free! No chains will ever bind us again!"

The folk let out a resounding, unified cheer. Three shadows flew past overhead—the griffin, manticore, and phoenix had been released, heading North towards the Hinterlands. Folk applauded again, cheering the creatures on with each flap of their wings.

Innesh's hand closed around the amulet. She murmured an order, and all of the iron collars shattered, falling into the grass.

Anja collapsed to her knees, praying up to the sky in ancient fae. Marai understood one phrase she repeated: *thank you, all-mighty gods. Praise you, Lirr.*

Smiling, Marai said to Innesh, "Take down the barrier."

Within seconds, the dark fog wriggled like a wall of worms, then evaporated, revealing a world beyond the Menagerie. A world of autumnal trees and grassy plains Anja hadn't seen in thirty years, Gunnora in seven. Anja put a hand to her mouth as she studied the dark countryside. Lights from the nearby town flickered in the distance.

Gunnora clasped Marai's hand, beaming. "We were right to place our faith in you."

Marai would have hugged her then, but they were running out of time. "If you're coming with us, leave everything behind. We travel light."

The folk dispersed. Some, like the green-skinned ogre, made for the forests.

Anja, however, didn't move. "I'm coming with you."

"Don't you want to go home to the Hinterlands?" asked Marai.

Anja frowned. "I told you that they never accept those who leave back into the court. They're no longer my people, and I have no home. You are my Queen, and after what you've achieved this night, my place is beside you." She lowered to a knee and kissed Marai's hand. "Perhaps I'll return someday, a long time from now, but until then, I shall serve you and your line until my last breath."

Moved by her words, Marai cleared her throat. "I need you to keep everyone calm and organized."

Anja stood and brushed the dirt from her ratty dress. She called to the others, gathering them into a clump around her, including Gunnora. Together, they hastened for the front of the theater.

Marai and Innesh went tent by tent, ensuring everyone got out safely. Marai untethered the unicorn from its tree, and it bowed its magnificent head to her in thanks before bolting off into the night. Marai only hoped the beautiful creature wouldn't be recaptured. Perhaps Anja was wrong, and the unicorn and other creatures would be welcomed back into the Hinterlands.

She then came upon Desislava chained to her tree.

"You've done the unthinkable, Faerie Queen," the vampiress said. "I'm impressed. Now set me free, as well."

"I'll release you," said Marai, "but I need your word that you won't attack me or any of our people here."

Desislava's red eyes bored into hers. "There's a whole village right over there, Your Grace. I have retribution to achieve." She smiled cruelly, revealing her fangs, reminding Marai so much of Nosficio that her heart ached at the thought of seeing him again.

Using the keys Innesh had stolen, Marai unfastened the locks chaining Desislava to the tree trunk. With a *click* and turn of metal, the lock fell to the ground. The vampiress disappeared in a flash and breeze. Marai had no idea where she would go, but she assumed that Desislava would not be joining them on the ship. Vampires and oceans didn't mix.

Lastly, Marai dashed inside Keshel's tent and grabbed his journal from beneath his bedroll. He'd strangle her if she left it behind.

Once all the folk had been gathered, unchained, and dispersed, Marai dared one final glance at the deserted Menagerie. Gathering her hatred into flames at her fingertips, she set the camp ablaze. The tents and cages. Bobo's commissary.

Good riddance. She gave herself a moment to watch it burn with a satisfied smirk. Once again, she was powerful. Once again, she was alive.

She turned her attention to the theater. Marai rushed back inside, stopping first in Cavar's office. She grabbed a torch from the wall and set fire to his organized papers. His books. His upholstered chairs. The artwork on the stone walls. The new rug he'd recently bought to replace the one she'd vomited on. Marai then ran up the stairs, setting fire to each employee apartment, guest and storage room.

In Acacia's, Marai didn't find the spoiled brat, but her fine dresses, curtains, rugs, and bedspread became excellent kindling for the bonfire. The coward had probably run at the first sign of trouble.

Marai's last stop was the theater, itself. Gathering up the final strands of strength and magic within her, she released a strike of lightning so powerful that the wooden planks of the stage burst apart into splinters.

Backstage was an inferno—fire snaked up the ropes towards the ceiling. Chunks of debris fell around her. The hellish prison would never function again.

Cavar no longer had any power over her.

Her anger was all-encompassing, but Marai's body was still weak from the effects of that dark poison in her body. She'd drained herself of magic, energy, and will. She fell to her knees, unable to stand.

The world was on fire around her. Blazing beams crashed down at her side. She needed to get out before she became trapped, but she couldn't get her legs to move.

Ruenen appeared at her side, as if he'd known she'd need his help. He scooped her up, dodged falling, fiery debris, and brought her safely outside the burning theater.

The air smelled of smoke, charred wood, sweat, and the iron of blood. Marai welcomed it all into her lungs. Dozens of bodies littered the ground. Most wore red or black vests, but some were clearly wealthy men, patrons who'd fought back against Ruenen. No women or children. In the distance, Marai spotted the panicked shadows of audience members running towards the nearby town.

"We waited until nightfall in the forest, and then attacked once the show started, when we knew people would be distracted," Ruenen explained as Marai took in the glorious sight of the dead Peace Keepers.

Aresti stood anxiously next to Bobo's wagon, biting her fingernails. When she saw Ruenen carrying Marai, she burst into tears, running over to embrace both of them. Aresti and Ruenen's arms were home to Marai.

"We don't have time for me to tell you all the ways I missed you," Aresti said through her tears. Marai couldn't remember the last time she'd seen Aresti actually cry. "But know that I will when we're on the ship, and you're going to grow sick of me telling you. And you'll need to tell me then why you suddenly have wings."

Marai let out a choked, laughing sob, and Aresti finally pulled away to mount her horse. Marai wasn't surprised to see Tarik and Yovel helping the tiny gnomes into the back of a wagon. They both saluted her with smiles, which she returned. Athelstan went over and shook their hands, introducing himself, grinning elatedly to be in the presence of fellow weres.

"Your Grace, it's an honor to meet you."

Marai turned to the male voice standing next to Ruenen, and couldn't believe her eyes at the sight of his green and ochre wings.

A full-blooded Astyean faerie? *Here?*

She was more than shocked when two other strange faerie males bowed to her, one of them also with wings. They stared at Marai reverently, as if their entire purpose of traveling with Ruenen was to see *her.*

"Later," Ruenen said, not unkindly, to the faeries. He carried Marai towards a second wagon, placing her next to Gunnora and Anja amongst the hay in the back.

"I can ride," Marai protested, already moving to climb out of the wagon.

"You know I never say no to you about anything, but this one time, I'd like you to listen to me and stay back here," Ruenen said, his hands lingering on her hips. "We have to ride hard. We're already going to be much slower now."

He glanced at Keshel, who was sitting with head in his hands, hay in his hair, against the wagon railings. Marai crawled over and took his hand; distress and confusion vibrated off him.

"I can't tell if this is a vision or reality," he said, breathing in short bursts. "Everything is spinning and flashing. The blood and smoke . . . and it's too loud. I can't . . . I can't make sense of anything."

"Look at me," Marai demanded, and Keshel timidly lifted his eyes to hers. "It's real. We're safe now. The Menagerie is finished."

"Is Cavar gone? Is the Lord of the Underworld defeated?"

"No."

Keshel slung his head back and forth. "Then we're not safe."

Marai handed him his journal. "Aresti and Ruenen came for us. We're going home."

"Home?" Keshel repeated, pupils oscillating between dilating and shrinking. He was still partially lost to a vision, even without the collar around his neck. He clutched the journal to his chest.

"Nevandia, Keshel. We're going home to see Raife and Thora. To Kadi and Leif."

Keshel smiled and closed his eyes. His head drooped onto Marai's shoulder. "Home."

The caravan lurched to life. Horses neighed and galloped onwards. Marai was only slightly aware of who rode with them in Ruenen's entourage. Elmar was there, dressed like a sailor. He couldn't seem to stop staring at the magical folk around him.

The wagon rattled and bumped along beneath Marai, far faster than the rickety old thing should have been going. Marai was surprised to see that almost all of the folk had decided to come along. Eno had been placed in a smaller steamer trunk, filled with water. For the first time, Marai was able to see her face above water, and the scales of her tail gleamed in the moonlight. Wilder and Dante ran alongside Ruenen's horse, as if they'd already become part of his retinue.

"So that's your King?" Anja asked, pointing up at Ruenen, sitting stalwart upon his mount at the front of the pack. "The man you love."

"I had no idea that you had so many attractive friends," Gunnora said, eyeing Tarik and Yovel, who were riding at the rear of the caravan behind their wagon.

Friends. Her friends had come. They'd traveled leagues and leagues of dangerous sea and road to rescue her and Keshel. Marai was lucky to have such courageous companions, despite barely knowing some of them at all.

The burning Menagerie grew smaller and smaller in the distance, the flames bright against the darkness. The folk stared and stared, until the Menagerie entirely disappeared behind the slope of a hill.

If she had any strength left, or knew anything about the geography of Andara, Marai might have tried to portal them to the dock, but her magic was drained, and she could barely stay awake, despite the jostling of the wagon. Her fingers remained interlaced with Keshel's. He mumbled incoherently, lost to dreams of his visions.

When the sun broke like a yolk across the sky, it didn't only signify a brand new day for the folk. It was the dawning of a new *life*. Their smiles and shining eyes were well worth the pain Marai had suffered. It had been a nightmare, and nothing would ever be the same for her, but Marai took comfort in the fact that, at least, the sun was still rising. The earth was still turning. The days would come and go, and she was now free to live them.

No sign of riders behind or in front of them.

He's waiting for us in Bakair. Preparing. Cavar had complete control of that city. He could bottleneck and trap them in the streets far easier than he could trying to chase them down on an open road.

Their fight wasn't over yet.

CHAPTER 33

RUENEN

Ruenen and his team hadn't slept in three days. They'd run all the way from Bakair to the Menagerie, battled against at least two dozen guards, and now rode day and night, only stopping twice to rest the horses and allow for brief respite. Ruenen was operating on pure adrenaline. Thank the gods Anja, the pink-skinned faerie, had the sense to scrounge up food from the Menagerie camp, otherwise they'd have nothing to sustain their rigorous pace.

He hadn't yet been able to have a conversation with Marai. In fact, she'd barely said much of anything since leaving the Menagerie, except to comfort Keshel and the folk. She was so pale, her bones so prominent. As strong as she was, Marai wouldn't have survived much longer in that place.

Seeing her upon that stage, a beautiful, sorrowful ghost surrounded by candlelight, deeply wounded Ruenen. Cavar had made her his slave, that collar subjecting her to his whims, forcing Marai to humiliate herself in front of a crowd of humans and their epicaricacy. She'd lived a life Ruenen couldn't begin to comprehend, and when he looked at her now, in the fleeting glances he dared to take, she wasn't the same person who'd danced with him on coronation night.

I should've gotten here sooner.

But he couldn't walk down that path of blame. Ruenen couldn't have gotten here any faster. It was by chance that he'd managed to find her and the Menagerie to begin with.

He glanced back over his shoulder at Marai in the wagon. Her eyes were closed, head leaned back against the wood, but her face wasn't relaxed with sleep. She was awake, every muscle in her body taut and ready to fight, despite the dark circles beneath her eyes. At least she had food in her stomach.

Once we get home, I'll help her heal. I'll do whatever it takes to bring her back.

Keshel's decay was worse than Marai's. Gone was that stoic, impenetrable facade; the subtle, commanding grace. His tall form shriveled, curling inwards, and he stared at his surroundings with an almost drunken glaze. He spoke in garbled ancient fae, mumbled riddles, metaphors, and prophecies. Ruenen didn't want to know the awful things Keshel saw.

Aresti spotted Ruenen staring at Marai and Keshel from his horse, barely paying attention to the road in front of him.

"What do you think they did to him?" she whispered, scrubbing at her face, her eyes, as if to wipe away the image of her weakened cousin. "I don't know that person. That male's a stranger."

Cavar had diminished Marai and Keshel to mere whispers of a being. Hands entwined, they'd bound themselves together through the horror they'd faced. Ruenen observed Marai placing her hand on Keshel's chest often, checking his heartbeat, as if to convince herself that he hadn't passed in his sleep.

"He'll regain his strength," Ruenen assured her. "Once we get Keshel home, he'll jump right back into working on magical relations."

Aresti gave him a hard look. "You truly believe that what's been done to them can be reversed?"

"Yes," Ruenen said without a moment's hesitation. He *had* to believe. "We'll need to be patient and give them the time they need to heal."

Aresti frowned, not hiding her skepticism, but Ruenen knew how distraught she was over Keshel's state. He couldn't blame her, especially since he was worried about the same thing.

The tattooed woman rode up next to Ruenen on her shaggy horse. She rode like she'd spent years and years racing along the beaches of Yehzig. "We're close to Bakair. We should stop here and plan our route to the harbor."

Ruenen halted the caravan. Bakair's outline, a shadowed mass against the pale blue sky, loomed in the distance; a bell from one of its towers tolled. He dismounted, signaling for his team to congregate around him and Innesh.

"This road funnels into the Central Quarter, and from there, we take the main causeway to the harbor," Ruenen told her.

"Yes, I know Bakair better than you do, Your Grace," replied Innesh coolly. "I was Cavar's personal slave for years, and traveled with him back and forth from Bakair and the Menagerie. While I don't know much about lower Bakair and the harbor, I do know the general layout of the city."

"We'd be playing into their hands to have us enter from this main road," Aresti said. "We should split up into smaller, more manageable groups."

"Any idea how many Guardians we'll be up against?" Ruenen asked Innesh.

"It's the bi-annual Meeting of the Governors. If they've all arrived by now, it could be hundreds," she said. "I bet many of them turned around, tail between their legs, when they felt their amulets warm. They're a craven bunch. We know Greguric's there, and he's a strong fighter, but the one you really need to worry about is Cavar."

Tarik glanced around at the folk, who were taking the pause in travel to stretch. "Most of them don't look like they're up for running half a league. I doubt any know how to fight."

"Is there a back way to get to the docks?" Ruenen asked Innesh. "Avoiding the main causeway and the Central Quarter?"

"There is." She pointed a brown finger at the craggy, beachy terrain that sloped downwards to their right. The place Hemming had said was too difficult to traverse. "Those hills go directly down to the docks, but there's no pathway, and the terrain isn't easy. We'll need to leave the horses and wagons behind, and go slowly on foot."

"Lead the folk to the docks that way, Innesh."

Marai stood on the outside of their circle. Her arms were crossed, and her face was sharp with calculations. Those strange, exquisite, incandescent wings fluttered once. Ruenen might never get used to seeing them upon her back, and he tried not to stare in fascination at the streaks of lightning cutting through the lavender and cerulean.

Finneagal and Elmar parted to let Marai into the group.

"Take everyone who cannot use magic," she continued. "These folk are defenseless against the amulets. Those of us who *can* use magic will enter through the city to keep Cavar and the Guardians' attention focused on us. If we should perish, at least the folk will stand a chance."

"As you wish, Your Grace," Innesh said.

Since when does Marai go by that title? The folk stared at her reverently, spoke to her with passion and respect, as if she truly had become their Queen. Ruenen met Marai's eyes briefly across the circle, a flash of amethyst fire, and then her gaze slid back to Innesh.

"You still have Acacia's amulet?" she asked, and Innesh nodded. Marai then looked back at Ruenen. "And you have another?"

"I do, and Nyle also has one onboard *The Arcane Wind*," said Ruenen.

If Marai was surprised to hear the name of the boat, she didn't show it. Her attention was already back on Innesh. "Use the stone, without question, if you encounter any Peace Keepers or Guardians."

"Who will be making the main assault, Your Graces?" asked Braesal, glancing between Ruenen and Marai.

Ruenen pointed as he went down the circle of faces. "You, Tarik, Yovel, Finneagal, Beck, Aresti—"

"Me." Marai pulled her long, white-blonde hair back into a low knot at the base of her neck. "And that's all."

Ruenen's stomach leaped. "Why not me? I have an amulet."

Marai's eyes narrowed. "Do you know how to use it?"

"I managed to bring down the barrier, didn't I?" Ruenen challenged her right back. It felt familiar, this back and forth dueling with words. "I'm going with you, whether you like it or not."

Marai's jaw ticked, but she said nothing else.

"What about those of us in the King's Guard?" Elmar asked.

"Go with Innesh and the folk," said Ruenen.

Elmar stepped closer to him. "Your Grace, we cannot let you go into danger without us. We're your Guard. We must be at your side."

"I need you to protect the innocents," said Ruenen. "I have the amulet, my sword, and five faeries around me. I'll meet you on the dock."

Elmar and the other three Guards replied with disgruntled agreements. They were men of honor. Ruenen knew this hurt their pride, but up against dark magic, they had no chance of survival.

Most of the folk were slight, trembling people who'd probably never held a weapon in their life. Ruenen was surprised that Marai didn't have Anja join them in Bakair, but the faerie female seemed like a gentle soul who'd probably never been to battle.

Suddenly, a high-pitched shriek cleaved the air. It was a chilling sound, one that made Ruenen shiver with a cold sense of dread.

"What in the Unholy Underworld is that?" he hissed, covering his ears.

Marai had gone still, the color draining from her already pale face. "That's Bellaya." She and Innesh exchanged a look, silent words passing between them.

Bellaya was a shrouded old woman, whose face Ruenen had not yet seen because she covered herself with the hood of her brown cloak. She stood in the middle of the wagon, hands reaching towards the sky as if the clouds were going to collapse upon her. The folk looked absolutely terrified.

"We should . . . we should get moving," Marai finally said with a swallow.

Ruenen halted her with a gentle hand on her shoulder. "What's going on with Bellaya?"

"She's a banshee."

"Alright, and why is she screaming like that?"

"It means someone will die today."

Ruenen quailed. *Well, odds are someone is going to die, if not many of us . . .*

Bellaya stopped shrieking. People began to move again, but seemed visibly shaken from both the wretched sound of her wailing, and what those wails foretold.

"We'd like to accompany you into the city," announced one of the horse-men. *Centaurs,* Ruenen had recently learned. "Wilder and I want to remain close to you, Your Grace."

Marai gave the dark-haired one a curt nod of understanding.

"We'll meet you on the ship," Anja said, briefly grasping Marai's hand. "Stay safe."

Ruenen and his team watched the Menagerie folk disappear over the hill with Innesh in the lead. Eno's water-filled trunk had to be carried by two of the Guard at the back of the pack.

"Go with them," Ruenen heard Marai ordering someone. He turned to see her addressing Keshel, standing next to the wagon. "You're in no shape to confront Cavar."

Keshel glared defiantly down at her, his skin a sickly gray color. He seemed to be gathering up his strength, pushing his shoulders back, although he slurred his words as he said, "I'm fae. I want to be with my people. I can help."

Marai's lips drew into a thin, aggrieved line. Ruenen had to agree with her as he watched Keshel's body sway unsteadily, his forehead pinch in pain, and his eyes cloud over.

"No, go with Innesh."

Keshel opened his mouth to respond, but Aresti clapped him on the back. "We'll meet you down there, cousin." The slight spark of life in him must have pleased her. She gave him a quick, one-armed hug, before she gently shoved Keshel at the hill path.

He glowered at her over his shoulder, but stumbled after the other Menagerie folk.

Marai and Aresti waited until he was out of view before they followed at the back of the team, walking the remaining distance past patchwork fields of crops to Bakair. Weapons were unsheathed. Faces hardened to steel. Tarik cracked his knuckles. Marai stated that Cavar would be standing at the city gates waiting for them.

She wasn't wrong.

Three rows of Guardians stood blocking the entrance to the Central Quarter like a small, well-dressed army. Ruenen counted roughly forty. Their amulets were already glowing with that eerie blacklight. Ruenen's responded with its own pulsating light, a thrum echoing in his bones. Although he held it by its bronze chain, Ruenen felt the amulet's heat. This time, the Guardians were also accompanied by four dozen red-vested Peace Keepers, their blades curved like a scythe, and shorter than the average broadsword. Some of them breathed heavily;

fresh cuts adorned their skin, clothes tattered, as if they'd already come from a fight.

Behind them, the city was quiet, practically abandoned. Not a single soul wandered the streets, leaving Ruenen to wonder if Bakair had been evacuated. Doors and shutters were closed, locking any remaining inhabitants safely inside.

One tall, regal man stepped forward, parting the Guardians and guards as if he was some sort of god. He didn't look physically powerful, or even slightly intimidating. If Marai hadn't stiffened at the sight of him, Ruenen wouldn't have given the man a second glance.

But Cavar's eyes were sharp as knives when he stared at Marai. So much hate in his expression, alongside far too much confidence. Marai's body was coiled and tense like a mountain lion waiting to pounce.

Cavar's amulet flashed.

Dark magic sped towards Ruenen and his team in the shape of a hundred flashing daggers. Marai flung up her hand, erecting an invisible barrier around the team. The daggers exploded into smoke on impact, unable to pass through, but Marai wobbled, dropping the barrier immediately after. She couldn't sustain that kind of magic yet.

Ruenen heard a neigh and galloping hooves from behind. He turned, expecting Dante or Wilder, but there instead was Koda, wincing and hobbling as he leapt from his horse.

Somehow, the bastard had caught up to them.

Fuck.

They hadn't counted on him and his immobilizing magic. The goal wasn't to fight against the Guardians in a city they didn't know. They could never compete against so many amulets at once. Ruenen had instructed his team to *run*.

So they did.

His team splintered apart, running off in different directions within the city. Aresti dashed behind a row of topiaries and shrubs. Braesal blasted a hole in the ground, creating a huge disturbance of dust and debris, providing cover as he and Finneagal took to the sky, flying above the city. Beck, Tarik, Dante, and Wilder scattered.

Ruenen and Marai went left, towards a skinny, steeply inclined side street.

Guardians and Peace Keepers dispersed, choosing a different pair to track. The Peace Keepers were faster, more athletic, and had no trouble chasing through the streets, shoving things out of their way, as the Guardians lagged behind.

Ruenen and Marai knocked over urns, stalls, and crates, spewing angry, squawking chickens into the path of the ten Peace Keepers on their tail. Cavar, of course, had sent the most people after Marai.

Ruenen dared a glance over his shoulder and saw black flames careening towards him.

He dove, shoving Marai to the ground, as the flames narrowly missed scorching them. The flames collided instead with someone's house, setting it ablaze. The innocent people residing inside screamed. A baby's wail pierced the air, squeezing a guilty fist around Ruenen's heart.

Ruenen glanced behind him again. Koda and a young male Guardian were hot on their heels.

"Give up, Marai," Koda taunted. "You'll never make it out of here. You belong to Cavar."

Further up the street, the Governor meandered slowly through the smoke, broken pottery, and chaos. He'd let Koda and the others do the dirty, difficult work of capturing Marai, but his cruel gaze spoke of dangerous promises awaiting her.

Koda snapped his fingers.

Ruenen expected something to happen, but nothing did.

"He's out of range," Marai said, scrambling to her feet. "Move!"

Ruenen dashed after her. His hands and elbows were skinned from the fall, and blood ran down Marai's legs from her scraped knees.

People poured into the streets. They'd decided to either join the chase, or were trying to vacate the city and far from danger. Ruenen had to shove a screaming woman out of the way. He leapt over a wooden box. Ran through a clothesline of wet laundry. Dodged a sleek knife thrown at his head by a guard.

Homes and market stalls around him exploded, spewing wooden splinters and rocks into the air. The young Guardian, who looked around Ruenen's age, shot black cannonballs of magic in rapid succession. The street became so clogged with people, escaped horses and goats, debris, and smoke, Ruenen could barely move or see.

Over her shoulder, Marai haphazardly tossed a ball of vermillion flames. She overshot, missing the ten Peace Keepers, but the resulting blaze halted Koda, the young Guardian, and Cavar behind them.

Marai's chest heaved. Sweat dappled her brow. *She hasn't recovered enough to be running and fighting right now.*

She stumbled and slammed into the chest of a man who'd leapt into her path.

He grabbed her arms, pinning her to him. "I got her, Governor, sir!"

Other citizens in the side street crowded around Marai, trapping her. Some of them held kitchen utensils and hammers in their hands, pointing them at her throat.

Ruenen yanked the sheathed sword from his back. He'd brought it for her, all the way from Nevandia, but didn't know if she was strong enough to wield it, and he couldn't fucking get it to Marai with those people surrounding her.

He called her name, and tossed the sword to her, high above their heads.

Please catch it.

Marai leapt and narrowly caught the hilt with three fingers, then ripped the sword from the scabbard.

Blood spurted and screams sounded as Marai cleaved through the hoard of Andarans around her. They disbanded, stumbling away as Death danced and twirled, her blade cutting through flesh and bone like butter.

Marai didn't look at the sword in her hand. She hadn't recognized it yet, too preoccupied with dispersing the crowd around her, when ten red-vested thugs finally caught up.

A curved blade sliced towards Ruenen, and he dodged, lowering to a knee. His sword slashed upwards, straight through the guard's gut to his ribcage.

The Peace Keepers and crowd further separated Marai from Ruenen, but he was able to glimpse her through the writhing limbs and blades. She was the Lady Butcher again, sawing off arms and heads as that blade sang through the air.

Ruenen almost stopped to watch her. *Lirr's Bones, she's brilliant.*

Koda, the young male Guardian, and Cavar were only a few steps away. Citizens chanted the Governor's name from the sidelines. Marai quickly erected another invisible barrier with a trembling arm as Cavar sent black, smokey daggers her way. The young Guardian clasped his amulet and pummeled her shuddering barrier with obsidian fireballs as she fended off Peace Keeper blades with only one arm.

Marai couldn't keep this up much longer. She was weakening, panting, fighting to stay on her feet.

But the foolish guards and Koda ignored Ruenen completely, not realizing he had an amulet in his grasp.

He lifted the stone and shot a blazing beam of darkness at the young Guardian. The man's body went up in black flames and blood-curdling screams. Within seconds, he was nothing but a pile of ash.

Ruenen blinked in surprise—he hadn't expected the amulet to be so powerful. A shiver coursed down his spine as a tiny voice in his head said, *"Do it again."*

Marai dropped her barrier, then ducked down a smaller side street.

Ruenen tried desperately to go after her, but Koda planted himself in his path.

CHAPTER 34

MARAI

Cavar and his five cutthroats were hot on her heels, and Marai's body was slowing down.

At least she'd lost Koda, but Cavar was more dangerous, no matter the distance between them. Whenever she could, she'd toss flames over her shoulder, knock down objects to block their way as she careened through the streets.

But those guards kept running, and Cavar stalked behind them, tireless and healthy, unlike her. Not a single hair on Cavar's head was out of place, and his long coat was only slightly singed from her attacks. He was *letting* her get away, enjoying the chase and her frantic struggle, because he knew he could stop her at any moment. Cavar was a cat playing with a mouse before devouring it.

Marai wouldn't let his mind tricks distract her. *Keep going. Don't stop.*

Three tall masts with white sails rose in the distance. Marai crested the hill and saw the glorious *Arcane Wind* waiting for her, ready to depart.

She was close. She could make it.

Marai tripped on an uneven stone in the pavement, and she fell, body skidding onto the street. Her head slammed onto stone. Black stars blinded her. Her exposed skin was scraped, stinging, raw, and bleeding.

"Grab her," Cavar ordered from afar.

Two sets of hands yanked her to her feet. The fog in her vision cleared, revealing Franulovic and Yelich's ugly faces. Marai's skull throbbed, her skin burned.

Cavar strode towards her, shaking his head, *tutting* and *tsking*. "You should have known better than to try this."

His amulet flared to life. A black ribbon of metal slithered out from the stone like a dancing serpent. *A collar.*

Marai struggled against Franulovic and Yelich's hairy grasp. *No! I won't go back to the Menagerie!*

The sword Ruenen gave her lay on the ground near her feet. If she could only reach it . . .

For the first time, Marai really *looked* at the sword.

Her heart fluttered. *It can't be . . .*

Silver and gold filigree twisted around the hilt in an elegant, intricate pattern. Ancient fae was etched into the metal between two fullers running the length of the blade.

With a mighty spin, Marai wrenched herself free from the guards' grasp and dove to the side. She narrowly avoided the ribbon of metal as it reached to wrap around her throat and harden.

Her fingers latched around the hilt of her fallen sword. The blade was light, agile in her hand, an extension of her arm. Holding it felt like coming home. Cavar didn't know Marai was skilled with a sword. He didn't know to be afraid.

She turned, and dragged Dimtoir straight across Cavar's gut.

He gave a strangled-animal shriek, and fell backwards, releasing his hold on the amulet. The ribbon of metal evanesced into wisps of smoke.

For a moment, Marai stared at Cavar, his blood and innards gushing from the deep wound. The scent of iron filled the air, along with a flurry of questions.

How was her father's precious sword, Dimtoir, the Protector, in her hand?

Stop thinking! Go!

Marai ran and didn't look back.

CHAPTER 35

RUENEN

Ruenen couldn't get around Koda. Cavar and five remaining guards had stalked after Marai, leaving Ruenen alone with the faerie male.

Fuck.

Ruenen sent his will into the stone, and a fog barrier shot up around him, blocking off the entire street and Koda's path to him. Until the barrier came down, Koda was stuck on the other side.

"That amulet doesn't belong to you," the faerie male said. "Give it here, and I'll only carve out one of your eyes."

Ruenen's fist curled tighter around the chain, trying not to lose concentration. "No, I think I'll keep it, thanks."

"I know your secret," Koda said, irises swirling with magic and threats. "Cavar will tell the rulers of Astye, and your beloved kingdom will learn you're a fake."

Ruenen's blood ran cold, even though he knew Koda was stalling. The silver-eyed male couldn't snap his fingers until Ruenen dropped the barrier. But the more time Koda isolated Ruenen, the further Marai ran from him.

"Even if you escape today, death awaits you back home at the hands of your own people," the male sneered.

His pulse sprinted at the thought, but Ruenen wouldn't let that happen. He turned, hoping the barrier would stay for a moment, and ran as fast as he could away from that street and Koda. But with each bound, Ruenen ran farther from Marai. He tried to turn down another narrow street to intersect her, but he only succeeded in getting himself lost.

Double fuck.

Ruenen hated not having eyes on Marai. He didn't want to be apart, not after he'd just found her again. But if he couldn't spot her, Ruenen hoped Marai would outsmart Cavar and make her way to the ship. He had to place his faith in her and her skills.

What about the others? Had they made it through the fray? Was the ship waiting for them in the harbor?

Over the crest of the hill, Ruenen finally saw the *The Arcane Wind,* ready to sail. As Ruenen ran, a long line of tiny figures appeared on the dock from the rocky hill nearby. Relief cascaded through him. *Innesh and the folk.* People on the deck waved and shouted down to those on the dock, and the gangplank lowered.

A group of red-vested men then arrived out of nowhere. They must've been lying in wait. Mayhem erupted on the dock as the King's Guard, Greltan soldiers, and crew fought back against dozens of Peace Keepers.

Through the bloody bedlam, Innesh corralled the folk, shepherding them onto the gangplank as men fought around them. Bellaya was shrieking again. One by one, the folk began to board the ship, Keshel at the rear. Two King's Guard brought Eno's trunk to the edge of the dock, and dumped her into the water. They unsheathed their swords and joined the fray.

Ruenen ran faster, his lungs ready to burst, a stitch stinging in his side. Aresti suddenly appeared from another street, racing towards the ship.

"Where's Marai?" she asked, as breathless as Ruenen, running alongside him.

"We were forced to split up."

Braesal and Finneagal landed on the dock, then Beck and Yovel appeared. Dante and Wilder galloped past Ruenen and Aresti, unscathed, save for a few scratches. Ruenen recognized Tarik's muscular form emerging from a street by the harbor, pursued by a small cluster of guards.

His team was all accounted for now, except for Marai.

Ruenen's feet touched the dock, and he leapt into action, cutting through Peace Keepers. Any moment, a Guardian could arrive.

"Get onto the ship," Ruenen shouted to Keshel, who lingered at the bottom of the plank looking confused.

"Where's Marai?" he asked in a daze.

More red-vested men, reinforcements, swarmed the boat. Folk screamed as Cavar's guards made their way up onto the deck.

Ruenen sliced his way through the throng towards the gangplank where Slate Hemming appeared, targeting Keshel, sword drawn. Somehow, the bastard had gotten out of the hold.

Keshel dodged Hemming's swing, falling to the ground. Ruenen lost sight of him as Hemming whirled and sliced with expert precision at an attacking member of his own crew. Covered in blood, Hemming effortlessly cut him down, but at least Keshel had gotten away.

Ruenen leapt into Hemming's path, and the Captain faced Ruenen with malicious glee.

"Give me that amulet, and I'll forgive you for locking me up on my own ship."

Ruenen's blade collided with his. "You double-crossed us."

Hemming blocked, then grabbed hold of Ruenen's sword-wielding wrist, dragging him closer. "You can't sail this ship without me. I'll take the amulet now as payment, or I'll sit down here on the dock, have myself a nice drink, and watch you all *die.*"

Ruenen wheeled back with his free arm and punched Hemming in the jaw. As the captain stumbled, Ruenen shoved him over the lip of the dock and into the water with a satisfying splash.

Someone from the ship deck cheered. Probably Mayestral.

Hemming shouted obscenities and curses as he swam back towards the dock, but it was too high for him to climb up without assistance. No one was aiming to help him.

Ruenen turned instead to Curly, who struck down a Peace Keeper nearby. "Can you sail us home?"

The enormous man nodded. "I've covered Brelioc for years."

Hemming shouted in the background. "You traitor, Curly. I'm going to *murder* you!"

To Ruenen's shock, Curly ignored Hemming, climbed onto the ship, and chucked a Peace Keeper over the railing into the water. The newly promoted Captain then assumed his position at the wheel as if nothing had happened.

The number of Cavar's guards dwindled; most had retreated back into the city, but the two captive Guardians, the bald man and shrieking woman, had also been liberated from the hold.

A sword sailed over Ruenen's head. He ducked just in time, and had no choice but to let the Guardians go. The attacking guard recovered quickly. Steel met steel, and Ruenen was locked into battle, stroke for stroke.

Closing in towards their King, Nyle and Elmar were the last two King's Guard still fighting on the dock.

Ruenen sliced his sword through the left side of the Peace Keeper. The man crashed into the water below, spraying blood into the air. Ruenen turned—

A blade cleaved straight through Elmar's torso.

Nyle released a wretched wail as loyal Elmar's severed body crumpled into a bloody heap on the dock. After cutting down his own assailant, Nyle went after the man who'd slaughtered Elmar. Within a few moves, Nyle dispatched him, and then fell to his knees next to his friend's lifeless, ravaged body.

Ruenen's frantic heart leapt into his throat. They'd been joined at the hip, those boys, and because of him, this mission had torn the friends apart. Elmar's life had barely started. He'd volunteered for this mission with the bravery of a man twice his age. Ruenen hadn't bothered to question the young knight about his life. His family. Regret pierced Ruenen's heart at all the things he never learned about him. Sir Elmar had served Ruenen and Nevandia honorably. *I'm so sorry, Elmar.* Tears stung Ruenen's eyes as Nyle reached for Yovel with a desperate hand.

"Help me haul him up!"

"There isn't time," the werewolf replied.

"Please, I can't leave him here," Nyle cried. "Elmar deserves to be buried in Nevandia. In the soil of our homeland, with the rest of his family."

Yovel's face twisted with guilt and grief. "We can't bring a body onto the ship. He . . . won't make it to Nevandia."

Understanding dawned on Nyle's tear-streaked face. He kissed his friend's forehead, then grabbed Elmar's sword. Yovel guided the young knight up the gangway.

Tarik and Braesal took care of the final Peace Keepers before joining everyone else on the ship. Ruenen was the only one remaining on the blood-stained dock amongst the limbs and bodies. He scanned the street, the crowds, the bodies on the ground, for Marai.

"Your Grace, it's time to leave," Tarik said from above.

Ruenen couldn't leave. He couldn't even breathe.

Aresti appeared at his side, sweating and wild-eyed beneath the blood spatter on her face. "I can't find Keshel. He's not on the ship." Her fearful gaze darted from body to body on the dock as she bit her thumbnail. Keshel wasn't among those slain. Aresti then grabbed hold of Ruenen's arm with a gasp. "I think he went to find Marai."

Ruenen's heart seized, as if someone had ripped it out of his chest and squashed it.

Marai and Keshel were lost somewhere in Bakair.

CHAPTER 36

MARAI

Marai crashed through someone's back courtyard, climbed over a fence, and came out onto the main road.

Is Cavar dead? Did I kill him?

Doesn't matter. Run!

Strength poured from her. Sweat dripped down her face and back. She stumbled over her own feet. But she kept on running—

Straight into Keshel.

They collided, falling onto their rears from the impact. Keshel was being pursued by three other Peace Keepers. And Koda.

"Thank the gods I found you," Keshel said, guzzling down air like a drowning man. Perspiration covered his face, along with a stripe of dirt across his cheek.

"*What the fuck are you doing here?*" Marai yelled at him.

"I'm your eyes," he replied in a trance-like daze. Keshel then leaned over and vomited black blood onto the street.

Marai took his trembling hands and heaved him to his feet. "We're almost to the ship. Move!"

But Keshel was slow, expelling black blood from his mouth as he went, tripping over a cobblestone. Marai's head pounded, and there was still so far to run.

"Hurry," she snapped, dragging Keshel along behind her. She was *furious* at him for entering Bakair. "Koda will soon be within range."

"I can't, Marai," Keshel wheezed.

"Yes, you can!"

With savage desperation, she pulled him harder. The ship was *right there*, sails unfurled.

A snap and a chill lifted the hair on the back of Marai's neck, but she could still move. Koda snapped again. Each time, the air turned colder as he closed the gap between them.

He's almost in range.

Keshel halted mid-step on the street. He whirled around to face Koda and the guards closing in quickly.

"What are you doing?" Marai asked, tugging on Keshel's arm.

But he was frozen. He'd planted himself firmly on the ground, immovable as a mountain.

She yanked again. "Keshel!"

Figures emerged from the crest of the hill behind Koda. Two Peace Keepers carried a severely wounded Cavar between them.

How in the Unholy Underworld is he alive?

Cavar's face contorted with wrath when he saw Marai and Keshel.

"Get her," he shouted, blood spilling from his mouth. He shoved his guards away, holding onto the wound in his gut, dripping ichor onto the pristine sandstone cobbles. The Governor refused to lose. He still assumed he was invincible.

Koda stopped his chase, looking now to Cavar staggering down the hill, torn and concerned about what to do. "Governor, sir—"

"Just get them," Cavar bellowed.

"You'll never make it off Andara," Keshel said softly to Marai, eerily, as if in a dream. Black blood crusted his lips, but Marai hadn't seen him stand so tall, appear so calm, in months. "You need more time to get the ship out of the harbor."

"We can make it, but you need to *move*!"

Keshel didn't listen. He raised his arms, and an invisible barrier snapped into place, creating a wall between Bakair and the entire port. "I can't hold it for long."

How did Keshel have enough strength to produce a barrier?

A wan, golden light surrounded him. *He's using Life Energy.* The seed of magic, of life, within every faerie. But Keshel had warned Marai never to use it because it would kill her. She'd almost died using Life Energy on the Red Lands, and had only survived thanks to Thora's healing magic.

Well, Thora isn't here now.

Keshel's barrier was flimsy—shuttering, fluctuating like ripples on water. Cavar's stone could shatter it instantly, but thank Lirr, the Governor had fallen to his knees, trying to hold in his organs.

Cavar glared up at Koda, who still hesitated, so the Governor slapped him. "I'll put a collar on *you* if you don't stop them!"

Koda reeled back, utterly stunned from Cavar's violent reaction, but he composed himself quickly and focused instead on Keshel's barrier.

"*Go,*" Keshel shouted at Marai, twisting out of her hold. "Get on that ship and sail home."

"Not without you," Marai begged. Her heart screamed as Koda and the guards slammed into Keshel's barrier. It flickered and warped from the impact. "I cannot leave you here to die!"

Keshel's face softened as his arms shook from the strain of holding up the barrier. "I'm fulfilling my purpose, Marai. This is what I'm supposed to do. My mind is shattered. I'm ruined. *You* must live, and see that the auburn haired girl succeeds. Guide her, or the world will be lost. Make sure that she's safe. Make sure that she's not alone." With one trembling hand, he reached into his vest and pulled out the tattered journal. He handed it over to Marai as he collapsed to one knee. "She'll rescue us from the darkness."

"How will I know her?" Marai asked, barely able to breathe from the pressure building in her chest.

Keshel smiled; a frail, bittersweet thing. "Because she is yours."

Marai's eyes flared wide. Then wider still. She clutched the journal to her breast as the word clanged through her. *Mine?*

Cavar flung a dark bolt of magic at the barrier. Keshel gasped in pain as the entire barrier shuddered. People shouted her name from the dock. Fat rain drops struck Marai's cheeks.

"The light, the dark, the eye, the shield," Keshel said through clenched teeth. His dark eyes swum with words he'd never spoken. Words of love Marai knew he felt, but had never dared utter because he understood that she'd never feel the same.

The rain continued to fall, as if the gods were weeping with her.

"Make the choice to be happy, Marai," Keshel said. "And to love. Even if your time is short."

Marai kissed his forehead. She wished she could give him her strength. She wished she could give him the life he deserved.

"Go, *now.*" Keshel turned his attention back to Cavar, Koda, and the magic pressing against his barrier.

Although her paper heart was shredding to pieces, Marai had no choice but to obey. Lirr was forcing her to say goodbye to yet another loved one, all for the sake of a girl in the future.

Marai dashed down the wooden planks of the dock, driving her weak legs as fast as they could go. She could practically taste her pulse.

Ruenen was at the end of the gangway, waiting for her. They rushed up just as the ship began to pull away from the dock. The plank of wood plummeted into the water—Ruenen had barely made it to the railing.

Marai's heart and mind strained as she tried to focus on her surroundings. Someone was shouting curses at her from below. Was that *Slate* in the water? Curly at the wheel?

"Where's Keshel?" Aresti asked, leaning over the railing, searching for Keshel in the water, but the only one down there was ex-Captain Slate Hemming, cursing and hollering up at the ship.

Marai couldn't answer. Aresti looked back to the street and spotted him, now a crumpled mess on the ground, long black hair spilling around him, but Keshel's two shaking arms still held the barrier in place.

Aresti called his name, raising a leg to climb back over the edge. Tarik pulled her away.

"He's granting us time. Honor his sacrifice," the werewolf said. His muscles flexed as he tried to hold onto a thrashing Aresti.

She let loose a wild, wretched scream. Keshel raised his head long enough to look at her. From a distance, Marai's fae sight saw him mouth a goodbye.

Cavar shattered the barrier. Keshel was flung backwards, and his body skidded across the stone. Aresti and Marai both screamed this time, as Cavar bared down. Keshel struggled to his knees, meeting his foe with valor.

"We're moving too slowly," Ruenen said, squinting as the rain continued to fall harder and harder. More tears, more sorrow, from Lirr. "Aresti, please!"

His voice shook something within her. With gritted teeth, Aresti drew herself up and called forth a titanic gust of wind. The sails fully inflated, propelling them further away and out to sea.

Still not fast enough.

Marai couldn't drag her gaze away from the dock. Keshel looked defiantly up into Cavar's face as the Governor drew back a hand.

The world around her dissolved. All Marai could see through the sheets of rain was the blacklight glow of the stone.

A bolt of magic, a long black spear, shot straight through Keshel's heart.

Marai nearly flung herself from the boat as she screamed. Innesh's arms wrapped around her, pulling her away from the edge, and Marai hadn't the strength to break free.

Keshel's body lay on the ground, blood pooling around him.

With Keshel and his blockade disposed of, Cavar made aim for the ship. He was grossly gray as he stumbled to the lip of the dock, clinging to his amulet with one hand and his wound with the other. He directed dark magic beneath the surface of the water, and Marai watched it slink, like spilt oil, towards *The Arcane Wind*. The ship listed dangerously to one side, and Marai was thrown to the deck. Ruenen crashed against the mast.

Braesal got unsteadily to his feet. His wings glistened in the rain as he drew the water around the ship into small waves, pushing and rocking them further out to sea. But they were still within Cavar's reach. Marai returned to the railing as more dark magic spilled into the water.

Eno's turquoise head popped up from the waves.

As a tidal wave of dark magic careened across the surface, its black fingers reaching out to ensnarl *The Arcane Wind*, the mermaid raised a wall of water. Dark magic crashed into it, spewing water in its wake, but Eno's power held, another kind of barrier, like Keshel's.

Curly spun the wheel, holding steady, as Aresti, Braesal, and the other fae worked in tandem, using wind and water to thrust the ship out of Cavar's grasp. Marai was useless, her magic spent. Even if she had the strength, she'd left part of herself behind with Keshel on that dock.

Eno ducked back under the water, and reappeared closer to the ship, forming another wall of water.

Cavar's wound finally caught up to him. He collapsed on the dock, bleeding out upon the planks. He pounded his fists and yelled as Koda and the guards tried to lift him. Marai doubted that he'd stay down for long. He could use the stone to heal himself, like Rayghast had, and once the Governor was fit, he'd set out to get back his prize. Cavar would come for her, and he'd make her pay for the damage she'd caused.

When at last the ship was far enough away from Bakair that Marai could no longer see its dock, nor the sandstone buildings, Eno swam up to the side of the ship. She stared at Marai and waved, beaming a pearly-white smile. She said something in mermish, something that Marai believed was her thanks. Eno then disappeared below the surface, and didn't come up again. Marai hoped she'd return home, wherever that was.

Someone draped a blanket around Marai's shaking shoulders. "Go inside."

Marai didn't move, not at Innesh's gentle push. She refused to look away from Andara, from Keshel's graveyard. She stood there as rain drenched the blanket, washing away the blood from her skin. She stood there, even when her legs wobbled and skull wanted to split itself open from the pain.

Strong arms lifted her, and carried her into the warmth and dryness of the captain's quarters. Ruenen laid her on the bed with aching tenderness. Anja, Gunnora, and Innesh had followed him inside, and they hovered at the double doors. Marai couldn't control her shivers.

"She needs to get out of those wet clothes," Anja said quietly, head bowed in Ruenen's presence.

Marai noticed Mayestral standing by the desk, pale and sweating with fear. *He came to rescue me, too?* If Marai's heart wasn't a dead thing sitting in her chest, she'd have felt appreciation at the sight of him.

The loyal Groom pulled himself together, and dug around in a sack of clothing. He handed Anja a few items.

"She also needs food," Innesh said. "She's barely eaten in weeks."

"We all do," added Gunnora. "You've got a shipload of sick and weary folk to deal with."

Mayestral nodded, color returning to his face. "Yes, come with me. I'll show you to the kitchen."

Innesh followed Mayestral out into the rain, and the cabin doors clicked shut.

Ruenen ran a hand through his sopping hair as Anja and Gunnora helped Marai sit up in bed. He approached, his wet boots loudly squelching as he walked. "Here, let me—"

"Forgive me, Your Grace, but we've dressed her for months. We can handle this alone," Gunnora said waspishly, as if the King of Nevandia was getting in her way.

Ruenen scratched behind his reddening ear. "Ah. I see. I'll grant you some privacy, then." He slid out of the cabin, back onto the deck, and Marai was sad to see him go.

But Anja and Gunnora removed her drenched gown, and shoved a clean, linen shirt that smelled like Ruenen over her head. They dried her hair and skin with a towel, and laid her back down again.

"I'm not tired," Marai snapped, knocking their arms away as she tried to get out of the bed.

"You really think we believe that?" asked Gunnora. "You can't even stand."

Marai's hands covered her shameful face. "I failed Keshel. I let him die, just like I failed Kadi and Leif."

The corners of Anja's eyes tightened, holding back tears. "He would not want you to blame yourself, Marai. He made his choice. He'd want you to get well again, and lead our people to a new life on Astye. You cannot do that if you don't get some rest."

Marai struggled once again. Anja's words were flimsy and brittle, like dead leaves on the ground after a frost.

"Please, don't hate me for this," Gunnora said. She whipped out a small tin from her apron, and blew a pinch of Koda's sleeping powder into Marai's face.

Marai coughed as the metallic drug did its work. Her vision went blurry, then dark as midnight.

Anja pulled the blankets up to Marai's chin. "Sleep now. We'll be right here." Her boney fingers smoothed Marai's wild, wet hair.

The last thing Marai saw before sleep took her was Keshel's broken body lying on the Andaran dock. Never to be seen again. Never to be honored at a grave that would never exist. He wouldn't be laid to rest next to Kadiatu and Leif, home where he belonged.

And she thought how cruel Lirr was to have given her back Ruenen and Aresti, only to take Keshel, her brother, her friend, *her eyes*, away.

CHAPTER 37

CAVAR

Koda, Franulovic, and Yelich carried him to the safety of a nearby house. They laid him upon a cot in the corner of the small cottage. Cavar was only mildly aware of the terrified family huddled in the background. He could do nothing but scream. Scream in pain. Scream in rage.

She'd escaped. She'd torn Cavar's life apart. Marai made him look weak in front of *everyone*. Made him look *mortal*. And because she'd injured him, he couldn't hunt her down immediately.

Cavar clenched his amulet with a shaking hand, and willed the stone to life.

Heal me.

At first, the magic didn't respond. Then, after multiple attempts by Cavar, it finally spoke to him in a voice filled with ire. *"You failed to contain her. You were supposed to keep Marai for me."*

The voice, the owner of the magic, wanted Marai alive, but imprisoned. Harmless. Kept safe, for some reason it never told Cavar.

I'll get her back, Cavar said. He could barely keep himself conscious.

"The only reason you have power is because I give it to you," the voice growled. *"I should never have entrusted Marai to you."*

The pain was unbearable, and his patience for the voice was wearing thin.

If she's so important, why don't you entrap her yourself? Cavar snapped. He was tired of feeling like a puppet to this bodiless presence. But if the voice withdrew its magic, Cavar would be powerless. He'd be nothing but a man once again.

My apologies. Give me another chance, Cavar pleaded. He never apologized to anyone for anything, but he couldn't risk losing the magic. *I weakened her. She won't be hard to capture again.*

"If you fail, I won't hesitate to dispose of you."

Cavar swallowed, the threat filling his lungs with ice. *Understood.*

The stone glowed, illuminating the cottage in blacklight, and Cavar's wound stitched itself together, with the help of a black needle and thread made of magic.

"How do you feel, Governor?" asked Koda tentatively, unaware of the conversation Cavar had had in his mind. Koda's cheek was pink from where Cavar had struck him. Thirty years old, and still such a child.

Cavar wasn't fully healed, but he refused to lie on that cot in that miserable cottage a moment longer. He sat up, wincing and gasping at the pain in his stomach. The wound was bright red and swollen; inside, beneath the surface, it burned. He'd finish the rest once he returned to his own clean, quiet townhouse, and didn't have so many eyes on him.

He stood, shoving away Franulovic and Koda trying to help him. He stumbled out the door, observing the devastation wreaked upon his city.

Bakair, once so orderly and pristine, looked as if a hurricane had plowed through it. Rain doused the flames, but smoke rose above ruined homes. Debris and belongings were scattered in the streets. Stray goats and chickens roamed free.

Cavar returned to where Keshel's body lay, contorted and peaceful in death.

Anger exploded in the Governor's chest. He kicked Keshel's corpse, cursing at him in Andaran. The male was dead, no physical violence or words could hurt him now, but Cavar unleashed a barrage against Keshel's body. It wasn't enough for the creature to die once. Cavar wanted to kill him over and over again.

Suddenly, the pain in Cavar's stomach cried out a warning. He doubled over, groaning, drenched from the rain.

Enough.

Keshel's body ignited in black flames, impervious to the downpour. Cavar watched until nothing remained of the faerie but soaking clumps of ash. It was far too painless an ending for what that vile creature deserved, but it was the best Cavar could do. At least Keshel's death would devastate the Faerie Queen.

"Governor, we should get you inside," Koda urged. He, Franulovic, and Yelich had tiptoed closer to Cavar while he'd raged.

"We'll go to Astye."

"Governor—"

"Begin the preparations. I want to set sail immediately."

"But we have no ships—"

"Then build them!"

"Governor, I insist we get you inside and out of the rain," said Koda, suddenly stern. He'd never taken that tone with Cavar before. "You need to heal. You're not invincible, sir."

Cavar froze. He didn't want to be treated like he was an elder. He wanted none of Koda's coddling. "I will not rest until Marai is leashed and punished for what she did!"

What he wanted was all-out revenge. Complete and total destruction of everything the Faerie Queen held dear. His fury was so potent that steam hissed from his body as rain touched his skin.

"I will go to Astye, and bring her back here to suffer for eternity," he continued through bared teeth, promising himself as much as the stone. "While I'm there, I'll kill that Nevandian King, but not before revealing to his country that he's a *liar*. I'll rip Marai's world to shreds. I cannot . . . *will not* let her get away with this."

CHAPTER 38

RUENEN

The storm that night was powerful, tossing the boat through waves like it was a bar of soap in a child's bathtub. Braesal, Aresti, and the other fae worked hard to keep *The Arcane Wind* afloat.

Marai slept through it all, comatose to the world.

Ruenen continually checked on her throughout the night, drenched and exhausted as he was from reefing the sails. He also made several trips below deck, nearly breaking his neck on the slippery stairs. The Menagerie folk huddled together in the hull of the ship, terrified, no doubt questioning their decision to make the dangerous journey to Astye.

Anja clung to Gunnora at her side. Athelstan, the gaunt werewolf, vomited into a bucket. Tiny gnomes were flung about. The only one who wasn't terrified or distraught was Innesh. She sat against the wall, silent and stoic, rubbing a salve on her ankles. They were bruised and covered with thick scars. She'd worn those shackles for a long while, Ruenen guessed.

Once the storm subsided and a sprinkle of rain dotted the deck, Ruenen studied both his and Nyle's amulets. A strange, alluring power thrummed through the metal, as if wanting Ruenen to use them again. This made him uneasy, and yet, for someone who didn't have his own magic, Ruenen had felt indomitable in those moments when he'd called upon their power. The amulets were certainly useful.

I could fortify Nevandia with this power. Protect my people.

But the amulet's easily-accessible dark magic was far too tempting to use for ill. His hands struggled against his mind, wanting to call upon their formidable power. If word of the amulets got out across Astye, other leaders would start a war to obtain one. Ruenen couldn't allow anyone to get their hands on the amulets. He didn't even trust himself.

He found a sturdy chest in the deepest part of the ship's hull. The place where Marai and Keshel had been shackled. A place no one except Tarik and Yovel went. Ruenen packed the amulets at the bottom of the chest, beneath layers of hay and unused blankets. He then locked the chest and gave the key to Innesh with no explanation.

"Hide this, and don't tell me where," he told her.

It was a failsafe. A way to ensure no one could access the amulets, including himself. When they returned to Kellesar, Ruenen and Marai would find a way to destroy them.

A weight lifted from his shoulders. Ruenen then stumbled into his cabin to find Marai exactly where he'd left her, curled up with a tortured expression. Beads of sweat dappled her brow. A tattered journal was clutched to her chest, as if it were a pillow.

Ruenen sat down heavily at the desk. He yanked off his water-logged boots, shrugged off his sopping jacket.

Marai tossed and turned, whimpering, gasping, crying. Her wings convulsed, as if she were trying to fly away from the pain. It was hard to watch her, suffering even in rest.

What does she see when she closes her eyes?

Would she ever be free of nightmares? Of the new scars given to her by Cavar?

Do I try to comfort her? Do I wake her? That might only make things worse. Ruenen didn't know if she wanted him there in the room, but he couldn't tear himself away.

He fell asleep sometime in the early blue hours of morning, lying across the desk, drooling a little onto a map. When he woke up, Marai wasn't in bed. He was used to Marai waking before him, but the sight of the scrambled, empty sheets left him momentarily fretful.

He quickly pulled on his boots, and stepped onto the deck. His gaze was immediately drawn to Marai standing at the stern, gazing out to sea, to Andara far away in the distance. She wore Ruenen's linen shirt, the hem stopping at her knees, the back ripped open to accommodate her beautiful wings. Someone had given her a pair of ugly, ochre knickers. The wind snatched at her white-blonde hair, lifting each strand in a chaotic dance. Her wings fluttered, drooping slightly. Ruenen still couldn't believe they were real. That her ears were now pointed. That she'd become *more fae*. He wanted to ask Anja or Innesh about it, but that felt like an invasion of Marai's privacy.

She still had that journal in her hands. Ruenen had never seen her write in one before. If anything, it was something Keshel would do . . .

Marai seemed peaceful in that moment, or, at the very least, momentarily steady. Ruenen didn't want to disturb that, to upset her. What did you say to someone who had been through such trauma? No words seemed right to him. None of them were justified or significant enough to encompass what he wanted to express. So he kept them all inside, swallowed them down like bile to stew and roil in his stomach.

She was far, far away from him. Despite finding her, rescuing her from Cavar's clutches, Marai was no closer to him than she was before. It felt like he was starting from the beginning again. That he no longer knew her and was meeting the Lady Butcher for the first time.

"Be patient," said a voice at Ruenen's elbow. It belonged to Gunnora, the tiny Greltan woman with curly brown hair and blue eyes. "She suffered more than the rest of us, though she was only there for a short while."

A short while? It had been months since Marai had been taken.

"Can you tell me what happened to her?" Ruenen asked through the lump in his throat.

"Not sure it's my story to tell," Gunnora said, "but I can tell you that she's earned our love and respect. That lioness-heart of hers is strong. She'll come around. Give her time."

Ruenen had been patient long enough, but for Marai, he'd wait a while longer. He'd be gentle. Give her space. He'd wait a lifetime if that's what she needed. He and Gunnora both knew that Marai would come to him when she was ready.

And I'll be here.

"You helped her in the Menagerie?" asked Ruenen.

This stout little woman had an air of capability about her. "She fought for us, every day, despite what torture Cavar put her through. Even if it wasn't her punishment to take."

Ruenen's chest warmed. *That sounds like Marai.*

"Thank you for being there for her." *When I couldn't be.*

Gunnora must have read the sorrow on his face, because she patted his elbow. "Never known a more stubborn girl than her. She'll come 'round, and when she does, she'll be glad that you're there." She smiled and curtsied. "And thank *you*, Your Grace, for setting us free. We know you didn't need to bring us rag-tag, sorry-faced lot with you. We're aware you came for Marai and Keshel, but for what it's worth, you've earned the loyalty of us Menagerie folk."

She walked away before Ruenen could respond, joining Tarik, Yovel, Athelstan, and Anja in conversation by the stairs leading up to the quarter deck.

Ruenen barely had a moment to study those in the Menagerie during the past few days. Looking at them, spread out in groups across the deck, he realized that the world was far vaster than he'd known. The diversity of the folk shocked him; so many different creatures, beyond his wildest imagination. And they now viewed Marai as their Queen. What Ruenen had been trying to achieve in Nevandia was nothing compared to the unity Marai had built within the Menagerie.

Aresti then approached Marai without any sense of caution. Ruenen envied Aresti of that. She wasn't afraid of Marai's reaction, or nervous about disturbing her calm. Aresti stood next to her in silence, breathing in the sea air. Ruenen sat down beside a barrel of mead and listened to them. Yes, he was eaves-dropping, but he was drawn to the sound of Marai's voice. The sound of her, there, present, *alive,* stole away his very breath.

"This is Keshel's," Marai finally said, cutting into the silence.

She handed Aresti the journal she'd been coveting, the last remaining fragment of a once-great male. Someone Ruenen had barely started to know before he'd been abducted with Marai. It was a regret Ruenen would always carry—that he hadn't tried harder to know Keshel before he died. Whenever he stood at Leif and Kadiatu's grave with Thora and Raife, he often felt the same. They were friends taken away too early.

Aresti flipped eagerly through the journal, as if searching for a message Keshel had scrawled for her. Her face fell the more pages she consumed. "What does any of this mean? They're ramblings . . . from a madman." She looked up at Marai, clearly troubled.

"His mind was . . . broken. Cavar's collar forced visions on Keshel," Marai said, and Aresti's face went ghostly pale. "They were unnaturally imposed on him, over and over again by dark magic, until Keshel lost his sense of reality. I doubt even Thora could have healed him. But he wrote down what he saw and what he learned as a guide for me."

"A guide?"

Marai took the journal back and tucked it into her chest again. "There's a prophecy written in these pages. It's my responsibility to decipher it."

A prophecy? Ruenen didn't like the sound of that. Keshel's visions were almost always bleak and vague. The last thing Marai needed was more trouble.

"He saw a girl, chosen by Lirr. She's the only one who can defeat dark magic for good, and I have to help her," Marai said, voice taking on a desperate lilt. Her stained fingers tightened on the journal's leather cover, shoulders hunched forward. "I cannot fail Keshel now. I cannot fail *her*."

"What have you failed at?" Aresti asked. When Marai gave no response, Aresti spun her around to face her. "Keshel's death was Cavar's, alone. Dark magic did that. Dark magic corrupted Cavar's mind, and manipulated him. And before you even start, you didn't fail Kadiatu or Leif, either. But if this chosen girl is truly the savior Keshel thought she was, then I will help you find her. We'll make sure she fulfills his prophecy, and then his death won't have happened in vain. We'll honor his sacrifice, and put an end to dark magic."

She then pulled Marai into a fierce hug.

Pain needled Ruenen's heart at the sight of Marai, so frail, clinging to Aresti. But he was also relieved, and *glad,* that she was talking. She was grieving with someone, even if it wasn't him.

Gunnora walked past, carrying a tray of food, and winked at Ruenen on the stairs, as if to say "I told you so."

Aresti and Marai sat at the stern all day, passing the journal between themselves, trying to understand Keshel's jumbled thoughts.

"I didn't know Keshel could draw," Marai said, pointing to a page. Her eyes glistened in the burnished dusk light.

"Oh, when he was younger, he was *always* sketching something," said Aresti, looking closer at the paper with a chuckle. "You probably don't remember that, do you?"

Marai shook her head. "I admit . . . there's a lot I didn't know about him."

"Don't be glum. He was my *cousin,* and most of the time he was a complete mystery to me, too." Aresti took a deep breath, calming her rising emotions. She returned her focus to the journal. "He stopped drawing after the massacre . . ." Aresti's eyebrows waggled as she tried to make sense of whatever was on the page. She flipped the journal upside down, squinting. "What are these? Fireflies?"

"I think so."

"What do fireflies have to do with anything?"

Marai shrugged.

"I don't think I gave him enough credit. For keeping us safe. Teaching you and Kadi to read and write, calming those squabbles between us," Aresti said, smiling softly. "Making us into a family, whether we wanted to be or not." She nudged Marai with a lopsided smirk.

A wan smile curled the corners of Marai's mouth in return, and she continued to reanimate as the sky's orange hues dimmed to a velvety indigo. Her face took on a fervent, determined expression. She even ate a bowl of fish stew at dinnertime.

But Marai never once looked Ruenen's way, although he'd been meandering the deck most of the afternoon. He decided to make use of his leisurely hours by speaking with each of the Menagerie folk, properly introducing himself. He memorized their names, and ensured that they were comfortable, fed, and getting the medical attention they needed. Those who spoke the common tongue wrung his hands, expressing their intense gratitude, offering *him* their services.

If he couldn't help Marai in that moment, Ruenen satisfied himself by aiding her people.

Newly-ordained Captain of *The Arcane Wind,* Curly, approached Marai after dinner. A kaleidoscope of emotions crossed her face when she looked up at the giant man. Her countenance grew cautious and tense at his arrival. Her fingers flexed, as if reaching for her sword on the deck next to her.

"I'm sorry for my part in your abduction," Curly said in his monotone, gruff voice. The man rarely showed much emotion, or spoke at all. He reminded Ruenen of a towering, stalwart Greltan pine tree. "I was wrong to be complicit. I regret my actions."

Marai's expression cleared as she blinked. "Forgiven."

She returned to devouring the contents of the journal, and Curly, satisfied, returned to the wheel. Ruenen tried to hide his smile.

The night was overcast, as usual in the Northern Sea. Dark clouds smudged over the stars and waxing moon, but the ship was more alive than before, so crammed with bodies that it was impossible to find a seat on the deck. Ruenen ate with Mayestral in his quiet cabin, then returned to the deck to secretly (or not-so-secretly) watch Marai.

He couldn't muster up the courage to speak with her, and she still wouldn't look his way.

Give her space. That's what she needs right now. But the thought of staying away from Marai, after he'd traveled across the perilous sea to rescue her, disheartened him.

His lute was suddenly shoved into his hands.

"Play for her, Your Grace," Mayestral said with a smile. "Play for us all." The Groom then sat down on a nearby barrel, perching his chin on his fist, and waited to be entertained.

"Subtle," Ruenen murmured to him.

Mayestral smiled innocently.

Ruenen's fingers hovered over the courses. *What could I possibly play for Marai and these other wounded souls?* "The Lady Butcher" certainly wouldn't do, and Ruenen didn't know any songs of healing.

So he wrote one. Right there.

He reached out and grasped their pain, their fear, their loss, and confusion, as if they were fraying strings in the breeze. Each emotion was a different color, a different melody. He searched inside himself for the thread of gray hurt and red panic he'd felt for those many months. Ruenen put it all into a melody, letting those colorful threads combine in harmony. He played the song softly, so as not to disturb, but the deck quieted anyway. Eyes of vivid fae, to human, to black and bulbous, watched him. Ears both round and pointed listened in.

Ruenen closed his eyes. His fingers had long ago memorized their placement on the strings—he didn't need to see to play. He could *feel* far more easily if he shut out the world.

But he sensed the electric tingle of a familiar amethyst gaze.

When he finished the tune, Ruenen returned to reality. Like a magnet, his eyes found Marai's locked on him, as if she'd finally registered his presence on the ship. As always, they were the only pair that mattered to Ruenen, and sent his pulse racing. He drowned in the sea of those swirling, wild irises. Everyone else onboard could have disappeared.

"Another, please," chirped a bearded gnome at Ruenen's side.

Bellaya the banshee wiped away tears with her cloak sleeve.

Ruenen cleared his throat, dragging his attention back to the rest of the crowded deck. He played for an hour or so, until his body and voice grew weary from lack of sleep. When he set his lute aside, folk approached to thank him, and compliment his skills. Those who didn't speak the common tongue expressed themselves without words by putting a hand to their hearts.

Cyrill, the goblin, was the most interesting to Ruenen. He lingered amongst the shadows, his long fingers stroking items of clothing he'd gathered from around the ship. Ruenen recognized his own vest in the pile next to the goblin, and wondered how he'd managed to snatch that away without anyone noticing.

"He's a hoarder," Gunnora hissed at Ruenen, pointing to Cyrill. "Watch out for your velvets and silks."

Her feet were silent on the wooden deck, but Ruenen knew Marai was behind him from the vibration in the air. The prickle of magic on his skin. He turned.

She picked her fingernails as she looked up at him. Her nervous tell. "How . . . how are you, Ruen?"

He stopped himself from grinning, but couldn't hide the relieved sag of his shoulders. The sound of his name on her lips was a melody he'd lost. "I'm well. And you?"

"Tolerable." Marai pursed her lips, then looked away, up at the clouded night sky. A pale flush came to her cheeks.

A smile consumed Ruenen's entire face. He didn't stop it this time—he'd missed her blushes. But he knew Marai was blushing now because she was uncomfortable and unsure of how to interact with him. That simply wouldn't do.

"I'm glad to hear that," Ruenen said, drawing her gaze back to him.

"And Nevandia? Is it . . . doing well?"

"We're rebuilding. It's slow but steady progress, yet I'm quite proud of what we've accomplished so far," Ruenen said, then gestured to Braesal and his group chatting with Dante and Wilder, the centaurs. "You've met our newest citizens."

"I didn't know there were any faeries but us left on Astye."

"There may be more, still. As word travels about the safe haven we've established in Nevandia, more may come." Ruenen looked around the deck, as co-mingling folk and humans began to make their way to bed. "Looks like we'll have more new citizens."

"I worry about integrating them," said Marai, frowning. "Nevandians might now be okay with fae and werewolves, but goblins? Centaurs? They're beings humans on Astye have never heard of before. Not only that, but these folk have been abused for years. Trust will be difficult for them."

"It'll be a challenge, but we've already changed many minds. We've proven that human and magical folk can coexist. I'm sure we'll find a way to work things out."

Marai's lips contorted into a wry smile. "You always were rather optimistic."

"I lost that part of me for a while," Ruenen admitted. He didn't want to say anything that would scare Marai away, but he had to be honest about how her absence had affected him. "When you were gone. Music, too, eluded me, and only recently did I get it back."

Marai's violet eyes pinned him in place. "And your Queen? How is she?"

Ruenen started. "My *Queen*?"

Was Marai being serious with such a question?

She picked at her stained fingernails again. "I know. I heard Mayestral that day . . . when I visited you in the daydream. He said the Queen was waiting for you." Marai looked down at the deck, as if not truly wanting to hear his answer.

Ruenen laughed so hard that tears welled in his eyes. "My *Queen?* Marai, you thought that I'd gone and married someone after you'd been abducted? I was worried *sick* about you every second of every day. The last thing on my mind was marriage."

Marai's entire face went beet red as she stammered. "But I *heard* Mayestral—"

"I was visiting Queen Nieve at the Glacial Palace. King Maes sadly passed away, and I attended the funeral service."

Is that why she's been avoiding me? Because she thought I'd married someone else? Relief, as strong as a tidal wave, washed over him.

"Well, how was I supposed to know that?" Marai snapped, glaring at him with those endearingly red cheeks. "I wasn't exactly thinking straight. And I know the Witan must've been putting pressure on you."

Ruenen loved Marai all the more for her embarrassment, for the defiantly haughty angle of her shoulders. He took a step towards her, closing some of the distance between them. "I refused the women the Witan recommended. I told them that I couldn't marry anyone until you were home safely. And if I hadn't found you for thirty years, I still would have waited."

The flustered challenge left her, and Marai's violet irises shimmered as she took in his words, relief smoothing out her features. Ruenen's spirits rose; his Marai was still in there. She wasn't lost. She was *recovering* and rediscovering, and he would wait, however many days or weeks or months it took for her to feel ready again.

She coughed awkwardly, took a breath, and said, "Right. Well, goodnight, then . . ."

"My bed is yours," Ruenen blurted, and then felt the heat climb into his own face. *Smooth.* "I mean, you can sleep in my room. It's far more comfortable, and you need a proper space to recuperate."

"Where will you sleep?" Marai asked, watching him intently. It always amazed Ruenen how bright her eyes were in the darkness, like two remote galaxies in the night sky, swirling with stars.

"Oh, somewhere else . . ." He hadn't really thought that far. Would she think him weird for sleeping at the desk? Or worse, on the floor?

I just need to be near her.

"You're a king," she said. As if that mattered to him at all.

"And you're a queen."

Marai stood a little taller as she said, "This is your ship. That's your bed."

"And I'm choosing to give it to you."

Marai stared at him, sizing him up, challenging him the way she used to. *Gods, I've missed her.*

Perhaps she saw that thought in his face because she immediately softened. "I accept, but only if you also have somewhere comfortable to sleep."

"I'll make up a bed on the floor. If you don't mind."

"I don't mind," she practically whispered.

He'd need to reign in the frantic gallop of his heart if he was going to survive the night in her presence. Marai followed Ruenen into his cabin, where Mayestral was laying out Ruenen's bedclothes and turning down the sheets.

"No need for any of that tonight," Ruenen told him.

Mayestral spotted Marai behind Ruenen. His eyebrows rose slightly as Ruenen pulled one pillow and blanket from the bed and set them on the rug. The Groom bowed, shooting Ruenen a knowing smirk, which Marai either didn't notice or pretended not to see. Mayestral then exited with the lantern, leaving the room in darkness and silence.

Marai crossed to the bed and slid beneath the sheets. Ruenen did the same on the rug, fluffing up the pillow.

"This reminds me of Dwalingulf," he said, staring up at the ceiling, "and the night you told me your name."

In that inn, Marai had given Ruenen her name, and in return, she'd unknowingly stolen his heart.

"You were so set on learning my name, or anything about me at all," she said, and Ruenen could hear the amusement in her voice.

At the time, the Lady Butcher had been a riddle he'd been trying to puzzle out since their first encounter in Gainesbury. Marai had been an elusive enigma that he'd studied and pondered, hoping to get a glimpse behind the scarf.

"Your name was never just a name to me."

No, when she'd whispered her name that night, it had been like discovering that the universe was made of songs, and her name was the only lyric that mattered.

He heard Marai expel a small breath.

"Goodnight, Ruen."

"Goodnight, Marai."

How many nights had he whispered those words into the darkness, hoping she would hear them?

Ruenen closed his eyes with a smile on his lips and the warmth of the sun inside his chest, because tonight, she was there. At least tonight, she'd heard them.

CHAPTER 39

MARAI

It was a strange, brittle thing to be back amongst those she'd known before. She kept waiting for the dream to crack, expecting to wake up in her tent, or in the terrible darkness of the crate. But each morning she rose and realized it wasn't an illusion.

She was beginning to come to terms with things. With Keshel's death. With Cavar and Koda standing, alive, on that dock.

There was a before, a during, and an after of the Menagerie. That was how Marai categorized her life three days later. It was difficult to put into words all that had occurred. Aresti wanted to know everything. She hovered around Marai like a gnat, often soundless, but very much present. Tarik kept giving Marai sympathetic smiles. Mayestral seemed to think Marai might snap in two at any moment, and treated her with a delicacy that was bordering on infuriating. Even Nyle and the King's Guard looked at Marai as if she were something to pity.

She hated it.

I don't want pity. I don't want sympathy.

"My Queen?"

Marai lifted her head from Keshel's journal to see a broad figure with wings blotting out the cloud-smudged sun. *Braesal.*

She was used to the Menagerie folk calling her Queen, but she couldn't comprehend why Braesal and his group of Astyean fae addressed her as such. They'd only just met her.

"I wanted to see if you know where you'll be settling once you return to Astye."

Marai was momentarily speechless by his blunt question. "I . . . I haven't decided."

"Wherever you decide to go, we of the fae will follow you," Braesal said.

"But why? You know so little of me. I may not be worthy of your loyalty." She glanced down at her stained fingertips. "Why choose to follow me when I have no land? No home?"

Braesal knelt before her. "Because you are a beacon of change for our people. You're proof that even through massacres and genocide, the fae survive. If one of the royal bloodlines can live against all the odds, then there is hope for us magical folk. There's hope for rebuilding. You symbolize a future, and that's a powerful thing."

Marai chewed the inside of her cheek. Braesal was exactly like the folk in the Menagerie. To them, Marai's existence was a symbol of hope. She was beginning to see that no matter where she went or what she did in the future, these people would follow and support her.

I'm not alone.

"I've spoken to the others from the camp," Braesal continued. "They told me that you defended them. Tried to take whippings for them. I don't know many kings or queens who would do that for their people. I believe you're more worthy than you think." He was a serious man. Marai had yet to see him crack a smile, but his face softened as he got to his feet. "We're entirely at your service, Your Grace, and we'll follow you to the ends of the earth, if that is what you desire."

"Thank you, Master Braesal," Marai said, feeling a stinging in her eyes. *Maybe I can forgive myself a little.*

Braesal bowed, then returned to Beck, Finneagal, and Zorish.

Marai's attention snagged on Ruenen, who was washing the ship's railings, his shirtsleeves rolled up to reveal his corded forearms. He was more muscular than before, and she'd noticed on Andara that his skill with a sword had improved. *He must have been training in my absence.* He wiped his sweaty brow with the back of his hand, tossing hair out of his eyes. He caught Marai staring, and she immediately stood and turned her back on him to shield her burning face.

Gods, why was it so impossible to talk to him? She'd seen him *naked* before, for Empyra's sake.

She let out a huff of frustration as she gazed out to sea from the stern. She'd barely left this location on the deck, except to sleep. In the Captain's Quarters. In Ruenen's bed. With him sleeping on the floor.

"You two are ridiculous," came Aresti's voice. She appeared at Marai's side, leaning back against the railing. Wind whipped her short hair and dangling earrings. "You're both acting like awkward adolescents, and it's excruciating to watch."

"Then stop snooping."

"Go talk to him."

"I'm not good with words."

Aresti shot her a bland look. "That man over there nearly lost his damned mind when you were taken. You were all Ruenen thought about. He sent out search parties across Nevandia and Tacorn. Lirr's Bones, Ruenen sent us into Varana and Cleaving Tides to look for you. He had Nosficio running up and down the continent *for you*. He defied his counsel over and over again *for you*. I'm not attracted to men, nor am I a romantic, but damn, even *I* swooned when he hired Cavar's own crew and *sailed across the sea* for you."

Marai swallowed. Aresti's words were a sledgehammer to Marai's walled off heart. She heard the joyous sound of Ruenen's laughter, and shot a hasty glance over her shoulder. He, Tarik, Gunnora, and Nyle were chuckling about something. Only a few days ago, it was a sound Marai thought she'd never hear again.

"All I'm saying is that man over there loves you, and you're an idiot to pretend that you don't love him back," Aresti said.

Marai wasn't pretending. All she'd wanted for months was to see his face. To hear his voice. To be held in his arms.

With a groan of exasperation, Aresti left her alone to contemplate the muted sunset.

Marai was scared. That was the true root of this uncertainty. She was scared to reach out for happiness, only to have it ripped away. She thought of Keshel then, and his melancholy parting words.

Make the choice to be happy, Marai. And to love.

"Alright, Keshel," she said into the howling gale. She reached a hand out over the railing, letting the wind twirl between her fingers, as if Keshel's were clasping hers back from the Underworld. "I'll make the choice to fight. I'll find the girl, I'll guide her to defeat the Lord of the Underworld. And I'll live. I'll live enough for the both of us. For Kadi and Leif, too."

That night was quiet because of the rain. Everyone was either below deck or in their cabins, if they had one. Marai had eaten with the folk in the hull, and then made her way up the stairs to Ruenen's quarters.

Her hand hesitated on the door handle. Although she'd been sleeping there, it didn't feel right to barge in. She knocked.

"Come in," said Ruenen from inside.

She opened the door and nearly shut it immediately when she saw Ruenen's bare back.

He whirled around, giving her a glorious glimpse of his muscular chest and torso, before his eyes opened wide. "I thought you were Mayestral—"

"I'm sorry—"

"Let me get a shirt on—"

"No, it's fine—"

Ruenen's hand froze, mid-reach, for the shirt lying on the bed.

You have to say this now.

Marai stepped further into the room and shut the door. Ruenen seemed suspended in time as a soft blush came to his cheeks.

"I wanted to . . . thank you," Marai managed to stumble out.

"For?" Ruenen finally lowered his hand.

For? Marai almost snorted.

"You sailed halfway across the world for me." Her stomach was full of wings as she stared into those gold-flecked eyes. "You braved death for me. You freed my people. You did the impossible, Ruen. I have a million reasons to thank you, and I'm sorry for not saying so sooner."

"I would cross every ocean, climb every single mountain, tunnel deep into the earth, to find you." Ruenen took a step towards her. His hands were shaking, as if he'd been holding back these words for days. "I would traverse galaxies. Through forsaken realms of the Underworld. *Nothing* could keep me from you."

The world tumbled away beneath Marai's feet as she released a tremulous breath. Her soul soared, higher than the highest wind. Ruenen was always so much better with words than she was, but Marai had decided that she would stop holding back, stop wasting valuable time. She wouldn't cower from the lyrics her heart was singing.

"Ruen, I will love you until the last breath leaves my body, and then, my soul will linger just to watch over you."

Something magical shimmered in the air between them. The taut cord that had tied them together since their first meeting quivered like a string on Ruenen's lute.

He closed the distance, and brushed away the tears on Marai's cheeks with a gentle thumb; tears she hadn't noticed she'd shed. "Please, can you say it again?"

"I love you," she whispered. "I love you, I love you, I love you—"

Ruenen's lips cut her off.

Her back collided with the wall, wings splaying behind her. She dove her hands into his hair, tugging him closer. There was nothing gentle in that kiss. It was wild and frenetic. The kiss spoke every word she still wanted to say.

She didn't want to be gentle. All that mattered in that moment were *his* hands, *his* lips, *his* gaze holding hers. Marai had forgotten what this felt like—the all-consuming heat and reckless joy that Ruenen brought with his touch.

His hand traveled up her side to her neck. One of his fingers stroked her pointed ear. He let out a small gasp against her lips, as if discovering something brand new about her, memorizing the changes to her body. Ruenen dragged his lips across her jaw to that pointed ear, and his breath against the shell of her ear sent a shiver down her spine.

Ruenen stopped then. He didn't pull away, but Marai sensed his attention on her wings.

"You can touch them," she said. She *wanted* him to. She wanted Ruenen to accept every new part of her, like he had with her old body.

Ruenen traced the pad of his finger along the outer edge of one wing. *Holy gods.* Marai's entire body was electric. That light touch was enough to send her reeling.

His face grew serious as he noticed the clipped hindwing. Ruenen took her hand, and brought it to his heart. "This belongs to you. All of me is yours. If you want the crown upon my head, you can take that, too, but I'd rather you wear one sitting on the throne beside me."

"The Witan—"

"Has no control over my heart. You've always been my Queen, even before you discovered your lineage. I would've married you without the royal blood. Without the titles. If we were still the Lady Butcher and Ard the Bard, and had nothing on earth but each other."

Beneath her palm, she measured the way Ruenen's heart pounded.

He then whispered the words she'd been aching for. "I love you." Between ravenous kisses, Ruenen uttered them again. And again. And again. Until the words were branded into her skin. "Say you'll be my wife."

The words slipped from Marai's mouth, as easy as any breath. "I will be yours until my bones are dust."

The last thread of restraint between them became untethered. Marai tossed aside her shirt as Ruenen's fingers untied the string of her pants. With one commanding hand, Marai pushed him backwards onto the bed. She straddled him, wings rising behind her.

Marai was powerful. She was in control. She dragged her mouth down the hard planes of his chest and taut stomach. Ruenen hissed between his teeth as Marai stroked him with a finger beneath the band of his trousers. She quickly unbuttoned them, and practically ripped them off his legs.

Her body may have been altered, but Ruenen still fit perfectly inside her. Marai never felt more complete than when she was with him. They moved together as one, in perfect harmony.

"I admire a woman who seizes control," he growled through his wicked grin.

In response, she leaned down and took his lower lip in her teeth, eliciting a deep moan from his throat that skated across her skin.

She wanted to live in this moment forever.

But then something tightened in her chest. A wound resurfaced. The scar on her soul began to burn. She almost had a very different future. She might have never seen Ruenen again. Been a prisoner for the rest of her life. The heartache came upon her so suddenly that she slowed her movement.

I'm here. We're together. I'm safe now. She wanted to be enveloped by the safety of his arms.

She rolled sideways, dragging him with her, until Ruenen was on top, bracing his arms on either side of her body. *This* was what she needed. Him shielding her. Protecting her.

Ruenen seemed to understand the shift, as he moved slower, planting tender kisses down her neck and breasts.

Once again, he whispered those beautiful words against her lips. "I love you."

And Marai shattered into hundreds of stars sent across the cosmos. Her universe was a sunburst, and Ruenen was its ardent sun.

A knock jolted Marai from her first nightmare-less sleep in weeks. Ruenen didn't stir, except to hold Marai tighter.

"Your Grace?" It was Mayestral, and it was morning.

Marai shook Ruenen's arm. "Mayestral's here. What's he going to think if he sees his King naked in the arms of a faerie?"

Ruenen groaned into her hair. "That his King is lucky. Mayestral can come back later." He sleepily kissed her bare shoulder, then burrowed into her neck, wings folded between them.

Mayestral was persistent. He knocked again.

But Ruenen was stubborn. He rolled on top of Marai, grinning mischievously at her concern, his hair adorably tousled. "Come back later!"

Mayestral seemed to get the message, because his footsteps disappeared.

"Good morning, my love," Ruenen said, rubbing his nose against hers. His beaming smile was cloyingly sweet, but Marai reveled in it. "There are a million things I've been dreaming of saying to you, and that's one of them."

"Good morning?" she asked with a laugh. It was such a simple thing.

"Because it means that I've woken up beside you, and that you're the first thing I see when I open my eyes."

Marai kissed him. Yes, "good morning" was a simple greeting, but how many times had Marai woken in that empty tent, wishing Ruenen was there with her?

"Good morning," she echoed, gently stroking the contours of his face.

They remained entwined beneath the sheets. Marai knew she really should get up and help with the daily chores, but she couldn't bring herself to vacate Ruenen's arms. Her stomach, of course, had other ideas. It released a mighty gurgle that made Ruenen chuckle.

"I suppose I should get my wife some breakfast."

"I'm not your wife *yet*," Marai reminded him, but she liked the sound of that word on his lips, and the way his eyes glimmered.

"Do you prefer to be called my betrothed? Or perhaps mine own heart's root? My peerless paramour? My sweeting?"

Marai shoved him off her with a laugh. "Uch, no. But yes, you can go fetch me breakfast."

Ruenen climbed out of bed and gave her a clumsy bow. "I have my Queen's command." He dressed in haste, then halted with his hand curled around the door handle. He looked back over his shoulder with that same mischievous smile. "What about lambkin?"

Marai threw a pillow at his head.

Ruenen returned shortly with a tray full of food. "I had to fight off Mayestral for this. He wanted to bring it, himself, but I figured you wouldn't want an audience."

Marai wasted no time in stuffing a slice of greasy bacon into her mouth. She'd forgotten what real food tasted like; she'd grown used to Bobo's slop.

Ruenen joined her in the bed, taking a swig from his tin cup of coffee. "So I've been thinking."

Marai raised her eyebrows.

"I think Curly should marry us today."

Marai choked on her bacon. "Today? Curly?"

"He's a captain. Isn't it true that a ship's Captain can perform marriage ceremonies?"

"I think that's a fiction, Ruen," said Marai, but she loved his enthusiasm just the same. *I'd marry him today if it was possible.*

Ruenen scratched the stubble on his chin. "*Someone* on this ship must be ordained."

"Is there a rush?"

"I don't want to spend another second of my life not married to you." Ruenen smacked a kiss on her cheek, nearly spilling his coffee. "But also, I think it's a good idea to marry before we get to Astye. And specifically Nevandia."

"Because of the Witan."

"I don't want to give them any ammunition to say that we cannot wed. I don't give a damn what they say, but they could certainly make our lives difficult. If we arrive in Nevandia already married, there's nothing they can do about it."

"I have a feeling they'll be most aggrieved that they weren't part of the ceremony. I imagine a royal wedding is a huge deal for them and the country."

"They've been pressuring me for a queen, so I can simply say that I took care of everything and made life easy for them."

Suddenly, Marai remembered. She let out a gasp, eyes wide, as she lowered her voice. "Ruen, Fenir *betrayed* you. He told Koda that you're not the child of Vanguarden and Larissa, that you're not even blood related to the throne. Cavar knows, and he's threatened to use that against you—"

Ruenen took another sip of coffee, nonchalant. "I'm already aware of Fenir's betrayal. He told me and Holfast everything, and he's currently under house arrest."

Marai frowned. "You don't seem concerned about Cavar having this knowledge."

"Cavar has no reputation on Astye. Who do you think people will believe? The King and his Witenagemot? Or a strange man writing letters from across the sea?"

Ruenen had a point, but it wasn't merely Cavar's knowledge that gave him power.

"He'll come after us, you know," said Marai. "He's not going to let me get away with destroying the Menagerie."

Nor will the Lord of the Underworld. He'd force Cavar to go after Marai, no matter what.

"Don't you think he's dead already? That wound you gave him . . . no one could survive that."

"Dark magic in the stone will heal him. He thinks of himself as an immortal god because of its power, but I made him look mortal in front of his people. I embarrassed him. *Ruined* him." Rage curdled Marai's recently eaten breakfast in her stomach. "He'll do anything to enslave me again. To make me pay."

Ruenen cupped Marai's cheek. "Then he'll have to face all of Nevandia, because you are its Queen. He'll have no power on our lands."

With the amulet's power, and the backing of the Lord of the Underworld, Cavar *was* limitless—he could wipe out whole cities and no one except Marai could stop him.

If I can stop him . . . she didn't know if she was enough.

Ruenen drew her into his arms, careful of crushing her wings. "Don't think about him today. Or tomorrow. Think about how much I adore you, Sassafras."

That was the only term of endearment she would accept.

Her eyes caught on the glinting steel in the corner of the cabin. She clambered out of bed, wrapping a sheet around herself for modesty, and grabbed the new Dimtoir by its hilt. It felt different in her hand. The weight was off, but not in a bad way. The metal now had a bluish sheen, and when Marai held it at different angles, the blade seemed to change colors. Different, but still beautiful.

"How did you get this?" she asked.

Ruenen scooted to the edge of the bed. "I reforged it."

Marai stared at him. She'd forgotten he was once a blacksmith's apprentice. "You *reforged* it?"

"After the Battle of the Red Lands, while you were recovering, I picked up every single shard of this blade that I could find on the moor. I brought it to a forge, and remade it using the original shards."

Love, unlike anything she'd ever known, curled around her heart like ivy. Marai pictured Ruenen, almost-king, crouching on the moor, healing from his serious wound from Rayghast, sifting through grass and dirt to find pieces of her beloved sword.

"I wanted to give it to you on the night of my coronation," Ruenen continued. "Consider it a wedding present. Of course, I didn't make it alone."

"What do you mean?"

"Aresti, Raife, Thora . . . and Keshel . . . they all put a drop of their magic into the blade whilst the iron was hot. Keshel had read a little on how the ancient fae made their blades. We tried to mimic the process as much as possible. I hope it's as strong as it was before. Keshel also told me that the ancient fae engraved on the original blade meant *'against the darkness, I ignite.'* He made sure the same words were written on this blade, too."

Tears overwhelmed Marai's eyes as her grip on the handle tightened. Keshel's magic *lived* in this blade. Her family's love, and Ruenen's own hands, had re-crafted her father's sword. No matter where she went, she would always carry a part of them with her.

Against the darkness, I ignite.

And she would, when she faced the Lord of the Underworld again.

Marai walked back to the bed and pressed her lips to Ruenen's. "This is the most beautiful gift I will ever receive."

"And here." Ruenen pulled the bloodstone ring out of his pocket. "It guided Aresti to you. I can get you a better ring, one less *cursed,* but I figured for now, a sword and your ancestor's ring would be appropriate for a proposal."

Marai laughed through her tears, and Ruenen slid the ring onto her left hand. He kissed it, then brushed his lips against hers.

"Who needs an officiant?" he asked, getting to his feet. "We have dozens of witnesses on this ship. Get dressed, Sassafras."

"Holfast will never accept an unofficial marriage. He'll want proof."

"Then we'll write up a document and both sign it. We'll have everyone onboard the ship sign it." Ruenen took her free hand, grinning like a court jester. "I'll marry you today if it's the last thing I do, and Holfast can pout about it later." He marched to the door and stuck his head out. "Anja, can I borrow you for a moment?"

He backed away to let Anja enter. Her jaw dropped when she saw Marai standing there wrapped in a sheet, holding a sword.

"Queen Marai will need to be properly outfitted for our wedding ceremony later today," Ruenen announced, puffing out his chest with pride.

"*Wedding* ceremony?" blanched Anja. Her white eyes grew to the size of walnuts.

"I'm entrusting her preparation to you, Gunnora, and Innesh. Don't get Aresti involved—she'll be a hindrance, not a help." Ruenen gave Marai a saucy wink before exiting the cabin.

Anja rushed over, beaming with effervescent glee. She clasped Marai's free hand. "Is it true? Are you getting married today to the King?"

"Apparently," Marai said dryly, but it was impossible to hide her grin.

Anja clapped, wings giving an excitable flutter. "Oh, this is truly a wonderful day! Let me find Gunnora and Innesh. A *wedding*? I haven't been to a wedding in thirty years. Oh, Marai, I'll make sure you're the most beautiful bride. Give me one moment. I'll be right back. A *wedding*!" Her feet almost didn't touch the floor as she danced from the cabin.

Marai didn't for a moment think about the old her, the one who shied away from love, who questioned at the coronation whether she wanted to be Ruenen's Queen. That woman had been transformed into someone new.

I will make my happiness a priority. I will live, Keshel.

Anja, Gunnora, and even Innesh radiated joy when they entered the cabin. Anja had brought sewing supplies in a basket, and a white billowy shirt she'd pulled from the clean laundry, possibly belonging to Slate or Captain Brelioc. The shirt was so large on Marai that it came to her knees. Anja cut holes in the back for her wings and styled the dress with a silver belt.

Gunnora brushed Marai's hair, and Innesh used the amulet chain to weave with the braid across her crown, pocketing the amulet itself. Marai refused to touch the awful thing, and had delegated its protection to Innesh. She had no idea what Ruenen had done with the other two.

Perhaps it wasn't the wedding a normal woman would aspire to. The dress was not a dress. She wore no shoes. She had no bouquet of lilies. But Marai was never a normal woman, and to her, this was perfect.

As long as it was Ruenen she made her vows to.

The deck had been cleaned and fully cleared of the usual mess of crates, barrels, and ropes. Every faerie, werewolf, gnome, goblin, guard, ex-slave, and sailor came to watch. Arm in arm, Marai and Ruenen climbed the stairs to the quarterdeck to stand before the massive wheel.

Marai was aware of the dozens of eyes and upturned faces staring at her, but she blocked out the nerves.

I'm Queen of the Fae. Queen of Nevandia. No longer can I hide in the shadows.

Ruenen leaned in and spoke into her ear, "The sight of you would make even the gods bow."

They whispered their vows to each other. Words and promises meant for their ears only.

In the faerie tradition, Marai wrapped a red strip of cloth, meant to be a ribbon, around their wrists, binding themselves to each other.

"These threads that bind us will never be severed," Marai said, and Ruenen's melodic voice echoed.

Marai's parents had performed this wedding ritual. Perhaps Raife and Thora had, as well, when they'd married in secret.

Ruenen took Marai's hand to dash through the cheering crowd and into the captain's quarters. There, beneath the sheets, closed off from the rest of the ship, they completed the wedding ritual.

And as they joined together, Marai could see those binding threads between them, transfigured into rays of golden, burning light.

CHAPTER 40

RUENEN

Was marriage so blissful for everyone? Because Ruenen couldn't imagine a time when he was more content. Waking in the morning next to Marai, curled up against him, making love to her, speaking with friends while doing the chores of the day, strumming his lute at night to a crowded deck. It was the most at-peace Ruenen had ever been, as if he'd finally figured out how life was supposed to work.

Here, he could be both King and bard, ruler and friend.

They'd made excellent time into calmer waters. The stormy skies disappeared, the weather warmed, and Ruenen and Marai watched each glorious sunset together. They'd stand at the stern for hours, locked in each other's arms, observing the soft glow of the moonglade on the Eastern Ocean.

Some evenings, they'd lie tousled in the bedsheets together, going through Keshel's journal, page by page.

"Keshel truly believed that this 'Chosen Girl' was supposed to be you?" Ruenen asked. Marai had filled him in on everything that had occurred in the Menagerie, and the strange prophecies Keshel had spouted.

"I had the tools, but never the guidance," said Marai offhandedly. "Once I called upon dark magic in Cleaving Tides, Lirr had to find someone new."

"Because you were 'tainted?'" Ruenen hated that description. Marai wasn't *contaminated* with dark magic.

"Because the person who defeats the darkness cannot have ever used it," she replied. "I must guide Lirr's new Chosen so she doesn't make the same mistakes I did."

Golden light. Glittering darkness. Eyes. Shields. Dark wielders. None of it made any sense.

In the journal, Ruenen's attention caught on a series of sentences. *A man, doubly marked. He is the key to her magic. He will shelter her from the Dark Wielder's lure.* Ruenen's gaze flitted down to the birthmark on his wrist.

"Do you remember when I asked you if a human and a faerie could be mates?" Ruenen had asked Marai that at the inn in Dwalingulf, when she'd first told him her name. His feelings for Marai had never been normal. He'd always, from the moment he'd first looked into her wild eyes, been drawn to her. "And you told me it wasn't possible."

Marai gave him a quizzical look. "Yes?"

"I think you're wrong."

She arched an eyebrow, ready to rise to the challenge. "How so?"

"If what Keshel says in here truly is prophecy, then this Chosen Girl is destined for this doubly marked man." Ruenen lifted his wrist, showing off the brown, sunburst smudge. "He'll be the key to her magic. If you were the original 'Chosen Girl,' then perhaps I was supposed to be your original 'key?' I am, after all, a doubly marked man."

Physically marked by that birthmark, and marked again by Rayghast's ire. Marked for the throne.

Marai pondered this for a moment as she traced a finger across his birthmark. "Perhaps you're right. Perhaps you really *are* my mate."

Ruenen blinked. He'd expected her usual type of scoffed response of "don't be ridiculous" or "that's impossible."

Marai brought his wrist to her lips, sending tiny electric sparks through his skin. "Or maybe you're just very lucky."

"Oh, I'm lucky, no doubt about that, Sassafras." Ruenen cupped her face in his hands. "But I know, deep in my soul, that I was meant for you. I was meant to help you discover your power. I was meant to be at your side."

"That doesn't bother you? You don't feel like a pawn in Lirr's game?" asked Marai, a crease worrying between her brows.

She considers herself a pawn.

Ruenen smiled. "If I was born with the purpose of being your key, then I consider that a great honor. I'm your gods-fated partner, and you cannot convince me otherwise. I'll go to my grave believing this."

Marai snorted, her brow smoothing. How long he'd ached for the sound of that ridiculous snort.

"Then I shall not argue with such stubbornness," she said with a playful haughtiness that had Ruenen chuckling.

His fingers traced up the side of her legs as he lowered her onto the mattress, and Marai said in a husky, quiet voice, "My love. My mate."

Marai didn't mention it often, but Ruenen knew she thought constantly about Cavar. He'd catch her freeze mid-forkful during dinner, face shrouded as the thought of Cavar crossed her mind. Ruenen would see it in the tense lines of her body when she'd stare out to sea, as if she was waiting for dark magic to come charging across the waters to devour her.

Cavar plagued her. The uncertainty of his fate, of his intentions, weighed on her.

Ruenen doubted that a severely wounded man would chase them to another continent, but Marai had witnessed more of Cavar's dangerous, obsessive nature than he had.

"He views himself as a god," she said to Ruenen and Aresti. "He *is* human, but thanks to that stone, he's virtually immortal."

In that, Cavar reminded Ruenen of Rayghast. The cruel king had thought himself all-powerful because of dark magic, and like Cavar, Rayghast would have sought Ruenen on any foreign soil to know he was truly dead. Cavar seemed to have that same neurotic mentality, with a strong need for revenge. As if something else, something deeper, was propelling him forward . . .

But would he follow Marai across the sea?

"Seems like a waste of his time," Aresti said. "Why bother with you when he can simply rebuild his Menagerie over there? It might take him a while, but he could keep kidnapping innocent folk from the Hinterlands. Not that I'm saying he *should,* but as a Governor and businessman, I think he'd find it far more convenient and cost-effective to stay on Andara."

As if waiting for him to suddenly appear, Marai kept Dimtoir sheathed at her side at all times. She and Aresti sparred every day.

"To keep loose", Marai said, but Ruenen knew it was the anxiety clawing at her. She couldn't sit still knowing Cavar was out there.

After a particularly long, grueling session where Marai schooled everyone else, she wiped the sweat from her brows, downed some water, and leaned against the railing of the stern next to Ruenen. They were a few hours away from making port in Yehzig. Seven days from Astye, and then *home.*

A strong gust of wind appeared. Something within it seemed to shimmer, as if the wind was somehow visible. It spun around Marai; her hair became a swirling nest of white-blonde strands.

"Is this yours?" Marai asked of Aresti, brow furrowing.

Aresti shook her head.

There was a whisper, the sound of a hushed male's voice, like the wind was *speaking.* Marai's eyes flared wide and her whole body stiffened. For several moments, that eerie voice whispered into Marai's ears.

Then the wind disappeared, as if its purpose had been fulfilled.

"What was that?" Ruenen asked.

Marai, visibly shaken, said, "A message on the wind. From Koda."

Ruenen's stomach tightened at the mention of the male's name. He didn't question *how* it was possible for someone to send a verbal message on the wind. Magic was mysterious and complex, and Ruenen would never understand it, especially since he'd never wielded it.

"What did he say?" asked Aresti, coming closer.

"It was a warning." Marai lowered her voice, fingers latching onto Ruenen's shirt as she looked up into his face. "Koda says that Cavar is coming for us. He'll attack Nevandia, and then establish Menageries across Astye."

"We won't let that happen," Ruenen assured her, placing his hands on her shoulders. "Nevandia won't submit, and we'll have the support of Grelta, as well."

"But Nevandia is still weakened from the war," said Marai, her pulse fluttering in the wrist Ruenen held. "It cannot survive an attack from Cavar and the Guardians. Not with all those amulets."

"We're assuming that Cavar will be strong enough to cross the seas. Remember, he'll need a whole new ship, a new crew." Ruenen tucked Marai's flyaway hair behind her ears. "Even if he does venture here, it won't be for several months, which means we'll have time to prepare for him. We'll make a plan, contact the other kingdoms, and warn them of Cavar's dark magic. I promise that you will never again be shackled, that none of the folk will be caged and tormented."

Marai's worry didn't ease, so Ruenen drew her into his arms and held her until she smiled again.

The ship pulled into Qasnal's Grand Harbor, and while there was a sigh of relief from the humans, the folk became noticeably skittish. A foreign land full of humans? A crowded port? Marai commanded them to stay out of sight below decks, and none of the folk objected. They were too recognizable, with their wings, hooves, horns, and bright-colored skin.

Ruenen was surprised to find Innesh down there with them. She tapped her foot anxiously as she stood cross-armed against a pillar.

"Isn't Yehzig your home?" he asked her.

"This place isn't my home. I ran away from here when I was fifteen, and swore never to return." Innesh then pointed to her bold facial tattoos. "I'll be identified instantly if I set foot on Yehzigi soil, and be taken to the Skelm. I have a debt with them."

Ruenen nodded. He didn't know what the Skelm was, but he could only guess based on Innesh's response.

"Although, I do miss the food," Innesh said pointedly.

Ruenen smiled. "I'll have some brought down here for you."

He sent Nyle, Tarik, and Yovel into the city to procure dinner for the crew and passengers. That evening, the entire ship dined on Yehzigi cuisine and local dark ale. Ruenen and Marai ate in the solitude of their cabin. She had a higher tolerance for spice than Ruenen—her eyes didn't water as she inhaled the spicy lamb kebabs, and her face didn't turn red from the heat of the bright orange rice.

Marai chewed pleasantly as she said, "Once we arrive in Baatgai, I think it would be wise to portal everyone straight to Kellesar."

Ruenen swallowed his lamb, then gulped down water to cool his fiery tongue. "I didn't think you were able to portal anymore."

She hadn't tried once while onboard the ship.

Marai glared at him. "I haven't lost my magic, Ruen. It took a long while to recover because my body was so weak, but I'm better now." She certainly *looked* healthy again. She'd put on some much-needed weight, and color had returned to her skin. "I didn't want to try portaling in case it didn't work, or something dangerous happened. I've never portaled at such a far distance before, and never over so much water, but once we get to Baatgai, I should be fine to get everyone through."

"And you don't want to have a caravan of magical folk parading through Syoto, I'm assuming."

"I think that's calling for needless harassment and trouble. The Emperor of Syoto would view that as instigation. Besides, we're all tired from this trip. Another two week trek to reach Kellesar sounds exhausting. I just want to get home."

Home. Ruenen had never heard her call Nevandia home before.

"Why are you grinning like that?" his wife asked, skeptically.

"No reason."

His wife. His Queen. Ruenen sometimes wondered how he'd become so blessed. After a traumatic, nomadic childhood, he found himself here, in this moment, with everything he could want.

Well, almost everything. There was one thing he and Marai had yet to discuss, but they were still newly-weds. There would be time for *that* discussion in due course.

"You can't show up as Queen of Nevandia wearing that," he said, indicating her rumpled shirt and baggy knickers.

"Where do you expect me to procure a gown onboard a ship?"

"We'll have Gunnora and Innesh buy you something once we get to Baatgai."

That might prove difficult since Baatgai was a tiny fishing village. When Ruenen had been there before, they didn't seem to have a seamstress or tailor establishment.

"Perhaps I'll simply wear *your* clothes, and shock everyone further by ignoring the 'women must wear dresses in Nevandia' rule," Marai said with a dramatic roll of her eyes.

"Well, as Queen, you have the power to change that." Ruenen nudged her foot with his toe.

Marai's face softened. "I'd like that. To change things for women, I mean. The way Nieve has in Grelta."

"Queen Marai of Nevandia: champion of women and magical folk everywhere." Ruenen said this with a sweeping gesture of his arm. "You and Nieve combined will be a force to be reckoned with. You'll have kings and emperors quaking in their boots."

A sly grin curled Marai's lips as she took a sip of dark Yehzigi ale. "Good."

Seven days later, the shadowed mass of land came into view on the horizon. As the ship approached, the mass became more distinct. Sloping hills and rocks, green leaves shifting into autumnal forests, a beach to the west. Nondescript masses solidified into buildings and boats docked at the tiny harbor village of Baatgai. Smoke from chimneys bruised the sky.

Marai practically ran to the bow, taking in the sight of her homeland. Although she often pretended otherwise, Ruenen knew she truly did care about Astye. He was also incredibly glad to see the continent. Sailing had been more enjoyable than he'd expected, but he was grateful to be on solid ground once again.

A dark-clad figure stood alone on the dock, waiting ominously like a harbinger of doom as *The Arcane Wind* pulled into port. His cape billowed in the wind. A facial mask covered all but his crimson eyes.

The crew tossed ropes down to the quay, and the gangway extended. Sailors went first, mooring the ship to the dock, then Marai bolted down the wooden plank, practically leaping onto the dock. She stalked straight to the cloaked figure; Ruenen could barely keep up with her.

"Your Graces," Nosficio said, bowing from the waist. "I came to greet you."

"How did you know we'd be arriving today?" asked Ruenen.

Nosficio glanced at him with little interest. "I can count, Your Kingliness. I estimated the number of days your journey would take, so I've been in the area for the past few days waiting." That searing gaze of his traveled to Marai. "And I could *smell* you approaching in the breeze."

He'd always loved the way Marai's faerie blood smelled, which sickened Ruenen, but he supposed it was in the vampire's nature.

Nosficio then studied Marai's wings and pointed ears, and something in his eyes shifted. "You have Aras' wings." His nostrils flared, as if picking up a change in her scent. "You truly are a sight, Faerie Queen. I'm glad that my efforts weren't in vain."

"I heard that you went through quite a lot of trouble to find me." Marai reached out her hand and spoke with warmth. "I wouldn't be standing here if it weren't for you. *Thank you.*"

Nosficio stared. Ruenen guessed Nosficio wasn't used to people thanking him (without his prodding), and he wished he could see the vampire's expression beneath the mask.

Nosficio's gloved fingers wrapped around Marai's. "I only did what Aras and Meallán would've expected of me." He dropped his hand, putting on airs again, but Ruenen heard the notes of falsity, the emotion, in his voice.

"You were right about Desislava," Ruenen told him. "She was there, in the Menagerie. Marai set her free, but she didn't come with us."

"At least there's some closure on that mystery," Nosficio said solemnly.

Ruenen *really* wished he could see the vampire's face beneath his mask.

"I've done as you asked, King of Nevandia, and watched over your Witan, and successfully frightened many of them. I will admit that my time in that chamber was a highlight of my long, arduous life. You'll be pleased to know that things are in good order in your country." The vampire gestured up at the ship, where dozens of non-human faces peered down at him in wonder. "I see that you've made some new friends. I was going to return to Grelta, but now I'm far too curious to see how this is going to work out."

Mayestral and the staff were busy unloading their supplies and belongings, along with the crew. The King's Guard and Greltan soldiers had also disembarked, and were now assisting the magical folk off the gangplank.

Innesh marched up to Marai and gave Nosficio a cursory once–over. She'd known Desislava, and probably recognized the vampiric crimson eyes. Without an ounce of caution, Innesh addressed him. "You have nice clothing. Help us find something for our Queen to wear."

Nosficio *did* wear the most luxurious of materials. The hooded cape around his shoulders was a stunning dark green, fur-lined velvet. *Where does he store all of his clothing?* Ruenen had never seen the vampire wear the same thing twice.

Nosficio eyed the Yehzigi woman, and Ruenen cringed when he saw the *desire* in the vampire's eyes. Innesh was yet another strong, unconventional woman like Nieve. One of Nosficio's few weaknesses.

Innesh, however, stared blankly at him, waiting for his response. "Did you hear me, vampire?"

"I suppose I can wrangle up something decent for *our* Queen. Do I have time, or are you intending to leave immediately?"

"We can stay for a few hours," Ruenen said. There were several loose ends to tie up in Baatgai, such as paying the crew their remaining fees, unloading supplies from the ship, and of course, establishing the intentions of the folk. Not all of them would decide to come to Nevandia.

Athelstan and Gunnora, for example, both wanted to return to their homes in Grelta.

"It's possible that my pack still lives there," Athelstan said, shaking both Ruenen and Marai's hands, then Aresti's and Tarik's. "If they've moved on, I'll come find you in Nevandia."

"Even if you do find them, bring your pack to Nevandia. We have plenty of room for more weres," Tarik said with a beaming smile.

Plenty of room? Ruenen didn't know where he was going to house the new refugees, but he didn't have the heart to say anything.

Marai and Gunnora shared a long embrace, which Ruenen found incredibly touching since Marai hardly ever hugged anyone.

"I *know* my family still lives in the mountains," Gunnora said. "They've lived there for generations. Please understand, Marai, that I must return to them. I wouldn't leave you if I didn't love them dearly."

"Of course you must go home," Marai said. "You never should have been taken from your family to begin with. Thank you for your kindness, Gunnora. I wouldn't be alive without you."

She leaned down so Gunnora could kiss each of her cheeks.

"You will make an excellent Queen. You're going to blaze new trails for all of us." Gunnora then looked up at Ruenen. "Thank you again, Your Grace. I wish you and Queen Marai a long and happy rule, and many, *many,* children." She winked, a little overdramatically, with a wide grin.

Ruenen was about to respond, but Nosficio interjected. "I'm sorry, are you *married?*"

Marai blushed, scowled, crossed her arms, and nodded.

Nosficio laughed. "You two are always so entertaining. No wonder I can't seem to stay away—you bring chaos and drama with you everywhere you go." The vampire seemed absolutely delighted.

Athelstan and Gunnora went on their way; Ruenen paid for a horse and pony for them to take, knowing how long their journey would be. Bellaya the banshee disappeared into the forest without much of a farewell, and Ruenen was silently glad. Of all the folk and creatures he'd met, she was the one who creeped him out the most.

The ship's crew was paid, and Ruenen granted Curly full use of *The Arcane Wind* for trading purposes. They struck a deal to share a portion of the profit with Ruenen, and their ship would fly under green and gold Nevandian flags.

Nosficio procured a dress from *somewhere.* Neither Ruenen nor Marai wanted to question where he'd gotten it, or whose body he'd stolen it off of. For all they knew, there was some poor woman running around naked in a village, having been bamboozled by the vampire.

Anja and Innesh quickly altered the dress for Marai's wings and stature, cinching the waist with a few pins. They styled her hair, and Innesh paid for a pair of slippers from a woman in a nearby cottage who seemed eager to help, if only to get rid of them from her village.

The plum dress was simple with a straight silhouette, a wide, horizontally cut neckline sitting off her shoulders, and long sleeves. Although she wore no crown, Marai still looked like a queen. She held her head high, rolled her shoulders back, unfurled her wings to full breadth, and secured Dimtoir at her hip. With commanding grace, she gathered the folk, staff, and King's Guard, now back in their golden armor, as they prepared to leave, but Ruenen sensed her nervousness from the quick rise and fall of her chest.

Ruenen took her hand and kissed it. "We will conquer whatever comes together. There's no you or me. There's only *us.*"

She didn't smile, but her amethyst eyes sparked at the promise. Marai raised her arms, and Ruenen sensed her magic before he saw it. Bright, multi-colored light shot from her fingertips, forming that electric portal. The signature ether, effervescent scent of Marai's magic drafted up his nose. Gods, he'd missed that heady smell.

On the other side of the shimmering portal, Ruenen recognized the slanted curves of craggy hills, green grass, and purple heather of the Nevandian highlands, the woody smell of thistle, and misty petrichor of wet rock. *Home.*

Aresti, Nyle, and the rest of the King's Guard went first, carrying Elmar's belongings between them. Then Daye and the staff, followed by a long line of timid magical folk, Innesh and Braesal at the helm, Nosficio at the rear. Tarik and Yovel came next, and finally Mayestral, who was reluctant to leave his King and Queen alone on the other side.

"We'll see you in a moment," Ruenen assured him, putting his gilded, emerald-studded crown on top of his head.

Mayestral nodded, unconvinced, but walked through the portal, staring open-mouthed at the magic pulsating around him.

Then it was just Marai and Ruenen. Arm in arm, as regally as possible, they walked through together. Marai's magic overwhelmed Ruenen's senses, so bright, so warm and static, zapping tiny pin pricks across his body. He shivered involuntarily. Marai had so much power. It was easy to forget when looking at her, but if Keshel was correct, Marai had been Chosen by Lirr. That power had been gifted to her by a goddess. She may no longer be Lirr's Chosen, but that deadly, inspiring power remained in her veins.

Pirate. Mercenary. Fae. Queen. Chosen.

Marai had been many things, but those titles weren't who she was. Not really.

When their feet touched Nevandian soil, and Kellesar towered above them, Ruenen smiled at her.

To him, she was his closest friend. The person he respected above all others. The echo to his own heartbeat. The courage in his bones. His wife. His mate. His heroine.

"Welcome home, Sassafras. Ready to cause an outrage and a scandal?"

A devilish smirk bloomed on Marai's lips. "Always."

CHAPTER 41

MARAI

Kellesar rose from the highlands, a moonstone mountain reflecting the sun's beaming rays, casting a golden glow upon the white city. The castle spires speared the sky, like fingers reaching out for the gods above. The Nydian encircling Kellesar sparkled as if it was a river of diamonds instead of water. Life bloomed around Marai, from the heather and gorse on the moor, to the sheep and cows in their paddocks, to fish swimming in the river. Autumn had begun to leave its gentle touch on the land. Yellow and orange leaves from the glen danced through the air on a breeze.

In that moment, Marai had never seen Kellesar look so beautiful. For the first time, she regarded the city, not as a place she lived, but as a *home.* These farmers on the moor were her people now. The tradesmen, merchants, nobles, peasants, women, and children inside the towering walls were her people, too. Would they respect her as they did Ruenen?

"I've never seen a city like this before. One that scales upwards," Innesh said at Marai's side. Marai's lips curled at the suppressed awe in Innesh's voice.

The Menagerie refugees gazed at Kellesar with hope, as if they could see the promise of their future waiting behind the walls.

"I think the folk should stay here, on the moor, until we know where to put them," Aresti murmured to Ruenen and Marai. "I'm worried that Kellesarans and the soldiers might get nervous seeing a whole retinue of magical folk parading through the city. Avilyard might bring the whole army down upon us."

"I'm inclined to agree," said Braesal. "One step at a time. These people have been through enough. They don't need to be jeered at again."

"Tarik and I will stay here and watch out for them," said Yovel. "Maybe leave a couple guards, too?"

It was a gamble, bringing more folk into Kellesar, and Marai could see that its current residents were uneasy.

"We'll send down food and drink as soon as we arrive at the castle," she said.

Food had been rationed on the ship, which hadn't been prepared for the influx of people onboard after Andara. Folk, staff, and guards alike needed a good, hearty meal.

"And some tents, perhaps?" asked Tarik. "Might take a while to find housing for them all."

"No tents." Marai bit the inside of her cheek. Those folk had spent years of their lives in tents. Setting up another camp would remind them of the horrors of the Menagerie. "We'll find somewhere else for them to stay tonight."

Braesal, Beck, Finneagal, and Zorish lowered to a knee before Marai.

"Do you grant us leave to return to our families, Your Grace?" asked Braesal. "I'm sure they're anxiously waiting."

"You've done quite enough. Please, thank your families for lending us your services," Marai said. "I wouldn't be standing here if you four hadn't rescued me."

The faerie males smiled.

"And for those outstanding services and for your courage, Queen Marai and I would like to reward you," said Ruenen.

Reward them? Marai had no idea what Ruenen was planning, but she agreed that those who'd volunteered for the journey should receive some extra compensation.

Braesal and the males each kissed Marai's hand, making her blush and squirm. *I'll need to get used to this . . .*

"What reward?" Marai asked Ruenen out of the side of her mouth as the faeries headed off towards the city.

"Oh, nothing outlandish," said Ruenen, in a voice that seemed to say the exact opposite of what he had in mind.

"I have a feeling it's something the Witenagemot won't like."

"They don't like anything. That's nothing new."

Anja came forward then, curtseying demurely in her homespun dress. "I should accompany Your Graces up to the castle. It's customary for the Faerie Queen, at least on Andara, to have her ladies with her at all times. I'd like to offer myself for that position, if you will have me."

Taken aback, Marai looked to Ruenen for confirmation. She hadn't thought about having ladies-in-waiting. There were still many things Marai needed to learn and come to terms with about being Queen. She didn't want anyone trailing at her feet like needy puppies, watching her every move, reporting back her habits and secrets to powerful men. No doubt the Witan would force wealthy, noble girls and women, their own daughters and nieces, on her. If Marai could at least balance that number with people of her own choosing, it might be bearable.

Ruenen shrugged. "It's entirely your choice who you have on your court."

Marai then squeezed Anja's hand. "Yes, of course. And Innesh, I want you to come, as well."

Innesh blinked, utterly perplexed. "Me? You want me as one of your ladies?" She certainly didn't look like the traditional lady-in-waiting, with her tattoos and sharp eyes, but that was all the more reason Marai wanted her. "I won't fit in, Your Grace. Your ladies must be of noble birth. I'm a gutter rat from Yehzig."

"I've no interest in people of noble birth," Marai said with a scowl. "Most of them are spoiled, ignorant, and pretentious. I'd rather have women I trust and respect in my court, than whoever the Witan might throw at me. You've been my friend and advisor through the worst of times. I would be honored if you'd accept."

Innesh's lips drew into a thin line before she slanted a rare smile. "It would be *my* honor, my Queen."

Marai's breath caught in her chest, nerves and emotions rising to the surface, but she focused on Ruenen's steady arm, which he held out to her. Marai looped hers through; a more formal gesture than merely holding hands, but he planted a quick kiss on the top of her head.

These next moments mattered greatly. This was Marai's first impression on the people as Queen of Nevandia. *What will happen when I walk through that gate? Will they remember me? Will I be rejected? Scorned?* Or would something miraculous happen, something to alter the continent for decades to come?

The King's Guard led the way over the marble drawbridge, through the iron gate. People noticed Ruenen immediately and began excitedly crowding the streets.

"Been a while since we've seen you out and about, Your Grace," said an older man with a cane. "Weren't you unwell?"

"I was, yes, but now I'm quite recovered. I've been kept busy by Lord Steward Holfast, working hard for Nevandia," Ruenen replied with a wave.

"I missed my favorite customer," said the woman who owned the hand pie shop. "But are you returning from somewhere, Your Grace? We didn't know you were gone."

Lirr's Bones, these people are so comfortable and friendly with their King . . .

Ruenen chuckled. "Fear not, friends. I snuck out to greet Queen Marai and escort her here."

Suddenly, the attention turned to Marai, arm-in-arm with Ruenen.

The hand pie woman blinked rapidly, startled. "Why, you're the faerie from the battle. The one who brought down Rayghast's army. I didn't recognize you, my lady." The woman lowered into a curtsy. "My apologies, *Your Grace,* Queen Marai. We're glad you've returned with our beloved King."

"All hail the King," shouted the old man, thrusting his cane into the air.

A blacksmith in a thick, leather apron, with hands smeared in soot, announced, "Bless this day, and his majesty King Ruenen!"

"Did you not tell anyone you were coming to get me?" Marai quietly asked Ruenen.

"Not a soul, except those who needed to know. My reliable Witan was supposed to concoct a reason for my absence."

Marai tried to mimic Ruenen's effortless smile, the congenial waves, his proud, purposeful walk, but she knew she'd never attain his approachable essence. It wasn't in her nature. Ruenen had a way with people that Marai could never master.

Kellesar was more vibrant than Marai had ever seen it. Every street had new shops, new faces, fresh paint, brighter colors, more lanterns beckoning her curiosity down streets she'd never noticed before.

There were many gawking faces, too. Not everyone looked pleased about Marai's arrival, and some seemed downright fearful of Anja and Innesh. There was no way to hide her ladies' unique appearances, so instead, Marai had instructed them to walk boldly, not to hide amidst the retinue.

Nosficio certainly wasn't—he relished the attention. Although his face remained hidden beneath the mask, his sleek, cocky gait told Marai everything she needed to know. Not even Ruenen adored attention as much as Nosficio.

Marai spotted familiar faces and wings in the crowd. Braesal was there, a small fae boy perched on his shoulders, cheering as Marai and Ruenen passed. There were perhaps fifteen faeries, standing there mixed amongst humans. Marai was shocked that most people didn't give them a wide berth. Only a few cast judgmental glances their way.

Have things really changed that much since I was taken?

A mass of people now trailed behind Ruenen's retinue by the time they walked under the portcullis of the outer castle walls. Marai wasn't surprised to see the Witan assembled on the stairs, along with the castle staff and remaining King's Guard; they'd been alerted to Ruenen's arrival in the city. Commander Avilyard, standing with his Guard, breathed a sigh of relief when his hazel eyes met Marai's from across the courtyard. Lord Fenir was noticeably absent.

The Witan, King's Guard, and staff bowed as one, in a move that looked far too rehearsed and formal. There were two new men on the Witan Marai didn't recognize. Ruenen whispered their names to her, saying these were once on the Tacornian counsel.

A lone woman stood off to the side, behind Lord Goso.

Rhia?

The ex-Tacornian Queen was dressed up like a present in an elegant emerald gown with a gold tiara on her head. Nevandian colors. A white patch covered the wounded side of her face.

Still reluctant of magic as ever, I see.

"Why is Rhia here, and why is she glaring at me?" Marai whispered to Ruenen as they approached the stairs.

"Oh. Right," said Ruenen, voice growing higher in pitch. "Well, Holfast tried to get me to marry her."

Marai's fingers tightened on Ruenen's arm. "Don't you think that's something you should have told me?"

"Probably," he said before Holfast stepped forward with open, welcoming arms.

"Your Grace, we're quite relieved at your safe return," the Steward said. Unlike Rhia, Holfast was actually smiling, a rare sight, indeed. Marai could feel the relief pulsating from the Steward. "And Lady Marai, I'm glad to see you well." His eyes tracked her wings and pointed ears; questions clouded his face, but he had never inquired into the mysteries of magic. Marai guessed that the less Holfast knew about magic, the more at ease he was. Besides that, Marai had no interest in explaining what had happened to her. "I'm certain you both would like to rest, but we of the Witenagemot were hoping for a quick debrief to discuss the new arrivals who are standing out on the moor."

"Naturally, Lord Steward," Ruenen said. "Nosficio informed me that you've done an excellent job keeping Nevandia safe in my absence."

Vorae, Corian, and the new Lord Wattling glowered at Nosficio, hovering innocently next to Marai, adjusting his cloak.

"Yes, Lord Nosficio was . . . quite insistent on being present for Witan meetings," Holfast said through a tight jaw.

Ruenen eased the tension with a heartfelt smile. "Thank you all for your dedication to our country." The Witan's chests swelled at the compliment. "But first, before we go inside, I'd like to make an announcement."

Marai stiffened. *Here? Now?* She tried not to let her nerves show. *Oh gods, what will their reaction be?*

"I'm pleased to present my wife, Queen of the Fae, and now also Queen of Nevandia."

As expected, Ruenen's words thrust the courtyard into startled silence. Goso blinked rapidly. Corian's jaw dropped. Cronhold scratched his head, perplexed. Even the impassive Holfast was momentarily caught off-guard; the smile froze on his face, and puckered.

Rhia, meanwhile, glared at Marai with hurt and worry in her eyes.

Ruenen reveled in the shock and growing anger of the Witan. He grinned back at them. "Now, with that out of the way, let's have our meeting, shall we?"

He gestured for Holfast to lead the way into the chamber, but the Steward hesitated, glancing between Ruenen and Marai. She cocked an eyebrow at him, daring him to challenge her in the public courtyard. Citizens at the portcullis heard the announcement and were already spreading the news into the streets. Holfast pursed his lips, then made his way into the castle. Murmurs of protest followed Marai and Ruenen inside as the rest of the Witan, guards, and retinue followed.

Once the heavy chamber doors groaned closed, the Witan unleashed.

"You cannot marry a faerie!"

"This is unacceptable! Against our laws!"

"Who performed this marriage?"

Marai's head spun from the noise echoing off the stone. Wattling and Corian were the two most vocal in the group, although Marai was surprised by Vorae's pensive silence. Usually, he was the most outspoken against Ruenen's antics, but Corian and Wattling seemed determined to steal the title from him.

Ruenen led Marai up the dais to his bone, wood, and gold throne, impervious to their shouts. There was no second throne. It wasn't traditional on Astye for a queen or empress to have her own.

Ruenen gestured for Marai to sit while he stood to the side. "I'll have another one made for you." Once she was seated, Ruenen whipped around, expression stern, as he addressed his Witan. "You forget yourselves, my lords. Is that any way to speak to your King?"

The room quieted. The Witan took their seats, disgruntled, upset, contemplative. Avilyard, however, wasn't trying to hide his smile. He gave Marai a nod that showed his approval, which she returned, glad to see the Commander looking well.

Holfast was the first to speak. "You've certainly surprised us, Your Grace. If I recall, you swore before leaving for your journey that you had no intention to marry anyone."

"That's because the women you were proposing weren't Marai. She was, and is, the only acceptable match for me." Ruenen donned his King-Persona like someone might wear a hat. Gone was the charming, smiling, soft husband. He played his character well, radiating confidence and authority. Marai inwardly smirked; he'd learned much in their time apart. "I've done what you wanted. I now have a queen, an honorable woman of royal blood, who's worthy to stand at my side."

Wattling's face grew red. "But she's a—"

"Faerie?" Marai cut in sharply. "Yes, I think, Lord Wattling, that we're all quite aware of that fact." For added emphasis, she fluttered her wings.

Wattling shut his mouth and glowered at her.

"Forgive us, Your Graces, but there are many questions surrounding this marriage," said Holfast. At least he acknowledged Marai's title and bloodline. He didn't *dislike* her. Why, it was only a few months ago that Holfast had practically encouraged Marai to become Ruenen's mistress and stay on as a member of the Witan. "Was this wedding officiated by a proper authority?"

Ruenen produced the marriage contract they'd made before their wedding on the ship, and handed the folded parchment to Holfast. "There were over seventy witnesses to our marriage, and although there was no officiant, it was nonetheless official. Their signatures, as well as ours, are there on the document."

"A piece of paper doesn't count," Corian said, tossing up his hands. "This marriage isn't valid."

"It's as valid as any other," Ruenen said sharply. "Citizens of Nevandia, my King's Guard and staff, as well as Greltan soldiers were witnesses to this marriage. They watched while Queen Marai and I exchanged our vows and signed this contract. They believe it's valid, and so should you."

"The document has no official seal," continued Corian, determined to ruin everything. "It wasn't performed by a monk or priestess. For Empyra's sake, your 'ceremony' wasn't performed on Nevandian soil. It's not valid, Your Grace."

"Well, put an official seal on the document now. Go find Monk Baureo and have him preside over us and we'll do it again, right here in front of you, if that makes you happy," Ruenen said with a roll of his eyes. "But Queen Marai and I *are* married."

Holfast read and reread the contract. He examined every signature. The lines of his face grew deep and rigid the more he thought.

"This has never happened before. There are rules that must be followed. We would need to make this official by Nevandian royal standards," he finally said, aggrieved.

"Holfast, you cannot possibly think to accept this," Corian said at the same time Wattling shouted, "We cannot have a faerie queen!"

"Why can't you accept a faerie as your Queen?" asked Marai, anger rising up her throat. She had to keep herself in check. The spark of magic tingled at her fingertips. "Am I truly any different than Queen Rhia? Or Queen Nieve? I defended this land and its people from Tacorn. My blood and sweat have seeped into the earth of this country. I will continue to defend Nevandia, with all the power I have within me."

"The truth is, Your Graces, that Nevandia is already under intense scrutiny due to our acceptance and housing of magical folk," Vorae calmly said. "I've spent enough time in Dul Tanen to have heard what people there think. Not only do we have our own countrymen to worry about, but we've become an easy target for other kingdoms who wish to invade. I don't say this out of prejudice. I say this because it's a fact. And now you have more folk, waiting out there on the moor, seeking refuge?"

"I disagree with you, Lord Vorae," Marai said.

Vorae's eyebrows rose.

Corian muttered a pleasant, "Why am I not surprised?"

"No other kingdom would be foolish enough to try and attack Nevandia now," Marai continued, ignoring Corian and his immature response. "You have *magic* on your side. Because you've embraced magical folk, you have an army of loyal citizens who possess extraordinary abilities. Other kingdoms might complain and judge, but they know it would be downright idiotic for them to try to fight with swords and arrows against magic. You saw how only seven fae, six werewolves, and one vampire managed to subdue the Tacorn and Varanese armies. Imagine quadrupling that strength. No human kingdom would attempt to invade us, unless they, too, had magic."

Like Cavar. If Cavar allied with another kingdom, he could easily defeat Nevandia, but Marai didn't want to mention him yet. Too many other things needed to be settled first. *Think about that another day.*

"I know that I'm new to this responsibility and title, but as your Queen, I will ensure the folk stay content here, contribute to our economy, and serve honorably," she said. "Think of what else magic can do? Our lands and industries will flourish with their help, and Nevandia will prosper. To rebuild, you need us as much as we need you."

Ruenen gave Marai a smile, gold-flecked eyes shimmering with pride. She was trying, trying *so hard,* to be worthy of this happiness, this title, and this second chance.

"I believe Queen Marai makes a valid point," Holfast said, inclining his head to her.

Corian and Wattling gaped at him, stammering in their disapproval.

"Excuse me, Your Grace, but have the two of you, uh . . . *consummated* this marriage?" asked ancient Cronhold with a wavering voice, shaking a decrepit finger in Marai's direction.

Heat seared her face at such a personal question. She didn't know how to answer without unleashing her fiery temper and unsheathing her sword, so Marai slammed her lips together in irritation.

"I think it's safe to assume that they have, Lord Cronhold," said Vorae, eyebrows still raised, seemingly amused by Marai's reaction.

Who is this man, and what has he done with Lord Vorae? Perhaps months living in Rayghast's gloomy, oppressive castle had changed Vorae's grumpy nature and made him grateful for having such a compassionate King.

"What about Queen Rhia?" Cronhold posed to Ruenen. "What does Your Grace intend to do with her? Send her back to, uh, Varana?"

"No, she doesn't wish to return to her father," said Ruenen, "and the only reason she would have agreed to marrying me was for her protection. I promised to keep her safe here in the castle. It would be wrong of me to recant and send her away when she's done nothing wrong."

An idea came to Marai, one she knew the Witan wouldn't like, but might mollify the Tacornian Queen. In fact, it was such a delicious idea that Marai's heart leapt within her chest.

To a guard at the door, she called, "Please bring Queen Rhia here."

Rhia had been hovering outside, clearly concerned about her fate now that Marai was Queen. No sooner had the guard left to fetch her, did he return with her in tow. Rhia curtsied low, her face a pale mask of cool impassivity.

"Congratulations, Your Graces, on your nuptials," she said, but her words came out strained.

"I understand that you don't wish to leave Kellesar," Marai said.

Rhia stood to full height, ready to defend herself. "Yes, Your Grace. I should like to stay on within the court, if you will permit it. I'll be no bother to you, and stay out of your way."

"I don't wish for you to hide away, Your Grace. I have another idea," said Marai.

Ruenen gave her an uneasy look, probably assuming she was angry that Rhia had been proposed as his Queen in Marai's absence. He had no idea what she was going to say. No one did.

That's what made Marai's announcement so satisfying, when she asked, "How would you feel about joining the Witenagemot?"

Rhia's jaw dropped, along with every other in the room.

Ruenen then released a laugh. "That's an excellent idea."

"Women aren't allowed on royal counsels, Your Grace," stated Corian quickly.

"I was briefly on the counsel, before I was abducted," Marai replied with a sharp look, "and you now have a queen who will oversee Witenagemot meetings alongside your King. Get used to the fact that women will be in the room. Queen Rhia has connections to both Tacorn and Varana. You want unification? Putting her on the Witan will show Tacornians how committed we are to that. It's about time women of intelligence were given a place at the table."

Wattling gaped. "But that's—"

"I accept," Rhia practically shouted. She calmed herself, trying to hide her enthusiasm. "Yes, Your Grace, I would very much like to join your Witan."

"Then take your seat," Marai said, gesturing to an open chair.

Rhia lifted her proud chin high as she sat between Corian and Vorae.

Ruenen leaned over and whispered into Marai's ear, "See? You're already breaking down barriers."

"We still have yet to settle the question of the validity of your marriage," Wattling said, redder than before. "You may have consummated your relationship, but that doesn't make anything official." He looked around the table for support from his fellow lords, gaze skipping over Rhia. "Kings can fornicate with any woman they please. That doesn't make each of those women his wife *or* a queen."

Ruenen's body went taut as a bowstring.

Before he could retort, Aresti cleared her throat rather loudly. Heads in the room swiveled to look at her, standing off to the side of the dais with the other King's Guard.

"Yes?" Holfast asked.

"I believe your lordships may think differently if you knew all the details," Aresti said, darting a glance back at Marai.

What's she up to? Marai's eyes narrowed in suspicion.

"I think you'd consider this marriage valid if a royal heir were involved," said Aresti.

Marai contemplated dying. Right there. Of embarrassment. Of anger and horror. She tried not to let the shock of the statement show on her face.

Ruenen stared at Marai, the question dancing in his eyes. She tried not to look at him, at the hope in his face.

"*Is* there a royal heir?" asked Holfast, suddenly far more attentive. He stepped closer to the dais. "Are you with-child?"

Marai gulped back her desire to give Aresti a thorough, public thrashing there in the chamber. Because it was a lie. Marai wasn't pregnant, but *saying* that she was gave her leverage with the Witan. She understood what Aresti was trying to do for her, but it was a huge thing to lie about . . . a lie that would eventually catch up to her if she *didn't* have a child soon.

"Is there any proof?" asked Corian, then turned a discerning eye to Anja and Innesh. "You two are her 'ladies'? What's the evidence of this?"

Innesh darted a glance first at Marai, then Aresti. "My Queen has missed her monthly bleeding."

Is everyone in on this now?

Ruenen squeezed her hand as hard as he could. Marai avoided his gaze. He was going to be so disappointed that it was a ruse.

"Call for the Royal Healer," Vorae ordered to one of the guards by the door. "She, alone, can give us a definitive answer."

"If you truly are with-child, Your Grace, then that changes everything," Holfast said with a resigned sigh. "If there's even a remote possibility of a royal heir, we cannot and will not ignore it. The birth of a royal heir solidifies the line of succession. Therefore, I will add the royal seal to this document, and arrange for Queen Marai's proper coronation."

Corian got to his feet. "But Holfast—"

"It's *done,* Corian," said Holfast with finality. "They're in love. There were witnesses to their ceremony, despite our opinions on the matter, and now there is an Avsharian heir. As soon as the Royal Healer provides confirmation, we'll publicly declare their marriage and the impending arrival of a royal baby."

Marai would have been pleased that this argument was now finished, but she was mortified by the lie she now had to make true.

"Perhaps we can continue our debrief later today?" asked Ruenen. "I believe my wife and I need to rest."

As Marai and Ruenen vacated the room, she made certain Aresti saw her deadly glare. Aresti, of course, merely shrugged in response, unaffected by her ire. She had a lot of explaining to do, especially to Ruenen, who Marai knew desperately wanted to be a father.

Marai was already jittery and nervous about the subject of children. She'd barely had time to consider being a wife and Queen, nonetheless a mother. Now it would need to happen *fast.* Fae fertility was notoriously difficult, which was why her people had begun mating with humans to begin with centuries ago. Who knew how long it would take to remedy the lie Aresti and Innesh had spun?

Ruenen led Marai to his own chambers. They'd discussed sharing the room, since neither of them wanted Marai to live in the typical Queen's apartments at the other end of the hallway. Ruenen politely asked Mayestral and the staff to wait outside; they'd already unpacked Ruenen's belongings, dusted the room, served tea, and lit the fire.

Ruenen closed the doors and whipped around to stare at Marai, who stood awkwardly in the middle of the room, picking her cuticles.

"I'm assuming by your reaction, it isn't true," he said, and the dismay on his face was heartbreaking.

"I swear I didn't ask Aresti to do that. I never would have said such a thing," Marai stammered.

"I know. I could see the shock in your eyes." Ruenen took both of her hands, stopping her picking and panicking. "The Witan is going to be furious when they realize the truth."

"We'll have to concoct another story . . ."

"Or we could just . . . *make* it true," Ruenen said, raising his eyebrows with an impish grin.

Marai could have laughed at his expression, his hope, but instead she said, "I don't know how to be a mother."

"I'm not sure anyone knows how to be a parent, Marai. I think it's something you learn over time. We'll make mistakes, but at least we'll make them together."

"How can my dirty hands hold an innocent child?" asked Marai, voicing the fear gnawing away at her. "What kind of role model would I be? I'm a cold-blooded killer, Ruen—"

He pulled her into his arms so that her ear was pressed against his chest. She curled into his warmth and the steady *thump* of his stalwart heart.

"You'll be a great mother," Ruenen said against her hair. "You're protective of everyone you love, and you can be incredibly gentle, understanding, rational, and grounded. When you want to be."

Marai smiled, and took a deep breath. "But what about Cavar, and dark magic—"

"The timing isn't great, yes, but should we put our entire life on pause because of Cavar? Forgive me, Sassafras, but I want to make every second with you count." Ruenen's lips caressed her ear. "And that means fixing Aresti's blunder, starting tonight."

Marai rolled her eyes and laughed

"Maybe a few times tonight," he added, and nipped at her neck, his arms tightening around her.

Insufferable.

But she had to wonder . . . what Keshel had said to her in Bakair . . . *Because she is yours . . .*

There was a knock at the door, and not a second later, it burst open.

Thora flew into the room, and Marai had never seen her move so fast. She flung her arms around Marai, sobbing incoherently, soaking the sleeve of Marai's dress. Aresti sat down in an armchair, and grabbed a teacake from the tray on the table.

"Oh, thank the *gods* you're home," Thora cried. "I was so scared, and I missed you terribly, and I hope you killed the bastard that took you, because if not, I'm going to wring his filthy neck!"

Marai laughed, and held Thora tighter. Gods, she'd missed her, too. Missed her scolding, her mother-henning, her tenderness.

Over Thora's shoulder, another golden-armored figure loomed. Raife smiled, the relief so transparent on his face, that he looked like he might fall down from it.

"Don't hog her," he said to Thora.

Thora didn't let go; she was still crying. Instead, Raife wrapped both of his long arms around his wife and Marai.

"I'm so glad to have you back. Nothing was the same without you," said Raife. "Aresti warned us about the, um, *physical* changes. You look good with wings. Being the Faerie Queen suits you."

Marai glanced at Aresti, who shrugged again as she chewed on the teacake. *Fine. I guess I'll forgive her.* Marai buried herself further into the warmth of Thora and Raife's embrace.

"I'm sorry we didn't come get you, ourselves," Raife said quietly. "It was the hardest decision I've ever had to make—"

"I understand why you couldn't," Marai mumbled against Thora's shoulder.

Raife and Thora finally disentangled themselves from Marai. She had to take a deep breath—Thora had squeezed the air from her lungs.

"You both look well," Marai said, gazing at them. "Ruen told me that multiple congratulations are in order." She gestured to Thora's slightly swollen belly.

Thora's cheeks were glowing and rosy; pregnancy only heightened her gentle beauty. She put a hand to her abdomen, smiling. "I have everything I've ever wanted, thanks to you and Ruenen." She then turned to the King of Nevandia, leaning casually against the settee. Thora let out a choking sob as she hugged him, too. "Thank you for bringing her home."

Ruenen patted Thora's back, and she released him with a sniffle.

"I'm sorry," Marai said quietly, and reached out to grip Thora and Raife's hands. "I'm sorry that I couldn't bring Keshel home, too."

Aresti's face darkened on the couch. She stared into the flames and swallowed.

Thora shook her head. "You mustn't say a word. Not today. No, today is a *happy* day. We'll speak of him tomorrow." She brushed off the tears, and put on her motherly, interrogating face. "Now, I was called here for a very peculiar reason."

Marai frowned. "I hate to ask this of you, but could you tell the Witan that I'm with-child, and we'll deal with it later?"

Thora put her hands on her hips. "This isn't something to lie about."

"Don't worry. We're working on it," Ruenen said, grinning like a fool.

Marai placed her hand on Thora's shoulder. "Since you're here, though . . . there's something else I want you to check."

Thora gave her a puzzled look, then had Marai lie down on the bed. The others came closer, buzzing behind Thora with curiosity.

"Do you all have to hover?" Marai snapped, and everyone but Thora took two steps back.

With ginger eyes closed, Thora's healing hands floated over every inch of Marai's body, assessing, sensing the blood, bone, and tissue beneath her skin. Thora's face scrunched, brow furrowed, when she reached Marai's torso.

"I've never seen anything like this," she said. "Small spots of darkness, like rot or scarring, on some of your organs."

Marai went cold. "It's from dark magic. Cavar, he . . . put it inside me."

Ruenen, Raife, and Aresti came closer again as Thora's eyes stared at Marai in horror.

"I thought Innesh got rid of it," said Ruenen.

"She did, but it appears to have left damage in its wake."

"Can you get rid of it? The darkness?" Ruenen asked Thora, serious now, and Marai wished she could take Thora's words back so he'd smile again.

"I can try, but I've never healed something of this sort before," Thora said. She closed her eyes again, and blue light appeared at her fingers. Healing magic seeped into Marai's pores and bloodstream, and her body warmed. Thora's shoulders and arms tightened as she continued to try to remove the rot. Eventually, Thora slumped in defeat. "I don't have the power to heal this kind of damage."

I'd thought as much. Marai tried not to let Thora see her disappointment. Instead, she plastered on a weak smile. "Perhaps you can experiment and research. Maybe Braesal and the other fae have suggestions."

"Does it hurt?" asked Raife.

"No, only a slight ache sometimes," Marai said, trying to keep things light. Ruenen's face was clouded with concern. This was supposed to be a happy day. She couldn't stand seeing her loved ones suddenly thrust back into worry.

Thora bit her lower lip. "I'm not going to sugarcoat it, though. If you *do* manage to conceive, it won't be an easy pregnancy, what with the damage done to your body. I don't know . . . I don't know if a babe would make it to term."

"We'll have to be extra careful, that's all," Ruenen said lightly, hiding the concern on his face. "Take it one day at a time." He smiled at Marai, before turning to Aresti and Raife. "Will you join us for dinner tonight? Not as King's Guard, but as our family."

"I won't say no to a royal meal," Aresti said with a smirk. "The food in the barracks is shit."

"We'll be there," said Raife, then clapped his hand on Ruenen's back. "Glad to have you back, as well, friend."

Ruenen and Raife shared a smile that warmed Marai's heart. In her absence, they'd grown close, and Marai was grateful they'd forged such a friendship when both of them were reeling from loss.

Once Thora, Raife, and Aresti left, Ruenen took Marai in his arms again. But this embrace felt different. Marai could sense his joy, but there was a certain underpinning of disquiet to the way his arms clung to her.

"No matter what happens, no matter the joy or sorrow that we encounter, we face it together," he said, pulling away to stare into her eyes. "Promise me that through every part of our journey, in light or darkness, we walk it together."

Marai rose onto her tiptoes and brushed her lips against his. "I promise you, Ruen, that I will hold your hand through the longest nights, and the brightest days, and every day in between. Come what may."

They fell into kiss after kiss, but Marai couldn't stop her eyes from glancing out the window.

Past the moor, to the sea, where darkness was brewing, and someone was only biding his time.

CHAPTER 42

RUENEN

Marai stared at herself in the mirror.

She'd been ready for an hour, and Ruenen now watched her with mild amusement while he adjusted his crown.

She wore a Nevandian gold gown with green vines crawling up the bodice, her hair woven and braided at the base of her neck. A white fur cape sat heavy on her thin shoulders, hiding her wings. She was stunning. Regal. But her brow furrowed the longer she stared at this new version of herself.

"Are you displeased?" Ruenen asked, smiling. "We hired the best seamstress in the country to make that for you. I think you look incredible."

It had been a scramble to outfit Marai's last-minute queenly wardrobe. She had nothing to wear except for that plum gown from Baatgai, and Marai refused to wait for more clothing to be made before getting to work. Seamstresses altered Queen Larissa's old gowns, making adjustments for Marai's wings. She'd worn simple dresses the past week to attend Witan meetings, and to visit Kadiatu and Leif's graves on the moor.

This dress was the most important one she'd ever wear, according to Rhia. Marai's coronation gown.

"I'm getting used to this reflection," she said, angling her chin down. Her fingers fidgeted with the fabric at her sides. Ruenen guessed she was trying not to pick at her cuticles.

"Wait until they put that crown on your head." Ruenen understood how Marai felt. She hid it well, but he often saw the churning emotions swirling around in her eyes. The sharp transition from nobody to royalty had been overwhelming for him, too. Honestly, he thought she was handling it better than he had.

She'd arranged for the Menagerie refugees to be moved into the army barracks until she could find a more permanent solution. Not only that, but Marai awarded those who'd gone on the rescue mission to receive a significant sum of money, and gifted Braesal and Tarik baronetcy.

The Witan had, of course, protested, but Marai shot them down with a strong and simple, "it *will* be done."

Ruenen had never seen Corian at a loss for words before, but watching the lord go silent with shock brought pure joy to Ruenen's heart.

In the past few days, he often caught himself staring at her. When Marai sat on her newly-crafted throne, addressing the Witan with her piercing gaze and razor-edged tongue, or eating dinner across from him in their private dining room, or curling up in front of the fireplace at the end of the night. The realization hit Ruenen over and over again. *That's my wife. That's my wife! And she's home.*

And that day, she'd officially be crowned Queen of Nevandia.

He approached his wife at the mirror and wrapped his arms around her. "How do you feel?"

"Nervous." She said it tersely, and Ruenen knew she didn't want to admit such a weakness. "I don't want . . . all those eyes on me."

Ruenen kissed her cheek, held her tighter. "I'll be right there with you. Keep your eyes on me, and ignore everyone else. All you have to do is repeat whatever Head Monk Baureo says."

"And not trip over my feet while dancing, or say something insulting to a foreign ambassador at the reception."

"You managed not to do either of those things at *my* coronation."

Marai scowled, making Ruenen's smile widen. "None of them want me to be Queen. They'd rather this be Rhia's coronation."

"That's only because they're terrified of you."

Marai shot him her seething look of death.

Ruenen laughed, turning her around to face him. "My love, you'll settle in your role as Queen, and the people will adjust and learn. Other kingdoms may fear you, scorn you, but no one will dare provoke the Faerie Queen. Not even Corian and

Wattling. I think you'll enjoy that part. You'll become a legend in the hearts of some—"

"And a monster in the eyes of many."

"It won't be long before people start giving you hand pies in the street, too."

Marai exhaled slowly, as if prepping her mind and body for battle. "I don't want to make any mistakes."

"You *will,* and that's acceptable. I make them all the time," Ruenen said with a shrug. "No leader is perfect. In fact, many are downright terrible. What matters is that we both work for the good of the country, and our people. I don't think you'll have any trouble doing that."

A knock came at the door, and Anja's face peered inside. "Your Grace, it's time."

Marai took another deep breath, steeled her face, and squared her shoulders. "I'm ready."

The castle monastery had been decorated the same as Ruenen's own coronation, but this time, he waited at the front, next to Monk Baureo, ready to receive his Queen.

Marai strode down the aisle, chin held high, fur cape trailing behind her. Her gaze latched onto Ruenen's, and never left, as she ignored the whispers, the gaping mouths, the judgmental and fearful stares. In fact, their murmurs only seemed to bestow upon Marai a renewed confidence. With each step forward, her body relaxed into a posture of strength. She was used to adversity. This was just another kind of battlefield, and Marai would always rise to the challenge.

Ruenen beamed, and pride warmed his chest.

The visiting Astyean nobles and ambassadors were balanced out with a healthy number of magical folk, as well. The fae were present, including young Holt and his friends, as well as every single member of the Menagerie. Werewolf friends of Tarik from Ain had arrived, drawn to the country by the Faerie Queen. And Nosficio, fully covered to avoid the sun streaming in through the windows, had a place of honor standing amongst the Witenagemot.

Marai's presence in the room was electric. The air crackled with intensity, promises of hope, and a small bite of danger. She lowered to a knee as Monk

Baureo recited the ancient texts, and placed a gilded, emerald-studded crown upon her head, the twin to Ruenen's own.

As she stood and faced her people, Marai, the newly crowned Queen of Nevandia and the Fae, *radiated* power. She looked confident, regal, *formidable*, sending a clear message to all opposed that she'd never cower, never yield, and never surrender.

A sly grin spread across Ruenen's lips as he imagined Marai wearing nothing *but* her crown and that formidable expression later that night . . .

Two months of peace settled across the land like snow flurries, soft and slow.

Tacorn's loyalist rebellions became few and far between, and a new cohesion had formed between each group of residents: Nevandians, Tacornians, and magical folk. Steady progress, and lots of hard work had gotten Ruenen and Marai to this point.

The burdens of being King didn't feel quite so overwhelming or stifling when shared with Marai. Ruenen settled into a rhythm, turning to music, or the training ring, or sometimes a blacksmith's forge, to refocus and reprioritize whenever he needed a break.

After a long day of meetings, Ruenen collapsed onto the bed, fully clothed. Marai was seated on the settee, thumbing through a proposal she and Rhia had drafted to grant Nevandian women the right to own, purchase, and inherit property.

Always working. Always fighting for someone.

"Why not come to bed?" Ruenen asked, rubbing the spot next to him, waggling his eyebrows. "You're working too hard."

"This is the first major law Rhia and I have drafted together, and we want it to be infallible." She twirled a stick of charcoal between her fingers, then jotted a note onto the page.

At her side sat Keshel's journal, opened to the page with a sketch of a little girl, ribbons adorning her wild hair. Ruenen often caught Marai rereading the journal in her downtime. Keshel and his prophecies were never far from her mind. Neither was Cavar.

The flames in the fireplace hearth heated their chilly bedroom, bathing Marai in a beguiling, gentle glow. She sighed in frustration, setting down her work.

"I can't concentrate." Marai stood and walked to the large window.

Her face clouded over as she stared at the city. Winter had arrived early. White flurries floated down from the sky, lightly dusting the roofs of Kellesar.

"What's wrong?" Ruenen asked, observing the sharpness of her gaze, the rigidity of her back. Her wings were taut with tension. "Is our friend flying around out there?"

The winged shadow creature, or *grotesque* as Thora liked to call them now. The white-haired, hawk-winged fellow never hurt anyone, and he wasn't around often, but sometimes Ruenen spotted him soaring above the castle spires, watching, learning.

"No shadow creatures in sight," she replied.

And there hadn't been since Marai returned to Astyean shores. The other creatures had gone to ground again.

"Then what's bothering you?" Something clearly was, and it must have been especially troubling for Marai to avoid speaking about it.

"Yesterday, I felt a shift in the air. A tremble in the earth. Something's coming."

On the bed, Ruenen sat up straight. "What do you mean?"

Marai glanced back at him, expression grave. "Cavar's finally on his way."

Blood rushed in Ruenen's ears, cold snaked under his ribs, as the statement crashed through him. "Are you certain? How can you tell?"

"I can *feel* dark magic coming closer, like an oppressive, suffocating weight sitting on my chest. I'm connected to it now. The force, the pressure, gets stronger every day, and sometimes, at night, I *hear* Him."

Ruenen stood, joining Marai at the window. His wife rarely spoke of such things. She never discussed her days in the Menagerie, the effects of dark magic on her body, but he could sense her fear in the atmosphere as if it were a vibrating string on his lute. He didn't need to see it on her face to know that the memories tormented her.

"What does He say to you?" he asked, hating the way Marai shuddered, as if she could hear the magic speaking to her even then.

"He calls for me. His voice grates against my bones, glides across my skin, like He wants to lure me deeper into the darkness. To use me. To claim me."

"Cavar's doing this?"

"I can sense Cavar's stone approaching, but it's the *magic* that's tugging on me. The Lord of the Underworld wants *me*, Ruen."

Heat traveled up Ruenen's neck. Anger smoldered at the fringes of his eyes. *I'll kill anyone who tries to take Marai from me.* Ruenen rarely had such murderous thoughts, but Marai truly feared this Lord of the Underworld and the power He had over her. Ruenen wouldn't let this maniac touch a single hair on his wife's head.

"In Keshel's journal, he spoke of how the darkness will always try to corrupt the 'Chosen,' to taint their magic, because once the Lord of the Underworld succeeds in claiming her, there'll be no stopping Him. His darkness already succeeded in luring me to use its power." Marai glanced down at her stained fingers. "He wants to use me for something terrible. To help him escape the Underworld. He wants my power."

Ruenen's body went rigid with controlled fury. "He will *never* take you away from me, or from Nevandia. You don't belong to Him."

"He's using Cavar to get to me. That must be why He planted that stone on Andara. Why He helped Rayghast. They were only puppets. He's been after *me* this whole time."

Ruenen bit his lower lip, calming his anger and fear. Marai didn't need him to get upset; she needed him to be practical, to stay focused. "We've prepared for Cavar's arrival. We have a solid plan to defend against him and Koda, and we still have Innesh's amulet locked away."

Marai and Raife's fire had destroyed the other two amulets Ruenen had hidden in the chest, but it took a lot of power to turn the amulets to dust. Both Raife and Marai had been exhausted from the effort.

"We don't know how many Guardians Cavar's bringing with him. It could be three or thirty." Marai picked at her cuticles. "Thirty amulets, Ruen. We only have one."

"We have *you*. We have Aresti, Raife, and Braesal, an entire army. You don't think we have the strength to beat a group of wealthy foreign lords who don't know this country, and have never fought a day in their pampered lives?"

"They don't need physical strength or numbers when they have those amulets." Marai backed away. A muscle feathered her jaw, and she took a deep breath. "Besides, I don't know how effective I'll be in a battle."

Ruenen scoffed. "You're jesting, right?" Lirr's Bones, Marai could do literally anything, defy the impossible, in Ruenen's mind, but the look in her eyes chased the smile from his face. "What are you not telling me?"

"I think dark magic isn't just calling for me," she said slowly, hesitantly. "It's calling for *her*."

Ruenen didn't need to ask who "her" was. They'd been talking about only one "her" for weeks. He waited for Marai to continue. Her morbid, eerie conjectures were starting to disturb him.

Marai's steady gaze pinned Ruenen in place, and he suddenly understood.

His eyes went wide. His heart kicked a frantic beat. "Are you sure? Are you really . . ."

Marai nodded with a nervous swallow. Shaking hands touched her flat abdomen.

"I'm going to be a father?" he asked in breathless amazement.

Marai nodded again, this time with a small smile.

A lump formed in Ruenen's throat as tears stung his eyes. "How long have you known?"

"A few days. I wasn't sure at first, and I didn't want to get your hopes up . . ." She fiddled with her cuticles again, speaking in a rush. "This wasn't how I'd imagined this reveal. I've been anxious and terrified for days. I wanted to deny the truths right in front of me, but I've been studying Keshel's words, and I know what I feel. Keshel told me she was mine, and I can *feel* her inside me. She's *ours*, Ruen. I know it. I know it so strongly that I can't think of anything else sometimes. I can already *feel* her magic growing."

It clicked into place then. The signs had been there for days. How she'd been picking at her food, how she'd looked paler, more tired than usual. Ruenen had thought she was overworked trying to prove to herself and the world that she could be a great queen.

Ruenen had prayed every day in the monastery for this. But gods, the news tore his heart in two. He was so incredibly happy, excited, and nervous, but this child was coming at the wrong time. Cavar was on his way, and Marai's scarred body might not be able to carry a babe to full-term.

And if Marai was right, Ruenen's daughter was already being summoned by the darkness before she was even born.

He pressed his forehead to hers. "This news makes me so happy, my love. I've wanted this for ages, and I cannot wait to raise our child together . . . but I'm scared. For what will undoubtedly be a difficult birth for you. That the *Lord of the Underworld* is going to come after *our* daughter."

Marai placed her hands on either side of his face and smiled. "I'm not afraid. Not of her. Not for us." Her smile vanished. "Cavar is another problem. We need to put our focus on him right now."

Ruenen dragged a hand through his hair. *This is too much to take in.* "How long before he arrives on Astyean soil?"

Marai's mouth twisted. "It's hard to tell. I don't know how long he's been traveling. We know we'd normally have at least a solid forty-seven days from when he set sail, although that might be more now that it's winter on the Northern Sea and the waters are rougher. Then, however long it takes him to travel here to Nevandia from Baatgai."

Roughly a month and a half. More if the weather slows him down. "We'll need to tell the Witan. Have Avilyard prepare the troops."

Marai shook her head. "There's no use pitting humans against those amulets. Cavar will decimate our forces. As with Rayghast, the only way to challenge someone with magic is *with* magic. We'll need shields, like the ones Keshel erected."

Marai had already taught Raife, Aresti, Braesal and the other fae to create those invisible barriers, but they weren't anywhere near as strong as Marai's or Keshel's.

"We'll need to pray that it will be enough," Marai said, her usual steely determination in the face of battle somewhat dwindling. "We'll need everyone with a drop of magic in their veins to fight."

"I think our favorite vampire might be able to assist," said Ruenen. "Maybe he can rally other vampires to join us, and the werewolves from the outer reaches. There might be more fae hiding somewhere."

"That's a long shot. Nosficio's social proclivities are rare amongst vampires. As a whole, they have little interest in collaborating with anyone, and he'd only have a month to find these folk and bring them back here."

"Then he'd better start today."

Nosficio was never far from Nevandia, unless he was visiting Nieve in Grelta. He enjoyed his place on the Witan, and the grand castle apartment that came with it.

Nyle stood outside their door, guarding the royal chambers, when Ruenen peeked his head out. "Send word for Nosficio, please."

The young guard's brown eyes widened, then he bolted down the hall; the sound of his clanging armor disappearing when he reached the stairs.

"We'll be ready," Ruenen said, turning back to Marai. "If we have to evacuate Kellesar, send everyone to Dul Tanen, we will. If we have to greet Cavar in Baatgai, before he steps off the ship, we will."

"We cannot bring an army of fae, vampires, and werewolves into another country," Marai said. "The Emperor of Syoto would view that as an invasion."

"I'll write to him. I'll warn him to prepare his own forces to block Cavar's entry into Baatgai."

"You wrote to Emperor Tetsuo before, and he wrote back a dismissive reply then."

"Yes, but that was under different circumstances," Ruenen said. "He had no interest aiding in the search for you. This time there's a threat to his own people, and I have a responsibility to warn him about a potential attack. Even if Tetsuo ignores me again, I will have done the right thing. You and I will do everything in our power to keep our people safe, regardless of what happens with Syoto. Hopefully, you can stay on the sidelines and avoid fighting at all."

Marai visibly recoiled. "I don't *want* to stay on the sidelines. I want to *fight* for my people, for my own freedom, for your safety . . . and our daughter's."

She wore the face of the Lady Butcher in that moment. The one that clearly told him he could go burn in the fiery hell of the Underworld. How could Ruenen compete against that ferocious expression? Marai had never scared him, even when she'd actively sought to in their early days, but no one was immune to palpitations upon witnessing that seething look of death and power.

And, well . . . it also made Ruenen want to tear off her gown and drag his tongue across her skin.

"I may be with-child, but I'm not weak. I'm not *fragile*," Marai continued. "I won't stay on the sidelines while my people sacrifice and suffer, because we both know that I'm the one he wants. I'll do what I must, Ruen. You know that there's no stopping me."

Ruenen huffed. "Oh, I'm well aware. But Lirr's Bloody Bones, I don't like it one bit."

Marai marched across the room and wrenched open the door. As she disappeared around the frame, dress whispering at her ankles, she shot over her shoulder, "It's war, Ruen. You don't have to like it."

CHAPTER 43

MARAI

Magic pulled at her. Two different textures, different shades, one light and one dark, battling for Marai's soul. They called to her, tugging on opposite ends of the string of fate wrapped around her ribs.

There was the building bellow of magic from across the sea; a dark current, deeper than the sandy depths. Every day it was stronger than the previous, coming closer, seeking Marai with its lethal intent.

I want you, it seemed to say. *Come meet me.*

It tugged at Marai's gut, like she was nothing more than a fish on a line. It slithered up her spine when she dreamed, a serpent made of nightmares and cobwebs.

Until Cavar and his Guardians were defeated, Marai would never escape the call of darkness. She had to destroy the stone to keep the Lord of the Underworld at bay. He'd find another way to get to her eventually, but Marai could at least subdue Him until the next 'Chosen' arrived to finish Him off.

Marai's daughter.

She was the second magic Marai felt.

The darkness from the Underworld was external, but this light was *inside* her. A gentle, fluttering magic. Rich, complex, vibrant; hues of gold and white shimmering sunlight. The incandescent magic of *life.*

Most fae babes were as ordinary as humans until childhood, according to Thora. But Marai had *sensed* this child, sensed her power, like a sprouting seed. Her daughter's magic was already manifesting. There was no question in Marai's mind that she was carrying Lirr's "Chosen." The girl with the auburn hair. The light that would vanquish the darkness forever.

Marai spent the last few evenings listening as she lay in bed. Feeling. Marveling.

She's powerful. She'll be far stronger than me. Her daughter's magic would only grow. She'd surpass Marai by her tenth birthday at this rate.

This babe would change the world, and the poor child would have a mountain of responsibility upon her tiny shoulders, but Marai would be there to guide her, along with Keshel's words. Marai would make sure her daughter steered clear of dark magic's allure. That she would be a stronger, better person than her mother.

But her daughter wouldn't be born at all unless Marai tackled the more pressing matter at hand: she needed to defeat Cavar.

"When female faeries are with-child, part of our magic goes into the growth of the babe. We're momentarily weakened," Thora had explained, rubbing her own swollen belly. "My healing skills won't return to full strength again until after the birth."

Marai now felt a portion of her own magic being siphoned away each day that the babe grew inside her. *How can I fight against Cavar and the amulets when I'm not at full power, whilst carrying a child, when my body is already damaged from dark magic?*

"Don't tell a soul about this pregnancy," she said to Ruenen, lying in their bed in the dark, cold hours of night.

"Why not?" he asked, tracing a finger up and down her naked arm.

"Thora will fuss and fret, and the Witan will find a way to isolate me. I don't want anyone treating me differently or standing in my way. Corian and Wattling will gladly lock me in the dungeon if they knew my intentions to fight Cavar whilst carrying the heir. All that matters to the Witan is that I have as many royal babies as possible."

The Witan still believed Marai's story that she'd been pregnant before arriving in Kellesar, but Holfast was definitely getting suspicious. His eyes kept darting to her stomach, expecting to see evidence.

"Alright, Sassafras, I won't tell anyone," Ruenen said, kissing her bare shoulder. "I hope you know how excited I am, despite everything. I want to shout it from the spires for the city to hear."

"Please, don't do that. You're likely to slip and fall," said Marai.

Ruenen laughed. "And you? Don't think about Cavar for a moment. Are you excited?"

Marai bit the inside of her cheek. "I'm worried that I won't be good at it. That I'm not ready. I'm still getting used to be Queen. To being married. Am I doing right by my people? Can I do right by my own child?"

"You're doing a brilliant job as Queen. Wattling and Corian aren't afraid of you anymore." Ruenen grinned. "I've never been happier, Sassafras. You will be an amazing mother, and you'll have the support of our whole family. Plus Braesal and River. They'll help us navigate parenthood."

There was no time to worry about the babe. She had to focus on defeating Cavar and eliminating those amulets.

Brick by brick, Marai built the stone wall around her heart. She was Queen. She wouldn't let her people sense her trepidation, her doubt. *Do not show fear.*

The next morning, she called the magical folk in Kellesar into the Witenagemot chamber, without the human Witan present. They'd interrupt and complicate everything, and Marai had no patience to deal with them. This conversation of war was only for those with magic in their blood. Nosficio was the sole representative of the vampire community, but all the adult fae, including Daye, Lilly, and Quinton, as well as members of the new werewolf packs were in attendance. Lastly, the gentle folk from the Menagerie lingered against the walls of the room.

"Forgive me for asking, Your Grace, but where's Commander Avilyard?" asked Finneagal. "Shouldn't the army be involved in this meeting?"

"A human army, no matter how large and well-trained, cannot succeed against those amulets," Marai said from the dais. Ruenen was seated beside her, one of only two humans in the room, besides Innesh. He was pensive, lost in thought, probably thinking about the babe. "You saw their power, Master Finneagal. You know Cavar alone can burn our army to cinders. We'll need to employ every skill at our disposal. What we did against Rayghast last time was successful, but we're without two of the major players this time around."

Keshel, who'd shielded the Nevandian army behind his barrier, and Kadiatu, who'd combated Rayghast's dark magic beneath the earth.

"We'll need to ramp up our training until they arrive," Raife said, gesturing to the other fae around him. "We know how to make the defensive shields, but we should continue to strengthen our offensive magic."

"Agreed," said Marai. "We must be able to fight and wield magic in battle as if it were any other weapon. Aresti and Raife, I'm placing you two in charge of that training, and it will be *mandatory* for all with faerie blood."

Thora scrunched her face, skeptical. She was five months along, and while she remained fairly active, she definitely wasn't ready for battle.

"Nosficio, what's the status of the vampires?" Marai asked.

The hood of Nosficio's ermine-lined velvet cape was drawn over his dreadlocks. It was overcast and snowing outside, but wan daylight still trickled into the room from the wall of floor-to-ceiling windows.

"The ones I've spoken to have no interest in helping," Nosficio said. "Vampires are not thinking of the bigger picture, that the amulets are a threat to their own safety. You know how my people are—selfish, indifferent."

Marai snorted. She could describe Nosficio as such most days.

"We'll see if anyone shows up." The vampire's bland tone revealed that he didn't believe that anyone would.

"Well, us wolves are prepared," Tarik said with a thumping fist against the table, and a resounding bellow of agreement rose around the room from the various packs. "We sent out the call, and more packs are bound to come."

"But will they arrive in time?" asked Aresti, fiddling nervously with her dangling earring. "It's Grelta all over again."

"Queen Nieve brought hundreds of soldiers," said Yovel. "We'll be lucky if twenty more wolves come."

"Could we ask Grelta for aid again?" Thora asked.

"As my brilliant wife stated, we don't need human soldiers," Ruenen stated, giving Marai a wink. "And besides, we can't always rely on Nieve's generosity. She's our ally, but we cannot abuse the relationship. As much as it grieves me to say, I think this is a problem only magical folk can solve."

"Can you sense how far away they are?" came Anja's soft voice from the side of the dais. Marai heard the fear, saw it in her thin face. "And how many amulets they're bringing with them?"

When Marai closed her eyes, she could feel the wall of darkness approaching. Cavar obviously had more than one amulet with him. The exact number was impossible to calculate, but it made no difference what the numbers were. One or one hundred, they'd prepare for the worst.

"They'll be here soon," was all Marai could say, and the room quieted.

"We need a concrete strategy," said Raife after a moment. "You've told us before about Koda's power of immobilization. We need to take him out first, or he can prevent us from doing anything."

From her position next to the dais, Innesh announced, "Leave him to me. *I* will kill him."

"No offense, because you're one rebel-ass lady, and I certainly wouldn't mess with you," said Tarik, "but you're also human. What makes you think you can kill him?"

Innesh uncrossed her arms and blinked at Tarik, as if he'd asked her the inanest question on earth. She pulled out a long, jagged knife from a holster at her waist, and touched the tip of the blade to her finger. "It's personal."

Tarik's mouth fell open, but then he gave her an impressed nod. "Should you feel the desire, my bedroom door is always open to you."

Innesh blinked again, but Marai swore she saw a slight twitch at the corners of her mouth.

Aresti groaned, placing a long-suffering hand to her forehead. "Can we stay on topic, please? Innesh can't handle Koda alone, but there's no point in trying to stop her. She'll need others with magic on her team."

"I can help," Anja said, head bowed. "It's personal for me, as well." She then lifted her head, a fire stoking in her usually kind eyes.

Koda had tormented her, too, but the female wasn't powerful. Marai had only seen Anja wield domestic, simple magic, such as lighting a fire, mending a hole in fabric with a swipe of a hand, and stirring a cup of tea with a twirl of her finger.

"Give me one of your knives, Innesh, and I'll stab the mealy maggot Koda with you," said Cyrill from a darkened corner. He shared a murderous smirk with Innesh that made Marai proud.

They'll get the job done with pure nerve and ire.

Brass and Zorish also volunteered for Innesh's team, and Marai bet that if Gunnora was there, she would've been the first to raise her hand to take Koda down, too.

"That leaves the rest of us for the Guardians and barriers," Raife said.

"See if we can isolate them as we did in Bakair," added Braesal. "Pick them off one at a time. Search out the weak ones, like lions do with elk."

"Then Marai can take on Cavar," Aresti said, as if there was no concern, that beating Cavar and his stone would be *easy* for the Queen of the Fae.

But it wouldn't be easy at all.

Her people assumed she could win. They'd witnessed her do remarkable things before, and *believed* in her, but Marai knew her limitations. She knew she'd be at half-power, and the amulets had no such limitations. An endless well of darkness writhed within Cavar's stone. Marai could very well burn out before defeating him.

The hasty glance Ruenen gave her meant that he could sense her wariness.

"As expected, I received a response from Emperor Tetsuo," he said, changing the subject. "The Emperor thanked me for my concern, but said Cavar has done nothing to bar him from anchoring at port. He doesn't think Cavar's a threat, and proclaims he's looking forward to welcoming Andaran visitors. In other words, he's refusing to send men to Baatgai."

"Fool. He's only going to get his own people killed," growled Braesal.

"You know Syoto: neutral to the last," Aresti said with a sigh. Her father and Uncle, Keshel's father, had been from Syoto. She never held much love for the country.

"We're on our own," Marai said, and brought the meeting to a close.

QUEEN OF THE SHADOW MENAGERIE 443

Kellesar was evacuated immediately. It was the obvious target for Cavar and his guardians, as the capital city and Marai's residence. Most people, when told an enemy with dark magic approached, fled to Dul Tanen. Only those too old, too sick, too stubborn to leave stayed behind. Holfast and half of the Witan also remained behind, including Rhia.

"I've no desire to return to Dul Tanen and that wretched fortress," she told Marai.

"You'll be in danger here."

Rhia gave Marai a hard stare. "I've grown accustomed to danger, Your Grace. If I'm to die, then I'd rather do it on my terms."

Fenir also remained, since he was still locked in his apartment and had no choice. Marai had barely seen him since returning from Andara. Ruenen hinted that he might grant Fenir clemency, but wanted to wait until the "Cavar problem" was dealt with.

The other half of the Witan led the evacuations to Dul Tanen, Vorae at the helm. The only magical folk who didn't remain behind in Kellesar were Quinton, as well as the gnomes and hobs, who were too small, and without an ounce of magic in their blood.

"We feel guilty leaving you to deal with Cavar alone," Gruper the hob said to Marai as she watched the evacuation from the drawbridge. "If there was anything we could do to help—"

"I'll be relieved knowing you're far enough away and safe," Marai said.

Mayestral was also incredibly resistant to leaving. "You *need* me, Sire. Who will bring you food? Draw your bath? Make sure your clothes are clean and pressed? My place is at your side."

Ruenen smiled, placing a hand on his loyal Groom's shoulder. "I can take care of myself for a few days, Mayestral. I survived two-and-twenty years without you, and I admit, they were rough ones, but I'll get by. Although, I can't promise that you won't be scandalized by the state of our chambers by the time you get back."

Mayestral's brown eyes had widened at the mere thought, but he joined Bassite, Quinton, and the other staff on the wagon headed for Dul Tanen. Marai's heart clenched watching them go.

I should go to Baatgai and meet Cavar on my own. I shouldn't bring the others into this fight.

But they'd follow her, she knew. If Marai tried to sneak away to the port, Aresti, Raife, Braesal, Tarik, and the other folk would be right behind her. They believed there was a chance to win. They placed their unwavering faith in Marai.

Stubborn fools.

Kellesar was a ghost town, eerily inert as Marai and Ruenen returned to the castle that night. Doors and shutters were bolted shut. Only stray cats and mice lingered in the snow-crusted streets. Marai spotted wan flickers of candlelight in between the cracks of some boarded-up windows. Whoever decided to stay, to ride out the upcoming battle, had been instructed to keep hidden. Hopefully, the glorious city Marai had come to love would still be standing in a week.

"This feels a lot like the battle with Rayghast," Ruenen said, undressing slowly, distractedly. "But with more snow and less people. I'm honestly more afraid than I was then."

Marai's hand froze, sharpening Dimtoir on the settee. It was a mindless activity, something to do while her body fizzed with energy, anxiety, and nausea.

"We're more prepared than we were then," she said. "We have more magic on our side, and we know exactly what those amulets can do."

Ruenen came and sat next to her. "But we also have more to lose." He removed Dimtoir from Marai's hands, setting it on his other side. He entwined his fingers with hers. "You aren't at full strength, and that's what frightens me the most."

"I know . . . I'm frightened, too," Marai admitted, and would only say such words to Ruenen.

"I think we've become accustomed to you saving us," he said, lips curling at the corners. "You always manage to defeat your enemies. I've grown complacent, believing that no matter what happens, you'll always win. Your power *amazes* me. *You* amaze me. But this time, you're carrying our child."

Marai wanted to scoff, wanted to pull away from him, but his fear mirrored the deep uncertainties inside her. Ruenen held onto her hands tighter, keeping his focus locked on her. There was a desperate gleam in his gold-flecked eyes.

"I don't have a choice, Ruen. I can't sit this one out. I have to give it all I have, or we're dead."

"I'm not asking you to stay behind. I'm saying that you should let the others pull the heavy weight first, stay back until absolutely necessary."

"And let my people die in the process?" Marai snapped, getting to her feet.

Ruenen stood, challenging her. "Don't take on Cavar by yourself. *Please.*"

"I'll do what must be done. Nothing more, and nothing less." Marai fumed, but the anger was misdirected. Ruenen wasn't wrong. She was frustrated because he was *right,* and there was nothing she could do to make it safer or easier for any of them.

A knock at the door. Avilyard entered, one of the last remaining humans in Kellesar. Helmet tucked under his arm, he bowed, expression grave, and Marai knew he brought bad news.

"Forgive me for disturbing you," he said, his voice a deep rumble of concern, "but I thought you'd want to know: Baatgai has been burned to the ground."

Marai's body went ice cold. "When?"

"Yesterday. Two large ships barely docked at port before black flames devoured the village and everyone in it."

"Fuck," Ruenen said, running a clawed hand through his hair. "Damn Tetsuo . . ."

All those villagers. Innocent men, women, and children, who'd done nothing wrong except live in Baatgai.

"The Emperor sent troops to retaliate, but hardly any of them survived."

Marai seethed with rage at Cavar's disrespect for life.

"How do you know this?" she asked Avilyard.

A carrier pigeon couldn't fly that fast.

"A female vampire delivered the message," said Avilyard, and judging by his sour expression, he wasn't too pleased. "Said she knows you. She's downstairs now. I can get her for you—"

"That won't be necessary," said a slick, cool female voice at the doorway.

She looked healthier now. Long midnight hair rippled down her back. Her skin was still starkly white, but no longer chalky and thin, and those red eyes blazed as Desislava cocked her head at Marai.

"Your Graces," the vampiress said, and curtsied with a flirtatious grin at Ruenen, showing off her fangs and blood-red lips.

"How did you get here?" Marai asked. The last time she'd seen Desislava, she'd disappeared on Andara.

"They hunted me, although rather pathetically," Desislava said, brushing past Avilyard and strolled about the room, examining the fine artwork and gilded mirrors. "With Cavar incapacitated and distracted, his Guardians didn't know what to do. I evaded them for months, hiding in the shadows, learning what I could." She grinned at Marai. "Oh, he's furious with you. Obsessed. Cavar had three brand new ships built for the voyage here. He spent an inordinate amount of money, had every craftsman within fifty leagues working on them around the clock. He forced anyone with sailing experience to crew the ships. Each ship quartered at least twenty Guardians."

Sixty Guardians. Marai had trouble in Bakair against only two.

"I snuck aboard one of these vessels, hid below deck amongst the supplies, living on the meager rations of rats and seagulls. But thanks to help from Eno, we downed a ship offshore before they could land here."

Eno. The mermaid. She'd swum a long way to help.

Desislava faced Marai directly, raising her chin. "Most onboard were already dead, courtesy of yours truly, before Eno crushed the ship with a massive wave. Unfortunately, the other two ships saw what was happening and defended against Eno. I'm not sure what happened to her, but at least you'll be fighting against one less ship."

Marai went to the window and closed her eyes against the swirling cloud of snow flurries. Her senses traveled through the storm, through the streets and across the howling moor. Through the forests, over the Syoton border, and to the Astyean coast.

Desislava wasn't lying—that inky, oppressive, cold fire, that cobweb sensation of dark magic, was closer now than before. And it was moving fast.

She whirled back around to see Desislava sniffing Ruenen. He inched away, closer to Dimtoir on the settee.

"They're on their way here, four or five days out. Cavar's moving quickly. The horses he stole from the village have collars around them, spurring them when they grow tired. He'll ride them until they die, poor beasts," said the vampiress.

"I would have followed them to keep track of their progress, but I decided the better use of my time was to warn you."

Marai would need to lead her small army from Kellesar to the Syoton border immediately.

She turned to Avilyard, still hovering at the doorway. "Send word to the others—be ready to leave at dawn."

Avilyard bowed and hastened from the room.

Desislava turned, making for the door. "By the way, I spotted a were tribe on my way here. They may arrive in time to join your fight."

"Thank you," Marai said. "You've given us time to assemble."

"You're welcome, Faerie Queen. I bid you farewell, and good luck."

"Won't you stay and fight with us?"

An additional vampire would be a huge asset.

Desislava paused, glancing back over her shoulder. "I think sinking a ship of Guardians pays for any debt I owe you. Surely, you, the Faerie Queen, the most powerful fae born in centuries, can handle Cavar. What difference would I make?"

"I've learned that one person can be the difference to tip the scales of favor in battle."

"That may be so, but I smelled another vampire lingering around here," Desislava said. "Rare to find one of my kind willing to help humans and fae. You have his skills. You don't need mine."

With that, she disappeared in a blur.

CHAPTER 44

RUENEN

Ruenen's chest felt like it would cave in on itself. That his heart was being eaten away by fear. That his strong, courageous, stubborn wife would sacrifice herself, or sustain injuries past the point of healing.

Neither of them slept. Marai was restless. Her legs twitched, she'd bolt upwards, eyes darting to the window, sensing Cavar and the amulets growing closer and closer. Marai dealt with a bout of morning sickness, and Ruenen held back her hair as she emptied her stomach into a bowl. When her nausea subsided, Marai crawled under the sheets again, exhausted, anxious. The dying flames in the hearth cast somber shadows across his wife's tense face as she lay back down, her pale cheek resting on the pillow.

How could she fight in such a state?

Ruenen lay his hand on her flat stomach. *Be safe, little one.*

Perhaps it was his imagination, but he felt something flicker, a tiny pulse, press against his hand. It was too early for the baby to quicken. Ruenen met Marai's eyes. She'd felt it, too.

Magic.

When the sun rose, they ate breakfast in silence. Dressed in silence. It wasn't as if they had nothing to say to each other. There were far too many things Ruenen wished to say, sitting at the back of his throat, nearly choking him, but Marai's face was drawn with concentration and deep focus. He didn't want to distract her with his fear, his protectiveness.

Marai helped Ruenen into his golden armor. She, of course, wore nothing but black gambeson and leather, Dimtoir at her hip beneath a thick, black coat. She would have worn less if it wasn't so cold. Hand in hand, they made their way out of the noiseless castle.

Avilyard, Holfast, and Rhia bid them farewell at the portcullis. They'd remain in Kellesar with a small handful of soldiers, maintaining an official presence in the hopes that the battle would be swift and life would resume as normal within a few days. Marai hadn't told the trio of the true dire circumstances of Cavar's arrival. Although their faces were somber, Avilyard and Holfast didn't understand that their King and Queen may not return.

But Rhia certainly knew the power of dark magic. Her voice wavered as she spoke to Marai. "Make sure to get rid of it for good, Your Grace."

Marai and Ruenen grabbed horses from the stables, and clip-clopped down the winding, empty streets. The fae, werewolves, Nosficio, and King's Guard waited for them on the drawbridge, equally as quiet. Thora sat in front of Raife on their horse, leaning back into his chest. It made Ruenen ill seeing her head towards battle, but their army needed her healing skills.

Gods, if you're listening, please protect my friends and family. Please spare them.

Ruenen gazed at the colorful congregation of folk and humans; roughly fifty people stood between Cavar and Nevandia. This wouldn't be a battle between vast armies, nothing like the war with Tacorn and Varana. Ruenen, in his fragile human skeleton, felt miniscule amongst such powerful beings, woven from magic.

What difference can I make in this battle? It wouldn't matter if he was there or not. He was probably more of a hindrance than a help, but Ruenen refused to leave Marai and his friends.

Their small army remained silent as they rode hard; fae, weres, and humans interspersed, horse hooves pounding against the earth. The sloping, snow-coated moor transformed as a dense, frosted forest came into view. This spot demarcated the border between Nevandia and Syoto. Marai sensed the magic coming from that direction; the same route Ruenen had recently traveled when he'd gone to Baatgai.

All that was left to do was wait and stare into the shadowed white of the forest. Trees creaked as wind moaned through their bare, gnarled branches.

Marai didn't move a muscle, so poised was she, standing there with Dimtoir at her hip and knives buckled to her legs and forearms. Wild energy vibrated off her, charging the air so that the hair on Ruenen's neck and arms rose. Her black clothing against the pearly-white snow made the colors in her wings all the more vibrant. They fluttered at her back, the only indication of her anxiety.

She refused to appear weak in front of her people, to let them know her uncertainty. If she crumbled, so would they. Ruenen tried to keep her same composure.

"Do you think Desislava will come?" he asked.

Marai's mouth tightened, but she didn't reply. The answer was clear: no.

Thora lingered in the back of the group, worrying her bottom lip and gripping the strap of her medical bag tightly. Her orders were to hide behind the large boulder behind them once Cavar appeared. She'd be on-hand in the event of an injury, but Marai didn't want her in the thick of it like last time. The fallen would be brought to her, safe in the shelter of the boulder. Thora had frowned at this. She'd bravely risked her life during the war, treating soldiers on the battlefield, with limbs and blood flying around her.

"Cavar would love to claim you," Marai said when Thora protested. "You have skills he'd prize. Stay hidden, and if the battle goes ill, take a horse and leave us. Get to Dul Tanen. Run. Hide."

Thora clamped her lips shut, glaring at Marai, but she, too, would obey her Queen.

Marai's fierce eyes slid to Ruenen. "You should join her."

"You expect me to leave my wife and friends to fight this battle alone?"

"I'm not doubting your skills, Ruen. There's absolutely nothing even the greatest swordsman can do against magic," she said, using the unfeeling voice of the Butcher.

"The King's Guard is here. Should I tell them to leave?" Ruenen challenged.

"They're soldiers, not the King of Nevandia." Marai's face softened for a fraction of a moment. "Those men aren't the father of my child."

Ruenen dropped the opposition from his posture, old habits of dealing with the Lady Butcher. But this was his wife talking, his partner.

"If you leave now, you could make it to Kellesar before they arrive," she said, quieter, with a slight waver. "Cavar isn't after you. Maybe he'll leave Nevandia alone if you leave. He wants me. He wants revenge."

Ruenen took her hand and brought it to his heart. "I won't let you leave this world unless I'm by your side. No, Sassafras, I'll stay with you until the end."

She squeezed his hand in acknowledgement.

"Marai . . . come see this," came Raife's voice, tinged with warning.

Ruenen and Marai rushed to his side, spotting the mass of figures, a smudge on the snowy horizon, heading towards them.

"Here they come," Marai said.

Shouts traveled down the line. Weapons were drawn. Metal slid from scabbards. Bows strings tightened with a creak.

Ruenen squinted, trying to make out the shapes of the people galloping towards them. They didn't *look* like approaching Guardians . . .

Anja's pale, fae eyes suddenly widened. "Wait—it's Athelstan!"

The lead figure in the front of the group waved from atop his horse. Anja waved exuberantly back.

Another pack of werewolves, ten strong from the Greltan White Ridge Mountains.

Athelstan jumped down from his shaggy horse and immediately hugged Anja. He looked far heartier than when Ruenen had last seen him. He'd put on weight and muscle, but his hair remained prematurely gray, and haggard lines still cut across his face. He smiled widely as he shook Ruenen and Marai's hands.

"Thank you for coming, and such a long way, too," she said.

Athelstan's sudden return meant a lot to her. Ruenen didn't need to see Marai's eyes crinkle in held-back emotion, or hear the way her breath stuttered, to know that.

"When my Queen calls, I answer," said Athelstan with a bow. The pale Northern wolves with him were his cousins and uncles, nephews, and one niece. Werewolf packs were typically tight family units, Ruenen had learned from Tarik.

"Where's Nosficio?" asked Aresti. Her two signature short swords were strapped to her back. She wore no golden armor today, and neither did Raife.

Armor wouldn't protect them from dark magic; it corroded even the toughest of metals.

"Scouting ahead," Marai replied distantly. "He'll meet us here when he feels like it."

The sun lowered from its apex, shedding a coppery glow across the snowy moor and canopy of the trees. The shadows in the forest grew darker, transforming it into shades of blue. Fat flakes of snow fell faster, creating another layer on top of the fresh blanket from the previous day. At this rate, no one would be able to see anything during the battle, but maybe that was Cavar's strategy. After all, he didn't have reservations about using his magic and accidentally hurting others. He'd come to kill or collect.

Marai stepped forward. Ruenen saw the formation of an idea brewing in her wild eyes. She addressed Tarik and the weres. "Would you be willing to turn?"

Tarik started, then frowned. "It's not a full moon tonight. Nothing to be done about it."

Innesh came to Marai's side and held up her amulet. "I bet this could help."

Marai trusted her to wield it in battle since Innesh seemed to understand best how it worked. Athelstan flinched away from the amulet. The mere thought of having that transformation forced upon the poor werewolf again made Ruenen queasy.

"Only those who wish," Marai said to him and the other weres, "but I think it could work, even without the collars."

Tarik's face grew dark. Brass fidgeted with the end of his long, braided beard. Yovel and the female werewolf from Athelstan's pack exchanged hesitant looks.

"I can't promise that it won't be painful," continued Marai, "but you'll be stronger and faster once you've turned."

"Sure, but we can't exactly control ourselves. We could attack you or anyone else here by mistake," Brass said.

"I could control that," came Athelstan's soft voice from the back of the pack. "I couldn't control when I shifted, but I learned how to switch off the wolf's brain and keep my own."

Tarik approached him, eyes alighting with intrigue. "How?"

"There's a part of your brain, right here—" Athelstan pointed to the back of his skull, "that I've always envisioned as a lever. It's not truly a lever or anything, just a form of consciousness or something. While you're shifting, imagine pulling the lever. It won't work once you've shifted, but if you do it while your human brain is still conscious, you'll keep your rational mind fairly clear."

Tarik's jaw dropped. "You're a genius."

Color flushed Athelstan's cheeks. "No, I've simply had far too much experience transforming, compared to the average were."

Five nights a week multiplied by seven years. Ruenen didn't need to do the calculation to know that it was an unheard of number for a werewolf.

"I'll do it, if it means we take down Cavar," Athelstan said, coming forward and drawing himself up to full height. "We need every advantage possible, and if my Queen asks it of me, then I'll oblige."

"How long will it last, Uncle?" asked the female werewolf, a pretty brunette about the same age as Daye.

"The collar controlled the timing, so I'm not sure. It may be a few minutes, hours, or forever, unless you use the amulet to stop it," said Athelstan.

Tarik lifted his chin. "If this is what you need from us, Marai, then we wolves will do what must be done. This battle's going to be unpleasant either way." He unstrapped the ax and sword from his body, then set them by the boulder, accessible if needed. The other werewolves did the same.

A dark blur appeared, stirring Ruenen's hair.

"They're nearly here," Nosficio said in a voice as hushed and heightened as midnight. "I'd hoped to kill some off as they traveled, but they have a barrier erected around them, impossible for me to penetrate."

Everyone stiffened, shifting their weight, focusing on the forest. Hands tightened on weapons. Fae fingers flexed, readying their magic.

"How many?" asked Marai.

Nosficio grimaced. After a beat, he said, "Enough."

"Any vampires?"

"None that I smelled," said Nosficio in disappointment.

Night fell steadily around them, drenching them in darkness.

"Light the bonfires," Marai ordered.

Raife sent jets of vermillion flames to the piles of wood they'd gathered earlier. Five bonfires exploded to life, granting some light on the moor. Above them, a half-moon crawled into the sky.

Marai turned to her small army of folk. "For too long, our people have wandered in the dark. Tonight, we make a stand. Tonight, we show the world we're not afraid. Remember—it's the amulets that hold magic. Get rid of the amulets, and the Guardians are powerless." Marai lowered into a fighting stance. Dimtoir's blue blade reflected both firelight and moonlight. "Their human eyesight will be hampered by the darkness. We'll have the advantage there."

Innesh raised one of her jagged knives as she glanced to Anja at her left, and Wilder at her right. "People of the Menagerie, let's show Cavar that we're not his property. We'll die before we let him take us back."

Wilder and Dante stomped their hooves in agreement. Cyrill rubbed his hands together in eager anticipation. Anja bounced up and down on the balls of her feet, wings anxiously flitting, as Athelstan shook hands with those around him.

Innesh then lifted the bronze amulet into the air, facing the wolf pack.

"Do it," Tarik said, his voice deep and determined.

Innesh willed her desire into the amulet, and it pulsed once with cryptic blacklight.

The werewolves buckled over in pain. Some fell to their knees in the snow, pounding the ground with their fists. Tarik grit his teeth, as if he refused to show weakness. Ruenen had never seen a wolf shift before, and he realized then that he never wanted to again. Their bones crunched and snapped sickeningly, growing, broadening, changing shape. Fur sprouted across their bodies. Vicious teeth elongated in their mouths, and fingernails lengthened to claws.

Brawnier and taller than normal wolves, they truly were a horror to be seen, with their wide, gaping maws growling and dripping saliva. It was nearly impossible to tell who was who. Two werewolves snapped at each other, standing too close together.

But there was consciousness in their eyes. No malicious intent to hurt as they turned their gazes on the others around them. Athelstan's description of the lever must have worked.

The largest of the weres, with wiry black fur and dark brown eyes, loped forward, assessing his enlarged pack. *Tarik.* He turned to Marai and nodded with his enormous head.

A twig cracked in the forest.

Heads snapped in that direction as the world went quiet.

Then a wall of darkness consumed them all.

CHAPTER 45

MARAI

M arai flung up her shield.

It snapped into place, making a concussive, ear-ringing sound, overlapping with Braesal and Finneagal's to fully surround Marai's miniscule army in a dome of invisible magic.

Darkness splattered against the barriers like black paint upon canvas. It slithered along, searching for cracks and chinks, blocking out light from the bonfires and moon above as it covered the dome completely. Marai couldn't see Cavar and his Guardians through the darkness.

"We can't hold this for long," Finneagal grunted, already shaking.

Marai could only see him thanks to the soft glow of his peach-and-maroon-colored wings. Finneagal and Braesal's barriers weren't as steady as Marai's, and hers was nothing compared to what Keshel had been able to achieve. Another sharp reminder of how badly Marai missed him. *Everything would be better if he was here.*

They could do nothing with darkness smearing across the barriers, blocking their view of Cavar. Who knew what he was doing on the other side?

"Get down and be ready to split up," Marai said over her shoulder.

At her side, Ruenen covered his head with his arms. *He shouldn't be here,* Marai thought for the hundredth time, but her husband was as stubborn and reckless as she was.

Marai addressed Braesal on her left and Finneagal on her right. "When I give the word, drop your barriers and duck like the others."

"Yes, Your Grace," they both echoed.

Marai gathered her power, felt it coursing through her in sizzling strands. "Down!"

Braesal and Finneagal dropped to their knees, their barriers disappearing with a *pop*. Marai's exploded outwards.

Lightning slammed against the black wall of Cavar's magic, igniting the night with white-hot power. The blast shattered the darkness like a pane of glass; shards of magic fell to the ground and melted the snow beneath it. The scent of something scorched hit Marai's nostrils. The acrid, sooty scent of decimated magic.

Marai had forgotten how *good* it felt to use this power. She hadn't accessed lightning since destroying the Menagerie, and her whole body tingled, relishing the magic and strength flooding her senses.

There, in the tree line of the forest, stood a closely clumped row of shadowed figures. Marai could make out fifty, perhaps sixty, bodies. She couldn't tell who was who. Cavar and Koda were camouflaged with the night, but no fog barrier surrounded them. They were vulnerable.

Marai's army scattered. Winged fae took to the skies.

Streams of fire, water, and wind sped towards the dark figures. Speed was Marai's main weapon. Her army was relying on the fact that the Guardians were slower, less trained for battle. Aresti, Raife, Braesal, and the other fae would attack swiftly and relentlessly, distracting the Guardians, keeping them occupied, while everyone else aimed for the amulets.

Guardians dodged their attacks, diving into the snow, behind trees and rocks. Raife ignited a row of rowans. A Guardian shot back a wave of their own fire to challenge. Black and vermilion flames clashed, spitting tendrils of fire across the moor. Both attacks burnt out after a moment; smoldering embers mixed in the air with floating snowflakes.

Normal elemental magic couldn't compete against the amulets for long. Marai's friends would deplete their power if they didn't end this quickly.

In the chaotic darkness, with fire, wind, water, and snow swirling around her, Marai searched for Cavar. The figures in the trees all looked the same from this distance. She gathered another round of lightning, hands glowing as two balls of crackling, flashing light appeared in each palm. She unleashed again, and lightning snaked towards the trees.

Within seconds, a barrier of thick, gray mist appeared.

That must be where he is. Cavar revealed himself, right smack dab in the center of everyone. The obvious, arrogant place to be.

Marai's lightning crashed against his barrier. Strands of electric splinters climbed up the wall of fog. Unlike the lightning, Raife's fire and Aresti's wind snuffed out when they collided with the mist. Their magic couldn't penetrate it, but perhaps Marai's could if she put more power behind her attack. She reared back, ready to strike again.

A warrior's roar sounded, halting her.

Dozens of figures burst through trees, fog, and snow. Swords glinted, reflecting the bright light of Marai's power, moon, and bonfires. Cavar's red-vested Peace Keepers joined the fray, rushing forward across the field. Gold-armored King's Guard met them halfway. Their blades collided in singing, clashing metal. Humans versus humans in a battle of magical wills.

And there, swinging his sword amongst them, was Slate Hemming.

Marai should have guessed the snake would slither his way back onto Cavar's crew. He'd probably captained one of Cavar's ships, the bastard.

As he cut down a King's Guard, Slate's blue-eyed gaze sought out Marai. He blazed a pathway of carnage towards her, revenge fueling his every swing.

Enormous wolves loped across the moor, followed by the galloping Dante and Wilder. Tarik, in the lead, leapt onto a Peace Keeper and tore him to shreds with his teeth and claws.

Marai couldn't focus on Slate. Someone else would hopefully kill him before he reached her.

She concentrated her attacks at the center of the barrier, a constant barrage of lightning aimed solely on Cavar. But nothing penetrated through the fog. At least four different amulets, not Cavar's alone, had to be producing that kind of barrier. Lightning spewed from her fingers in white-hot strands, but she couldn't burn a hole through that fog.

Marai released a frustrated growl. *I'm wasting power.* She needed to conserve energy, but she'd never get a chance to eliminate Cavar if they couldn't get the damn barrier down.

Out of the corner of her eye, she spotted the dark outlines of a massive wolf, two sets of faerie wings, a tiptoeing hunched figure, and two humans running together across the moor. Innesh's team of Anja, Brass, Cyrill, and Zorish was on the prowl, hunting for Koda. Marai hadn't sensed a tingle from the faerie male yet. He was hiding, somewhere behind the fog, waiting for his turn.

But who was the second human with Innesh?

Marai's body clenched as she made the realization. She dared a glance over her shoulder.

Oh, Lirr's Bloody Fucking Bones.

Ruenen wasn't there.

CHAPTER 46

RUENEN

He hadn't planned on joining Innesh's group, but Ruenen felt useless standing safely behind everyone else, including Marai, as they did all the work. He was a trained fighter. He wasn't helpless.

Besides, he had his own personal vendetta against Koda. The bastard knew Ruenen wasn't the rightful King of Nevandia by blood. Ruenen had to ensure the male went down so that no one would know the truth.

"Can Koda do anything else besides his immobilizing trick?" Ruenen shouted to Anja as they ran towards the far right side of the fog barrier.

"Usual fae magic—igniting a flame, messages on the wind, but nothing strong," she panted back. "His magic focuses on freezing the nervous system. We cannot let him snap his fingers."

Ruenen's hand curled around the pommel of his sword. *Then we'll need to cut them off.*

Innesh roared into the night, legs pumping as she approached the fog. "Koda, you fucking dog, show yourself!" Two knives glinted in her fists. The heightened magic in the air had Innesh's long hair rising around her like a black halo. She was a fierce sight to behold, as intimidating as the Lady Butcher, with her bared teeth and black tattoos stark against her brown skin. "That's right, hide behind your master, you groveling piece of shit!"

Ruenen and Zorish exchanged glances. *Lirr's Bones, I never want to be Innesh's enemy.* No wonder she and Marai got along well.

Someone materialized out of the fog, mist curling around him as he strolled, hands in his pockets, in an unhurried way. His confident molten-silver eyes gleamed like moons in the night. A sword sheathed at his belt was his only weapon.

"Looking for me?"

Quick as a whip, that easy-going exterior vanished. Koda's hand shot out from his pocket.

Zorish threw up his arms, erecting a barrier around the team right as Koda's fingers snapped.

The sound of the snap seemed to echo amongst the swirling snow.

Zorish's shield worked. Ruenen could still move. *But the others . . .*

Ruenen held his breath as he glanced to Marai, Raife, and Aresti fighting across the moor. None of them had been affected by Koda's magic, which meant that the radius of his abilities was smaller than Ruenen had originally thought. Good news for Innesh's team.

Koda smirked, eyeing Zorish, who was already struggling to hold the barrier in place. "Smart, but for someone of full-blood, you're rather weak. I can outlast you. Best to give up now and come quietly."

"Not if I saw off your head first," Innesh said, steel flashing as she twirled a knife in her hand.

The cockiness drained from Koda's stance. Something like hurt flashed across his face. "Why are you doing this, Innesh? Why are you making me your enemy? I've protected you—"

Innesh bristled, hackles raised, accurately mimicking Brass in his wolf form. Ruenen took a tiny step back from her.

"You allowed Cavar to enslave me for fifteen years," she snarled, "and you never once tried to release me. You stood by as he imprisoned and abused me, after you swore you'd care for me." Innesh scoffed. "Foolish, adolescent promises from a weak-willed craven."

"I had no choice! Cavar will lock those shackles around me, too, if I don't follow orders. I do what I have to do to survive, Innesh. This isn't a kind world to people like us. I thought you understood that."

Ruenen chuffed. *Is he still in love with Innesh? The bastard had a dumb way of showing it for fifteen years.*

Koda refused to back down. "Cavar would have killed you by now if I didn't have his ear. I've convinced him to keep you on, despite your impertinence, and I've never been unkind to you, have I? Never abused my status over you."

His words only infuriated Innesh more. "You're the lowest of low. No curse, in any language, is good enough for you."

Koda flinched at those words, and took a step closer. "Innesh, please. You mean so much to me. Though you've scorned me, every day I got to see you in the Menagerie was a blessing because we were still together. Cavar has no quarrel with you. He wants you to come back. *I* want you to come back."

"Is he serious?" Ruenen murmured to Cyrill.

The goblin shrugged in response.

How could Koda claim to care for Innesh when he'd allowed her to suffer for fifteen years? That wasn't love. That wasn't kindness.

Or was this a ruse to weaken Innesh, diminish her fury, because Koda viewed her as a threat?

Koda's eyes shimmered. He held out an inviting hand. "Come back with me, Innesh, and we can talk this through. We can start again, maybe even as Guardians on Andara. If you stay here, you'll die with *them*."

He jerked his chin to Marai and the others across the moor, still flinging their power at the unrelenting fog.

Ruenen heard the honeyed manipulation in Koda's voice. Innesh did, too. If she had any magic in her veins, Ruenen bet Koda's body would be on fire from the raging inferno dancing in her eyes.

"I'd rather die," she stated, her tone promising violence.

Unfortunately, Koda was right—Zorish couldn't keep his hold on the barrier. It gave way with a *pop,* leaving them all exposed to Koda's magic. Innesh threw her knife straight at Koda's chest, but her ex-lover was fast. Koda dodged the blade as his thumb and middle finger touched.

Ruenen's breath caught in his chest again.

But Anja was faster. She tossed a ball of blue flame at Koda. It landed at his feet, engulfing his shoes. He leapt back, dowsing his smoldering boots in the snow. Innesh closed in, crowing a warrior's yell. Brass' furry body launched itself at Koda, slobbering maw gaping wide.

Koda slipped, regained his footing. "Dammit." His fingers snapped before Innesh or Brass could reach him.

Ruenen held his breath yet again.

No one froze. Innesh and Brass crashed into an invisible barrier. To Ruenen's left, Zorish had flung his arms up again. Sweat dripped from him as Zorish's body heaved. This barrier wouldn't last much longer than the first.

Innesh used the momentary pause wisely. She hurled insult after insult in Koda's face. Ruenen had never heard such a spectacular array of curse words before. Some were in the common tongue, but others were in Yehzigi and Andaran.

As each insult landed, Koda grew angrier, more upset. His body tensed, his silver eyes flared. He snapped, over and over, waiting for the moment when Zorish would drop the barrier from exhaustion. Each time, Ruenen felt the impact of his magic against the barrier, like a pounding fist trying to get inside by breaking down the door.

"I can do this for hours," Koda taunted as he snapped again. "You'll die where you stand. Frozen. Helpless. But you'll still feel the pain. And when I'm done, I'll immobilize Marai. Cavar will put a new, stronger collar around her neck. She'll be his slave for eternity."

"That's my *wife* you're threatening," Ruenen said, coming to the edge of the barrier with his sword unsheathed.

"Oh, that's tragic," said Koda with a laugh. "You came all the way to Andara to rescue Marai, only to have her stolen away again. This time, you won't get her back. Not when Cavar and I tell everyone on Astye your little secret."

Ruenen stiffened.

Koda looked to the others behind the barrier, grinning in triumph. "Did you know that the King of Nevandia really isn't Vanguarden's son? He's not even blood related. He *lied* to you. Everything about this kingdom is a sham. Once the people of Tacorn learn about this, they're going to burn it down, and kill those loyal to him."

Ruenen waited for the accusations to start, for the shocked and angry expressions upon the faces of his friends, but they never came. Instead, Brass snarled at Koda, teeth thrashing.

Anja stepped closer to Ruenen in support. "He's our King, no matter what lies you spout."

Innesh began her barrage of curses once again, and Cyrill held up a rude gesture at Koda. Perhaps it wasn't the right time, but Ruenen was incredibly grateful in that moment for their unwavering friendship.

Koda hadn't expected loyalty. He hadn't expected honor, since he, himself, had neither. His face contorted into a sneer as he watched Zorish fall to his knees, the male's whole body shaking, blue wings quivering with the effort.

"I gave you a chance," Koda said. He raised his fingers, meeting each of their eyes.

One pause.

One moment.

One held breath.

Zorish's arms fell. He slumped forward, on all fours, in the snow.

The shield disappeared. Koda's fingers began their slide a millisecond later.

Snap!

Ruenen's body went rigid as ice. He couldn't move. Not to blink or take a breath. Next to him, Anja, Innesh, Brass, and Zorish had suspended in time, as well; their expressions frozen masks of terror and shock.

A victorious grin bloomed on Koda's face. He unsheathed the curved sword at his side, and pointed it at Ruenen's heart.

This is it. This is how I die. Frozen like a statue, unable to defend himself, was a terrible way to go. Ruenen couldn't even turn his head to look at Marai one final time.

Goodbye, my love. Win this for me.

A black blur whizzed past Koda, so fast that Ruenen wasn't sure he'd truly seen it. A trick of the wind? A shadowed slant of firelight?

He heard the sick sound of steel slicing through flesh.

And suddenly, Ruenen could move again. His body collapsed from his frozen pose. He sucked in a mighty breath of frigid air as he observed the scene before him.

Koda's hands flopped into the snow at his feet, severed at the wrists, leaving two gaping wounds of blood and bone. He screamed, stumbling backwards, growing paler by the second as blood poured from his wrists.

Desislava stood next to Koda, holding Innesh's missing bloody knife in her pale hands. Her crimson eyes blazed as she crooned, "On behalf of the Shadow Menagerie, *fuck you.*"

CHAPTER 47

MARAI

Desislava had come. Momentary relief rushed through Marai as she cut down a Peace Keeper. Then another.

She'd been ready to abandon her own mission when Koda had immobilized Ruenen and the others. Thanks to Desislava, her husband was still breathing and moving. Marai tried not to be distracted by him and the scene playing out on her right, but she couldn't tear her eyes away.

A black-clad goddess of terror, the vampiress stood above Koda's bleeding body. A fanged smile spread across her lips, like a cat who'd stolen cream. Desislava gestured to Innesh, giving the former slave the final kill.

Innesh charged forward, knife raised above her head. The woman released a primal, vanquishing yell.

Koda fell backwards onto his rear, stained in blood and perspiration. He lifted his stumped arms as Innesh bared down on him, trying to block her blade, but he had no defense anymore. He relied too heavily on his magic.

Innesh's knife plunged deep between his ribcage. Koda let out a pained squawk as she sawed with the jagged edge, in and out of his chest. Cyrill jumped on him, like a spider, and joined in the carving.

Desislava bent down and picked up Koda's hands. She *sucked* on the wound, draining the hands dry of blood. Marai's already rocky stomach churned with nausea at the repugnant sight.

Another Peace Keeper hurled himself at Marai. She barely blocked in time; his curved blade sliced into her left arm. Marai hissed in pain, then whirled, and struck him down.

Stay focused.

Ruenen and the others were unscathed, but Zorish's magic was tapped out. His cyan and aquamarine wings drooped against his back, exhausted from the effort of holding that small bubble.

They'd beaten Koda, but he was nothing compared to the threat that lingered on the other side of the fog. Marai didn't know how many Guardians hid with Cavar. He'd brought plenty of guards with him, enough to occupy the weres and King's Guard. There could be reinforcements hidden behind Cavar's shield. Marai *hated* not knowing the true strength of an enemy.

Amidst the fray of battling bodies, Yelich spotted Marai. He ran for her, sword raised.

She rolled into the snow, dodging Yelich's downward slice. Marai leapt, cleaving Dimtoir straight through Yelich's gut. His body collapsed in a gory heap. Marai grimaced at her stinging wound. Blood dripped down her arm as she dragged her focus back to the fog, to her own duties.

Bring the barrier down.

The Peace Keepers were distracting her. Cavar had clearly instructed them to go after Marai, no matter the cost. Tarik lunged forward, ripping the head off an attacking guard. He planted his massive paws in the snow, blocking the path to Marai.

She didn't have time to thank him. *Focus.* Lightning ignited in her veins once again. She raised her arms and slammed magic against Cavar's barrier.

Nosficio appeared at Marai's side. He'd been running around the perimeter of the fog, trying to find a hole, a weak point, a way to break through.

"You're the only one who can bring that down," he said, Aresti's wind snatching at his dreadlocks and cloak.

"I'm aware," she snapped back. Another strike of lightning lashed the barrier. "Don't you think I've been trying?"

"You're not digging deep enough." Nosficio's eyes narrowed, and he stepped dangerously close to her, to the point where he could get electrocuted by an errant filament of lightning. "You gave everything you had in that battle against Tacorn when you tapped into your Life Energy. I know you're holding back because you're afraid of losing that child in your belly."

He'd smelled the shift in her scent. Marai couldn't hide such things from him, but Nosficio didn't know that the baby was Lirr's Chosen. How could he? Marai had never shared any details of Keshel's journal with him.

"You won't survive if you don't end this now," the vampire continued, letting his fangs show. "We'll *all* suffer the consequences if you don't break through that barrier. *Now.*"

Marai tensed. She couldn't risk harming her daughter. But she'd already failed Lirr once. Marai had made so many mistakes. The auburn haired girl was the chance for Marai to make up for calling upon the darkness. Keshel had spent the final weeks of his life ensuring Lirr's Chosen would have the guidance to do what she needed to do.

Marai couldn't fail Keshel. She couldn't fail her daughter.

Aresti staggered closer to Marai's side. "I can't keep doing this," she shouted above her swirling wind, creating a funnel of snow aimed straight at the barrier. Her body sagged as she kept pulling from within her shrinking well of magic.

Marai risked a quick scan of the moor.

Raife's fire sputtered at his fingertips. Braesal and Finneagal, flying high above the battle, could barely draw precipitation anymore, despite how saturated the air was with snow. Their wings struggled to stay aloft. The fae drained their magic to take down the barrier, but their efforts were *wasted*. They'd have nothing left to defend themselves when Cavar finally attacked. The King's Guard dwindled down the number of Peace Keepers, along with the help of ravaging werewolf fangs and claws. Nosficio savagely bit into a guard's neck, draining him of blood in seconds.

Slate, of course, still lived, drawn into battle with Nyle. The young knight could barely defend against Slate's sword skills, and the Captain wasn't even trying. His attention was utterly fixated on getting to Marai.

Everyone else was doing their part, except for her. If she didn't rally, the people she loved and cared for would be shackled and imprisoned for life. Ruenen would be executed by an angry mob of Nevandians and Tacornians.

Get Cavar's stone, Marai demanded of herself, clenching her teeth. *No one will lay a finger on my family.*

As she was about to tunnel deeper into her well of power, darkness finally made its appearance.

"*Oh, Marai . . .*" called a taunting, eerie voice in her head. "*You're losing.*"

Her body seized as a smokey talon stroked across her consciousness possessively.

"*Use me.*"

Marai took a deep, shuddering breath, trying to block out the alluring sound in her ears. Her magic kicked within her, like a heartbeat, in response.

The Dark Wielder was unperturbed by her rejection. "*I can save the babe in your belly. I'll shatter the barrier. I'll kill all those humans for you, my darling, including the Governor and Captain. Just use me.*"

Marai squinted, begging, *Go away, go away.*

This villain, the Lord of the Underworld, had already lured Marai away from the light once. Did this wielder, somewhere down below her feet, beneath layers of rock, shale, and mantle, still believe Marai was Chosen?

His desire saturated the air around Marai like a miasma. She felt it in the deep recesses of her mind. If Marai gave in to him, He'd have the power to destroy mountains, bring forth floods and earthquakes to wipe life off the planet. Maybe defeat the gods, themselves.

Marai couldn't let that happen.

"*Take my hand, Marai. It will be painless. We'll be One, as we always should have been. Our powers are meant to combine. Darkness and light create balance. You can become Queen of All.*"

Marai gagged. *Get out of my head.* She spat on the ground.

The darkness recoiled, as if its wielder was insulted. Its smokey residue disappeared from her brain, but His invasion left her shivering. He'd return to haunt Marai the longer this fight dragged on. She had to end this. No matter what it took, Marai couldn't allow Cavar to win, and she couldn't let the Lord of the Underworld have his way with her.

I hope you're strong enough, girl, she thought to the child in her womb. *Please, hold on.*

Marai dug deep into the untapped well of power within her. Like the birth of a star, it flashed to life with a cataclysmic explosion inside. Her body began to glow with blinding white light.

I'm Queen of the Fae, she shouted to the villain in the darkness, *and I'm more powerful than you.*

Marai swore she felt the Dark Wielder quail a little in surprise.

Fighting on the field halted. King's Guard, folk, and Peace Keeper alike shielded their eyes from the light and heat radiating from Marai's skin.

Against the darkness, I ignite.

Vengeful power fulminated from her pores. A tremendous *boom* and *crack* sounded as an eruption of lightning crashed into the barrier once more.

Marai burnt up every coil of fog and wisp of mist. Smoldering ashes of incinerated trees and Cavar's barrier rained from the sky. The forest was on fire.

She stumbled to a knee, body heaving from the effort of such an attack. During the pause, Marai glimpsed sixty human shapes running from the forest's edge. Blacklight steadily pulsed from the amulets at their necks. Some had fallen over from the impact of Marai's attack. Bodies were engulfed in flames, flailing and rolling in the thick snow to douse them. Hopefully, some were dead.

Cavar's army of Guardians was distracted.

Marai's army charged.

The younger, weaker fae and werewolves who'd been waiting in the wings, back by the boulder with Thora, rushed forward, joining the others. Daye and Lilly, dressed all in white, practically blended in with the snow, creating a successful sneak attack on a female Guardian who'd run too far onto the moor. The sisters brought her down in two strikes with their knives made of thorns; their white outfits now soaked with bright red blood.

The folk wreaked glorious chaos.

But Captain Slate Hemming wasn't giving up yet. He bludgeoned Nyle across the face with the pommel of his sword. The young knight went down, still alive, but unconscious. Slate left him there in the snow and prowled towards Marai.

She got to her feet, and raised Dimtoir, lightning sparking off the blade.

Fury detonated across Slate's scarred face. "I won't stop until I spear my sword through your head."

Marai flew at him. Dimtoir crashed down upon his blade, skating across the metal as Slate deflected. Lightning burned through the fabric of his jacket, searing the flesh of his arm. Slate reeled backwards with a yelp.

She didn't have time to waste on him. Cavar would take advantage of her distraction. Speed was her one advantage over Slate's sword skills.

Marai pummeled him with attack after attack, weaving and twirling like she was made from the rushing wind. Every attack he blocked, she returned with another, changing up her targets and angles, leaping and dodging his swings.

Slate was on *her* turf. He wasn't used to fighting in snow.

Marai tumbled away from his strike, and gathered up snow in her fist. She chucked the compact ball; icy snow hit Slate square in the face. His feet slipped as he tried to wipe the snow from his eyes, spewing frantic curses. Marai rammed her shoulder into his chest, knocking him down.

Slate dropped his sword. His fingers desperately reached for it, as the other hand reached for Marai's throat. His legs bucked to get her off, but Marai held on, releasing her inner hellion, and punched him in the face.

Slate roared in anger. He thrust his hand up under her jaw.

He's trying to break my neck.

The tip of Dimtoir slid into his stomach, and up beneath his ribcage. Slate emitted a shocked, strangled sound as he gazed, bug-eyed, at the fatal wound.

But Slate Hemming had returned from the dead far too many times. Marai wouldn't take any chances. She sent a wave of electricity through the handle. Slate's insides were charbroiled. His jaw clenched as his body violently convulsed.

Satisfied, Marai withdrew her magic, releasing him from the seizures. Blood spurted from Slate's mouth as he coughed.

Marai leaned forward, lips inches from his ear. "This time, Slate dear, stay dead."

She rolled off him, ripping Dimtoir from the wound. Blood gushed and Slate Hemming went still, blue eyes wide with shock.

Marai backed away, panting. Her ears hummed. Vision blurred. Reality and time caught up to her, swarming her brain. She stared, unblinking, at his body.

Slate was nothing more than a corpse, lying in a pool of crimson.

Marai let out a rasping, victorious laugh. *Finally.* He'd never haunt her again. Touch her. Torment her. Tears stung her eyes as Marai gave her younger, innocent self peace in this triumph. She gave that girl vengeance.

One devil down.

She wiped Slate's blood on her pants.

Focus.

Marai set her sights on Cavar.

CHAPTER 48

RUENEN

Dark magic leapt towards Marai's rushing army.

Visibility was difficult in the nighttime snow squall, and Ruenen could barely see what was happening around him. Bitter wind lashed his face. Ice stabbed his lungs with each breath.

One of the weres, Ruenen couldn't tell who, was devoured by a sheet of darkness. It wrapped around the werewolf's body like a blanket and burst into black flames. In seconds, there was nothing left of him but a pile of ash.

Four King's Guard were knocked off their feet as a wave of darkness submerged them. Ruenen cringed, heart stampeding in his chest, at the sound of their tortured screams.

Death by the power of the amulets wasn't painless or swift.

Ruenen ran towards the nearest Guardian. The man had fallen onto his fleshy rump, and was distracted by Wilder galloping past. Ruenen charged towards him, sword raised. The Guardian stumbled to his feet, tripping over his long, silk coat, and dropped his hold on his amulet.

Before Ruenen could get to him, Nosficio appeared, and ripped the Guardian's head clean off with a sickening crunch. Ruenen slowed to a stop. He'd intended to take the Guardian prisoner after collecting his amulet. The man had posed no threat without its power.

"I could've handled him on my own," Ruenen said to Nosficio, looking away from the gruesome sight.

This battle was vicious. Savage. Made worse by the snowstorm, which created a perfect blank canvas for the bright red of gore.

Nosficio plucked the amulet from the snow, and tossed it to Ruenen like it was a chicken bone. "Destroy it, wield it, whatever you want. But there's no sense in trying to spare lives tonight, Your Grace." He disappeared, onto his next victim.

Ruenen stared at the amulet in his grasp. He *could* use it against the Guardians... It began to glow in that strange, deep mauve light, sensing Ruenen's sudden interest. The temptation became stronger the longer he stared at the three-pronged symbol on its bronze surface.

Slapped by sanity, Ruenen came to his senses. The amulet *wanted* him to use it. It pried into his mind, luring him with temptations of power. Ruenen wouldn't become like Cavar. He dropped the amulet into the snow and swung his sword down upon it with a mighty strike. Cracks splintered up his blade, and the amulet remained unscratched, still glowing.

A blade couldn't destroy them. It had to be magic.

Movement in the sky snagged Ruenen's attention.

The winged shadow creature soared in circles above the battlefield. Braesal and Finneagal didn't seem to notice the vulturous stalker looming above the fray. His focus seemed glued on Marai. Not with the intent to help, but his wings beat steadily as he observed.

Ruenen waved his arms. "Oi! Bird-brain!"

The creature's head whipped to Ruenen.

"How about lending a hand? Or a wing?" called Ruenen.

The creature turned his attention back to Marai without a response. *Whose side is this thing on?* Ruenen gave the grotesque a rude gesture. *Bloody, overgrown chicken.*

Darkness hurtled towards Ruenen from the fringes of his vision, drawing his attention away from the creature. His chest seized as an ink-black beam of magic rushed closer.

Ruenen didn't have time to dodge that. He raised the amulet, ready to counter—

Someone knocked him to the ground.

Air rushed from Ruenen's lungs as Raife swept fire around them both like a vermilion cloak. Heat stung Ruenen's skin, making him sweat, but not a single tendril of flame or darkness touched him. The beam of dark magic burnt up on contact with Raife's fire. Once it was gone, Raife pulled back his magic.

"Thanks," Ruenen said, breathless.

Raife wiped his brow, cheeks red from the heat and stinging snow. "I don't know how much longer we can last."

They weren't losing. Not yet. But it felt imminent, knowing that the amulets' powers were endless, and the fae were starting to tire. Peace Keeper bodies littered the moor. Hemming had been butchered, and Ruenen suppressed a jig of joy at the bastard's demise.

Desislava appeared out of nowhere next to Raife. Without a word, she thrust four amulets into his hands, having disposed of their owners, before disappearing again.

Raife's body spasmed. He dropped the amulets into the snow, gasping for breath.

"What happened?" Ruenen asked, searching Raife's shaking hands for signs of injury.

"The power in those . . . it's too much for me to hold," Raife said. "I could feel it grating against my mind."

Ruenen picked up the amulets by their chains. "I'll hold onto them for now. Maybe Marai's lightning can destroy them."

When she's not battling for our lives . . .

He glanced at his wife, a blazing star in the middle of the battlefield. She glowed from the bottom of her boots, to the ends of her hair, to the tip of Dimtoir's blade. Her wings were incandescently white, as if she'd become lightning, itself.

A goddess dressed in faerie skin.

The sight of her took Ruenen's breath away. The winged grotesque gaped at Marai, too, from his position above. Proving she'd been gifted a goddess' power, Marai's lightning was locked in a battle with an unstoppable wave of black flames. Ruenen traced the darkness back to its wielder. Cavar stood in the tree line, grasping his stone with long fingers, muttering his will.

Ruenen shoved the five amulets inside the breastplate of his gold armor.

"With all of those, you're going to become their main target," Raife said.

"Don't worry about me. You take down the Guardians. I'll follow behind and collect the amulets."

Raife hesitated. "Be careful." He then rejoined the fray.

Ruenen stayed in the shadows of the trees, darting from one to another, watching, waiting. Another Guardian fell, blasted back against the trunk of a pine by Braesal's torrent of water. He struck his head on the bark. Ruenen dashed forward to claim his amulet while the man lay disoriented on the ground. Ruenen turned, tucking that amulet into his breastplate, and spotted Aresti, fiercely battling a man Ruenen recognized from Bakair. *Greguric,* Marai had called him later.

Aresti collapsed on the field, magic entirely spent. Greguric, seeing his opponent now weakened, barreled towards her. But he didn't reach for his amulet. Instead, he unsheathed a long, curved, fiendish sword with teeth. Aresti didn't have time to stand before he was upon her. She blocked his strike with one of her short blades. Greguric pushed with all his strength against Aresti's sword. He was a large, muscular man, and clearly a well-trained fighter. Aresti bared her teeth, sword-arm shaking as she struggled to hold him off.

Ruenen left the sanctuary in the trees, rushing to her aid.

Aresti's blade glided along Greguric's as she deflected, rolling on the ground away from him. She leapt to her feet, unsheathing her second sword. Ruenen reached her side as they faced down the Guardian.

"You're a foolish king to throw your lot in with them," Greguric said.

"And you're a bastard for enslaving magical folk," Ruenen shot back.

"You're only going to die in the end," said the Guardian. "Stop this folly now, pull your troops out, and let us finish off the folk. We can come to a financial agreement and make your kingdom a lot of money. Cavar already plans for Nevandia to become the first location of the Astyean Menageries."

Ruenen's stomach felt leaden down by jagged rocks. "I would *never* allow such an atrocity to happen anywhere on my land."

"That's only for as long as you're alive." Greguric turned his attention back to Aresti, appraising her up and down. "Your magic is too good to waste. A fair piece of pretty flesh, for that matter. You'll make a nice addition to one of the new Menageries."

Aresti's shoulders shook as she snarled. "Go ahead and *try* to capture me, you pus-filled boil. I'll skin you alive before that happens."

Greguric smirked. "So be it."

He attacked with the force of a Greltan white bear.

Ruenen and Aresti fought the Guardian, stroke for stroke. But Aresti was exhausted. Her attacks slowed, growing clumsier as the fight dragged on. Greguric knew how to use his body as a weapon. While blocking Aresti's blade, he managed a fierce uppercut to Ruenen's jaw. Ruenen's teeth clanged together, biting his tongue, his vision momentarily speckled with white dots.

While Ruenen was distracted, Greguric kicked out Aresti's legs from beneath her, and placed his blade to the skin of her neck.

At an impasse, Ruenen spit the blood from his mouth. That's when he realized that the collected amulets had fallen from his breastplate into the snow.

Greguric's eyes alighted. "You've got quite a hoard there."

He clasped his amulet as Ruenen tried to gather them back up. With a magnetic pull, the amulets flew from Ruenen's hands straight into Greguric's. They glowed in each other's presence, pulsating in an eerie rhythm. Greguric shivered as power coursed through him. He rolled his shoulders with a series of cracks.

His dark eyes seemed to glow with the stone's blacklight as he reared back, ready to take off Aresti's head.

A bolt of bright fire slammed into Greguric's back. The scorched Guardian roared in pain, staggering as he whirled.

Raife stood, panting, a glove of fire swirling around his wrist. The flames then guttered out, and Raife sagged. He tried to call forth his fire again, but only sparks spurt from Raife's fingertips.

Greguric cursed in Andaran, and returned fire with a matching bolt of obsidian flame. The flames were too fast, too widespread.

Raife ran. Fire licked at his heels. Miasmic smoke blocked Ruenen's view as Raife continued to run.

Faster! Faster!

Raife's boots were on fire. Black flames climbed the leather, dancing at the hem of his pants—

Ruenen's heart stopped when suddenly, Raife disappeared.

Gone. Winked out of existence with a gust of wind.

Greguric extinguished the flames, frowning.

Raife hadn't been . . . the flames . . . he hadn't been *incinerated*, had he?

Aresti shrieked his name, panic flooding her face.

A breeze ruffled Ruenen's hair. Nosficio appeared next to him, and set Raife down as if he weighed nothing. His crimson eyes met Ruenen's, silently admonishing, *Be more careful.* The vampire then blurred in a dark, smudgy haze. Gone again.

Raife was unharmed, other than the smoking of his charred boots, but there was no time for relief. Another crashing wave of onyx came barreling across the moor, straight towards them, sent by Innesh and her amulet.

Greguric turned, gaping as dark magic ascended upon *him*. Black flames slammed into Greguric, instantly cremating him and the amulets he carried.

But the magic wasn't done yet. It careened towards Ruenen, Raife, and Aresti. They dove to the ground, sliding in the wet snow, barely missing the cold, devouring darkness.

Innesh called off the attack with another message to the amulet.

"*Be careful,*" Aresti shouted at her.

"You're welcome," Innesh huffed in response.

Innesh had little experience wielding magic. She didn't have the precision of Cavar, whose magic sliced at Marai like a thin, black blade. He was a better wielder than Rayghast had been, so practiced and creative with its uses.

Marai used Dimtoir to block Cavar's attacks. Lightning twisted around the blade like a dozen galvanic snakes. The few strikes Marai didn't block or deflect continued onward, finding other targets to hit. They sliced through a boulder only a few paces from Thora, splitting it in two.

Aresti's anger at Innesh was cut short when one of Cavar's errant blades of darkness carved its way across the moor towards them. Her feet slipped in the snow as she tried to stand. Aresti didn't get up in time to dodge the blade.

Ruenen froze as darkness sliced right through her.

CHAPTER 49

MARAI

S creams rattled her eardrums.

Screams Marai recognized.

Screams of those she loved.

The memories of the Red Lands moor, when Kadiatu and Leif had been slain, and of Keshel holding the barrier in Bakair, were raw, ragged wounds Marai knew would never fully heal.

She could do nothing but watch as a blade of darkness sliced through Aresti's calf.

Thank the gods Aresti maneuvered around the blade, shifting enough to avoid severing her leg completely. But now the back of her calf revealed a gaping wound, straight to the white bone inside. Blood soaked the ground. Aresti remained lying in the snow, clinging to her injured leg.

That was all the time Marai could afford to watch. She had no choice but to yank her gaze away from Aresti, and continue the raging battle with Cavar.

He changed tactics. Instead of quick, flashy blades of darkness, Cavar formed a wall, as sturdy as stone. Marai erected her own wall of lightning to match. The two forces pressed against each other, grappling for control. The stone's never-ending power shoved against Marai's wall of lightning. Each laborious step Cavar took had Marai's numb feet sliding backwards in the snow. He crept closer, gaining ground.

Cavar, however, also began to show signs of fatigue. The muscles of his face were taut with focus and strain. How long could he continue pouring his will into the stone? How long before his concentration broke?

Marai was waiting for that one second to strike. One second was all she needed, and Cavar knew it.

A thousand black daggers sheared through the air at Braesal and River, swooping overhead. The pair blocked many, but River's arms covered her face as the remaining shards of darkness darted past her, slicing and nicking at her flesh. A shard lodged itself deep into River's shoulder. Another in her leg and left wing. She screamed, tumbling from the sky.

Braesal caught her before she slammed into the earth. River remained limp; one dangling arm dripped a trail of blood as Braesal ran her to Thora's boulder. Marai could only hope that Thora would be able to heal wounds made by dark magic.

The truth was glaringly clear: although Marai's army had cut the number of enemies in half, they were still losing this battle.

Bold-hearted Lilly leapt into action against Guardian Kovacevik. Blood-stained Daye followed. The sisters poured their combined, weak magic against the darkness. But they were no match for such power.

Marai's heart stuttered as Kovacevik's amulet created a dark, parabolic void. Its gravitational pull sucked the snarling vines and brambles of Daye and Lilly's earth magic in, dragging the girls along. They couldn't seem to release their magic; the tug on the vines from the void was too strong, swallowing snow and rocks inside its event horizon.

The sisters' small, struggling bodies, sent waves of scorching heat through Marai's arms and fingers.

She took a chance. With one arm still holding the lightning wall, Marai sent a bolt at the cavernous void. It imploded, disappearing with a ground-shaking explosion. Kovacevik and the girls were blasted onto their rears as the force nearly pressed Marai off her feet.

That distraction cost her.

Cavar edged closer. He was now halfway across the field, close enough that Marai would be able to see the detailed embossment of his coat if magic and snow didn't distort her vision. Cavar's wall of dark magic had widened, overshadowing Marai's barrier of crackling, hot light. Their powers clashed with impressive, earth-shuddering strength.

Dark magic from another Guardian chased down Dante as he galloped past Marai. One second, he was there, a dark brushstroke against the pearly-white background. Then, gone. Black smoke evaporated, revealing no trace of the centaur except his hoofprints in the snow.

"Give up, Marai," Cavar called, his strained voice echoing through the air. "Your selfishness will be the death of your friends."

Have I been selfish? Will he spare my family if I give in? Cavar's crazed expression answered for her—no, he wouldn't. He'd collect her family and friends, and add them to his new Menageries across Astye. And he'd tell the world the truth about Ruenen.

Snow lashed Marai's face. Frozen tears crusted her eyes. She was too aware of everything happening around her—every agonized cry, frightened shout, rush and whorl of black flame, each spurt of blood. The pristine snow of the battlefield was stained red and black.

Marai's arms trembled. Her finger joints locked and cramped. *I can't hold this much longer.* Her legs turned to jelly beneath her. Sweat froze on her temples, hair hardening to icicles as the spark, the fire within Marai, began to die.

CHAPTER 50

RUENEN

He hoisted Aresti into his arms. Her blood slid down the contours of Ruenen's gold armor, and he cringed at the sight of her exposed tibia, a gruesome wound. Aresti's tan skin grew sickly gray as the gash turned black. The scent of burning, singeing flesh made Ruenen's stomach roil.

Aresti was taller and heavier than Marai, and flailed about in protest as he carried her. Ruenen almost dropped her twice.

"I'm not some damsel in distress," said Aresti, pounding a fist on his back. "Put me down!" She then let out a howl of agony as she shifted her injured leg.

"Stop wriggling. You're going to be fine," Ruenen said. He was already breathless from running with her across the moor, dodging werewolves, faeries, and dark magic. "Thora will heal you."

Anja crashed into him, running the opposite direction, away from a pursuing Guardian. The impact knocked the wind from Ruenen's lungs. He dropped Aresti into the snow, and she bayed a slew of furious curses as she landed on her injured leg.

"I'm sorry, *I'm sorry,*" Anja wailed, tears and panic in her eyes.

The pursuing Guardian barreled closer. The snarling woman had a gash on her forehead, oozing blood into her eyes and hair. The Guardian, not much older than Ruenen, began to call upon her amulet.

Aresti shoved a knife into Ruenen's hands. "I can't make the shot." Her leg quivered of its own accord; more skin had turned black. Aresti's aim wouldn't be steady.

Ruenen wasn't skilled in knife-throwing. In fact, he'd barely tried it.

Aresti lifted her arms, taming the wild, whipping wind so that Ruenen had a better chance.

He sent a desperate prayer to Laimoen, God of War, as he drew back and flung the knife.

The metal glinted in the air, rotating, over and over. The Guardian was concentrating on the black flames climbing from the ground around her feet. She didn't see the knife heading for her stomach until it was too late. The blade lodged into her gut. Flames mushroomed into wisps of smoke. The Guardian toppled to her knees, and she fell face first into the red snow.

Ruenen gave himself five staccato pants, one moment of stillness, before hefting Aresti into his arms again, with Anja's help, and carrying her to the boulder.

The number of bodies scattered behind Thora's shelter had tripled: King's Guard, fae, werewolves, the little blue oni, all with varying degrees of injuries. Some lay deathly still on the ground, eyes closed. Ruenen couldn't tell who was dead and who was unconscious.

The sight of blackened lacerations on River's body was especially horrific. She was always bright and full of smiles. Now, River lay in the red snow, motionless and pale, lips turning blue. Her vivid hair seemed to dull, as if color leached from her, along with blood.

Braesal clutched her limp hand to his chest, whispering prayers and words of comfort to his partner. Ruenen's heart twisted in pain for Braesal. If that was Marai, he would have been inconsolable.

Ruenen placed Aresti as close to the bonfire as possible. Thora sucked in a breath when she saw the calf wound. She didn't need to ask if Aresti's injury was made from a blade or magic; the black, necrotic flesh spreading around the wound was evidence enough.

"Can you heal it?" Aresti asked her, eyes glazing over. She'd already lost a lot of blood.

Thora bit her lower lip. "It's not as simple as healing a regular blade wound." Her ginger eyes flashed to River. "Her lacerations won't heal. The blood won't clot. I need to remove the dark magic first."

"Can you?" pressed Ruenen.

Thora hadn't been able to remove the damaged tissue inside Marai's body.

She must have read the thought on Ruenen's face, because Thora said, "These are fresh wounds. I don't think the poisoned magic has had enough time to sink into the bloodstream yet. I'm hoping the damage is mostly external right now."

"What's the delay, then?" Aresti asked. Her head fell back against the ground—she couldn't hold her body upright anymore. Her chest rose in shallow breaths, puffing out like smoke in the frigid air, her brow creased with agony.

Thora leaned into Ruenen's ear. "If I do this, if I take the time to remove dark magic from Aresti and River's wounds, I'll drain myself completely. I'll have no magic left for at least a day. This means that if anyone else requires my help, regardless of the severity of their injury, I'll only be able to treat them the old-fashioned way."

With balms and ointments, stitching and cloth. A harsh reality that, without Thora's magic, most of Marai's army would already be dead.

Thora was leaving the choice up to Ruenen: deplete herself to save two, or reserve her power to save others, and let Aresti and River's wounds fester?

Already, since Ruenen had arrived with Aresti, the charred flesh around River's cuts had spread. Snowflakes stopped melting on contact with her bluish skin. Aresti lay in the powdery snow, face contorted in torment. She grew colder, weaker, by the second.

This was an impossible decision. Ruenen would be damning others if he told Thora to use up her magic to heal Aresti and River.

Ruenen watched Marai, her whole body alight, lightning crackling and snaking around her in a corona of power. She'd made an impossible decision only hours ago. She continued to make impossible decisions, by draining her magic against Cavar, by not giving up. The light around his wife grew dimmer. She was shelling out everything she had, struggling against the indomitable power of the amulets.

Thora will run out of magic soon, regardless. At least if Aresti and River were healed, perhaps they could rejoin the battle.

"Heal them," Ruenen said to Thora.

Marai would never forgive Ruenen or Thora if they let Aresti suffer and die from dark magic, especially if there was a chance to save her.

Thora nodded, face set. She started with River, hands hovering over the unconscious female's injuries. Braesal released his partner's hand as Thora's cerulean healing magic covered River's body in warm light, melting the snow around her. Thora's eyes narrowed, her jaw tensed, shoulders rose with focus and strain.

Slowly, curling ribbons of black smoke oozed from the wounds. Thora drew out the poison, and Ruenen was surprised at how much had burrowed into River's body in a matter of minutes. The smoke dissipated amongst the snow flurries. The black around and inside the lacerations disappeared as flesh stitched back together, leaving nothing behind but pale pink scars on River's skin.

Thora dropped her arms, sitting back on her heels. She closed her eyes, and released a harsh exhale, rubbing her swollen belly.

"Are you all right?" Ruenen asked, fearing for her babe.

"I can manage," she replied, but her voice was thin from fatigue.

River shuddered, and her blue eyes creaked open. "Am I dead?"

Braesal planted kisses across River's cheeks and forehead, her chapped lips, once again pink. "Not yet, my beloved. We'll be home with Holt and Fina soon."

Not yet. Ruenen exchanged a look with Thora. Her ginger eyes told him everything, how exhausted she felt, how fragile her hope was. Her chest rose and fell as she steeled herself for Aresti.

As with River, Thora's magic sucked the darkness from the grisly wound on Aresti's calf. Color returned to Aresti's cheeks, the tortured grimace on her face eased.

"You're a blessing to humanity," Aresti uttered as muscles, tendons, and tissues reformed her calf and the new skin around it.

Thora's magic sputtered out. She smiled weakly before falling sideways in a faint; Ruenen caught her before she hit the ground. Aresti yelped, clutching Thora's hand in panic.

"She's completely spent, that's all," Ruenen said, feeling Thora's steady pulse in her wrist. "Now it's her turn to heal."

Braesal shrugged off his coat, and draped it over Thora.

The injured oni crawled over, and said in a thick accent, "I watch her."

"Thank you." Aresti struggled to her feet, using the boulder as support. "Let's go."

"You need more time to rest," Ruenen said.

Aresti tossed her short hair from her face and speared Ruenen with a haughty glare. "There *isn't* time. Marai's almost empty, and there are too many Guardians still standing."

Most were dead or had been taken prisoner, defenseless without their amulets.

Aresti winced as she put weight on her newly healed leg, and Ruenen reached out to help her.

"I'm fine. It's just sore." Aresti hobbled a few steps, sucked in a breath, and dashed onto the moor, hiding the limp.

Following her lead, Braesal leapt back into the sky to rejoin Finneagal, Zorish, and the other winged fae shooting arrows down on the Guardians below. *Please, don't die, my friends.*

The night grew colder. Darker. Polar winds bit at his nose, whipped through the crevices of Ruenen's armor, as snowflakes fell in wet, heavy clumps, splattering across his frigid face.

Marai's army was on its last legs. The fae had no magic left. Most had resorted to weapons, but no blade could block the darkness. No arrowhead could pierce through the wall of magic. All the fae could do was dodge and leap to avoid getting hit.

A dozen Guardians congregated around Cavar in the middle of the field. They had the upper hand. They knew Marai's army was beaten. Most of the Guardians stopped fighting against the folk on the field, and used their amulets instead to reinforce Cavar against Marai.

Marai.

Thirteen Guardians against only her. Marai's light was so dim that Ruenen could barely see her through the nighttime storm.

Ruenen adjusted his numb fingers on his sword and ran. He couldn't stop Cavar. He was running to his death, but if he was to perish, Ruenen wanted to be at his wife's side. He was Marai's key, after all. If he couldn't help her, no one could.

Ruenen fought his way to his mate in the heart of all the madness.

Where darkness and light clashed in an epic battle for the fate of magic, itself.

CHAPTER 51

MARAI

*L*irr *gave me the power to defeat the darkness.*

I may no longer be Chosen, I may be stained, but I still have that power inside me.

I must win this.

Marai's blood was on fire from the constant usage of her magic. Heat radiated from her skin. At any moment, she wondered if she might burst into flames. Marai hadn't taken a breath, hadn't stopped for a moment. Her eyes were nearly blind from looking into the irradiant, white lightning.

Armor clattered behind her. She couldn't risk looking to see who it was, although her brain made a passing guess.

"I'm here, Sassafras," came Ruenen's voice.

The sound of him, so comforting, so full of love, stabbed her in the heart.

"No," she huffed through chapped lips and bared teeth, "get away." Marai couldn't afford to speak. She needed every scrap of energy she had left.

"I'm not going anywhere," Ruenen said, his voice closer now, just out of range of her corona of lightning.

Stubborn fool, but Marai was glad he was there. *If we're going to die, at least we'll be together.*

A gust of dark wind, and Nosficio appeared, covered in bloody viscera from mouth to the tip of his expensive leather boots. He tossed Ruenen a few amulets of the Guardians he'd killed.

"Too many remain. What's your plan?" he asked Marai.

Her army was falling back. Werewolves limped to Thora's boulder; most of them had shifted back already. Athelstan had to be carried there on Wilder's back. The fae drained the final remnants of their magic, congregating together, never once turning their backs to the enemy. Anja and Aresti ran hand-in-hand, seeking the safety of the boulder. Raife and Thora clung to each other, shivering from cold and terror. Soon, it was just Marai, Ruenen, Nosficio, and Innesh left on the field facing twelve unrelenting Guardians and Cavar.

Innesh, the madwoman, was combating four Guardians by herself with her own amulet. She stood her ground, surrounded by a pool of glowing blacklight, wind snarling her hair. Marai had never known someone with a stronger will, except perhaps Cavar. Innesh might have won against the Guardians on her own if Cavar wasn't there.

But his will was iron, forged by a blacksmith of the Underworld.

"I have no plan," Marai growled back at Nosficio. Her only plan was to continue expending magic until she ran out. There was no other option. "Get Ruenen out of here!"

Her husband jolted away from Nosficio, sword raised in defense. "No! I'll stay with you until the end."

"You're a distraction the Queen cannot afford," Nosficio said. "It's up to Marai and Innesh now. Desislava and I can't reach those Guardians when they're in a clump together, with magic flying every which way."

Marai's head echoed a carousel of curses she hadn't the energy to voice. It really was up to her and Innesh alone.

"Both of you need to leave *now*," she shouted over her shoulder.

Marai's knees buckled. One foot slipped in the snow. She fell onto all fours. Lightning fizzled out, leaving Marai, Ruenen, and Nosficio entirely exposed.

Cavar was ready. A beam of dark magic careened towards them, devouring snow and rocks in its path.

Marai called upon her magic, but nothing sprang to her fingertips. She tried again in desperation, but she was empty. Marai had no defense, no barrier, as that beam of darkness headed straight for her.

Nosficio couldn't gather Ruenen up fast enough, especially with her husband struggling against the vampire's arms, shouting her name.

Not like this!

Darkness was an inch away. Marai could see death lurking around its edges, in the corners of her vision. And death was cold. Lonely. Frightening and eternal—

A shadow blurred into existence in front of Marai. Long black hair fanned out around Desislava as dark magic plowed forward.

Marai didn't have time to shout her name. To reach for her. Desislava flashed a self-satisfied smirk at Marai before darkness engulfed her.

Blacklight sparked upon impact with Desislava's body. The vampiress shrieked, the sound of gut-wrenching, soul-devouring agony, and disappeared into wisps of burning smoke.

Marai choked on shock and fatigue. Desislava had sacrificed herself for Marai. For all of them. She'd blocked Cavar's attack. Nothing remained of the vampiress, who hadn't owed Marai anything, but had given up her immortal life. Marai couldn't move. It was as if she'd been turned to ice, immobilized by Koda's magic.

But Koda was dead. So was Slate. And Desislava, Dante, Elmar . . . and Keshel.

Black iron chains sprung from one of Cavar's hands, wrapping around Nosficio's arms and legs, searing into the vampire's skin. Nosficio staggered away from Marai, snarling as the burning chains tightened.

"*Release him,*" Marai cried.

Cavar stalked forward, his cruel smile curling with smugness, as his Guardians followed closely behind him, amulets at the ready. "Stop this, Marai. The loss of such potential pains me."

"Potential for what?" barked Ruenen. "Revenue for your new Menagerie? Potential performers for your sadistic show?"

Cavar ignored Ruenen. "Desislava was the perfect attraction. She wasted her life so flippantly." He regarded Nosficio, still struggling against the burning chains. "You'll be an excellent replacement, though."

"I'll rip out your shriveled heart, bastard, because your blood is too fetid to drink," snarled Nosficio, more vicious and wild than Marai had ever seen him.

Cavar was unperturbed as he kept striding forward. "Precisely the kind of bestial ferocity I'm looking for."

Marai struggled to her feet; Ruenen grabbed her arm to assist.

"You want me," she said to Cavar. "You're after me, so take *me.*"

Ruenen's fingers tightened on her body. His furious breath a hiss in her ears. "Marai—"

"Let Nosficio and the others go. If you promise to leave them unharmed, then I'll come with you to Andara, and I won't fight."

Cavar considered, angling his head to the side, placing his fingers on his chin in mock thought. "That's an interesting idea, but what use is one faerie queen?" The stone pulsed around his neck. "I must rebuild from the ground up, and restock my entire Menagerie." He gestured to the boulder where faeries, werewolves, goblins, onis, centaurs, and more stood shaking. "I have everything that I need right in front of me." Another set of chains lashed out and captured Raife around the ankle, reeling him in like a floundering fish. "Such as a fire wielding faerie the ladies will swoon over."

Thora shrieked as Raife clawed at the snow, searching for purchase, trying to crawl back to his wife. Aresti dove forward to catch his hand, but chains claimed her, too.

Fear consumed Marai as Raife and Aresti were pulled closer to Cavar.

"The one with the healing powers will be useful," said Cavar, observing Thora sob by the boulder. "I'll make a fortune off her abilities."

"*No,*" Marai shouted, but her legs couldn't support her.

Another set wrapped around Thora's wrists, but didn't drag her. Resigned, she walked forward as the chains slowly reeled her towards Cavar.

"And look, she has a babe on the way. How sweet." Cavar's smile grew. "Audiences will want to see it."

Marai wouldn't let Thora and Raife's child grow up a prisoner in the Menagerie, but she had nothing, *nothing* left to stop him.

Cavar gestured to his Guardians. Marai recognized some of their faces, but the terror inside her was too strong, she could concentrate on nothing else as more chains sprung from their amulets.

One by one, those black chains pulled Marai's struggling, flailing friends onto the field. Tarik, the only remaining were to remain in his wolf form, thrashed with all his might against the chains, but he lost the battle as he transformed back into a man, covered in cuts and bruises.

The pain of knowing her people, her friends, her family, were doomed to a lifetime of imprisonment and abuse was worse than a thousand lashes on Marai's back. Worse than slicing open her veins, one by one, and bleeding out into the snow. Worse than the pain Cavar had brought forth with Marai's dormant blood.

Marai couldn't protect them. She wasn't strong enough. She'd failed *everyone*. It was as if she was seeing Keshel, Kadiatu, Leif, and her parents die all over again. Each one another dagger in her heart.

"I hope you're happy, Marai," Cavar said, grinning maniacally at his horde of prizes. "Because of your rebellious selfishness, you offered up your friends and family to me on a silver platter. All it took was a little power and perseverance. I'll bleed them dry, like I did with Keshel."

A rivulet of black escaped his palm, weaving through the air and snow. The ribbon of darkness wrapped itself around Marai's neck, solidifying, squeezing, a python strangling its prey. Her heart screamed as the last ember of magic within her ebbed away. Marai clawed at the collar, pulse ratcheting to a frenzy.

"No!" Ruenen tried to pull the collar off with his fingers as she gasped for breath. His arms shook from the effort, his face a mask of horror, reddening as he pulled in vain.

Marai clung to him; she could feel her face turning purple.

"My Faerie Queen, back where she belongs," continued Cavar. "Any folk who *aren't* present . . . well, I'll go door-to-door in your kingdom and drag them out by their pointed ears."

The Guardians lifted their hands, amulets pulsating against their chests. Collars locked around the necks of every faerie, werewolf, and creature.

Ruenen gave up on trying to remove Marai's collar. He wrapped his arms around her and trembled. Even in his embrace, Marai couldn't feel safe. She could only think about her unborn daughter. She'd never get the chance to live, to grow up, and step into her power. Marai would never hold her.

I'm so sorry, she said to the babe.

Innesh charged Cavar, amulet blaring blacklight and magic in front of her. "Let them go!"

Cavar whispered into his stone. Within seconds, chains appeared around Innesh's ankles and wrists. She stumbled, and fell into the snow, dropping her amulet.

"Foolish woman," Cavar said, looming over her. "You're nothing more than a gutter-rat slave." He snatched up the fallen amulet.

Innesh cringed, folding in on herself, tears streaming down her cheeks as she gazed in horror at her shackled limbs.

This is my fault. My fault. I'm failing again! "Stop, please," Marai begged.

Cavar's fingers squeezed into a fist. At the same time, the iron around Marai's neck heated, searing the tender flesh beneath.

"Know. Your. Place," Cavar said. Obsidian flames flickered in his light eyes.

Ruenen lunged at Cavar with a swing of his sword. "Release my wife!"

Marai reached out to stop him, too late.

Cavar's magic brushed the blade aside, then slammed into Ruenen's stomach like a massive, gauntleted fist. His body went flying.

Marai released a wheezing, breathy scream as Ruenen crashed to the ground with a horrible crunch of metal armor. Her heart wouldn't start again until he moved. She couldn't breathe, her lungs had entirely frozen.

Ruenen finally coughed, spitting blood onto the ground. He lifted his head. Tears welled in Marai's eyes as he found her gaze. His gold armor, now dented, cracked, destroyed, had shielded him from the worst of the blow. The front of it had corroded away, the metal charred black.

Cavar *tsked,* shaking his head at Ruenen. "You don't seem to comprehend, Your Grace. I want Marai. You? Disposable."

Ruenen tried to get to his feet as a Guardian stalked towards him. The man kicked Ruenen in the jaw. Then the stomach. Marai heard his bones breaking. Ruenen grunted with each impact, and Marai's desperation became a blinding, all-consuming thing within her.

The other Guardians wrangled the fallen folk, pummeling and beating them. Thora wailed as a man backhanded her, then gripped her by her sable hair, dragging her further away from Raife. He roared, reaching for his wife, but couldn't move—a different Guardian stood on Raife's rib cage.

Slavery awaited Marai and her people. Her family and friends. Death awaited Ruenen.

Marai looked up at the night sky, ready to pray, plead, and beg to the gods.

The winged shadow creature hovered above. With one pale finger, he pointed to the ground. "Call."

The word, spoken in common tongue, rang through her. *Call.*

The gods weren't going to help her. The creature had given Marai the answer. Was it better to damn them all . . . or just her own soul?

Marai grit her teeth as she dropped to her knees. The Dark Wielder wanted her. She could bear the shame, shoulder the burden, as long as the others lived.

Because she wasn't a hero. She never had been.

Her fingers dug into the snow, and she *called.* She *pulled.*

Help me.

No response.

Ruenen swung out a leg on the Guardian's next kick, sweeping the man's feet out from under him. The man toppled, but whipped out a long, curved dagger. He plunged down, narrowly missing Ruenen's neck.

I need you.

A talon of darkness stroked the inner curtain of her mind. He enjoyed her begging.

Marai closed her eyes. She called louder. *Grant me the power to defeat the amulets.*

A shadowed face formed in her mind. A dark eyebrow rose. *"Where are your manners, Your Grace?"*

For Lirr's sake, please!

"I don't answer to Lirr or any god."

Help me save my family!

"You want me to kill the humans? Use my own power against myself? After your rudeness?" The voice was fucking toying with her.

Yes, she replied impatiently.

A slow, cat-like grin spread from His lips. *"Very well. But you owe me, little queen."*

Power flooded from deep underground into Marai's hands, up her arms, rippling, consuming, claiming.

The magic was intoxicating. Dark, slick, syrupy as molasses, yet as thin as cobwebs. Hot and cold at once. It was magic like she'd never felt before. How could she ever have thought to defeat this kind of power? Not even Lirr's Chosen could be stronger than what was now taking hold of Marai.

On her tongue, she tasted dusk and danger, that telltale scrape of pepper in her throat. The edges of her vision darkened with smoke. Black flames sprouted at her feet.

"Marai, no!" Ruenen knew what she'd done.

To save him, to save them all, she allowed dark magic to consume her, to control her in this battle.

The collar around her neck cracked and shattered. Marai guzzled down air as more power surged through her. Chains snapped, setting her people free once again. They quickly scattered, Guardians chasing after them. Raife rushed to Thora and pulled her away.

Cavar paled. He stepped backwards. Because the Governor recognized the orbs of blacklight in Marai's hands. Her lightning, once white and incandescent, was as pitch black as a moonless night.

"But I've done everything you asked," Cavar stammered, and Marai knew he wasn't talking to her. "I recaptured her. Marai was contained for you!"

She heard the sinister voice's response in her own head.

"Marai came to me of her own accord. She welcomed me. I no longer need you, Governor."

Cavar blanched. His eyes bulged.

Marai had no control as that foreign magic exploded. Bolts of onyx lightning shot through the skulls of the remaining Guardians. Cavar had enough sense and skill to put up a barrier before that tainted lightning crashed against the fog, sparks and embers skewed in all directions.

The desire for *more* power seized Marai, a dark cloud encompassing her every thought. She felt unstoppable.

QUEEN OF THE SHADOW MENAGERIE

"Together, you and I can surpass the gods," said the Lord of the Underworld. She could almost feel his cool breath against her ears. *"You could always have this power. Whatever you want, I'll give you. You need never be powerless again, Marai."*

The words intrigued her. The magic was as intoxicating as liquor, and Marai was becoming drunk with the obsession of it.

But Marai watched, a passenger in her own body, as black stains inched up her hands, her arms past the elbows . . .

The Chosen child in her womb, Marai's daughter, released a feeble pulse of magic. A warning. A farewell. Something warm and wet trickled down Marai's legs.

Pain and pleasure battled within her. *More power, more, more!* At the same time, her heart was shrieking.

Stop! You said you could save her!

The Dark Wielder laughed in response.

Lightning bored a hole in the fog, and Cavar's barrier finally broke.

Darkness struck him, melting the flesh from his bones in a gruesome, nightmarish image that would be branded into Marai's eyes forever. Cavar's hair and clothing burst into flame. The stone around his neck shattered, dissolving into dust.

Marai had destroyed the enemy, but she knew with certainty that the real enemy was the magic she'd allowed in.

Darkness released its hold on her, lifting away like the wings of a villainous angel. Marai collapsed to the ground. Skin sizzling, magic and energy spent. Empty. Damned.

"I'll be back for you, my Dark Queen," the Lord of the Underworld cooed. *"Another time, another place."*

Like the charred snowflakes falling around her, Marai's consciousness began to drift away. Darkness vanished to the Underworld, from whence it came.

"Because you're mine now." The Dark Wielder smiled again. *"And always will be, Marai."*

CHAPTER 52

MARAI

The emptiness was there when she awoke, warm in soft bed sheets.

It was a hollow emptiness, the kind where something essential felt like it had been torn away.

For Marai, she'd lost more things on that battlefield than she could count.

The scent of burning wood and smoke from a fireplace filled her lungs. The crackling of flames was the only sound.

She didn't want to open her eyes. Because then she'd see the evidence. By the slight chill in her fingers, toes, and limbs, she sensed where darkness had stained her. Half of her body, now blackened, served as proof of how she'd sold her soul.

That was the first thing she'd lost, along with her self-respect, and perhaps the respect of others.

Then the deceased came back to haunt her. Desislava, Dante, and so many others gave their lives to beat Cavar. Their deaths had at least been honorable and valiant, but Marai had tarnished their memories when she'd used dark magic that night.

Her mind turned to Kadiatu and Leif, how disappointed they'd be of her actions. If their ghosts lingered in the castle halls, they probably despised the sight of her. And Keshel . . . the mere thought of him had Marai's throat closing off with grief and self-loathing.

She finally opened her eyes.

Ruenen sat in a chair at her bedside, hair tousled, face unshaved, eyes red-rimmed and bruised from lack of sleep and spent tears. His shirt was rumpled and untucked. Thora had healed his injuries from the battle, but there remained an air of fragility about him. The image of a man at the edge of his sanity. An untouched plate of food sat beside him on the bedside table.

When he noticed Marai was conscious, Ruenen bolted from the chair, knocking it over.

"Oh, thank the gods," he choked out. His urgent hand brushed back her tangled hair, stroking Marai's cheek, as if desperate to touch her. "I thought you'd been taken from me again. Thora couldn't wake you." Ruenen nuzzled his nose against hers, kissed her brow, breathed in her scent. "I've been so frightened, my love."

Marai had used dark magic to save him, but the cost was heavy on her heart. How could she regret her actions when doing so had protected Ruenen, Thora, Raife, and Aresti?

As she met his gaze, Marai was struck by the sorrow reflected in his brown eyes. Ruenen's overt pain opened the floodgates to Marai's own emotions. Tears cascaded down her cheeks. Ruenen pulled her to his chest, cradling her as she sobbed into the crook of his neck.

"I lost her," Marai uttered. Shame and misery, almost unbearable, climbed up the knobs of her spine. Would Marai ever escape a life of grief and loss?

Not now. Not after what I did.

"I know, love."

"I *lost* her!"

Marai's hands moved to her stomach, to the gaping, heartbreaking hole in her womb. Where once she'd felt the gentle pulse of magic, of life, she now felt nothing. Silence.

She'd lost her child. Her daughter. The auburn haired Chosen One would never come. Yet again, Marai failed Lirr, and in doing so, she'd failed Keshel. No one would be able to stop dark magic now. The Dark Wielder would rise and consume the world, shrouding everything in darkness, and he would make Marai his puppet. Millions would die because of her weakness. Because she decided to value the life of her friends and family above the purity of her soul and the fate of civilization.

"There was nothing you could do to prevent that," Ruenen whispered, swiping away one of her tears with his thumb. "You had to make a terrible choice, one no mother should have to make."

"I *killed* our daughter! I'm sorry, Ruen. Please, forgive me." Sobs wracked Marai's body. She couldn't stop shaking.

Ruenen held her tighter. "There's nothing to forgive, my love."

"How can you say that?" Marai asked, drawing back from him. There was a silent scream of grief in her head that she couldn't let out. "I've doomed us all, and I lost our child."

"You *saved* us, Marai. And then you collapsed, and I thought I'd lost *both* of you." Ruenen's expression crumpled. He brushed away the tears. "My darkest thoughts, my greatest fears, have been eating away at me. I prayed to the gods that if they spared you, if you lived, I'd do anything, *give anything*. They heard me, Marai. They answered. They brought you back to me."

Ruenen's words, his love, wrenched at Marai's heart. And yet, panic bubbled up inside her. "Cavar may be dead, but the Dark Wielder lives. He'll find a new puppet, a new enemy for us to face, and we won't be able to defeat them next time. It might even be *me*. Darkness will claim more of the land, more magic, and soon, this world will be plunged into an eternal night full of death."

Ruenen took Marai's ghastly stained hands and held them to his lips. She shrank away from the sight of her blackened skin, a permanent paint that inched halfway up her biceps. Marai had used a substantial amount of that forbidden power on the battlefield to incur such rapid consumption.

"I don't care about the world, or prophecies, or Chosen Ones," said Ruenen. "My love, the only thing I care about is *you* . . . that we lost a child, and you were forced to sacrifice yourself—"

"I sold myself to a demon. I've damned my soul, and I killed our child—"

Ruenen became gravely stern. "You did *none* of those things. You didn't kill our child. And no one in this godforsaken universe can *claim* your soul, damned or not, because it's already intertwined with mine." He placed Marai's hand upon his unfaltering, beating heart. "I feel it here, Marai. Your soul resides *here*. As long as I live, I will protect it."

She wanted to hate herself, and perhaps she wanted to see that hatred and disappointment reflected on Ruenen's face, but of course, she didn't. His beautiful, gold-flecked, brown eyes were lined with silver.

"You're the bravest person I know," he continued softly. "No one else has fought harder for their loved ones, for the innocent, for equality and freedom, bringing peace and safety to these lands. Your soul, your heart, your very existence, has been wounded so many times, but *still* you choose to protect. To sacrifice. To love." Ruenen smiled; tender, melancholy, and exquisite. "Your soul has wings, and soars above us all."

Marai let his words wash over her. She allowed herself to hear them.

Ruenen had always seen the darkness inside her, the scars and sharp edges, and never balked, because he'd discovered and illuminated her *light*. He'd shown her that she was worthy. Perhaps he was right. Perhaps she was regressing to the time when she thought herself worthless and tainted, nothing more than a heartless butcher trying to survive. She'd come a long way since then.

But could she ever look at herself in the mirror and accept the woman staring back? Could she forgive herself, knowing that her decision to protect others had cost her a child?

"I *wanted* her," Marai whispered. "I loved her, before setting eyes on her. Before holding her. I didn't realize how fiercely I loved until now that she's been taken from me."

And the emptiness was a barren field, a dried up river, a skeleton of bleached bones, inside her. A hole that could never be filled. When Marai closed her eyes and thought about a little girl with wild auburn hair and Ruenen's smile, the image threatened to shred her heart to tatters. It was a raw blister in her brain.

Ruenen pressed his forehead to hers. "I loved her, too. I wanted to hear her laugh, and chase her through the gardens. To ride with her across the moor. To teach her about music. I grieve the loss of who our daughter could have been."

Sharing her grief with Ruenen eased some of the pain. She wasn't alone.

"We can try again," Ruenen said. "When we're ready. When the time feels right."

Marai didn't know if she'd be able to conceive again, not after the new damage done to her body. Dark magic would continue to spread and claim more of her. But she didn't want to vanquish Ruenen's hope.

"Please, don't shut me out," Ruenen said, voice breaking, recognizing the signs of her withdrawing. "I'm here. We can be enough. Let us be enough together."

Marai buried her face in his chest. They grieved the loss of their child together. She let him feel her pain, and he, in turn, shared his.

No, she wouldn't erect those walls and shields again.

I will not withdraw. I will not hide my sorrow. I will not cower.

"I created more shadow creatures, didn't I?"

"Quite a few, unfortunately," said Ruenen slowly, "but they scattered, including our winged friend. None of us could bother to go after them, not when we had so many dead and wounded to carry home."

The winged creature had been the one to suggest to Marai to call upon the darkness. *He's in league with the Lord of the Underworld.* All of the creatures were. That's why the winged one had been watching her, and why they'd stalked and attacked Ruenen. Because the creatures knew Ruenen was a link to Marai's power. He made her stronger. The creatures used her love for Ruenen to pressure her, and they served their Master well. Marai had let the darkness in, and the Lord of the Underworld would never leave. She'd created an inescapable link to Him. Even now, a fingernail scratched at her mind like someone rapping at a door. She'd hear Him in her head forever, and He'd have access to her magic.

Marai gasped, eyes flaring wide. "He could use me against you. He could take control of me, like Cavar's collar, and I could kill you, destroy the city—"

Ruenen took her face in his hands, forcing her to meet his gaze. "You would never harm me or anyone you love. I do not fear the power inside you. I never have. This wielder cannot take you from me. From your people. You're stronger than Him."

Marai pursed her lips. Her brain whirred, racing in leagues and leagues of circles, trying to formulate a plan.

There was a knock, yanking Marai from her thoughts. Sweet, loyal Nyle poked his head inside.

"Forgive the disturbance, Your Graces. You have guests. Shall I allow them in?"

Marai nodded, and Nyle fully opened the double doors. Thora, Raife, Aresti, and shockingly, Nosficio, entered solemnly.

Marai's heart leapt at the sight of her friends, unharmed, but she stuffed her hands beneath the sheets. She feared them seeing her stained skin, of what they now thought of her.

"Nosficio heard your voice from outside the door, and came to get us," Aresti said. "Thank Lirr you're finally awake."

"How are you feeling?" asked Thora, sitting on the bed next to Marai.

The thing was, Marai felt physically fine, other than the cramping in her abdomen and her chilled limbs. She may never feel truly warm again, thanks to the cold fire of dark magic circulating in her veins. She was well-rested. Any minor injuries she'd sustained in battle, Thora had healed whilst Marai slept. Her magic seemed replenished, but Marai dared not check to see, in case she awakened the Lord of the Underworld.

"I tried removing the darkness inside you, but it wouldn't budge. It's not the same as what happened to Aresti's calf," Thora continued. "Then Innesh tried her amulet before Raife destroyed it—"

"There's a difference between *choosing* to use dark magic, and having it used on you," Marai murmured.

Thora's delicate hand inched forward and covered Marai's stained knuckles. "Thank you for saving us. We know what it cost you. We're so sorry. I . . . I can only imagine . . ." She choked off the remainder of her words.

Marai couldn't stop her lip from trembling. Thora gathered her into an embrace. Marai sobbed again in the arms of her older sister, the one who'd raised her, had always cared for her.

Another set of arms draped over both of them, and Marai was fully ensconced by the love of her family. Aresti's calloused hand rubbed Marai's back, up and down.

Raife sat down next to Thora at the end of the bed. "We're here. We'll always be here," he said, green eyes glistening. "And Keshel, Leif, and Kadi are here, too. They're always watching over us. Can't you feel them?"

Raife smiled, and Marai closed her eyes.

Yes, she could feel them. Their souls were hazy, golden orbs floating around her head.

"Whatever you need us to do, Marai, we'll do," Nosficio proclaimed. His solemn voice lacked its usual silken drawl.

Marai glanced through Aresti and Thora's hair and saw the vampire standing next to her bed. His red eyes were dimmed, lips thin and sullen. She reached out through the tangle of limbs around her and took Nosficio's gray hand. He sucked in a small, surprised breath, eyes widening. Vampires ran cold, but with Marai's new state, he felt slightly warm in her grasp. He stared at their conjoined hands as if he'd never seen anything quite like it.

She hoped he could sense how much his words, his friendship, meant to her.

Nosficio gently squeezed it back.

Once Aresti and Thora disentangled themselves from Marai, cheeks wet with tears, Nosficio studied her black skin more closely.

"You're going to need to be careful with your magic from now on."

Marai wasn't startled by this news. She'd already guessed that it was something else she'd need to worry about.

Raife frowned. "Why? Thora said she's stable."

"It doesn't matter if she's stable. The darkness inside her is alive." Nosficio's piercing gaze was full of messages and warnings. "This happened with Meallán, as well. She let the darkness in once, and it slowly took over. Why do you think she created a cursed ring? She would never have done that if she wasn't being controlled by a darker power."

Marai's ancestor had been lured by the darkness, too. That weakness must lie within the bloodline. Or had Meallán also been Lirr's Chosen, and failed? Was the Dark Wielder hunting down Lirr's Chosen, one by one? The thought made Marai shudder.

Ruenen saw the movement, and took her hand, rubbing his thumb across her wrist.

"When Aras was killed, darkness fed on Meallán's grief," Nosficio continued. "She wasn't the same person once she let it in. I think it spoke to her, dragging her deeper."

"What will happen if Marai uses her magic now?" asked Raife.

QUEEN OF THE SHADOW MENAGERIE

"The darkness will spread faster, and you'll become more of a danger to us, and to yourself," the vampire said mournfully to Marai. "It could eventually kill you."

"Then I won't use it," she stated, and her family's faces blanched with shock and pity.

It hurt deeply to admit that Nosficio was right, but she felt the darkness crawling around inside of her like a bed of worms beneath a rotten log. She had to live to protect her loved ones. She had to protect Nevandia at all costs. Marai couldn't let Him use her, as He promised He would.

She steadied her breath.

"I won't risk any of you. Or this country." Marai sat up taller in bed, lifting her chin. "I don't need magic to be a queen. I have a duty to my people that I must uphold. I have a voice. A vision. I still have far more to accomplish." She turned her head, meeting Ruenen's soft gaze. "Magic doesn't make me powerful."

Ruenen smiled. "No, it doesn't."

Marai placed a hand on his cheek, then kissed him lightly.

She closed her mind to the darkness. She slammed the metal door in its face. The possessive hand massaging her brain evaporated into smoke, but she couldn't keep Him away forever. She was still His prize, for as long as she lived. He'd always find a way in.

"We'll help you shoulder the burden you carry," Raife said. "We'll keep these lands safe."

"And if He comes for you, we'll fight Him," said Aresti, taking Marai's hand. "We won't let you slip into the darkness."

"There are still Guardians remaining in Andara," Marai said, "and I'm certain Cavar had a stockpile of those amulets. Andara will remain a threat until all of them are destroyed."

"Do you think they'll come back here?" Thora asked, tensing.

"Doubtful, without Cavar to lead them, they'll stay across the sea," said Marai. "But we can never forget those amulets are out there. And when I tapped into that dark magic, I spawned more shadow creatures on the moor."

She shoved down the shame. *No, you did what needed to be done. No one is blaming you for anything. You need no one's forgiveness but your own.*

"We'll hunt them down," said Raife. "It might take some time, but we can handle them."

"We'll search for any signs of dark magic, too," added Aresti. "Keep our ears open for rumors of a new wielder."

Darkness wasn't gone. He was merely biding His time. This was only one wave in the larger battle. He'd recuperate, revise, and return. She'd shut Him out for now, but the Dark Wielder slinked below the earth, watching, listening.

Marai didn't know if this was her battle to fight anymore. Someone else would need to take over. Someone stronger, who wouldn't be tempted by His dark allure. Someone who would make better choices than her.

Thora, Raife, Aresti, and Nosficio left later in the evening, granting the King and Queen of Nevandia a few moments of privacy.

Marai stared out the window, lost in thought, looking back on her life, the path that led her here.

I forgive. I don't just accept my choices, I forgive them.

The weight she'd been carrying, for months, years, lifted from her shoulders, taking flight.

Ruenen came up from behind, wrapping his long, muscular arms around her. "I don't think she's gone forever."

"Who?"

"Our girl with the auburn hair. She'll come."

Marai turned to look up into his sincere, handsome face. "How can you possibly know that?"

"Because if she truly is Lirr's Chosen, then Lirr will find a way." Ruenen tucked a strand of Marai's hair behind her pointed ear. "And if the girl's part of your blood, then she's bound to be too stubborn not to complete her task. She'll demand life."

Marai snuggled closer to the man who'd pulled her from the darkness, healed her scars, and taught her to believe.

Perhaps he was right. Maybe Lirr kept creating a new Chosen when the previous failed. Had Marai been born to correct Meallán's mistakes? Marai's bloodline was the pathway. If she and Ruenen managed to have a child, even if they weren't the Chosen One, perhaps that meant she was only a generation or two away.

Then the world won't have to wait long to be exhumed.

"No matter what happens, Sassafras, you and I face life together. We won't let this land fail. We'll protect those we can, provide a safe harbor for magical folk, and if the darkness comes, I'll fight against it with every bone in my human body. We won't let it take away what we love. I will hold you until the last light of this world blinks out of existence."

Marai had spent her life wandering alone in darkness, but Ruenen had always been the candle, the luminous flame, guiding her home.

Guiding her here, to this moment, in his arms, gazing out at the kingdom they shared. He'd pulled her into the sunlight and reminded her that good was worth fighting for.

The key to her heart. A friend when she'd lost faith in herself.

The man who'd tamed her storms, and empowered her to ignite.

I am worthy. I am powerful. I am not alone.

And I will light up the world.

EPILOGUE

The garden is alive.

And it's empty, save for the little girl humming a lilting melody.

She pirouettes, barefoot in the grass, leaving flowers in her wake.

A gentle breeze curls around her, dancing and twirling through her wild hair. Strands of auburn escape from silk ribbons. She giggles as the friendly wind strokes her cheeks.

She passes a fountain, and the water sparkles, rippling in response to her presence.

The girl, so young, is already one with the earth. Life surges around her.

She can taste magic in the air, in every bloom and ray of sunlight. The magic is golden, and glittering, and beautiful. She loves to reach out her fingers and watch as golden threads wreath between them, like aureate gloves.

She continues her barefoot frolic through the grass, singing to the birds in the branches over her head.

But with each step she takes, a strange magic calls beneath her.

A dark shadow, one that filled the girl with dread the first time she'd felt it. She cannot understand why, or how she knows, but this darkness wants her. It has its eyes on her.

A stern woman calls from the other side of the garden. The little girl's name on the woman's lips is as sharp as the crack of thunder.

Disappointment rushes through the girl with the auburn hair. Her time outside, being *herself,* has come to an end.

The stern woman, her Nurse, waits at the doorway, tapping her toe on the ground. She shakes her head at the girl, whose feet and dress-hem are coated with grass and earth. The woman's cold eyes narrow at the sight of the briar-patch-state of the girl's tresses.

The girl slides her feet into the slippers she'd left on the stone path, and steps foot inside the austere estate, leaving the ghost of herself at the door. She becomes the quiet, obedient child the world expects her to be.

She says goodbye to her magic, farewell to the music, and bids adieu to who she longs to be, who she knows deep down that she intrinsically *is*.

A candle in the darkness. An indestructible light. A flash of lightning in the sky.

She has a purpose out there. She *knows* it. Something far greater than palace walls, royal courts, and a world of "no."

Because she has been Chosen.

THE STORY CONTINUES...

Darkness returns.
The Lord of the Underworld will rise.
And Lirr's Chosen will discover her destiny.
Dark Magic Series: Underworld
Book 1
Coming 2025

Never miss a release day, cover reveal, or giveaway–sign up for J. E. Harter's
monthly mailing list on her website:
https://jeharterauthor.wixsite.com/j--e--harter-author

GLOSSARY

AIN -□□□(Ay-n) Kingdom in the Southwest on the coast of Astye

ANDARA -□□(An-dar-uh) Far away, mysterious country

ASTYE -□□□(Ah-stye) The largest continent, home to The Nine Kingdoms

BAATGAI -□□(Bot-guy) Port village in Syoto

BAKAIR -□□(Buh-care) Capital port city of Andara

BAUREAN SEA -□□(Boar-ee-an) Body of water in the South

BENIEL -□□(Ben-ee-ehl) Kingdom in the Northwest of Astye

BURSGAMI -□□(Buhrs-gah-mee) Smaller island off of Qasnal

CASAMERE -□□(Kaz-uh-meere) Large country off the continent

CHIOJAN -□□(Chee-oh-jan) Capital city of the Kingdom of Varana

CLEAVING TIDES -□Prosperous port city in Henig, the Southernmost point of Astye, wealthy area above in the hills called High Tides, harbor and beaches called Low Tides

CLIFFS OF UNMYN -□(Un-min) On the Northern Coastline, part of the White Ridge Mountains

DUL TANEN -□□(Dool Tan-ehn) Capital city of the Kingdom of Tacorn

DWALINGULF -□□(Dwah-lin-gulf) Large logging town in the lower North

EHLE -□□(Eh-leh) Kingdom in the Southwest of Astye, known for its deserts and canyons of red dirt

FENSMUIR -□□(Fens-mee-ur) City in the Kingdom of Ain

GAINESBURY -□□(Gains-buhr-ee) Small village in the Northern White Ridge Mountains

GELANON -□□(Gel-uh-non) Holiest day in the entire year, a winter holiday known for fasting, throwing minerals into fire to show colors for gods to see for blessings

GRELTA -□□□The Northernmost and largest kingdom on Astye, cold and snowy most of the year

HAVENFIORD - □□(Haven-fee-ord) Large town on the border of Grelta and Tacorn

HENIG -□□□Kingdom in the Southeast, busy harbors and port cities

HINTERLANDS -□□Territory of magical folk on Andara, hidden behind the Veil

INIQUITY -□□□Town of criminals, also known as the Den, the Nest, Vice, etc.

KELLESAR -□□(Kell-eh-sar) Capital city of the Kingdom of Nevandia

LIRR -□□(Lear) Goddess of Creation and All Living Things & Fertility

LIRRSTRASS — (Lear-strah-ss) Capital city of the Kingdom of Grelta

LAIMOEN -□□(Lie-moh-en) God of Destruction and War, Lirr's partner

LISTAN -□□□(Lee-stan) Small, sandy country off the continent

MIDDLE KINGDOMS -□Name for the two middle countries on Astye–Tacorn and Nevandia

NEVANDIA -□□(Nev-an-dee-uh) Kingdom in the middle of Astye, in a bitter forty-year war with Tacorn

NYDIAN RIVER -□□(Nid-ee-an) River that stretches East to South on Astye

PEVEAR -□□□(Pev-ear) Town on the outskirts of Tacorn, once the site of a bloody battle

QASNAL -□□(Kaz-nal) Capital port city of Yehzig

RED LANDS -□□Nickname for the Middle Kingdoms–a land so covered in blood

SILKEHAVEN -□□Small town in the Northern White Ridge Mountains

SYOTO -□□□(See-oh-toh) Empire in the Southeast of Astye

TACORN -□□□(Tay-corn) Kingdom in the middle of Astye, in a bitter forty-year war with Nevandia

UKRA -□□□(Oo-kruh) Country off the continent

VARANA -□□□(Vuh-ron-uh) Empire in the Northeast of Astye

WHITE RIDGE MOUNTAINS -□Large Northern mountain range made of obsidian rock

YEHZIG -□□□(Yeh-zig) Small, tropical isle off the continent

ACKNOWLEDGEMENTS

Every time I write this section, it feels surreal. I wrote a *trilogy!* I'm not sure that I'll ever get used to being published, and having people read and enjoy this story and these characters. Writing this third book was a journey in itself. I honestly doubted myself as a writer at the beginning during the first and second drafts. I felt so much pressure to make this third book better than the previous two. But then, by draft three, the magic reappeared, spewing from my fingers like Marai's lightning, and "Queen of the Shadow Menagerie" came alive. I'm so proud of this book, and for pushing through my own doubt and self-consciousness. I cried at so many moments writing this, because Marai and Ruenen are a part of me, and I love them dearly. Finishing this chapter of their story was cathartic. Finishing a *trilogy* was an enormous feat. But, as always, I couldn't have done it alone.

Thank you once again to my amazing editor Erin Young. You are always in my corner, helping me find ways to make moments in my books sparkle, and shining light on the areas that need fixing.

I don't know how you do it, Miblart, but every time you design a cover for me, it sets the tone and aesthetic perfectly. Thank you for creating unique and eye-catching covers for the Dark Magic Series. I love them all.

My critique partner Addison—I don't know how to thank you properly for all the things you've done for this trilogy. You've been part of this journey since its early stages, before I even decided to self-publish "Butcher," and I know this series wouldn't be what it is without your guidance. Thank you for your work on "QotSM," but also for the nearly two years of advice and email conversations. Meeting you in person earlier this year was truly special!

Alex, Nicole & Sam, my fabulous beta reader team—I can't thank you three enough for being loyal readers and supporters of Marai & Ruenen. I appreciate all of your work & feedback on "QotSM," and this book would not be the same without you. Thanks for helping tie together loose ends, clarify battle scenes, and spot those tricky grammatical errors!

My PA Tay—there are a million things to thank you for! Thank you for being an amazing cheerleader for me and other indie authors. For your work with the Fantasy Author Legion, for all your organizing, and promoting, and outreach. For driving me to and from the Glastonbury B&N event. And of course, thank you for helping me navigate the marketing side of self-publishing, and teaching this old woman about social media.

To my family and friends for supporting me every step of the way. I know my whole writing career came as a big surprise to you all, but I hope you know how much it means to me that you think this is kinda cool. You don't often get to hear me talk about the fun stuff, so thank you for listening to me rant about my difficulties, confusion, and doubts, and for celebrating each win, no matter how small.

Lastly, thanks to you, dear reader, for falling in love with Marai and Ruenen. For rooting for me and for them. For your support and kind words. I write for myself, but I also write for you. I want to write words that move you, stories that keep you glued to the page, and characters you claim as your own, as part of your heart. You make my struggles worthwhile. Thank you.

ABOUT THE AUTHOR

J. E. Harter is a lover of music, theatre, beaches, cats, and books (obviously). "The Butcher and the Bard" is her debut novel. She lives in NYC with two fluffy children Simon Catfunkel and Ziggy Starcat. When not authoring, she is (hopefully) inspiring young performers as a youth theatre director. Visit her website to sign up for her monthly newsletter:

https://jeharterauthor.wixsite.com/j--e--harter-author

Instagram: @j.e.harter

TikTok: @j.e.harterauthor

Facebook: J. E. Harter Fantasy Author

Also by J. E. Harter

Made in the USA
Monee, IL
08 January 2025

209c4b7c-5bcb-4c65-97ac-fa69ac883c9bR01